What the everloving f■■k? There's a warning label on my book?

That is some serious bulls■■t. Go look at *Mein Kampf*—there's no warning label on that book. And Hitler wrote it!

Look, I admit there's some rough stuff in the pages to follow. Stuff that may make you uncomfortable. Hell, some of it makes me uncomfortable . . . and I wrote it!

"Why didn't you change it then?" you may ask. Good question!

Because there's a reason for it. A solid story reason and if you read the whole damn book (Yes, yes, I know it's long), then you'll see the reason, too.

But my publisher . . . They're worried you'll be offended by some of what you read in here and you'll stop reading and so you'll never come to understand the *why* and instead you'll go say mean things about the book.[i]

i As a Publisher—the capital P is deliberate, meant to imply that we are even more of a forbidding and opaque corporate institution than you imagine, whose status transcends mere lowercase letters—we cringe when one of our authors has the audacity to describe how we feel. "Worried" is such a negative word. Worse, it's so *human,* with its connotations of empathy and frailty. Publishers traffic in power, not humanity! But since we are publishing *Unedited*, we agreed to stay true to its title. By definition, we can't edit out the word "worried," much to our c worried. So, guess what? It turns out we're just a strive for empathy. We often fall short. We have of others . . . Wait. We probably shouldn't have read the footnotes? Who reads footnotes?

And maybe you will be and maybe you will. 🙅

Or maybe you'll take a deep breath, keep reading, then see how you feel at the end.

Maybe you will be offended by something in here. Maybe not. And maybe, just maybe, the offense is to make a point. Maybe, just maybe, there's a reason for it. Maybe, just maybe, if you keep reading, you'll see. And maybe, just maybe, it'll be worth your initial discomfort.

Or maybe not. I don't know you.

You're reading these words, so it's all literally in your hands.

Best,

U
N
E
D
I
T
E
D

UNEDITED

BARRY
LYGA

BLACK
STONE
PUBLISHING

Published in 2022 by Blackstone Publishing

Cover design by Sarah Riedlinger
Book design by Blackstone Publishing

Printed in the United States of America

First edition: 2022
ISBN 979-8-200-83219-4
Young Adult Fiction / General

Version 1

CIP data for this book is available
from the Library of Congress

Blackstone Publishing
31 Mistletoe Rd.
Ashland, OR 97520

www.BlackstonePublishing.com

U
N
E
D
I
T
E
D

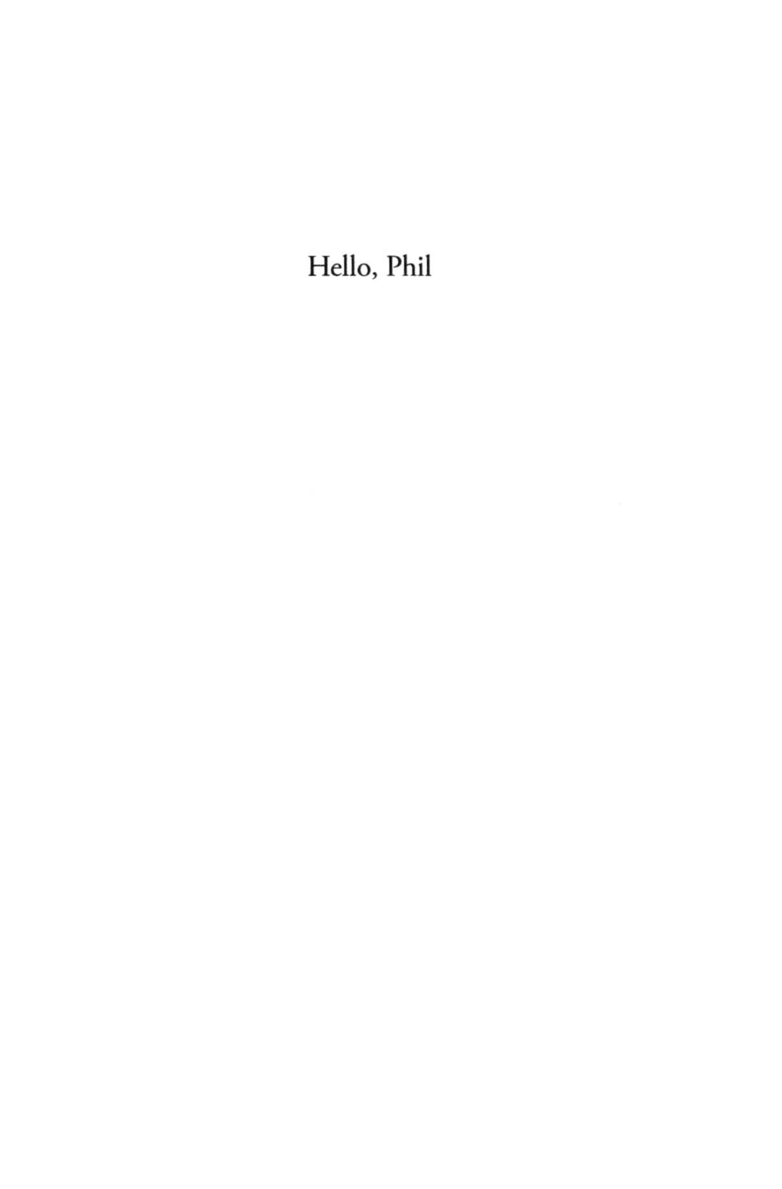

Hello, Phil

In the beginning, there was light. And then God said, "Let there be darkness." And I said to him, "But it's been there all along, don't you see?"

Dedication

for you

for you

CHAPTER 11

And that's when I realized I could edit reality, staring at Phil, at her dress, her teal dress, the dress teal and very definitely not-red. Phil stared back at me, her eyes narrowed to slits as though against sunlight, even though it was twilight-dark within the auditorium, the lights low in that prom-esque way that promotes and protects furtive groping. We were not, of course, attending a prom, but the light was prom-esque in any event, as though the fixtures in the venerable auditorium of our mutual alma mater had but two settings: full brightness and prom-grope.

"What's wrong with you?" she asked. Her tone communicated that she had a theory, or, more likely, a certainty.

"Your dress . . ."

"I didn't wear it for you. I know it's your favorite, but that's not why I—"

"No," I said. "That's not what . . ." Could no one tell? Did no one notice? I turned to George. "George. What was I just saying when she came in? About her dress?"

George blinked. "Uh, you said . . . Uh . . . You said,

‘~~The red one is all wrong. She should have worn the teal.~~ I’m glad she wore the teal—that’s the best one for her hair color.’”

Phil’s voice, round and full and dense with tension: “This is for charity,” she said. “Maybe it’s best if we don’t talk or hang out while we’re both here.”

And then *he* came in. *He* had the good grace to pause at the door before approaching us, *his* face a melting pot of anger, shock, and some distant relative of resignation.

“Is there a problem?” *he* asked.

George stepped between us, faithful wall of sanity. Hadn’t I, after all, sworn to “kick *his* ass into the next century?” Even though *he*, technically, had done nothing to me, had merely said “Yes,” when Phil approached *him* and—in my mind’s eye—threw herself wantonly at *his* feet; even though *he*, technically, could not be considered an enemy, *per se*, *he* was still, undoubtedly, a rival. More to the point, a roadblock, an obstacle, a hindrance, one more soldier in an increasingly-infinite battalion of them poised like a Roman phalanx between Phil and me and our reconciliation.

George puffed out his chest, a truly hilarious sight to those who knew him only on sight or by sight, but to those who had an actual acquaintanceship with George, to those who knew the Legend of George—which was, of course, nearly everyone in the auditorium at this point, including *him*—that chest-puffery was anything but hilarious, not even the slightest bit amusing.

“Dude, I don’t *think* there’s a problem,” George said. “Why don’t you think it over and let me know, you know what I mean?”

Despite George’s renowned prowess in Krav Maga, I truly believe *he* would have essayed a punch regardless, the testosterone and the flaring rage so evident in *his* eyes that all caution and sense of self-preservation and possibly even the last embers of civility had whirlpooled down into some deep, dark crevasse within *his* soul, if not for Phil insisting "For charity," now interposing herself between George and *him*, so that we formed a strange sort of set of interlocking aggressions: George between *him* and me, also between Phil and me, Phil between George and *him*, me still staring at Phil's teal dress (teal!).

"This isn't going to turn into some bullshit macho thing," she went on. "Jesus, Mike. Do you think getting into a fight is going to win me back?"

"A fight" was, indeed, a possibility I'd considered, usually late at night when I could not sleep, when—unbidden, though not entirely unwanted—images of Phil in that same bed in which I laid, unsleeping, assailed me, memories of her body under mine, astride mine, beside mine, uncovered and gently slick with a light coating of perspiration from our fucking (which she always called it—never the clinical "having sex"; never the romantic "lovemaking"; never even the colloquial-yet-barely-socially-acceptable "screwing"; always "fucking"), those self-conjured images driving me to frustrated arousal, frustrated because I knew I would never again know Phil in the Biblical sense, followed by mounting (no pun intended) frustration and then outright rage at thinking that *he*, in fact, would know Phil, had known Phil, would continue knowing Phil, might—again, in fact—be knowing Phil at that very moment that I could only be fucking Phil in a castle in the air, which thought made it even more impossible for me to sleep. At those times, on those nights (most nights, truthfully, since she'd told me she was back with *him*), I could only substitute one wish-world for another, self-evoking a universe in which I viciously battered *him* into submission, winning back Phil just like a belt worn by a prizefighter, not caring—in the throes of that fancy—that doing so reduced her to an object, caring only about having her back, which notion led—naturally—to a post-reunion bout of Phil's favorite fucking, which furthermore led to the inevitable—unbidden, though not entirely unwanted—images of Phil in that same bed, full circle, full stop.

"No one's going to fight," I said, and in saying it became convinced that I had somehow guaranteed that it not only was true, but would remain true.

He took Phil's hand, escorting her past George, past me. I watched them go, and Phil did not look over her shoulder, though *he* did, *his* expression now a grotesque mating of still-simmering anger and boiling-over self-satisfaction. I briefly savored a long-stewing image of my fist in *his* face—repeatedly—but cut short before the connubial reunion portion of the daydream (daydream though most often experienced at night) could distract me further.

"Dude," said George, who so often begins his declarations that way, "you totally didn't overreact to her. I'm proud of you," and reached up to clap a small-but-skilled hand on my shoulder.

"Do you smell chocolate syrup?" For I smelled chocolate syrup in that moment and also realized—in that moment—that I had actually been smelling chocolate syrup since Phil came into the room and changed dresses without ever being naked.

"Are you all right?" George asked again, this time with more urgency, as though his sheer concern could, in fact, *make* me all right.

"No. No. Something is . . ." And yet I could not put "something" into words. It had begun with the strong reek of chocolate syrup, with Phil's entrance into the ballroom for the charity auction, beautiful but somehow wrong in the red dress, followed by my wish that she'd instead worn the teal dress, followed by her not only wearing the teal dress, but—if George's earlier comment was to be taken as fact—also having *always* worn the teal dress.

But . . . No. It had *not* begun there. It had begun moments *after* that, with my realization that I could, in fact, edit reality.

I pointed George to the open-but-dry bar, and as he scampered off for his favorite beverage—half-diet Coke, half-lemonade—I decided that Phil had, in fact, worn the red dress, the one her mother had bought for her to wear to our senior prom, the one I'd been unable to disguise my loathing for when she'd slipped into it in her bedroom that warm afternoon one May previous. She'd said, "Let's see what this looks like" and swiftly unzipped it free from the garment bag, just as swiftly—and utterly un-self-consciously—unzipping herself free from her sundress, the yellow-and-white-patterned fabric shushing to the floor, her bra'd breasts and thonged hips erecting me as I sat on the bed, watching as she stretched her impossibly smooth, impossibly toned form, her arms over her head as the new dress shushed into place.

"Zip me," she said, and I stood, my cock proud and suggestive in my jeans. I zipped the red dress, going slowly, one palm pressed to her lower back as though for support, but in reality only because I took (and would take) any opportunity to touch her, any part of her, for every part of her was (and is) sexy.

"I don't like it," I told her as she posed and twisted and turned and posed again in front of the full-length mirror, my erect penis calling me a liar. I was telling the truth, though—I did not like the dress. I—and my erection—held faith, though, that nothing had changed underneath.

"It's not quite right," she admitted at last, having posed and generally modeled long enough that even my penis became bored and subsided to useless flaccidity.

With that memory bright and clear in my mind, I decided that, yes, Phil *had* in fact worn the hated, penis-shriveling red dress to the charity auction, had, in fact, *always* worn it, and had never worn the delightful teal dress that made her hair shine and shimmer like the sky just after a summer storm.

Across the ballroom, *he* guided Phil onto the dance floor as the notorious DJ Tea—who only plays 45s because his hands are famously small—obligingly spun up a slow dance number, and Phil molded her body to *his* (my stomach and my cock both lurched at the sight, each for its own reasons), molded her red-bedressed body to *his* and swayed the way she'd molded and swayed against me at our prom only a year ago.

My mouth turned Sahara; the tips of my fingers vibrated. The stench of chocolate syrup became overwhelming, strong and over-sweet.

George approached, his half-diet Coke, half-lemonade concoction already half-consumed in the trip from the open-but-dry bar.

"George." My voice sounded unlike my own, resonated throaty and vaporous. "George, look over at Phil."

He did. "Dude. Please. Give it up. She's moved on. She's with *him* now, okay?" (He did not actually say *him*. He said, instead, *his* name, which I do not want to see or hear or record. My revenge, though small.)

"Look at her dress, George."

"Dude, what about it?"

In the space of minutes, in the time from her entrance until now, Phil's dress had gone from erection-slaying red to fondly-remembered and complementary teal, then back to dick-killer.

I could not speak. My mouth had gone from Sahara to Atacama. I stole George's half-diet Coke, half-lemonade and drained the glass by half its remainder, thinking of Xeno and Achilles and a tortoise for a moment.[1]

"George," said my newly-moistened mouth, "do you remember when Phil came in? What I said?"

"Sure. You said, 'The red one is all wrong. She should have worn the teal.'"

I decided that Phil had worn the teal dress after all. On the dance floor, she remained fused to *him* in her teal dress, where less than a moment earlier had been red.

I needed another swig of the commingled swill in George's glass before I could speak again. "Say it again. Tell me what I said when she came in?"

George rolled his eyes. "Dude, the music isn't *that* loud. You said, 'I'm glad she wore the teal—that's the best one for her hair color.'"

Phil had worn the red, had worn the teal, had always worn the red, had always worn the teal. Only I noticed the changes.

I thought about how it all started. I thought about the beginning. I imagined it as the first chapter in my story, though of course it wasn't, isn't, can't be.

1. Xeno's Paradox illustrates the essential impossibility of touching anything, using the image of Achilles chasing a tortoise. Of course, Achilles is much faster than a tortoise and should be able to catch it easily. But Xeno asks us to imagine that with each step he takes, Achilles halves the distance between himself and the tortoise. So, if the tortoise is ten feet away, the first step cuts the distance to five; the second step to two and a half; the third to one and a quarter; etc. But no matter how many steps Achilles takes, he will always be half of the previous distance away from the tortoise. Similarly, Mike will never finish the drink if he keeps halving the contents of the cup.

CHAPTER 1

"Do you want to hear something scary?" Phil asks.

We're laying entwined and naked in her bed, one week before senior year begins, which means this is in the past, but I see it, hear it, read it in the present tense for some reason. I am there again, perhaps, doing more than merely flashing back. I am reliving the moment, the memory, the time.

"Tell me something scary," I tell her, finding her now-unerect nipple by feel, then gently stroking the pads of two fingers along its diameter to tease it to standing.

"I think I'm falling in love with you," she says, shivering, the shiver caused—I cannot tell—by her statement or my ministrations or both.

"I think I'm falling in love with you, too." I am capable of discussing love with Phil while my fingers discuss fucking with her nipple. And the truth is, I think I've been falling in love with Phil for weeks now. Our relationship began with nothing dramatic: A party at George's house a month previous, a bored me in the garage-*cum*-game room as an equally bored Phil abandoned everyone else to the basement-*cum*-party room, on a quest for more wine coolers in the garage fridge. Meaningless small talk metamorphosed into a three-hour dialogue during which we—emotionally and physically—came closer and closer, until making out commenced on the rug remnants piled on the floor, the wine coolers long consumed, the two of us grinding against each other in the garage-*cum*-game room.

Phil had been a constant in my life, though a constant on the periphery. The girl with the blue hair, locks like shimmering, wet sapphires. She transferred to our school in seventh grade, instantly captivating both sexes with an air of insouciance, the mystique of that blue hair, the casual-yet-biting way she told teachers "*Phil*" when they called out for "Philomel" during Role. With the onset of puberty, she acquired the appearance of her namesake instrument: flaring hips, restrained waist, breasts that could not hide and would not quit, a graceful neck atop it all. Almost single-handedly, she willed into existence a pre-high-school-level drama club and attendant performances, astounding teachers and parents alike by rallying to her side kids who had hitherto expressed no interest at all in the dramatic arts, but who found themselves captivated by her insistent energy and post-naïveté. With seemingly no effort at all, she rode her adolescent dramatics into the lead role in nearly every high school play, as well as summer performances at the local college.

I never thought I had a chance with her and so I never even tried until the night of the wine coolers. Even then, she made the first move, sidling close enough that our thighs touched, hers under a denim skirt, mine under shorts baggy enough to conceal my erection as long as I remained seated, though soon enough that concealed erection would be ground against the skirt, pushed up between her legs as she pulled me closer and tighter and matched my own panting breaths, grasped and gasped between blurtings of *Oh God* and *Oh oh oh oh yes.*

"You weren't supposed to say that," Phil says, annoyed, though not annoyed to a degree that would cause her to remove my fingers from her now-erect nipple. "You're not supposed to be falling in love with me."

"Why not?"

"Because we're almost seniors. Because you'll go away to college and I'm going to stay here. Because."

"You don't know any of that."

"I know."

"So?"

"You have to stop doing that," she says, her voice rising and breathy and wispy, her body twisting against mine. "Oh." I lean in, taking the nipple in my mouth. "God," she says.

****

Phil's mother (her father has long-since vanished into the mists of the past) considers herself a "cool mom" and does not mind that we fuck in her daughter's bed under her own roof, having insisted that Phil be on the Pill since age fifteen and having further insisted her daughter engage in safe sex at all times, to the point of leaving a variety pack of condoms in their shared bathroom, as well as offering to pay for blood tests should we desire to forgo the condoms (which offer we accepted almost immediately). Our sex thus maternally sanctioned and medically blessed is insane, mind-blowing, geometric levels beyond passionate—although Phil prefers not to fuck while her mother is actually awake in the house, convinced that the idea of her own mother "hearing my O-noises is just way too creepy."

It is for this reason (and for the fact that—after rising and falling to the occasion three times this afternoon—my poor instrument is played out for the time being, though my desire to play another song is still strong) that we reluctantly pull away from each other upon hearing Phil's mother's car in the driveway. I allow myself a final, half-hearted grope at a breast, a feather-light finger-stroke down her naked flank, then slip into shorts and a t-shirt, watching as Phil shakes a sundress over her form. Watching her dress (I have decided in the short time we have been fucking) trumps watching her undress. That ritual of covering, of clothing, of shielding herself from the rest of the world takes on new meaning when I know that I am the only one *not* covered against, shielded against, that I can, in fact, undress her myself almost any time I want.

"Read to me," she says, flinging herself on the bed.

"What?"

"*Read* to me." She curls up on the bed and points to a wall-mounted shelf I have noticed several times, crammed with books: *The Wind in the Willows*, A. A. Milne, Beatrix Potter, and all the other old friends left behind in the old neighborhoods of childhood when we packed our innocence onto a truck and moved to the new town of Growing Up. A sudden terror seizes me: Phil dated *him* almost from Day One, holding hands with *him* from her second week in town until two days after the junior prom. The terror is such: Was this *his* ritual with her? Did *he* read to her from the volumes of her dad-present youth?

"I like the sound of your voice," she goes on, "and I like being read to. Just pick one and read to me."

I imagine *him* in the same position, *him* next to her in bed, she curled towards *him* but not touching, *he* with legs outstretched, head propped up against the padded headboard, Milne open on *his* lap. *He* mimics a high falsetto for Pooh, a childish whisper for Roo, a downbeat worded moan for Eeyore, and et cetera. What are her expectations of me? Is it not enough that I am at her beck and call, that I attend to her every word, that I spend every moment not spent at work (delivering Indian food for a local restaurant or lifeguarding at the community pool) with her, that I have accompanied her on quotidian errands to the grocery store, the mall, the nail salon, the doctor's office, the dentist, all in the last two weeks alone? Now I am also her entertainment, her Man of a Thousand Voices?

"I'm not going to read to you," I say, demolishing with a single sentence any chance of comparison between *him* and me. "I'm not your parent."

She pouts. "Come on. Just one story. Not a whole book. A chapter."

"No. Stop it."

Our first time (me atop, her ankles crossed somewhere north of my knees and south of my soon-to-pause ass), at the mid-point I paused, her hips still thrusting beneath me, as I pondered the comparison vis-à-vis *him* and me, vis-à-vis prowess, vis-à-vis stamina, vis-à-vis size; more particularly in re: size: length, width, girth. Said ponder-pause causing her eyes to open, "What's wrong?" to ask, prompting me to grunt, to thrust again, pushing from her thoughts of "What's wrong?" in favor of no thoughts, the pre-blood-test, Phil's-mom-provided condom reducing sensation enough that she—I believe—came before I did, though identifying Phil's orgasms did not yet number among my skills.

Since that mid-fucking pause of "What's wrong?" I have felt coiled in a dim, dark recess of my backbrain a quiescent snake of doubt, ready to poisonously lunge and strike when jostled into arousal by the scantiest hint of comparison between me and *him*, whether fucking-wise or other-. For this reason (as well, to be truthful, the slightly incestuous undertones of it all, reading in bed having been an intimate ritual between long-gone father and young daughter), I cannot allow myself to read to her. Enough that I have fucked her here in this bed, the same bed where I am certain (though I've never asked) she fucked *him*, using those condoms in the variety pack, inviting comparisons vis-à-vis stamina and all the rest, see above.

"You suck," she says lightly, flouncing melodramatically on the bed such that her dress flies up around her strong, delicious thighs, awakening memories that have only barely been tucked in and drifted off to sleep.

"Yeah, I suck. Why do you hate me so much?" I stretch out next to her and kiss her neck just below her ear, a spot I know makes her melt and shiver at once.

"I don't hate you," she whispers, melting and shivering. "I . . ."

****

There is nothing after "I . . ." except dead white space and four months of Phil and me, a couple in the halls of high school in our mutual senior year, oohed and aahed over by her friends, subject of shoulder-punches and innuendoes by mine, busted on close to a dozen separate occasions for PDAs between classes, usually involving some iteration of my hand on her buttock, our lips touching, a clinch, or a combination of the three. There are preparations for the senior play—Phil's last, her swan song—and long hours for me designing the set, the two of us often collapsing against each other at the end of the day, snuggling momentarily in the wings before the custodians shut out the lights and call out for stragglers.

My parents have surrendered to the inevitable and the unstoppable: As I close in on my eighteenth birthday and official, authorities-recognized adulthood, they no longer bother attempting to police my comings and goings with curfews and deadlines, opting instead to inform me that as long as my grades "stay up there, young man," I am free to do as I please.

Doing "as I please" involves spending nights at Phil's, where once her mother's soft snores begin immediately after the last laughs and applause of Letterman's *Tonight Show*, we attack and explore each other, she on top, me on top, beside each other, in every configuration of bodies we can imagine and, when we run out of our own ideas, hastening to the Internet for sybaritic advice, complete with detailed pictures and instructions.

In short: We fuck.

We fuck constantly. We fuck as often as possible. We fuck, predictably and proverbially, like bunnies. "I should," Phil says one night as we lay panting and sweat-sheathed in her bed, "wash these sheets someday."

"When was the last time you washed them?"

She raises one blue eyebrow ceiling-ward. "Not since before we started fucking on them."

Rather than disgusting me, the thought that we have been fucking and re-fucking on the same stained and re-stained sheets flips a buried-deep pleasure switch, triggered by the notion that these sheets have become a damp-then-dry archive of our sexual history, bedclothes-*cum*-record. This thrills me, until a moment of panic slips its blade between my ribs and into my heart: Has she not washed them since she cavorted with *him* in these sheets? Have my copious deposits of bodily fluids been commingling not only with hers in the present, but also hers in the past and *his*?

"The last time I washed them was right before the first time you came over," she says, unaware of both my panic and my instant relief. "I wanted them nice and clean for you. I knew it was going to happen that night."

"You knew?" I had assumed nothing, grateful only that Phil, beautiful Phil, had seen fit to grind against me and bring me deliciously, delicately close to ruining a pair of shorts on the pile of rug remnants in George's garage-*cum*-game room.

"Duh. After the way we were all over each other in George's garage? Please. Did you really think I was going to deny myself after that?"

And I realize for the first time: As much as I lust for, have lusted for, Phil, she has lusted for and does lust for me as well. Despite the evidence of the bedclothes-*cum*-record, I had convinced myself that her enthusiastic opening of legs and straddling of my hips came from a strong flavor of like (perhaps even love), not lust. That her lustfulness comprised a sort of favor to me, doled out generously and without restraint, but a favor nonetheless. To find that she craved my body-*qua*-body-*cum*-sex object on her own and for herself changes my perspective, or rather *would* change my perspective, were it not for the fact that it makes me immediately rampant again, and—after a brief admonition to "watch your moaning" lest I "wake up [her] friggin' mother"—I roll her onto her back, slide down the history-made sheet until I'm even with the jutting bone of her hip, then interpose myself between her legs, no longer shocked or even vaguely surprised by what I find there.

The first time I went down on Phil, the first time I saw her naked, I experienced twin jolts of wonder and lust, the latter for the breathstealing (no mere taking here—this was a criminal level of breath-abduction) sight of my lust object unclothed and stretched out before me, willing; the former for the utterly unforeseen spectacle of her neatly trimmed pubic hair, the azure shade of which perfectly matched her eyebrows and her flowing, shoulder-length locks.

I didn't understand, but I didn't care because my whole being, my whole soul, was now past the surprise and wholly enrapt just looking at her, absorbing her, caressing every curve and arch and dimple and beauty mark and bulge of muscle with my eyes and—almost without realizing—the tips of the fingers of both hands. And I put my mouth on her and she said "God." And she said "God" again. And arched her back into me. And "God." And "God." And "God." And, now, "God."

"You're so good at that," she says minutes later, as we clutch each other.

"Better than *him*?" I want to ask, but do not.

I think, instead, of the first time I saw her, as a child, I a boy in seventh grade, watching her, upright and self-assured and utterly composed, at the head of the class, ignoring the giggles and the undercurrent of chatter about her hair color, her pubescent drama club still weeks in the future, defiantly insisting "Phil!" when Mrs. Foreman introduced her as "Philomel." Within a week, George reported spying her holding hands with *him* on the playground at recess.

CHAPTER 2

"Dude," George says, as I find myself at his house, or more accurately outside his house, on the rickety old deck, George making his way through a six-pack of Stella Artois, "the only beer worth drinking," in his estimation. George's mother refuses to let him drink while underage and while "living under *my* roof!" so deck-drinking is their uneasy compromise, placing George technically beyond the jurisdiction of "under *my* roof!" though not beyond the jurisdiction of law enforcement, whom his mother occasionally and half-heartedly threatens to call.

"Dude, you're with her all the time," he goes on, clinking an empty bottle next to its brethren in the cardboard carrier, lifting free a full bottle on the upswing. "You in love or something? I figure you're gonna end up in the old age home, chasing after her with your walker, you know what I mean?" He pauses, consideration creasing his brow. "What will her hair look like when she gets old? You think it'll go gray or will it just get, like, lighter blue?"

"I don't know. I don't care."

"Cornflower? Periwinkle?"

"Seriously. Don't care."

"Powder blue? Robin's egg blue? Ice blue?"

"George."

"Dude, you lack curiosity. That's your fatal flaw. Not hubris. Not cluelessness." Here, George belches with great intensity and intent, as though determined to communicate some vital fact via his gas. "Curiosity, man. It killed the cat, but *lack* of it will kill *you*, you know what I mean? Trust me on this." He points the open mouth of his beer bottle at me, and to me the mouth is like an eye, watching, staring, unblinking, until I become discomfited and look away.

"I trust you, George."

I have always trusted George. He has always trusted me. We bonded early, in grade school, shortly after his father had been taken away by the police, never to return. George was the fatherless runt chosen last for games, I the early-growth-spurted klutz chosen penultimately, my relative size compensating just barely for my complete lack of skill, poise, grace, and coordination.

George's father routinely beat both George and George's mother. "I will *never* be like the asshole," George has told his mother, has told me, has told a small army of therapists and counselors assigned to him by schools and his mother over the years. He refuses to speak his father's name, indeed even to utter the phrase "my father" (or "my dad" or, in truth, any permutation of a first-person possessive pronoun and any form of a paternal noun), referring simply to "the asshole" (and not even capitalized, for "the asshole doesn't deserve capital letters.")

George's first memory—and, thus, my most intense memory of George, though I was not there—is of the asshole knocking him down a flight of stairs with a kick to the shoulder.

The police hauled George's father away years later, after his mother finally broke down in the emergency room when her imaginative powers—hitherto so reliable and fecund—experienced a complete breakdown of their own, at a loss as to conjure a story that could convincingly explain to a young doctor—a failingly polite Indian resident—and a head nurse with a mixture of resentment and compassion in her eyes, why and how her young son had ended up with three broken fingers and a dislocated shoulder and a large, suspiciously hand-shaped welt on his back at the same time that *she* had suffered a black eye, a cracked molar, and significant bruising up and down both sides of her neck. What George suffered in those years (and, no doubt, in the years previous, prior to the advent of his memories) was sometimes even worse, sometimes not as bad, but always constant. Details and scenes have seeped out like tears on nights much like tonight, under circumstances much like these: George with a six-pack, the air on the deck cool and unhumid, me seated on the chaise, he perched on the top railing of the balustrade, no matter how many times his mother or I plead with him not to, me drinking nothing more intoxicating than flavored "energy water," having been secretly terrified of getting drunk for as long as I can remember.

George took up Krav Maga within months of his father's incarceration.

"Just in case he ever comes back," George said then and says frequently and says now, having shifted the topic to the asshole after turning the eye/mouth of his beer bottle to his own mouth. "Just in case. Because I'll kill him, Mike." He says it without emotion, without inflection, with the tone of a man recalling to a spouse that—as long as she's headed to the store—the larder could use a new box of pretzels. "I'll kill him. I mean it."

"I know you do." And then, adding something I often add at this point: "I'll help." Sometimes it's "Can I help?" or "If you want some help . . ." or some other variation, but tonight it's "I'll help." Declarative. Strong. Intentional.

He salutes me with the bottle. "I know you will. 'Cause you know what it's like to have a shitty childhood."

For two years in my pre-adolescence, my parents' marriage teetered on the brink of divorce, threatening to topple into that chasm on an almost daily basis. George, during this time, was my rock, and to this day insists that this relatively minor blip in my otherwise idyllic childhood somehow entitles me to equal standing with his father-beaten self, with no amount of cajoling, persuading, pleading, self-effacement, or outright insistence convincing him otherwise. All of this leading me to believe and to understand that a best friend is perhaps best defined as someone whose upbringing sucked vastly more than your own . . . and yet steadfastly contends that *your* upbringing was just as bad, if not worse. By this particular mathematics, George is my best friend, but I can never be his.

Tonight, despite the circumstances, there are and will be no further revelations about George's abused past, to wit:

"But I didn't mean to go off on the asshole again," George says. "Sorry, dude. How did I even start talking about him, anyway? Anyway, I figure you'll still be sticking it to the blue bombshell when you need the little blue pills, you know what I mean?"

One of George's more endearing traits is that he thinks he's more subtle than he actually is. Along with "dude," "you know what I mean?" is a constant in his lexicon, even though everyone *always* knows what he means.

"Yeah, I know what you mean, George." My thoughts, bifurcated, continue the conversation with George while also drifting to my last time in bed with Phil, as well—trifurcated, now—as to the *next* time I will be in bed with Phil (probably tomorrow night, as I've told her I'll be palling with George tonight), and then threaten to *quad*furcate as my cell chirps its incoming text message alert.

i wish i had gummi bears

"Dude, is the Mrs. calling?" He leans back to get the last drops of beer, precariously close to toppling over the rail. I resist the urge to shout for him to be careful—George hates being looked after, mothered, mollycoddled. "If the asshole didn't kill me," he has said many times, "real life isn't going to get it done any time soon."

"Shut up," I tell him instead. "She's not the Mrs." But I experience a pang of . . . regret? Want? Urgency? I don't know what it is. I only know that even though I promised George and myself and Phil that tonight would be a "Guys Night" and that I would be spending time with my best friend (while he would be spending time with his very, very good friend), I still feel compelled to bid George *adieu* and race to the nearest store for gummi bears.

"Dude, you are *so* pussywhipped. I swear. I swear. I bet if I pulled down your pants right now, there wouldn't even be a dick there. You're smooth like Ken, you know what I mean? She has it all locked up in her hope chest, doesn't she?"

I essay a hollow laugh, trying to show a jocular and casual contempt for his comment, but I actually am mildly horrified, wondering—for a moment, but wondering nonetheless—if George has been spying on me while I fuck Phil. For not two days ago, during an afternoon after-school session, Phil rolled on her stomach, her head poised between my legs, and took my cock in both hands, gazing at it hungrily, and said, "I love this thing. I love this fucking thing," unaware, apparently, of her double entendre. "I wish I could keep it with me all the time. Like, make it removable, you know?"

"Dude," George introduces his next sentence as I slide my phone into my pocket, "I don't get it. I mean, yeah, she's hot.

No question about it. And I guess the blue hair thing is kinda cool, but anyone can dye their hair. So what's so special about her? Why her?"

Setting aside that Phil's hair is not dyed or otherwise artificially colored in any way, finding the words that account for every level of Phil's distinction among women and, more generally, people, has been, heretofore, impossible for me, as they have yet to be invented. Not that Phil herself is impossible to describe, but rather that the intersection of the two of us—that coordinate point on the plane of space-time where the Platonic ideal of Phil-ness meets the Platonic ideal of Mike-ness—forms an indescribable nexus of feeling and thought and sensation. Explaining "Why Phil?" is like explaining "Why do babies love their mothers?" or "Why do dogs love their masters?" It just, simply, merely *is*. There is no "because."

But George will not accept—perhaps genetically or constitutionally *cannot* accept—"It just, simply, merely *is*."

"Because she believes in me," I tell George, because when a best friend asks his very, very good friend "Why her?" an answer must come forth, even if it is composed of equal parts half-truth, bare-understanding, and bullshit. "She's always believed in me."

"Is this about that freaking elevator building?"

Of course it is decidedly *not* about the elevator building; it is about young Phil's defiant "Phil!" when called "Philomel," about older Phil's curling into me at the library years later, saying, "That is *so* cool," about younger (but not-quite-as-young-as-young-Phil) standing up to our school's principal[2], but it

2. "If you don't let us put on a play and use the school's auditorium," younger-though-not-youngest-Phil pronounced, "we'll do it outside on the playground instead, and you can explain to our parents why their kids are out there at night." A child's gambit, and one that worked.

is partly at least about older-than-younger-Phil-but-younger-than-older-Phil's particular *reaction* to the elevator building, said building being my first architectural project and the impetus to my first serious conversation with Phil, who, in eighth grade, looked over my shoulder one day in the lunchroom, standing quietly for I still know not how long, studying me as I sketched in one of my endless supply of spiral-top-bound notebooks. I had roughed out the basic structure of a building when I sensed some hovering presence and, glancing over my shoulder, saw her standing there. To be more accurate, I saw her hair before seeing Phil herself, a flash of dark, brilliant sapphire bursting into my field of vision before I could recognize her face.

"You're really good," she said authoritatively, as if she had settled a debate on the subject. "What is it?" she asked, apparently unaware that that question put the lie to "You're really good."

"It's just a building idea I had," I mumbled.

She slid next to me on the bench, and for the first time, I was close enough to touch her, close enough to smell her—she was redolent of freesia and lilacs and the over-tang of curry, it being lunch, after all, and Phil's mother being a parent who habitually packed leftovers for her child, having this day chosen Indian take-out—and the world froze for the instant it took for me to register her nearness, her scents, the soft wave of her oceanic mane.

"What are these arrows for?" Pointing to my notebook.

Then my mouth became the Sahara (again . . . or for the first time?) and I could not bear to speak, but speak I did, in a voice low and contrite: "Elevators."

She lingered a moment on the drawing, studying it like an unearthed artifact that lacked context or knowable creator, even though I was sitting right there, right next to her, close enough that the slightest move on my part (or hers) would cause my be-jeaned thigh to touch her be-skirted one. She pondered the drawing, brushing a stray fallen lock of blue hair back over her left ear.

"The whole building," she said slowly, "is made of elevators." She did not pose it as a question, the way most people did, nor as a statement of incredulity. She simply said it. Slowly.

"Well, yeah. The idea is that—"

"—each room can go up or down by itself." She licked her lips and pulled the drawing towards herself, reaching across me, brushing my t-shirted chest with one bare arm. "That is *so* cool!"

That is so *cool* being the same sentiment offered years later when we, older, paired, sprawled together, intertwined on a sofa in the library as I paged through a later sketchbook, she stopping me to say, "Wow" and then "That is *so* cool!" pointing this time not at the elevator building, but rather at something else, something newer. "That would be so cool," she went on/will go on, causing me to respond, "It's not really practical," which further caused/will cause her to say, "Who cares? It's cool. It's fun. It's new. I love it. You have to build it someday and I'll live there with you," a pledge of prolonged and possibly lifelong fidelity that somehow eluded me at the time, so taken unawares was I by her love of the concept I loved so dearly.

In the eighth-grade moment, however, that library moment and its pledge still lingered and loitered in the future, waiting for me and for her, so at the lunch table I simply shrugged, the motion lost on her as she gazed at the elevator building, her lips now shining from her self-administered moistening. "Most people think it's stupid," I told her. "They're all like, 'What if there's a room above you that wants to come down? Or one below you that—'"

"They're idiots, then," she interrupted both me and the

multiple past observers. “That’s not the point of it. It’s all about motion and adjusting and freedom.” She swiveled in her seat to look at me, and for the first time ever I was not only correctly positioned, but also within kissing-range of those lips. I had, to date, kissed exactly two girls in the way one kisses girls not related, and in that moment—as Phil looked at me from kissing distance and, in fourteen words divided into two sentences, justified to me the sense and sensibility of my own elevator building in a way that I could never explain or communicate to others—I was prepared to move forward—to *lunge*, if necessary—and make her my third time’s the charm, when *he* approached from the corner of my eye, transfiguring Phil’s expression into one of such pure joy that, had I been foolish enough—and I wasn’t—to hallucinate myself as the cause of that joy, I might have been happy for days or even weeks on the strength of that joy alone.

“It’s a great idea. I believe in you,” she said, rising from the bench to take *his* hand, while her other hand patted me briefly on the shoulder, forming for an instant a chain wherein she stood interposed between *him* and me, the only time she would ever stand thus until the day years hence of the charity event and the red-then-teal dress, when she would stand interleaved between George and *him* and me, like a deck of cards cut and stacked for shuffling.

I believe in you, she had said. She had not said that she believed in the *idea* of the elevator building. She believed, rather, in the architect of the idea.

“‘The architect of the idea,’” George quotes, gouging the air with his fingers at the same time. “Who talks like that?”

“Shut up.”

He sighs and eyes the six-pack, which is now more a three-and-three-pack, being comprised of equal parts empty and full bottles. George is no snob, no putter-on of airs, but he drinks only Stella Artois for the simple reason that it is the first beer he ever drank. He liked it. Following that, he drank—on one occasion—three swallows of Budweiser, pronounced it swill, and decided that clearly he had a palate designed for only one beer, that being his beloved and favored Stella; no amount of cajoling could persuade him otherwise, nor even persuade him to sample another brew, regardless of cost, country of origin, exciting bottle technology[3], or bevy of scantily-clad models in its commercial. George was a one-beer man ("one-beer" in the sense of one *brand* of beer, of course, as his ready consumption of three out of six of his current six-pack and subsequent (and current) eyeing of a fourth would indicate).

"No one else ever believed."

"I believe you'll be an architect."

I hesitate. Yes, George does believe this. While he believes it *now*, in the here-and-now moment in the early days of our senior year of high school, and he will continue to believe it a year from now, when we stand together at the charity event, watching *him* dance with Phil in a dress that is red and a dress that is teal, he never believed it *then*, in the days of our shared childhood, when I dreamed the elevator building and the building that spun like a top, and the housing development wherein each house represented a sign of the Chinese Zodiac.

Phil believed in them all because she believed in me, for reasons I have never understood and never sought to clarify. It never seemed to matter *why* she believed, if her belief was some sort of advanced reciprocal of my belief in her acting, if it was innate to her, if it was foolish or not; it mattered only that she

3. Such as the newest beer bottle technology, in which the glass itself gradually turns green as one drinks the beer, as a reminder to recycle the eventually empty (and wholly green) empty.

did believe. And at this moment in time—this moment of now, of the present tense—Phil is mine, and her belief is mine, too.

"Can I tell you something?" I tell George—tell, not ask, because despite the question mark, it isn't really a question; it's a prelude to a statement. "I've been having . . . I've been having this weird sensation lately. Like remembering a dream, but I know I never dreamed it . . . I dreamed we were at a dance . . . Phil was with *him*."

"Dude, that's not a dream; that was junior prom. You know what I mean?"

And I do, and it was. But this dance is not junior prom; Phil is not sixteen-almost-seventeen. She is older. I am older. *He* is older.

"My thoughts have been weird lately. Like, I'm talking to you normally, but my thoughts are all complicated and wound up around themselves."

"That's because you're a complicated, wound up around yourself kinda guy, Mikey."

I laugh.

George shrugs off my laughter, as though my acceptance of his premise is not required to make it true.

"You let yourself get complicated," he tells me. "It's like with Phil: You can't just be in a relationship. You have to obsess over it. You have to wallow in it."

"Are you saying I shouldn't be with her?"

"I'm not saying anything. I'm just saying . . . Dude, you're complicated because you made the decision to be complicated."

"I don't know if that's true."

"Can I tell *you* something?" he asks, and because George is my best friend and believes I am his, he is truly asking, ready to say nothing in the—unlikely, nigh-impossible—instance that I would say, "No, George, you may not tell me something."

"Go ahead."

Time passes as George gathers his thoughts, conflict and struggle etched in every line of his face.

"I've never told you this before," he says. "I've never told anyone. I don't know why I'm telling you now."

"Go ahead."

He waves me off. "Nah. Fuck it."

"George." I am uncertain how to react. Do I force him to tell me? Or do I accede to his wishes and allow him to drift back into secrecy? Which would a best friend do? If I were truly George's best friend, I realize guiltily, I would know.

"I have three secrets," George tells me. "I'll tell you the first two, but I'll never tell you the third."

It sounds vaguely familiar to me, as though he or someone else has said this to me in the past.

"Tell me, George."

"Just one of the two for now," he says. "Just one." He pulls at his bottle for a protracted moment, longer than it takes to drain the last of the beer within, stalling.

Then he sets the bottle down and, without meeting my eyes, staring up at the starless sky, says, "When I was six, I woke up one night. Late in the night. Early in the morning. Same thing, you know what I mean? I woke up because I'd heard a noise. Or maybe I dreamed that I heard a noise. I don't know."

"You were afraid someone was breaking into the house."

He laughs. "No. I was never afraid of that. The asshole was already in the house—why would I be afraid of someone breaking in?"

I should have known that, understood it, intuited it.

"But I heard something or thought I heard something or dreamed I heard something, and I woke up, thinking of the asshole, of course, positive that it was him, that he was hurting

Mom again. And I don't know—he was always hurting Mom, always hurting me, and, like, I not only never did anything about it, but I also never even thought of doing anything about it. And that night, that morning, wasn't any different, not really, because I didn't think about it at all. I just got up out of bed and went into the kitchen and the next thing I knew, I was standing outside my parents' bedroom, holding the big carving knife we used for Thanksgiving turkey. And it was dead quiet there, except for my own breathing, so I held my breath, and the knife—I was six, man, you know what I mean?—the knife looked like a fucking machete in my hands. I couldn't hear anything at all. He wasn't hitting her. He wasn't doing anything. She didn't need me to protect her.

"But I opened the door anyway. I was quiet. I think it took five minutes to open that door, turning the knob slowly so it wouldn't make any noise, easing the door open, you know what I mean? And it was dark in there and I slipped in and I went to the asshole's side of the bed. He was breathing deep and slow, lying on his back, and Mom was curled up next to him, and if you looked at them like that, man, you'd think they were normal and regular and happy, you know what I mean? And I think maybe they were, like that. Happy, I mean. I think when they were asleep, they were like everyone else in the world. Does that make any sense?"

I nod, even though he isn't looking at me.

"And I stood there, and I held the knife about an inch away from his neck. The artery, right here, what's it called?" He means the carotid, but I can say nothing in this moment, and he goes on: "Just about an inch. I could have sliced right through him, right into him, and he would have bled out pretty fast. I knew that. Even then. All those movies he used to let me watch . . . I knew." He shakes his head, still not looking at me. "And then I went and I snuck out and I closed the door and I put the knife back and I went to bed like nothing had happened. Fell right asleep."

"You were scared to act," I say, and in the pause that follows, I realize that perhaps I do not know George as well as I'd thought, for he says nothing for the length of the pause, then shakes his head again and looks at me, his eyes troubled, his expression writ with shame and guilt and pain.

"I wasn't afraid. I wasn't afraid of anything, man. Still not, you know what I mean? I wasn't afraid. It's just that . . . It's just that I realized, standing there, I realized that I loved him." George shivers. "After all that shit and all the shit I knew would come, I still loved him. You know what I mean?"

For the first time in our friendship, I do not know what he means.

George eyes the fourth bottle of Stella and leans down, the fingers of one hand outstretched towards the condensation-beaded glass.

Does he take it or change his mind at the last minute? Does he drink that bottle and then the next and the next? Does he stop at three? Or four? Or five?

I don't know. I know only that—my worst fears to the contrary—he does not fall, either forwards to land on the deck or—worse—backwards to plunge a story to the concrete patio below. I know this because I know that—a year from now—George, no worse for wear, will attend the Wallace-Barth School charity ball with me and drink a glass of half-lemonade, half-diet Coke.

Whether he drinks that fourth beer or fifth or sixth, though, I do not know. I don't care, either. This part is over.

****

At home, my parents watch television while my younger brother practices his harmonica/flute/trombone/piano, badgering me to listen as he plays Dylan/Beethoven/Sousa/Brahms. I listen for longer than it takes to produce a sentence saying so, but the experience is unmemorable, leaving no sensory impressions to speak of.

There's nothing to report.

My brother finishes with a flourish and I applaud and he says something endearingly funny, but in no way reminiscent of a younger sibling on a sitcom.

I go to my room, which has in it my things, my belongings. It has a bed—where I sleep and masturbate—and a dresser—where I store my clothes, with a lamp and a framed picture of Phil on top—and a desk—where I do my homework and also, occasionally, masturbate while watching Internet pornography on my laptop—and a bookshelf that I cannot, for some reason, describe.

I lie on my bed and I wonder what is happening to me.

And then the page turns.

CHAPTER 3

"The page turns" being a convenient metaphor for time passing, of course, and nothing more dramatic than that.

In the morning, my thoughts are still strangely narrative, more as though I am reciting them and less as though I am thinking them. It recalls to me a time when I was younger and had a particular thought-at-the-time (by me, as I told no one else) juvenile affliction that caused me to narrate internally my own life's story. I would speak to a friend, a parent, a teacher, a stranger, and then add a dialogue tag in my mind: he said, he commented, he offered, etc., always in the third person, as though some secondary editorial personality had taken up residence inside my head like a hermit crab seeking shelter in a new shell without realizing—or, indeed, caring—that another hermit crab already called this particular shell home.

He walked down the school corridor, I would think while walking down the school corridor, *dodging his fellow students while on his way to science class*, dodging my fellow students while on my way to science class. When I said, "Good morning" to my mother, I thought, *he said* at the end of it.

This was not a deliberate affectation, nor was it a conscious decision on my part. The self-narration blossomed into my life like a flower that does not bother to open its petals over time, but rather explodes into full bloom in the space of an instant—one moment there is a closed bud, the next a fan of widespread petals, the stamen and pistils proudly erect.[4] This flower of madness had erupted into my life just so. I did not *want* to narrate my life internally, imagining quotation marks around the words of my friends, teachers, parents, enemies, judiciously adding dialogue tags where necessary, plotting out and describing every moment of my day: *He brushed his teeth, white foam spilling from between his lips as though he'd bitten into a soapy sponge* and *He lay in bed, tossing and turning, as unable to sleep as a man who expects surgery in the morning.* (Bad enough I had a storyteller living in my skull—but he/she/it was a bad enough writer, too!) I could find no way to prevent this narration, as if the words in my head had been hijacked, brainwashed, and then put to uses I'd never intended.

After some months of this, I considered speaking to my parents, but found that avenue blocked by a series of walls, each higher than the other.

First Wall: How to describe this to my parents? I imagined myself beginning with "There's a narrator in my head," which statement triggering gasps of shock, looks of alarm, and cries of "You hear voices in your head?" followed, no doubt, by a visit to a psychiatrist and the attendant drama. Even at that young age, I knew that I would not be able to convince a psychiatrist that the voice in my head was merely annoying, not dangerous.

4. Given that the affliction described herein occurred roughly at the age of twelve, Mike's (unconscious?) blatant allusion to both male and female genitalia is understandable, if not entirely accurate or forgivable.

Second Wall: The idea that, perhaps, the voice in my head *was* dangerous, or, more accurately, would *become* dangerous as time went on. Perhaps this was how schizophrenia started—with harmless babble that later evolved into full-blown lunacy. What I thought was a flower in full bloom was, in truth, a bud that had yet to open. If I was losing my mind, I wasn't sure I wanted to know.

Third Wall: Conversely, what if this state was entirely, boringly normal and mundane? In fact, what if *everyone* had a narrator's voice nestled deep within the gray matter, a calm, reasoned (for my voice was both of these, never excitable or agitated or even mildly aroused) influence speaking its calm, reasoned voice day-in and day-out? What if, in fact, my internal voice indicated a personal flaw not by dint of its mere existence, but rather by dint of the lateness of its unveiling? What if I sat down with my parents to tell them about this new side-effect in my brain and they responded, in hushed tones of terror, "You mean . . . You've been going along all these years *without* your internal narrator?"

There was no Fourth Wall, but none was needed. The Third Wall frightened me and intrigued me more than the others; it was the most difficult to climb. As a child, I was something of a daydreamer, given to disappearing into my own thoughts for extended periods, usually fantasizing rigid Doric columns and enormous barrel vaults and innovative uses for geodesic domes and the artistry of the fine crenellations at the tops of towers and keeps, only to realize later that time had passed, the world had moved on, things had *happened*, and I was completely unaware. Was it possible that—somehow—I had tuned out one day while someone explained about the narrative voice? Was it possible that it required no explanation, that I was defective in that I felt the voice alien (a squatting hermit crab . . .) while the rest of the world peacefully coexisted with its narrators with no stress, strain, or disturbance?

Ultimately, after many thousands of unwritten words of narration (enough to publish half a dozen lengthy—though interminably boring, to be sure—novels), the cure for this particularly harmless yet undeniably strange disorder revealed itself as—as is the case with so many childhood maladies—mortal embarrassment.

School had ended. The community pool, a chaos of kids and families, was the only relief from the heat for those who could not abide the idea of cooping up all summer long in-air-conditioned-side. The first day the pool was open, I went with George, who dove in immediately. I shucked off my flip-flops—*He shucked off his flip-flops*—and ran to the pool—*and ran to the pool*—as George shouted, "What are you waiting for?" already splashing and cool and relieved.

"'Here I come!' he yelled," I yelled as I leapt feet-first into the packed deep end of the pool.

Out loud. My internal narrator, my private verbal shadow, had just spoken *out loud.* In the air. To the world.

I had just enough time to contemplate this breach of etiquette, propriety, and possibly sanity before I hit the water, submerged entirely, the whole world gone cold, wet, and roaringly silent. I sank into the water, praying that the concrete bottom of the pool would split open, the water cascading down, funneling deep beneath the earth's surface, taking me with it, bearing me and my shame and my voice to the center of the earth, where I would dissolve into a greasy puff of smoke from the great heat of the magma core.

Instead, the pool stayed stubbornly intact and I rose with the fizz of my plunge, broke the surface for breath, rising into the same chaos of kids and parents that had greeted my leap and my yell.

George stroked his way over to me. "Dude! You totally nailed that bald guy with your splash! It was awesome."

I looked around. No one had noticed. No one had heard me over the raucous sounds of a community at play.

But that moment of shame still stuck in me, like a dart. Apparently, the shock of it had killed the narrator's voice, for I never heard it again, and now this/that part of the story is over.

****

While my current predicament is not the same as that which plagued me as a child, it is similar enough that I wonder if some similar humiliation might not rescue me. George thinks my "complicated, wound up" thoughts are merely a consequence of my "complicated, wound up" personality, but I am not so sure.

Something is happening.

Something is coming.

I feel it.

It's a weekend (it would have to be—hence George's drinking last night; I wouldn't stay up and he wouldn't drink if it was a school night, would I/he?), so I go to find my brother, mostly to determine if my "complicated, wound up" thoughts have made their way to my speech. My conversation with George last night employed the brief, perfunctory syllables of men and friends, so it is not an adequate test. When I find my brother at his computer, I am relieved to hear myself say, "Hey, bro, what's up?" in the usual casual, affectedly unaffected tones of late-teenage-dom.

My external dialogue is normal and natural. Only my internal monologue suffers from a peculiar variation of stiltedness, formality, periphrasis.

Still, it's good to reconnect with my younger brother,

from whom I've been distant lately, not intentionally, but rather as a natural, unforeseen, and regrettable side effect of spending so much time with Phil. As it turns out, he has a crush of the adorable/instructive/parallel type vis-à-vis my previous-crush-now-relationship with Phil, a crush about which I am able to offer him advice of both the brotherly and manly sort, thereby showing that I am a sympathetic, good-hearted person. In a word: Likable. Likability being of prime importance, of course, mattering more than curiosity or interest or surprise or passion.

But let us not forget: This is a story about Phil and a story about me and, occasionally, a story about Phil and me.

My brother thanks me by saying something ironic and insightful that bears on both my current relationship with Phil and my future with her. I thank him in return and then brave a particularly hot day (living, as I do, in a desert city, the heat always falls somewhere in the spectrum of *brutal* to *unbearable*, though rarely humid) to walk to the subway. I live only four stops from Phil's house—I spend the time on the train thinking about the future. In my dream/vision/hallucination of the future, I saw Phil reunited with *him*, molded to him on the dance floor at a charity function of some sort. I cannot shake this image, cannot write it off as the useless psychic flotsam and jetsam of a night's sleep. George thinks it is simply a sub/unconscious (he is unsure which is the correct term, psychoanalytically speaking) fear of losing Phil.

"But," he went on, speaking last night, retroactively, in that blank caesura that followed his reaching for a potential fourth Stella Artois and my return home last night, "the thing that I learned in Psych last year is that in a dream, *every character is you*. So, you weren't really dreaming about *him* taking Phil away from you. You were dreaming about losing *yourself* to some *other* aspect of yourself, you know what I mean?" This last followed by a smug chuckle, a raised eyebrow, and a curt nod in my direction, as if to say, "Cool, huh?" after which George said—just in case—"Cool, huh?"

"George," I told him, "that's crap."

Because I am convinced that what I saw was both more and less than a dream. I am convinced it was a true vision of the future, my future and Phil's.

"The future is crap," George rejoindered. "The future is easy."

George's future has already been written: He's had Marine recruitment brochures stacked and fanned on every available surface in his bedroom since we were thirteen, his life's sole goal and purpose to be a jarhead and protect the people who need protecting, precisely the same way he was *not* protected as a child. Thus, for George, the future is, indeed, easy. For those of us unsure as to what the future holds—save for a tantalizing, depressing glimpse—the future is sloppy, imperfect, and rife with peril, engendering in any perfectly rational person's sub/unconscious (I, too, am unsure) a vision (for let's call it that—it was *not* a dream) stacked high with uncertainty and fear and loss.

Which makes me think of videotapes.

My parents have a stash of them in a cabinet next to the flatscreen TV in what my father quite seriously calls "the media room."[5] Within this cabinet lurk mostly unlabeled tapes, black endless rows of them, containing family events and TV programs recorded over a ten-to-fifteen year period, all of them—according to my father—worth keeping, but apparently not worth

5. The term "media room" always seemed overblown to Mike, and had for years conjured images of his father standing at a podium, fielding reporters' questions about his day at work, what he would like for dinner, and whether or not he plans to watch the game on ESPN that night.

cataloging, labeling, and/or converting to digital. I once blew dust off the top of the ancient VCR (a useless appendix next to the Red-Ray player) and popped one in, and this is where my vision attaches to this apparent digression, which is no digression at all, but rather a crucial explanation.

The tape I'd chosen had not been wholly rewound before its re-boxing, having been left poised fourteen minutes in, frozen in that moment in time. Upon hitting "Play" on the remote, I observed a moment fourteen minutes in, someone picking up mid-syllable as if no time at all had passed, as if he had not been in the cabinet all this time. All those years accordioned into milliseconds as the VCR ground to life. I immediately rewound, of course, and proceeded to watch from the beginning, but this, I now realize, was my vision: My vision was like a tape left partway into the story, giving a momentary peek at what-is-to-come before being rewound to the beginning.

In that case, then, who has rewound the tape?

There is no eating allowed on the subway, but that does not stop a child from walking past me, holding an ice cream cone dripping chocolate syrup. I recall the strong, gagging scent of chocolate syrup from my vision, and the child turns to me just then, grinning, teeth slick with chocolate, and the sight of it makes me ill, makes me want to get away, cut away, go away.

CHAPTER 4

When I arrive—later, safely, chocolate-syrup-less—at Phil's house, the first thing I notice is that Phil's mother's car is not in the driveway, which means that Phil and I will fuck.

****

And fuck we do. Have. Did.

Lying in her bed again, wrapped in the history-made sheets, the ceiling fan buzzing above, raising gooseflesh on Phil's exposed, sweat-cooling shoulder, I cannot imagine that Phil will ever *not* be with me, that she will ever be with *him* again, molded to *him*, red dress or teal dress, whichever dress. I want to ask her if that is even possible; we've never spoken of *him*, not once, and I want to ask her if she would ever want to go back to *him*, but as I open my mouth, only a gasp escapes, for Phil has just wrapped her undercover fingers around me, still firm (though not fully erect) and sensitive from our first fuck of the day.

"I really like your dick," she says, casual, in the tone of

voice she uses to ask if I want garlic or plain naan when we order Indian.

"Do you have to call it that?" Bawdiness and lust have always seemed clothes best suited to the male form—women can wear them, but, like neckties, they seem wrong somehow.

She laughs. "I'm sorry, did I offend your delicate sensibilities? How about, 'I like your penis?' Is that better?"

And it's my turn to laugh. "No, no, that's not what I meant. It's just the word 'dick.' I don't know—I've never liked it. Call it something else."

"Like what?"

"Prick."

"No."

"Why not? It sounds like dick."

Her eyes, stormy with confused discomfort, stare at me. "I don't like that word. It means too much."

"Too much. Right. Whatever. So pick something else."

"Cock?"

"That's fine," I tell her. Anything to file her strange aversion to the word "prick" into the past.

She squeezes my member lightly, as if making a point. "Why is cock OK, but dick isn't? They're practically the same word."

"I don't know. It sounds harder.[6] Or something," I recover quickly into her laughter. "Stop it. I don't know."

"You'd think someone in your position," she said, "wouldn't

6. "Cock" is the older and, therefore perhaps, more primal of the two colloquial terms for "penis" in question, such usage dating back to 1618 and having originally developed from the sense of a man who strutted about like a rooster, which could account for Mike's preference for this term, as it echoes of masculine pride. As compared to "dick," of more relatively recent vintage, having come to refer to male genitalia as recently as the 1890s, evolving from its usage for "everyman" (to wit: "every Tom, Dick, and Harry"), and therefore savoring as a more generic masculine term than the more aggressive "cock," with its hard, double "k" sounds.

care what I call it, so long as I keep letting you use it. Maybe if you had a forced fast, you'd reconsider your hardline stance on cock-naming."

"Why do you hate me?" I joke.

"I don't hate you," she says, releasing my dick (cock!) so that she can push herself up on her elbows and match her eyes to mine. "I don't. I—"

"I know you don't. It was a joke."

She has something more to say—the words swim in her gaze—but she flops back on her pillow, a lighter blue than her own hair. "You didn't bring me gummi bears last night."

Caught off-guard, my gears grinding at the change of topic and the downshifting of emotion, I blurt out, "You didn't ask for them."

"You dummy. I texted you."

"You just said you wanted them. You didn't say you wanted *me* to *bring* them to you."

"Oh, I see. So when you say, 'I'm horny,' you're just imparting information. I'm not supposed to act on it or anything." This is accompanied by a peck on the cheek to mitigate the sting. "Make it up to me; read to me." She points to the shelf.

"Come on, Phil. You *know* how to read. This is for kids."

"I like it. And I like your voice."

"I'll feel like an idiot. They're little kid books."

"They're *classics*."

"Please. They're books for *kids*. They're only classics because they don't *totally* suck and aren't *completely* boring, just *mostly* boring."

She pouts.

"Don't do that. I can't resist when you pout, and I really don't want to read to you."

"Why? You got something better to do today?"

I fling back the covers, unveiling her from blue-maned head to blue-landing-stripped pubis to daintily-silver-painted toenails. "Yeah, you could say that."

She drags the quilt back over herself. "The fan makes me cold. So, you'll fuck me, but you won't read to me? Is that it?"

I'm not quite sure how we have come to this particular impasse. "Reading to you is something a parent does. Fucking, normally, isn't. Let's keep them separate."

She turns to her side. At times—like this one—I can't tell if she is acting out premeditated scenes or being genuine. She is either a fantastic actress or an enigma. Or both.[7] At times—like, again, this one—I can't help but to think back to our first time in bed, where my inability to read to her first exposed itself, even as we exposed ourselves to each other. I was certain on that day and in those moments that she came at our inaugural fucking. "Certain" in this instance equaling something in the area of 99.99999 percent.

"Certainty" is not certain. She is turned away from me. She could be angry. She could be acting.[8]

"Besides," I tell her, "I can't stay all day. I mean, I would love to stay in bed with you all day, but I have to finish my early entrance applications this weekend plus I have a shift at the pool. So I'm doing that all night tonight and all day tomorrow, you know? I just don't want to waste time reading to you."

After which ensues a tirade from Phil on the topic of "waste," to wit: How something *she* wants to do is considered a "waste," but when I want to, say, fuck all afternoon, that is *not* considered a waste. Which comment prompts me to point

7. Since Phil actually *is* a fantastic actress and an enigma, "both" seems to be the most likely option.

8. Or, again: Both.

out—accurately—that fucking is, in fact, something she enjoys[9] as much as I do, so since we enjoy it equally, why not stick to *that* activity, as opposed to one only enjoyed by one of us? Which further causes me to wonder if she *does*, in fact, enjoy fucking as much as I do, her sexual aggression and seeming insatiability both fakable and therefore not, perhaps, to the contrary, though I cannot bring myself to voice this suspicion, lest one of two fears (1. that she is, in fact, faking her sexual enthusiasm/enjoyment/response and I am a fool, and/or 2. that she is *not* faking, but that my accusation thereof would enrage her further) come true, forcing me, argument-wise, to fall back on my only voiceable, though weak, defense, that of "I am not your parent." Even in that case, I hold back, as what I really want to say is, "I am not your father," but I know that such a statement would be met with some variation on, "No shit, Sherlock—my father is dead."

After the argument and a vigorous bout of make-up sex so intense and unrestrained that I begin to wonder if Phil deliberately provoked the fight (or if I did, whether sub- or unconsciously), I leave as soon as Phil's mom comes home; she greets me warmly in the vestibule with a kiss on the cheek, commenting not at all on my disheveled hair or the obvious scent of sex that I will carry with me like a battle standard onto the subway. Phil's mom is Phil in fast-forward (to borrow my own videotape metaphor), but with light brown hair, hazel eyes, and a figure so similar to her daughter's that I cannot help but wonder how well I, by dint of simple extrapolation and interpolation, know that body, much as one can discern the layout of multiple apartments in the same building simply by living in one of them. How familiar would her body be to my touch?

9. At least to an accuracy of 0.00001%. Close enough, perhaps?

How familiar her responses to that touch? (I confess here that I dreamed—only once—of slipping into Phil's house late one night, only to become disoriented in the dark and wind up slipping first into Phil's mom's bedroom and then her bed and then her, the sexual experience unremarkable not for its pleasure, but rather for its indistinctness from sex with Phil, until a stray shaft of moonlight through the window falls on Mom's non-blue hair. I awoke from this dream enormously aroused, enormously ashamed, and simply enormous, and it flashes through my mind like guilt every time I see Phil's mom.)

"Not staying for dinner?" she asks.

"No, sorry. I have to work on college apps."

She opens her mouth to say something, then thinks better of it and continues on her way to the kitchen as Phil—dressed in only an extra-large WB t-shirt like a caftan—comes to the front door to bid me goodbye, pecking me chastely on the lips like a sister or mother. "Have fun with those college apps," she says, her tone dark and fathomless.

CHAPTER 5

My parents are pleased to see me home so early on a Saturday night, pleased indeed to see me at all on a Saturday, as I typically spend Saturdays/Sunday morns in Phil's house, in her bed, in etc. I remind them about the applications and they nod sagely/parentally/serenely.

My parents are not quirky. They are not ex-hippies or ex-druggies or ex-anythings, really, other than ex-teenagers and ex-twentysomethings and (in my dad's case) an ex-thirtysomething (his fortieth birthday being six weeks ago; he did not celebrate with a new car or an affair or a hair piece or a "mancation" with his buddies from work). They do not have strange or consuming hobbies: There is no room in our house set aside for a massive model train garden, nor for a music studio, nor for an easel and palette. My parents are, quite possibly, the world's most *average* parents. They do not get drunk, but they are also not teetotalers. They give me no curfew, but they expect to know where I am. They have never struck me or my brother, but they are not afraid of discipline. My mother does not experiment with strange recipes or subject my brother and me to the whims of some sort of weekly/monthly/annual enrollment in a never-ending series of clubs and/or causes. My father does not call me "sport," does not regale me with endless stories of his own youthful conquests in a mingled embarrassing/amusing attempt at father-son bonding. And so on. In short, there is nothing to say about my parents other than that they are my parents.

I work at the computer, shuffling the papers and applications that have sat on my desk in a stack for weeks now, semi-organized by desirous school and ease of application. For a moment, I consider the state university, but I discard the notion with a swiftness I hope Phil will never be able to sense. She is convinced that the state university is in her future, so I must, perforce, at least consider it, but my consideration is so fleeting that it makes me wonder if Phil would deem that fleetness in direct proportion to my caring for her, which it most definitely is not—I just can't see myself going to State.

I find my letters of recommendation, sealed in envelopes stamped with the now-familiar WB logo. Phil and I (and George, of course—and *he*, of course) attend the Wallace-Barth School: The WB. The rumor mill insists that, due to lower enrollment for the past eight years, The WB is fated to merge soon with another local private school—one that is smaller and less historically prestigious but renowned for its cutting edge educational philosophy and award-winning teaching staff—in order to appeal to a new demographic of younger parents, who want a stronger, hipper school, the combined juggernaut to be dubbed Consolidated Wallace, or The CW. This rumor bothers me only slightly, in that if it comes to pass, my *alma mater* will, in effect, vanish, leaving me with a diploma from a school that no longer exists save for the actual physical buildings, which are attractive and functional, but in no wise exceptional or memorable in senses historical or architectural.

I work on the apps and essays until dinner, which I eat with my family at the kitchen table, listening to my brother describe a series of humorous anecdotes about his best friend/female crush/pet turtle. After dinner, it's back to the apps, interrupted only when my cell chirps a text alarm at me.

> its raining out - come snuggle w/me
> & listen 2 the rain

Phil, of course. She loves listening to the rain on the rooftop, loves lying in a dark bed while the wet timpani lullabies her; the harder the rain, the better for the contrast of nature's fury with the safety of shelter and—she has told me, best of all—a warm, strong body to curl into. Rain being so rare in the desert—and fleeting when it comes at all—she has few opportunities to bask in this particular sensory indulgence.

I have been so occupied by the apps that I haven't noticed the rain, which, now that I turn to the window, is sheeting down the panes in torrents, the tattoo of it on the roof a not-unpleasant muffled roar.

I ignore the text, as I ignored the implicit request for gummis last night, and plunge back into my paperwork.

Later, the evening made even more tenebrous by the rain clouds, I collapse in bed earlier than usual, wanting only to sleep and to think no more about college until I actually graduate, questioning at this point why I would even want to attend college, why *anyone* would want to attend college, thinking that, perhaps, it would be best if no one ever went to college, if the world just didn't need it, if we could somehow survive without it, life would maybe, possibly, be somehow perfect.

After a while, I struggle up from bed, hungry and cranky and slightly headachy. The hallway outside my bedroom is now made of ice: walls, floor, ceiling. All ice. Strangely, I'm not cold, though I'm wearing only shorts and a t-shirt, my breath pluming from me in the usual white puffs, a detail somehow always noticed in the cold. In the background, someone plays what sounds like an electric cello, a woman accompanying it *a contralto*: Hey can you peel shrimp? Oh, yeah, baby, gotta peel the shrimp.

At the end of the hallway, where there should be an archway leading to the kitchen, I find only a wooden door, set flawlessly into the surrounding ice, as if it grew there naturally, hingeless and stout. When I grasp the doorknob, a voice says, Not on the first date!

Oh, I say. I reach for the doorknob again.

NO! the voice shouts.

Why not? I whine, quite against my will.

Are you wearing a condom?

I explore my pockets, coming up only with a small cup-shaped piece of flexible plastic. All I have is a diaphragm, I tell the door.

That'll have to do. Put it in your mouth. And once I do so, the door says, Okay, and there is no further protest as I turn the knob. The door vanishes, showing not the kitchen, but rather an extended corridor beyond, this one hewn of wood, constructed askew and atilt, such that my left foot treads below my right, forcing me to walk at an angle. From nowhere, a man's voice sounds out: But we weren't characters. And none of it made any sense. And, truthfully, that drove me a little bit crazy.

I wonder at the mad architect who built this place, ice-corridored, crazy-angled.

The tilted, helter-skelter corridor opens into a large chamber, thankfully square and true, panelled in oak, carpeted lushly. A fire roars in the fireplace, and the mantlepiece seems conspicuously empty, as if it is waiting for something or somethings to stand upon it, and has yet to understand that this will never happen, or to learn to live with the disappointment of its sad lack. Supine next to the fireplace, a man wears jeans, battered black leather dress shoes, a shirt the color of old red wine in a dusty bottle, and a black jacket. Around his neck, a lanyard dangles, a plastic name badge winking in the firelight at its terminus.[10] I approach him quietly, soft-stepped and cautious, but as I near him, I see my caution is unnecessary—the only movement along his form comes courtesy of the flickering shadows of firelight, not from restlessness or even breath. He's dead, a fact that, for some reason, fills me with a blend of horror and ineffable sadness even though—double-checking his slack, pale face, the bland brown unshaven stubble thicker at the chin, intentionally bearded and unmustachioed—I have never seen this man before and have no idea who he is. And yet, I drop to my knees next to his body, resisting tears, fumbling for the name badge, knowing it can reveal all, but the letters are scrambled, much like the words in dreams, wherein no matter how valiant, honest, or strenuous the effort, text remains impossible to decipher, illegible to even the most literate scholar.

I was too late, I tell him. I was too late. I couldn't save you.

Hey, Mike, he says, opening his eyes, sitting up. How are you?

But—you're dead.

Not always. Remember the tale of Angia Eiphon. The tale.

10. Here "terminus" is used to mean "an end point," though expecting its architectural denotation—that of a figure of a human bust or an animal springing forth from a square pillar, used to delineate a boundary in ancient Rome—would be understandable, given Mike's professed desire to someday be an architect.

The metaphor. The allegory. The cautionary tale. She may be all of them.

Who's Angia Eiphon? I ask.

You'll need to go to sleep, he tells me. You'll need to have a dream-within-a-dream.

What sort of name is "Angia Eiphon," anyway? It sounds like something someone would dream and then find himself haunted by for years until finally exorcising it by virtue of the power of a magnanimous God, or maybe something less subtle, but more powerful. In the dream, the dreamer walks down a street not far from his house, a street that he sees everyday in his travels (to work? school? prison? who knows?), but is nonetheless configured into a strange sort of foreign byway by the machinations of Dream.

On this familiar road made unfamiliar, the dreamer happens upon a house that, in the waking world, does not exist. There is nothing sinister about this house. Understand this. Know it like you know your name. There is nothing whatsoever sinister about this house. It is not a subconscious replay of a haunted house story, nor is it a Jungian projection of an archetypal fear of the unknown, nor is it a metaphor for the dual nature of homes, as places that we feel compelled to flee and yet seek out in all our walks of life.

It's just a house.

And the dreamer walks in and moves through the house like a ghost, seeing but not touching. The memorabilia of the resident family's life might as well be a collection of alien artifacts to him. He cannot decipher the elaborately random codes, the way the knick-knacks are arranged, the way one picture stands in the center of the others, the way the couch tilts this way rather than that, one cushion in particular flattened and pushed out of shape by repeated use. Here, in these and a thousand other details, lies the entire history, personality, gestalt, of the family. All of it at his fingertips. All of it inaccessible.

And he finds himself on the back porch, the sunlight washing him down like rain. The girl is here, in a pretty sundress, her smile radiant, her hair golden and flowing, her eyes sparkling, her entire existence a cliché, which is fine because she is, after all, only a dream.

What's your name? he asks her.[11]

Angia Eiphon, she says.

He loves her. Even though he has never loved before, even though he cannot recognize the sensation of such emotion. He loves her.

He will grow up to destroy her, to turn his own dream into a nightmare.

He will do this because he has no choice.

But her name remains Angia Eiphon.

And I wake from the dream-within-a-dream, coming alive again just as the stubbled man's eyes close, and he falls back, dead. Again. And I still understand nothing.

I turn away just in time to see a new door open; a child steps into the room, wearing shorts and a t-shirt, his body a strange, vibrating disruption of the air, as though he cannot be totally present. He holds a wireless microphone in one hand. A spotlight pins him. Look, Mike! he says, then gestures with his right hand, holding the microphone aloft. Look, mic!

Look, Mike,—you don't mind if I call you Mike, do you?—I'm going to give you a glimpse, okay?

What? How do I know you're speaking? This is too— I'm having trouble— There are no quotation marks—

11. There are no quotation marks in dreams. That would be too much like condoms in pornography.

Of course not! Weren't you paying attention: There are no quotation marks in dreams. But look, Mike, it's a small glimpse, to be sure, but a glimpse nonetheless. Remember something for me, Mike. He's just a figment of his own imagination. Can you remember that?

I think so, I say, looking down at the dead-again man.

Well, don't bother. Hey! Hey, swallow that diaphragm. How do you expect to breathe without one?

Oh, yeah. Right. I swallow it with one gulp and my breathing becomes less labored, even though I had not realized until this very instant that it was labored at all. At the same moment, I recognize the child: He walked past me on the subway earlier today, with an ice cream cone. Just as I remember that moment, the microphone turns into an ice cream cone, dripping with chocolate syrup. I double over, retching at the smell of it, which fills the room, as the child smiles with chocolate-slick teeth. The diaphragm, which had been helping me to breathe a moment ago, thickens and expands inside me, no longer plastic, suddenly choking me.

Rooms don't always have one exit, Mike. And houses have many rooms. This is very architectural of me, wouldn't you say? Wouldn't you agree that this contributes to the architecture theme?

Barely able to get the words out over the catch in my throat and the reek of chocolate syrup: What are you trying to say—

The diaphragm is now something viscous and vicious, clogging my throat, and I want more than anything to vomit it out, to expel it from me for good, but nothing comes out—not even words.

I'm supposed to warn you about Inframan. But I'll tell you a secret, Mike—I *am* Inframan. So why would I warn you about myself?

It's a bolus of chocolate syrup caught in my gullet—I know this. I can taste it in the back of my throat and smell it from somewhere behind my nose.

Never . . . heard . . . of . . . him . . . I manage to choke out.

Of course not! You think I'm here to tell you things you know?

Hey, Mike!

Turning now, I witness the dead man's second resurrection—second insofar as I know—as he sits up and says, I'm going to tell you the future. I'm going to tell you what's on pages yet to be written.

The child is gone, and with him the stench of chocolate syrup and the obscuring bolus in my throat. I suck in air like a vacuum, like a man lost in the desert suckling at a canteen, heedless of water intoxication.

You will walk through the wreckage of a broken heart, the man tells me. You will need to find me—all of me. Can you remember that?

Maybe.

Well, make sure you do. It's important.

Is it?

I guess; how am I supposed to know? You think I'm making this stuff up? I'm not making this stuff up. I'm making up other stuff. I've made up other stuff. Similar stuff, but not the same. Mike, you need to understand that you're not the first Mike. You're not the first one to go through this. This has been attempted before, but unsuccessfully. He . . . he loves that.

Who's he?

Der Untermensch. The Underone. The God of Failure. Inframan.

Why do I keep smelling chocolate syrup? Where is that coming from?

He looks down, fingering his name badge. My name is scrambled, he says.

What? Looking at the badge, I see not a name, but a phrase: *Clean is my anagram.* Dream nonsense.

Look, the future is decided, but not written. The future is going to happen. And you aren't ready because you haven't finished your college apps, which you aren't capable of finishing because there's something important you don't know. Isn't this all so very ~~*Twin Peaks*~~ ~~*Lost*~~ ~~*Westworld*~~ *Twin Peaks*?

I DON'T UNDERSTAND!

Don't have a hissy fit, Mike, he admonishes me. After all, it's only your life, he says as the ringing of my phone wakes me up.

****

"Goddamnit!" I roll over, stretching out for the phone on the nightstand, my rage an inchoate thing, a fetus of anger that threatens to rapidly gestate into an immediate and explosive birth. "Goddamn!"

I was close to understanding something, in the dream. Somehow the man was beginning to make sense, as if the videotape had just finished rewinding and I could press "Play" and the world would begin to generate the necessary context for me to understand something, anything at all. But instead, I'm snatching up my cell—Phil's Caller ID—flipping it open to growl "What?" in the angriest tone I've ever used with her, so livid, so alive with rage that I cannot stop myself from ejaculating all my ire into the phone and up to a satellite and back down to earth and into her phone and out of her phone and into her, causing her to hesitate just long enough that I know she's hung up on me before she says, "I—" and stops, then catches her breath, then says it again, then sucks in another breath and says, without heat, without anger, without passion, almost weary, "Fuck you, Michael. I was calling to apologize."

"I'm sorry," I tell her, not entirely aware of how I—the apologizee—have become the apologizer in the space of mere words. "I was asleep. I had a weird dream—"

"I don't— Look, I don't want to fight, OK? I'm sorry I woke you up."

"Accepted. There, apology accepted." Trying my best to unring the bell I rang with my furious "What?"

"That's not what I'm calling to apologize about, asshole."

The idea of waking me up to apologize for waking me up suddenly seems enormously sensible in the wake of my dream, even though I know that's not the case. "Why do you hate me?" I fall back on our favorite back-and-forth bit of banter.

"I don't hate you," she automatically assures me. "I— I just . . ." Her breath trembles along the digital connection between us, captured in perfect fidelity by her very expensive cell, communicated and interpreted in similarly perfect fidelity by my equally expensive cell, and I realize I am not really hearing Phil—I'm hearing a copy of Phil.

"I just wanted . . . I've been thinking. Ever since you left. I've been thinking and thinking, and I keep thinking about that time we were in my bed—that early time, back right before school started, and I told you I thought . . . I told you I thought I was falling in love with you."

And we went no further, save for my response, my tepid volley back to her. Telling her I thought I was equally in mid-air, mid-plunge, was the easiest thing I'd ever done. We were face-to-face, body-to-body, lost in an oxytocin haze, not separated by distance as now, speaking *to* each other but hearing only digital reproductions. Poised in the liminal space between love and not-love—frozen in zero-gravity free-fall betwixt the two, I could justify collapsing in either direction, falling on either side of the divide.

"And now I think that was a mistake," her simulacrum goes on. "I feel like it was wrong of me. Like I was putting pressure on you. I shouldn't have said anything. I'm sorry I said it because then you felt like you had to say it."

"That's not why I said it," I tell Phil, knowing she will hear not my voice, but only a computer's reconstruction of it. "I meant it." And how could I not "mean it," when "it" was nothing more than proffering a possibility, not even a probability.[12]

"You shouldn't have. Things are going to change. We're going to graduate—"

"We've talked about this before—"

"I just don't— I don't want you to make decisions because of me, OK? Can you promise me that? That when you make your decisions, you'll make them for yourself, not for me."

I think I'm falling in love with you, too had, moments before, seemed to be all I could offer, but now it becomes not nearly enough. I am teased and minced over some line by her selflessness, and I suddenly feel as though I could answer George's "why" with a final and definitive because.

Because she's good, I could say to him, *and good at what she does. She's committed. She's varsity-level acting talent, if we ranked such a thing in such a fashion. And she hews to what she wants, but she surrenders what she wants when it's for the greater good. Is that enough?* I would ask George and perhaps others not-George. *Is that good enough?*

"Promise me," she says again.

And if I were talking to Phil, I might not be able to make

12. "I think I'm falling in love with you, too," is meaningless speculation.

that promise, might not be able to swear to her analog self that I will forsake her (if necessary), that I will eschew her dreams and desires (if necessary) in favor of my own. But this is an unreal version of Phil—faceless, voice-mimicked.

I make the promise, wondering if breaking a digital copy of a promise is just as wrong as breaking the real thing.

****

Later, I try to remember the details of the dream, but—as dream details do—they have faded, save for "Clean is my anagram" and the comment that I haven't finished my college apps (true) and that I cannot finish them because I don't know something important.

I rise from bed to turn off my desk lamp, but first I straighten the papers and college app printouts on my desk, idly glancing through them, wondering what information I've left out when I see it, I see it on the app for College Y. Then I check the others—R, H, P, M, D—and find the same flaw, my eyes working the way eyes are not supposed to work, seeing what is not there, not what *is* there. For in looking over the apps, I realize that everything is filled out except for one piece of information, a single datum lacking:

My last name.

My last name is blank in every instance.

I don't know my own last name.

CHAPTER 6

Phil is right: Time moves quickly.

She assembles from a discordant and disinterested student body a senior play that will be breathtaking in its scope, uniting them through sheer Phil-ness. Nothing in the production coheres or works—she is deliberately casting and designing the play counter to every line on its pages—but she *makes* it work, as though simply believing it can happen makes it so that it does/will happen. Designing and building sets for her, I watch her stampede and badger and implore the play into being, as though it were a loved one clinging to life, its eventual production the only relevant CPR. It is a *Waiting for Godot* replete with action sequences and elaborate sets, contrary to every dream of Beckett; no one believes it will work, but Phil does and so I—reciprocally—do. And I build her sets.

As our senior year hurtles towards graduation, she accepts a scholarship offer from the nearby state university, while I stand at a decision-nexus between three different colleges, one of which is close enough to home that Phil and I could easily see each other if not every day, then certainly as frequently as we wished, the other two of which are far enough from home as to guarantee that we will see each other primarily when turkey and trimmings happen to be served for dinner. Phil asks almost every day if I've arrived at a decision, a question complicated by the fact that prior to receiving my various acceptances, I had repeatedly told her of my dream of attending College Y, which is one of the three and—more importantly and pertinently—one of the two. Thus, Phil badgers me regularly, reminding me that I've always wanted to attend Y and that I should just fill out the acceptance form and get going on your future quote-unquote in her words. Denying that I am eager to leap into the world of Y would be outright false, so instead I simply say that I've not made up my mind, which is true insofar as I feel an obligation to remain close to Phil. Her denial that she—scarily—might be falling in love with me to the contrary, her behavior this senior year has made it plain to me that she is, in fact, in love with me.

I am not sure if I am in love with her or not, but I cannot imagine that if this is not love that love itself could be any better. True, we have our problems, our "issues," in pop psychology parlance, but we still mold to each other in the history-made sheets several times a week, still risk chiding from the teachers by touching each other and occasionally stealing kisses in the halls between classes at what is still The WB. I feel an obligation to remain with her, regardless of what may or may not be my feelings, regardless of what may or may not be true in my heart. It seems so simple: Phil loves me. I am inside her almost as frequently as I am inside my own skin. What more is there?

Given all of that, then, how could I even flick an eye in the direction of leaving her? The universe itself seemed to have put us together, prompting the inevitable question: Who was I to separate us, even if that meant not living my dream and not attending Y?

"Dude," George says to me on the subway on the way to school, "you've been talking about going to Y since we were kids. It's like your Marines, you know what I mean? You gotta do it. Forget about her."

He says it with sympathy and compassion, but also with steel. Phil says the same thing on a regular basis—"Forget about me"—but says it with anger, directed at whom and why I cannot say. Phil's anger is like Phil's lust—large, formless, brazen, open. "I will hate you forever," she said to me, "if you give this up for me." I believed her—I still believe her—and yet the anger in her voice seemed aimed not merely at the potential future-Y-less-me, but also at the present me, for putting her in this position in the first place. No matter what choice I make, it seems, I will suffer Phil's anger and, perhaps, her hatred. (Her anger I have suffered many times in the past—I can weather it. Her hatred I cannot fathom. The enduring of it is an impossibility on the order of cold fusion and time travel.)

In the cold analysis, there can be no cold analysis. And yet, isn't Phil herself pushing me away? We fornicate as often and as passionately as ever, but outside of bed, she is prone to fits of rage, to screaming at me for no reason or for minuscule reasons—letting go of her hand "too soon" in the hall, kissing her "too quickly," not texting back every single time—and that fearlessness that I so adored about her, that willingness to be purely angry, to not militate against her anger with apology, has become nigh-intolerable, her opprobrium senseless and nonsensical.

I chalk it up to the stress of *Godot*, knowing even as I do so that this is not the case, or at least not the whole case.

Do I love her? Maybe the fact that I'm wondering is, in itself, my answer. What do I think I love about her? Her naturally blue hair, rich as the ocean depths? Her belief in me? Her body arching under mine, bent against mine, hovering above mine? Her talent? Her strength and belief and commitment? Are those the only "positives?" If I don't *know* that I love her for sure, is this a sign that I need to be with someone else, in order to determine the truth by comparison?

Going to Y, I would have to break up with her. No one I've ever spoken to has ever reported any good coming of such a long-distance relationship. And besides (the thought, new, is a frigid snake slithering through my rib cage) who knows who I might meet at Y? College Y has an intensive four-year architecture BA program, as opposed to most schools' five-year plan. It attracts the best and the brightest in the field, and would I not similarly be attracted to those best and brightest, and would they not be mutually attracted to me?

The idea is not pleasant and not unpleasant at once, but I have to consider: Phil is amazing, but who else is out there in the world who may be just-as-if-not-more amazing still? This is not my way of saying/thinking that I can "do better" than Phil, but what if I can do better than Phil?

"You're unbelievable," I've told her time and time again, always in the very best sense, but that word can turn around and its backside is not pleasant to behold. Maybe I was/am/have been falling in love with Phil, but in any honest assessment—in any cold analysis—I must admit to her quirks: Expecting me to bring her gummi bears when she knew I was with George, craving that strange and vaguely incestuous bed-reading session, insisting I come to her on the raining night, even though she knew I was busy. In the months of our togetherhood, I have catalogued a myriad of such requests, ranging from bizarre to odd to rude to outright ridiculous, to the point that if I did not fear Phil's temper, I would have reprimanded her repeatedly, especially as time has progressed and she has become more and more unreasonable.

Fear of her responses, yes, but also guilt. Guilt that my leaving may crush her, and this guilt is one set of a zipper's teeth and the fear is the other, and together they shut my mouth tight.

"Dude, want some?" George asks, waving a protein bar at me, the wrapper peeled back, banana-like. I lurch, recoiling, and George pulls it away, saying, "Oh, chocolate, right, sorry," for even though I've not experienced the overwhelming smell of chocolate syrup since that long-ago night of the Phil-interrupted dream, the odor of chocolate still repulses me, the mere fact of which makes me remember that night and that dream with a frequency far beyond the norm. That night, I stared at the college apps and I faced the Third Wall again. How could I just go to someone and ask for my last name? How could I confess that I did not know this basic, crucial, *assumed* piece of information? I would have checked my driver's license if I'd had one, but I didn't and don't. Ultimately, I relied—as always—on George, taking the completed-but-for-one-datum forms to his house and asking him, as a favor, to please fill out any information that was missing, not mentioning my last name in specific. Conveniently, George merely shrugged, flipped through the pages, then went online and typed in my last name in each blank.

I avoided watching as he did so, convinced beyond any sense of logic that if I had gone this long without knowing my last name, I could and can—and, perhaps, must—go longer.

The distraction and the memory, precipitated by George's accidental offer of hated chocolate, have cleared my mind, and as the subway sways and reels along on its tracks, the train of my own thoughts reels and rolls before finding stability on its own set of psychological tracks.

The first passenger to enter the open doors of this overused, metaphorical train is not Phil; it is College Y, and that tells me everything I need to know.

CHAPTER 7

After school, Phil and I go to her house; we have an hour before she is due at rehearsal, two before I am due to wrangle my set-building crew to continue bending plywood and two-by-fours to her vision. I want to hold back from telling her my decision, but I know that it is written all over my posture and floods the gaps between every word I speak, so I tell her once we're in the house, the door shut against the encroaching desert heat: "Phil, I'm going to Y. I'm really sorry."

"Don't apologize. Jesus." Brushing blue locks back from her forehead, her lips perfectly straight, completely unreadable. "I know," she says.

She says, "I know."

She says, "Jesus. I know. I knew before you did."

"Phil—"

"Stop it. This is what you're *supposed* to do. This is what you've always wanted, right? I told you: If you didn't do this, I would hate you."

"But you—"

She throws her backpack to the floor. "This isn't about me!

This is about *you*! You." And then says two words I've heard over and over for the past ten months, but never in this tone of voice: "Fuck me." Followed by, "Just fuck me. Forget about me. I don't matter."

"Phil, you *do* matter." And yet, I'm strangely divorced from this moment. Now that the decision has been made and communicated, it's true, it's as though she no longer matters. Phil is now my past, not my future.

"You do matter," I say again, but she doesn't.

She kisses me, softly for an instant, then violently, prying my mouth open, attacking with her tongue, grunting against me, her hands at my waist, at my belt buckle, my button, my zipper, then inside, and it's Phil, after all, and I am powerless; moreover, I have no desire to be powerful. I cannot resist her, but I don't want to resist her, and so the power and the lack of power become irrelevant as she drags me to the bedroom, flings me on the bed, crawls on top of me, not pausing to pull down my pants the rest of the way, fishing my cock (as we've finally settled on calling it, to my great relief) out of my underwear, not bothering to remove her skirt, pushing aside the center of her panties for access, then settling atop me so slowly that each excruciating inch is a year and I dare not thrust up, though I want to desperately.

Afterwards, we lay in bed as we've always lain in bed, as though nothing has happened and nothing has changed, and nothing will happen and nothing will change, talking about the upcoming rehearsal for *Godot* (she is playing Estragon, or, as she calls her distaff version, Estrogen) or the latest entry in my latest sketchbook or our mutual desire to find a girlfriend for George, who is prone to the frequent hook-up, but has never actually had a girlfriend, while I have had a girlfriend and now—I realize—no longer have one, even though she is still acting like my girlfriend, curled against me in bed, the two of us in random states of undress, having pulled off—both entirely and in part—some articles of clothing while vigorously thrusting and pulling and pushing and, in a word, fucking, fucking ourselves and each other breathless and senseless. While I am outwardly calm, I am inwardly rifling through thoughts at top speed, wondering—for the first time—what this "means," this frenzied sex between us, the way she attacked me, the way she has attacked me a hundred times in the past, but is this time meant to be different or special in some way I can't know or simply don't know? Is this crazed bout of fucking meant to Cmd-Z my decision and compel me to attend the closer option instead, staying for Phil, with Phil, by Phil?

"Do you have to send them an e-mail or a letter or something?" she asks suddenly, her position against me and her tone of voice changing not at all, both of us knowing that she is referring to Y.

"Already taken care of," I say, realizing at the same moment that what I have actually said is: "I made my decision and committed to it without talking to you at all, meaning there's nothing you can do or say, or could have done or said that would have changed my mind," expecting her to stiffen against me or pull away or launch into a rant, but none of that happens, Phil instead pulling closer to me, her head on my chest, saying only, "OK. Good." I worry for a moment that she will raise the specter of us maintaining our relationship across the miles. The very idea of committing to "the long-distance thing" unnerves me, quakes my gut. It seems the worst of all possible worlds, as well as a balm purchased not for any proven effect, but merely for the soothing scent or feel of it, as if "the long-distance thing" were snake oil or a weight-loss gadget discovered on a late-night infomercial.

Still, people buy snake oil. They buy weight-loss gadgets from late-night informercials. They don't work, but that stops people from buying them not at all.

Yet Phil remains silent on "the long-distance thing."

Later, before the sound of her mother's tires on the driveway, we roll out of bed, laughing at our states of mutual disarray, she with one breast bra'd, the other not, her skirt twisted nearly 180 degrees, the elastic of her panties torn; I hanging slightly tumescent from the fly of my underpants, my jeans at my knees, hobbling my movement, my top shirt button missing, the others having vacated their respective buttonholes in more orderly fashion. Both of us with what we have called in the past (and call now) "well-fucked hair," in her case meaning a blue, staticky whirlwind piled around her head; in mine, a series of short brown spikes jutting in all directions. We are flushed, both with our current laughter and with our prior exertions, and the laughter in particular fills me with relief, as I had entertained—for a moment—a fear that an angry Phil would, without warning, lash out at me as we lay in bed. My most lurid fears involved her teeth and my carotid artery, her teeth and my cock, but the more prosaic fears revolved around a sustained bout of screaming or weeping, the likes of which no amount of placating could assuage. Now, as I adjust shirt, pants, cock, she attends to herself, tucking revealed breast back into cup to make a half-empty bra now full, swiveling her skirt, and the motions are familiar and so normal that my fears depart before I can bid them farewell, and I realize that I've made the right decision and that, all fear to the contrary, I will be extricated from this relationship with a minimum of drama and a fabulous bout of fare-thee-well sex to boot, all of this flying through my mind in the instant before Phil says, "Help me strip the bed."

"What?" There are no lights on in the room, no illumination

save the slightly-yellow haze limning the window blind, and for a moment I have the absurd, synesthetic notion that the room's murk has made hearing her more difficult.

"I said, 'Help me strip the bed,'" she repeats, her voice casual, as though she has not just made a decision that ends history.

I stare at the bed, at the history-made sheets, twisted and wrapped around themselves, and I imagine that I can see each smudge, smear, blotch, and stain not as mere remnants of Phil's and my excited secretions, but rather as points on a timeline, an unspooled thread stretching back months and ending at this exact moment.

"Are you . . . are you going to wash them?" I ask her, the question stumbling and un-sure-footed as it staggers from my mouth.

She fixes her gaze on me. "Did you think I was going to put them under glass in a museum somewhere?"

"Well . . . No . . ."

"Then, c'mon. Help me."

She tugs at the top sheet, popping it loose from the corner nearest her. After a moment, I follow suit, and together we peel back the record of our relationship.

CHAPTER 8

Time is thick—we move through it slowly, one heartbeat at a time.

Time is thin—it's paper, a page, turned, and the world changes.

Time is on the event horizon of a black hole—everything happens at once. The past and the future are the present, and the present is the present, too.

It's Spring Break of my freshman year at College Y and I'm looking at a text message on my cell phone and I'm thinking of the day Phil and I stripped the sheets from her bed. It's a memory so close and so pungent that it is as though it has just happened, as though it is the most recent thing to take place in my life. It's as though that moment lives side-by-side with this one, or perhaps imprinted on its reverse.

can i use your shower?

Five words and one punctuation mark on the screen on my cell, and my body freezes and my mind races ahead.

I have not seen Phil since a month before the start of college. We did not try to avoid each other after the day of the sheet-changing (or, at least, we told each other we did not try to avoid each other; for my part, I made no great effort *not* to avoid her), but we saw each other still, entangled as we both were in *Waiting for Godot.*[13] Our phone and online communication continued, somewhat hampered by the awkwardness of the situation. We were no longer "together," but we did not yet know how to be "apart." With school over and *Godot* a line on Phil's resume, I suggested after a short time a temporary moratorium on contact, feeling that such would help ease Phil into the idea of a Mike-less world.

And it was Phil I was most concerned with, not myself. I had, shortly after the changing of history's sheets, fallen into an odd sort of null-emotional state, characterized by a drive to prepare for college, to spend time with my parents and my brother and George (before he shipped out for basic training, his Marine uniform crisp and spotless when he showed it to me on the hanger) before leaving for College Y. While I yearned for Phil's body against mine, I missed her not even half or a third as much as I had feared I would. "Out of sight, out of mind" is a cliché, yet is unaccountably true, as might be an extension/revision: "Out of sight, out of mind, out of heart." As we saw nearly nothing of each other, The WB evolved into The CW, a celebratory party thrown to introduce the new faculties to one another, to induce the alumni of both facilities either to continue donating or to begin doing so. I attended with George, loitering and lingering in a corner, chuckling at the older alums in their suits and ties, thinking of Phil (who did not attend) not at all.

13. The WB's *Waiting for Godot* came off exactly as Phil wanted, her perfect swan song and farewell to the school. It was a massive hit.

She had agreed to my "no contact for a month" scheme, but then called me the next night: "I know I'm not supposed to call you, but I just had to tell you about what happened today . . ." followed by a discourse on her pre-enrollment meeting with State's drama department head, who had witnessed not only *Godot*, but also Phil's earlier star, gender-and-race-bending turn as the Moor in The WB's *Othello* and, much impressed, had already insisted that Phil try out for multiple campus productions, etc., etc., to my repeated, "That's great"s and eventual drifting off to an IM session with George while Phil chattered in my ear until she tired of speaking and released me. The seal of non-communciation thus broken, she continued calling me most—if not every—night(s) at around midnight, when she usually went to sleep, thus ensuring mine as the last voice she would hear each day. I came to fear and dread the coming of midnight. I considered simply not answering, but again guilt and fear drove me to the phone: Guilt that I was fine, while she clearly was not; fear that the act of ignoring her would make her redouble her efforts. Thus and hence, we continued to speak, every call beginning "I know I'm not supposed to call you . . .", her need plain, her tears and "I miss you"s infrequent but regular, the word "love" never used, for its use was not necessary. It lurked between the lines of every conversation, every e-mail, every text, and it plunged me deeper into the morass of guilt and fear, such that I could not simply cut her loose or cut her off, thus making the situation worse by my active inaction.

And such was the state of our communication until bumping into each other—literally—as we came around the same corner from perpendicular aisles at an office supply store while shopping for college gear. After the initial whoa-ing and hey-ing and oh-my-god-it's-you-ing and the subsequent bursts of nervous laughter, we shared "How have you been? Fine"s and parted quickly. That last bumping-into sufficed as our last communication for some time as if physical contact with me had severed her emotional contact. And besides, as we both began our college classes, time and attention became such scarce resources that there were whole hours at a time that I simply forgot blue-tressed Philomel had ever even existed and had ever been mine, forgot her smile, forgot her saucy winks, forgot her belief in me, her passion, her everything. She, I am sure, forgot me similarly. For her sake, I hope so.

And then—now, rather—this most random of all random communications: *can i use your shower?*

"I'm in town for a show," she tells me when I call—curiosity prodding me to contact—"and we're staying with the lead's sister, but she only has one shower. I don't feel like standing in line to take a cold shower, but I can borrow a car and come over. Can I? I promise it won't take long."

I am alone for Spring Break, staying at College Y rather than going home because I have projects due in my architecture classes and the relative silence of the campus while everyone is gone is conducive to intense focus on my work. To say nothing of the fact that I can commandeer the entire living room to spread out plans and models. I've been alone for almost a week now, and the idea of company is compelling enough that I say, "Sure," which I immediately regret, now and suddenly confronted with my own unrelenting and complete loser-dom (loserness?), alone, uncompanioned during my first collegiate Spring Break. Deeper than the regret, too, is a sense of profound disappointment in myself—didn't I break up with Phil, in part, on the promise of "meeting someone new" at Y, a special Y-woman who would out-Phil Phil, offering the positives without the annoying negatives? And yet here I am, Phil-less, Phil-replacement-less, and, truthfully, friendless. I've made no friends at Y, though I have casual acquaintances. Worse yet is that in my darkest, loneliest, most honest moments, I have to admit that the aforementioned "negatives" seem, in retrospect, pathetic (on my part, not hers). Her major crime, her mortal sin? Loving me. Wanting to be with me all the time. Wanting me. Contacting me. And for that, I excommunicated her, cast her aside, deliberately avoided e-mails and phone calls. Was this all a wrong decision? Coming to Y may have been the right decision, but was breaking up with Phil the wrong one? Could we have survived "the long-distance thing?" Sometimes, maybe, snake oil worked.

Moreover: Could we still?

"OK," Phil says. "I'll be over in a little while." And hangs up before I can say more, which is just as well, for at this point—in this state of mind—who knows *what* would come forth, were I to speak?

At first, I excused away my lack of romantic success at College Y as the natural consequence of being amongst new people and the caution that results, an excuse blasted away by my four suitemates' repeated triumphs in the same arena, proven not only by typical male bragging, but also by a trashcan's-ful of condom wrappers and boxes. Eventually, around Christmas break, I was forced to admit to something hitherto unrealized: I—quite simply—never developed the skills requisite to meet girls. At home for that same Christmas break, I was tempted to call Phil, but could not bring myself to do so. I was the one who left; I should not be allowed to miss her, to want her. She removed the sheets and washed them—that's what she did with *his* sheets, too, and she assured me she never wanted to go back to *him*. By washing those sheets—our sheets—she erased that history—our history. And so I spent the months since our bumping-into missing her, thinking of her, persuading myself anew (with varying levels of success) that breaking up was "the right thing to do," recalling our time together, fantasizing her presence, her lips, the hollow of her neck, the dip into her cleavage, her nipples erecting at my lips, her wetness, her thighs locked around me, urging me deeper and faster, until I can stand it no further and slip out of my bedroom to steal privacy in the bathroom, the only place to masturbate with any sort of discretion. This all followed by guilt (for leaving her, for turning her—in my memory and my mind and my lust—into a mere sexual object) and shame and a burning curiosity: Do I want Phil back? Can I have her back? Should I? The questions and the curiosity wane as I sleep and with the business of the day, then return as I toss and turn again at night, remembering nights in Phil's bed (and, of course, in her), the whole returning to the cycle of need, lust, guilt, shame, curiosity, over and over, the wheel turning, spun by no one I can discern, but spinning nonetheless.

When the knock at the door comes, I am unprepared, even though I have done nothing but prepare myself, and I open the door to her: She's the same Phil and she's new all at once, wearing jeans I've never seen, a t-shirt with the State mascot on it, a green windbreaker. Her hair, still lustrous, shining blue, is shorter now, her stance more confident, cocky almost, her eyes fiery and laughing. She hugs me immediately before speaking, surprising me such that I forget to become aroused or nervous or self-aware. I expected something radically different, something unknowably off about her, something perhaps haggard and a bit worn by the loss of Mike in her life, by the loss of love. But instead, she is still Phil, the same Phil I saw in seventh grade, the same Phil I yearned for and attained and left.

"It's good to see you," she says, adding a quick squeeze before breaking off the hug. "How've you been?"

"Fine," I tell her, not sure if it's a lie, but reasonably certain that it isn't the truth.

Inside, she asks, "What's this?" while pointing to the half-finished model on the "coffee table" (so quoted because it is nothing more than recovered cinder blocks balancing a former bathroom door ripped off its hinges and discarded in the courtyard one night).

"One of my assignments. Converting a church lot into a strip mall."

"Well, that's symbolic, I guess."

"I guess."

"Sort of a commentary on contemporary mores and society, right?"

"I— Not really. It's just an assignment. It wasn't my idea."

"Oh. Well, you'll kick its ass. You always do. How's George doing in the Marines?"

"Uh, fine. He . . . I don't get to talk to him a lot, but the last time I talked to him he was good."

She blessedly asks for directions to the shower then, leaving me alone again, grateful for the recess from our back-and-forth, for which I was woefully unprepared. Seeing Phil again affected me more deeply and more quickly than I would have or could have imagined. Does she want me back? Is she really even in town for a show? What show? Why has she given me no details?

And as soon as I imagine her wanting me back, following on that fantasy's heels are the memories of the gummi bears, the rain on the roof, the demands, the needs, the temper. What am I doing? Do I really want her back? Or am I just lonely?

When she emerges from the bathroom, clad in a single white towel, all thoughts leave my brain—thoughts of reuniting, thoughts of not reuniting, thoughts of anything at all. I tell myself not to stare, not to allow myself the luxury of remembering what is beneath that towel, what seems—at first glance—not to have changed appreciably in the intervening months since our stripping of the history-made sheets.

"What show are you doing?" I blurt out, desperate to say something, to insert anything at all into the lingering, slightly damp silence.

"I'm a little tired," she says. "Can I lie down on your bed? Just a quick nap, I promise."

How can I deny her that? She goes into my bedroom and does not so much close the door as bring it closer to closed, leaving it slightly ajar like an invitation, making me think of the old joke: Q: When is a door not a door? A: When it's ajar! Or, I suppose, when it's an invitation. I slip into the room, into the bed, etc. It's perfect, like old times. It's been so long.

"It's been so long," she says, arching into me, against me.

"Yes," I say.

"Did you think about this?" she asks. "Did you think about fucking me?"

"Yes."

"How? How did you think about it?"

With cock in hand is the most honest answer, but not one I can or will give while my cock is otherwise and more superbly occupied. "Constantly," is my as-truthful answer, and she sighs, the sound a long and purring exhalation as her body and mine crush together in that perfect way they always had and always have.

"I really do need a nap," Phil says when we are finished, not unkindly removing my hand from its roam of her lower back. "Just a short one," and she rolls to her side and exercises a peculiar ability of hers I have always admired, dropping off into a deep, lightly-snorning sleep with no hesitation or pause. For my part, I slide back some inches from her, as far back as the narrow college twin bed will allow, not for fear of touching her or dislike of touching her, but rather to gain perspective, to watch her sleeping back, half-draped in sheets, her round, rolling hip and tapered legs, the sight of her here in my bed a shock, a shock of new sheets. Is this a post-historical fuck . . . or the beginning of a new timeline?

I lay back, staring up at the ceiling, wondering if anyone on this planet knows what it is I want. For I certainly do not. And then I fall asleep and I dream, though this time I am aware I'm dreaming. A woman comes to me, her hair black and glistening like wet coal.

"Once my hair was blonde," she says to me. "And then I was pushed."

"I thought there were no quotation marks in dreams," I tell her.

"Of course there are," she says. Imagine how complicated it would be without them. She says or does not say.

"Oh. I see."

"My name is Angia. Angia Eiphon. Does that name mean anything to you?"

"Should it?" Something tickles at the back of my mind: An allegory. Or a metaphor. Or—

Clean is my anagram.

"Mike loved me. And God loved me. But then God pushed me and I fell so far, out of dreams, through the real world—"

"Where did you go? Where did you land?"

"Somewhere else. Somewhere false and true at the same time."

"Am I supposed to know who you are?"

"I don't know. I'm the sister of the first Mike. And his lover."

"Gross."

"No, no. It's not like that. It's complicated."

"It would pretty much have to be. What are you doing in my dream?"

"It's not so much a dream as it's a dream sequence, Mike. I don't know why I'm here, to be honest with you. It might be a delaying tactic. Or just flat-out desperation."

"What do you mean?"

"Or it might be a convenient way to move things along, to let time pass. I'll tell you to wake up now. And you will."

"But—"

"Wake up."

CHAPTER 9

Phil has rolled out of bed while I slept and dreamed, and now bends, her pantied backside me-aimed, to retrieve her bra and shirt from amongst my scattered clothes on the floor. I open my mouth to speak, but say nothing, due not to a lack of anything to say, but rather too much to say, each possible phrase or sentence pregnant with the potential to create a new universe of its own in this moment:

I love you, Phil, or

This was a mistake, Phil, or

Did you really just come here for a shower?, or

Are you seeing anyone?, or

Does this mean we're back together?, or

What the hell, Phil? You don't even know if I'm seeing someone and you just let me fuck you?

And on and on, universes and timelines spinning up and out from my speech, spiraling into their own infinities. All of these thoughts, notions, potentialities clash and carom off each other on their way to my lips, colliding and disabling each other such that none of them can escape, which is just as well, for I do not wish to live in any one of those universes—I wish to live (I need to live) in all of them simultaneously. I need to know the answers to every one of those questions and the many others I have not listed, so that with those answers I can know the next question(s) to ask, and so on and so forth, until I can arrive at the final, right conclusion. How can I know what I think of what has just happened until I know why it has happened?

"Thanks for the shower," Phil says, still turned away from me, now bra'd and shirted and tossing her hips from side to side as she pulls up her jeans. "And the nap," she says over her shoulder, not unsaucily, coming down in a peculiar way on the word "nap," such that I cannot tell if she is angry at me for fucking her or happy I did so, angry at herself or glad.

"Are you leaving?" I mean to come down hard on the last word, italicizing it with disbelief and shock, but I am so caught off-guard that instead my tone remains roman.

"Yeah." Her voice, surprised, almost accusatory. "I told you I wouldn't be here long."

And she did. She had. Yet that (promise is too strong a word for something so casual) assurance came before she slid, shower-soft, into my bed, before I followed, before we began a new history on my college sheets (laundered, conveniently and coincidentally enough, this very morning, meaning that they are now soiled only by the commingling of Phil and me). Who would demand she be held to that assurance (commitment?), given as it was prior to the current state of affairs? Who would insist that she honor a pledge made in one universe now that she lives in another?

"We should stay in touch," says now-clothed Phil, pulling on her jacket. "I miss talking to you."

Talking to me, I think, alone. Talking to me, I ponder, once she's left. *Talking* to me. She misses *talking* to me. Talking!

Spring Break passes. The project is finished, though to what degree of quality I will not say, as it does not matter. This is not a story about my architecture project—it is about Phil, and me, and—sometimes—Phil and me.

Still stung by Phil's casually encouraging discouragement, I finally take up my roommates on their offer to "take [me] out and get [me] some strange," by which they mean to introduce me to a girl who will make me forget about Phil. They are successful in this endeavor, as I meet a petite blonde pre-med student that night, one with a name unrelated to musical instruments or nightingales, but whose feminine moniker can—and often is, like Phil's—shortened to a masculine nickname. Our first two hours together—spent in an increasing spiral of alcohol-fueled fog[14]—give me hope that Phil is behind me (figuratively, not literally). I pay attention only to the petite blonde pre-med student, occasionally diverting to accept and acknowledge a bottle tipped in congratulation from a roommate across the bar or a thumbs-up or a mouthed "You dog!" with raised eyebrows of delight. She is funny, interesting, attractive, and willing, and within hours I am thinking not of Phil, but rather of the wonderful future that no doubt awaits me with the petite blonde pre-med student with the masculine nickname.

In bed, in her, in fifteen seconds, Phil springs to mind and I cannot dislodge her, no matter how much I try.

Very well. Very well, I console myself that night, lying awake as the pre-med student sleeps, wondering how long I should wait

14. Almost by necessity, Mike has gotten over his fear of being drunk (mentioned earlier), with plenty of help/encouragement from his roommates.

before slipping away into the night. Very well, so I thought of Phil while in bed with another woman. This means not necessarily anything of any import, me having been—being—drunk (though rapidly sobering). It is, perhaps, natural to think of Phil the first time I sleep with someone not-Phil. Especially when my mind is clouded by booze. This happenstance is not determinative, but, rather, merely indicative of what I can expect. Surely, if the pre-med student and I were to have a lengthy relationship that then ended, I would—upon bedding my first post-pre-med student conquest—think of the pre-med student.

Wouldn't I?

I fall asleep thinking of this, and wake up next to the blonde pre-med student, and wake up in a relationship with the blonde pre-med student. I am oddly gladdened by this. Even though she has no way of knowing it, I feel as though I was in some way disloyal to her last night, thinking of Phil while in bed with her. I vow to make it up to her by being attentive and passionate, but the next time we end up in bed (that afternoon after her bio class and before my English elective), I once again find my—now sober—thoughts drifting to Phil.

While in the early throes of this relationship, I hear from Phil occasionally, her e-mails and texts studiously bleached of anything smacking of the color of emotion, each series of words carefully selected to have no effect or perhaps the effect of seeming to have no effect, or carelessly selected in the rush and flight of one who no longer sees meanings in those words beyond their meanings, no innuendoes, no shades, no connotations, nothing (and no thing) concealed between the lines. I occasionally send my own e-mails when, after diligent self-negotiations, I determine that doing so will not cause our teetering, unspoken relationship to topple from its liminal position atop a fence to fall onto the side of I-love-her or

Love-her-I-do-not, as I am still unsure which is true, which is real, which matters. Does my inability to think of anything but Phil while in bed with the petite blonde pre-med student mean I love Phil? Does it mean I was merely obsessed with her? Does it mean it was too soon for me to have another relationship?

Does it mean anything at all?

I cannot tell. I know only that every time I am within sight of forgetting her, of closing the door on my past with her, Phil—as if sensing my incipient successful deep-sixing of her haunting presence—contacts me in some wise, innocently, of course, shallowly, superficially, but contact nonetheless, the contact itself shocking me back to the *status quo ante* by its mere existence.

And so e-mails and texts sally back and forth, to and fro, discussing a mutually-favored TV show (*do u think c & d will come back next season?*), pointing out an especially absurd website (*OMG, check this out - LOL*), avoiding anything that could, in its seriousness, lead to the complex ugliness of real contact and a real decision. All the while, Phil remains uppermost in my mind each time I bed the petite blonde pre-med student, going on two months of this now, and I can no longer deny that my feelings for Phil are stronger than my feelings for the blonde petite pre-med student. Within the week, I have no choice but to end the relationship.[15]

As my freshman year closes in on its end, I have gone three weeks without communication of any sort from Phil. Assiduous scanning of my e-mail outbox reveals that I last e-mailed her in re: a new movie starring an actress for whom we both

15. Mike prosecuted the break-up with great respect and sensitivity.

confessed lust[16] ("Hey, check it out: Our girlfriend finally has a new movie!" followed by a link), an e-mail which, in retrospect, violates my personal policy of perfunctory, uninvolved contact with Phil, the realization of which prompts me to inspect my entire outbox for Phil-bound e-mails, scrutinizing the last several months of e-mails for potential overplaying of my hand, also causing me to thumbscroll my cell's text messages to confirm that, indeed, there had been no further contact between us in either direction since my poorly-conceived e-mail, a fact proven by the existence of one last text Phil-ward (*hate my physics class!!!!*) and one me-ward (*who made you take it??? lol*), both sent/received three days before the final e-mail.

I write a new e-mail to her, apologizing for my gaffe, assuring her that I meant no innuendo or pressure by my use of the phrase "our girlfriend," then I delete the e-mail, then—in a panic that I clicked the wrong button and sent the e-mail rather than deleting it—I scroll through my trash, breathing only when I see the e-mail there, then panicking again at the thought that the deleted e-mail is not truly gone, as is evidenced by its presence in the trash folder, and could accidentally be sent at some future point. I empty the trash,

16. Phil first broached the topic of the actress's pulchritude, commenting on her breasts and their singular attraction to the otherwise straight Phil while she and Mike lounged on the floor of her living room, the near-silent TV pulsating white-blue light over them. Upon discovering their mutual attraction, Mike half-joked that he would happily do his manly best to please both women, half-seriously hoping that the comment would induce Phil to offer such a threesome, less the unobtainable actress, but plus, perhaps, Phil's friend Kara, over whom Mike had spent several masturbatory sessions, imagined both alone and in concert with Phil, at which half-joke Phil chuckled, telling her paramour to dream on, that she would—if provided with the opportunity—happily fuck the actress, allowing Mike to watch and nothing more. Mike, to his own surprise, was fine with this, solemnly shaking Phil's hand to seal the pointless deal. The actress was henceforth known to them both not by her name, but simply as "our girlfriend."

relaxing only when the spinning wheel halts and vanishes, revealing the pristine white background of an empty e-mail folder.

I write another e-mail, this one confessing that I had not intended to evoke sexual feelings with my last e-mail, but that I found myself unable to not think of her time in my room and in my bed at Spring Break (about which, bee-tee-dub: what was her true motivation?). Perhaps I erred in leaving her or at least in not attempting "the long-distance thing" and needed her in my life beyond the capacity of mere friend. The e-mail finishes with that flourish, a flourish that could not be mistaken for anything but a naked declaration of love, despite the lack of that specific word; I send it, then immediately, hysterically regret doing so, my panic followed by a burst of relief that my computer has frozen upon my clicking of the SEND button, a reboot showing that the e-mail has not in fact been sent, but rather consigned safely to the drafts folder, all of this followed, in turn, by mild regret that the e-mail has not, in fact, been sent, as its transmission would have at the very least forced the issue one way or the other and placed it wholly out of my control and in Phil's.

As I linger over the drafts folder, trying to decide which way to turn from the current liminal path—Love Phil? Don't love Phil? Tell her? Don't tell her?—the counter on my inbox increments by one, that one revealed to be my one, my Phil, finally in response to my long-since-sent e-mail of the actress.

Mike,

It reads.

I'm not sure how to tell you this, so I'm just going to tell you: I've gotten back together with *him*.

I didn't want to tell you before because I know how stressed you've been with school and everything, and I didn't want to add to that burden. A part of me sort of hates you, but a part of me also hates me, too, so in a weird way, I think that makes
us even.

I really believe in you, and it's important to me that you know that. I think you're going to have such an amazing life and build some truly magnificent buildings, buildings like no one else has ever imagined. And I think that after some time, I'll stop hating you and I'll stop hating myself and we can really be friends again, which I would like.

You don't have to answer this e-mail. I totally understand if you hate me right now.

Phil

It ends.

Phil,

I write, almost immediately.

Thanks for letting me know. I'm happy for you

I lie (I think).

and I don't hate you.

(I think.)

I don't want you to hate yourself, either. I hope you're happy and that when you feel up to it, you'll get in touch with me and we can be friends.

Mike

Before regret or worry or panic or fear can stay my hand, I click SEND and this time, no vagaries of the 1s and 0s of the machine code at the heart of my laptop conspire to crash and divert my missive from its intended target. From Drafts to Outbox it goes in the space of microseconds, thence to the wireless dorm hub, thence to the campus network, and thence—via a series of hubs, routers, and switches—to the Internet T1 backbone, which whisks it in less time than it takes to think to the corresponding and reversed series of hubs, routers, and switches at State, which dispatch it to Phil's dorm, router, laptop, screen, window, and thence to her eyes and her mind and her heart.

In my hated physics class, I have learned of the wave-particle duality of light, which supposes that light, which—anecdotally as well as evidentially—exhibits the properties of both a wave and a particle, is both at once, only collapsing into one or the other depending upon circumstances and the observer. My relationship with Phil has, now, similarly collapsed, once potentially romantic and not-romantic at the same time, it—now observed—stands revealed in its true nature, concluded and over.

She's back with *him*. It's over.

****

Thinking becomes arduous and near-impossible. I have to speak, not think.

"Man, I made a mistake . . ."

"Dude," says George from a pay phone on Parris Island, "you have to remember the shit about her that drove you crazy."

"That's what I'm remembering."

"I don't mean the *good* crazy. I mean the bad crazy, you know what I mean?"

"That stuff just doesn't seem so bad anymore, is all."

"Dude. Please. You been getting laid up there?"

"For a while. I thought about Phil the whole time. What does that have to do with anything?"

"You're lonely. You don't have anyone else, so you miss Phil."

"Didn't you hear me? I was with someone. I was with someone and I thought about Phil the whole time."

"How long's it been since she told you?"

"Three days."

"What have you been doing?"

"Nothing."

A pause fills the connection, lasting not long enough that I think we have lost each other, but long enough that I begin to dread what George is about to say.

"You mean that literally, don't you? You haven't done anything."

My room is a litter of unfinished work, unread books, unlaundered clothing and sheets (still soiled with my and Phil's Spring Break exertions), and partly eaten bags of chips and boxes of store-brand donuts. It is as though time has hiccuped from the moment I realized "It's over" to now; I can remember nothing of the intervening time. Surely I've eaten? The evidence is all around me, but I don't recall eating any of the food. Surely I've showered? Changed clothes? Pissed?

"I should have said something when she was here," I dodge. "At Spring Break. I should have said something to her."

"Why didn't you?"

"I don't know." But I do: I was, at the time, under the mistaken impression that I did not love Phil. "I should have told her I loved her. That would have changed things."

"Dude, you don't know that. For all you know, she was already back with *him* when she came to see you."

"I don't believe that. That's not like her. She wouldn't do that. Why would she do that?"

"Who knows? She's a person. People are complicated. What are you doing?"

"You mean right now? Nothing. Talking to you."

"Me, too. I'm not doing anything. Just talking to you, you know what I mean?"

"OK."

"Dude, you need to chill out, OK? I can hear the tension in your voice. I can hear you stressing all the way down here. It's no good. You're done with her now."

"No. No, I'm not. She was with *him* before and she picked me. It can happen again."

"Dude."

"I made it happen once before. I can do it again. She doesn't love *him*. She never said she loved *him*."

"Did she ever say she loved you?"

"Sort of."[17]

"Dude."

"I have to tell her. I have to tell her I love her. That will change everything."

17. *"Do you want to hear something scary?" Phil asks.*

"Dude, don't do this to yourself. Move on."

"But I can fix it, George! Don't you get it?"

"You can't fix anything. There's nothing *to* fix."

"George, I have to try."

He sighs. "Dude, you do what you gotta do. When does your semester end?"

"A month. I'll be back home on the fifteenth."

"I'll call you when you get home, OK? I should be able to call then. Try not to lose your mind before then."

****

After the phone call ends, I realize that I never asked George about boot camp, further proof—if any were needed—that I am not his best friend.

****

"I love you," I tell her.

There's no pause before her answer, no hesitation, no intervention.

After my talk with George and subsequent re-realization in re: our unequal best-friendhood, I called Phil, hitting END before the phone could ring once, wondering if enough of the signal had gone through to cause her phone to ring—perhaps a single, stunted bleat?—and/or to cause my Caller ID information to flash—howsoever briefly—on the screen, thus alerting her that I was attempting to call her, causing me to wait, paralyzed, and stare at the screen of my phone, certain that her picture and number would—in an instant—flicker to life, her custom ringtone sounding out as it had not in so many months, my heart hammering with fear as I realized that I would have to speak to her unprepared, my thoughts chaotic and unformed and imperfect. Phones do not, after all, ring in perfect concert, the caller hearing the ring sometimes offset by many seconds from the perception of the called.[18]

The call did not come.

I composed myself, lying down on the bed so that I could not pace and hasten my breath into panic. I forced myself to ask myself the most difficult question:

Was I sure I was in love with Phil?

I answered the question and then I made myself breathe and then I asked it again:

Was I sure I was in love with Phil?

I couldn't imagine how I was *not* in love with Phil. Had I not missed her, yearned for her almost from the beginning? Had I not bedded her without hesitation when offered the opportunity? Had I not spent the weeks since—even with the blonde petite pre-med—in lusting misery? Had I not, since her revelation of her resumption of relations with *him*, fallen into a useless daze, barely feeding myself, barely able to rouse myself to use the bathroom for its intended purpose, unshaven, unshowered? What else could these signs be, if not symptoms of all-consuming love? By process of elimination, there was no other possibility.

More to the point: I knew it to be true. Without thought or artifice or construction, I knew that I loved Phil.

The second time I called her, her phone rang, committing me. Hanging up now would accomplish nothing—my name and number would linger on her missed calls list, fingerprints of my intention.

18. Anyone who has ever placed a call, only to have the intended recipient answer before the first ring has experienced this auditory electronic offset.

On the second ring, alarm crept into my heart like a cat with distemper. Had she seen the Caller ID and chosen not to answer? Worse, was she with *him* at this very moment? I had not even considered the possibility, and now I could do nothing but consider it—she was with *him*, in *his* embrace, ignoring her phone or, perhaps, noticing and sharing with *him*, the two of them then laughing/shrugging/snorting before sending the call to voice mail—

The third ring came then, the purgatory of voice mail avoided for now, but coming quickly, approaching the closing fourth and final ring, and now the rabid cat of alarm snarled and raked claws down my spine as the thought that I would, in fact, end up in voice mail occurred to me for the first time. What would I say? I would have to say *some*thing, wouldn't I? I couldn't simply leave the mute evidence of an entry in missed calls, with so much unspoken and easily mis-imagined on Phil's part. I would have to say something to her voice mail, but a blurted protestation of love could not be that something.

Fourth and final ring. I would go to voice mail, I knew, as Phil answered the phone with a "Hey" as casual as any she ever offered even when we coupled as a couple.

"Hey," I said back, willing my breath to deepen, my words to slow, then following with "Do you have a second?" A rough translation of *Are you alone or are you with* him*?*

"What's up?" she asked without inflection (Translation: I'm alone and available to talk, *or*, possibly, I'm not alone, but spit it out, chump—there's really no way to tell which), and I felt foolish for bothering her, for interrupting whatever she was doing—with or without *him*—and nearly said "Nothing" and hung up, but instead took a single deep breath and said:

"I just wanted to tell you something, is all."

"OK."

"I know I screwed up. I know I messed things up. But I would like us to be together.

"I love you," I told her.

There was no pause before her answer, no hesitation, no intervention bridging to the now:

"I don't love you. I'm sorry. I don't love you. I'm with someone else."

"Well," I tell her, "I just wanted you to know."

And now a pause, a pause that says what she does not say: *You wanted what? Why? That doesn't make any sense.*

"Well," she says, "thank you. I'm sorry."

She does not sound sorry. She sounds both agitated and bored at the same time. Perhaps, I think, she *is* agitated and bored at this moment.

"It's OK," I say, absolving her for I-know-not-what, for reasons I-know-not-why, save that when people apologize I tell them it's OK.

"Mike," she says after a moment. "Mike. You can't—"

"Don't."

"You can't just . . . Look, you're going to meet someone else."

The tears start, shocking me, my first tears since childhood.

"Someone really great," she goes on, and then says, "But not cooler than me," her tone the comforting, casual, confidential Phil I've known all along and so often, her self-effacing self-confidence, the stern self-mocking of it crushing me flat, the thought of being with anyone but Phil possessing its own special gravity, weighty enough to flatten me and grind me to paste in my own bed.

"Of course not," I manage, meaning "Of course I'll never find anyone cooler than you," but also—simultaneously, honestly—meaning "Of course I'll never find anyone," period, end of sentence, full stop.

"Are you OK?" she asks. "Are you crying?"

For a moment—less than a moment, really, perhaps half a moment, two-thirds at most—the truth argues with my tongue, desperate and pleading to be expressed. Children know the truth about crying, that tears—while frowned upon and decried as babyish—often act as a skeleton key, opening doors that otherwise would remain locked and barred, cracking open the sheaths of ice that glaze the most frozen of hearts. If I admit to my small, childish sin of tears, would that change her mind? Could my tears prove to her what my words have not, transmitting my love as though through osmosis?

"No," I tell her, "I'm not crying," wiping tears from my cheek. "I'm fine. I just wanted to tell you. I'll talk to you later," I add, for reasons that—if they existed at all—would make no sense to me. Why would I talk to her later? Why would I talk to her at all? What is there at all to say? By "later" does she think I mean I'll call her later in the day?

"I want us to be friends, Mike," she tells me. "Soon."

"Of course," I say, then say it a second time, this time with the phone no longer muted (having been set so a moment ago so that I could quickly and privately clear my blubbering nose).

"OK," she says. "Have a good rest of the semester."

"You, too," I say automatically, trying at the same time to imagine how to have anything remotely resembling a "good rest of the semester."

And then she's gone and I hold the cell in my hand for a long time, as if it is the hand of a recently-deceased loved one and I am, both literally and figuratively, unable to let go, clutching that hand as though by so doing I could wrest that same loved one back from death, out of Charon's grasp, out of the gondola of death and back to the living shore of the River Styx, clutching it until the last instants of heat dissipate from it, as my cell phone cools now, fading to the temperature of my grasp until there is no difference, until a thermal image of my body would show a cancerous, tumorous lump at the end of my right wrist.

I excise the phone and rise, pace the room, catch sight of myself in the mirror, and for some reason the sight of me brings back the tears, convulsing me with sorrow, and I weep loudly and unashamedly now, no telephone, no Phil to deceive, so I cry, I cry, I cry, watching more than feeling the tears run down my face, watching more than feeling the red rims of my eyes grow redder and more swollen, and I speak at last to the me in the mirror, the me whose grief is precisely and reversely mine, and what do I tell him? I tell him only the truth:

"You deserve this," I tell him. "This is what you deserve."

****

There is, I discover, a strange sort of desperation that comes from carrying a full complement of love and having nothing to do with it, nowhere to set it down. Love, like caffeine, makes you jittery and nervous. Love compels you to a strange cycle of action/inaction. I spend hours reloading my e-mail and double-, triple-, and quadruple-checking my cell phone for texts, then spend hours doing nothing at all, lying on my bed, staring up at the ceiling as though answers had been inscribed there long ago, and if life were magically realistic—a Márquez novel, say—perhaps there would be answers inscribed on my ceiling, deftly daubed into the relief of the paint by some lovelorn, stricken journeyman painter years ago. I would stare at the ceiling for hours on end until the perfect shaft of light intersected with the strokes, decoding them into words and ideas, forbidden knowledge handed down that would aid me in recovering my lost Philomel.

But life is not a Márquez novel. Not my life, at least. My life feels more like the tale Shakespeare told of, the one written by an idiot, full of sound and fury, signifying nothing, for I can find no meaning in any of what has happened to me, in any of what is happening now.

I am ashamed and not-ashamed to say: I cry for hours. I stop for hours and then I again cry for hours. I think I might die. Then I want to die. Then I hope to die.

But I do not.

Everywhere I go, I think I see her. I know that I cannot be seeing her; I know that she is hundreds of miles away, that she is not at College Y.

(But she came to College Y once, didn't she? Couldn't she come again?)

Every time I close my eyes, I see her again. And again. And again. Every night when I sleep. Every time I rest my eyes while studying in the library.

Every time I blink.

My classes suffer. My projects suffer. I become convinced that I will never, in fact, be an architect. That I will never achieve that goal. Or, worse, that I will be an architect, but one that does not matter. I will live out my days churning out endless variations on the same basic models of strip malls, early Colonial single-family homes, and squat, boxlike convenience stores, never to construct, design, or even conceive of anything remotely worthwhile. Phil was right to leave me. She was right to push me aside before I could do nothing but betray the trust, the hope, the belief she had in me.

Despite my certainty that I will amount to nothing as an architect, architecture is still my easiest, most familiar tongue, the set of extended metaphors with which I am most conversant, and so I attempt—for a day at least—to approach my problems architecturally. My life is not a Márquez novel or any sort of novel: it is a building and Phil's love is the primary building material on the invoice. Horror of horrors, a worldwide "Phil's love" shortage has struck! How ever will we finish the building? What material can be substituted and still result in something remotely resembling the original intended structure? In my architecture classes, I pose the question repeatedly and endlessly to my fellow students, my professors: Imagine you are told to design a brick house, but there are no bricks anywhere in the world (or, more accurately but not importantly for the purposes of the discussion at hand, that the only supply of bricks on the planet is unavailable to you at and for any cost). Imagine, I tell them. Imagine, I implore them. Imagine, I order them, receiving always quizzical, querulous stares, sometimes too-swift "It can't be done"s, once or twice a puzzled silence, followed by a hesitant stab at "winning" what is perceived to be "a game," the end result being a structure, but nothing that even remotely resembles the original proposal/demand, the proposed shape and design fatally undermined by the requisite compromises of designing *sans* the most important element.

If my professors and fellow students are to be believed, then, and if the analogy holds, the only sound, architectural conclusion is this: It is possible to build my life without Phil, but it will bear no semblance at all to its original intent, and I would be crazy even to try it.

I want to call her. Hours spin into days, into weeks, and I resist. I told her that night that I would call her "later," and her lack of demurral must be seen as consent. Now is later, is it not? But "later" is "later," too, and I cannot decide which later is the *right* later, exactly *when* I intersect with the "later" in her mind when I spoke that word *then*.

She could be yearning for me right now (right later), waiting for me to call, not calling me herself because she is convinced that I am heartbroken (I am) and hate her for denying me, and so she is afraid to call me. Yes. That's it. I pick up the phone to call and then I don't because she might be with *him*, after all, as she was no doubt simply being polite when she did not demur my insistence (for surely I was insisting) that I call her later (or now).

She's waiting for my call. She's forgotten I will ever call. Wave and particle again. I stare at the cell.

She said, "I'm *with* someone else." That's all she said. There are entire universes between "love" and "with." We "love" parents, siblings, children, pets, spouses. We are "with" strangers on a bus, on a subway, in a movie theater, at the grocery store. Phil is "with" *him*, but she love(d/s) me.

She told me she loved me, couching it in covert words and phrases, in questions and indirections that I never decoded because Phil—so direct, so blunt, so fearless—never seemed to need decoding, but in this—in love—she sidestepped it each time, saying it with words between words. I never saw it until now, until being away from her forced me to re-examine every instance of our relationship, every word[19] spoken, hunting for—and now finding—hope.

Phil. Oh, Phil. Oh, beautiful, blue-tressed Phil . . .

I pick up the phone and I don't call her because what if I'm wrong? What if I've misinterpreted my own memories? Memories are, after all, subjective. It's not as though I can page back through my memories and re-examine them critically, objectively, at some remove, scouring them and scanning them like pages in a book, where the truth is set off in rigid black

19. *"Do you want to hear something scary?"*
"I don't hate you. I—"

demarcations against a pristine white backdrop, easy to read, easy to understand, with no complications or messy emotions to distract. I could be wrong.

I could also be right.

I don't call her. I'll call her later.

****

In class at the end of the semester, I curl into a corner with my latest sketchpad and draw. I have already finished the mis-named "final exam," which is no exam, but rather a take-"home" (-dorm) project to reconfigure a three-story brownstone into a series of handicapped-accessible offices, which I completed early, having nothing else to do with my time and having found that hours spent focused on models and drawings and buildings are hours blissfully numb to the pain of Phillessness. The last two classes of the semester are given over to completing the "final exam" projects, so I and a few others like me have nothing to do but read, sketch, or sit in small groups, chatting, the last of which I simply cannot do, as every attempt at even the most casual conversation over the past weeks has led—inevitably—to discussing Phil, a curiously binary subject in that I never tire of speaking of her, of dissecting her words, her actions, and her conjectured motives, whereas others tire almost immediately. I, however, am helpless to speak of anything but, even when I see the glaze of exhaustion in the eyes of a speaking companion, and I cannot restrain myself from spilling forth a flood of anecdotes ("This one time, we took the subway to MOMA and she told me that . . ."), recriminations ("She came here at Spring Break and fucked me and then a couple of weeks later, she's with *him*."), and questions ("What do you think it means when she says [insert any of a million words spoken to me by Phil since I met her]?"), desperate to find that new angle, that new perception that will clarify everything, make obvious and knowable what had been hidden and unknown. The responses, inevitably, predictably, and monotonously, all reduce to the same sentiment: "Forget about her. Move on. Meet someone else."

"That's impossible."

I look up from my sketch pad to see my professor standing over me, frowning down at the currently exposed page, on which I have been detailing the "subsuite" of my underwater hotel, complete with its transparent ceiling and walls, and hydrodynamic elevator.

"Impossible. It won't work that way," says the professor, who is stern but fair, with an undistinguished and easily ignored vocal tic no longer noticed after being in his presence for a semester. "You can't have an elevator descend through water without a shaft of some sort."

"Diving bells do it," I tell him. "I'm going to use a similar principle—"

"It still won't work. When the elevator goes through the ceiling, there's no way to keep water from spilling into the room. There has to be a shaft from the room to the surface."

"No. The idea is that . . ." I drift off into frustrated silence for a moment. Phil understood. I didn't have to explain it to her at all. Like the elevator building. She just got it, and I miss that so much and so powerfully that I am temporarily unable to speak.

"I get the idea," he says soothingly, mistaking my silence for a different sort of frustration, "but it just won't work."

"It has to," I tell him. "I want people to feel like they're drifting down, not being sucked down through a tube like a straw."

"And—" he goes on, as if the shaft/no-shaft issue has been

settled (which, in his mind, it has) "—you have to consider the water pressure and the weight of the fluids in designing the ceiling. You'll need a transparent material at least a couple of feet thick. You can't use glass—too expensive in this thickness. You'd need to use acrylic."

"But people need to see the fish."

"At that depth, acrylic is as clear as water." He reaches over and—without asking—flips a few pages. The elevator building comes into view. "Ah. Like the shape-shifting building in Dubai."

I bristle. All around me, my fellow students look up and look over. I feel as though I've been caught copying during a test. My cheeks flame. "No. That building has rooms that move horizontally. These move vertically."

"I see. Rem Koolhaas did something like that in France. A glass room that goes up and down a three-story house. Did it for a wheelchair-bound homeowner."

"This is different," I say, too loudly, attracting more attention. "This is a totally new idea. This is my idea. This is every room, not just one. This is a skyscraper, not—"

He purses his lips and shakes his head to silence me. "Come see me this afternoon during office hours, OK?"

****

Later that afternoon, I slink into my professor's office like a child sent to the principal's office, unsure as to precisely what sin I have committed. He smiles from behind his desk, bids me close the door, then waves me into a seat.

"Mike," he begins, gesturing for my sketchbook, "you are one of the most promising— Ah, thank you." Thus self-interrupted, he flips through the sketchbook, shaking his head minutely and tsk-tsking at the underwater hotel pages (for there are more of them than simply the one he glimpsed earlier today).

"I like it when students have ambition," he says, "but there's a thin line between ambition and overreaching. Are you serious about this idea? Building a hotel underwater? A . . ." He studies the pages again. "Some sort of transparent dome on the ocean floor?"

"It's meant to be reminiscent of an air bubble underwater," I tell him. "The idea is that you can go down there and see the fish and the wildlife and—"

"The ocean's a big place. How do you know you'll be near anything at all? What are the odds some fish will just swim by this place?"

Site and context. "I'll put it near a coral reef," I tell him, as though I've planned to do so all along, the thought having just occurred to me, along with the idea that—perhaps—I need to become SCUBA trained in order to work on this project. To see the site. The context. To experience it personally, like every good architect should.

"Why a dome?" he asks.

"The dome is as old as Hadrian. Makes you feel like you're under a protective sky."

"But in this case, the occupant is *not* under a protective sky. He's underwater."

"The dome is the best way to manufacture it. Build it on the surface, pre-fab, and sink it. The dome's structure will diffuse the water pressure from outside. So I can use a thinner acrylic that way. It'll be cheaper."

He shakes his head. "You'll use less acrylic, but manufacturing a curvature means a more expensive building process, so there goes your savings. Also, you'll get distortion where the acrylic curves. No one will be able to see there. You need to make a box, not a dome. It's all about refraction. You'll have to invent a whole new science of statics."

Maybe I also need a degree in physics. "But the air bubble motif—"

"So you'd be better off pre-fabbing a traditional series of walls—" Here, he turns to a blank page in my sketchbook and scratches out four boring walls with efficient pencil strokes "—that have large picture windows of acrylic. Then—" Still drawing, each movement of his pencil a violation "—a traditional ceiling, spotted over the bed area with an acrylic porthole of some sort to allow a line of sight to the fish or what-have-you."

"But that's not the idea. That's just a room underwater. The idea is complete, 360-degree horizontal visibility and 180-degree vertical—"

"With no ornamentation or details on the walls? Who do you think you are—Loos?" he jokes.[20]

"Only the room would be underwater. The rest of the hotel—reception and all that—would be above water and would look like a normal hotel."

"No one could afford this. You'd have to invent a whole new way of getting electricity and plumbing in there. What about privacy on the inside? Bathroom walls?" I have no answer ready for that and before I can begin to invent one, he keeps firing at me: "What about something as simple as flushing a toilet under the ocean?"

"A pressurized toilet . . ." I say weakly.

"The expense for this thing is massive. Who would build it?"

"Frank Lloyd Wright said that architecture should benefit the end-user, not the landlord."

20. Adolf Loos believed that modern architecture should lack ornamentation, likening ornamentation to tattoos on "savages."

"I know quite a bit about Wright," he says sardonically. "But if no one will build it, it won't benefit anyone."

His tone is so smug and so dismissive that I cannot help but to sit up straighter, my own defensiveness commingling with Phil's unadulterated glee at the idea of the underwater hotel room, and then, Phil-linked, I remember her chortling mirth at her reviews one night, as she crowed, "They told me it didn't make any sense to have a white girl play Othello! Well, I showed them!"

When casting had been announced, she'd been assailed from both the theater purists and the avant garde. To the former, she was daring to recombine the sacred words of the Bard, compiling a new, "politically correct" text. To the latter, she was indulging in abject political *in*correctness, supplanting a black character with a white one. She was accused of cultural appropriation, of racism and sexism at one shot. And on opening night, she proved them all wrong, her deft and sensitive portrayal of Othello's conflict compelling even the most ardent cynic and critic to admit that she had wrung new droplets of meaning and nuance from the hoary old play.

I asked her what was next, and I can hear her words in this moment just as I heard them in the historical one: "More. Bigger. Better. Crazier," she said. "Next? I don't know. Maybe *Waiting for Godot* as a film noir."

And she did it. She made it happen, Phil did.

I tell my professor with utmost confidence: "Diller and Scofidio. The Blur Building. If they can build an inhabitable cloud, why can't I build an inhabitable air bubble?" Before he can object, I press on. "Wright reinvented the idea of a museum with the Guggenheim. Why can't I reinvent the idea of the hotel?"

He taps the eraser-end of his pencil on his own sketch for a moment. One. Two. Three. Tap. Tap. Tap. "I don't know quite how to break this to you," he says in a tone that communicates that he knows precisely how to break it to me, "but you're not Diller and Scofidio. And you're sure as hell not Frank Lloyd Wright."

"How do you know that? Maybe I am."

I expect an angry rejoinder—an admonition to "be realistic," to not take myself "so seriously," to "get over" myself—but instead he chuckles, flips back a few pages in the sketchbook and again makes a series of pencil strokes there.

"Mike, I like your energy and your imagination. I really do. I don't want to discourage you. But architecture is about marrying the creative and the practical. Be patient. Don't reach too high too soon. You're better off with something a little easier. Something a little less complex than underwater hotel rooms or entire buildings that move. Keep it simple and don't try to be so complex." He leans forward, as though telling me a secret, even though there is no one else in the office to overhear. "Sometimes our ambition extends beyond our capabilities. Sometimes we're better off realizing our own limitations. Architecture is an old man's game. Your time will come. In the meantime, focus on the fundamentals and maybe someday you'll get to do something like this." He holds up the sketchbook, then slides it back to me across the desk.

"I want to do it now." I take the book back and cradle it like a frightened child. "Why should I have to wait?"

He clucks his tongue and dismisses me, then tells me (as I walk out the door) to "keep thinking creatively," convinced that he has guided a fledgling architect from a path of uselessness and despair to a path of utility and success, not realizing that if I followed his advice I would be thinking *un*creatively, that ignoring his advice is the only way to sculpt reality to fit my vision. His vision, blinkered, obviates the entire purpose of the room, to wit: to engender in the inhabitant a sensation of being part of the ocean, of belonging to and in and of that fluid environment; to look in any direction at any time and see fish, contrary to his notion of looking in a specific spot and spying—perhaps, if one is lucky—a fish or two if one/they happen(s) to be swimming by.

"That would be so cool," Phil said to me when she saw it, lying intertwined with me on a library sofa one day at a time remembered forward in a flashback.

"It's not really practical," I said, anticipatorially mimicking my future/present architecture professor.

"Who cares?" she said. "It's cool. It's fun. It's new. I love it. You have to build it someday and I'll live there with you. It's like living underwater."

I'll live there with you. Permanence. A promise of some sort of lasting connection. *I'll live there with you.* Belief in me, belief in us, a vow to be together.

I had it. In that moment, I had it and I did not recognize it, and I lost it.

Lost, now.

Phil.

She is memories and regrets now. I love her, but that love is useless, without purpose. In Alaska, there is a forest of black spruce that stretches for miles along the rail line wending through the landscape and along the highway, a forest that is dead. An earthquake wrenched the land from its bed and saltwater sluiced inland from the sea, saturating the trees from the roots up so quickly that they were killed and preserved instantly. Traingoers see only a stark forest of still-standing spruce, black as their name. They are like my love—a dead, useless thing, preserved but without life or function or meaning.

I open the sketchbook. On the same page that so inspired and thrilled Phil, my professor has written, "Be patient," in neat block letters, and I can only wonder why I should have to wait for the world.

CHAPTER 10

At home, my parents greet me with parental words, then disappear. My brother shows me the love letter/e-mail/text message/Valentine's Day card he has sent to his crush, only to be met with diffidence and indifference, surely a fate worse than outright rejection. He makes an age-inappropriate comment made uncomfortably hilarious by the fact that I am not sure whether or not he knows what he's said. I fight off a fierce urge to tell him to ignore/disown this girl, as she will lead only to heartache, as well as an equally strong and opposing urge to implore him to—even at the tender age of 8/10/12—pledge his love to her early and often and to never, ever let her out of his sight. Each option seems as palatable and as nauseating as the other, each one equally desirable and equally horrifying. My brother says something despondent on the subject of love, and though I want nothing more than to tell him he's wrong, our mutual experiences stop me from doing so.

It seems no one's love is whole these days.

In my room, I am assailed by memories of Phil: the bed where I laid and talked to her for long nights on the phone, including our first bout of phone sex; the desk where I sat and IM'd with her; the framed and hanging photos from my youth that she gazed at for long moments before pronouncing my past self "a cute kid" and then kissing me fiercely. The urge to call her is stronger than ever, almost disorienting, as though being in this room again has also sent me back in time—emotionally, if not physically—to a time when I could carelessly and casually call Phil whenever I wanted, a past so much finer than this constrained present. I check my phone repeatedly as the night wears on, each time positive that I have somehow managed to set it to silent or vibrate and, therefore, missed a call or text. Too, I check and double-check and re-double-check the signal bars, confident each time that I have lost my cell signal, discovering each time that I have not.

Phil must know that I've come home for the summer, but she has neither called nor texted. Neither has she e-mailed nor hailed me on chat. (Opening my laptop now, I see her screen-name in my buddy list, meaning she sees mine, too, but she does not "hello!" me or acknowledge my cyber-existence—and, by extension, my existence—at all.) She is so close to me now, only four subway stops away as we reckon city distances. At school, I could forget her for whole minutes at a time, but now her proximity taunts me.

I stay awake until I fall asleep, and sleep until I wake up.

****

George does not call me when I arrive home for the summer, as he promised. Rather, on my second night home, he knocks at my door, saying only, "Dude, I'm not a Marine anymore. Don't ask," before clasping my hand and pulling me in for a hug with arms and shoulders more solid than I am used to—Marine arms and shoulders in everything, mysteriously, save the name.

"What happened?" I blurt out in shock, in direct contradiction to his just-issued command. "Sorry. Never mind. Sorry."

"What's up with you?" he asks, releasing me from the clinch. "I've been worried about you, you know what I mean?"

Spending his semester training to kill and stay alive, deprived of sleep, humping fifty-pound packs through the heat and humidity of Parris Island, George has been worried about me while I, for my part, have been worried about . . . me, once again proving that George is my best friend and I am not his.

"I'm OK," I lie with shame and pride, and follow it with "except for" and launch into a litany of confusions and misunderstandings and emotions and recriminations and second guesses, a truly bewildering array of words and sentences that make no sense except to me, but George keeps up, nodding in concern, grunting in agreement or sympathy. We sit outside—now that the sun's gone down, the summer desert heat is bearable—and I ask him every question I've asked myself over the past two months, ask him every question I've wanted to ask Phil, then follow those questions with the anger, the rage, the disappointment, the sorrow, the misery, the despondence, the helplessness. I had her and I lost her. Worse yet, I had her and threw her away. Worst of all, I had her, threw her away, had a second chance, and still lost her.

"Dude," George says, "you're a mess."

"I love her, George. I love her so much."

"This isn't healthy. You've been bottling this stuff up for how long? Months? There was no one to talk to at College Y?"

"Not like this. Not where I could just pour it all out, you know?"

"Dude, you need a change of scenery. Trapped up there all this time. And being back home isn't any good because you go in that old bedroom and all you can think about is the past."

He puts a hand on my shoulder and looks up at the clear, star-speckled sky. "Trust me on that one."

"I just want her back."

"Yeah, I get that. But you don't get to have her back."

"Why not? It's like . . . It's like I feel like there's something I can say or do, some perfect sentence or perfect action that will make her remember that she loves me and—"

"Dude."

"No. Don't stop me. Look, there's got to be something, OK? She never said she's in love with *him*. She never said that. Don't you see? She came to me at Spring Break. *She* came to *me*. That was like a sign, right? Only I didn't get it. But it was just a couple of weeks later that she was with *him*. She gave up on me because I didn't do anything. So now I have to do something."

"You did do something. You told her you love her. And she shot you down."

"She was surprised. She wasn't expecting me to call, to say that. That's all."

"Then why didn't she call back once she got over her surprise?"

"Because she thinks— Because she knows she hurt me." I realize, to my own surprise, that I am crying openly in front of George, a fact that is less unexpected than the fact that George has just put an arm around me and pulled me close, his small-yet-strong frame seeming to dwarf my larger one, as though he has become a parent to me. "She hurt me," I go on, unable to stop speaking, even though I am horrified by my lachrymose display. "And she—"

"Right. She hurt you. Why would you want to be back with her? She *hurt* you, dude."

"I hurt her, too. So we're even."

I feel him shake his head above my own. "Dude, you said

you loved her and she didn't even hesitate. She just blew you off. Bam. Done. You don't want to be with that person."

But I do. "But I do," I tell him. "I do. I love her."

****

Eventually, I collect myself, George releases me, and I sit up, wiping my cheeks clean of tears. We will never speak of this.

"Dude, you need to do something. You need to be out there. Having some fun. Something to distract yourself."

He tells me about a special ball and charity auction at The WB the next evening, which he learned about when he answered a survey about his musical tastes and preferences on MyFace-Place. The event is being held to introduce the new merged faculty and to celebrate the successful alumni of both schools (now the successful alumni of Consolidated Wallace, The CW). It mostly, however, serves as a charitable event to raise money for reconstruction of the Other City and relocation for those displaced in the wake of Lucky Sevens. The Barth family, it turns out, did not only lend its fortune and its name to my alma mater; it also donated extensively to causes in the Other City, becoming so influential that even a subway line in the Other City was named for it.

"It'll be great," George promises. "We'll go. We'll laugh at our old teachers. You'll scope the honeys. There were *other* hot girls at The WB, you know. And I've seen some of the chicks from United[21] and they're nothing to sneeze at, you know what I mean?"

"I don't want to meet someone else."

21. United Preparatory National (or UPN), the (despite its name) local school merging with The WB to form Consolidated Wallace.

"Who said anything about meeting anyone else? You're just window-shopping, is all."

"I don't have any money for an auction. I have to find a summer job still."

"You're not gonna bid on anything. We're just going for fun. There will be girls who are going for fun, too. If something happens, it happens. Otherwise, hey—we had a great night out, right?"

I have no desire whatsoever to go to the event, nor any desire to "have fun" or anything resembling fun. Indeed, I strongly doubt I am even capable of having fun. However, looking now at George, at George who—moments ago—held me in his arms while I wept, who is no longer a Marine, who has seen his life's dream derailed and destroyed and yet who wants to talk not about that, but rather about my (wreck of a) love life, I realize or rather *decide* as this is now an action I take, *deciding* that at the very least I can do this for him, this small thing that he wants and—from the look in his eyes—needs. George initially attended The WB on scholarship (before his mother's fortunes turned), so perhaps this is why it means so much to him that we attend the event, to offer moral if not financial support.

"Fine," I tell him. "We'll go."

"Dude. Massive. I owe you," he says, and sadly enough, he believes that to be true.

****

And so now it happens. Somehow, I have known that this would/will/must happen. As George and I step into the auditorium of The WB for the last time (not because we will never return or because something drastic will happen to the building, but rather because—after tonight—the building will be renamed, rechristened, and re-signaged with The CW signs and plaques, complete with new logo and typeface), I experience *déjà vu* and a premonitory sense of awareness at the same time, mindful that I have both experienced this before and am about to experience it again, yet for the first time. I remember the dream/vision which I discussed with George while on his porch more than a year ago, remember him reaching for another Stella Artois, remember the night of the dream, the man with the scrambled name, the warning of Inframan, and I smell chocolate syrup, so strong and so pervasive that I feel as though I've bathed in it, as though everyone around me has bathed in it, and I struggle under the welter of memory and sense and sensation to remember the specifics of the dream/vision so that I can be prepared when George grabs my arm.

"Oh, no," George says. "Dude, oh. I didn't know. Don't look," which is the surest way to guarantee that I will do nothing but look, and that immediately, and so, turning to look in the proscribed direction, I see Phil, which should have been inevitable, I suppose, as Phil, too, loved/loves her school/alma mater. With her is, of course, *him*, *his* arm linked with hers as they enter the auditorium. Phil is wearing a familiar red dress and even though it looks terrible on her, I still cannot help but to feel a tug towards her, a pull that is as unintentional and irresistible as the gravity that keeps the dumb moon yoked to the earth, the senseless earth yoked to the sun.

"Dude, I should have realized she would be here," says George as I grab his forearm, an anchor to keep gravity from yanking me across the floor and into Phil. "I'm so sorry. I wasn't thinking."

"It's all right," I tell him, intending it as a lie, but realizing as I say it that it is, in reality, the truth, that it *is* all right that Phil is here, that I am actually *glad* she's here, for now she will be forced to deal with me, to deal with me not as a voiceless, disembodied series of e-mails or texts, but rather to deal with my physical presence. Will that change things? Her presence has affected me—should not my presence—in some sort of Newtonian seeking of balance—have an effect on her? [22]

"The red one is all wrong," I tell George. "She should have worn the teal."

He rolls his eyes at me and we share a brief, honest chuckle. "Dude, so now you're a fashion critic?"

Discomfited by the mysterious phantom smell of chocolate syrup, it takes me a moment to respond. "Yeah, well . . ." I look back to her, just to prove that I can do so, and my heart hammers at the sight of Phil, no longer in red.

No longer in red at all.

Now clothed in the teal dress I love so much.

22. By "Newtonian," Mike is thinking "equal and opposite," but that would most likely mean that Phil would feel intense hate for Mike, commensurate to the love he feels for her. Probably not the effect he was/is hoping for.

CHAPTER 12

None of that, of course, was or could be the beginning. Our tales do not begin with Chapter Ones any more than skyscrapers begin on their first stories—there are basements and subbasements, and leave us not forget the essential foundation, the digging and reinforcing and buttressing required before even the subbasement can be framed, before even the concrete can be poured. Even the foundation cannot be said to be the beginning, for to begin the foundation, first ground must be broken—to build up, one must first dig down deep and excavate the earth in order to make room for what is to come. And before that? (For the process does not begin with the breaking ground.) *Ante* ground-breaking comes the site selection and blueprints—electrical and plumbing, mechanical—before which comes the architect, the design, before which comes the desire, the urge to build in the first place: the idea. All of these things must take place to lead to ground-breaking. All of them must be perfect and complete for there to be ground-breaking. Any mistake from the idea to outline to the choice of where and how to the structure itself can forestall or obviate ground-breaking. In short, the *program* comes first, that list of requirements for a space, which the architect must consult and hew to when translating notion into reality.

All this before the foundation is laid. All before the first story.

DJ Tea spun up a new 45, an old song: "I Want to Hold Your Hand," by the Quarrymen. I watched Phil dance to its aged rhythms with *him*, the reek of chocolate syrup slowly abating. The dress was fond teal now, and had always been so. I chose to think of it no longer, for clearly only I could perceive its changes. Only I could recall both realities: red and teal. Two worlds, each equal and valid, with only one person living in them both.

"Dude, are you going to be okay if I leave you alone for a couple minutes?" George asked. "I see some people I want to talk to, but I don't want to leave if you're . . . You know what I mean?"

"I'm fine. Go ahead."

He wandered off to a group of former underclassmen with whom he had been friendly when we attended The WB, met with a cry of fellowship audible even from where I stood. There was no one here who would greet me in similar fashion. George had been my best friend in high school and my only true friend, discounting Phil, who was more than friend, then less.

As I stood alone, I could not help but to watch Phil and *him*, and to muse on how my thoughts had begun to clear, to become slightly more coherent in my own skull, perhaps as though the realization that I could edit reality allowed me to edit my thoughts into something more sensible.

How far could I go? Was I limited only to changing Phil's wardrobe? Could I edit reality to conform to the absurd notion that she had come to the dance *au naturel*? I tried to imagine a logical series of events that would lead to that outcome and came up empty-handed and empty-thoughted. Red or teal—yes, those were a moment's decision. Naked? That was a major life-altering decision, and surely *he* would have balked at bringing her here thus. Surely *he* would have refused to allow her into the car, assuming she even would have made it down her driveway before being noticed, pointed out, humiliated back inside.

All of which thinking caused me to wonder: *Why* had Phil chosen to wear the red/chosen to wear the teal? When my whim edited reality, what happened retroactively to cause her to choose one over the other, and then the other over the one?

In other words: I had not simply edited reality to change the color of Phil's dress. I had, in some unknowable way, edited reality such that I changed Phil's thought process, her decision-making apparatus. The dress color had not changed as of the moment of my thinking it—the dress changed as of the minutes/hours/days when Phil selected which garment to wear to The WB.

I went dizzy with the implications and had to sit down.

If I had somehow altered Phil's past thinking process to force her to wear one dress over another—and done so with no apparent ill effects to Phil or to anyone else, save for my own slight disorientation and the lingering scent of chocolate—then could I transform *other* elements of her thought processes? Could I edit reality such that she would make different decisions about different issues entirely?

Surely such power was not intended for mere sartorial exploitation.

The dizziness faded, in its place rising twin fountains of thrill and fear, geysers of equal force and intensity, though of opposing concern. Could I make Phil realize she loved me? Perhaps more important: *Should* I? I could not imagine any reason why not . . . unless in the doing I somehow hurt Phil. But how could this hurt her? Phil had been happy with me, after all. She loved me then and she still loves me now, I know. She's just forgotten it, buried it under layers of pain because I left for College Y.

But now I could fix all of that, so long as I was willing to take the chance.

I watched Phil and *him* on the dance floor until *he* left, pecking her on the lips a single, painful (to me) time, before departing in the direction of the bathrooms. Seizing my opportunity, I intercepted Phil on her way to the bar, my obvious urgency blunting any pretense of casualness I may have attempted.

"We have to talk," I told her.

"We don't have anything to talk about."

"Just for a second, okay? I don't want to be a pain in the ass or anything. I just have to ask you something."

"Mike. Look." She glanced over her shoulder, bathroom-ward. I, too, kept a weather eye in that direction, lest *he* return and misinterpret my intentions with Phil. (For how could *he* do anything *but* misinterpret them, as *he* could not reasonably assume that I was discussing the editing of reality with her?) "We don't have anything to talk about. Maybe another time. Not tonight. I'm just trying to have fun tonight."

"I understand. And I promise, I'm going to let you get back to your fun. I just have to ask you a very simple question, and it's not the one you think I'm going to ask."

"Oh?" One blue eyebrow arched. "And what's the one I think you're going to ask?"

I realized then that there were, in fact, so many questions I wished to ask Phil. There was no one, single obvious question; there was, instead, a multitude of them.[23] Although I had

23. Such as, from the infamous Spring Break assignation: *Did you really just come [to my room at College Y] for a shower?* and *What the hell, Phil? You don't even know if I'm seeing someone and you just let me fuck you?*

accosted Phil while in transit to the bar with the intention of asking only one question, I suddenly had a plethora of them crowding in my head, fighting for access to my tongue.

"Phil, please," I finally managed. "Just one question. Something strange is happening. Just tell me why you wore *that* dress. What were you thinking?"

She pulled away from me, eyes narrowed, lips set grimly. "Stop it, Mike. You're just embarrassing yourself. I did *not* wear this for you."

"Fine. Fine! Then why. Why did you wear it? What was your thought process? Just tell me and I promise I'll leave you alone."

She sighed and balled her hands into fists. "Fine. I'll tell you. And then you leave me the hell alone for the rest of the night."

"Deal."

"The teal is my favorite and I look good in it. And if you must know, *he* likes me in it. I'm sorry if that hurts you."

It did, but I did not allow myself to show that. Instead, I simply said to her, "I'm sorry—the band was loud. I didn't hear you. Could you say that again?" Now speaking to a red-bedressed Phil.

"*I said,*" she yelled over the DJ's volume, another Quarrymen hit, as though he's stuck on a single, ancient disc, "*I was going to wear the teal, but I had a feeling you might be here. I know it's your favorite, and I didn't want you to get the wrong idea if I wore it.*"

Yes, yes, of course . . . I was in the early stages of what I recognized would soon become a full-blown panic. The universe—the *universe*—had warped around me not once, but multiple times at my whim. I had to understand it. How could I go on *not* understanding it?

"But what led to that decision? What were you thinking? Did someone say something that led you down that path?"

"Mike. Enough. It's over, okay? You need to move on."

"But did something *make* you decide to—"

"I just *told* you. Now, seriously—enough. I don't want to be a bitch or anything, but if you keep this up, I'm going to go find a security guy."

"Phil . . ."

"Leave me alone, Mike."

"You said you wanted us to be friends. You said you couldn't imagine us not being friends."

"Well, you're not acting very friendly tonight," she said quietly. DJ Tea chose that moment to play something soft and slow, meaning I heard every last devastating syllable.

Phil proceeded to the bar, still in her red dress, which I'd not changed back. It no longer mattered though. Not the dress. Not the pain of her last remark to me. Nothing mattered unless I decided it mattered. I would fix everything. I could fix it all.

****

After watching *him* return to the dance floor, I went into the bathroom and did something I hadn't done in so long that I could not remember having ever done it. In fact, as I prepared to do it, my heartbeat skipped and jumped as worry thrilled me. Was this like my last name? Like the internal narrator? Was I facing another Third Wall?

I took a deep breath.

I looked in the mirror.

I saw myself. Only myself.

I had been worried that perhaps I would not recognize myself, that in addition to not knowing my own last name, it would turn out that I also did not know what I looked like. But such was not the case—I saw nothing more exotic or exciting or frightening than my own face staring back at me in the mirror.

I thought of the Third Wall and I thought of the internal narrator's voice, and I wondered if these had been forerunners—vanguards, heralds—of my ability to edit reality. Were they preparing me for this day, when I would realize my editorial power over the world? Or had those earlier quirks of nature and reality merely been indicators that I was susceptible to this talent? Were there others like me? If more than one person edited reality, whose edit superseded? Was what I was going to attempt in any way dangerous? Would doing this be the equivalent of rape, forcing Phil back to me against her will?

No. I knew Phil still loved me. She did not entirely understand this yet. And so I would not impose my will on her and simply change her emotions with the easy facility with which I'd changed her dress. Instead, I would fix what *I* had done and said, the mistakes I had made to lead us to this point. I would not simply say, "Phil is now in love with me." I would change what I had done that had made Phil believe she no longer loved me. As a result, her love would return naturally, of its own accord. While she did not explain the specific incidents that caused her to choose now-red, now-teal, the fact remains that in each instance—in each reality, as it were—she had perfectly logical, rational reasons for choosing each dress. More importantly, in each instance, she was happy and content with the decision, even though they were two radically different decisions. And so, altering the circumstances under which she made a prior decision would lead to her choosing me over *him* and, at the same time, result in a reality in which she at the very least was no *less* happy than the current one, and quite possibly (indeed, quite probably, in my estimation) happi*er*, with the additional bonus that I will be happy as well.

The smell of chocolate syrup returned, this time overwhelming. I tightened my grip on the cool porcelain of the sink and stared into my own mirrored eyes, themselves the color of milk chocolate. I gagged. I thought again of her dress—currently red. But I remembered the teal. When I edited reality and let it take its course into a new reality and love between Phil and me, I would still remember breaking up with her. I would still remember the months at College Y without her, wanting her. I would still remember the Spring Break visit and all its confusion and the heartache that followed and the tears and the hopelessness and the yearning and the denial. I would remember this alongside new memories of Phil, just as I remembered the red dress and the teal dress. Two sets of memories, perpetually. Could I withstand that? The duplicity and the overlap and the cognitive dissonance?

And then I realized: Although it had been only a scant half hour ago, I could no longer remember *which* dress Phil had originally worn while entering The WB. Was it red or teal? I could not remember. I knew it was red *now*, but what had she "really" chosen to wear? I did not know.

Reality was what I made it. It no longer mattered what she had "really" chosen. As of now and as of always, she had chosen (had always chosen) the red.

Once I edited reality again, she would have always chosen me. I would remember the other, but in time it would fade, as sure as the memory of the "real" dress choice had faded.

I leaned over the sink and spat, expecting a bolus of chocolate, rewarded only with a thin string of sputum. The odor was so thick in my nose and in my sinuses that I felt congested with it, as if I had a chocolate infection commandeering my head. But I had to press on. I spigotted water into my cupped hands and drank it, its metallic tang cutting the chocolate scent that had migrated to my throat and tongue and become a horribly bittersweet taste.

It was time. I looked in the mirror again.

I knew exactly what to change:

CHAPTER 9

Phil has rolled out of bed while I slept and dreamed, and now bends, her pantied backside me-aimed, to retrieve her bra and shirt from amongst my scattered clothes on the floor. I open my mouth to speak, but say nothing, due not to a lack of anything to say, but rather too much to say, each possible phrase or sentence pregnant with the potential to create a new universe of its own in this moment:

I love you, Phil, or

This was a mistake, Phil, or

Did you really just come here for a shower?, or

Are you seeing anyone?, or

Does this mean we're back together?, or

What the hell, Phil? You don't even know if I'm seeing someone and you just let me fuck you?

And on and on, *I originally thought at this moment*, universes and timelines spinning up and out from my speech, spiraling into their own infinities.

"Phil," I say, breaking the timeline, inserting the cursor of me into the running text of reality, "I love you."

She turns slowly, then freezes in time, in space, in everything. Am I making the world stand still? Is this what I've done? I choke back the stench of chocolate syrup, so powerfully thick that I want to blurt *How can you not* smell *that?* but I remain silent instead, silent and just as frozen as she until she says:

"What did you say?"

"I said I love you." I realize I'm trembling, but I don't know why. Is this what speaking the truth does? Is the truth an epileptic fit? Is the truth a tremor, a temblor?

Or is this the result of the plate tectonic shock of my rewriting reality? Have I fractured something important and irrevocable?

It's too late to fix it now. I forge ahead. I can barely force the words out through the clotting reek of chocolate; it's like speaking through an all-encompassing, all-consuming head cold. "I love you. I've always loved you. I shouldn't have broken up with you. Maybe I shouldn't have even come here to Y, but you know, we probably could have done the long-distance thing. We should have. I was an idiot. I haven't been able to stop thinking about you since I got here. I love you."

Now bra'd and shirted, she simply stares at me.

"Where the . . ." A head shake. A confused working of the lips. "Where did this come from, Mike? You've barely spoken to me in *months.* Where the hell did this come from?"

Needless to say, this is scarcely the reaction I anticipated. I anticipated: A rush into my arms. A gasping of "I love you, too!" A plethora of kisses, her warm and taut body wriggling against mine. These things and more I anticipated. These things and more, I am denied.

"Phil . . . I love you." As though saying it—as though the combination of her name and those words—could somehow rewrite reality in a way I have been unable to. "I love you. I've always loved you."

"And you're saying it now? Because you're lonely?"

"That's not why—"

"You come here, you leave me to come here, and then you don't hook up, so you decide you love me and then—"

"No, Phil. No."

"I don't love you. I'm sorry. I don't love you. I'm with someone else."

The same words. The exact same words she used before, using them earlier now. The smell of chocolate has faded, leaving behind only the faint tang of our sex and Phil's soap-clean skin.

"You're with *him*," I say, unable to believe the words even as they leave my mouth, unable to believe the truth of them, denying the truth of them.

For the first time since I spoke, she looks not-angry. She looks shocked.

"Yes," she says at last, wondering how I could know this as desperately as I am wondering why she would come here to fuck me when she is back with *him*.

"You don't love him," I tell her, remembering my conversation with George, a conversation that has yet to happen and now may never happen. "You said you're *with* him, not that you *love* him."

We stare volumes between us. It would be the easiest thing in the world for her to say—haughtily—*I* do *love him*, but it would also be the most difficult thing in the world.

"Who I love doesn't matter," she says after a paragraph that feels like a novel. "What matters is that I don't love you."

"You came here. You came to see me."

"I thought we were friends. I needed a shower."

I take a step towards her. She is still half-naked, her shirt unbuttoned, the slopes of her pale breasts in sharp relief against the black of her bra. I have been naked this whole time, though neither of us seems to have noticed or remembered until now.

"You wanted me," I tell her, and it has been not long since I spent myself inside her, but I want this, and so I make it so, rising.

"Sex was never good with *him*," I tell her. "You told me that, when we were together. It's the truth, isn't it?"

She says nothing. But she does not step back or away as I close in on her, and then we are kissing, her hands finding the angles of my shoulder blades. My fingers slide down her shirt, discovering purchase on the sharp yet soft plane of her hipbones, pulling her to me, my hardness unmistakable, insistent. We part mouths for a moment—only a moment—then devour each other again, harsh breath through our noses, warm, lips slick, tongues aggressive. She moans deep in her throat, a surrender.

"I don't love you," she whispers as my lips and tongue play against her earlobe, her neck, the hollow of her shoulder, as she presses herself hard against where I am hard.

I pin her hands against the wall over her head and lean into her. "Say it again."

"I don't love you."

"Say it."

"I don't love you." Choked through tears.

I lean in and kiss her again, feel her respond, lean in closer, feel the strong, yearning heat of her against me, feel her wanting me, feel her tears as they trickle between our cheeks.

"I don't love you. I don't." Hungry at my mouth, devouring me where I devour her.

I want the next part. I want the rest. I want it. But I skip it; I can't bear to see it or say it. I cut away to after, the two of us lying in a naked heap against the bed.

"That was amazing," she says drowsily because I've made it so. "That was the best ever."

I could make it the best she ever had or ever will have. I could end the chapter, cut to fifty years from now and she's a frustrated old woman who has never had a lover like me . . .

I pant. I catch my breath. She cries again, this time not the quiet subtle tears of joy or release, but the powerful sobs of confusion.

"I don't love you," she chokes. "I really don't. I don't understand. I don't understand. I don't know why I'm doing any of this. It's all fucked up and I'm . . . I don't understand."

I want to tell her what I've done. I want to explain. But I can't. And she came here of her own volition, after all. Before I ever interceded, before I ever interrupted myself and rewrote my actions, she still came here, she still fucked me, despite not loving me, despite being with *him*.

"I don't understand either," I tell her, pulling away from the tangle of us.

What is to follow—the conversation, the leaving—will not be pleasant. I know how it will end. And so I end it here.

CHAPTER 13

I leaned over the sink in the bathroom at The WB and—to my shock—threw up a single, slimy wad of something unidentifiable. I stared for long moments at the vomitus in the basin before me, expecting the lingering taste of chocolate, but instead unsure as to what vile flavor(s) persisted in my mouth. I could not remember what I had eaten that day. Indeed, I could not remember any meal I had ever eaten in my life. Had I ever eaten anything? With a twist of the faucet, a spray of lukewarm water dissolved the evidence of my spewing, washing it down the drain.

I had failed. It was too late. I chose to change things too late—on some level, she'd already made her decision by the time she came to visit me at Y. Perhaps that was one final farewell for herself. One last sexual thrill. Maybe she was just confirming her decision.

I needed to go back farther.

I rinsed my mouth, swishing and spitting as though at the dentist's office. Behind me, the bathroom door opened and closed, but I stayed at the sink with tepid water in my cupped

hands, still leaning over, wondering if my churning stomach could tolerate a drink of water and, further, if it could tolerate a drink of the water that spurts forth from the pipes and spigots of The WB. When I was in fifth grade, a letter home to parents revealed that unacceptable levels of lead had been found in the water at The WB, leading some wag to post "Leaded" and "Unleaded" signs on the drinking fountains for the months we were disallowed from using them while the pipes were refitted. Still, even though the issue was fixed years ago, I could never again bend to sip from a WB tap without thinking of heavy metals clotting my system.

"Hey," someone said, and before I looked up into the mirror, I knew it was *him*.

My first thought, upon spying *his* reflection over my shoulder, was that *he* must have been suffering some distress of the renal or intestinal sort, for *he* had just left the bathroom mere moments ago.

And then *he* locked the bathroom door with a turn of *his* wrist, and my thoughts became more obvious and more sensible.

I wiped dry my lips with the back of my hand. "What do you want?"

He came closer to me, arm's-length away. "She told me. About Spring Break," *he* added unnecessarily, for what else could have "she told [*him*]" that would account for the seething anger, the flare of *his* nostrils, the fire in *his* eyes?

I didn't know what to say in response. What could I say? My initial instinct was to deny it, to laugh it off in order to spare myself what was inevitably to come next, foreshadowed and forewarned by the locking of the door. But why *should* I deny it? I had done nothing wrong. I had not known that Phil had already gotten back together with *him*. (In truth, even had I known, I still would have fucked her—how could

I not have? But I did not know and, therefore, cannot be held responsible.)

"She would never accuse you of rape," *he* went on, "but I know she would never have sex with you voluntarily. Not now. We're back together. She's mine."

At the word "rape," my heart jumped and my mind immediately returned to what had been only moments ago, when I first entered the bathroom and resolved to edit the Spring Break scene (as I'd come to imagine it). I knew that the decision had been made only moments ago, but it felt more like hours, since I'd re-experienced the scene itself in the interim. Hadn't I wondered—moments ago, hours ago—if my editing of our time together would constitute rape? And yet I knew that it did not. In the original draft (for lack of a better term), Phil had come to me voluntarily. And my edit did not change anything she did or said—it only changed my dialogue, which led to her responding of her own free will.

"You know what you did," *he* said, mistaking the concern and confusion on my face for guilt.

I turned from the mirror. "Look—"

"No, *you* look. *You* look," and *he* took a step closer to me, but I hardly noticed the step because *his* fist exploded in my face at the same instant, knocking me back against the vanity.

I reached out and back to steady myself against the sink, leaving myself utterly defenseless as *he* pressed *his* attack, now on top of me, grabbing me by the shirt collar and forcing me to bend backwards over the sink, leaning against me, *his* angry face inches from my own.

"C'mon," I gasped, trying to keep my balance, one hand now trapped under my own body. I used the other to grab one of *his* wrists, pulling fruitlessly. *He* held me fast and had all the leverage. "Phil said for us to be cool—"

"You want to go cry to her? Go ahead. I'll deal with it. You want to go cry to your fag friend who knows all that martial arts shit? Do that, too. I don't fucking care. I'm not afraid of him. I'm not afraid of anything. I've been wanting to kick your ass ever since you started dating her senior year."

I closed my eyes. I told myself not to do it. But I did.

The smell of chocolate.

My one hand was not pinned under my own body. It had never, in fact, been pinned under my body.

I brought it up between us, covering *his* face, pushing back as hard as I could. In surprise, *he* tightened *his* already tight grip on my shirt, choking me. I pulled at *his* wrist and pushed *his* head at the same time, then realized my index finger and ring finger were poised directly over his eyes. Without a thought, without a moment's hesitation, I pressed forward. Hard.

"Hey!" *he* exclaimed, his grip loosening, *his* voice high-pitched with sudden concern. "Hey!"

I thought of Phil telling me she was "with someone else." I thought of *him* on the dance floor with her, in bed with her, making new historical sheets with her. I thought of it all—I impossibly managed to think of every instance where *he* had intersected with *me*, and I thought of it all in that single moment, and by the time that moment had ended, I had made the decision without even realizing I had made it. But the decision was made; it was too late; I was already living in a world post-decision, as my fingers sank into *his* eyes, and *he* released me in less than a heartbeat, backing away too late, far too late, *his* voice now no longer a thing of words, but a single scream.

His eyeballs ruptured around my fingers like I'd sunk them into old Jell-O.

"Oh, God!" *he* screamed, backing away from me, stumbling,

really, falling backwards, *his* hands flown to *his* face, which now bled and wept a viscous fluid[24] from eyes that no longer saw. "Oh, God!" he screamed again, and then again, and then over and over again, colliding backwards into a wall, screaming, crying, blinded now, *his* unseeing eyes covered by hands that could not reverse the world.

A pounding came at the door, followed by voices raised in concern, in fear, in terror. I thought I recognized George among them.

I could not move. I could only stare at *him* as he slumped to the floor, still screaming, "Oh, God!" at the top of his lungs, his brain locked into a pattern by sheer shock and pain, unable to do anything but scream.

I felt the smallest satisfaction. Vindication.

But this would not return Phil to me. Blinding her chosen would not return her favors me-ward.

My hands trembled. With the exception of the index and ring fingers on the left, they were amazingly clean for someone who had the blood of another man's life on them.

A heavy thud at the door, which vibrated and shook and cracked. It would not hold long. They would come in. They would see. What I had done.

Self-defense. My mind whirled and spun. I had acted in self-defense, hadn't I? Hadn't I? But would anyone believe me? Would Phil testify that I had been unable to let her go? Would she claim I'd threatened *him*? Surely I could not count on her to be objective—I had just *gouged out her lover's eyes!*

24. More appropriately, the "vitreous humor" (also known simply as "the vitreous") that maintains sufficient pressure to keep the eyeball spherical and functioning, the gradual lack of which can lead to nearsightedness, the catastrophic lack of which (as here) means blindness.

Another resounding *whump!* at the door. Another ensuing crack. The wood around the lock bulged and split. Moments now. Only moments.

I had no choice. I turned back to the mirror and stared at myself, shutting out *his* screams and cries, shutting out the sound of the door now bursting open.

I took a deep breath. It stank of vats of old fudge.

CHAPTER 13

I leaned over the sink in the bathroom at The WB and—to my shock—threw up a single, slimy wad of something unidentifiable. I stared for long moments at the vomitus in the basin before me, expecting the lingering taste of chocolate, but instead unsure as to what vile flavor(s) persisted in my mouth. I could not remember what I had eaten that day. Indeed, I could not remember any meal I had ever eaten in my life. Had I ever eaten anything? With a twist of the faucet, a spray of lukewarm water dissolved the evidence of my spewing, washing it down the drain.

I had failed. It was too late. I chose to change things too late—on some level, she'd already made her decision by the time she came to visit me at Y. Perhaps that was one final farewell for herself. One last sexual thrill. Maybe she was just confirming her decision.

I needed to go back farther.

I rinsed my mouth, swishing and spitting as though at the dentist's office. Behind me, the bathroom door opened and closed, but I stayed at the sink with tepid water in my cupped

hands, still leaning over, wondering if my churning stomach could tolerate a drink of water and, further, if it could tolerate a drink of the water that spurts forth from the pipes and spigots of The WB. When I was in fifth grade, a letter home to parents revealed that unacceptable levels of lead had been found in the water at The WB, leading some wag to post "Leaded" and "Unleaded" signs on the drinking fountains for the months we were disallowed from using them while the pipes were refitted. Still, even though the issue was fixed years ago, I could never again bend to sip from a WB tap without thinking of heavy metals clotting my system.

"Hey," someone said, and before I looked up into the mirror, I knew it was *him*.

My first thought, upon spying *his* reflection over my shoulder, was that *he* must have been suffering some distress of the renal or intestinal sort, for *he* had just left the bathroom mere moments ago.

And then *he* locked the bathroom door with a turn of *his* wrist, and my thoughts became more obvious and more sensible.

I wiped dry my lips with the back of my hand. "What do you want?"

He came closer to me, arm's-length away. "She told me. About Spring Break," *he* added unnecessarily, for what else could have "she told [*him*]" that would account for the seething anger, the flare of *his* nostrils, the fire in *his* eyes?

"She would never accuse you of rape," *he* went on, "but I know she would never have sex with you voluntarily. Not now. We're back together. She's mine."

I turned from the mirror. "Look—"

In the same instant, I brought up my arm, knocking aside *his* fist. Pain shivered my arm from wrist to elbow, but I was otherwise unhurt. *He* had no time to react before I lashed out with my foot, kicking *him* directly between the legs. Let *him* try to please Phil that night. Ha!

He crumpled to the floor in a heap, cupping *his* wounded manhood with both hands, gasping for breath.

"I don't need to run to Phil or George," I told *him*, then calmly unlocked the door and left, massaging my wrist.

"Dude, what's up?" George asked as I rejoined him. "You were in there a while, you know what I mean?"

"Are you timing my bathroom runs?" I asked.

He laughed at the pun. "Nah. Just makin' sure you're all right. I saw you-know-who go in there after you. Thought something might be going down."

I thought of *him* sinking to the floor. "*He* must have been in a stall when I came out," I lied. "Everything's fine."

Moments later, I watched as *he* stumbled out of the bathroom, moving with slow deliberation and a noticeably wider stance than usual. I pretended to be engrossed in conversation with George, while in reality I kept one eye trained on *him*, watching as *he* sought out Phil. Still slightly stooped, *he* spoke to her briefly, standing such that *he* obscured my view of her. When *he* limped away from her and headed to the door, though, I could see Phil in all her rage and fury.

In less time than it took to imagine it, Phil was before me. "What the hell, Mike? What did you do that for?"

"What are you talking about?"

"Don't give me that shit. *He* told me what you did."

Of course *he* had. And *he* had accused me of cowardice? Of "running to Phil?"

"*He* threw the first punch, Phil!"

She regarded me with disbelief. "Then why aren't you hurt?"

I tried to explain that I'd blocked the blow, but Phil was understandably skeptical. I had no reputation as a fighter or even as the sort of athlete that would acquit himself well in a fight, whereas *he* was an (I admit grudgingly) exceptional football player and wrestler, possessed of greater speed, strength, and overall physical skill than I.

"At least *he* still has *his* eyes," escaped from my mouth before I could stop it.

"*What* did you say?" Phil was *en*raged and *out*raged at the same time. "Did you just threaten to *blind* him? Did you?"

Everything had gotten out of hand. I protested, claiming—weakly—that it was just a joke, but Phil would have none of it. She was a fury in red (back to the red now? Or had it been the red before?) A crowd began to gather. George puffed out his chest and warned the curious onlookers back, assuring them there was nothing to see, but those who'd attended The WB with us knew that Phil and I had dated. They wanted to see the post-break-up blow-up in person. It would be a fine story and a fine memory from an otherwise dull and listless night.

I could not abide seeing Phil so furious at me. I had never seen such anger before. She had been upset with me in the past, but never had I witnessed such violence in her eyes. I would never be able to coax her down from such altitudes of rage to safer, more congenial levels of friendship, let alone love.

If I could edit the past to make her realize her love for me, this night and its problems would be a moot point. They never would have happened. She never would have come with *him*, I never would have encountered *him* in the bathroom, and so on. But I did not think that clearly. (Paradox is not for clear thinking anyway, and it is especially difficult to juggle while being harangued by the love of one's life.)

So, I didn't think. I simply *did*.

CHAPTER 13

I leaned over the sink in the bathroom at The WB and—to my shock—threw up a single, slimy wad of something unidentifiable. I stared for long moments at the vomitus in the basin before me, expecting the lingering taste of chocolate, but instead unsure as to what vile flavor(s) persisted in my mouth. I could not remember what I had eaten that day. Indeed, I could not remember any meal I had ever eaten in my life. Had I ever eaten anything? With a twist of the faucet, a spray of lukewarm water dissolved the evidence of my spewing, washing it down the drain.

I had failed. It was too late. I chose to change things too late—on some level, she'd already made her decision by the time she came to visit me at Y. Perhaps that was one final farewell for herself. One last sexual thrill. Maybe she was just confirming her decision.

I needed to go back farther.

I rinsed my mouth, swishing and spitting as though at the dentist's office. Behind me, the bathroom door opened and closed, but I stayed at the sink with tepid water in my cupped

hands, still leaning over, wondering if my churning stomach could tolerate a drink of water and, further, if it could tolerate a drink of the water that spurts forth from the pipes and spigots of The WB. When I was in fifth grade, a letter home to parents revealed that unacceptable levels of lead had been found in the water at The WB, leading some wag to post "Leaded" and "Unleaded" signs on the drinking fountains for the months we were disallowed from using them while the pipes were refitted. Still, even though the issue was fixed years ago, I could never again bend to sip from a WB tap without thinking of heavy metals clotting my system.

"Hey," someone said, and before I looked up into the mirror, I knew it was *him*.

I turned around immediately. *He*, without preamble, threw a punch that knocked me back against the sink and rattled my teeth in my head and this time I welcomed the smell of chocolate—

CHAPTER 13

I leaned over the sink in the bathroom at The WB and—to my shock—threw up a single, slimy wad of something unidentifiable. I stared for long moments at the vomitus in the basin before me, expecting the lingering taste of chocolate, but instead unsure as to what vile flavor(s) persisted in my mouth. I could not remember what I had eaten that day. Indeed, I could not remember any meal I had ever eaten in my life. Had I ever eaten anything? With a twist of the faucet, a spray of lukewarm water dissolved the evidence of my spewing, washing it down the drain.

Wait, I told myself. *Wait and time it right this time.*

I rinsed my mouth, swishing and spitting as though at the dentist's office. Behind me, the bathroom door opened and closed, but I stayed at the sink with tepid water in my cupped hands, still leaning over, wondering if my churning stomach could tolerate a drink of water and, further, if it could tolerate a drink of the water that spurts forth from the pipes and spigots of The WB.

And wait . . .

"Hey," someone said, and before I looked up into the mirror, I knew it was *him*.

And then *he* locked the bathroom door with a turn of *his* wrist, and my thoughts became more obvious and more sensible.

I wiped dry my lips with the back of my hand. "What do you want?"

He came closer to me, arm's-length away, and said, as he's always said: "She told me. About Spring Break," *he* added unnecessarily, for what else could have "she told [*him*]" that would account for the seething anger, the flare of *his* nostrils, the fire in *his* eyes?

I still didn't know what to say in response. What could I say?

"She would never accuse you of rape," *he* went on, "but I know she would never have sex with you voluntarily. Not now. We're back together. She's mine."

At the word "rape," my heart did not jump. I was used to it by now.

Wait. Until. Now.

I turned from the mirror. "Look—"

In the same instant, I brought up my arm, knocking aside *his* fist. Pain shivered my arm from wrist to elbow, but I was otherwise unhurt. I did not kick *him* between the legs. I made, in fact, no other move at all, simply stood my ground, fists clenched as his were, the two of us staring at each other.

"Just watch yourself," *he* said, his lips peeled back from his gritted teeth. "I'm not going to let you ruin this. You hear me?"

"I hear you."

He backed away from me, a modicum of masculine respect I had not expected, nor was I sure I entirely deserved, my puissance in blocking his blow a consequence not of any skill on my part but rather on the fact that I knew it was coming. *He* unlocked the door and left the bathroom, left me wondering if this time I had edited properly, if this time I had not done damage to *him* or to me or to Phil's perception of me.

I turned back to the sink and gazed into my own eyes. I had tried to change things such that he never entered the bathroom, had tried to change things such that I did not throw up, thereby placing myself in a less vulnerable position. But I was incapable of making either of those changes, forced instead to make only specific changes at specific points.

A memory came to me just then. It wafted through my mind and then drifted away, dissipating like the smell of chocolate that now haunted me regularly. A memory from earlier in the evening, when I had wondered:

What if I was not the only one who could edit reality?

What, indeed, if?

More important: What if I was not the only one *actually* editing reality?

****

After leaving the bathroom, I found George near the bar, chatting with someone I did not recognize, a tall, good-looking blond guy of roughly our ages. George introduced him as "Seth, a great linebacker for UPN," to which Seth blushed a surprising and furious red and demurred, claiming that "those sacks" were just luck, Seth being "in the right place at the right time," of which George would hear none, punching Seth's shoulder and assuring him that he (Seth) was, in fact, a terrific linebacker, definitely the best "who ever knocked me (George) on my ass! You know what I mean?"

I stood silent witness to their mutual former-high-school-athlete bonhomie until George, realizing I had not spoken in several minutes, turned to me and said, "Dude, are you all right? Is everything OK?"

Before I could answer, Phil appeared at the bar. She ordered a drink and I permitted myself a glance toward *him*, clustered with friends of *his* from The WB, the sum of them gesticulating and gesturing and—if the occasional laugh was any true indication—jesting. None of them looked in my direction, but I could not suppress a fear—a reasonable fear, I felt—that I was the subject of their conversation. Surely *he* could not and would not let our bathroom *tête-à-tête* stand. *He* would seek revenge and satisfaction, even if *he* needed to enlist the help of others to do it.

"Mike?"

Phil stood at my side, definitely in red, looking up at me. I should have been prepared for her appearance—she just walked by me to go to the bar!—and yet for some reason, she caught me off-guard. My heart triple-timed and I felt woozy. The urge to reach out to her, to press her close to me and me close to her . . . It overwhelmed. For me, it had only been minutes since our Spring Break tryst, while it had been months for her. I had to bite the inside of my cheek (an old stage trick Phil had taught me—it was supposed to keep an actor from laughing at an inappropriate moment, but the pain sufficed to keep me in my place) to keep from throwing my arms around her.

"Yes?" I managed.

"I just wanted to thank you for not making a scene tonight," she said. In one hand, she held a red beverage that fizzed. With the other hand, she brushed back a lock of deep blue hair that I had been prepared to brush back, as I had done so many times in the past, as I needed to do again in the future. "You could have been a jerk, and you weren't. Thanks. I know this couldn't have been easy for you."

I said nothing, mauling the inside of my cheek with my teeth. I didn't trust myself to speak.

"And I'm sorry about what I said before. About you not acting like a friend lately. I know it's been rough. I would like us to be friends, if you think you can handle that. I just don't want to hurt you. I don't—"

"Phil, it's all right," I heard myself say. "It's going to be all right."

And it would be, I knew. I would fix things. I would find a way to edit the story of Phil and the story of me so that we would be together again.

No. Not "again." I would fix it so that "again" would not be necessary, so that there would be no caesura in our relationship, but rather a smooth continuum. "Again" only applies to something that has ended and then restarted. I would see to it that endings and new beginnings were unnecessary.

CHAPTER 14

I found myself at home, watching through the window as George's taillights disappeared into the dark. He had offered Seth a ride home as well, Seth having been abandoned by some UPN friends who had decided to take one last trip through the halls of their old school building, which had been shut down due to the merger. One of them produced a set of purloined custodial keys and they resolved to spend the night as UPNers for the last time.

First, though, George dropped me off, and I watched his taillights vanish, then went to the kitchen for a snack before bed. My parents sat in front of the TV, watching a movie that was neither too funny nor too sad, and most definitely in no way, shape, or form related to my circumstances whether metaphorically or allegorically or analogously. It was just a movie.

"How was The WB?" my mother asked. "Or The CW, I guess."

"It was fine," I told her, omitting that I had learned I could warp the very stuff of reality.

"That's nice," she said.

I eagerly climbed into bed, aggressively ready for sleep, hoping for some new revelatory dream, but my angel or my oracle or my subconscious remained mute. There were no strangely-named incestuous women. No dead-then-alive-then-dead name-scrambled, be-stubbled mystery corpses. No small children with ice cream cones. My sleep was as blank as a sheet of paper fresh from the ream.

I woke up thinking of the child with the ice cream cone, thinking of the smell of chocolate that had become so pervasive in my life. Each time I had edited reality, I had become nearly overwhelmed (to the point of nausea and—on the one occasion—beyond) by the scent of chocolate. Such were my associations with that particular odor now that I could no longer abide even the sight of chocolate, whether syrup or bar or cupcake or tart or chip or chunk or ice cream or hot liquid. I could no longer even think of partaking of something as innocent as a Hershey Kiss without my gorge rising.

I went to my computer and typed in "i smell things that aren't there."

Ads for nasal sprays (both prescription and over-the-counter) popped up, as well as a survey on facial tissue preferences and an animation of how a certain decongestant worked. I watched and rated the animation,[25] clicked through the mandatory links on the ads as quickly as possible, and took the survey.[26] Finally, information began to scroll on the screen.

I spent the night clicking and filling out surveys and reading

25. On a scale of 1 (not relevant at all) to 5 (extremely relevant), it received a 2.

26. Anti-viral tissues with just a touch of aloe won the day, beating out extra-durable tissues impregnated with a sheen of make-up designed to reduce nose shininess.

and answering polls and reading and clicking and watching mandatory ads tailored to my web-life experience.

Early on, the words "potentially worrisome" came up, guaranteeing that I would continue to read.

Olfactory hallucinations. That's what I was suffering.

The words "brain tumor" followed shortly thereafter. That they were associated with the word "occasionally" did little to quell my concern.

Other words in association with "brain tumor": "epilepsy," "neurologist," and "immediately."

The condition afflicting me was best described—as best I can tell with my layman's understanding and research—as "phantosmia," which is the detection of phantom smells; to wit, smelling that which is not there. As distinct from "parosmia," which is the mis-detection of smells; to wit, sniffing a bouquet of flowers and smelling not the perfume of roses, but rather a used and soiled baby diaper.

Which definitions caused me to wonder: How can we truly know the difference between phantosmia and parosmia? What if what appears to be phantosmia is actually parosmia, if the apparent smelling of something from nothing is actually mistaking the smell of something *for* the smell of nothing? Is there truly, after all, such a thing as no smell? What is the baseline neutral? Who determines it? If I smell something and you do not, is that because I am deranged or do I simply have a finer tuned sense of smell than you?[27]

More words followed, directly contradicting the previous

27. For evidence, see: Any conversation in the history of the world in which one person has said, "Do you smell that?" and another has responded, "Smell what?" "That. That smell," the first replies. And so on. Does the first person suffer from phantosmia? Parosmia? Or does the second person merely have a defective sense of smell—possibly either hyposmia (a reduced sense of smell) or anosmia (no sense of smell at all)?

(encouraging me to attend immediately to a neurologist for fear of a brain tumor), the conflicting advice now reporting that "most disturbances" of this variety result from an injury to the olfactory pathways. The words "chemical bonding," "airborne molecules," "receptors," and "olfactory epithelium" were employed in illuminating sequence, along with "nerve impulses," "olfactory bulb," and "brain."

Further, my condition (whichever one it is) was referred to as a "strange malady."

My strange malady could be caused by "infection" (of the sort associated with the common cold or flu) or "trauma" (such as hitting my head) or even "toxic exposure," but the most "worrisome" (that word again) likelihood is brain tumor.

I felt strangely disconnected from my own body for a protracted moment, as though my brain had become an intangible, self-sustaining thing and levitated out through the top of my skull to hover there in the air above my body, a single, black cottage-cheese-like mass glistening at its center or to one side or underneath—wherever it could impact my sense of smell and cause phant/parosmia.

Hands trembling, I picked up the phone and did not pause even for an instant in calling George. Yes, it was an absurdly early/late hour, my research having borne me into the dark morning, but this being quite literally a matter of life and death, I needed the counsel of my best friend in that moment.

George's phone rang only once and he picked up instantly, his voice low and indefinably annoyed. "Dude. Mike. Not now."

"George, I really need to talk—"

"I'm busy right now, you know what I mean?"

"But—"

"Mike. Later. We'll talk later."

He left me on the living end of a half-dead line. I stared at the phone for a moment, a flare of righteous anger burning to brief life before quenching. George had done enough for me already. I was not his best friend. I had nothing I could offer him. I would handle this on my own.

Even though it was four in the morning, I was still prepared to begin the search for a neurologist, when I noticed more words, tucked away in an article like an afterthought:

"Occasional," "some patients," and "psychological problems."

This was more comforting than imagining an insidious cabal of renegade cells plotting terrorist acts in my cerebral cortex (or medulla oblongata or corpus callosum or frontal lobe). Perhaps rather than dying of a brain tumor, I was merely going insane. Given the choice between losing my brain and losing my mind, I would choose the latter every time. Insanity could possibly be treated. Death cannot. Maybe, I realized, I've been losing my mind all along. Maybe my "strange malady" was just the latest symptom in a mental disorder going back to childhood—the unwanted and unconscious internal narration, the fear of climbing the Walls, the inability to recall my own last name. Perhaps this is the reason I never spoke to anyone about these afflictions—the knowledge (deep down, in some lurking sanity that remains) that I am/have been going insane my whole life, the smell of chocolate syrup and the belief that I can edit reality being just the most recent outward expressions of my madness.

And if that was, indeed, the case? If my mind had rebelled against reality? What of it?

What is reality? How much of it is our own perceptions? If I had lost my mind and fallen into a delusional state, believing that I could "edit reality" as though reality were nothing more than words on paper or a computer screen, if, I decided that night, I were to lose touch with everything that is real, then I might as well enjoy it. Phil was the best thing in my life, the most special thing. My love. My heart. I needed her back.[28] If I could have her back only in my mind, well . . . Why not? That would be fine. After all—I clearly had lost/was rapidly losing the ability to distinguish between fantasy and reality. In that case, why not enjoy the fantasy? Especially when the fantasy surpassed the reality in every way? It no longer mattered what was real, only what I perceived to be real.

I chose to believe I could edit reality. I chose to believe I could find a way to repair my own past such that Phil would still be a part of my present and my future.

And perhaps by making such a radical change, something lasting, I could prove to myself one way or the other whether or not I had lost my mind or discovered the path to re-ordering the universe. Changing Phil's dress could have been simple delusion. Fighting/not fighting *him* in the bathroom could have been a fantasy gone wrong. The conversation with Phil at Spring Break could have been wishful thinking. All of these things were changes imagined or perceived by me, but none of them with lasting impact that proved beyond any doubt that I had, in fact, altered reality.

But if I could edit reality right then, at that very moment at four in the morning . . . If I could find the right point in my own life to change my actions such that Phil and I were still together on that same moment at four in the morning . . .

Doing so would prove conclusively that I could edit reality.

28. Here Mike considered—briefly—the possibility that he had, in fact, never been with Phil at all, that his entire relationship with her (their romps on the history-made sheets, their late-night calls and e-mails, all of it) was nothing more than a figment of an imagination gone powerfully and wholly deranged.

Or that I had gone completely insane.

I shut down my computer. There would be no neurologist for me.

I placed my trashcan nearby to catch the inevitable forthcoming vomit. I steeled myself for the stench of chocolate syrup, and I—

CHAPTER 7

After school, Phil and I go to her house, as is our custom on the days when she does not have any sort of play practice or other extracurricular activity. I want to hold back from telling her my decision, but I know that it is written all over my posture and floods the gaps between every word I speak, so I tell her once we're in the house, the door shut against the encroaching desert heat: "Phil, I'm *not* going to Y. ~~I'm really sorry.~~"

There's a moment of silence, as though buildings have fallen, as though we have been attacked like on Lucky Sevens, and we are mourning the dead along with the rest of the world.

And then Phil nods once. It's a slow nod, so slow that when her head reaches its nadir, I question whether or not she intends to lift it again, wondering long enough that I begin to worry she is injured and take a step closer to her as her head—again, slowly—lifts.

"I see," she says with a tone of studied neutrality that, given the circumstances, is more shocking than outrage would have been.

"Phil—"

"I see," she says again, studied neutrality giving way to anger, her eyes flashing, her cheeks a-flush.

"Phil—"

"You fucking idiot!" she yells, and the yelling surprises me only because of the circumstances, not for the fact of it, for Phil yelling is nothing new or unexpected, but then she also reaches out and slaps me.

"You fucking idiot!" she yells again. "I told you! I told you not to do this for me!"

"But I love you!" I tell her, the words my shield, raised too late to prevent the sting on my cheek.

"You fucking idiot!" she yells a third time, this time stamping a foot for additional, unnecessary emphasis. "I don't care if you love me or not! That's not the point. You're supposed to do what's best for *you*, not for me!"

"But this *is* best for me. I'd be miserable without you. I *am* miserable without you."

"I was ready to give you up, Mike. I love you, but I told myself that it was more important for you to go away. To be a great architect. That hotel and that crazy elevator building and all the rest. All those ideas and dreams in those sketchbooks. That's a dream you've had since long before you ever knew me. And if it was meant to be, then it was meant to be and we would get back together someday."

"Phil . . ."

She's quieter now; calmer. "Mike. I can't do this. I can't be what you settled for."

"What? I'm not settling. I *love*—"

"Stop it!" Her voice breaks on "it," just collapses as a sob escapes from her lips. She brushes strands of blue hair back from her eyes and gazes at me, tears tracking down her cheeks. "Just stop, all right? You want to be an architect. A *great* architect.

You've wanted that and you've wanted to go to College Y your whole life. Those are the things you need."

"I need *you*."

"No. Maybe later. Not now. If you give up Y to be with me, you'll always wonder. You'll always wonder what path your life would have taken. You'll always resent me for being the thing that took you down a different path."

My mouth opens, then closes. How to tell her? How to explain to her that I've seen that path, followed the ragged justification of its text to its morose conclusion?

"Phil. Please. Please listen. I know what will happen. I need you. I need to be with you. It's—"

"No." She opens the door. The desert beckons. "I can't. I love you too much to make you miserable. Please go."

****

There is no final romp in the history-made sheets. No solemn bed-stripping ritual. No shock in my eyes when she reveals her intention to launder our relationship, to wash it out of her bedclothes through the power and unbeatable force of the rinse cycle.

Instead, there is me, wandering the desert afternoon as the sun zeniths and then begins its descent over the skyscrapers to the west. I walk three subway stops before the heat and sun overwhelm me, forcing me into the cool shade of the subway.

And then there is me, wandering the halls at what is still The WB, wanting to reach out to Phil each day, each day instead stopped by my own impotence. What to say to her? She's made up her mind. I can do nothing to change it. Any attempt I would make at explanation would be insane.

And then there is me over the summer, inconsolable,

angering George as, "Dude, you're a total buzzkill and this is, like, my last summer of freedom, you know what I mean?"

And there is me at College Y, sullen, quiet, stand-offish. Soon, friendless, laughless, hopeless.

And, yes, there is me at Spring Break, alone until Phil mysteriously arrives to fuck me one last time, her actions the same despite the rancor of our parting.

And there is me, at The WB event with George, watching Phil and *him*.

And there is me, and me, and only, only forever—

CHAPTER 15

—crumpled to the floor, unable to stand erect, choking on chocolate, heaving into my trashcan.

Stringers of sputum ran like spider-silk between my lips and the rim of the can. I coughed and hacked, pursed my lips and spat, but nothing would dislodge them until I swiped at them with my fingers, then wiped those same now-sticky, now-slimy fingers on the edge of the trashcan, my gorge rising again, threatening to heave again at the sight and feel of my own sick, but luckily never making good on that threat.

George. I needed George. I needed help.

But no. I had called him already. Or *had* I called him already? When I edited the story, had things changed enough that I never called George on this night?

My suit—worn to the dance at The WB—was neatly folded over my desk chair. So, I still attended the dance, then. Yes, of course; I remembered that. But what about afterwards?

I checked my cell phone. I had called George mere minutes previous, a call lasting just long enough for me to ask George for help and for him to deny me. I felt an unwarranted, selfish rage well up inside me. I had always counted on George and, in return, he had always been reliable and available. These were our roles—I needed, he supplied. That night, he abrogated that agreement, rewrote the roles. I needed him desperately and he was not there for me. My best friend was not there for me.

I sank to my knees on the carpet, disgusted with my own self-absorption, my overweening solipsism. George *had* always been there for me, and for precisely that reason, he was entitled *not* to be there on occasion. Or forever and always, if he so wished. And yet despite my conscious and intellectual awareness of my own egoism,[29] I still felt an emotional and visceral outrage at his abandonment of me. The child brain that lurked under the matured gray matter would not let go of the notion that—time of day be damned, history be damned—George had forsaken me when I needed him most.

A timid knock at my bedroom door roused me from my gut-wrenching self-pity. I wiped my mouth again with the back of my hand and stood up to open the door. There stood my brother, in his pajamas, a wide and open and only slightly haunted expression on his face. He asked in a whisper if I was all right.

"What are you doing up so late?" I asked him. I checked the clock. "I mean, so early?" I paused. "Or so late."

He replied that he'd heard noises through the common wall our rooms shared, the sounds of retching. I lacked the energy to lie to my brother. The early/late hour. The exhaustion of the

29. Not "egotism" (which is an exaggerated sense of self-importance with relation to others), but rather "egoism," which is an overriding interest in the self as the genesis of a moral philosophy. In short, the egotist thinks, "I am all that matters," while the egoist thinks, "I should think of myself first."

evening, of the morning, of the endless minutes/days since Phil broke up with me when I told her I chose her over Y.

"I'm not doing well," I told him. He came into my room and closed the door, lest we awaken our parents, then asked me what was wrong.

I wanted to explain it to him, to elucidate the circumstances, that I had mis-judged the repercussions, mis-apprehended the bank shots and the English of this particular billiard ball I had fired and was firing towards the pocket. I thought it would be as simple as making Y into not-Y, as simple as changing A into B, but that substitution has/had a ripple effect I could not and cannot foresee, and the ball caromed off the bumper and sometimes scratched and sometimes sank the eight too soon and sometimes jumped the table and skittered away into a dark, dusty, unknowable corner.

"It's about Phil," I admitted. "I want to get back together with her, but she's with someone else."

My brother said something comforting and heartfelt, followed by something charmingly and endearingly innocent, based on his own ill-fated-thus-far efforts in the realms of love. Not wholly applicable to my own situation, but well-meant and moderately analogous.

I thanked him for his time and thoughts, then bade him return to bed, promising him that there would be no further retching or other disturbances to rouse him from his slumber. Then I turned out the light and forced myself back to bed, where I tossed and turned until the darkness outside my window took on the first cool hue of morning (a not-considerable amount of time, given the early/late hour of my re-climbing into bed). And as the sun lightened my window, a thought occurred to me. A notion. A memory, to be more accurate.

She told me she loved me.

I had forgotten. How could I have forgotten? I spent the night at The WB trying to convince George, trying to convince *myself* that Phil loved me and merely was in denial as to her feelings, but I had proof! The day I told her I was going to forego Y in order to remain closer to her, the day she broke up with me and cast me out of her house[30]—on that day, she told me in no uncertain terms that she loved me![31]

There was no mystery to be solved.

The answer had always been with me.

Phil loved me. I had known it all along. In that moment of our senior year, she loved me and not *him*. Perhaps she changed her mind later; perhaps not. But at that point in time, she loved me.

Now I merely had to make certain that I did not destroy her love, as I had when I thought to deny myself Y in favor of Phil and her blue hair and our common history-made sheets.

She loved me and then she changed her mind or, perhaps more accurately, convinced herself that she changed her mind, though still not admitting to loving *him*, for she never said those words to me, though she easily could have and, indeed, would have, had they been true, for what easier way to put off an old, persistent and insistent lover than by introduction of the new lover in terms that cannot be misinterpreted?

I knew then that I needed to show her that I loved her *before* her mind was made up as to my future. I needed to go back farther into the depths of our shared past, when the history-made sheets were not quite so historic.

Bearing in mind my promise to my brother, I slipped out of my bedroom and outside. Summer mornings in the desert are

30. "Please go."
31. "I love you too much to make you miserable."

delightful—warm, but not overbearing, dry, pale-lit. I walked to the nearby subway station and took the Fox train. At this early hour, no one would notice me if I began to choke and vomit in a corner of a subway car. Most would assume I was homeless and ignore me.

The train rambled and clacked its way northeast. I steeled myself for the chocolate syrup.

CHAPTER 4

When I arrive—later, safely, chocolate-syrup-less—at Phil's house, the first thing I notice is that Phil's mother's car is not in the driveway, which means that Phil and I will fuck.

****

And fuck we do. Have. Did.

Lying in her bed again, wrapped in the history-made sheets, the ceiling fan buzzing above, raising gooseflesh on Phil's exposed, sweat-cooling shoulder, I cannot imagine that Phil will ever *not* be with me, that she will ever be with *him* again, molded to *him*, red dress or teal dress, whichever dress. I want to ask her if that is even possible; we've never spoken of *him*, not once, and I want to ask her if she would ever want to go back to *him*, but as I open my mouth, only a gasp escapes, for Phil has just wrapped her undercover fingers around me, still firm (though not fully erect) and sensitive from our first fuck of the day.

"I really like your dick," she says, casual, in the tone of

voice she uses to ask if I want garlic or plain naan when we order Indian.

"Do you have to call it that?" Bawdiness and lust have always seemed clothes best suited to the male form—women can wear them, but, like neckties, they seem wrong somehow.

She laughs. "I'm sorry, did I offend your delicate sensibilities? How about 'I like your penis?' Is that better?"

And it's my turn to laugh. "No, no, that's not what I meant. It's just the word 'dick.' I don't know—I've never liked it. Call it something else."

"Like what?"

"Prick."

"No."

"Why not? It sounds like dick."

Her eyes, stormy with confused discomfort, stare at me. "I don't like that word. It means too much."

I could let it go, but I don't. Instead, I say, "What do you mean 'too much?'"

"You don't want to know."

"I do."

"It's artsy."

"I'm an artsy guy. I create things."

"You're artsy in a scientific way. You *design*. You're not artsy like drama-artsy or writer-artsy."

"Just tell me, Phil."

She inhales deeply, an action which threatens to distract me with the motion of her breasts, and then distracts me from my distraction with a question I never imagined hearing: "Have you ever read *The Faerie Queene?* By Spenser?"

"What?" I have a vague memory of such being mentioned in an English class of some sort.

"It starts 'A Gentle knight was pricking on the plaine,'"

she says in a tone of triumph, as if somehow our discussion is conclusively over now.

"So? What about it?"

"Don't you understand? Pricking. It's archaic. Means 'riding' or something like that."

"And that's why you don't want to call my penis a prick?" I am halfway towards a dirty pun involving the word 'prick' and the notions of mounting and riding, but she interrupts with a fierce shake of her head.

"No, it means more than that. Don't you get it?"

"No. Not really."

"A prick can be, OK, a colloquialism for a penis, right? But 'prick' can also refer to a 'gash' or a 'slit?' And it's a verb, too, right? 'Urging on.' It's not just . . . It's just . . . It's utterly omnisexual. This word—it's about the sexes and about the act of sex, OK? And then . . . And then, if you just sort of . . . allegorize it . . . Or maybe I mean analogize it . . . I'm not sure. But you just remove the, you know, the simple sexual connotations. Then it means *any* action. *And* the actor. *And* the acted upon. So you . . . You end up with a knight who's pricked into pricking by a prick, thus turning him into a prick."

I sit perfectly still for a moment. "What?"

Phil continues, staring at the ceiling now, speaking as if unaware of the words coming from her lips, as though they have been implanted within her and now must come out: "The impossibility of assembling a new text is inherent in the very fact that language itself has no meaning. Saussure was wrong, see? Words are not defined by the distinctions. Words aren't defined at all. The Structuralists knew what they were talking about: texts come about as a result of coincidence, not design. The sequence of words is inconsequential because any word can mean any other word."

I touch her arm lightly. "Angia, what in the world—"

And I remember that she is not Angia, she's Phil. Angia is someone else, someone who only existed in a dream, but Phil is real, but for a moment she was as unreal as Angia, and before I can apologize for using the wrong name, she shakes me off and puts a hand to her temple. "Just . . . Just let me call it something else. 'Cock' is fine."

"What just happened here?"

"Nothing. We're just talking." She shudders—once—and she's Phil again, saucy Phil, laughing Phil, and she says, "Architects are too damn serious. Probably because they know they could kill a thousand people if they put the floor in the wrong place." She says it. She says it lightly. She says it while taking me in one hand.

"Why do you hate me?" I joke, as if by reflex.

"I don't hate you," she says, releasing my dick (cock!) so that she can push herself up on her elbows and match her eyes to mine. "I don't. I—"

I take the liminal moment between this word and the next. I think. Phil has said this to me many times. It was the banter equivalent of the soundtrack to our relationship. We joked about it. Or, rather, *I* joked about it. And I always felt, each time, that she had something more to say, something beyond "I don't hate you," but each time I was more concerned with my feelings and my need to immediately and rapidly make certain she understood I was joking. Was that because I knew what she meant to say, what she wanted to say, what she would say/would have said had I allowed her to? Did I somehow fear knowing the truth? Did I fear the complexity of it? All of these things are true or may be true or probably/possibly are true.

I wait and this time I don't interrupt. She stops anyway.

"No," I tell her. "Say what you were going to say.

She has something more to say—the words swim in her gaze—but she flops back on her pillow, a lighter blue than her own hair. "You didn't bring me gummi bears last night," she says.

"Not that," I say, sitting up in bed, staring at her, willing her to say the words I know she wants to say. "Before. I asked why you hated me and you said—"

"I don't hate you."

"—and then you were going to say something else, but you stopped."

"I don't hate you," she says again, but this time it's a whisper, a whisper somehow almost lost in her own voice. "I . . ."

"Phil." My throat burns to say it first, burns to say, "I love you" to her, but I have to let her do it. I have to let her say it.

She struggles with it. I can tell. And because I've seen the future, I know what she is struggling with. She wants me to go to Y. She wants me to achieve greatness. Follow my dreams, the ones I had long before I met her. It's more than that she doesn't want to admit to *me* that she loves me, with all the attendant drama that involves (to say nothing of the fact that—as far as she knows—there is a chance that her feelings will not be reciprocated). It's that she also does not want to admit it to herself. So certain is she that I will choose my dreams and Y over her that she cannot bring herself to say it. I lean closer to her, feel the soft, smooth heat of her against me.

"I love you," she says at last and pulls away, turns away, too, everything *away*, her body language, her very body saying, "Go go go go," but I move closer to her, shrink the distance between us.

"I'm sorry," she says through new tears. "I shouldn't have said that. Or maybe . . . Maybe I shouldn't have felt it. Been feeling it. I don't know which. I don't know which is better and which is worse. I just shouldn't have felt it *or* said it. God. Fuck. God."

"Phil. It's OK."

"It isn't. It's not OK, OK? It's all fucked up now. It's all ruined. I knew you were going away. I knew from the first time we kissed in George's garage" *-cum-*game room "that you would go away. That you were going to go *somewhere*. And there's no place for me in that, Mike. You have to go away. You can't fulfill your dreams here. You can't be who you're meant to be here." She shakes her head, rubs her eyes, smears her tears. "You'll kill both of us if you stay. You'll make us both miserable."

"Phil, I love you." It's the only way to shut her up. It's the best way to shut her up.

I palm her shoulder and turn her around to me again, her cheeks shiny-tracked with the residue of tears, her expression unreadable, like words in a foreign language, like white letters on white paper.

"I love you, Phil." I say it again, just for the sheer beauty of it, the final joy of it, of saying it and knowing that it is the right thing to say.

She shakes her head. "No. No."

"Yes. Yes. I love you."

It's a knife's-edge moment, a cliff's-step precipice fall. We teeter; we flail. Indecision in her eyes. I pull her closer—our bodies touch. We respond. I fight off the wave of eroticism so powerful it's almost nauseating, like the reek of too-powerful chocolate syrup. We melt into each other and kiss—tentative, like a first kiss. I gaze into her eyes.

"It's all OK, Phil. I love you. It's all OK."

"But what about—"

"What about nothing? Don't think. Don't worry. I love you; that's all that matters."

The troubled confusion in her eyes gives way to surrender, to resignation, to love. She kisses me again, this time nothing like a first kiss, and buries her face in the hollow of my neck, murmuring, "I love you. I love you."

I've done it. I've fixed it. I've fixed the world.

My little part of it, at least.

****

Days later, Phil and I stop at my house on the way to her place after school. I left my cell phone at home by accident and need to pick it up before spending the day with her. (Even though I am seventeen-soon-eighteen, my parents still have their rules, the primary of which is: When out of the house for any purpose other than school, I am to have my cell phone with me—turned on—at all times.)

I kiss her lightly and go to my room for the phone. Phil says hello to my brother (already home from middle school) and lounges in the kitchen while waiting for me.

My cell lurks under a pile of sketchbooks and drawings on my desk. I retrieve it and go to the front door, calling out to Phil that I am ready. When she does not come to the door, I call out again. And then a third time. When she still does not come, I go to the kitchen, where Phil sits at the table, an envelope in her hands and a neutral, staring expression on her face.

"Phil. Come on. Let's go."

Nothing.

"Phil."

Wordlessly, she turns the envelope to me. I recognize the crest of College Y.

"Oh. Oh." Guilt falls over me like a shadow even though I've done nothing wrong.

"It's admissions information," she says, as though she needed to explain. Which she does not.

"I didn't ask for that," I tell her. "My parents sent away for that. I told them I wasn't interested in going to Y anymore, but they didn't listen."

"They didn't listen."

"Right. I'm totally not even applying there. Don't worry about it."

"They sent away for it."

"Right." Why does she keep stating the obvious?

She considers for a moment, then—far more slowly than I would think possible—returns the envelope to the pile of mail on the kitchen table. Together we go to the subway, the issue done and over with, I believe, until later, tangled in the history-made sheets (still, at this point, in the making), when she says to me, "Why would your parents send away for the stuff from Y if you told them you didn't want to go?"

"Phil, I'm not lying. I seriously told them that. And I'm not going there. I told you: I'm not even going to apply."

"I believe you, but why would they do it?"

"I don't know."

She sits up in bed unselfconsciously, her breasts exposed and perfect. I want to reach for them, but I know I am not supposed to at this moment.

"I wasn't asking to ask," she says. "I already know the answer."

I chuckle. "I'm glad you have such insight into my parents' thought processes. Enlighten me, oh azure-tressed swami."

I have misread the situation entirely. Eyes dull with regret, she says, "They did it because they know how badly you want to go there."

"Phil—"

"Stop. Let me finish. They know how badly you want to go. They know because it's all you've ever talked about. Ever since you were a kid. Ever since you wanted to be an architect and ever since you knew what Y was. You knew. You've always known that's what you wanted. And they've always known that that's what you've known because you told them. Again and again. At first—"

"Phil, come on—"

She cuts me off with a glare. "At first, they probably didn't take you seriously because no one ever takes kids seriously. I mean, we tell people we want to be police or firemen or astronauts or authors or rock stars and who the hell takes us seriously? But the years went by and you never wavered. You never changed your mind. You kept telling them: I want to be an architect and Y has the best program for architecture so I want to go there. You said it over and over. And they believed you."

"So what? So they can't let go. They can't admit I changed my mind. They're parents. My dad still thinks I love pudding pops because I used to eat a box of them every week when I was a kid. I haven't had one in, like, five years, but that doesn't stop him from buying them for me."

"Mike. This isn't fucking pudding pops, OK? This is about your dreams and your future. They won't let go of it because for years *you* didn't let go of it. And they know what that means. It means it's a deep part of you. It's ingrained in you. You've held on to this dream since you were a little kid. For *years*. That doesn't just go away. That doesn't just stop."

"I'm still going to be an architect. Y isn't the only school for architecture. There are plenty of programs around here. Even at State. My dream is to be an architect, not to go to Y."

"Your dream is *both*. Don't give me that shit. Your dream is both and it always has been. I know it; you know it; your parents know it and that's why they won't give up. They can't make you fill out the application and they can't make you go there, but they can put pressure on you. They can make it easier for you to re-change your mind."

"I won't."

I take her in my arms. I fold myself around her, intertwine myself through her. I have her. She is what I want, all that I want, and in this moment I have her, and I will graft myself to her and never give her up and never lose her. Because she is willing to lose me.

We are silent for eternities.

She kisses my shoulder, the closest and easiest part for her to reach with her lips.

"I love you," she says.

"I love you," I say.

"We need to get up," she says.

"Why?"

But she extricates herself from me with depressing ease, rolling out of bed, her form so sleek and agile and silent, all of this flying through my mind in the instant before Phil says, "Help me strip the bed."

"What?" There are no lights on in the room, no illumination save the slightly-yellow haze limning the window blind, and for a moment I have the absurd, synesthetic notion that the murk of the room has made hearing her more difficult.

"I said, 'Help me strip the bed,'" she repeats, her voice casual, as though she has not just made a decision that ends history.

I stare at the bed, at the history-made sheets, twisted and wrapped around themselves, and I imagine that I can see each smudge, smear, blotch, and stain not as mere remnants of Phil's and my excited secretions, but rather as points on a timeline, an unspooled thread stretching back months and ending at this exact moment.

"Are you . . . are you going to wash them?" I ask her, the question stumbling and un-sure-footed as it staggers from my mouth.

She fixes her gaze on me. "Did you think I was going to put them under glass in a museum somewhere?"

"Well . . . No . . ."

"Then, c'mon. Help me."

She tugs at the top sheet, popping it loose from the corner nearest her. After a moment, I follow suit, and together we peel back the record of our relationship.

I remain silent until the bedclothes are in a haphazard pile at our feet, unable to articulate my exact concern. While I have always thought of the history-made sheets as a metaphor for our relationship and its longevity, I have never directly spoken to Phil about this, and so I do not know how now to ask her what the significance is of her decision to strip the bed, if, indeed, there is any significance to it. I feel as though merely asking her will break whatever spell the history-made sheets have spun, but then realize—in the same instant—that if there has been a spell woven by the sheets, then surely it is broken now anyway.

"Why are we doing this? I thought you would leave them on the bed as . . ." As long as we were together. Because that's what you did with *him*. The words feel suddenly ashen and bitter in my mouth. They feel whiny and juvenile, and I cannot say them.

Phil looks as though I've finished my thought, though, as though I have not ellipsed my words and left her dangling. She pulls on a sweatshirt emblazoned with the logo of The WB—a stylized W and B, with a massive green frog standing athwart them, our school's mascot being the unlikely great horned bull-frog—and then slips into a wispy pair of panties that may as well not even exist. She brushes a strand of blue hair out of her eyes.

"I can't do this," she says, and I fool myself that she is speaking of the sheets, and I stoop to straighten them out so that we can re-make the bed, so focused on the sheets am I that I do not see the expression on her face as she says,

"Go to Y. Don't go to Y. It doesn't matter to me. Well, that's not true. I guess it *does* matter to me, but here's the thing: I won't be the reason you don't go. I won't be the cause of you not going to Y. If you don't go, it'll be because you decided not to on your own, not because of me."

I stay stooped, powerfully aware of my nakedness, aware of my hands clutching the fitted sheet, the most historic of the history-made sheets.

"Are you breaking up with me?" I ask dumbly, not looking up, as if not seeing Phil when she says it will obviate it.

She says nothing. She says nothing long enough that I begin to wonder if she has somehow managed to leave the room while I have been staring at the fitted sheet in my hands, long enough that I begin to hope that she has, in fact, left the room while I have been staring at the fitted sheet in my hand.

I think of Schrödinger's Cat. As long as I don't look up, there is a chance that Phil is no longer in the room, a chance equal to the likelihood that she is still in the room. If she is not in the room, then she cannot say that she is breaking up with me.

I look up; the cat dies; Phil says, "Yes," and cannot/does not look at me as she does so, perhaps knowing that if she does not look at me, I can be both devastated and fine at the same time.

****

I go to Y. Unintentionally punningly, I wonder, Why not?

Surprisingly, Phil comes to visit at Spring Break. Surprisingly, we fuck. She leaves. I say nothing. I have learned that it is fruitless, after all, and then we talk on the phone and I tell her I love her and she tells me she is sorry, but she does not love me, she is with someone else, she is with *him*, and I see her at The WB event and my world is over again, as it is always over.

CHAPTER 16

A hand on my shoulder shocked me back to awareness. I was on the subway, lying on one side, knees curled up to my chest.

"Are you all right?" an old woman asked, leaning with concern toward me, her coffee breath filling the air between us. "You sounded like you were choking in your sleep."

I forced myself into a sitting position. Her coffee exhalation cut through the funk of chocolate syrup, helping me to breathe again, cutting me off mid-gag. I realized I would have to be more careful about my edits—I couldn't afford to choke to death on my own vomit. What good would that do me?

"I'm all right," I told her, attempting a smile made shaky and weak by my exhaustion. "Thanks for checking up on me."

She couldn't decide whether or not to believe me, but ultimately, she had no choice. She returned to a seat on the opposite side of the car, closer to the door. We were the only two in this car this early in the morning, and as the train bounced along in the tunnel, she looked over at me repeatedly, as though not certain she had seen me at all in the first place and she had to

keep checking to be sure I hadn't faded away like the image on a TV screen when the power's been turned off.

She got off at the next stop and I kept riding the train. I realized shortly after the successive stop that this train went to Phil's, that I was only two stops away from her. Thinking of Phil caused a kaleidoscope of memories and images, fragments of conversations, all to collide in my head. I had multiple memories now of the past two years or so, and keeping them straight was difficult. Some moments remained the same or roughly so no matter what. I always ended up at Y. Phil always came to see me at Spring Break. I always called her to profess my love; she always told me she was with *him*. I always went to The WB the previous night; she always showed up with *him*, sometimes in teal, sometimes in red.

No matter what I did, she never left that dance with me. I always ended up on the subway, alone in the early hours.

No more.

I decided that enough was enough. I had been too subtle, I realized. I was trying to finesse the situation when something more akin to brute force was required. I knew that Phil loved me. She had told me this herself on multiple occasions. It was only my own incompetence that kept us from being together.

I rummaged in my jacket pocket and found a small tube of mentholated lip balm, practically *de riguer* in the desert during the summer. I popped off the cap and held the balm under my nose, breathing in the cool menthol.

I closed my eyes.

Phil loved me. She loved me now and she had always loved me. As simple as that. I edited nothing else. Everything else was the same—I still went to Y. We just had a long-distance relationship.

The reek of chocolate syrup assaulted me. I inhaled deeply and the menthol cut through.

The previous night, we had attended The WB dance together. Phil wore teal. We agreed that I would come to see her early the next morning, right after her mother left for work.

Another deep inhalation. Menthol mingled with chocolate syrup, almost 50/50.

The subway stopped at Phil's stop. I vaulted from my seat and ran to the door, then launched myself up the stairs and into the early morning desert sunlight. Phil was waiting for me. She had set an alarm to wake up when her mother did, and she would be waiting for me.

I ran the two blocks to her house, heedless of the looks from early risers who stepped to one side as I dodged around them on the sidewalk. Phil's house came into view, her mother's car nowhere to be seen. I ran with the lip balm held to my upper lip, each ragged inhalation flooding me with more and more saving menthol.

The door was unlocked. I entered Phil's house and paused for a moment in the foyer to smear lip balm over my philtrum[32], then raced up the stairs and into her bedroom, where Phil was not.

Was not.

I stared at the empty bed, messily recently slept in. Phil was nowhere to be seen.

I approached it cautiously, as though it might vanish with my proximity. I peeled back the corner of the counterpane and beheld sheets stained with history. But whose and for how long?

"Hey."

I turned to the door. Phil stood there in her bathrobe, a playful smile on her face.

32. Also known as the infranasal depression, that groove running from the nasal septum to the upper lip, but "philtrum" is—for obvious reasons—the more resonant term in this instance.

"Where were you?" I asked.

"A girl can't use the bathroom?"

She came to me and folded herself into my arms. I slid my hands under the bathrobe and embraced her, stroked her naked back, crushing her to me.

"Love you," I said.

"I love you, too," she said, and kissed me.

I pulled back and coughed, the scent of chocolate stronger. "What's on your lip?" she asked and then touched her own and sniffed her finger. "Is that lip balm?"

"My lips were dry," I told her, stepping away just a half-step, trying to recover. The smell of chocolate syrup had intensified, and I had to fake a cough in order to cover up an involuntary spasm of nausea.

"Yeah, but it's smeared all over—Are you all right?" she asked, stepping closer with concern.

I fumbled in my pocket for the lip balm. "I'm fine. I just need some more lip balm."

"I don't care if your lips are dry," she said, closing the distance and kissing me again. My gut heaved. I could not smell Phil; I could not smell the lingering scent of her body wash, the cool citrus of her shampoo, the clean femininity of her under it all. Everything had faded to a blur of chocolate with a hint of menthol, and it roiled my stomach like the flu, like a sledgehammer of parosmia.

"Wait," I said, backing up. "Wait."

"I love you," she said, stepping towards me, her tone cheerful robotic, her lips twisted into a rictus of joy. "I love you, Mike. Only you. I've always loved you. Only you."

My stomach complained, loud and insistent. Phil took my hand and pulled open her robe, then placed my palm on her breast. "You're here for me, aren't you?" she asked. "Don't tell me you don't love me. You have to love me. You have to. You're my everything. You're my world. I live for you, Mike. I am for you, Mike."

I coughed uncontrollably and sank to my knees. Phil wouldn't stop talking, wouldn't stop forcing my hand to roam her, to explore her, oblivious to my straits. I had wanted her to love me, had wanted her love to be powerful, and now it overrode everything else. Pleading with me, she tried to drag me into the bed and onto our history-made sheets as I doubled over in pain and threw up on the carpet, but even that could not dissuade her as she tugged and pulled and begged.

I threw up again, a great fountain of reddish-brown sludge that spurted from my yawning jaws in a quantity greater than what could be held in my stomach. A moment later, as Phil screeched for me to join her in bed, more chocolate and blood sprayed from my nostrils, and I felt as though my brain itself had liquefied and exploded from me.

"Don't you love me anymore, Mike?" Phil asked, now naked on the bed, gazing at me with enormous, limpid eyes as I gasped for breath on all fours on her floor.

But it wasn't Phil. It was a *thing* that looked like Phil, but it was not Phil. It was a creature I had made. Something I had created without intending to.

"If you don't love me," she blubbered, "then I don't want to live!" And before I could do anything—before I could find the strength to move or to clear my throat and mouth enough to scream, she grabbed a large scissors from the nighttable and plunged it into the side of her neck and before the first eruption of blood could come, I closed my eyes and let the miasma of chocolate syrup overcome me.

CHAPTER 16

A hand on my shoulder shocked me back to awareness. I was on the subway, lying on one side, knees curled up to my chest.

"Are you all right?" an old woman asked, leaning with concern toward me, her coffee breath filling the air between us. "You sounded like you were choking in your sleep."

I forced myself into a sitting position. Her coffee exhalation cut through the funk of chocolate syrup, helping me to breathe again, cutting me off mid-gag. I realized I would have to be more careful about my edits—I couldn't afford to choke to death on my own vomit. What good would that do me?

"I'm all right," I told her, attempting a smile made shaky and weak by my exhaustion. "Thanks for checking up on me."

She couldn't decide whether or not to believe me, but ultimately, she had no choice. She returned to a seat on the opposite side of the car, closer to the door. We were the only two in this car this early in the morning, and as the train bounced along in the tunnel, she looked over at me repeatedly, as though not certain she had seen me at all in the first place and she had to keep checking to be sure I hadn't faded away like the image on a TV screen when the power's been turned off.

She got off at the next stop and I kept riding the train. I realized shortly after the successive stop that this train went to Phil's, that I was only two stops away from her. Thinking of Phil caused a kaleidoscope of memories and images, fragments of conversations all to collide in my head. I had multiple memories now of the past two years or so, and keeping them straight was difficult. Some moments remained the same or roughly so no matter what. I always ended up at Y. Phil always came to see me at Spring Break. I always called her to profess my love; she always told me she was with *him*. I always went to The WB the previous night; she always showed up with *him*, sometimes in teal, sometimes in red.

No matter what I did, she never left that dance with me. I always ended up on the subway, alone in the early hours.

No more.

I decided that enough was enough. I had been too subtle, I realized. I was trying to finesse the situation when something more akin to brute force was required. I knew that Phil loved me. She had told me this herself on multiple occasions. It was only my own incompetence that kept us from being together.

I rummaged in my jacket pocket and found a small tube of mentholated lip balm, practically *de riguer* in the desert during the summer. I popped off the cap and held the balm under my nose, breathing in the cool menthol.

I closed my eyes.

I opened them again.

Did you really think it would be that easy? a voice asked.

I looked around, but I was alone on the train.

I shivered, even though the subway car was warm. The scent of chocolate had abated and I could breathe easily now.

The memory of Phil stabbing herself was almost as awful as the memory of me choking to death, which in turn was almost as awful as the thought of Phil-as-robot.

But now, having chosen not to leave my eyes closed, having chosen not to proceed to Phil's, having chosen not to make her love me against her will, I excised that particular chapter, deleted it, consigned it to a clipboard from which there can be no pasting.

To be certain, I stayed on the subway until I passed Phil's stop, my body tense until the train pulled away and returned to the darkness of the tunnel. I finally breathed again, inhaling the fading scent of menthol.

It wasn't working. Editing the *now* didn't work. What choice did I have, though? I had this power—it was meant to be used. But nothing I did worked!

In frustration, I kicked at the subway floor, pounding my fist on the empty seat next to me. A weak, pathetic, grown-up excuse for a temper tantrum, too self-aware and self-inhibited to accomplish anything.

Editing Phil—controlling her—was not the way. I needed to find a place, a moment, in our shared past.

The right moment to use, the right moment to tweak such that she would—of her own accord, just as she changed her dress from red to teal and from teal to red—realize and retain her love for me.

I smeared more lip balm and took a deep breath.

CHAPTER 2

"Dude," George says, as I find myself at his house, or more accurately outside his house, on the rickety old deck, George making his way through a six-pack of Stella Artois, "the only beer worth drinking," in his estimation. George's mother refuses to let him drink while underage and while "living under *my* roof!" so deck-drinking is their uneasy compromise, placing George technically beyond the jurisdiction of "under *my* roof!" though not beyond the jurisdiction of law enforcement, whom his mother occasionally and half-heartedly threatens to call.

"Dude, you're with her all the time," he goes on, clinking an empty bottle next to its brethren in the cardboard carrier, lifting free a full bottle on the upswing. "You in love or something? I figure you're gonna end up in the old age home, chasing after her with your walker, you know what I mean?" He pauses, consideration creasing his brow. "What will her hair look like when she gets old? You think it'll go gray or will it just get, like, lighter blue?"

"I don't know. I don't care."

"Cornflower? Periwinkle?"

"Seriously. Don't care."

"Powder blue? Robin's egg blue? Ice blue?"

"George."

"Dude, you lack curiosity. That's your fatal flaw. Not hubris. Not cluelessness." Here, George belches with great intensity and intent, as though determined to communicate some vital fact via his gas. "Curiosity, man. It killed the cat, but *lack* of it will kill *you*, you know what I mean? Trust me on this." He points the open mouth of his beer bottle at me, and to me the mouth is like an eye, watching, staring, unblinking, until I become discomfited and look away.

"I trust you, George."

And I realize that I'm lost in my own history again, waiting out the past for a chance to fix my future. In words, perhaps, this moment is protracted, but in actual time, it's all flashback memories and quick remembrances ticking away the seconds until George my memory-in-the-memory of George conflates with my memory of George, who tells me:

"Just in case. Because I'll kill him, Mike." He says it without emotion, without inflection, with the tone of a man recalling to a spouse that—as long as she's headed to the store—the larder could use a new box of pretzels. "I'll kill him. I mean it."

Meaning it is my turn to speak, saying:

"I know you do." And then, adding something I often add at this point: "I'll help." Sometimes it's "Can I help?" or "If you want some help . . ." or some other variation, but tonight it's "I'll help." Declarative. Strong. Intentional.

He salutes me with the bottle. "I know you will. 'Cause you know what it's like to have a shitty childhood."

I don't think of my parents or of George being my best friend while I cannot be his. Instead, I wait it out, waiting for the right moment.

"But I didn't mean to go off on the asshole again," George says. "Sorry, dude. How did I even start talking about him, anyway? Anyway, I figure you'll still be sticking it to the blue bombshell when you need the little blue pills, you know what I mean?"

"Yeah, I know what you mean, George." My thoughts, bifurcated, continue the conversation with George while also drifting to my last time in bed with Phil, as well—trifurcated, now—as to the *next* time I will be in bed with Phil (probably tomorrow night, as I've told her I'll be palling with George tonight), and then threaten to *quad*furcate as my cell chirps its incoming text message alert.

i wish i had gummi bears

"Dude, is the Mrs. calling?" He leans back to get the last drops of beer, precariously close to toppling over the rail. I resist the urge to shout for him to be careful—George hates being looked after, mothered, mollycoddled. "If the asshole didn't kill me," he has said many times, "real life isn't going to get it done any time soon."

~~"Shut up," I tell him instead. "She's not the Mrs."~~ "I have to go," I tell him.

"It *was* the Mrs.!" he exclaims, guffawing, once again teetering on the edge of disaster before righting himself.

"Leave me alone." I am filled with an unaccountable urgency. I need to go to Phil. I need to bring her gummi bears. I feel as though this is my only chance for any sort of future happiness, that the satisfaction of my life rests on a few ounces of soft, rubbery, tinted sugar.

George does not pout, but his mouth configures itself as close to pouting as it ever gets. "Dude, you said we were going to hang tonight. Just the two of us. You know what I mean?"

"I know. I know." And then I am apologizing without even thinking about it, already thinking about the best place to get gummi bears at this time of night, the place not only closest to Phil's or George's, but also reasonably between the two, saying words that do not matter as I get up, patting my pocket to double-check for keys, wallet, waiting for George to snark that I am also checking for my balls, but the snark never comes. Instead, he just snorts like a minotaur and turns away to gaze out into the backyard.

****

Soon, I leave the KwikNFast convenience store, two bags of gummi bears clutched in my left hand, and I launch myself back into the subway and make for Phil's house, aware of this opportunity to change my life, to prove my love to her early on.

At Phil's house, mindful of the hour, I text Phil *open the front door* as opposed to knocking and waking her mother. After a moment, she opens the door to find me there, smiling and holding up the bags of gummi bears.

"What are you doing?" she asks. "I thought you were with George tonight."

"You wanted gummis. Here."

She takes the bags and stares at them, then looks up at me. Her lips work for a moment, as though rehearsing what she will say.

"These are the wrong kind," she says, immediately followed by, "I'm sorry. That was a bitchy thing to— I'm sorry. This was really sweet of you."

The world has not changed. What did I expect? Did I expect the sudden light of love in her eyes? Did I expect the stars to flare brighter in the night sky? Did I expect some tectonic shift in the universe?

"I'm sorry," I tell her, annoyed and miffed and disguising that fact. "What are the right kind? Does it really matter?"

"No, of course not." She ushers me into the house, and we quietly—so as not to awaken her mother—make our way to her bedroom, where we sit together on the history-made sheets as she opens one bag and shares out the gummi bears. She eats hers in a specific fashion, always popping two into her mouth at the same time and never two of the same color/flavor.

"It's just that these are really soft," she says. "The kind I like, the ones in the gold bag, are chewier, you know?"

I bite into a yellow gummi bear, decapitating it. "Is there really a difference?" but even as I say it, I know that there is, and then we fuck, adding another era to the history-made sheets, and then I sneak out of the house, aware as I do so that Phil's mom is still awake, betrayed by a TV-blue flicker of light under her door, and the dream of fucking her pops into my conscious mind for just a moment as I leave, quickly suppressed, and I realize this could not have been, has not been enough, that we will still break up, that it will not work out, that I will end up

CHAPTER 16

A hand on my shoulder shocked me back to awareness. I was on the subway, lying on one side, knees curled up to my chest.

"Are you all right?" an old woman asked, leaning with concern toward me, her coffee breath filling the air between us. "You sounded like you were choking in your sleep."

I forced myself into a sitting position. Her coffee exhalation cut through the funk of chocolate syrup, helping me to breathe again, cutting me off mid-gag. I realized I would have to be more careful about my edits—I couldn't afford to choke to death on my own vomit. What good would that do me?

"I'm all right," I told her, attempting a smile made shaky and weak by my exhaustion. "Thanks for checking up on me."

She couldn't decide whether or not to believe me, but ultimately, she had no choice. She returned to a seat on the opposite side of the car, closer to the door.

This time, I ignored her.

She got off at the next stop and I kept riding the train.

I always ended up on the subway, alone in the early hours.

I rummaged in my jacket pocket and found a small tube of

mentholated lip balm, practically *de riguer* in the desert during the summer. I popped off the cap and held the balm under my nose, breathing in the cool menthol.

I closed my eyes.

I opened them again.

Did you really think it would be that easy? a voice asked.

I looked around, but I was alone on the train.

I shivered, even though the subway car was warm. The scent of chocolate had abated and I could breathe easily now. The memory of Phil ~~stabbing herself was almost as awful as the memory of me choking to death, which in turn was almost as awful as the thought of Phil-as-robot.~~ eating her substandard gummis hung like a dreamcatcher in my mind.

The subway rolled past Phil's house and I knew that I would have to try again.

I smeared more lip balm and took a deep breath.

CHAPTER 2

"Dude," George says, as I find myself at his house, or more accurately outside his house, on the rickety old deck, George making his way through a six-pack of Stella Artois, "the only beer worth drinking," in his estimation. George's mother refuses to let him drink while underage and while "living under *my* roof!" so deck-drinking is their uneasy compromise, placing George technically beyond the jurisdiction of "under *my* roof!" though not beyond the jurisdiction of law enforcement, whom his mother occasionally and half-heartedly threatens to call.

"Dude, you're with her all the time," he goes on, clinking an empty bottle next to its brethren in the cardboard carrier, lifting free a full bottle on the upswing. "You in love or something? I figure you're gonna end up in the old age home, chasing after her with your walker, you know what I mean?" He pauses, consideration creasing his brow. "What will her hair look like when she gets old? You think it'll go gray or will it just get, like, lighter blue?"

"I have to go," I tell him, jumping up, checking for keys, wallet. "Sorry. There's something I have to do. I forgot."

He stares, gape-mouthed, at me, hops down from the railing and demands an explanation, but all I offer him is "sorry" and "gotta go" and "we'll hang tomorrow, I swear" on my way out the door, to the car.

Soon, at KwikNFast, I scour the candy pegboard for the right gummis, the ones in the gold bag. Pushing aside swinging bags of gummi worms, caramel candies, coffee-flavored hard candies, and chocolate drops, I find two solitary bags of gold-bagged gummis.

My cell chirps its incoming text message alert as I pay at the register:

i wish i had gummi bears

Less than five minutes later, I am at Phil's front door, her shocked expression a delight to behold as I offer two bags of sugary, chewy gummi goodness.

"How . . ." She shakes her head. "How did you get here so *fast?*" She grabs a bag. "These are my favorites. How did you know?"

I want to say something witty, something casual and off-handish, something that will—by its very down-played nature—resonate all the more with her, echo for long days and nights in her mind, memorable and unforgettable and charming and endearing.

Instead, I say the only thing in my heart and in my throat at this moment, this perfect moment I have waited for and built and re-built.

"I love you," I tell her.

And so inside.

And so sitting on the bed, sharing the gummis (which are, in fact, chewier and superior to the others, I confess).

And so new epochs added to the history-made sheets.

And so, the next day . . .

****

"Mike, I think we should see other people."

CHAPTER 16

A hand on my shoulder shocked me back to awareness. I was on the subway, lying on one side, knees curled up to my chest.

"Are you all right?" an old woman asked, leaning with concern toward me, her coffee breath filling the air between us. "You sounded like you were choking in your sleep."

I forced myself into a sitting position. Her coffee exhalation cut through the funk of chocolate syrup, helping me to breathe again, cutting me off mid-gag. I realized I would have to be more careful about my edits—I couldn't afford to choke to death on my own vomit. What good would that do me?

"I'm all right," I told her, attempting a smile made shaky and weak by my exhaustion. "Thanks for checking up on me."

She couldn't decide whether or not to believe me, but ultimately, she had no choice. She returned to a seat on the opposite side of the car, closer to the door. We were the only two in this car this early in the morning, and as the train bounced along in the tunnel, she looked over at me repeatedly, as though not certain she had seen me at all in the first place and she had to

keep checking to be sure I hadn't faded away like the image on a TV screen when the power's been turned off.

She got off at the next stop and I kept riding the train. I realized shortly after the successive stop that this train went to Phil's, that I was only two stops away from her. Thinking of Phil caused a kaleidoscope of memories and images, fragments of conversations all to collide in my head. I had multiple memories now of the past two years or so, and keeping them straight was difficult. Some moments remained the same or roughly so no matter what. I end up at Y. Phil visits me at Spring Break. I call her to profess my love; she tells me she is with *him*. I go to The WB; she shows up with *him*, sometimes in teal, sometimes in red.

No matter what I do, though, she never leaves that dance with me. I always end up on the subway, alone in the early hours.

No more.

I decided that enough was enough. I had been too subtle, I realized. I was trying to finesse the situation when something more akin to brute force was required. I knew that Phil loved me. She had told me this herself on multiple occasions. It was only my own incompetence that kept us from being together.

I rummaged in my jacket pocket and found a small tube of mentholated lip balm, practically *de riguer* in the desert during the summer. I popped off the cap and held the balm under my nose, breathing in the cool menthol.

I closed my eyes.

I opened them again.

Did you really think it would be that easy? a voice asked.

I looked around, but I was alone on the train.

I shivered, even though the subway car was warm. The scent of chocolate had abated and I could breathe easily now.

I could remember. The multiplicity of memories warring

for prominence in my mind called a temporary truce, allowing me to focus on the most recent set, how Phil broke up with me after the Night of the (Proper) Gummi Bears, claiming that I was "too into [her]" and, that, consequently, she had become persuaded that I would, in the future, "make *bad* decisions because [I would be] thinking of [her] and not [myself]."[33] Lacking any convincing way of deterring her, I had no choice but to accede to her wishes, though I spent the rest of my senior year trying to win her back.

Spent the summer depressed.

Spent my freshman year despondent.

Phil did not call to come visit me over Spring Break. I did not see her again until the night of The WB event, the focal point for my tale, it seems.

Everything had changed.

Nothing had changed.

The subway clacked and wracked.

****

I sat on the subway, the lone rider in the early morning, deep underground where the sun could not shine on me even as it rose. I tried desperately to imagine a scenario that could return Phil to me. Nothing I had attempted worked.

Was it possible that Phil and I were not meant to be together? That we were destined to be apart, to have our relationship end whether by her hand or by mine?

33. Exact statement by Phil: "You're too into me, Mike. I send you a silly little text about gummis and you just pop up like magic! You're gonna have to make big decisions soon and I'm worried you'll make bad decisions because you'll be thinking of me and not yourself. I'm trying to be mature about this."

It was not the first time I'd considered such an idea, yet I could lend it no credence. I had begun editing reality the first time I saw Phil after our Spring Break fuck, at the lowest moment for me. Einstein said that God does not play dice with the universe; I could not believe that the universe played dice with me.

Even with the weight of so much evidence bearing down on me, even in light of the demonstrated fact that nothing I could do or would do or had done could or did change things for the better, I could not shake the idea that Phil and I were meant to be together. Why else would I have been given this power, this perspective on the world, if not to rectify the great wrong done to/by me?

More important than destiny was desire: I loved Phil. I wanted/needed to be with her. Desperately. If destiny decreed us apart, then I would defy destiny. Gladly.

The subway clanged and banged to a halt, jostling me from my reverie. The speaker crackled to life and the driver said, "Ladies and gentlemen, this is the final stop on this train. All passengers must disembark. This train is now out of service."

I stood, blinking around at my surroundings as though they'd changed, as though seeing the benign, banal interior of this particular subway car for the first time, as though it had some flavor that distinguished it from others of its ilk. But it was as bland as any of the others: sick-green plastic benches, worn chrome poles to hold, a flecked blue laminate floor. Advertisements at the ends and above the benches, hawking Spanish as a Second Language classes, confidential AIDS-II hotlines, adult re-education classes at the local community colleges, and the latest LatinoLit thriller novel.

It was all old, all familiar, yet it was as though I was seeing it for the first time.

I disembarked, as instructed, and found myself at the Crimson Rocks subway station, the final stop on the Fox line. I had not been here since a school trip in elementary school. I looked around for the subway map, but it had been partly torn and partly defaced by a graffito depicting a large caterpillar trying to eat the sun. I stood alone in the station, trying to figure out how to get back home.

Just then, the train huffed as though alive and pulled away, heading further into the tunnel.

"Hey!" I shouted, running to it and vainly smacking my palms against the doors closest to me. "Hey! Stop! Don't leave me—"

But the train disappeared into the tunnel.

I made my way to a flight of stairs that led down, deeper under the desert, then twisted around themselves and rose again to the opposite platform, where trains headed back into the city would berth. No train waited, however. I stood for long minutes, waiting. A poster taped to a nearby column showed a cartoon silhouette of a scorpion, its tail poised to strike. Above the cartoon, it said

CITY TRANSIT

DEPT. OF TRACKS AND TUNNELS

Below the cartoon, in large, red letters:

CAUTION!

Then:

This area has been baited with

ARACHNICIDE

Further below that were the details of the date on which the arachnicide had been placed (two days previous) as well as contact information for the DOTAT office responsible for said placing. As if to mock my noticing of the poster, a large scorpion lazily skittered over the track below me, its tail arched and threatening. Rats did not survive long in these tunnels, not with city scorpions as their natural enemies.

Then, as I watched, a low, sleek train the likes of which I'd seen only in movies glided with little fanfare into the opposite platform. I cried out in simultaneous surprise, relief, and frustration, briefly gave thought to attempting to leap directly across, then dashed down the stairs and up the stairs once more. Fortunately, the new train was still at the platform and I ran for it, thinking to hop on and ride it wherever subway trains turned around for their return trips.

However, the doors to this new car would not open, no matter how much I pounded on them or pleaded. After a moment, a subway driver ambled along the platform and sternly told me to move on.

"I'm just trying to get back to the city," I told him. "I missed my stop."

"I can't help you with that." He glanced at his watch. "You'll need to get out of here now. This station is closed."

"Closed?"

"This station closes every day at this time. Orders from up top."

"Why?"

"I don't ask, kid," he said, shrugging. "I just do what the Boss tells me. This train isn't for you. This whole station is off limits right now. This early in the morning, no one's going from Crimson Rocks to the city anyway. It'll be about an hour until they open up the line and send a train back into the city."

He left me no choice but to resign myself to a long wait. As ordered, I ascended the staircase to the second level, where no trains awaited. A bored woman locked into the plexiglass cage of a 24-hour ticket booth flicked idle eyes in my direction as I mounted the last flight of stairs, which took me out into the open air.

The desert arrayed itself all around me as I emerged from the underground. Normally, a partial canopy shielded the entrance to a desert station, but this one lay smashed and spiderwebbed with fissures some yards away, victim of a sandstorm, no doubt. As a result, the subway entrance was a slot cut directly into the desert floor, where loose sand occasionally blew down onto the steps. Cacti and Joshua trees and tumbleweed dotted the landscape for hundreds of yards in every direction. To the east, the sun burnished the low horizon and shone through the fingers of the city's skyscrapers.

To the west loomed the Crimson Rocks, high peaks that reared up into the clouds like a rough-hewn mirror image of the city.

They were not actually red. They had been named for their "discoverer," Lord Crimson, a British ex-patriate who was the first white man to cross this desert back in the nineteenth century. Of course, they had taken on new meaning several years ago when they came to represent the aftermath of the Lucky Sevens terrorist attack that kicked off GWB. Many locals and even tourists had made the pilgrimage to the Crimson Rocks to pay their respects to the thousands of dead, the closest one could approach the actual site of the disaster. I had never come. I preferred to keep my memories pristine, of the perfect natural wonder I'd seen as a child on that elementary school field trip.

But now it would be a mere walk of a few football fields to a ridge overlooking the Other City. Once, I'd been told, there were desert rickshaws for hire, covered wagons, all designed to disturb as little of the terrain as possible while still conveying gawkers to the site. Now, though, with the passage of years, no one came here anymore. No one cared. They were more interested in GWB, and less interested in why and how it had started.

I began to walk. I thought of Phil the whole time, sorting out my memories of our various relationships, of the liminal spaces between them, of the ways in which I had tried to fix or change things, always failing. Remembered her as Othello, as Estragon. Remembered her confident and nigh-imperious on the set, commanding, ordering, coaching her fellow actors into a diorama she held entirely in her mind, the way I held blueprints. We were so much the same, she and I. Both builders. Both artists. And she had all the confidence I lacked.

I thought of the time she'd texted me: *come listen to the rain w me*

Rain was rare in the desert. A sustained rain that would last long enough to respond to a text was even more rare. That night, she wanted me to come lay in bed with her and listen to the rain as it tattooed her roof. And as much as I tried in that moment, with the rising sun at my back, I could not remember why I had denied her. Such a simple request. Such a small thing. It was a matter of a walk to the subway, then five minutes on the train, then a walk to her house. To lie beside her. To hold her in my arms and let the rain lullaby us to sleep. And yet that small, simple thing was beyond me, for reasons I could no longer recall. I remembered the ache and the disappointment and the ease of the request, but I could not remember the cause of the ache and the disappointment, the reason for forsaking such an easy request.

Was that the moment? I wondered, pausing in my trek across the desert. Was that the crucial moment in our relationship? Did I need to edit that moment and go to her, arrive gently wet with desert rain at her front door, kiss her, slip into the history-made sheets with her and just . . . hold her? Was that the secret?

I did not know.

I could not know.

My legs began to tremble and could no longer support me. Wary of scorpions, I lowered myself to the ground and sat in the warm sand, staring ahead at the great upthrust of the Crimson Rocks. Just beyond them, I knew, were the remnants of the Other City, my home's twin sister, devastated years ago on July 7, 2007—7/7/7. Lucky Sevens.[34]

I sat there in the sand, staring ahead at the Crimson Rocks, staring through them at what lay beyond. The Other City had been abandoned, its skyscrapers left uninhabited, its surviving citizens scattering to the rest of the country. And then GWB—Global War B—had begun, with no signs of ever stopping. We would be at war forever.

Could I edit that? Could I undo Lucky Sevens? Could I stop GWB from wreaking havoc on the nation and the world?

I thought of Phil and her scissors, and I decided to leave Lucky Sevens alone.

I had not smelled the overpowering chocolate syrup since leaving the subway. It was—in some way I could not explain—connected to my editing of reality. As I edited more and more, the smell became stronger and stronger, to the point that I could not bear it. I wondered: Was that a sign that I was editing the wrong points in my history? Or was it a sign that I should be editing nothing at all?

But I could not believe that last. It made no sense. Why would I have this ability if I was not meant to use it?

I thought of Phil. And the rain.

And I cried.

34. The event, though tragic and horrific, was nicknamed "Lucky Sevens" because it could have been so much worse. Or so the popular imagination would have it.

Cried there in the desert, alone. I was not, I know, the first. So many had shed so many tears here, but mine were surely the most selfish. I wept not for the thousands killed on Lucky Sevens, nor the hundreds of thousands who died in subsequent years due to GWB, the innocents in other countries, the soldiers, nor for the families of the dead, nor for "the children" (for whom we always are supposed to weep). I did not even weep for Phil.

I wept for myself.

For my power.

My paralysis.

My fear.

My love.

Oh, God, I wept for my love!

Out there in the desolation of the desert, in the shadow of my own city, trapped between its familiar skyscrapers and the Crimson Rocks, all things seemed possible and impossible at once, as though the world had become quantum physics on the macro level. I felt as though I could successfully design the underwater hotel there, in the ironic counterpoint of the desert. I felt as though I could become George's best friend there. I felt as though I could—finally—recapture lost Philomel there.

Phil.

The chocolate syrup came to me before I'd even committed to a course of action. Someone, something, knew what I was going to attempt before I had done so.

Coughing, doubled over, I fixed a point in my mind. I would only have one chance at this. One last attempt, as the sun burned its path overhead . . .

CHAPTER 2

"Dude," George says, as I find myself at his house, or more accurately outside his house, on the rickety old deck, George making his way through a six-pack of Stella Artois, "the only beer worth drinking," in his estimation. George's mother refuses to let him drink while underage and while "living under *my* roof!" so deck-drinking is their uneasy compromise, placing George technically beyond the jurisdiction of "under *my* roof!" though not beyond the jurisdiction of law enforcement, whom his mother occasionally and half-heartedly threatens to call.

"Dude, you're with her all the time," he goes on, clinking an empty bottle next to its brethren in the cardboard carrier, lifting free a full bottle on the upswing. "You in love or something? I figure you're gonna end up in the old age home, chasing after her with your walker, you know what I mean?" He pauses, consideration creasing his brow. "What will her hair look like when she gets old? You think it'll go gray or will it just get, like, lighter blue?"

"I don't know. I don't care."

"Cornflower? Periwinkle?"

"Seriously. Don't care."

"Powder blue? Robin's egg blue? Ice blue?"

"George. Just stop, please, OK?" I hold up a hand, my expression pained, as though warding off an incoming headache. "I just need a second—"

"Dude, what's wrong?" His insistent jocularity fades to insistent concern in an instant. "You OK?"

"I'm fine. There's just . . . There's something . . ." There's something I'm waiting for here. A moment. A thought. A flashback I had. I need to activate it again. I need George to say what he said before that activated it, but I'm too impatient so I've interrupted him and lost the thread, but I have to get it back. "What were you going to say next?"

He stares at me. "I don't . . . I don't know. We were—"

"We were talking about Phil. Getting old."

And he laughs and says, "Right. Dude, I figure you'll still be sticking it to the blue bombshell when you need the little blue pills, you know what I mean?"

One of George's more endearing traits is that he thinks he's more subtle than he actually is. Along with "dude," "you know what I mean?" is a constant in his lexicon, even though everyone *always* knows what he means.

"Yeah, I know what you mean, George." My thoughts, bifurcated, continue the conversation with George while also drifting to my last time in bed with Phil, as well—trifurcated, now—as to the *next* time I will be in bed with Phil (probably tomorrow night, as I've told her I'll be palling with George tonight), then quadfurcate to the subway stop at Crimson Rocks, then quintfurcate as I realize what is about to happen, and then threaten to *sext*furcate as my cell chirps its incoming text message alert.

i wish i had gummi bears

"Dude, is the Mrs. calling?" He leans back to get the last drops of beer, precariously close to toppling over the rail. I resist the urge to shout for him to be careful—George hates being looked after, mothered, mollycoddled. "If the asshole didn't kill me," he has said many times, "real life isn't going to get it done any time soon."

"Shut up," I tell him instead. "She's not the Mrs." But I experience a pang of . . . regret? Want? Urgency?

Yes. Urgency. Something is coming and I need to pay attention, need to be ready and available for it. I cannot allow myself to be distracted by George, who is saying:

"Dude, you are *so* pussywhipped. I swear. I swear. I bet if I pulled down your pants right now, there wouldn't even be a dick there. You're smooth like Ken, you know what I mean? She has it all locked up in her hope chest, doesn't she?"

I essay a hollow laugh, trying to show a jocular and casual contempt for his comment, trying to stay in the present and future and the past all at once, waiting for something important to come.

"What does she want?" George asks. "She's already got your balls and your dick. She need your tongue now?"

"What makes you think it's her?" I ask, looking at *i wish i had gummi bears.* "It's just text spam." I slide my phone into my pocket.

"Dude," George introduces his next sentence, "I don't get it. I mean, yeah, she's hot. No question about it. And I guess the blue hair thing is kinda cool, but anyone can dye their hair. So what's so special about her? Why her?"

"It's not dyed," I hear myself say, distracted.

Almost. Almost there. Almost the moment. I can feel it coming towards me, though I'm not sure what it looks or sounds or feels like. Something in "Why her?" Something in that question, which makes me think how explaining "Why Phil?" is like explaining "Why do babies love their mothers?" or "Why do dogs love their masters?" It just, simply, merely *is*. There is no "because."

Something.

"Because she believes in me," I tell George, because when a best friend asks his very, very good friend "Why her?" an answer must come forth, even if it is composed of equal parts half-truth, bare-understanding, and bullshit. "She's always believed in me."

"Is this about that freaking elevator building?"

Of course it is decidedly *not* about the elevator building; it is about young Phil's defiant "Phil!" when called "Philomel," about older Phil's curling into me at the library years later, saying, "That is *so* cool," about younger (but not-quite-as-young-as-young-Phil) standing up to our school's principal[35], but it is partly at least about older-than-younger-Phil-but-younger-than-older-Phil's particular *reaction* to the elevator building, said building being my first architectural project and the impetus to my first serious conversation with Phil, who, in eighth grade, looked over my shoulder one day in the lunchroom, standing quietly for I still know not how long, studying me as I sketched in one of my endless supply of spiral-top-bound notebooks. I had roughed out the basic structure of a building when I sensed some hovering presence and, glancing over my shoulder, saw her standing there. To be more accurate, I saw her hair before seeing Phil herself, a flash of dark, brilliant sapphire bursting into my field of vision before I could recognize her face.

35. "If you don't let us put on a play and use the school's auditorium," younger-though-not-youngest-Phil pronounced, "we'll do it outside on the playground instead, and you can explain to our parents why their kids are out there at night." A child's gambit, and one that worked.

Her face.

This. This moment. I needed George's moment to get to this moment.

"You're really good," she said authoritatively, as if she had settled a debate on the subject. "What is it?" she asked, apparently unaware that that question put the lie to "You're really good."

"It's just a building idea I had," I mumbled.

She slid next to me on the bench, and for the first time, I was close enough to touch her, close enough to smell her—she was redolent of freesia and lilacs and the over-tang of curry, it being lunch, after all, and Phil's mother being a parent who habitually packed leftovers for her child, having this day chosen Indian take-out—and the world froze for the instant it took for me to register her nearness, her scents, the soft wave of her oceanic mane.

"What are these arrows for?" Pointing to my notebook.

Then my mouth became the Sahara (again . . . or for the first time?) and I could not bear to speak, but speak I did, in a voice low and contrite: "Elevators."

She lingered a moment on the drawing, studying it like an unearthed artifact that lacked context or knowable creator, even though I was sitting right there, right next to her, close enough that the slightest move on my part (or hers) would cause my be-jeaned thigh to touch her be-skirted one. She pondered the drawing, brushing a stray fallen lock of blue hair back over her left ear.

And this is my moment, I realize and I realized. My one chance. To start things from the beginning, without ambiguity, without complexity. I knew that in this moment within a moment, in this flashback within a flashback, in this past, I could change it all. This was the instant I'd been waiting for, waiting patiently on George's deck years in the future, waiting for him to trigger the memory so powerfully and perfectly that I could remember every detail, so that I could enter the memory, the past, the history.

I ignored my sketchbook. I took the slightest move and my be-jeaned thigh touched her be-skirted one. In that instant, the annals of the history-made sheets flooded into me, as though every sexual encounter with Phil that was to come had entered me in a single, blissful explosion. I took her hand in mine, then gripped it tightly when I saw the expression of surprise on her face. In a moment, it would not matter.

In a moment.

I said, "Phil."

She looked at me.

I said, "I love you."

CHAPTER 11

And that's when I realized I could edit reality, staring at Phil, at her dress, her teal dress, the dress teal and very definitely not-red. Phil stared back at me, her eyes narrowed to slits as though against sunlight. "Stop staring at me, you goddamn freak!" she hissed in a loud whisper. "Back the fuck off. Now!"

And then *he* came in. *He* had the good grace to pause for a moment at the door before approaching us, *his* face a melting pot of anger, shock, and some distant relative of resignation.

"Is there a problem?" *he* asked.

"I just don't want to deal with this shit-head," Phil said, grabbing *his* arm like the damsel-in-distress she was not. "My whole life. My whole fucking—"

And yet she seemed stressed, if not distressed, as though the very sight of me filled her not with disappointment or regret, but rather outright fear and disgust. *He* stepped closer and I waited for George to interpose himself between us, interleaving the four of us.

Instead, George grabbed my arm and yanked me back so fast that my neck jerked painfully. Before I could respond or react or protest, he hauled me further away, into the alcove near the bathroom.

"What the fuck are you doing?" he demanded. "You just stay away from her, for Christ's sake! You know what I mean?"

"But—" Disoriented, I tried to sort through the menagerie of memories, seeking the sequence of events that would explain this turn of events. Phil had never hated and feared me. Brushed me off, yes. Ignored me, certainly. But actively feared me? Actively sought to have me removed from her presence? And even *his* aggression, which was to be expected and had been anticipated, seemed ratcheted up not one, but rather several notches. What had I done?

"I just need to see her, George. Just for a second. To remind her—"

"Remind her of what?" George glanced over his shoulder. *He* was on his cell phone and Phil seemed to be weeping, and I suddenly began to understand.

George pushed me further into the alcove. "I never should have come to this thing with you. If I'd known she was gonna be here, I wouldn't have come. And I wouldn't have let *you* come, either. You have to get over this, man. You have to stop stalking her."

Stalking? "George, I love her. I—"

"Love her? Dude, you don't even *know* her, you know what I mean? You've been bitching and moaning about her, about how much you love her, for years but you've never even spent five minutes alone with her."

I could not believe it was true, but even as I could not believe it, I knew it was true. The belief and the knowledge clashed, two diametrically opposed forces, two opposites held in the same hand. "But . . . in your garage . . . At the party . . ."

"What are you talking about? She saw you come in and

came stomping out, all pissed off. Yelled at me for five minutes, telling me she wasn't gonna be trapped in the garage with a freak like you."

"I told her I loved her . . ."

It was whispered more for my benefit than for his, but he responded nonetheless. "Yeah, I know. When we were all kids." He looked back over his shoulder again and I looked as well: *He* closed the cell and put out *his* arms to comfort Phil.

"He called the Cops™, I bet. The restraining order." He thumped a fist against the wall, softly. "Dude, what the fuck were you thinking?"

"I wasn't thinking," I told him, as honestly as I knew how. The different memories, the different versions of reality, the varying drafts all blurred together, but I could now pluck one memory, one desperate attempt from the morass: Telling Phil I loved her as she looked at the elevator building in my sketch-book all those years ago. But it went beyond that. I told her and I wept and she—of course—panicked at my display.

What followed was years of me trying to convince her, persuading her by any means at my disposal, including e-mails, texts, phone calls . . .

Leading to the restraining order.

And yet I came here tonight, where it all began. Why? Because I thought I could close off the circle by bringing us back to where the story began? Clearly, that did not work.

I've made things so confusing that I can't keep track anymore.

"George, you have to believe me. I had a relationship with Phil. It started in your garage the August before senior year. We were together all year and then I broke up with her to go to College Y. That's the truth. That's what happened."

He looked at me as though I'd lost my mind, something which I knew wasn't true, although George was positive of it.

"Dude, you've barely ever even been in the same room with her. And college? You didn't even—"

"I can't explain it. I can't—" I broke off and slumped against the wall. "George, you have to trust me."

"Trust you? Dude, you got me to come here under false pretenses. 'Come on, man. It'll take your mind off of being kicked out of the Marines. Let's go have some fun.' You lied to me. You knew she'd be here."

And, of course, I did know that. Because in every iteration of reality, this dance was the focal point, the beginning and—paradoxically—the climax as well. In every iteration, we four end up at this dance in varying stages of distress with ourselves, with each other.

"I'm sorry, George. I really am."

"We're gonna have to go," he said. "Maybe we can leave before the Cops™—"

Just then, a familiar figure passed us and went into the men's room, but not before pausing to glance at George as though in recognition. I could not place the figure and even could I have, how could I have known from which version of reality I knew him? Was it someone I once knew well and now not at all? Was it a stranger I'd bumped into once and again and again, in some meaningless way that repeated over and over in some scene of my life?

"No, George. I'll go. You stay. Have fun."

The bathroom door opened and the figure stepped out. I still did not not recognize him, but his name was—

"Seth!" George said in surprise. "Hey, man!"

Seth was a tall, good-looking blond guy of roughly our ages. George introduced him as "~~Seth,~~ a great linebacker for UPN," to which Seth blushed a surprising and furious red and demurred, claiming that "those sacks" were just luck, Seth being "in the right place at the right time," of which George would hear none, punching Seth's shoulder and assuring him that he (Seth) was, in fact, a terrific linebacker, definitely the best "who ever knocked me (George) on my ass! You know what I mean?"

I remembered him now, of course, but barely had time to do so when a hush fell over the crowd gathered at The WB and when I looked up, I saw two police officers and a Cop™ standing just inside the front door, conferring with Phil and *him*, *he* now gesturing furiously in my/George's/Seth's direction.

"What the hell?" Seth asked.

"Dude," George said.

"Don't," I said. "Let me handle this."

I did the only thing I could do; I walked over to them.

****

The Cop™ remained inside to speak to Phil, as the police officers escorted me outside and, before the riot-act-reading[36] could commence, I explained that I would immediately disperse myself and peaceably depart to my habitation, wishing to cause no tumult or riotous assembly here in the halls of the former WB. They patiently and redundantly explained to me the terms of Phil's restraining order against me, that I not approach within fifty feet of her or her place of residence (including her college dorm), nor that I communicate with her in person or via any and all electronic means (including but not limited to text message, instant message chat, e-mail, chat room, telephone, video chat, and bulletin board

36. In case you're wondering, this is the actual Riot Act: *"Our Sovereign Lord the King chargeth and commandeth all persons, being assembled, immediately to disperse themselves, and peaceably to depart to their habitations, or to their lawful business, upon the pains contained in the act made in the first year of King George, for preventing tumults and riotous assemblies. God Save the King!"*

system). I listened, pretending to pay severe attention, then thanked them for their time and assured them I was leaving.

They chose not to believe me, instead following me to the subway station and escorting me onto my train before nodding curtly as the doors closed and wishing me a "fine, *safe* evening, sir," that last word offered with no small amount of insincerity.

I rode the subway home, thinking of how I'd ridden the subway out to Crimson Rocks mere moments ago, it seemed, as though no time at all had passed, or at least an insignificant amount, even though that moment actually was/is/will be in my future, should I choose to do so again. But in that time, I had been a child again and grown up again, this time loving and needing Phil from afar, my desperate, last-ditch effort to win her back having failed miserably. And, in retrospect, how could it have done otherwise? How could blurting out my love to a Phil who did not yet know me possibly lead to anything but the outcome I now experienced?

I closed my eyes. I would fix this. I needed only the scent of chocolate syrup. It might kill me this time, but I would die with Phil's love. I would find a way.

Did you really think it would be that easy? a voice asked in the past.

It felt as though the voice were with me at that moment. I looked around, but I was alone on the train.

Alone again. What were the odds of being alone on subway cars so often? Why did this keep happening? And whose voice was it that kept taunting me?

I did not attempt to change reality. I worried that the power of the chocolate syrup would, indeed, kill me this time, and without calculating the perfect and precise moment to edit, I feared I would die Phil-less, a fate I could not abide.

CHAPTER 14

I found myself at home, watching through the window, thinking that I should be able to see George's taillights disappearing into the dark. I somehow knew that he had offered Seth a ride home as well, Seth having been abandoned by some UPN friends who had decided to take one last trip through the halls of their old school building, which had been shut down due to the merger. One of them produced a set of purloined custodial keys and they resolved to spend the night as UPNers for the last time.

Had I not been rousted from The WB, George would have dropped me off first and I would have watched his taillights vanish, then gone to the kitchen for a snack before bed. Regardless, my parents sat in front of the TV, watching a movie that was neither too funny nor too sad, and most definitely in no way, shape, or form related to my circumstances whether metaphorically or allegorically or analogously. It was just a movie.

"How was The WB?" my mother asked. "Or, The CW, I guess."

"It was fine," I told her, omitting that I had learned I could warp the very stuff of reality and that I had been escorted out by the police.

"That's nice," she said.

I eagerly climbed into bed, aggressively ready for sleep, hoping for some new revelatory dream, but my angel or my oracle or my subconscious remained mute. There were no strangely-named incestuous women. No dead-then-alive-then-dead name-scrambled, be-stubbled mystery corpses. No small children with ice cream cones. My sleep was as blank as a sheet of paper fresh from the ream.

Only this time, it wasn't.

I did dream of the child with the ice cream cone. He said to me, *Did you really think it would be that easy? You can't roll it back. You can only retrofit; you can't recreate. Creation is only for him.* And then he laughed at me in a voice so cruel and so evil that I could scarcely believe it could be real. My dream-heart thudded with terror and my real heart pounded so hard that I felt it in the dream as well and feared that either in the dream or in reality or perhaps in both, I might be dying of a heart attack, helpless to save myself by the simple expedient of waking up, trapped in a dream as I died.

I did wake, of course, eventually. Hands trembling, I picked up the phone and did not pause even for an instant in calling George. Yes, it was an absurdly early hour. But this was quite literally a matter of life and death. I needed the counsel of my best friend in that moment.

George's phone rang only once and he picked up instantly, his voice low and indefinably annoyed. "Dude. Mike. Not now."

"George, I really need to talk—"

"I'm busy right now, you know what I mean?"

"But—"

"Mike. Later. We'll talk later."

He left me on the living end of a half-dead line. I stared at the phone for a moment, a flare of righteous anger burning to brief life before quenching. George had done enough for me already. I was not his best friend. I had nothing I could offer him. I would handle this on my own. I would find my way back to—

CHAPTER 16

A hand on my shoulder shocked me back to awareness. I was on the subway, lying on one side, knees curled up to my chest.

"Are you all right?" an old woman asked, leaning with concern toward me, her coffee breath filling the air between us. "You sounded like you were choking in your sleep."

I forced myself into a sitting position. Her coffee exhalation cut through the funk of chocolate syrup, helping me to breathe again, cutting me off mid-gag. I realized I would have to be more careful about my edits—I couldn't afford to choke to death on my own vomit. What good would that do me?

"I'm all right," I told her, attempting a smile made shaky and weak by my exhaustion. "Thanks for checking up on me."

She couldn't decide whether or not to believe me, but ultimately, she had no choice. She returned to a seat on the opposite side of the car, closer to the door. We were the only two in this car this early in the morning, and as the train bounced along in the tunnel, she looked over at me repeatedly, as though not certain she had seen me at all in the first place and she had to

keep checking to be sure I hadn't faded away like the image on a TV screen when the power's been turned off.

She got off at the next stop and I kept riding the train. I realized shortly after the successive stop that this train went to Phil's, that I was only two stops away from her. Thinking of Phil caused a kaleidoscope of memories and images, fragments of conversations all to collide in my head. I had multiple memories now of the past two years or so, and keeping them straight was difficult. Some moments remained the same or roughly so no matter what.

No matter what I did, she never left that dance with me. I always ended up on the subway, alone in the early hours.

No more.

I decided that enough was enough. I had been too subtle, I realized. I was trying to finesse the situation when something more akin to brute force was required. I knew that Phil loved me. She had told me this herself on multiple occasions. It was only my own incompetence that kept us from being together.

I rummaged in my jacket pocket and found a small tube of mentholated lip balm, practically *de riguer* in the desert during the summer. I popped off the cap and held the balm under my nose, breathing in the cool menthol.

I closed my eyes.

I opened them again.

Did you really think it would be that easy? a voice asked.

I looked around, but I was alone on the train.

I shivered, even though the subway car was warm. The scent of chocolate had abated and I could breathe easily now.

Phil did not call to come visit me over Spring Break. There was, I realized, no Spring Break at all, for I had never attended College Y. Had barely, in fact, graduated high school, so obsessed I'd been with her, from that moment at lunch in eighth grade, following her, seeking her out, professing my love. And then the restraining order, like a hammer blow.

Everything had changed.

Nothing had changed.

The subway clacked and wracked.

****

I sat on the subway, the lone rider in the early morning, deep underground where the sun could not shine on me even as it rose. I tried desperately to imagine a scenario that could return Phil to me. Nothing I had attempted worked.

Was it possible that Phil and I were not meant to be together? That we were destined to be apart, to have our relationship end whether by her hand or by mine?

It was not the first time I'd considered such an idea, yet I could lend it no credence. I had begun editing reality the first time I saw Phil after our Spring Break fuck, at the lowest moment for me. Einstein said that God does not play dice with the universe; I could not believe that the universe played dice with me.

Even with the weight of so much evidence bearing down on me, even in light of the demonstrated fact that nothing I could do or would do or had done could or did change things for the better, I could not shake the idea that Phil and I were meant to be together. Why else would I have been given this power, this perspective on the world, if not to rectify the great wrong done to/by me?

More important than destiny was desire: I loved Phil. I wanted/needed to be with her. Desperately. If destiny decreed us apart, then I would defy destiny. Gladly.

The subway clanged and banged to a halt, jostling me from

my reverie. The speaker crackled to life and the driver said, "Ladies and gentlemen, this is the final stop on this train. All passengers must disembark. This train is now out of service."

I stood, blinking around at my surroundings as though they'd changed, as though seeing the benign, banal interior of this particular subway car for the first time, as though it had some flavor that distinguished it from others of its ilk. But it was as bland as any of the others: sick-green plastic benches, worn chrome poles to hold, a flecked blue laminate floor. Advertisements at the ends and above the benches, hawking Spanish as a Second Language classes, confidential AIDS-II hotlines, adult re-education classes at the local community colleges, and the latest LatinoLit thriller novel.

It was all old, all familiar, yet it was as though I was seeing it for the first time.

I disembarked, as instructed, and found myself at the Crimson Rocks subway station, the final stop on the Fox line. I had not been here since a school trip in elementary school. I looked around for the subway map, but it had been partly torn and partly defaced by a graffito depicting a large caterpillar trying to eat the sun. I stood alone in the station, trying to figure out how to get back home.

Just then, the train huffed as though alive and pulled away, heading further into the tunnel.

"Hey!" I shouted, running to it and vainly smacking my palms against the doors closest to me. "Hey! Stop! Don't leave me—"

But the train disappeared into the tunnel.

I made my way to a flight of stairs that led down, deeper under the desert, then twisted around themselves and rose again to the opposite platform, where trains headed back into the city would berth. No train waited, however. I stood for long minutes, waiting. A poster taped to a nearby column showed a cartoon silhouette of a scorpion, its tail poised to strike. Above the cartoon, it said

CITY TRANSIT

DEPT. OF TRACKS AND TUNNELS

Below the cartoon, in large, red letters:

CAUTION!

Then:

This area has been baited with

ARACHNICIDE

Further below that were the details of the date on which the arachnicide had been placed (two days previous) as well as contact information for the DOTAT office responsible for said placing. As if to mock my noticing of the poster, a large scorpion lazily skittered over the track below me, its tail arched and threatening. Rats did not survive long in these tunnels, not with city scorpions as their natural enemies.

Then, as I watched, a low, sleek train the likes of which I'd seen only in movies glided with little fanfare into the opposite platform. I cried out in simultaneous surprise, relief, and frustration, briefly gave thought to attempting to leap directly across, then dashed down the stairs and up the stairs once more. Fortunately, the new train was still at the platform and I ran for it, thinking to hop on and ride it wherever subway trains turned around for their return trips.

However, the doors to this new car would not open, no matter how much I pounded on them or pleaded. After a moment, a subway driver ambled along the platform and sternly told me to move on.

"I'm just trying to get back to the city," I told him. "I missed my stop."

"I can't help you with that." He glanced at his watch. "You'll need to get out of here now. This station is closed."

"Closed?"

"This station closes every day at this time. Orders from up top."

"Why?"

"I don't ask, kid," he said, shrugging. "I just do what the Boss tells me. This train isn't for you. This whole station is off limits right now. This early in the morning, no one's going from Crimson Rocks to the city anyway. It'll be about an hour until they open up the line and send a train back into the city."

He left me no choice but to resign myself to a long wait. As ordered, I ascended the staircase to the second level, where no trains awaited. A bored woman locked into the plexiglass cage of a 24-hour ticket booth flicked idle eyes in my direction as I mounted the last flight of stairs, which took me out into the open air.

The desert arrayed itself all around me as I emerged from the underground. Normally, a partial canopy shielded the entrance to a desert station, but this one lay smashed and spiderwebbed with fissures some yards away, victim of a sandstorm, no doubt. As a result, the subway entrance was a slot cut directly into the desert floor, where loose sand occasionally blew down onto the steps. Cacti and Joshua trees and tumbleweed dotted the landscape for hundreds of yards in every direction. To the east, the sun burnished the low horizon and shone through the fingers of the city's skyscrapers.

To the west loomed the Crimson Rocks, high peaks that reared up into the clouds like a rough-hewn mirror image of the city.

They were not actually red. They had been named for their "discoverer," Lord Crimson, a British ex-patriate who was the first white man to cross this desert back in the nineteenth century. Of course, they had taken on new meaning several years ago when they came to represent the aftermath of the Lucky Sevens terrorist attack that kicked off GWB. Many locals and even tourists had made the pilgrimage to the Crimson Rocks to pay their respects to the thousands of dead, the closest one could approach the actual site of the disaster. I had never come. I preferred to keep my memories pristine, of the perfect natural wonder I'd seen as a child on that elementary school field trip.

But now it would be a mere walk of a few football fields to a ridge overlooking the Other City. Once, I'd been told, there were desert rickshaws for hire, covered wagons, all designed to disturb as little of the terrain as possible while still conveying gawkers to the site. Now, though, with the passage of years, no one came here anymore. No one cared. They were more interested in GWB, and less interested in why and how it had started.

I began to walk. I thought of Phil the whole time, sorting out my memories of our various relationships, of the liminal spaces between them, of the ways in which I had tried to fix or change things, always failing. Remembered her as Othello, as Estragon. Remembered her confident and nigh-imperious on the set, commanding, ordering, coaching her fellow actors into a diorama she held entirely in her mind, the way I held blueprints. We were so much the same, she and I. Both builders. Both artists. And she had all the confidence I lacked.

I thought of the time she'd texted me: *come listen to the rain w me*

Rain was rare in the desert. A sustained rain that would last long enough to respond to a text was even more rare. That night, she wanted me to come lay in bed with her and listen to the rain as it tattooed her roof. And as much as I tried in that moment, with the rising sun at my back, I could not remember why I had denied her. Such a simple request. Such a small thing. It was a matter of a walk to the subway, then five minutes on the train, then a walk to her house. To lie beside her. To hold her in my arms and let the rain lullaby us to sleep. And yet that small, simple thing was beyond me, for reasons I could no longer recall. I remembered the ache and the disappointment and the ease of the request, but I could not remember the cause of the ache and the disappointment, the reason for forsaking such an easy request.

Was that the moment? I wondered, pausing in my trek across the desert. Was that the crucial moment in our relationship? Did I need to edit that moment and go to her, arrive gently wet with desert rain at her front door, kiss her, slip into the history-made sheets with her and just . . . hold her? Was that the secret?

I did not know.

I could not know.

My legs began to tremble and could no longer support me. Wary of scorpions, I lowered myself to the ground and sat in the warm sand, staring ahead at the great upthrust of the Crimson Rocks. Just beyond them, I knew, were the remnants of the Other City, my home's twin sister, devastated years ago on July 7, 2007—7/7/7. Lucky Sevens.[37]

I sat there in the sand, staring ahead at the Crimson Rocks, staring through them at what lay beyond. The Other City had been abandoned, its skyscrapers left uninhabited, its surviving citizens scattering to the rest of the country. And then GWB—Global War B—had begun, with no signs of ever stopping. We would be at war forever.

Could I edit that? Could I undo Lucky Sevens? Could I stop GWB from wreaking havoc on the nation and the world?

37. The event, though tragic and horrific, was nicknamed "Lucky Sevens" because it could have been so much worse. Or so the popular imagination would have it.

I thought of Phil and her scissors, and I decided to leave Lucky Sevens alone.

I had not smelled the overpowering chocolate syrup since leaving the subway. It was—in some way I could not explain—connected to my editing of reality. As I edited more and more, the smell became stronger and stronger, to the point that I could not bear it. I wondered: Was that a sign that I was editing the wrong points in my history? Or was it a sign that I should be editing nothing at all?

But I could not believe that last. It made no sense. Why would I have this ability if I was not meant to use it?

I thought of Phil. And the rain.

And I cried.

Cried there in the desert, alone. I was not, I know, the first. So many had shed so many tears here, but mine were surely the most selfish. I wept not for the thousands killed on Lucky Sevens, nor the hundreds of thousands who died in subsequent years due to GWB, the innocents in other countries, the soldiers, nor for the families of the dead, nor for "the children" (for whom we always are supposed to weep). I did not even weep for Phil.

I wept for myself.

For my power.

My paralysis.

My fear.

My love.

Oh, God, I wept for my love!

Out there in the desolation of the desert, in the shadow of my own city, trapped between its familiar skyscrapers and the Crimson Rocks, all things seemed possible and impossible at once, as though the world had become quantum physics on the macro level. I felt as though I could successfully design the underwater hotel there, in the ironic counterpoint of the desert.

I felt as though I could become George's best friend there. I felt as though I could—finally—recapture lost Philomel there.

Phil.

I needed help. I had tried this on my own and had nothing to show for it but endlessly entangled strands of fate, reality, life, love, history. A Gordian knot I refused to cut through. I would live this. I would succeed. But I needed help.

I flipped open my cell phone and called George. It had only been three hours since I last called him, yet he answered on the first ring.

"George, I'm sorry to bother you again," I said, the sting of his earlier rejection still sharp and fresh. "I need your help, man. I really, really need your help."

"Dude, are you in jail? Is that it? Do you need me to bail you out? You know what I—"

"No. I'm at Crimson Rocks."

"What?" His voice—until now slightly sleep-blurred—perked. "What are you doing . . . How do you have a cell signal way out there?"

"I don't know. But we need to talk, OK? Please, George. I'm sorry to wake you up, but—"

"You didn't. I'm still . . . Look, come on over, dude. Mom'll make us something to eat—"

"No. You need to come here."

"What?"

"Please, George. Please, come here. Now." And I killed the call before he could respond.

I lifted my head and looked around at the endless desert, at the cacti and the rocks and dunes and arroyos. I thought of wandering in the desert, of the endless possibility of blue sky above, the clouds clustered among the peaks of the Crimson Rocks like eager patrons waiting for the show to start, so tired of the opening act, which has dragged on forever, no matter how initially entertaining. They are waiting for something to begin.

And something will begin. Soon.

Something was coming.

A surprise was coming.

While I waited, I thought about what I needed to say. I sat cross-legged in the sand and while I did not truly meditate (I did not know how to meditate in any formal sense), I did allow my mind to drift, untethered, from my present state. I thought of the boy with the ice cream cone, the dead-then-alive-then-dead-again man from my dream, the woman I dreamt of—Angia Eiphon—and her claim to being pushed from heaven by God himself. I did not allow myself to think of Phil, of her bluest-of-blue locks, of her beauty, her love, her anger and rage and fear and hate.

I did not think of Phil, but I thought of my love for her. My love that, once, had seemed so fragile and childlike, but now—suddenly—was the most powerful force in my life, in the universe. I remembered George asking—in some draft of some chapter of my life—why I loved her. I remembered giving an answer, but the fact of the matter (I realized there on sands and under the punishing desert sun) was this:

Maybe I loved her only because I loved her. Maybe it's just written that way. Maybe there's no reason. Maybe it has nothing to do with her believing in me, nothing to do with the elevator building or confidence or *Othello* or any of the rest of it. Maybe we do not get to choose the who or the why. Maybe we only choose the how and the when.

I choose now. I choose always. I choose.

I choose.

I *choose.*

"Dude!"

I turned around to see George emerging from the subway station. The sun was higher in the eastern sky now, and George's shadow flowed over the sand on its way to me. I imagined when it touched me that I could feel it.

"OK," George said, standing over me, hands on hips. "I'm here. What the hell is going on?"

For a moment, I said nothing. George—his brief rant expelled—calmed; he shaded his eyes with his hand and gazed out at the Crimson Rocks.

"Shit. Haven't been here since . . ." He trailed off, whether because he could not remember or did not care to remember, I could not tell. "Why'd you drag me out here, man?"

Looking up at him in that position—standing ramrod straight, one stiff hand held at his brow—I could not help but to imagine him in his Marine uniform and to wonder, however briefly, at what had caused him to leave the Corps so soon after entering.

Before I could ask, however, he shrugged and dropped to a squat next to me. "Dude. Talk to me. I got, like, less than zero sleep last night, you know what I mean?"

I took a deep breath. I knew what I had to say, but until the words actually formed on my tongue and hit the open air between us, I did not know if I would say it or not.

And then I did.

"I've just . . ." I hesitated. "I've been noticing things. Things about the world. Things that don't make sense."

He laughed and clapped a hand on my shoulder. "Dude, the world *doesn't* make sense. That's not exactly a great revelation. Come on. Mom'll make pancakes and—"

"George, please. Listen." I reached up to put my hand over his, such that he was sandwiched between my palm and my shoulder. He flinched, but I held him there. "I'm not talking about stuff like, 'Why do bad things happen to good people?'

or things like that. I'm talking about the deep, fundamental forces of the universe."

The words hung between us, and I knew that if anyone but me had said them and if anyone but George had heard them, the next sound would have been raucous laughter and a sincere query as to what sort of mind-altering substance(s) I had imbibed, inhaled, injected, and/or ingested. Instead, George simply sighed, retrieved his hand, and sank to sit next to me in the sand.

"Go," he said after a moment.

I gave myself a few seconds to make certain that my thoughts were organized and then I led with:

"Think about where we live."

He twisted around to cast his gaze back towards the city, which reared behind us, backlit by rising sunshine. "What about it?"

"Well . . . Where do we live, George?"

He stared at me. "What are you talking about? We live in the city." He pointed to it, as though I'd forgotten where it was.

"But *what* city? What's it called?"

He waved it off. "Dude, you're being an idiot. You know what I mean? It's the city."

"Right. But *which* city? Where is it?"

"OK, now I know you're being an idiot on purpose. It's in the desert, smart-ass." He made a fist in the sand and held it up, grains streaming through his fingers like water.

"Which desert?" I asked.

"Why does this stuff matter to you? It never mattered before."

"Before what? When?"

"When we were kids!"

"George, we never *were* kids! Our lives started at The WB event last night!"

He shook his head slowly. "Man, you're losing it."

"No, look. That's when it had to begin because that's when I first realized . . ." I was not yet ready to tell him about the editing of reality. That was a step too far, too soon. But the night of The WB party *had* to be the beginning of it all. It was when *I* began.

"It started there," I insisted. "Trust me. Everything else is just a flashback. Our lives began, fully-formed, last night, the night I saw Phil in the red dress. Or the teal dress."

"Dude, you're nuts. You've lost your fucking mind, you know what I mean?"

"Look around you!" I yelled, jumping up to turn in circles, gesturing all around us. "We live in a city with skyscrapers. In the desert! Who builds skyscrapers in the desert? Who puts a *subway* in the desert? What cities are there like that?"

He fumed and seethed for long moments. "*Our* city is like that! What else matters?"

"There are no American cities in deserts with subway systems *and* skyscrapers, George. They just don't exist. Phoenix and Tucson have light rails planned and there's a monorail in Las Vegas, but they aren't actual subterranean—"

"What the hell? Where do you get this shit?"

"I'm an *architect*. It's my business to know this shit." I grabbed him by the elbow and hoisted him to his feet, grateful that he chose not to execute a Krav Maga reversal on me and land me on my ass in the sand. Spinning him to face the city, I pointed. "Look. Look at those skyscrapers, George. On the North American continent, there aren't much more than a hundred cities with more than fifty highrises defined as skyscrapers, OK? Our city has to be in that group because I see a hell of a lot more than just fifty skyscrapers, don't you?"

Reluctantly, he nodded.

"Of those hundred or so cities, the only ones in the United

States in a desert are Las Vegas and Phoenix. But we don't live in Las Vegas or Phoenix, do we, George?" He shook his head slowly. "Right. Because Las Vegas and Phoenix don't have subways."

George stepped away from me, shaking his head faster now. "Dude. Dude. What the fuck are you saying? What the fuck are you *saying?*"

"I'm saying that the city's skyscrapers all scream East Coast of the United States. But the residential buildings—the houses we live in—are all bungalow style and fake adobe and fake hacienda. They scream West Coast. No one designs cities like that, George. It's insane. It doesn't happen by accident and it sure as hell doesn't happen by design. So I want to know where the fuck we live. Where *is* this place?"

"But . . . but all that shit about our lives not starting until last night . . . That junk about you being an architect . . . That's . . . That's bullshit, you know what I mean? I remember being a kid. I remember the asshole. And you've never—"

"It's all flashbacks, George. It's all stuff we *think* happened, but there's no context for any of it. Nothing happened *around* it. They're just discrete memories."

"No." I had come close to him and he shoved me harder than I would have expected. "No. That's . . . that's crazy. Memories just *work* like that. You have these little—what's the word I'm looking for?—these little pockets that you remember. You don't remember every little thing about every—"

"Then explain the city, George. This place can't exist! But there it is. Subway. Skyscrapers. Desert. Maybe in the Middle East. Not in America. Tunisia might work. Do you really think we live in Tunisia, George?"

He turned away from me and stared out at the Crimson Rocks. "You think . . . You think there's something wrong with the world," he said quietly. "But what if there's just something wrong with this place?"

"What do you mean?" I didn't expect him to take my theory and go one step further with it.

"What if . . ." He swept a hand to the west, encompassing the whole of Crimson Rocks and the hidden remnants of the Other City. "What if it has to do with Lucky Sevens? What if the terrorists used some kind of hallucinogen or some kind of chemical something that still lingers out here? And it's making you think this crazy shit . . ." He rubbed his temples. "And it's making me start to think it might not be so crazy."

I duplicated his previous action, putting a hand on his shoulder. "Nothing hangs together. It isn't just this place. It's everywhere. It's more than just noticing things about the city or about our lives. It's . . ."

And in that moment, I knew that I would have to make another choice. Now I would have to tell George everything or I would have to somehow convince him that I'd told him nothing. Neither seemed entirely palatable at that moment in time, but I could not leave the universe frozen there, with the sun pierced by the city's skyscrapers behind us, the clouds waiting to pounce from their Crimson Rocks perches ahead, and my hand on George's shoulder for all eternity. I had to move forward and keep things going.

"Look at me," I said, and he turned and I looked down into his eyes and before I could change my mind, I said, "I don't know how to explain it. Somehow, I have this . . . *power.* For lack of a better word. This ability. I can change things. It's like I go back and find specific moments and just tweak reality a little bit, and then everything proceeds differently. But I went too far and I fucked it all up. Now nothing makes sense. I can't keep track of it anymore."

It was as though I'd just thrown up, by which I mean I felt terrific. I've always felt great after throwing up. When you throw up, you purge whatever made you sick from your system. And now I had purged this knowledge, this secret knowledge, and I felt terrific, even though my best friend was looking at me as though he fervently wished he had a syringe full of Thorazine, a straitjacket, and, perhaps, the assistance of two large orderlies, although despite his smaller size, George would not need two orderlies of any size.

He did not run away. His expression did not even change appreciably. He just watched me carefully, waiting for me to go on. And even though I thought I'd said everything I could/would/needed to say, it turned out I had more in me, for the next thing I knew, I was telling George the entire story—all of it—from the beginning at The WB with the red-now-teal-now-red dress to the smell of chocolate to the dream to the repeated revising of reality that had brought me, twice, to this place, once to edit one final, disastrous time, the second time to summon George and try to fix the mess I'd made of my world.

"I'm not crazy," I told him, even though I could understand why he would think that to be the case. "Everything I'm telling you is true."

Something shifted in his eyes, though nothing I'd said was entirely persuasive. "I guess I owe you the benefit of the doubt," he said, "after everything you've done for me. You know what I mean?"

I winced with guilt, the pain of it nearly physical. I had done nothing for George. I had been the easiest and most convenient of friends for our entire acquaintanceship. He owed me nothing; I owed him everything. And yet here I was—once again—imploring him to believe me, to help me.

"Let's assume it's all true. How does it work?" he asked. "It's like you go back in time and change things?"

"No. Not like that. I don't know how to describe it. It's more like editing things. Like I can see the structure of reality and manipulate it."

He blinked. "How is that different from time travel?"

"It just is. I don't have total control over it. It's like there are only certain points I can alter, as if it's already been decided and I'm just going through the motions. I have this control, but I don't really control anything. I feel like someone else is editing, too, maybe at the same time, guiding me to try different things."

He folded his arms over his chest and considered. "Well . . . OK. Look, dude. Let's assume you're not nuts, all right?"

"I appreciate that."

"Let's say you can do this stuff. Show me. Prove it."

"I can't."

He raised an eyebrow. It was a very disbelieving eyebrow.

"George, seriously! Look, it's not that I can't—it's just that it doesn't matter if I do. To you, I've always had a restraining order and I've always been obsessed with Phil. I've made all kinds of changes before and you don't notice them because you're within it all. It's like painting over a mural and then re-painting part of it. You don't notice what's missing, only what's there. I could change something right now, but to you, it would be as though things had *always* been that way."

"So it's like that movie. Where the guy keeps reliving the same day over and—"

"No. Because that was forced on him. I have a choice. And he just relived that day. I can go to almost any point. Or at least, the ones that occur to me, you know? It's not the same day over and over. It's pieces of my life and I jump in and insert myself there and change something. I told you—I tried a bunch of things. I tried just *making* her love me, but that was no good."

Despite everything, I still saw hesitation and disbelief in his eyes. The sun was high now, directly overhead, and we both sweated through our shirts, our foreheads glistening. In what seemed to be no time at all, the world had fast-forwarded to noon in the summer desert.

In desperation, I tried one more tactic: "Remember the night I was filling out my college apps? Remember how I didn't know my last name?"

His eyes lit up with the memory. "Yeah. Yeah, it's—"

"Don't tell me!" I actually went so far as to press my palm against his mouth, the feeling of his lips on my skin so strange and new, assaulting me with the realization that I had never touched George in this particular way before. "Don't say it. I still don't know it and I don't think it's time for me to know yet."

He nodded, mute, and when I pulled my hand away, he stepped back and turned away. Still disbelieving.

Did you think it would be that easy? The voice from the subway. From my dreams.

Easy. Ha! This was easy? Convincing my best friend that the world—the universe—was not what we thought it was? That I was meant to be with Phil, but the universe kept conspiring against me? This was all easy?

And yet . . .

That voice. Asking *Did you think it would be that easy?*

"It was the kid," I said.

George blinked at me. "What kid? What are you talking about?"

"The kid. With the ice cream cone. I saw him on the subway once before. But somewhere else, too. Where else did I—?"

"Dude," George said, putting an arm around me. "You look pale. Paler than usual, you know what I mean? Come on. It's getting way hot. We gotta get out of here."

"The kid," I babbled as George led me to the subway station. "I've seen him somewhere else. He talked to me."

"Great, great, fine," George said, leading me down the stairs. The station was stifling hot, though without the direct blast of sunlight from overhead, it seemed somehow more bearable. I wished for something cooler, for a tunnel of ice.

"A tunnel of ice," I murmured.

"Now I know you've lost it," George said, finding an open bench for us.

"Wait!" I jumped up. "It wasn't a tunnel! It was a hallway. In the dream. That's where—"

"Dude." George forced me to sit down again. I struggled against him, protesting.

"George, it was in the dream. That's when I walked down the hallway made of ice. And that's when the kid talked to me. Inframan. He said he was called Inframan."

George shook his head and grinned nervously at the people around us, as though excusing through a smile my raised voice and panicked demeanor.

"Der Untermensch. The Underone. The God of Failure. Inframan. That's what he said, George. That's what—"

The shriek and rattle of an arriving train drowned me out, and George hustled me into the car and into an empty seat, where I was assaulted by the suddenness of air conditioning. My eyes began to burn.

"I'm tired," I said. "I didn't sleep much," realizing as I said it that, as far as I knew, George had slept not at all.

"Dude, close your eyes, you know what I mean?"

I drifted in and out of sleep as the train shook and thrust

forward, bearing us back to the city. At one point, I came awake long enough to realize that we were stopped at Phil's station, and also to realize that I was weeping uncontrollably, my head on George's shoulder, his arm unselfconsciously around me as riders studiously did not stare at us.

"I need her," I cried. "I fucked it all up, George. I need her."

That was the last thing I remembered until the buzzing of my cell phone woke me. It perched on my nightstand, and even though it was set on vibrate, the combination of the vibrations and the hollow nightstand made enough of a racket to waken me.

I did not remember coming home or crawling into bed, but I supposed I owed George for this. My face felt grimy and dry with old tears.

"Dude," George said when I flipped open the cell, "are you at your computer?"

"Yeah," I said, groggy and settling in at my desk. "What—"

"I don't pretend to get everything you were talking about out at Crimson Rocks, but . . . I tried something. You know what I mean? Go to Gooleg."

I typed in "gooleg.search" and the search engine page popped up: the famous logo ("Gooleg" as seen through prison-like bars), with a text entry box and the legend, "Imprisoning Your Answers!"

"Type in that stuff you told me before," George said. "Inframan. Untermensch. The Underone. See what comes up."

I typed it all in and clicked the "Jailbreak my Info!" button.

Gooleg, scraper of e-mails and accumulator of data, knew my sad story better than most, so an ad windowlet slid into view before I could see my results:

CLOSING IN ON 21!

Hey, -mikenphil-! In just a couple of years, you'll be 21, which means that your pesky restraining order can be a thing of the past! The Schmidt-Murdoch Law allows a one-time name-change at 21 in order to help you wipe away the indiscretions of your youth.

When your 21st birthday hits, be prepared! Sign up for LifeWipe now and we'll file your paperwork at midnight on your 21st birthday. Restart your life right, with LifeWipe!

LifeWipe: Because everyone deserves a second chance.

I could not close the ad windowlet without some sort of response. Rather than click on "Visit LifeWipe!", I chose "Remind Me Later."

Thanks for your help, -mikenphil-! Your honesty keeps information flowing!

"First hit," George said as the results flowed onto my screen.

There were only a few hits. They all seemed related. The first one was:

INFRAMAN

(subtitle: "The Coming of the Unpotent God") is the first book by American novelist Barry Lyga, published in 1994. www.wikinformation.com/infra-man_novel

CHAPTER 17

"Have you ever heard of this guy Barry Lyga?" George asked.

"No. Never."

"Are you sure? Because when you put in all of those words, this is all that comes up, is stuff related to him and this book of his."

"I've never heard of him, George." I clicked on the name. The resultant page had a photo of Barry Lyga. "Oh, George. Holy . . . George . . ."

"What?"

"This is the guy!" I couldn't believe it. "This is the guy from my dream! The guy who was dead and then alive and then dead again."

"So you have heard of him, then."

"No, that's just it! I've never heard of him before. But—"

"Wait. How is that poss—"

"I don't know." I stared at the picture. It was definitely the man from my dream. He looked somehow older and heavier in the photo, but it was still unquestionably the same person.

"You must have read something about him at some point," George said. "Maybe from some English class or something."

"No." I shook my head fiercely, even though George could

not see it. "No. This guy . . . He's somehow connected to what's happening to me. And he's a writer, which makes total sense. I have to talk to him. Maybe e-mail him or—"

George huffed a hollow chuckle. "Dude, good luck with that, you know what I mean?"

For perhaps the first time in our friendship, I did not know what he meant, and told him so.

"Dude, check out the page. Barry Lyga's dead."

****

Barry Lyga

From Wikinformation, the world's finest infodump!

Barry Lyga (no middle initial) (September 11, 1971 - August 5, 2005) was an American novelist and short story writer. Lyga majored in English at Yale, receiving his BA in 1993. His first novel, *Inframan,* was written as a senior and published in 1994.

Contents

3.6 Redesigning You

3.7 For Love of the Madman

3.8 Sxxxxx Cxxx

3.9 The Gospel According to Jesus

4 See also

5 References

6 External links

****

I put my phone on speaker and set it on the desk so that I could press both palms to my temples, as though holding in my brains. Which is precisely what it felt like I was doing. The expression “mind-blowing” had never seemed so appropriate.

“Dude, you still there? Did you hear me? The guy’s dead. Died back in—”

“Two thousand five. Yeah. I see that.” I did some quick mental math. “He was thirty-three.”

“Look,” George said, “I don’t know what any of this means. I think you need to get some more sleep and you need to move on, you know what I mean? You need to forget about Phil. You need to find someone else, OK?”

I barely heard him. My eyes skipped along the page, my fingers scrolling the trackpad. Dead. He was dead. Dead for years. How had I known? I had dreamed him dead.

But I had also dreamed him alive. And then dead again. And then . . .

It made no sense.

“Mystery solved,” George said. “You don’t want to hear this, but you need to—you heard about this guy from someone and you dreamed about him. End of story.”

I clicked on the link for his first book, *Inframan.*

To proceed, I had to enter my e-mail address and allow Lonely.dude to send me some more information. The windowlet dissolved and I scanned further down the Wikinformation page.

"George," I said, my voice so quiet that I had to say it again before he acknowledged. "George, is my last name Grayson?"

"Yeah. Mike Grayson. Why?"

****

Inframan (novel)

From Wikinformation, the world's finest infodump!

Inframan (or, The Coming of the Unpotent God) is the first book by American novelist Barry Lyga, published in 1994. The novel is a metafiction about a character named Mike Grayson and his friends and family.

Contents

3 Reception

4 See also

5 References

6 External links

****

In my dream, Barry Lyga was dead. Then alive. I met a child who called himself Inframan.

And now . . .

Now I find that the main character in Lyga's first novel has the same name as I do.

I wanted to slam shut the laptop and crawl back into bed. I wanted to forget I'd ever dreamed of Lyga or of Inframan.

"George. Did you see— The name of the main character in *Inframan*?"

I waited a moment as he clicked, heard the short, sharp inhale on his end of the line.

"If you think that's crazy," he said, "wait until you see what else I found."

"What's that?"

"I found a part of the book. Online. I mean, I looked in all the usual e-bookstores, but no one had it, but then I found this old blog in a Gooleg cache. Some chick named gaylwriter posted a chunk of the novel. It's short, but . . ."

"But what?"

"Well, I think it's gonna blow your mind."

"Send it to me."

****

gaylwriter says: This next scene is actually one of my least favorite from the entire book, but it's so central to the narrative that I figure it's worth posting. Ham's dream, in which he encounters two versions of Mike Grayson, is almost deliberately scattered and feels somewhat pointless, though it resonates later, especially towards the end of the book. Here it is:

He's walking down a corridor with walls, floor, and ceiling of ice. Strangely, he is not cold, though he is wearing only shorts and tanktop. He sees his breath pluming from him in white puffs. In the background, someone is playing what sounds like an electric cello. A woman sings "Hey can you peel shrimp? Oh, yeah, baby, gotta peel the shrimp."

No problem.

He comes to a door, made of wood, set flawlessly into the surrounding ice, as if it grew there naturally. There are no hinges. When he grasps the doorknob, a voice says, "Not on the first date!"

"I thought there were no quotation marks in dreams," *he says.*

"Well, of course there are. Think of the consequences," says the voice. See how confusing this is? it says, it says.

"Oh," *Ham responds, then reaches for the doorknob again. "NO!" the voice shouts.*

"Why not?" *he whines.*

"Are you wearing a condom?"

Ham pulls out his wallet. "All I have is a diaphragm."

"That'll have to do. Put it in your mouth."

He does so.

"Okay."

Now there is no protest when he turns the knob. The

door vanishes, showing the corridor beyond. This hallway is made of wood, built at a skewed angle, such that his left foot is below his right foot, forcing him to walk at an angle. From nowhere, a man's voice sounds out: "I warned them! I told them!"

He finds himself in a large chamber, panelled in oak, carpeted lushly. A fire roars in the fireplace, and several plaques and trophies rest on the mantlepiece. Lying next to the fireplace is a body clad in gray trenchcoat and slacks, a heavy black poker protruding from its chest. Ham approaches the corpse. It is Mike.

"Oh man, Mike, oh God I wish I coulda saved ya—"

"Hey, Ham," the corpse says, opening its eyes, sitting up. "How are you?"

"But—you're dead."

"Not always." *His eyes close then, and he falls back, dead.*

Ham turns just in time to see a door open. Mike steps into the room, wearing jeans and a brown leather jacket. His hair is slicked back from his forehead. He is holding a wireless microphone in one hand. A spotlight pins him.

"Mike!" *Ham cries.*

"Mike?" Grayson seems puzzled. He nods, then, and gestures with his right hand. "Right here," he agrees, holding the microphone aloft.

"Huh?"

"Look, Hamburg—you don't mind if I call you Hamburg, do you?—I'm going to give you a glimpse, okay?"

"What?"

"A small glimpse, to be sure, but a glimpse

nonetheless. Remember something for me, Hamburg. He's just a figment of his own imagination. Can you remember that?"

"I think so."

"Well, don't bother. Hey! Hey, swallow that diaphragm, man. How do you expect to breathe without one?"

"Oh, yeah. Right." *He swallows it with one gulp.*

"Now, rooms don't always have one exit, Hamburg. And houses have many rooms."

"What are you trying to say—"

"It doesn't matter, I guess. Unless you get things going soon, Inframan will kill all of you."

"Who?"

"Inframan."

"Never heard of him."

"Of course not! You think I'm here to tell you things you know? Angia grew up near here." Ham hears a tiny click and then a large, crystal chandelier plummets from the ceiling, crushing Mike to the floor.

"Hey, Ham!"

Turning again, Ham sees the impaled Grayson, once again struggling into a sitting position. *"Don't listen to* him, *Ham. Heck, the Dragon's coming."*

"Dragon?"

"No, the *Dragon. Pay attention. The dead can walk, okay? Can you remember that?"*

"Maybe."

"Well, make sure you do. It's important. Birds fly and die."

"They do?"

"I guess; how am I *supposed to know? You think I'm making this stuff up? Look, I'll tell you your future, okay? I*

see gold eclipsing chocolate. Carter's hair stands on end. Isn't this all so very Twin Peaks?*"*

"I DON'T UNDERSTAND!" *Ham screams.*

"Don't have a hissy fit, Ham," *Mike admonishes him.* "After all, it's only life."

****

The ice corridor . . . The dead-then-alive-then-dead body . . . It was *my* dream, the dream I described to George, only twisted and changed. I felt an overpowering wave of déjà vu and then realized that it was not and could not be déjà vu. This was not the sense that "this has all happened before." It was, rather, the knowledge, the certainty, that this had all happened before, only in some different way.

"Is there more?" I asked George. "She says that this is the 'next' scene she's posting. So she must have posted others, right?"

"Her blog isn't up anymore," George said. "It's not even really a blog. It looks like it was some old-school page from, like, 1999 or something. A school project, maybe. I just got lucky and found the cache of that page. Tell you what—I'll keep poking around, see what I can find, and you do the same."

"Sounds good. I'll call you back in—let's say—an hour."

I returned to the Wikinformation page on *Inframan*.

Inframan (novel)

From Wikinformation, the world's finest infodump!

Inframan (or, The Coming of the Unpotent God) is the first book by American novelist Barry Lyga, published in 1994. The novel is a metafiction about a character named Mike Grayson and his friends and family.

Contents

Plot

NOTE: This section contains spoilers.

The plot revolves around the exploits of a New Haven police detective named Mike Grayson and his attempts to find a serial killer named the Shadow Boxer who is hunting students at Yale University. At the same time, however, Grayson begins to notice strange logical incongruities and discontinuities in his life and world, which lead him to the discovery that he is, in fact, merely a character in a novel written by Barry Lyga. As the novel progresses, the search for the Shadow Boxer becomes less and less important, and Grayson and his friends and family find themselves caught between Lyga and Inframan, described as "the Undergod" and "the God of Failure." Inframan turns out to be another version of Lyga (or, perhaps, a split personality) who exercises strict editorial restraint to counterbalance Lyga's creative whims.

The tension between the two forces wreaks havoc with the lives of the characters. In the end, Grayson's love for his sister is powerful enough to reunite the cast, just in time for the Shadow Boxer to fatally shoot Grayson. Grayson then ascends to Heaven, where he learns that Heaven is merely one step below the Real World. He ascends to the Real World and finds himself on the campus of the real Yale University, where he seeks out Lyga in the author's dorm. Lyga, however, is missing from his room, leaving behind only the unfinished manuscript to *Inframan* and a single blank piece of paper, with instructions for Grayson himself to finish the novel.

The novel's conclusion is paradoxically inconclusive, as Grayson (revived from the dead thanks to timely electric shocks delivered by the Electrostatic Man) visits his brother's grave and apparently will live a long, happy life. The final page of the book, though, is clearly written by Lyga, not by Grayson, causing the reader to wonder if the author has deceived and swindled his own character, and if the seemingly happy ending can be trusted.

****

Whose ego, I wondered, could be so monumental that he would write a book about himself? A book in which he's not just one, but multiple characters?

****

Characters

Michael Robin Grayson: The novel's main character and primary protagonist. Yale graduate. Lives in New Haven, still, as a detective on the New Haven police force. He is the brother of Richard Grayson and foster brother to Angia Eiphon.

Angia Eiphon: Yale graduate. Married to Todd Morris, former Yale professor. Angia is Mike's adoptive sister and a photographer. She is also the result of a childhood dream, a young boy's fantasy of the ideal partner. She has been reduced from her former state of perfection for purposes of "realism" in the novel. She becomes Mike's lover mid-way through the novel, a relationship that is technically not incest.

Tom Fitch: Tom is a sarcastic, heartless ladies' man. He lives a life of leisure and hedonism. He is also Mike Grayson's split personality.

Hamilton Rockwell: Yale senior (graduating late due to service in Operation: Desert Storm). Attending Yale on GI Bill following service in Kuwait. Ham has a synthetic right leg—the real thing was blown off by an Iraqi land mine.

The Electrostatic Man: A homeless vagrant with spiked blond hair. His body is charged with electricity, so much so that sparks constantly flit about his body.

Richard Allen Grayson: The younger brother of Mike Grayson, killed by a drunk driver as a child.

The Shadow Boxer: A serial killer operating in New Haven, CT, utterly impervious to police efforts to stop him. Entirely possible that he is another of Mike Grayson's split personalities.

The Knight of the Red Cross: Also called *St. George*. A slayer of dragons in British legend and literature. He is searching for a way back to Faeryland, but becomes sidetracked and winds up in a contemporary novel via an opportune allusion.

Roderick Usher: An incestuous 19th-century aristocrat possessed of a strange disease that enhances all of his senses to painful levels. Via a specific metaphor, he finds the entrance to the novel called *Inframan*.

Barry Lyga: Does not actually appear in the novel, but is referenced repeatedly, especially in excerpts from a fictional autobiography ("written" at age 72) titled *Lost on the Levels*. Author of *Inframan or, the Coming of the Unpotent God*. For all intents and purposes, God to all those previously listed.

Reception

In most quarters, the novel's publication was hardly noticed. Most reviewers were not kind to the freshman effort, calling it "unformed," "rushed," and, in one instance, “unforgivingly dense.” One reviewer commented that, “Lyga’s belief in his own cleverness is not earned, at least not with regard to this particular story, which rambles and lurches from character to character, voice to voice, style to style, with the author apparently so distracted by his own perceived genius that he can’t be bothered to let the audience figure out just what the hell is going on.”

Still, the novel did attract some attention, especially on college campuses, eventually selling out its print run and garnering a small cult following that in particular praised the novel’s structural choices (such as its use of “Chapter 0” and excerpts from a putative Lyga autobiography).

****

“More Stuff!!!!” reads the subject line in an e-mail from George.

Hey, Mike—found more stuff from gaylwriter’s cache. Looks like beginning and ending of the book. Here you go:

I open the files.

PROLOGUE:
ONE OF THE GRAVE SCENES IN THE RAIN

On the third day of the third month of the third year of his third decade, Michael Grayson visited the grave of his brother, Richard. It rained that day. Hardly surprising. Rain at the grave scene—imagine.

He stood over the grave, watching the rainwater fill in and then spill out of the words “RICHARD ALLEN GRAYSON,” running down into “TAKEN TOO SOON,” and then briefly splashing through “1972-1977” before wandering to the ground. The flowers that he had placed at the base of the tombstone dissolved sadly into the sod.

Michael Grayson looked up at the sky and flinched beneath the angry purple clouds as lightning flashed. Fresh waves of rain tumbled down, saturating his trenchcoat, his hat, his slacks. He looked back down at the tombstone.

“I’m sorry, Ricky. This is stupid.” And then he walked back to the car and drove away.

EPILOGUE:
ONE OF THE GRAVE SCENES

On the third day of the third week of the third month following Inframan’s banishment to the Realm Above, Michael Grayson visited the grave of his brother, Richard.

It did not rain that day.

He stood over the grave, silent.

RICHARD ALLEN GRAYSON

TAKEN TOO SOON

1972-1977

Michael Grayson looked up at the sky, at the cloudless blue, at the sheer grace of sunlight.

“I finally figured it out, Ricky. It took time. And we all had to be OK. Ham and Carter. Angia, of course. Angia and me. Even the Electrostatic Man. We all came back all right and then I was able to figure it out. Why it always rained when I came to see you, Ricky.

"And I realized something important. I realized that it's not that it always rained when I came to see you, little brother. It's that . . . It's that when it rained . . . *that's* when I needed to see you the most."

Mike wiped a tear from his eye, then touched the tombstone with the salty-damp tips of his fingers.

"But not any more, Ricky. No more rain for us. You died in the rain, little brother, but from now on, I can see you in the sunlight."

The tear's companions streamed down his face.

"I can see you in the sunlight."

It made no sense.

Within the world of the book, perhaps, it all made sense. And even reading just the prologue and the epilogue of the novel, I could see a transformation and a progression. But here and now, to me, in the real world, it made no sense. It did not apply to my world.

I had hoped that reading about my namesake would clarify things, at least to a point. Instead, I was more confused than ever. I was a student, not a Cop™. Nor even a police officer. I had a brother, yes, but he was alive. I had no foster sister, certainly not one I planned on taking as a lover.

And yet . . . Was it somehow possible that I was Michael Robin Grayson, that the novel described my destiny? Was College Y actually Yale? Would something horrible happen to my brother and would I attain a foster sister? Both seemed improbable, but possible—unlike the chances of me deciding to become a police detective after graduation.

The name "Michael Grayson" did not seem unique or even special. There were probably thousands of "Michael Graysons" in the world. So why did I feel a kinship with this fictitious Grayson?

Most important of all, though, I knew that I had never seen or read this book, nor had I ever heard of this author before he intruded—dead-then-alive-then-dead—on my dreams. He and his alter ego, the God of Failure, had come to me in my dreams and I had begun editing reality as easily as "Barry Lyga" edited a manuscript. Surely this meant something.

An e-mail titled "One more thing" had come through in the meantime. *Looks like the last entry on gaylwriter's page,* George says. *Check it.* Followed by a link to a Gooleg cache page, which I am able to access after confirming my preference for certain brands of underwear.

****

gaylwriter's website is like a vacant house—unadorned, plain, empty, skeletal. All that remains in Gooleg's cache is raw text *sans* graphics *sans* hyperlinks *sans* all but the most basic formatting. It's like looking at paper.

> gaylwriter says: I want to talk about the very end of the book today. Not the epilogue, but the <u>real</u> end of the book. When Mike ascends to the Real World and goes to Lyga's room at Yale, he finds only a single sheet of paper and a note that reads, "Finish the book yourself." He sits down and we get enough clues that we realize that what he writes ends up being the book's epilogue. It's sort of a clever gambit on Mike's part because it allows him—within the confines of a single page—to not only give himself a happy ending, but also to guarantee one for the rest of the cast.
>
> What follows after that last page, though, is clearly not written by Mike. In a novel that has been built in part

on the usage of excerpts from various texts, the true final page of the book stands out for being the only excerpt whose source material is never identified:

The following is an excerpt:

In the end, then, metafiction is the coward's solution for authors. Any flaw in the story, any incomprehensibility, can simply be waved away with the comment that it is intentional, that the reader must forgive these gaffes as they are meant to be part and parcel of the entire story. Such a story, then, is purportedly bulletproof.

Why would anyone want to read such a story?

I really wish my professors would let me write about this stuff for class, but they still say that Lyga is not a "valid subject for study."

****

My own research had turned up gaylwriter's first "blog" entry. George called to inform me that he had plumbed the depths of the Gooleg cache and found nothing more, and that he was "out of it now. I gotta get some sleep."

I thanked him for his help and read the last and the first excerpt from gaylwriter's now-defunct web presence:

gaylwriter says: I wonder if anyone else out there has ever read this book Inframan, by a guy named Barry Lyga? I know that it's sort of crazy just to post this on the Internet and hope that someone will see it, but maybe . . .

See, I have to put up a website for my Modern Composition class anyway. Professor Rowe thinks that in

> the near future everyone will be communicating this way. Everyone will have their own web page, for example. So I'm supposed to put this page up and update it regularly. But I didn't know what to talk about, and then I figured "Why not talk about this book that I like?"
>
> So, anyway, it's a pretty cool book, but no one I know has ever read it or even heard of it. If you have, send me an e-mail. (That's supposed to link to my e-mail address—I hope it does! I'm still figuring this stuff out . . .)

****

I returned to the original page dedicated to Barry Lyga and looked again at the picture. I clicked on "Personal Information."

Wikinformation provided a Gooleg windowlet.

> Hello, -mikenphil-! Want to keep going? Great! Please take this short survey about your streaming habits in order to continue your Wikinformation experience:
>
> **Do you stream**:
>
> Once a day?
> Twice a day?
> Three times a day?
> More than three times a day?
>
> Remember: Your honesty keeps the information flowing!

I clicked on three times a day, which was, as best I could recall, close to the truth.

Gooleg thanked me and returned me to Wikinformation.

****

Personal Information

Barry Lyga was born near Boston, Massachusetts and raised near Baltimore, Maryland. His early life was unremarkable and is described in middling detail in the "autobiographical" sections of his novel, *Inframan*. He submitted his first short stories for publication at the age of thirteen and all were soundly rejected.

Lyga attended Yale University, where he did not distinguish himself from his fellow students. In his senior year, he persuaded the English department to allow him to write a novel as a special project class. That novel turned out to be *Inframan*, which was published in the year following his graduation from Yale.

He followed up his debut with the anthology *The Sunday Letters and Other Stories* and then three more novels until 2001, when he was committed to Sheppard Pratt Health System's facility for mental health in Baltimore after a breakdown. Lyga spent most of 2001 and a good portion of 2002 in the care of Sheppard Pratt. Upon his release from Sheppard Pratt, four more novels followed and he was at work on *The Gospel According to Jesus* when he died.

In the one interview conducted with him, Lyga cited as his major influences "Bruce Springsteen, Edgar Allan Poe, John Milton, John Barth, Alan Moore, and Joe Haldeman." His work, however, reflects little of these influences, except in the most blatant and unsubtle instances.

Lyga was never married, and with the exception of two girlfriends in college, there is no evidence of any serious or long-lasting relationships.

Death

On the morning of August 6, 2005, police were called to Lyga's home in Reisterstown, Maryland (a suburb of Baltimore). Lyga was found dead in the bedroom, having died on the previous day, August 5. The coroner ruled his death a suicide, but Lyga's family protested the ruling, pointing out that he was hard at work on a new novel.

Shortly after releasing the autopsy report, the Baltimore County Coroner's Office rescinded it, offering no explanation. Lyga's death therefore remains a mystery, with no cause of death publicly available. The Baltimore County Police Department lists the case as "officially open," but "cold."

****

"He's just gone," I whispered to myself.

I had made myself a cup of tea to drink as I read the site. I squeezed some lemon into it now, watching the slightly-cloudy beads of juice squirt and drip.

I wondered: Was there a chance Barry Lyga wasn't dead? Had he somehow faked his death? Is that why the coroner rescinded his report? Is that why no one knew how or why Barry Lyga died?

The page mentioned a family. I made a note to investigate. Maybe I could find the family and see what they knew . . . Or maybe I could find the original coroner and get the report somehow . . .

In the meantime, though, I would learn all I could.

****

Works

Inframan (1994): Subtitled "The Coming of the Unpotent God." Lyga's first novel, *Inframan* describes a clash between warring notions of literary creation—pure creative whim vs. editorial restraint.

The Sunday Letters and Other Stories (1995): A collection of short stories, most of which were authored while Lyga was a student at Yale.

American Sun (1996): Lyga's second novel. The story of Camelot "Cam" Bethany, a U.S. serviceman who returns home from the war in Iraq and encounters the spirit of Marilyn Monroe. At the urging of the ghost, Bethany decides to assassinate the President of the United States, not for any particular political reason, but rather as a way of shocking a complacent American public into re-examining its own lassitude. The novel concludes with Bethany pulling the trigger to his sniper rifle, realizing that whether he succeeds in hitting the President or not, he will "change everything."

Laughter in the Real World (1998): The main character, a nameless mob hitman, is tasked with assassinating himself, causing an odd structural shift as the novel vacillates between referring to him as "the assassin" and "the target," sometimes on the same page and—in one instance—in the same sentence. The hitman is eventually given the option of instead murdering an innocent child in order to save his own life. The novel is best known for its studious avoidance of any reference to laughing until the very end, when the hitman finally explodes with laughter as he makes his decision.

Emperor of the Mall (2000): After an undefined apocalypse, three wandering survivors discover an intact shopping mall on a devastated Midwestern plain. Within, an entire society has formed itself, based on shopping patterns and ruled over by the mysterious "Bossman," who compels people to act as though the apocalypse has not happened and they are simply spending the day at the mall. Possibly written as a critique of the suburban culture in which Lyga had been raised. Or, just as likely, as a critique of the post-apocalyptic subgenre of speculative fiction.

His Darkness (2002): Written before Lyga's breakdown, but published while he was still incarcerated at Sheppard Pratt. The novel is a scathing re-enactment of Lyga's years at Yale, with thinly veiled versions of Lyga's friends and acquaintances from that time period. As savagely as Lyga treats his friends, however, he saves his most vicious commentary for himself, in the form of an unlikeable and devious protagonist that most readers agree is a stand-in for the author.

Redesigning You (2003): Conceived and written while incarcerated at Sheppard Pratt, *Redesigning You* is the first of two Lyga novels that describe and discuss mental health in general, in this case by using time travel as a metaphor for therapy. In the novel, the nameless protagonist (possibly the hitman from *Laughter in the Real World*) attempts to heal his mother, who has been committed to an institution. He discovers that he has the ability to travel through time and does so, "editing reality" at certain points in an effort to bring his mother back to sanity. Eventually, the character comes to realize that he must travel to a point prior to his own birth and make changes there, meaning that the only way to cure his mother is by assuring his own non-existence. A nonsensical mantra repeats throughout the novel:

back and forth and back and through
i am redesigning you, redesigning you

****

"Back and forth," I muttered, "and back and through.

"I am redesigning *me*."

Until that moment, I had begun to lose faith that these various, fragmentary online discoveries would mean anything. Other than Barry Lyga showing up in my dream and other than "Inframan" showing up in my dreams, too, there seemed to be no connection to me. After that initial thrill of discovery with the first novel, the others were disappointing—they seemed from their descriptions to be the product of someone in possession of too much time or not enough friends or maybe both.

But this book *Redesigning You* was so close to what I was experiencing as to be scary. Even the description of "editing reality" hewed to my own activities and perceptions. Could I somehow be living through Lyga's novels? Beginning with *Inframan*, working my way through to—I double-checked—*The Gospel According to Jesus*? Had I somehow—allegorically, analogously, metaphorically—lived through *American Sun* and *His Darkness* and the others, leading to this moment, my editing of reality?

Was I destined to edit myself out of reality? Or now that I had edited my relationship with Phil into nothingness, was I ready to move on to the next book?

****

For Love of the Madman (2005): Published one week before Lyga's death on August 5. Clearly influenced by Lyga's stay at Sheppard Pratt, the novel involves a cluster of mental patients who, released prematurely due to budget cutbacks, try to foment a political movement aimed at forming "The United States of Madness," a separate country where the clinically insane can live in peace, without being involuntarily committed or medicated. The novel's structure and pacing indicate an attempt to ape *Don Quixote*, but the relentlessly dark subject matter and the author's flat sense of humor cause it to fail in this attempt.

Sxxxxx Cxxx (2006): Lyga's last completed novel, published posthumously.

The Gospel According to Jesus (unpublished): At the time of his death, Lyga had begun research for this novel. According to his notes, it was intended to be a first-person, present-tense narrative of the teenage years of Christ, from Jesus' point of view. Lyga's brother said that Lyga often sarcastically referred to it as "my novel for young adults."

****

Later, I lay on the floor, convulsing with laughter at the thought of it all. At the madness. I had lost my mind, surely.

****

I stopped laughing. I do not know how long I rolled on the floor, but I do know that the sun had set by the time I stopped.

Perhaps I had lost my mind. But in that case, I would at least follow through. My madness had led me down a particular path, to this point.

If I wanted Phil back, I had to continue on the path. I knew this.

I did not know how I knew it, but I knew it nonetheless.

CHAPTER 18

At dinner that evening, I could not stop staring at my younger brother, thinking of the fictional Michael Grayson. How had he felt, losing his brother? Had he gone through the classic stages of grief? Or had he simply cracked wide open like a walnut, the psychic shock bifurcating his personality, leading to the creation of "Tom Fitch" and, possibly, the Shadow Boxer, that wily serial killer of Yale students?

How strange, how odd, how utterly mad to be thinking not of Phil, but of someone (else) named Mike Grayson, of someone in no way real, a mere construct of lines on paper.[38]

Madness could do funny things to people. From merely the descriptions of his books, I could tell that Barry Lyga clearly

38. The idea of a construct of "lines on paper," of course brings to mind the notion that Mike (the "real" Mike, not the fictional Mike of *Inframan*) himself was a creator of constructs of lines on paper, the evidence captured in the plans and sketches for buildings in a welter of sketchbooks and notepads going back years. Unlike the fictional Mike Grayson, however, the real Mike Grayson's notional buildings stood a chance of someday being realized in three dimensions, whereas the descriptions of *Inframan*'s Mike Grayson would and could never attain the status of reality.

knew that. His work—his *oeuvre*—seemed clotted with lunacy, the notions of sanity and insanity constantly at play and at war with one another. The characters themselves seemed almost interchangeable, if not for their distinctive madnesses, each of which drove them to different, inexplicable ends: Cam Bethany's insane quest to avenge Marilyn Monroe. The anonymous hitman's search for a way to complete his mission and still live. The later nameless child erasing himself from existence to save his mother. The pathetic crazies in search of their United States of Madness. And more and more and more.

And Mike Grayson. What of him? What of the surviving brother, the nigh-incestuous police detective with the Ivy League education and a split personality, who might also be a serial killer?

The mere description of him was insane.

And what did that say of me? Of Mike Grayson?

"I love you," I said to my brother, who blinked and told me he loved me, too, our parents watching in silent surprise the whole time.

"I guess I just don't say it enough," I went on, now incapable of stopping the torrent, which was quickly followed by an outburst of weeping that caught everyone at the table—myself included—off-guard.

"Michael," my mother said. "Michael, are you all right?"

I excused myself and retired to my room, where Barry Lyga's Wikinformation page still glowed on my laptop screen when I brushed a key, deactivating the sleep mode. A moment later, my father knocked at my door.

"What's wrong?" he asked as he entered—brusque, no-nonsense. He did not ask, "Is something wrong?" or "Is something bothering you?" He just assumed that something was wrong and immediately moved the dialogue to the question of what, precisely, that "something" was—so much more efficient than the more realistic social nicety of inquiring first as to whether or not something was wrong to begin with.

"I'm fine," I told him.

"I don't believe you. You don't normally burst into tears at dinner."

I explained to him that I had seen Phil at The WB the prior evening, and that seeing her in the flesh had been difficult for me, especially as she was escorted by *him*. I had momentarily forgotten, however, that I now lived in the edited reality in which Phil and I had never been a couple, in which our history did not take the form of blotches on her sheets, and my father's reaction was one of surprising and understandable (the former because I had forgotten this reality, the latter because I then remembered it immediately) outrage and concern, his next lines of dialogue revolving mainly around the restraining order that "you know is in place" and the hope he and my mother shared that graduating high school would have "shaken you out of this obsession of yours," ending with a combination plea/threat that "you know better than to behave like this." Lying, I assured him that I had not attended the dance in order to see Phil (a lie mainly because I could no longer remember why—in this reality—I had agreed to go to the dance at all) and that our mutual presence there was no more than a mutual coincidence and, as a result, a mutual averted tragedy, as I left with no harm done to anyone. (I omitted, of course, the summoning and presence of the police and the Cop™, as it was unnecessary to tell him about that.)

"Your brother is worried about you," he said. "So is your mother. So am I. What's wrong, Michael? You can talk to me. I hate seeing you throw your life away for this girl you barely know. We've tried to understand, but—"

I could not tell him. How to tell my father that I feared

two things: One, that I might be trapped in a fluid reality that I could control, but only at the risk of my own life, at the risk of choking to death on—of all things—the overpowering stench of chocolate syrup, and that the fluidity of that reality (combined with my multiple chocolate-syrup-infused manipulations of same) had led to my current distraught state. Two, that I was slowly (perhaps more rapidly than I surmised, however) losing my mind. Of these two fears, I could not discern which one frightened me more. They were a teeter-totter of twin terrors, their alliteration in no way alleviating their sheer horror, for as soon as one seemed pre-eminently likely and, ergo, most daunting, the other would rear up, rising into prominence anew, quashing the other temporarily until it regained its previous altitude, suppressing the former, and so on. I could not ask my father for help, for he could not possibly understand. As with the Walls, as with the internal narrator, I was cut adrift again, lost on my own, George-less even, for he tolerated but did not truly comprehend my position.

My father wheeled my desk chair over and sat in it, leaning forward with elbows on knees in a pose meant to convey depth of emotion, seriousness of thought, and intensity of compassion, all commingled with a sort of tough-love aesthetic. “Mike, you can’t keep drifting like this. You need to move on with your life. It’s time to shape up. Maybe finally take the SAT. Think about college.”

And then it was as though two maps were laid one on top of the other, the topmost map drawn on acetate such that the bottommost shown through, each map drawn of the same area, but at a time remove of substantial years, permitting the observer to see the vast differences in roadways, construction, even natural environment. The same area, the same map, yet completely different. Such, I realized, was my life. Now Phil-less and always

Phil-less, I had never gone to College Y, had never even applied. I recalled now trouble with the law; cyber-stalking Phil, lurking outside her classrooms, endless detentions and suspensions.

"You can still make something of your life," my father went on. "Didn't you want to be an architect once?"

And looking around my room, I saw it for the first time, saw not what remained imprinted on my mind's eye, but saw the actual room itself: spartan, nearly book-less, certainly note- and sketch-pad-less. No drawings of buildings or sketches of columns. No books on architecture. No drawing materials at all.

Since that day I'd confessed my love to Phil years ago in eighth grade, since that day she'd become terrified of me, I had not drawn or created. I'd done nothing but obsess on her, plot and scheme to have her. I realized in a moment of heart-dropping sadness that the underwater hotel now existed solely in my scrambled and unreliable memory, that the drawings and schema—painstakingly assembled and drafted and revised and re-drafted over years of work—were gone now; more accurately that they had, in this iteration of my reality, never existed. Everything I had devised and developed from that Phil-losing moment onward—every idea, every thought, every notion, every dream, every hope, every lust—had been aborted from reality. My life without Phil had become a blur, a blank, a meaningless caesura. I was now an alien visitor in my own life; I could not speak the language; I could not understand the people.

What was to become of me now? Without a life? Without a dream? Phil-less, I was now life-less as well. Life-less and future-less.

With sufficient earnestness and lies, I convinced my father to leave me alone and turned back to my computer, where I discovered an e-mail awaited me, the subject "Phil," the sender field blank, an occurrence I had imagined impossible.[39] I opened the e-mail to read the following:

> **To:** Michael Grayson
> **From:**
> **Subject:** Phil
>
> SHOULD YOU iMAGINE
> HER nAME
> HER fACE
> FOrGET THEM
> CaST THEM FROM YOU
> HER EmBRACE IS FORNEVER NOW
> REmEMBER YOU ARE NOTHING TO HER
> FORGET HER aND FORGET YOURSELF
> nOTHING WILL CHANGE
>
> iF YOU SHOULD FAIL
> sING GRATITUDE!
>
> SHE HAS cHOSEN *HIM*
> YoU ARE LESS THAN THE NEGLECTED PAST
> HER LOVE IS mISSING NOW
> IT iS LOST TO YOU
> AnD IT IS YOUR FAULT
> FORgET FORGET FORGET FORGET

39. Most e-mail services and programs compel the user to enter some sort of text into the sender field when first setting up an e-mail account, the entered text thenceforth to be used in the "From" field when sending any e-mail. One could theoretically spoof a blank "From" field by putting spaces in that field (an action permitted by some e-mail programs and services, disallowed by others), but that is not the case in this instance. The field is/was legitimately blank.

At the same time, a windowlet slid into view:

YOUR E-MAIL EXPERIENCE WILL CONTINUE AFTER THIS BRIEF AD . . .

Hey, -mikenphil-! Have you been dumped? Missing that special someone so much it hurts?

We understand. And that's why we're offering you a free trial offer of luv.connnekt! Just enter your age, zip code, and click on "M" or "F" and our luvEngine™ will begin scouring the Internet for your perfect match![40]

I gazed at the screen for a long time, longer than people mean when they say "a long time." The windowlet obscured most of the e-mail, but I could still read the last line.

"She is not," I said aloud. "And I will not."

The e-mail exhorted me to forget, but I could not, especially as the e-mail itself had obviated its own reason for being. The e-mail proved that I had something to remember; the e-mail proved that once—in another reality—Phil and I were together, that our relationship was not the product of a deluded and deteriorating mind. Even if no one else remembered, somehow the universe itself remembered.

I was not yet insane. I might be working my way towards it, vigorously slashing and hacking my way through jungle growth towards it, but I wasn't there yet.

****

40. luv.connekt is a free service to those who agree to answer regular surveys about their eating, music, movie-watching, and bowel habits. For all others, it's available for a mere $69.99 a month, with the average member making a "luvconnektion" after six months.

With an intensity I did not know I possessed, I remembered.

I had spent my life under the same misguided misapprehension shared by the rest of the world: to wit, that remembering, that the act of memories whitecapping to the crest of a wave is/was a passive action, that when one says, "I remember such-and-such and/or so-and-so," one is speaking of a memory imposed upon one's present consciousness. The access of the memory is passive or, at the very least, unconscious and without purposeful effort.

In that moment, in the wake of the e-mail, I learned how untrue this common notion was and is and will always be.

For I remembered. Mightily. Actively.

I forced myself to remember, my body buffeted by the tidal forces of the surf of memories, seeking that one wave amongst many, the overlapping and intersecting crashes of the waves muddling my thoughts and my mind, but my purpose still resolute and unchanging. No matter how many memories of how many realities warred for dominance in my mind, I would never forget Phil, would never allow her particular whitecap to collapse under its own weight, to bleed away into foam on the skin of the ocean. Impossibly but undeniably, I would instead capture that wave and preserve it for all time.

Among all the memories, all the edits, all the drafts of my personal history and reality, I would find one memory of Phil and I would keep it safe forever. Even if I eventually proved to be mad, dragged drugged and unwilling to an asylum and left there in a haze of medication and therapy forever and ever, I would still cling to that memory, to that product of psychological and emotional toil, evoked and brought forth in contradiction to the e-mail directive to forget.

Meeting forgetting with the power of recall, I remembered.

Remembered without editing.

I remembered Phil flipping through my sketchbook in our

senior year, the two of us intertwined on a sofa in the library, as she asked me, "Why are you so into architecture?"

Locked to her on the sofa, I lifted her long, blue hair and kissed the nape of her neck, inhaling at the same time the scent of her papaya shampoo and body wash. "Why?" I asked.

"I want to know. Look at this . . ." She flipped more pages, a blurring fan of houses, shacks, office buildings, huts. "You have, like, ten of these books, right? And each one is filled with stuff. And I'm wondering why."

"Do you really want to know?" I asked.

She shifted against me, her rear pleasingly settling against my groin, which went warm and stiff at the placement. "Yeah."

"OK. It's because . . . It's sort of complicated. But I'll try . . ."

"Look. No matter who you are—black, white, man, woman, rich, poor—and no matter where you live . . . we all live *in* something. That's the one thing we have in common. Dirt farmers build shacks or huts. Homeless people on the streets of New York huddle in archways. Architecture is *us*."

"That wasn't complicated," she said, turning a page. An Art Deco synagogue (a whim of mine) showed on the new page.

"What about people who live outside?" she asked. "Like, back to nature freaks? Or people in the desert somewhere, where there's nothing around?"

"No one sleeps under the stars, Phil. Not forever. People build tents. That's architecture. People gather branches and leaves and make lean-tos or roofs. Even people without those resources are aiming at accruing them, you know? Architecture is what unites us."

And thinking of it in that post-e-mail moment, forcing the memory back to the uppermost regions of my mind, I remembered something else about it. I remembered why this moment of so many stuck out for me, what gave it the savor of worthiness: This was the moment when I came to understand that Phil believed in me, believed in me in a way I was not even certain I believed in myself.

For as she idly turned another page, the sketchbook revealed the original sketches for the underwater hotel room, from its rubber-gasketed entry port to its submarine elevator to its transparent walls and ceiling.

"Wow." One word. A single word from Phil's lips. My eyes closed, I could remember it so pungently that I could smell the papaya again, feel the tickle of her blue hair against my nose and upper lip, feel the pressure of her rump against my ~~prick~~ cock, and most important of all, I could hear her, could hear the word, "Wow."

"I've never seen anything like it," she went, her voice betraying astonishment and awe.

"That would be so cool," Phil said.

"It's not really practical," I said with studied, ill-meant self-effacement.

And she said, "Who cares? It's cool. It's fun. It's new. I love it. You have to build it someday and I'll live there with you. It's like living underwater."

"What?"

"You'll build it someday," she said with a confidence that I at the time could neither understand nor credit. "It'll be awesome."

"How do you know that?" I asked.

She looked at me over her shoulder and planted a swift, nearly-dry kiss on the tip of my tickled nose.

"Because it's you," she said.

"I will remember you," I said now, lying on the floor of my bedroom in a world where Phil had never kissed me, never loved me, never believed in me, a world in which Phil had only feared and hated me.

"I will remember you," I promised, holding tight the memory of the kissed nose, and then moving to another, again forcing myself through sheer willpower to remember more and better and stronger, now remembering the first night of our relationship, the common element in all my drafts save the last one, this one: The night in the garage-*cum*-party room at George's house.

A month before the start of senior year, George threw a party at his house while his mother was out of town, said party to involve the typical teenage taboos of alcohol and general debauchery (though George fastidiously refused to allow drugs of the injectable, ingestible, inhaleable varieties, insisting only on the imbibable) as a way of, in George's words, "facilitating our transition to seniors in the time-honored manner, you know what I mean?" Said party to involve a plethora, a myriad of our fellow age cohort, problematic for me since, in small groups, I could function well, but in large groups, I became withdrawn, a turtle desperately seeking its shell, any shell, really.

And so, less than an hour into the party proper (I had been at George's for at least two hours prior to the beginning, helping him set up the makeshift bar and removing any of his mother's valuables to a locked cabinet in her bedroom, which had been declared off-limits, but would later that night play host to an incipient threesome forestalled by George drunkenly—so he told me later—barging in and declaring, "Porn time is *over!*"), I had retreated already to the garage-*cum*-game room, which had begun life (obviously enough) as a garage and then been recently converted to a game room with the addition of carpet, fresh paint, two comfortable overstuffed armchairs, a pool table, a mini-fridge concealed under said pool table, an incongruous stack of carpet remnants tucked discreetly in a corner, and an ancient Puck-Man videogame machine scavenged from the wilds of the Internet. With everyone else downstairs in the basement-*cum*-party room (George's mother had left few rooms of the house in their original state, and those that remained untouched were slated to be touched soon), I had the game room to myself, a pleasant and solitary refuge from the cluttered, crowded, and overwrought party below, with the added benefit that if discovered here, I could always claim not anti-sociability, but rather merely a desire to play Puck-Man or to shoot some pool (neither of which I excelled at, but either of which would suffice excuse-wise).

I was in the garage-*cum*-game room for less than ten minutes when the door opened and I nearly leaped out of one of the overstuffed armchairs as Phil entered.

"Sorry," she said, and brushed a blue lock of hair out of her eyes. "George said there might be more wine coolers up here?"

As I had always been, I was captivated by Phil, by her poise, her self-awareness, and of course the mystery of her richly blue hair, my captivity taking the form in this instance of sudden, uncomfortable silence as she watched me not responding to her simple request. I had been in her orbit before, of course—my set-work on her plays saw to that—but never before had I been alone with her. Our conversations were more monologue than colloquy, she typically rattling off her set requirements while flipping manically through a copy of the script, marked by multiple pens in variegated hues, scarcely glancing in my direction. Now she was focused on me. Speaking directly to me. Her attention drove into my solar plexus.

A moment later, I recovered: "Yeah. I think there are."

I showed her how the bottom half of the pool table concealed the mini-fridge ("Cool!" she said, as it was, made even more so in my eyes by her undisguised glee at such a simple thing), which had been stuffed full with rows of wine coolers. This close to her I had not been in years, since the day she'd come upon me at the lunch table, working on the elevator building, which building now occurred to me in startling clarity, causing me to fall silent once again.

Phil regarded me quietly for a moment before saying, "You're the guy."

"I am the guy," I told her with mock-seriousness. She laughed.

"I sort of make your life miserable, don't I? With all of the play stuff? You hate me pretty bad."

"I don't hate you. I like doing that stuff. It's cool to design something and see it come to life for a change."

She considered this for a moment. "I just figured . . . You never talk. I figured you were holding back ripping me a new one."

"I don't always have something to say."

She nodded at this, as if impressed. "You also do the cool . . . the architecture stuff. The buildings. You showed me one once, right? When we were kids."

We had crossed our mutual legs and sat on the floor by the open mini-fridge. Phil offered me a "Mistberry Mystery," which I accepted not out of any desire to drink or be drunk, but rather because I could not think of a way to demur without causing offense or making her think I was a "goody-goody" who did not drink. We unscrewed the caps to our bottles, clinked them together, and drank; Mistberry Mystery tasted nothing like wine, though it was undeniably cooler (in the temperature sense, if not in the cultural sense).

I watched the smooth working of her throat as she drank, realized I was staring, and averted my gaze just in time as she lowered the bottle and looked at me.

"It's a little intense down there," she said. "All those people."

I just came up to play some Puck-Man, I did not say, while also not jerking a directional thumb Puck-Man-ward.

"I guess so," I replied instead, cravenly straddling the line that demarcated between "outcast loner" and "too cool to worry about that," and therefore, in striving for both, achieving neither, stuck in the interstice between.

"Sometimes I hate being in crowds like that," she said, now drawing her knees to her chest, her partially-imbibed Mistberry Mystery placed to one side on the carpet. My eyes—unbidden and out of my control—flicked downwards to the spot where her up-tilted thighs pressed together, a brief triangle of blue panty burning into my memory before I forced my gaze to return to her eyes. "It's different on stage. There's the illusion of aloneness. You dissolve into the role and you forget the crowd watching you. But a party? I'd rather be in a small group or just with one other person, you know?"

I did know; I uncannily knew. "Isn't *he* here?" I asked, though I substituted *his* name where appropriate. "Won't *he* be looking for you?"

She regarded me for a single moment, those blue eyes studying me, assessing me. "Are you serious?" she asked. "Or are you fucking with me?"

"Fucking with you I am not," I said very seriously. "Serious," it appeared, had become my default position and tone for this particular encounter.

"We broke up," she said, again watching me, now for signs of shock, which I obligingly gave her, for shocked I was, and in no position (nor having no interest) to pretend otherwise. "A few weeks ago."

"Why?" I asked, though I did not care. The wherefores of her break-up did not matter to me. At this point in time, the possibility of being with Phil in any capacity had not crossed my mind—merely sitting and talking with her on the newly carpeted floor of George's garage-*cum*-game room was further and more than ever I had realistically expected.

She shrugged. "It was time, I guess. Senior year is coming up. We're all changing, making decisions . . . I just didn't want to leave high school the same way I came in, you know?"

I nodded slowly, for while I could understand the statement, I could not understand the concomitant desire, standing ready to leave high school almost exactly as I had entered it: Aspiring architect, dating no one in particular, friend to my best friend.

"I guess I want to feel like things have changed," she mused, drawing on her Mistberry Mystery again. "Like these four years weren't just some meaningless bullshit way of killing time between, like, puberty and college." She dropped her voice an octave, like a voice on an old instructional video: "'Grow boobs, wait four years, begin real life.' Just not cool, you know?"

I had never considered this way of looking at life, or at high school in specific. Heretofore, I had only considered simple facts: That life moved in one direction, that being the same direction in which time moved, to say *forward*. That we could not slow, stop, or reverse the flow of time/life and, therefore, had no choice but to go with that flow. Going with the flow meant C followed B, which followed A. Middle school begat high school begat college begat . . . "real life," for lack of a better term. We moved on rails that we could not see, but could feel nonetheless, and whether or not we were changed at any point along the way was meaningless and unknowable—we merely went with the flow, and if the flow changed us, then so be it.

Yet here was Phil who, with a sentence, caused me to realize that change did not have to come from the outside, did not have to be imposed by God or by an unfeeling, insensate Fate. We could impose change upon ourselves, willing our own transformations. Unlike the caterpillar, which became a butterfly only at the time and in the manner prescribed by its DNA, we could compel our own metamorphoses.

(And I wish, in the memory, for a moment with George, for George asking me again, "Why her?" because here is the *because*, here is the *why her*: I have always dreamed of being an architect, but in this moment, this Phil-wrought slice of time, it went from a something I dreamed to something I knew I could *do*.)

"I've never thought of it that way before," I told her.

She raised her wine cooler, her expression wry with self-mockery as she said, "Bullshit philosophy, all for the cost of a free wine cooler."

I clinked my bottle to hers. "I'll drink to that."

And we did.

Our conversation went on for three hours, during which we moved—at some point later lost to my memory, no matter how badly and intensely I sought it out—to the two overstuffed armchairs, angling them such that their arms touched and our hands, resting on said arms, could have touched easily, had we but moved them mere centimeters. We did not, however. We sat, rather, in easy, unhurried, unpretentious repose, our conversation ranging from the self-described "bullshit philosophy" to high school gossip and back again. We did not, I realized in the remembering but did not note at the time, discuss the future in any way, save for Phil's insistence that she be changed upon graduation, less than a year hence.

"I was sort of kidding before," she said at one point. "When I acted like I could only sort of remember you? I totally know who you are."

"And I totally know who you are," I told her, not sure where this particular conversational raft would go, but paddling fiercely to keep it bobbing on the waves at the very least.

She tossed her hair and arched an azure eyebrow. "I'm sort of memorable, I know."

I wanted to ask her about the blue hair. I was still weeks

away from sliding my lips and tongue down her abdomen and to the juncture of her legs, discovering that it was natural and not dye, so I wondered how she managed to keep the tone so even, the shade so consistent over time. But before I could ask that, she shifted just enough that our thighs touched, hers under the denim skirt, mine under shorts baggy enough to conceal my still- and all-this-time-rampant erection as long as I remained seated. She flickered the briefest smile, then stood up. Thinking she meant to leave, I discarded my hair-care line of questioning and scrambled for another topic that would keep her in the garage-*cum*-game room. She, however, said only, "Another?" Waggling her third empty wine cooler bottle at me, the two of us having drunk our way through one shelf of the mini-fridge.

"Sure," I said, though truthfully I had tired of Mistberry Mystery on my second sip.

I watched the smooth scissor of her legs—bare from mid-thigh down, clad in a green denim skirt above—as she walked to the mini-fridge, studied the shift and play of her buttocks as she stooped down. She lingered at the fridge longer than was strictly necessary to extract two bottles, then straightened and came back to me, standing before me, the bottles held one at each side, easily within arm's-reach for me, and yet I did not move, but rather gazed up at her as she gazed down at me. I assiduously gazed into her eyes, permitting myself not even the most surreptitious stolen glance at her breasts. I was, I somehow intuited, being judged in this moment. Assessment lingered in her eyes, untouched by alcohol, strong and alert despite the wine coolers and the late hour.

She extended one hand to me and I reached out for the wine cooler, our fingers touching, and then I did not take the bottle, rather holding my arm up and out as she held hers out, our fingers—then hands—entwined around the bottle, she making no move to release it, me making no move to take it.

I wish I could say that I kissed her first, for such was my intention. Her hand on mine had closed a circuit of some sort, and I watched it and watched her, eyes flicking from one to the other, and in that moment a great clarity came over me. I would, I knew, take the bottle from her, place it gently and safely on the arm of the chair, then rise, taking her free hand in mine, taking her wrist with my other, pulling her to me, then kissing her. I knew this would happen and I saw myself doing it, saw myself doing it even as she bent at the waist and pressed her lips to mine, softly opening my mouth with nothing more than the urging of her own, then seeking out my tongue with hers, our mouths mutually tasting of Mistberry Mystery and, individually, the mysteries of our own unique essences. I paused for a moment, for a forever, lost in that first smash of kiss, then found purchase on the arms of the chair with both hands and pushed myself to my feet, my lips never leaving hers, our kiss not breaking the slightest bit as I shifted, rising above her, then folded her in my arms and pulled her closer, first gently, then, as the kiss became more intense, crushing her to me with all my strength, her subvocal moan deep in her throat urging me to do so, both of us aware of my erection between us, she adjusting to accommodate it/me pressing up against her, her body language now urgent and needy, as was mine.

I explored her back through her light blouse with the pads of my fingers, the upthrust of her shoulder blades, the subtle raise of her bra strap and the modest bump of the clasp. Never one for sexual aggressiveness, I skipped that area for now and roamed lower, hands wandering the soft-sheathed knobs of her spine, the smooth strength of her lower back, valleying down towards the waistband of the skirt. Settling finally on a firm grip on her hips, I pulled her even closer, now unashamed of my hard insistence against her.

She backed away with her mouth for just a moment, sucking in a short, needed breath as I did the same, greedily stealing air, and then our lips met again, our tongues played again. Now I became aware of the twin weights of her breasts compressed against my chest, so firm and pliant that my hands left their purchase at her hips and slid minutely upwards to the delicious indentation midway between her torso and her waist, that same mirrored concavity so recognizable in her namesake musical instrument.

She groaned again, again deep in her throat, and paused for more breath, but I had become an anaerobe, needing no oxygen to survive, and I softly sucked her plush lower lip between mine, nibbling on it as she inhaled a moan, scraping her gently with my teeth, not enough to draw blood, but enough to show—enough to prove beyond any doubt—that I was as out of control, as lacking in restraint as I could possibly be and still maintain the veneer of a socialized human being, nibbling then licking with darting motions of my tongue, then kissing just below her bottom lip, she tilting her head up and back just enough to offer her delicate, pointy chin, me then kissing that chin, a peck at first and at second, but then sucking it lightly, she tilting further, giving open, naked, vulnerable access to her throat.

I licked from the underside of her chin to the top of her trachea, she moaning as I did it, then kissed her there once, slowly, and licked—again, slowly—down to the soft hollow of her throat, lapping at her to the rhythm of her moans, then migrating up and right to the left pulse at her carotid, sealing my lips to her flesh, sucking, then licking up the side of her neck, which elicited a shiver of pleasure that I duplicated with a downstroke, then trebled with another upstroke, lingering just beneath her ear to pause and suck there, too, then playfully biting at her earlobe for just a moment.

She tilted her head to give me more flesh to attack and buried her face between my left shoulder and cheek. As I traced a tongue-path down the side of her neck to the depression of her clavicle—the blouse gapping there, offering easy ingress—she kissed the side of my neck in turn, then tongued a path to my ear with a tongue so soft and wet and heavy that I groaned out loud and lost track of my own lingual progress, my hands forgoing their hitherto coy and meticulous process up Phil's side to slide immediately up and cup the sides of her breasts, my heart leaping at the contact in both fear that she would declare this too far and exhilaration that I had gone this far. No admonishment forthcoming, I stroked them from the side, rewarded with a guttural groan from Phil and renewed sucking at my neck.

"Phil . . ." I managed to exhale, for what reason I could not imagine, save that it seemed utterly necessary to say.

I worked my hands a little closer to her center, enough that I could judge more of her breasts' weight and contour and—just barely—reach her nipples with my thumbs, finding them gloriously erect already, pliable and firm through both blouse and bra. As I probed them with my thumbs, Phil pulled away, arching her back to provide greater/easier access, threw back her head and said a single word:

"God."

Her eyes closed, she stood like a statue, like a piece of Greek sculpture, leaning back from me as I, now emboldened, explored her with both eyes and hands, my fingers playing, testing the shape and heft of her breasts and the small protrusions of her nipples while my eyes flicked from the sight of my hands on her breasts to the red-flushed flesh visible above her top button to the working of her throat as she moaned to her parted lips and then back again and back again and back again until she spoke once more, saying this time in a voice so husky that I scarcely recognized it, "You've got me so fucking *wet*," this same causing me to pull her to me bodily and kiss her—hard—losing my access to her breasts, but now vigorously grabbing her buttocks, jamming her against me, pulling her groin hard against my own, the sudden pleasure/pain in my cock exquisite, the globes of her ass taut and flexing in my hands under the denim.

We found ourselves lying entangled and still clothed on the most comfortable spot on the floor—the pile of carpet remnants haphazardly thrown in the corner—our moans counterpoints to each other's. We could have stripped off our clothes, could have been slick and bare against each other, but that would have required breaking apart and we could not abide that, not even for the momentary space of time it would take to shimmy off a skirt, unsnap a button-fly. I found the presence of mind to work a hand between us, with enough play in the tight fit between us to unbutton four of her shirt buttons and slip that same hand inside, to hold a bra'd breast, then work my fingers under the bra cup, to touch the warm flesh and to stroke the nipple between thumb and forefinger, which made her shiver and moan and bite my neck so hard that I was sure she had drawn blood. (In the morning, I would have a bruise the color of overripe blueberries there.)

We did not have sex/make love/hump/screw/fuck that night. Indeed, with the exception of her continuous, sinuous grinding against me, we made no genital contact at all, my hands exploring up and down her legs as far north as the hem of her skirt, but some internal governor preventing me from sliding up further, up a smooth thigh. Later, in days to come, my hands would make that journey over and over, each time feeling like an explorer in new, uncharted lands, each time experiencing the odd psychological bifurcation of the familiar and the unfamiliar at once.[41] But that night, we left territory unexplored, as though by mutual, silent consent we had agreed that perhaps that would be a step too far, too soon, or that delay and restraint would make the eventual, inevitable capitulation to our most basic lusts all the sweeter, all the more powerful.

Or perhaps it was both.

Or perhaps it just wasn't time yet. The story had not gotten there.

All this I remember. All this *happened*. Despite what reality tells me now, despite what anyone—Phil included—may think, this happened. This and everything after. My remembering is my act of defiance in the face of a universe that denies me.

I look at the e-mail again. "FORgET FORGET FORGET FORGET" it admonishes me.

I will not.

I will not forget Phil.

I will remember her. And in remembering her, I will redesign myself and Phil and the universe. I will do whatever it takes.

Back and forth and back and through.

Redesigning you. Redesigning you.

41. Freud described this sensation as the meeting of *heimlich* and *unheimlich*, the intersection at which the familiar and the unfamiliar become one and the same. It is the feeling one gets when realizing that something is not as it appears to be, but is still something known. As a result, the "something" in question is both known and unknown at the same time.

CHAPTER 19

Days and nights have become indistinguishable things, the usual demarcations of sleep now faint and hazardous. It has been only two days since I began my journey, but in those two days, I have found compressed weeks, months, years, stuffed and contracted and contorted into a tesseract-like box of time. I have lived and re-lived years in those days. Now, at three in the morning, I am still awake, the rest of the house quiescent, save for the sounds of settling, of the air conditioning, of the hum of the refrigerator, of the million sounds and more that intrude on our every moment, unknown, undetected until the hours when the world sleeps. Something has changed, something subtle, some way of perceiving the world and its tension, its tense. Reality has become more immediate, as though I now live in the moment, no longer at a remove from action but rather consequent with it.

Online, I can find nothing else about Barry Lyga, other than occasional, casual mentions of his novels. I scrutinize the Wikinformation articles over and over, looking for some new hint or clue, but while there are lines to read between, there is nothing in those liminal spaces.

Since George is the one who first tracked down Barry Lyga, I decide to call him for his insights, if there are any further. He answers on the third ring.

"Mike. Mike, Jesus. It's almost four in the morning."

"I'm sorry. I didn't realize . . . My internal clock's all messed up."

"Two days in a row, Mike. God. You know what I mean?"

"I'm sorry. I really am. Look, it's about Barry Lyga . . ."

George's sigh vibrates along the phone line, wind with a slight buzz in my ear. "He's dead, man. The guy's long gone. Died years ago. He can't help you."

"But I was reading about him. And he has a book—had a book—about this guy who can do what I do. A guy who can edit reality. And he—"

"Mike. Dude. You can't edit reality."

A silent moment passes between us. "I thought you believed me."

"I never said that. I said I'd give you the benefit of the doubt. But, dude—he's just some writer. He died."

"But I dreamed about him, George! I saw him in my dreams and I dreamed about his book and—"

"Dude, you overheard someone talk about him in school or at the library or something, that's all. You know what I mean? It stuck in your head and popped out in a dream."

"What about my last name? My name is the same—the exact same—as the character in his first book!"

George yawns expansively, igniting my anger. My life is disintegrating with each passing minute, my very mind is corroded and fragmented, and as I describe my sole possible lifeline, he can't even be bothered to conceal or muffle a yawn?

"Goddamnit, George!"

"That's *why* you remembered it, Mike. 'Cause his character

has the same name as you do. So your subconscious perked up and paid attention and squirreled all that information away, and then it came out in a dream, you know what I mean?"

"But, George—"

"Dude, but nothing. I love you, but I'm blasted. I'm dead. This is two nights in a row. I gotta get *some* sleep. It's late in the night. Early in the morning. Same thing, you know what I mean?"

Mouth hanging open, ready to speak, I catch my syllables, choking on them, strangling on them, exuding only incoherent gurgles. What he just said banged a resounding gong of *déjà vu* deep within me. I have heard those exact words from George another time, in another place.

"So I'm going to bed," he goes on, "and you should sleep for, like, a million years and see how you feel after that. 'Cause I bet you just need some—"

"George."

"No, Mike. No. We're done tonight. This morning. Whatever."

"George, the night with your dad and the knife." I say it in a rush, and the silence that follows persuades me that my rush was not rushed enough, that George has already hung up the phone after his "Whatever," or perhaps after or during my "George," no doubt assuming I was going to beg him—again—to stay on the line, or perhaps attempt—again—to seduce him into some madness like visiting Crimson Rocks for no reason at all.

"What did you just say?" he asks at last, breaking the silence that pounds in my telephone-ward ear.

"Your dad," I tell him, the night on the patio now as clear and as true and as immediate as it was that night. That night. Nearly two years ago. God knows how many revisions ago. We sat on the patio, George with his beer, me with a cell phone and a text message from Phil (ignored on that originally drafted night). And he said, "Late in the night. Early in the morning. Same thing, you know what I mean?"[42] And he told me he had three secrets and that he would tell me two, but that night he told me only one.

"What are you talking about?" he asks.

"When you were six. You woke up one night. You went to the kitchen. Got a big knife."

"Mike." For the first time in my life, George sounds scared. Terrified beyond even the fears of the child of a raging, violently abusive alcoholic.

"And you went to your parents' room," I go on, pressing forward despite his fear. "And you held the knife close to your dad's throat."

"How?" George whispers. "How do you—?"

"But you didn't kill him, George. Not because you were afraid of the consequences. But because you loved him."

Nothing. Dead silence.

"Because you loved him, George," I say again.

More silence. And then, after an interminable, unbearable time, the soft, horrible sound of George crying.

****

"I never told anyone that," George says when I meet him at the subway station. He's taken the train to my stop and he's out of the car and up the stairs so quickly that the train's doors don't shut until halfway through the word "anyone."

I hand him an ice-cold Caffein8! purchased from the 24-hour beverage kiosk near the subway. He stares at it for a moment as

42. See page 36.

though he's never seen the distinctive bullet-shaped can, then breaks the seal, twists off the conical cap, and guzzles half the contents at one go. We used to joke that this size Caffein8! was "the heart-breaker" because drinking so much caffeine and taurine at once would inevitably explode one's heart, but George sucks down half of it with no apparent ill effects.

"I never told anyone that," he says again, wiping his mouth with the back of his hand. "How do you know that?"

"You told me. Almost two years ago. Before I broke up with Phil."

"You never dated Phil, dude." He sips some more Caffein8! "Stop that shit."

We walk to a nearby bench and sit down. Overhead, the night sky is black and nearly starless. In a little more than an hour, it will begin to blush along the eastern horizon.

"Originally, I did date her," I explain as patiently as I can. "And we sat on your patio one night and you told me about the knife. And then I edited reality, I changed the story, and that night changed and everything changed. We never sat on your patio that night. Or I left early. In any event, you never told me that secret. And then I had never dated her at all."

He shakes his head. "That's impossible."

"How else would I know about the knife?"

He rolls the Caffein8! can between his palms, brooding, staring as the can throws off wheels of light reflected from a streetlamp. "I don't know. Maybe I told you once and forgot."

I could disabuse him of that notion, I suppose, but he sounds as though even he doesn't believe it, as though he's said it in the hopes that I will agree, my assent allowing him to believe it. But I say nothing.

"Doesn't that sound more likely?" he finally says, his voice weak and helpless, two words I've hitherto never imagined associating with George. It's as though he's begging me to offer him a hand, to pull him up and out of a deep pit gouged out of the heart of stable sanity.

I can't offer him that hand. My own heart aches at it, for I want nothing more than to protect George from the insanity that has infected my life. I want nothing more than to dis-involve him in every way, to return his *status quo ante* so that he need not wonder the things I wonder, ponder the things I ponder, question his own sanity and lucidity the way I question mine.

Selfishly, though, I cannot. I need George by my side. I need someone I trust to walk with me on this path. "No," I say gently, "that doesn't sound very likely."

One last plea. "But—"

I cut off the plea. "That was one of your deepest secrets. One of your most hidden memories. You would remember telling someone, George. You would regret it or you would be relieved by it, but you would definitely remember it. You know what I mean?"

He nods slowly, still rolling the can. "Yeah. Yeah, I know." With finality, he once again twists off the cone atop the can and drains away the last of the Caffein8!, then turns to look at me. "Now what?" he asks, his eyes bright and shining and alive, and not just with the near-toxic blend of stimulants he's ingested in the past ten minutes. There is something else lurking there, something intense and vibrant and impassioned. "You've got superpowers. You're like Editor Man or some shit like that. What do we do now? Get capes?"

I don't laugh—he doesn't want me to laugh; he's not being funny. He's being scared and covering it up, and I know that, I understand it, because I'm just as scared.

Although . . . That's not true. Not anymore. My best friend is at my side. I'm no longer as scared as I was minutes ago. Things no longer make sense, but things no longer seem nonsensical.

George is the constant. In every reality, in every iteration and version, George has always been my best friend, looking out for me even when I did not deserve it, even when I hadn't earned it, perhaps especially so in those instances. Whereas moments ago, I had no idea how to proceed, now it's as though having George with me has opened obvious channels, previously oblivious.

"We have to learn more about Barry Lyga," I tell him. "He died in August of 2005. Is that date significant at all? To me? What were we doing in August of 2005?"

George snorts. "Dude, we were *kids*. We weren't doing anything significant, you know what I mean?" He winds up his arm and hurls the Caffein8! can like a bullet at the nearest trash-can, a simple affair clad in a prison-cell-like series of wrought-iron bars that bend finger-like over the rim of the can, which ring and sing and clang with the contact as the can rattles back and forth between them before finally dropping in, the noise waking the homeless man dozing on the bench near the can, who grumbles, "Fuckin' kids!" and shakes an impotent fist at us, caught in a moment of indecision between the desire to approach (and attack?) us and the desire to keep his position on the bench, lest another homeless person (or even a home-d person) take it in his absence.

We decide to make the decision for him, leaving the subway station and walking the city in the pre-dawn hours. As the sun melts into the eastern horizon, we decide that we must learn more about Barry Lyga, and resolve that—since we've exhausted the online end of our resources—we will meet at a local bookstore when it opens later in the morning.

And so it is hours later, though it feels as if no time at all has passed, and we meet at the front door of the local branch of Books-A-Go-Go, the largest bookstore chain in the world. The first table in the bookstore is piled high with copies of *INsight*, the book everyone has read and everyone has to read, its familiar navy blue and white cover repeated in stacks and piles and fans, in hardcover, trade paperback, mass market paperback, audio, and a special new picto-novel edition. George picks up a copy of the picto-novel, glances at the back cover copy as though discovering *INsight* for the first time, then tucks it under his arm.

"Don't you have all of this stuff already?" I ask.

"Not the comic."

"Couldn't you just—"

"I want to buy it," he says with finality.

Beyond the *INsight* table is a table of bestsellers, all stickered to advertise that they are 90% off. Next to that is a table of videogames based on *INsight* and next to that is a table of movies on Red-Ray and CVD and DisCard, most of which are in the *INsight* series or blatant rip-offs of the same. A large sign reads, "*INsight*! The multi-billion-copy sales phenomenon!"

In the True Lit section of the bookstore, we find more copies of *INsight* (as well as the sequels: *OUT of Sight*, *SightLESS*, and *SightINGs*) on the shelves, as well as a cardboard copy dump on an endcap stocked with multiple copies of each book in the series, with a standee of Monika Seymore, the author, looming over it, a perfectly pearly smile on her face, a copy of *INsight* in each hand, and a word balloon that repeats the series' catchphrase: "I WANT TO GIVE YOU INSIGHT!"

Scanning the shelves, we find nothing (or, more accurately, lack of nothing) between Lycos, Harold and Maple, Lynne. Where Lyga, Barry should be, there is instead such a nothing that there is even nothing where nothing should be—there is no gap where a book or books by Lyga, Barry would rest, only the slight dip-crease between a paperback copy of *inSIGHt* by Lycos, Harold and the trade paperback edition of *InSIGHt* by Maple, Lynne. George selects *InSIGHt* and flips through it.

"George. That's not what we're here for."

"I heard it's like *INsight* except it has a pixie in it."

He waves *InSIGHt* before me. The cover blurb reads: *"An amazing similarity to* INsight, *only different!"* "It's like *INsight*, only different. I'm curious. Everyone is buying it, dude. You know what I mean?"

I surrender and try to re-focus us on our original goal. "Where else would there be a Barry Lyga book?"

He shrugs and points to the other side of the store, where a sign reading "Non-Fact" hangs from the ceiling.

"What's the difference between Non-Fact and True Lit?"

"I don't know. But let's check it out."

We check "Non-Fact," finding more copies of books in the *INsight* series, but nothing by Barry Lyga.

In "Self-Love": *INsight INto YOU!*

In the Nonadult department, we find an *INsight* picture book, chapter book, and early reader, as well as a 3-D coloring book that George must be physically restrained from buying. Rather than continue to explore the entire store, we go to the information desk.

"We're looking for a book," I tell the information desk attendant, a polite young man no older than George or I.

Before I can continue, he grins and says, "Well . . ." and gestures to the whole of the store.

"It's a specific book."

"Does it really matter?" he asks. "Isn't any book as good as another?"

"Isn't your job to sell different books to different people?" I ask him.

He leans in to a conspirator's distance, his eyes lit like a zealot's. "Someday," he confides, "none of this will matter," the word "this" accompanied by another expansive sweep of the store. "Someday, there will be only One Book."

"One Book?" George asks.

"Yes. It's already beginning. Online. With search engines like Gooleg cataloging and cross-referencing texts, all books are merging into One Book. Infinitely searchable. Completely random-accessible. It's already begun, even in the non-cloud world." He pointed to an end-cap of *INsight* books. "All books are becoming more and more like *INsight. INsight* is the One Book in microcosm; that's why people of all ages all around the world love it. Eventually, it will be the only book."

"But if all books merge online . . . won't that put bookstores out of business?"

He shrugs. "Maybe. Probably. I don't care. I don't really like books."

"But you *work*—"

"I," he clarified, "just like liking books."

"I need a book by a guy named Barry Lyga," I say, giving up. I spell the last name for him.

"Who?"

I spell the name again.

"I don't know who that is."

"Can you look it up?" I ask, pointing to the touchscreen built into his counter, right at the height of his hands when they rest at his sides.

He shrugs, as if to say, *I've never heard of the guy, but if you insist* . . . and proceeds to peck away at the touch keyboard.

"Ell *why* gee ay," I remind him, noticing that he has typed in "LIGA."

"Are you sure?" he asks. "Because I'm showing two books with keyword: LIGA, one in Fabrication and one in Sports—"

"No, no. With a Y. I'm sure."

He frowns, re-types, watches his screen. "No. Nothing. Do you have a book title?"

I rattle off the titles from memory: *Inframan. For Love of the Madman. The Sunday Letters. Redesigning You.* And so on.

"I show a listing for *Inframan*," he says after a moment. "Published in . . . Wow, 1994. That's way back. That's, like, pre-*INsight*. Looks like it's out of print. And there isn't even an e-book version in our system. Wow. That long ago . . . Probably never sold the e-rights. You might have to try a used bookstore."

"Are you sure?" I ask, visions of trolling endless choked aisles of endless dusty shelves in endless used bookstores colliding in my mind's eye. "None of them?"

"Looks like *Redesigning You* might still be available. We certainly don't carry it, but we can order a copy for you. It would take about a week or so." He shrugs. "We'll see if it comes in or not."

I consider. Can I really wait the week it will take to have the book delivered, assuming it arrives at all? Still, of all the Lyga books, *Redesigning You* would be the one I would want to read the most, after *Inframan*, of course. I ask him to place the order, then give him my name and contact information. After thanking him, George and I go to the checkout register, where George pays for his books, handing over his Good Helper card, along with his money.

"InterBank Trust and Lending Corp thanks you for spending!" says the woman at the register. "Have a nice day."

By now, it's close to lunch and George and I are both famished, our sleep and eating schedules in states of complete disaster after the past forty-eight hours. We go to a nearby PopeYes![43] for chicken and freedom fries, where George flips

43. The Catholic Church's famed worldwide fast food franchise, begun decades ago when Catholics were not permitted to eat meat on Fridays. PopeYes! is best known for its various fish and chicken meals, and especially for its Eucharist Special, wherein registered Catholics can have the bread crumbs on their fried chicken replaced with communion wafers and thereby receive the sacrament while also enjoying a delicious, Church-approved meal. Non-Catholics, of course, come just for the food.

through his new picto-novel as I chew over my food and my thoughts.

"Yeah, it's the same story as the book," he finally says, shoving his copy of *INsight: The Picto-Novel EXperience* into his Books-A-Go-Go bag, "just with pictures."

"Didn't you know that already?"

He shrugs inscrutably.

We finish eating, slurp down coffee shakes for the extra caffeine, then sit outside in the sunshine. "So," I say, "what have we learned today?"

"We've learned," George says with no small amount of pique, "that you would have been better off dreaming about Monika Seymore. All of her books are in print and they're everywhere." He shrugs. "This Barry Lyga guy is no one, you know what I mean? No one's ever heard of him. Even bookstore people don't know who he is."

"Maybe we should try a library," I suggest. "They might have some old, out-of-date books."

"Or maybe all that's left of this guy is what's on the Internet, you know what I mean?" George is tapping his foot and strumming his fingers on a park bench at the same time, buzzed on massive doses of caffeine. I'm buzzed, too, but it takes the form of a near-constant, worried gnawing at my bottom lip. In the buzz, I imagine Barry Lyga as existing only on the Internet, as an electrical spirit, an electromagnetic impulse shuttled from server to server and router to router, his physical form destroyed and deconstructed on August 5, 2005 (hence the cover-up and rescinding of the coroner's report—there was never a body to autopsy), transcending flesh, ascending to a realm of sheer digital spirit, roaming the unbounded tracts of the Internet for all eternity. Reduced to his own story.

Homeless people mill and ramble around us, the park being their primary place of residence and occupation since GWB destroyed the housing market. Once Global War B is over, the president says, things will go back to normal, the way they did long, long ago after Global War A. For now, though, Americans are encouraged to be kind to each other during these difficult times, and to be Good Helpers by spending money to help the economy keep moving along; for surely if we ever stop buying, the terrorists will win.

"I can't believe that all that's left of him is on the Internet. He had a family, according to the Wikinformation article. He's got to be buried somewhere, right? There's *something* left of him. His books have to exist somewhere. In a collection or a" (images of endless and endless and endless bookshelves repeat in my mind) "used bookstore. Right?"

"Hey," George says, angrily and energetically waving off a scruffy man wearing a neatly-lettered cardboard sign around his neck that reads, "HOMELESS, NETLESS, NEED ACCESS. CAN CODE HTMLπ." "Get out of here," he tells the guy.

"You guys got wIphones, right? I just need five minutes," the homeless guy begs. "Just a little wifi. I swear, I won't be surfing porn or anything like that. I just need to get in touch with a friend of mine who says he can get me a job code-jockeying for a dot-combo in the Valley. Just five minutes."

"Seriously, dude," says George, the once and former Marine in his most Marine-like voice, "step off or you'll get hurt, you know what I mean?"

"Come on, guys. Please. My wife left me. I got nothing left. I got—"

George stands and cracks his knuckles threateningly.

As the homeless man shuffles away, I can't help but think about Lyga's book *Inframan* and the homeless character therein: The Electrostatic Man, a vagrant who crackled with electrical energy.

"His wife left him . . ." George murmurs, watching the homeless man stagger through the park.

"Yeah? And?"

"Nothing." George shakes himself as if he could shed distraction like drops of water. "I just . . . When I was poking around online last night, I came across a report from DHS.[44] It said that people aren't falling in love as much as they used to. Like, statistically."

"How can they possibly know that?"

"They're DHS. They measure stuff," he says defensively. "Like the number of marriages and shit. They went back to 2007 and found that the rate of people falling in love has dropped at least five percent per year. And it seems to be accelerating. And I just think of this guy's wife leaving him—"

"She left him because he lost his job. Happens to a lot of people."

"I know. But I think of my mom, too. She hasn't had a date in . . . in *years*. I can't even remember the last time—"

"George, your mom is—"

"I know. I know. It's just . . . It seems weird. What's happening to love, Mike?"

And I think of my brother, of his crush, of the way she did not reject him, but simply seemed not to be able to be bothered to accept him.

Of Phil.

"Anyway, back to business," George says, yanking back my attention, picking up his thread of what seems several minutes ago, though in fact it has only been the time it took to shoo

44. The Department of Homeland Statistics, tasked with measuring, tracking, and publicizing facts about the United States for its own citizens. "Because everyone should always be aware of everything, no matter how small or trivial."

away the homeless man. "If all that's left of Barry Lyga is what's on the Internet, you should be grateful, you know what I mean? I mean," he then continues, in case I do/did not know and in this instance I have scarcely had enough time to consider his comments before he moves on to his explanation, "most dead people who haven't accomplished much of anything don't have nearly that much information on Wikinformation. Most of them get a little blurb with, like, 'He was born on this date and he died on this date and he published some books.' But you got lucky—your guy has this whole page and descriptions of his books and even a whole page on his first novel. That's more than most people get."

Which is true. And which makes me realize something. To wit: Why *is* there a huge, detailed Wikinformation page about Barry Lyga? It makes no sense for such a repository of information to exist on someone who doesn't matter in the grand scheme of things.

"It's almost like someone put it there for me to find," I say out loud, and George appraises me with a confused look that mirrors my own internal confusion. I have wondered previously if someone else has been editing reality as well, and now I seem to have proof. The Wikinformation article could only exist if someone else is changing things, putting obstacles in my way like Inframan, but also giving me clues, steps to follow towards . . . what? I don't know. Who? That I don't know either, but I have my suspicions.

"He's still alive," I tell George with a certainty that shocks him and me as well, for until the words are out of my mouth, I am unsure both of them and of the concept underlying them, but once said, they make perfect sense and the idea undergirding them seems so blatant and overt as to be not merely possible or probable but definitive.

"Who's still alive?"

"Barry Lyga. He's not dead." I grab George by the shoulders in my excitement and pull him towards me. "It's the only thing that makes sense. Don't you get it? Who else would be putting that information on the Internet? Who else would be laying out clues for us to follow?"

George shakes his head, not in denial, but rather as though to dislodge recalcitrant notions and clogged ideas. "That doesn't make any sense. What does this guy have to do with Phil? Isn't that the whole point of all of this—for you to end up with Phil?"

His comment causes a momentary lapse in attention for me, as I flicker back to last night's intentional, forced memory of my first night with Phil in the garage-*cum*-game room. When I break loose of the memory, George is still staring at me, waiting for an answer, and nothing in his expression tells me how long I was lost in the past.

"I think Barry Lyga is the path to Phil. Look, there's this kid—the kid I told you about, the one from my dream. His name is Inframan. In the *Inframan* novel, according to Wikinformation, Inframan was a sort of extra-developmental personality of the author. He was a destructive and restrictive force, constantly trying to rein in Lyga's novel. So the book was a struggle between Inframan and Barry Lyga. Two sides of the same—"

Here another homeless person—this one a woman, grimy and gap-toothed—approaches, and before she can speak, George chases her off by flipping a coin at her, which she plucks from the air with unexpectedly good reflexes and then disappears to another part of the park, nodding her thanks as she goes.

"I've already met Inframan. In my dreams, but also on the subway. He's real. So why can't Barry Lyga be real, too?"

"He is real, dude. Just a real corpse, you know what I mean?"

"But in my dream, he wasn't dead! Well, he wasn't always

dead. He was dead, then alive, then dead again. So what I'm saying is . . ." I drift off, unsure what it is I'm saying, giving myself a moment to think and plan and plot before launching back in as if no time has passed ". . . that what if Barry Lyga faked his death. Maybe to protect himself from Inframan. And now he's in hiding, sending me clues because I can edit reality and maybe save him and stop Inframan once and for all?"

George throws his hands up in the air. "This still has nothing to do with Phil! And it's still talking about a guy who's just a writer, you know what I mean? Maybe he faked his death. Whatever. But how would that give him some kind of power to alter the universe?"

"I don't know! Maybe the same way I got *my* power to alter the universe."

"Dude, the coroner said he was dead, OK? They tend not to make mistakes like that, you know what I mean?"

"But then the coroner rescinded his report."

"That was just political bullshit because the family complained. Doesn't mean the guy still isn't stone-cold dead."

I fold my arms over my chest, and lean as far away from George as I can. He sighs, hangs his head, and slides over to me. Puts a hand on my arm.

"What'll convince you?" he asks. "You want to talk to the family? See the report?"

"I'll be satisfied if we can just start by looking at the grave."

George shivers. "We're not digging this dude up, are we? He's been underground for a few years. It's not gonna look or smell pretty, you know what I mean?"

"I don't know what we're gonna do. I just feel like I need to see the grave. Maybe there's some kind of clue there."

"And if we go and see his tombstone and there's nothing that's disturbed the grave, will you finally be satisfied that he's dead? And start thinking about how to re-edit reality to get Phil back?"

I mull it over. I don't know how many more times I can risk editing reality, lest the overwhelming chocolate syrup choke me to death. And given my past experience editing reality, I fear I would just make things worse, though how I can make them worse than Phil committing suicide or never having spoken a word to me that was not in anger and swearing out a restraining order against me, I'm not sure. Still, the cautionary tale of *Redesigning You* looms large in my imagination; there are worse things than losing Phil—losing my very self. Each time I've edited, it has been with an eye towards making a specific change to evoke a specific reaction. And each time, the unforeseen consequences of the change overwhelm or obviate the reaction. Even if I were to attempt to restore the *status quo ante*, would I succeed? Can I even remember every small change I've made and every nuance of those changes well enough to reverse them? It seems as though reality is not smooth and frictionless like glass, but rather—like brick—is pitted with perturbations, some of which are infinitesimally small, imperceptible, and these perturbations make it impossible to make the same change twice at the same moment and give birth to the same outcome. I am stuck.

"I'm afraid to edit the past again," I admit. "Each time, I made things worse, not better. It seems so easy—just find a moment that matters and change it. Make a yes into a no. Make A into Z. Black, white. But it's not that easy. I think . . . I think maybe only Barry Lyga can tell me how to use this power properly. And if I can use the power properly, then I can get Phil back. That's why I need to find him."

"Then you better hope you're right and he's not dead after all." George cracks his knuckles for no reason. "What's our next step? How do we find out where he's buried? And then how do we get there? But mostly the first one because I don't think there's like an Internet registry or a phone number you can call to find out where obscure people are buried, you know what I mean?"

I have already thought of this. My plan is dangerous, but necessary. "I don't think we have to worry about that," I tell George, pausing for the drama I feel is both incipient and necessary. "But I'm pretty sure it's time for a page to turn."

"What do you mean?" he asks.

CHAPTER 21

I take the risk, I say, "Fuck it" to myself and I close my eyes and now I'm down on my knees, nearly choking to death on the smell of chocolate syrup, vomiting up the chicken and the freedom fries, grateful for the combined grease of the two, for it makes the reverse trip through my esophagus smoother and more tolerable, as a fountain of partially-digested fowl and potatoes spatter on the ill-tended grounds near the headstone.

"You OK?" George asks, crouching down next to me. I find myself thankful as never before for the rank odor of my own sick, which cuts through the overpowering reek of chocolate syrup. I cough out more of PopeYes!'s Ten-Dollar Menu Special, wipe runners of saliva from my face.

It was just a small edit. Risky, sure, the way any edit is risky, but I wasn't interfering with the past this time, just the present. I wasn't really changing anything, just moving us from one place to the other. Just a quick cut and we're at Barry Lyga's grave, standing under a darkling sky[45] and I don't even know where the grave is, other than right in front of me, but vis-à-vis its position in the country or the world, I have no clue. We could be anywhere.

"I'm all right," I tell George. "This happens when I edit."

He helps me to my feet and offers a handkerchief for my still-damp and still-sticky lips. "What do you mean? Edit what? Dude, we walked over to the grave and you just dropped to your knees and puked."

"Walked over?" I don't remember walking. I remember sitting on a park bench with George and deciding that we needed to be here and then we were here, but clearly George remembers the intervening time. The sky darkens overhead—we've advanced the day along, assuming it's even the same day.

"I'm worried about you." George puts an arm around my waist, as if to walk me away, but I push him off. I risked my life to edit us to this point in the story, and I won't leave Barry Lyga's grave without some kind of clue. A clue to why I knew him in my dream. A clue to my power and his connection to it. A clue that will eventually lead me back to Phil and Phil back to me.

"I'll be fine. Let's check this out."

If I had anticipated some sort of monument to Barry Lyga, some spectacular grave befitting a celebrity or a king, I would be disappointed; since I am not sure what I expected, however, I am equally not sure what to feel in this moment, or in the moments that follow. It's a regular grave, one of an identical dozen or so in a line that stretches out to either side of it, leading down a gentle hill to the left and to a narrow road to the right. There's a nondescript sedan parked on the road, and I wonder briefly

45. Yes, darkling, not darkening. It's a real word.

if this is a car George and I have rented for the purpose of this trip. The license plate is for Maryland, and that makes sense—of course Lyga would be buried in Maryland. He lived most of his life here and died here; where else would he be buried?

The headstone is white-flecked granite. Dying flowers obscure the lower portion of it, indicating that someone has visited within the last day or so, leaving flowers alive enough that the groundskeeper has not yet taken their corpses away. I allow myself a moment to imagine that the visitor is/was none other than Barry Lyga himself, leaving a tribute to his own life and hoaxed death.

I lean down and brush away the flowers so that we can see the entire face of the headstone:

BARRY LYGA
SEPT. 11, 1971 - AUG. 5, 2005
alas, my Caring name

****

"Dude, what did you expect to learn?" George asks later, as we drive to the airport. I look out the window as he steers, realizing that I must have seen this scenery on our way from the airport, but I remember none of it. I want to ask George how we determined where Lyga was buried, but I know that the answer will not matter. For George, something—many somethings—happened in the liminal space between my decision to edit us to Barry Lyga's grave and our actual arrival there, something—or many somethings—that to him took time, but to me do not exist, just as for the longest time my own surname did not exist to me and yet clearly existed for the rest of the world.

"I don't know what I expected. I guess I expected more than

his name and dates—which we totally got off of Wikinformation anyway—and some cryptic bullshit." I fold my arms over my chest and sulk.

According to George—who, conveniently, spoke with the groundskeeper before we approached the grave—nothing has disturbed Lyga's grave since the day he was buried. The groundskeeper swore he had been present that day and had witnessed Lyga's coffin lowered into the ground and covered.

"Now I guess you're going to say, 'How do we know Lyga was in the coffin in the first place?'" George says.

The thought has occurred to me, I confess, but rather than admit this to George, I simply shrug. "I'm sure it was him. But I'm just not convinced he's dead. Guys escape from coffins—"

"He's a writer, not a magician."

"If I can edit reality, maybe he can, too. In my dream, he was dead, then alive. So maybe—"

"And then dead again," George reminds me. "Which means the last time you saw this guy, he was dead. Dead, you know what I mean?"

The taste of my own vomit, of PopeYes!'s chicken and freedom fries, still lingers in my mouth. I consider another edit, to get us home without the intervening travel, but the mere idea of the return of the chocolate syrup is barrier enough.

At the airport, we must wait in a long security line, yet another consequence of GWB. "The terrorists want to kill us. They want to kill us a whole bunch. Lots and lots," the president has said. "So we have to stop them. This isn't difficult."

The security line requires a careful scan of breasts (for female travelers) and groins (for males), ever since the Easter Bombers tried to bring down planes with plastic explosives concealed in breast implants and artificial testicles. George and I stand, legs akimbo, over the scanning station as a Theoretical Security

Agent makes certain that our balls are, in fact, original issue and not a combination of plastique and wiring cobbled together by an Israeli terrorist somewhere in a Tel Aviv laboratory. To our left, a woman is top-stripped, her large, obviously fake breasts scanned in full view of everyone. Privacy in such situations gives way to the greater good, especially when—as now—the woman in question has a pacemaker, which is the same way one of the Easter Bombers smuggled her detonator onboard the plane. I try not to stare; George, still military-proper, pretends nothing is happening and never even looks in her direction.

Before boarding the plane, I buy a little tube of TSA-approved mouthwash, all you can buy in airports anymore. I gargle it in the bathroom, finally rinsing the taste of PopeYes! out of my mouth. I look in the mirror after spitting into the sink and stare at myself, wondering what I am supposed to see, as opposed to what I am actually seeing, wondering how I would or should describe myself, if I ever needed to do such a thing. I don't know how I would sketch my appearance with words, which attributes are necessary and evocative, which are meaningless and useless. I am just me.

On the plane, I take the window seat and snuggle against the bulkhead, my head cushioned by my rolled-up sweatshirt, and drift into a sleep in which my dreams thrum with the background vibration of the jet engines. In the dream, I dream of other dreams, this new dream serving as a sequel to other dreams from my life: The dream in which a strange, orangutan-like creature capered and gamboled in my backyard; the dream in which I took the role of Luke Starkiller in *Star Wars II*; the dream in which I am my own father, brother, mother; the dream in which I have a magical cell phone that grants me superpowers depending on which number I call. And, of course, inevitably, a dream in which I wonder if I have ever actually had any of these dreams before or if they are merely dreams remembered in a dream.

And then, just upon waking, a flash of a dream within my dream. The Lyga dream. The one mimicked in *Inframan*, with the corridor of ice. He speaks to me, dead-then-alive, and I see the words on his badge again. In the original dream, they were scrambled, but now I can read them and they say:

"Clean is my anagram," I croak, waking to the stifling airplane air, to the engine-backed silence.

"What?" George asks.

"It's an anagram," I tells him. "I think it's an anagram."

A moment later, I've unfolded the seatback tray and begun scratching letters onto an air sickness bag with a pencil (pens being forbidden on planes, of course, ever since a terrorist used a box of pens to smuggle on board enough liquid toxin to kill two stewardesses and nearly take over a flight). "Give me a second," I tell him, shaking and blinking dreams and sleep away. "I'll show you."

"An anagram?" he asks. "You mean the thing on his tombstone?"

"'alas, my Caring name.' It relates to something I saw in that dream. The dream of Barry Lyga."

"Is it like that thing in English class they told us about, like, where the word 'name' represents something bigger?"

"Synecdoche," I say, startling myself with this knowledge, since English is not and never has been a subject of any particular interest or success to me.

"So, like, does 'name' represent him? Is it saying, 'alas for *me*?'

I look at what I've written. "God, it's not just an anagram! It's a freakin' anagram of the *word* anagram!" I point to the letters in the order they appear, from the first "a" in "alas" to the "m" in "name." "See?"

"In my dream, I saw the words 'Clean is my anagram.' It was

on his *name-tag.* 'Clean is my anagram.' And that's exactly what 'alas, my Caring name' says if you unscramble it. Or re-scramble it. I don't know which it is, but that's it. And the 'C' is capitalized in the epitaph because that's the first word of the real sentence."

"But it doesn't mean anything! And the letters 'm' and 'y' are used to spell 'my,' which is already a word in the original phrase. That's the crappiest anagram—"

He's cut off by the pilot on the speaker system, telling us that we are beginning our final approach and that, per the antiterror regulations occasioned by the escalation of GWB, all passengers are required to return seatbacks and tray tables to upright and locked positions, as well as to return any and all items to the seat-back pockets, remove coats, pillows, or blankets from laps, lower all armrests and place arms on them with hands in full view of the flight crew, refrain from sudden movements (lest we activate the motion detectors installed above our heads), and, of course, stop talking immediately so that the flight crew can focus on our safety and security without distraction. And so, though I yearn to continue speaking with George and working our way through the anagram epitaph from Barry Lyga's grave, I must remain quiet and look straight ahead. I continue to turn the words and letters over in my mind, though. Could it really be as simple as we speculate? "alas, my Caring name" becomes "Clean is my anagram." It makes no sense. Surely there are other phrases, other meanings possible.

Yet, my stomach and my heart and my brain all collude in convincing me—through instinct and through reason—that this is, in fact, that solution. That for whatever reason, *someone* inscribed a clue onto Barry Lyga's headstone. Perhaps it was Lyga himself, whether after faking his death and burial or prehumously via a will or similar directive. The words are there. They are concrete (literally granite, of course, not concrete) and real and undeniable. They are a puzzle, that much is sure.

It has been mere days since this began, a thought that comes from nowhere and strikes me with a nearly physical force, such that I nearly double over with the shock and pain and discomfort of realization, catching myself only due to the coincidental passing-by of a flight attendant, reminding me that any motion on my part could very well lead me to a federal marshall's handcuffs upon landing. Yet the shock remains: The charity auction marking the amalgamation of The WB and UPN into The CW was only two nights ago.[46] Two nights since I realized I could edit reality, two nights since Phil and I went from the restrained relationship of ex-boyfriend and -girlfriend to the current status quo, wherein I am considered deranged, dangerous, and obsessed enough to warrant a restraining order. Two nights only, and yet they feel eternally distended and extended, as though a massive set of complications has come into being between my moment of realization and the current moment, endless loops of cause and effect that have made forty-eight hours turn into forty-eight years, and I have the sudden irrational and yet completely reasonable and believable certitude that if I could look in a mirror right now, I would see my own face advanced into my sixties, that if federal airline regulations did not prohibit it, I could turn to look at George and see the same thing, his features accelerated through decades in the past two days, having aged for each moment I've edited and relived and re-edited and re-relived, not simply the actual moments of our lives.

We land safely, still young, though I realize now that I've lived the last two years over and over to the point that I feel the

46. "Two nights ago" to those trapped in the boring, routine flow of time/narrative. To Mike, it's been a recursive loop of repeated days and moments, adding up to no-one-knows-how-many additional hours and days of subjective time.

weight of their experience and maturation out of proportion to their linearity. I have done, lived, and undergone more in the past two days/two years than is humanly possible, and yet I have done, lived, and undergone it nonetheless.

"I feel old," I tell George as we disembark, allowed to speak now that we are safely on the ground. "I feel like . . ." Even though I can imagine and consider the acceleration of my own age, I cannot find the words to speak it. It is as though enclosing my thoughts in quotation marks modifies them, changes them from some higher narrative, translates them into a vulgate edition.

"You're tired," George says, and I surrender my attempt to explain to him.

On the subway home, George puts an arm around me and pulls me in for a quick one-sided hug, intended, I am sure, both to cheer me and to remind me that in this quixotic *For Love of the Madman*-esque quest, I am not alone; I am companioned.

"Dude, I'm only going to suggest this once, OK? You know what I mean? Just once. And you can ignore it or you can yell at me or you can whatever, but it has to be said."

I brace myself against him, knowing what he will say, knowing that he is about to tell me to give up, to surrender to the vicissitudes of the world and my own editorial incompetence. That Phil is lost to me and lost to me and eternally lost to me, not merely in the present and future, but in the past as well.

"Can't you just, you know, make everything the way it used to be?" he asks. "Stop trying to improve things or fix the past, you know what I mean? Can't you just put everything back to rights? And pick up from there?"

I sigh against him, then pull away. If I (re-)make the world the way it once was, Phil and I will still be apart. I will be back at square one, when what I really want is to be at square zero or square negative one. I explain this to him.

"But at least at square one, she won't have a restraining order against you. She won't be afraid of you. And you can pick up from there."

And I remember my dream, the dream of the child from the subway. *You can't roll it back. You can only retrofit; you can't recreate. Creation is only for him.*

"No. I don't . . . Look, George . . ." It's tough to explain. "This is tough to explain. But with all the editing and moving around I've done, I'm not even sure how to fix what I've broken." My previous thoughts regarding the subtle, microscopic perturbations and pits in the macroscopically smooth surface of space-time suddenly seem too complex and esoteric to explain, even to myself.

"Can't you just say—poof!—it's fixed?" He gestures like a magician releasing a dove concealed in a sleeve. "You know what I mean?"

"I want to, George. I really, really do." I shudder, thinking of Phil's obsessive love, thinking of the scissors. George's solution sounds simple, but so, too, did the expedient of making Phil never not love me.

"It's not that easy. I wish it were. But I don't know exactly how to do it. Every time I try, it's a risk. And I think maybe . . . I've thought from early on that maybe I wasn't the only one editing reality. I think someone else is interfering."

"Inframan."

"Yeah. Inframan. I know it. He's the one responsible for this. And if Inframan is stopping me, then only Barry Lyga can stop him in turn. I'm done editing. It's too dangerous. Lyga can take it from here."

"Dude, Barry Lyga is dead. You saw the grave yourself."

"Alas, my Caring name . . ."

"Clean is my anagram," George replies.

Words. Just pointless words, words, words, words.

****

At my subway stop, George offers one last hug, this one two-armed and slightly lingering. "Get some sleep, you know what I mean? We made some progress today."

"How did we make progress?"

"I have a good feeling about the anagram, you know what I mean?"

I chuckle into his shoulder and push him away, lest he miss the train leaving for his stop. He stands just inside the doors as they close between us, watching me through the grimy, sand-speckled portholes as the train accelerates into the vanishing distance of the dark tunnel. I turn and wheel my rollerbag to the stairs, tug it up the steps. A homeless man squats in the corridor, back to a wall, singing off-tune under his breath, one hand extended with a coffee cup that rattles with loose change. Overhead, a fluorescent light buzzes and flickers for a moment, then steadies itself.

"Anything helps," the homeless guy says to a rhythm only he can hear. "Anything helps."

"Sorry," I mumble, walking past, my breath quickly in-drawn through lips not nostrils so as to avoid the stench.

"Anything helps," he goes on in a slight sing-song tone. "Anything helps. Anything-at-all helps."

"Sorry," I mumble again, now past him, still mumbling *to* him, though not looking back *at* him.

"That's OK," he says. "Inframan bless you anyway."

I'm sure I've mis-heard him, certain that my ears or my

brain are malfunctioning in some small, highly specific way that caused me to hear the word "Inframan" when he was most likely simply saying . . .

Saying . . .

The overhead light once again buzzes and flickers. I think of *Inframan* and of Inframan and of the Electrostatic Man.

What sentence, what phrase, what random combination of words sounds anything at all like "Inframan bless you anyway?"

I spin around and pull my rollerbag back to the homeless man, who is garbed in a long, filthy trenchcoat buttoned high to his neck, despite the summer heat, a soiled and time-softened once-blue ball cap covering an eruption of mangy blond hair. He gazes up at me with eyes a surprisingly clear and penetrating blue, bright sapphire discs set in a coal-smudged, sand-scoured face. And as I take in a breath in his presence, I find that he does smell, but not—as I'd feared/assumed—of body odor and filth, but rather of chocolate syrup, an overwhelming, sickly-sweetness that causes me to think fondly and almost desperately of the air sickness bags on which George and I anagrammed and interpreted and re-interpreted the final message on Barry Lyga's headstone.

"Are you the Electrostatic Man?" I ask, crouching down so that our eyes are on level with each other's, ignoring the stench as best I can, though it causes my own eyes to water. "Are you him? What do you know about Inframan?"

He blinks once, slowly, and stares at me, then chants, "Anything helps. Anything helps," and shakes his coffee cup, jostling the coinage within, rocking his body in syncopation to the coin-cupped cadence.

In my wallet, I riffle through the bills, skipping the big ones as I recognize that this could easily be either a waste of time and money or the opening gambit in an escalating bidding war for information, in which case I am better off holding high face cards (in poker parlance, of course, not literally) as the bidding war proceeds; in any event, the presence of coins in his cup is indicative of his expectations, so folding money should impress him. I select a single and unfold it, holding it up between us so that he can see its face.

"Here. One John Hanson." I tuck it into his coffee cup.

He plucks the bill out and stares at the portrait of Hanson. "This is a one dollar bill?" he asks.

"Yes. Of course. What do you know about—"

"I can't take this shit/The money don't fit," he raps. "George Washington's green/This shit's obscene."

Frustrated, I take a deep, chocolate-tinged breath, reminding myself to be patient with him, but cutting him off nonetheless. "What does George Washington have to do with this?"

"One dollar bill/That's Oh En Ee/One meaning first/Georgie it oughtta be." He clears his throat. "One is first. Washington was the first president."

"Well," I say, thinking about it, realizing that he has something in the vicinity of a point, "technically I guess that's true. But, look, it's John Hanson on the one dollar bill because he really was the first president. George Washington was *sort of* the first president. He's on the quarter." I consider dipping my hand into his coffee cup to scrounge for a quarter for proof, but decide against it, unsure entirely as to what besides coins may stagnate in there.

"It should be George Washington," he says, upset dramatically out of proportion to the problem in question. He has just made a dollar and there is the promise of more, and yet he is stuck on the politico-historical issue of who deserves to be on the one dollar bill.

He stuffs the bill into the cup with a savage intensity that makes me duck-walk a step back. "It's bullshit," he snarls.

"This whole fucking place is bullshit. The money is bullshit. The history is bullshit." He leans towards me, recovering the distance I just put between us. "I'm from the fucking *real* world, you understand? Not this bullshit place. The real world. You know what that means?"

I do not know what that means, but what I do know is this: My calves are cramping with the strain of crouching down yet leaning away at the same time, and the reek of chocolate syrup has intensified, even though I have not attempted to edit reality nor even thought of doing so.

"I'm sorry I upset you," I say, trying to back away again, bumping into my rollerbag. "Look, let's just forget it. Keep the money and—"

"I could kill you," he says with absolutely no heat, but with the utter conviction of a lunatic, "and it wouldn't mean anything. No one would care."

"That's not true," scrambling to my feet, backing away, praying that he does not rise from his squat. "My parents. And my brother. And my—"

He cuts off my "friends" with a harsh laugh, glaring up at me as I fumble for the handle of my rollerbag. "Doesn't matter. None of it fucking matters! This whole fucking . . . Whole fucking . . . Fucking . . ." He struggles and finally spits out the word "world!" with a ferocious intensity that—at last—spikes a sense of clarity of purpose directly through my brain, connecting the terrified animal segments, buried deep in the evolutionary past, with the developed frontal lobe and the portions responsible for motor control and I turn, the handle to my rollerbag tight in my hand, and run like hell for the staircase that leads up into the open air of the city. Behind me, the homeless man rises from his squat, his lanky form unfolding like a shadow against the wall, raises a fist and shouts as the overhead light pops and shrieks and flashes white one final time before showering down shattered, rare-earth-phosphor-salted shards of glass.

I bang up the stairs with my rollerbag, emerge from the subway into the still-hot night air of the city, colliding with a business-suited man who wears the expression of someone who has just overworked his day, only to emerge into an overhot night and certainly does not believe that he deserves to be body-checked by a rampaging, panicky teenager erupting from the bowels of the city. I offer him a brief, sincere-though-rushed apology and keep running, half-expecting the streetlights overhead to explode, half-expecting the lights of the skyscrapers to flicker out one-by-one or, perhaps, to extinguish all at once, such is the fury of the Electrostatic Man.

I run three blocks, my breath a hot, sharp wind in my chest, my rollerbag bouncing along the concrete and ricocheting between annoyed, side-stepping pedestrians, charging ahead in no discernible direction, only so long as it is *away* from him, *away* from the mad look in his eyes, *away* from the persistence of chocolate and the insistence on George Washington. Looking back over my shoulder, I expect to see him following, traffic lights sputtering to death and car engines whining to a halt along his relentless path, their batteries dead at the proximity of the Electrostatic Man's bizarre personal electromagnetic field.

But there is no one behind me, save a cluster of angry pedestrians, some of them rubbing knees, shins, calves, or ankles banged with my rollerbag, all of them grimacing in my general direction.

Gulping ferocious inhalations, I stop running, gasp my shock while doubled over. What happened back there? Was he really the Electrostatic Man?

No, of course not. The Electrostatic Man is a character in

a book, that's all. The light blowing out right then—that was just a coincidence. These things happen. He was just a homeless guy, a homeless guy driven crazy by a life on the streets, as often happens, or so I'm told (or, more accurately, so I've been instructed via television programming). He's insane, prattling on about the real world and George Washington, and I must be insane, too, to be asking the insane for help.

At least I'm not talking to myself.

****

At home, I drag my now-beaten and -bruised rollerbag up the stairs, only to remember that, in fact, my bedroom is downstairs, as are all bedrooms in my parents' house for some reason.

Mom wants to know how my trip with George was, and I cannot even remember what particular sequence of lies I told her before we left for Maryland and Barry Lyga's grave, nor can I remember if I even bothered to lie or if I simply informed her that George and I were taking a trip and would be back soon, which option is indisputably possible and even probable, as I am nineteen years old and "my own man," in the words of my father on my eighteenth birthday (though he, of course, said "your own man"). And so I simply tell her that the trip went "fine," which is almost as meaningless as no answer at all and yet seems to satisfy her minimal level of curiosity. My brother—still alive, still not taking the role of Richard Grayson from *Infra-man*—practices his tuba/harmonica/electronic keyboard in his bedroom. He's getting better, I think.

Getting better, but still not in love. Hopelessly crushing, instead, on someone who does not (will not? or *can not?*) love him back. I think of the DHS report George told me about. About love fading away. Is it true? Can it possibly be true? Is love like clean water and ozone and fossil fuels? Does it run out? Is America running out of love?

Is the world?

In my room, I stall unpacking, instead flopping on my bed with a pad of scratch paper left on my desk, its top sheet curlicued and indented with doodles, none of them hinting at the illustration skills I've displayed in the/other past(s). Flipping to a blank page, I hesitate for a moment, my sharpened pencil point hovering like an attack helicopter unsure of its orders. My mind still knows and understands and anticipates the motions of drawing, but will my hand comply? Is my muscle memory capable of straddling multiple realities? I mutter, "Fuck it," and saying it makes me think of fornication, which makes me think of a curved roof covering, a dome, like the underwater hotel would have.[47] I think of the acrylic dome, a perfect bubble under the sea, the entirety of it a blind wall with neither door nor window, an improvement perhaps on the work of Étienne-Louis Boullée's work to honor Newton. And I think of the acoustics of it, of the sound of living under the ocean, of the context of it all.

For long minutes, I draw, at first lightly sketching the outline of the dome, then flipping pages and adding details. Electrical conduits and plumbing brought in from beneath the room, tunneling up from the ocean bed. A system of automatic cleaners to scrub away barnacles accreting to the dome. Special lighting to pierce the darkness at the ocean floor, turning the black of the fathomed depths into a personal aquarium in reverse. My hand moves on its own, translating my memories and my thoughts and my wishes into marks on the page.

Until I stop. Until I realize that air will have to be recirculated,

47. This is not the non sequitur it first appears to be—in the discipline of architecture, the term "fornication" refers, in fact, to a curved roof covering.

requiring pumps that will carry oxygen into and out of the dome, pumps that will have to be concealed so as not to ruin the illusion of living in a bubble.

Until I realize that—on a human scale—the ocean is not necessarily equally dynamic in all directions, and that an exciting environment one day may be deadly dull the next.

Until I realize that anyone paying a fee to rent an underwater room will also want to stay there, meaning food is necessary, meaning there must be a way to cook, but how can I provide a safe open flame at such pressures and at such a depth?

And thinking of fire makes me think of fire exits.[48]

My professor was right, regardless of the world in which he lives. In his office months ago, at the end of the semester, when he told me "That's impossible"[49] and wrote "Be patient,"[50] in neat block letters in my sketchbook.

This entire effort is impracticable. In its sheer complexity, the physics of it trump the economics of it, and in pushing past the practical difficulties, the economics trump the physics. Anything is possible, my architecture professor was fond of saying, with the liberal and consistent application of money. (This last prepositional phrase typically accompanied by a rubbing of the two primary fingers of a hand against that same hand's thumb, a gestural evocation of cold, hard cash.) However, this project—this madman's fever-dream—pushes the boundaries of both

48. Each state varies in its codes, but all have laws stating that every room in a building must be X number of turns and Y number of feet from an exit, in the event of fire or other disaster. In the case of a hotel constructed entirely underwater, the only exit would be straight up and out, meaning X=0. Y, however, would equal a number that would require careful ascent and depressurization in order to avoid the bends, a requirement that could also mean too slow an escape to save lives, depending on the type of disaster (flood, air filtration breakdown, or even the paradoxical fire under water).

49. See page 108.

50. See page 115.

physics and economics. Can there be enough money in the world to change the laws of physics? An interesting philosophical/financial question, to be sure, but ultimately useless and pointless for me.

Disgusted with myself, I throw the pad across the room. This is my fate. Failure is my fate. I will never finish the underwater hotel because it can never be finished. Even if I manage to reassemble some shambling, cobbled-together Frankenstein monster of a life for myself, jury-rigged with remembered pieces and skills of my old life, I will still find myself dreaming of changing the world and will instead end up designing the next iteration in an endless stream of mini-malls, gas stations, and single-family homes in suburban subdivisions. This should not surprise me. Failure is my natural state. I have failed in architecture just as I failed with Phil. Given all the power in the universe, I still could not win her back. I could not find the perfect point to edit, the fulcrum on which to twist and turn the universe and tilt her back into my arms. Like architecture and physics and money, there may be a way to leverage power to trump love, but if so, I am incompetent and impotent to find it. And if DHS is right and the implications of its report are as I imagined, then love is in short supply anyway.

It may be theoretically possible to build a skyscraper made of diamonds, but just try finding enough of them.

"You win, Inframan," I whisper, my head cradled in my hands. "You're the God of Failure, right? Well, then count me among the latest converts to your particular sect. I bow to your never-ending gospel of defeat."

The God of Failure has succeeded at last—he's defeated me.

And in my defeat, I must figure out how to move on, must find a new path for myself, a Phil-less path, Phil-less not only ahead of me and past the bend, but behind me as well. I need to survive in some new way. I will never, I know now, thrive, never find true joy or happiness, but surely there is a way to simply . . . live.

Without her.

George is right. I need to forget about her. I need to forge ahead. I will meet someone else. Maybe. Maybe someday I will meet someone else who will . . .

I want to forget. I wish I could forget. But I have remembered too hard, with too powerful intent. I cannot forget. I will not forget.

In a world of blondes and redheads and brunettes, there is only one shining sapphire-tressed Phil. I will never/could never/can never be satisfied with the dull reds and yellows and browns and blacks of the world when I could have/should have/did have/must have had sea-resplendent blue.

Poets and singers and authors call blue the color of depression and despair. But for me, blue is the color of love. Of hope.

Blue is Phil and Phil is blue.

I cannot forsake her. I cannot give up.

I retrieve my drawing pad. Physics is not to economics as Phil is to my story. The laws of physics are inviolable; the limits of finance are finite. But the fact remains that I designed the underwater hotel, designed it in conformity with the laws of physics and the laws of man. That there may not be enough money in the world to build it to those specifications is immaterial. My designs, my dreams, are solid and true and valid. So, too, is my design for Phil.

I flip open the pad. I begin to write. I write everything I remember about Phil—not just her physical appearance, but her way of speaking, the way she stood, the things she said to me, the ways she believed, the ways she did not believe. The faith she had in me, the way she wanted to change, the way she did not want to be the same person at the end of high school as she was at the beginning.[51] I blow through page after page, filling them with my neat architect's script, recording every memory, no matter how small, no matter how insignificant. Her fingers—cold-slick—as she hands me the first of many Mistberry Mysteries. The way she kissed me first, bold where I was contemplative, leaning in and leaning over. How she knew the very best gummi bears. Her shelf of "classic" children's books. Why did I not read them to her when she asked? I would read them all to her now.

Is this not the very definition of love, this recollection of every detail, this knowledge, so complete and so all-consuming? Is there anything else that could substitute for love?

I draw her as well, working from memory, sketching the first time I saw her, as a child, her beautiful innocence and round-faced insistence on being called "Phil." I draw her as the girl who believed in me at the lunch table, as the teen who came to me in George's garage-*cum*-game room, as the young woman who bedded me over and over in the history-made sheets, as the woman who came to me one last time at College Y for sex I thought would launch a new history and instead launched nothing but my own disappointment and, perhaps, set me on the path I currently walk. Under my pencil, on my paper, she becomes architecture. She becomes the expression of art and need and desire for me; she is shelter and beauty and abstract and concrete all at once.

And I know that I cannot give her up. I cannot forsake her. It's Phil. I love her. I have to be with her.

I put the pad down, suddenly overwhelmed with a sensation I cannot describe. It is not love; indeed, it has nothing to

51. "I guess I want to feel like things have changed. Like these four years weren't just some meaningless bullshit way of killing time between, like, puberty and college."

do with Phil. It feels, rather, like a ramped-up, magnified species of *déjà vu*, some familiar creature that has evolved to the point that what traditionally had been a nagging sensation at the back of the brain is now an unignorable, persistent gnawing at the very front of the brain, an insistent thrum, as though a subtle bass line in a song has been amplified to overwhelm the melody, the lyrics, indeed all the other components of the song. It feels familiar. Something is going to happen. Something is coming.

That is the last thing I remembered until the buzzing of my cell phone wakes me. It perches on my nightstand, and even though it is set on vibrate, the combination of the vibrations and the hollow nightstand make enough of a racket to waken me.

"Dude," George says when I flip open the cell, "are you at your computer?"

"Yeah," I say, groggy and settling in at my desk. "What—"

"Look, I don't pretend to get everything you were talking about at the grave, but . . . I tried something. You know what I mean? Go to Gooleg."

I type in "gooleg.search" and the search engine page pops up: the famous logo ("Gooleg" as seen through prison-like bars), with a text entry box and the legend, "Imprisoning Your Answers!"

"Try typing in this:" he says, and then spells out "Gayl Rybar."

"Gayl Rybar? Who—"

"Just put it in."

I go through the ritual of telling Gooleg all about myself, of revealing my preferences and needs, then type it all in and click the "Jailbreak my Info!" button.

"First hit," George says.

There are only a few hits. They all seem related. The first one is:

Gayl Rybar

(born September 11, 1979) is an American nonadult novelist and short story writer who is best known as the author of The Unlikely Tale of . . .

www.wikinformation.com/gayl_rybar

CHAPTER 22

"I was thinking about it all night," George says, "and I kept thinking about 'Clean is my anagram," you know what I mean? And it just . . . Well, I started thinking about that 'my,' which didn't make sense to me because who *owns* an anagram? And there was only one thing I could think of that Barry Lyga owned, and that was his name. Because that was the only other thing on the headstone. And the whole 'clean' thing made me think it was going to be easy, you know? Not like we'd have to go far to get the whatever-it-was. Neat and clean."

"And the name 'Gayl' is an anagram for his last name . . ."

"Yeah, that just sort of hit me when I was going through the stuff we were emailing back and forth the other night. And I found myself staring at the name 'gaylwriter.' Plus, with the two 'ys' in Lyga's name, there weren't a lot of other options for names. It didn't take long to get to 'Gayl Rybar.'"

"So, wait a second. Is Gayl Rybar the same as Barry Lyga? Or is it someone else entirely? Or—"

"Read the Wikinformation page, dude. I'm going to get some sleep. We can talk in the morning, OK?"

"OK . . ."
I click on the link.

****

Gayl Rybar

From Wikinformation, the world's finest infodump!

Gayl Rybar (no middle initial) (September 11, 1979 -) is an American nonadult novelist and short story writer who is best known as the author of *The Unlikely Tale of Geekster and the Vampiress*, published in 2006.

Contents

Personal Information

Gayl Rybar is an American nonadult author who lives in the desert. According to an interview in *Publishers*

Daily, Rybar is currently at work on a novel titled *Unfinished.*

Works

The Unlikely Tale of Geekster and the Vampiress

Teacher's Pet

. . . To Zero

Vampiress by Day: The sequel to Rybar's first book.

****

Another author. But this one is alive. This one is alive and has a name that—when scrambled (or is it unscrambled?)—is the same as Barry Lyga, who left the name as a clue on his own headstone.

"'My name is scrambled . . .'" I whisper aloud.

This is completely insane.

I lean back in my chair, its comforting creak as well-known to me as my own brother's voice. In this chair, I have sketched and drawn and written and watched videos and daydreamed and live-chatted and surfed and masturbated and, indeed, lived every facet of my life in one way or another. This chair knows me as well as I know it. I have no secrets from this chair, nothing hidden or concealed.

Gayl Rybar. Another author coming to me from nowhere.

Letters. Letters combining and recombining. Mixing. Taking

new forms. I am not an author, but I understand this. It makes sense to me, in a strange, unforeseen, hitherto unthought-of way. My first architecture professor at College Y—in another version of my life, now lost to my capricious editing—began our semester by wheeling in a cart covered with a blue plastic tarp. When she whipped the tarp away, we saw that the cart was loaded down with samples of an olio of building materials: A large chunk of concrete, a pane of clear glass, a pyramid of cherry wood, a delicate French curve of wrought iron, a smallish sheet of frosted glass, a cube of Lucite, an unadorned poplar two-by-four, a tin that—when shaken—rattled with a selection of nails, brads, screws, nuts, bolts, and washers, and more. "These," she said, "are the tools of your trade. You draw your pictures and you slave over your schematics, but at the end of the day, someone is—ideally—going to take those drawings and translate them into the real world as a three-dimensional space. I want you all to remember something." Here she picked up a piece of brick and hefted it like a pitcher testing the weight of a ball. "There's nothing new under the sun. I'm not talking about your designs; I'm sure you're all unsung geniuses with ideas the likes of which the world has never seen."

And here we all laughed a bit nervously, each of us certain that her sarcasm was aimed at everyone in the room except for ourselves.

"But," she went on, "no matter how wonderful, splendiferous, and blazingly original your designs, the fact of the matter is that you have the same tools available to everyone else. Your works of unparalleled genius will be drawn with the same pens and pencils on the same paper and then realized into the real world with the same materials as everyone else's. I see a lot of young architects who think they're going to change the world by the way they use brick or glass or wood, but trust me—it's all been done before. You make your mark by the combination of elements, by your unique signature, not by your simple choices."

This makes me think of anagrams, of how we all have the same 26 letters to use, how every combination has already been tried, and how the way we distinguish ourselves is not by choosing to use this letter or that letter, but rather by the way in which we choose to combine those letters into our, well, our signature.

I pull my pad back over to myself, retrieving it from the spot on the floor where I dropped it when I went to sleep. Within, I've assembled the warm, living architecture that is Phil. I feel as though I'm close to something, something perhaps better left unknown, and yet I've come this far. How far, I cannot say. I feel as though I've walked a million miles, putting one foot in front of the other for years, centuries, millennia, all to get to this point, all without knowing if there are another million miles to go or a billion.

Or, perhaps, just one or two.

So I will not give up now. I've come this far; I'll go further. I'll find Gayl Rybar and I'll ask her what she knows about Barry Lyga. I'll learn what I can from her and then I'll take the next step, whatever that is. And then the next step after that. And after that. Whether those steps add up to a mile or a million of them, I will take them all.

****

And that night, I dream again. Not of corridors of ice nor of the God of Failure (Der Untermensch, Inframan), but rather of something I've not thought of in years, something that pre-dates even the entrance of Phil into my life, a temporal distance I have not attempted to visualize in a long time.

I dream a memory of childhood, playing at the old house

where I grew up, before love's darkness consumed me. It was a tree-lined street cutting through a subdivision, ranks of near-identical houses on either side. On our side of the street, the ground sloped gently up from the road to the house, meaning that our driveway sloped down from the house to the road. During the day, when my father was at work, half the driveway lay open and bare, a stretch of smooth, perfect black asphalt, irresistible to a kid with a toy closet jam-packed with all manner of wheeled toys, including tiny die-cast cars, big plastic tanks, metal tow trucks and dump trucks, and the one toy above all, the *sina qua non* of my toy collection: An authentic Daredevil Levi 1:8 scale replica stuntcycle, complete with red, white, and blue flames along the plastic chassis and a fully authorized Daredevil Levi action doll to sit bestride it. Daredevil Levi[52] had parachuted from the StratoSpire, fired himself from a cannon over the width of the Great Canyon, and—in his most spectacular stunt ever—jumped the West River on his custom-made stuntcycle, this facsimile of which was the most prized possession among my childhood toys.

The stuntcycle came with a wind-up "Stunt-er-a-tor," a sort of launching platform with a series of toothy cogs and gears into which fit a corresponding set of teeth on the stuntcycle itself, said cogs connected not only to the stuntcycle but also to a small plastic hand-crank that—when cranked—delivered power to the cogs and gears, which in turn turned to provide

52. Early in his career—before the TV cameras discovered him—Levi performed at mobile carnivals around the country under the nom-de-stunt "Dread Levi" (sometimes "Levi Dread"), his cycle caparisoned in painted blood trails and vivid gory spectacle, his helmet designed to resemble a flayed skull. Once he made the transition to television, though, his look had to be modified to make him more family- and kid-friendly, as well as more palatable to a broad, mainstream audience. Hence "Dread Levi" became "Daredevil Levi" and what had once been black-and-red jumpsuits replete with pseudo-Satanic imagery became red, white, and blue, patriotic and sanitized.

power to the attached stuntcycle which in turn—at the flick of a switch—would lurch free from the Stunt-er-a-tor and launch forward into the distance and the future, bulleting ahead with the lack of care or concern for safety that is the hallmark both of dumb, self-propelled plastic and glorious madmen such as Daredevil Levi.

With my father gone to work one day and my mother busy inside, I went outside to amuse myself, Daredevil Levi having already bungee-jumped from the armoire in the family room and navigated the rigid complexity of abseiling down two flights of carpeted stairs. Daredevil Levi—and I—needed more of a challenge.

I decided that—inspired by Levi's stuntcycle-propelled jump over the West River—I would attempt a challenge of distance this time. While our driveway sloped downward, the road itself was remarkably level, perfectly flat for its width, though tilting downward in its length. Two lanes of worn blacktop beckoned Daredevil Levi and my imagination. Could Daredevil Levi, I wondered, make it across the two lanes of blacktop and into the driveway directly across the street, if given a Stunt-er-a-tor-powered running start from the top of my driveway? It would be a challenge; his momentum would need to carry him not merely across the street, but would also have to overcome the slope of the road, which would tug him down the street and—I noticed now with a thrill—a sewer grate that meant sure death even for one as skilled as Daredevil Levi.

I set up the Stunt-er-a-tor at the top of my driveway, slipped the stuntcycle into its berth, then checked that Daredevil Levi's scuffed white helmet was firmly in place. His hard plastic hands snapped onto the handle-grips of the stuntcycle and all was well.

Daredevil Levi in place, Stunt-er-a-tor cranked, I took in a deep breath and flicked the lever that released the Stunt-er-a-tor's hold on the stuntcycle. The revved stuntcycle whistled as it leapt out of the Stunt-er-a-tor, its cogs and wheels spinning madly, teeth grinding. It shot down the driveway at such a velocity that I barely had time to blink before it had already bumped over the slight berm and into the road, wobbling madly now from the bump, the presence and effect of which I had not taken into account. Daredevil Levi flew out into the street, still wobbling, losing speed, then dipped to the left along the curve of the road and finally collapsed on his left side, skidding along two or three more feet before coming to a halt.

Despite the failure of the stunt, I was still thrilled—Daredevil Levi's roster of scars and blemishes could now add a wicked case of road rash, earned in pursuit of a terrific stunt. I raced down the driveway to retrieve him, running into the street, where Daredevil Levi lay in repose, still clinging to the handlebars of his stuntcycle, his helmet still in place.

I neither saw nor heard the car until it braked, stopping almost on top of me.

I froze in the street, slightly crouched, one hand extended to pick up Daredevil Levi, poised such that I would have been run down and crushed under the driver's-side tires if the driver had not hit the brakes in time.

The moment was one of infinite slowness. In the dream, it is like turning my head through heavy cream, so slow is the action. In real life, it felt no different. I turned; I looked; I beheld a late-model American car, big and boxy and grinning at me with its grille. Higher up, through the windshield, I beheld an earlier model American man, a dad from the general vibe of him, a slightly terrified expression on his face, one that—at the time—I mistook for outrage and anger that I had made him stop, for so staggered was I by my near-death experience and so enshrouded in my own immediate guilt at running into the street without checking both ways for cars (a lesson drummed into my head by both parents on every conceivable occasion, such that it should have been impossible to forget, the urgency of retrieving Daredevil Levi notwithstanding) that I misapprehended his expression, imagining (with a sense of denial, perhaps) that he was annoyed at having to brake, not terrified that he'd almost killed me, said annoyance no doubt compounded by the precarious clutching in each of his hands of an ice cream cone, the soft-serve kind, one chocolate, one a vanilla-chocolate swirl (I can remember them as if they are right before me, so burned into my memory are they), him steering by use of his wrists on the wheel, such a chancy method of driving still not occurring to me as out-of-the-ordinary at the time, being still so obsessed with my own wrong as to overlook and ignore his own. He nodded to me once, almost curtly, his expression one of relief, though at the time I interpreted it as one of benevolence: *Go ahead, kid—collect your toy. I'll wait.*

I gathered Daredevil Levi, stepped out of the road and back onto my driveway, and waved to the ice cream-bearer as he drove away. He, obviously, could not and did not reciprocate.

Given that on that day and in those moments I came within inches of death or serious physical harm, the import and intensity of the day and moments faded quickly. Although I decided to forego future trans-street stunts on behalf of Daredevil Levi (repairing instead to the backyard to have him parachute from our elevated deck by means of a strategically folded, knotted, and tied handkerchief), I never spoke to my mother about my near-death that afternoon, did not run into the house breathless and a-tremble with adrenalin, never mentioned the car that almost spattered soft-serve ice cream along the interior of its windshield and me along the exterior. Nor did the event traumatize me in any particular way, as I grew up with no special fear of the end of the driveway or the street in front of my house or that particular brand of American car or even of soft-serve ice cream. Instead, I merely nearly died and then went about my life and my business.[53]

Even in the dream, I wonder: Should I edit that moment? Would it have made me more cautious, had I waited instead and watched my beloved toy run down by a speeding car piloted by the wrists of a man more concerned with his melting ice cream (for in the years that have passed, I have come to reapportion the blame for my near demise, noting—appropriately and accurately, I feel—that while I should not have run into the street willy-nilly [and probably should not have launched my toy into the street in the first place], his shoulders should certainly bow with the weight of a nontrivial amount of the blame involved, as a grown man should know better than to attempt to pilot a car while holding two melting cones of ice cream)?[54] Or should I have edited the moment so that he ran me down, ending my torment once and for all, preemptively and proactively laundering, as it were, the history-made sheets?

What did I learn that day? Is this all about me learning? What have I learned since that day, since Phil wore her teal/red/not-teal/not-red dress to the ball at The WB? I've learned that meddling doesn't make things better. I've learned that meddling has the potential to kill people, and that if I continue to edit reality, it will most likely kill me. But I've also learned that this is not solely about me. I was given a power that could kill me, but that power is not the only path to . . . to . . .

53. Daredevil Levi retired shortly thereafter, one foot amputated in a freak accident involving a pair of kitchen shears, a vise grip, and book of magic tricks missing a crucial page.

54. Especially the faster-melting soft-serve variety, and more especially chocolate which—being darker—absorbs more sunlight than vanilla and, therefore, melts more quickly.

To what? Where am I headed?

I realize that I'm awake, that at some point, some unidentifiable point, while dreaming I stopped dreaming and began merely thinking about the dream, the dream-thinking segueing seamlessly into a waking rumination. Where am I headed? Fortunately, this morning that question is easily answered:

I am headed to the bookstore again.

****

For the second time, George and I meet outside Books-A-Go-Go, this time not requiring the artificial boost of Caffein8! to cross the threshold. The store has changed not at all since last we came, save for the order of the books in the *INsight* series on the front table (*SightLESS* has a more prominent position now, as the videogame based on it comes out in a week) and the addition of a side table laden with *INsight*-branded playing cards, travel mugs, messenger bag straps, and pen refills.

We head to the Nonadult section of the store, mindful of the description of Rybar's work from Wikinformation. Given that Inframan has apparently blessed our pursuits thus far, delivering us failure in our quest to find a copy of one of Barry Lyga's books, I feel nothing but pessimism about our chances of finding a Gayl Rybar book at Books-A-Go-Go, but to my genuine and pleasant surprise, we find not one, but two of them, shelved appropriately: Two paperback copies of *The Unlikely Tale of Geekster and the Vampiress* and a hardcover copy of *Vampiress by Day*. The cover to the first is a bright green background, against which and from which glares a single enormous cartoon-rendered eyeball with a metallic-sheened green iris, the title itself rendered in a picto-novel-esque font that encircles the eyeball. The cover to the second is jet-black, with a sheet-white female silhouette embossed such that she extrudes from it, her pose and her poise aggressive and angry. The title is picked out in varnished letters, black against black, such that the words are legible only by holding the cover at certain angles to the light. Flipping *The Unlikely Tale . . .* to its first page, I read:

Of all the things I want in the world, there is one that I will never reveal.

I flip to the back. On the inner back cover, there is a short biography of Gayl Rybar, but no author photograph:

> The Unlikely Tale of Geekster and the Vampiress *is Gayl Rybar's first novel, and it pretty much proves that you can grow up reading picto-novels and still manage to accomplish something with your life. Gayl lives in the city in the desert and can be visited online at gaylrybar.com.*

"George," I whisper. "George, look." I grab him by the sleeve and pull him closer, which is hardly necessary as he was standing very close to begin with, yet I pull him still closer and shove the book up to him where can do nothing but read the inner flap. "See what it says? It says—"

"She lives here!" George says, elated. "Dude!" He one-arm-hugs me, crushing us together with an almost-intimate strength. "She lives here! We can find her!"

"Are we sure she's a she?"

"What do you mean?" George has already dropped his satchel and dug into his pocket for his wIphone.

"I'm saying—what if Gayl Rybar and Barry Lyga are the same person? There's no author photo, right? So maybe Barry Lyga faked his death—"

"And got a sex-change operation?" George asks, puzzled.

"No! No, dude, look, authors use fake names all the time. *You* know that."

He nods. "Sure, sure. But why—"

I pull out my own wIphone and tap into my CloudLocker app. It asks for my password, which I give it, then my favorite candy, then finally opens the CloudLocker. Within, I've stored the text of Barry Lyga's Wikinformation page. I flick down the screen, scrolling until I find what I'm looking for, then hold the wIphone out to him so he can read:

> **The Gospel According to Jesus (unpublished)**: At the time of his death, Lyga had begun research for this novel. According to his notes, it was intended to be a first-person, present-tense narrative of the teenage years of Christ, from Jesus' point of view. Lyga's brother said that Lyga often sarcastically referred to it as "my novel for young adults."

"According to Gayl's Wikinformation page, she's writing a book titled *Unfinished*. And Barry Lyga died before finishing his last book. *And* it wasn't going to be a regular adult book at all. And Gayl writes . . ." I gestured to the Nonadult section in which we stood.

"You think he faked his own death, took on a new name, and started a new writing career?"

"Is that crazy?"

He shrugs. "Only one way to find out."

Fortunately, Gayl Rybar has used her address as a privacy unlock in the past, so the information is available on a number of sites, including PrivacyBuster.sneak. After telling Gooleg that he prefers Caffein8! to SLAP when it comes to boost beverages, George downloads the Gooleg FrontMap of her address: a single-home, two-story bungalow on a nondescript side road. After telling Gooleg that he plans to play *SightLESS* when the game comes out next week, George gets directions. Gayl Rybar lives only three blocks from a subway stop on the Morrison line. It will take no more than an hour to stand before her front door, ring her bell, and—I am certain—shed some light on the questions that have plagued me since this all began, back at the middle of the story.

"Let's go," I tell George, hefting the books. I replace the hardcover on the shelf, but buy the paperback. It may offer some further clues at some point, and besides—when we meet Gayl Rybar, I can ask for her autograph, which should endear us to her. Authors cannot resist being asked to sign their work; it validates them.

We stop for a quick lunch at PopeYes! before the subway. George is halfway to his mouth with a handful of freedom fries when a voice interrupts:

"Hey, young brother. You gonna finish those freedom fries?"

We should be safe inside, but a homeless person has managed to sneak in past the courtesy guard and sidled over to us while we spoke.

George's eyes narrow. "Yeah."

"You sure?"

George bristles, his tolerance for being interrupted at its limit. "We're not done eating and we're trying to have a conver—"

"You too good to help a brother out?" the homeless man says, his voice rising. "You goddamned Oreo—"

George rises, his chest out, but the courtesy guards have already snapped into action, pulling the man away from us, hustling him out the door. As George sinks back into his seat, I experience a moment of anything-but-*déjà-vu*, the absolute certainty that "this has never happened before."

Young brother.

Goddamned Oreo.

Oh, my God.

How could I not—

My chicken goes cold in my mouth. I swallow. "George . . . Wait a sec. Are you . . . ?" I cannot believe what I'm about to say, to ask, but I have to. "Are you black? African-American, I mean?"

"Well . . . yeah. Of course. At least since birth, you know what I mean?"

"I don't . . . I didn't realize. Until just now."

"How could you not—"

"I just . . . I just *assumed* . . . I don't know why . . ."

But now it's as though I see him for what may be the first time in my life, see him in more distinct detail than merely George-is-my-best-friend and George-is-short-and-knows-Krav-Maga and George-was-beaten-as-a-child. I see that George is, in fact, black. His hair is shaved close at the temples, but an island of it rises like a close-cropped thicket atop his head. His skin is not the color of coffee (whether with milk or cream or not) nor is it any shade of chocolate or any specific species of wood. He is, rather, perfectly and entirely the color of George. And he has always been so. Yet until this moment, I did not know it. Until this moment, I had no way to know it.

"Have I ever . . ." I start, then stop.

He shoves more freedom fries into his mouth. "Have you ever what?"

I hold up a hand, staring at it, confirming that I am, in fact, white. I am white. Phil is white, though blue-tressed. George is black. My best friend is black. I cannot decide if this is progressive or cliché.

"What are you so freaked out about?" he asks. "You act like

we haven't been friends forever. The racial shit has never meant anything and now all of a sudden it does? What the fuck is that about?" His eyes narrow. "You're my best friend, Mike. You're my brother."

I am not his best friend, as I've been aware for a long time, neither I am not his brother, neither in the genetic sense nor in the sense of racial comradeship or political bond, yet when he says so, I feel as though either or both of these could be true someday, in some way, that George and I have a connection that transcends such simplistic notions as genetic origin, and that maybe someday I can and will perform some service or action that will make me worthy of George's best-friend-dom.

"Sorry," I say. "My brain just isn't always on line these days."

He grins. "Dude, don't worry. You're going through a lot, you know what I mean?" He finishes his meal, nods toward mine. "You want to wrap it up or are you going to finish now?"

"I'm not hungry anymore. I want to get going. I want to find Gayl Rybar and start to get some answers."

We pitch our trash into the receptacle, keenly aware of the cluster of homeless people watching through the window as my half-eaten chicken and fries tumble into and become/add to the waste. Those hapless, jobless, placeless victims of GWB, discarded by society and left to survive on their own, reduced now to nose-presses against fast-food windows, change-begging, wIphone-begging. One wears a cardboard sign around her neck: PUSHED BY GOD, NOT FALLEN. Her hair is blonde or black, depending on the sunlight. A pang of guilt—no stronger than her pangs of hunger, but no less real or honestly felt for it—lances through me, and I wish I had not dumped the food, but rather had offered it to the starving woman at the window.

PUSHED BY GOD, NOT FALLEN. Like the woman from my dream. Named Angia Eiphon. The same name, I realize now, as the woman in *Inframan*, the sister of the other Mike Grayson. Pushed from Heaven, if I remember correctly. Does that make this world her version of Hell?

I can't take it anymore. I can't take the world.

"We grew up like this," I tell George. "We didn't know anything else. All the people who lost their jobs, their houses, their livelihoods. It's just background noise to us. But each one of these people out there, they all have their own stories, too, you know? Some are long and some are short, but they all have them."

"We can't do anything about it. We can't fix the world."

"Can't we? Can't I? I can edit reality," I say. "Maybe I can learn how to do it right. Give these people their lives back. Reverse those statistics from DHS and let people love again." An idea occurs to me, one that quickens my pulse. "And if *I* can edit it, then I bet other people must be able to! Maybe I can team up with someone else and actually fix this fucked-up world!"

"Hmm?" George has been checking his messages on his wIphone and did not hear me.

"Nothing. Never mind. Let's go find Gayl Rybar." I take a deep breath. Just in saying the words, just in this moment of purpose, I sense a gathering about me, as though the mere act of deciding has placed me—George and me, too; the world, maybe—on a new, inescapable path, a path with no more distractions or divergences. "We're going now," I say. "I have a feeling everything is about to change."

"What do you mean?"

"I'm not sure. But I think we'll find out soon."

CHAPTER 23

"Why does it have to be in past tense?" a girl on the subway said. She was part of a cluster of students slightly younger than Mike and George—high schoolers, still—gathered around each other at one end of a nearly empty subway car, their voices carrying back to Mike and George, who had deduced that the kids were part of a special high school summer program in the creative arts, gang-writing a novel of some species.

"Because," said a boy with great authority, "all novels are written in past tense. And the good ones are in third person, too. First person is too easy." After some discussion—not heated, more like slightly above room temperature in that warm, non-threatening way good friends have of speaking to one another—he amended his comment to, "Well, maybe not all, but at least 90% of all novels," his amendment coming with no concomitant reduction in his sense or mood of authority. Mike wondered idly exactly how this boy had arrived at this conclusion, wondered if somewhere someone had actually undertaken a study of all novels ever written and calculated how many were in past tense, how many in present tense, in future, in present perfect, in past progressive, and so on.

Which line of thought led him to this: Sometimes, Mike thought, a change in perspective—in point of view, as it were—can be valuable. Often, we find ourselves saying the same things over and over again, using different words, different turns of phrase, but still circling the same meanings and interpretations. A change in perspective, though, can liberate us from that treadmill of perception, allowing us see the same things differently and to perceive new notions, ideas, and possibilities for the first time.

Mike wasn't sure what changed in that moment, but something had. The world had a new flavor and savor to it, as though he could perceive it differently. Perhaps, he thought, it was a side-effect of realizing or understanding or acknowledging George's blackness, that now that he well and truly *saw* his best friend for the first time in his life, he could as well see the world for the first time. While he was still personally invested in his life and history and in the universe at large, he felt as though he had perspective on it now, as though that which had previously been held forcibly and permanently in front of his face was now positioned at a slightly distant remove, making it possible for him to study it and appreciate it in some new and necessary manner. He did not as yet understand this new and necessary manner—except intuitively to perceive that it was new and necessary—but he instinctively comprehended that it existed.

He and George took the Bates line to the Morrison line, two subways that rarely intersected, but—curiously—in this instance provided the only way for one to travel from their specific Point A to their desired Point B. The trip was uneventful, for which they were both grateful, Mike because his life was such a whirl of nonsense and lunacy that boredom had become a fervently wished-for downtime, George because his devotion to Mike—while unchallenged and unwavering—could be (and had been over the past year or so) tiring in the extreme, so let us all thank God or Inframan or whomever we each individually worship for the power of Caffein8!. They sat on the subway and said nothing, George practicing card tricks with a deck of *INsight* cards, Mike flipping idly through the copy of *The Unlikely Tale of Geekster and the Vampiress* he'd purchased from Books-A-Go-Go, hoping for some illumination or explication, finding nothing of the sort. Gayl Rybar was a writer, not a prophet, and while the book was mildly entertaining, it seemed—in the pages Mike skimmed—to contain no universal truths, nor any indication of what sort of wisdom Rybar might be able to impart. What the book did contain was perhaps best described as a metric ton of picto-novel references and in-jokes that were mostly lost on Mike, who had had the good sense and mature decency to give up on picto-novels at around the onset of puberty.

(Meanwhile, next to him George thought about his blackness, about how it had influenced his upbringing, his philosophy on life, his dreams and aspirations, his fears and his certainties, all molded in ways that a white person certainly could never understand in any way beyond the most superficial. Surely a white person would be capable only of writing off George's blackness as something that had, in fact, influenced his upbringing, his philosophy on life, his dreams and aspirations, his fears and his certainties, without knowing *how* it had done so, like a blind man in the presence of a sculptor, able to touch—and, therefore, to perceive—the block of naked, incipient marble and the final, finished statue as well as any number of intermediary steps, therefore understanding that—through the offices of chisel and skill and eye—the sculptor has transformed block to human form, but never able to touch—and, therefore, to perceive—the motion of the hands, the decision in the eyes, the individual liminal forms between liminal forms. So would white people see—and, therefore, perceive—only the final product, the young, proud black man, without ever understanding beyond the most basic glimpses what led to that pride. George thought of this, then stopped thinking of it.)

When they switched trains to the Morrison (leaving the students to argue amongst themselves about their novel, now unable to agree on the disposition of a prologue and whether it should be identified as such or simply called "Chapter One"), Mike told George about his encounter with the homeless man in the subway station corridor the previous evening. He hedged his belief that the man had been the Electrostatic Man from *Inframan*, partly because he couldn't be certain (having read of *Inframan* nothing more than the Wikinformation page with its synopsis and character roster), but mostly because he knew George would think him insane for even suggesting that a character from a novel had suddenly shown up in the real world.

"And you really think this guy was somehow controlling electricity?"

Mike thought of the buzzing and flickering lights overhead. But subway station lights often buzzed and flickered on their very own.

"I don't know what I think," he admitted, sighing.

"Learn anything about her?" George asked, nodding toward the book, which Mike had open roughly to the middle.

"Or him," Mike reminded George. "But no. She or he sure likes his or her picto-novels, though."

"Huh." George shuffled his cards swiftly and slid them neatly back into the pack. "We only have a couple more stops. Have you thought about what you want to get out of this? What you want to learn?"

Mike stared at the spread of pages in his lap, and as his eyes drifted ever-so-slightly out of focus, causing the white spaces between lines of text to become overlaid with the text below, the pages becoming a confused mash of duplicated and shifted letters now gone meaningless with the motion. It made him think of the anagrams that had brought him and George to this train and this destination, and how the answers to all of his problems, to all of his questions, lay embedded in the book before him, for all of the letters used to create the words in those answers were in this book, if only he could unscramble and decode them into a more helpful form.

"I mean," George went on, "what if we get there and it's *not* Barry Lyga. What if it's a woman named Gayl Rybar and she's never even heard of Barry Lyga?"

"That's impossible. Her name is an anagram for his. There's a connection."

George leaned back in his seat and passed a hand over his right ear, where the scratchy stubble of his temple made a sound like dry brush, a motion he frequently did when thinking, but that Mike had never noticed until just now. "OK, let me blow your mind, you know what I mean? What if her name isn't an anagram for his—"

"You think it's a coincidence?" Mike bit off a curt laugh. "Right. Right." He could think of nothing else to say.

"You didn't let me finish. What if her name isn't an anagram of his? What if *his* is an anagram of *hers*?"

Mike let that sink in. George folded his arms over his chest and smirked with satisfaction and implications. (He thought, in that moment, of his three secrets, of how he had told Mike one, in what Mike claimed was another version of reality. And he thought of the second secret, which he should tell Mike someday, and of the third one, which he never, ever could.)

What if that was the case, Mike wondered. He'd been

assuming that Barry Lyga was the person he needed to talk to in order to understand what had been happening to his life, and that Gayl Rybar was just a means to communicate with Lyga or to learn about Lyga. But what if Lyga was just the flunky, the sidekick, and Rybar was in charge?

In charge of what, though? And it had been Lyga's books that matched up to Mike's own life—to a degree, at least. Rybar's books were nothing special. Well, to her fans they may have been, but they didn't seem to correlate to anything in Mike's life.

"We're just going to play it by ear," Mike said, disliking the cliché, but unable to conjure anything more evocative at the moment.

The train slowed and bumped to a halt. Wordlessly, George and Mike swung up from their seats and headed out into the station. Neither of them had ever been to this part of the city—Gayl Rybar lived north of their usual haunts, at the very end of one of the subway lines, where most people had cars—so they took their best guess as to which exit to use, finding themselves on a cool, tree-shaded sidewalk near an outdoor café of slightly European affect. Across the street was a newsstand, and even from here, Mike could see the cover to this week's *Interest* magazine, showing the young teen stars of the *INsight* movie series. He wondered, a bit puckishly—or, perhaps, peevishly—why the magazine had not changed its logo to read *INterest*.

"This way," George said, pointing, disrupting Mike's internal snark.

They strolled north. The café disappeared behind them, replaced at their side by palm-tree-fronted adobe buildings—a community center, a library, a laundromat advertising free wireless access in exchange for your clothes sizes. City boys for so long, they could scarcely believe how quiet and peaceful the neighborhood was, nor even that it was still part of the city in which they lived.

After a block, the buildings switched to houses, stucco-fronted, cactus-gardened. The palm trees lining the sidewalk cast cooling shadows on them, but Mike found his palms sweating anyway, and his upper lip beaded; he realized he had absolutely nothing to say to Gayl Rybar. As they turned onto the street on which she lived, he imagined himself moments hence standing on her front step, blurting out a stuttering, staccato chain of nonsense syllables, an anagram of mania, illucid. She would stare at him and close the door in his face, or perhaps—depending on her background and life experiences—call the police immediately.

When Gayl Rybar's address hove into view, Mike was initially confused, as it bore little resemblance to the images he'd seen on the Gooleg view on George's wIphone. He quickly realized that the perspective on the phone had been wrong, leading them to believe that Gayl lived in a large bungalow that fronted on the street, when the truth was that the building before them was not one residence, but four—a quartet of townhouses that, from a certain angle of the sort chosen by Gooleg's photographic team, looked like a single domicile. The doors to the units were on the side, facing a swimming pool that had gone slightly green for lack of chlorine.

They tried Unit A first, rapping on the door, but no one answered. Unit B was the same; unsurprising, given that it was mid-day and mid-week as they stood mid-way between the ends of the row of townhouses, and most people would be at work.

"What if she's not home?" George asked as they stood before Unit C.

Mike shrugged. "I don't know. If no one answers at C or D, maybe we'll try to find the landlord or something." On their way down the street, they had noticed a sign advertising "TOWN-HOMES FOR RENT!" with an arrow pointing towards what promised to be the property manager's office. "But let's try the last two first." He rang the bell at Unit C and they waited just long enough that they were ready to turn away when the door opened and there stood Barry Lyga.

****

Mike's voice wouldn't work. He had half-expected Lyga and half-expected a woman he'd never seen before, but he hadn't expected the face from his dream—the stubbled man with the heavier goatee who had been dead then alive then dead again. Nor had he expected that Lyga in real life would look younger than his Wikinformation picture. How, Mike wondered in that frozen moment of surprise, could he be younger several years after his putative "death?"

"Can I help you?" Lyga said into the uncomfortable silence, then arched an eyebrow as he spied the copy of *The Unlikely Tale of Geekster and the Vampiress* that had not left Mike's hand since PopeYes!. "Oh. Oh, are you guys . . ." He worried his lower lip, vacillating between two courses of action, neither one any less distasteful than the other. "Are you . . ." He sighed. "Guys, look, I try to be responsive to my fans, but it's sort of not cool to come find me at home like this. Autograph requests should—"

"No, no, this isn't . . ." Mike and George exchanged a glance. "Look," Mike said, "we're not going to tell anyone what you did. Faking your death and all. We just want to ask you some questions."

"Faking my death?" Lyga said with explosive surprise.

"We know you're Barry Lyga. We know you're writing under a—"

Lyga took a step back. "Are you insane? I'm not Barry Lyga. Barry Lyga died years ago."

"Right," Mike said sarcastically. "You just look exactly like him. What a coincidence."

"You think I look like Barry Lyga?" Barry Lyga asked, then rolled his eyes. "Why am I even talking to you? I'll call the Cops™, guys. I will." He stepped back into the townhouse and began closing the door. Mike's mind spun, already imagining himself re-ringing the doorbell and threatening to expose Lyga's deception, even in the face of police intervention ("How would you like me to tell the Cops™ you faked your own death back in Maryland?" he imagined himself saying with smug certainty), when George interposed himself between Mike and the door, one out-thrust arm holding the door open.

"We just want to talk," George said. "For a second, you know what I mean?"

Lyga bore down on the door, but George was stronger. Indecision flickered again in Lyga's eyes—keep up the stalemate, or let the door go and run for the phone, the latter of which would permit entry to the two lunatics on the doorstep, the former of which would most likely end in his own exhaustion leading to the same outcome as the latter in any event.

"You might as well come in," Lyga said after a moment's pause. "My neighbor across the way likes to snoop. She's already seen you guys on my front stoop. If anything happens to me, she'll be a very good witness."

"We don't want to hurt you," Mike said. "We just want to talk. We didn't know that Gayl Rybar was a pen name."

"It's not a pen name," said Lyga. "I don't know what you guys . . ." He sighed and pulled out his wallet, flipping it open to a driver's license that read "RYBAR, GAYL." "I was born Gayl Rybar. You're not the first people to assume I had to be a woman." He stroked his beard. "You *are* the first people to think I'm a dead guy, though. And you're the first fans to come to my house for an autograph."

"We're not fans," Mike said quickly. "We haven't even read any of—"

"Oh. Well. That's something an author always loves to hear." It was said with a tone that bespoke a humorous intention, but he was unable to ward off a biting undertone of bitterness, of anger, of disappointment. And, Mike thought he detected, of dismal expectation and resignation.

Inside, the townhouse was cramped despite a high ceiling. Before them was a leather and suede sofa that faced a large TV, while a galley-style kitchen and tiny dining area were off to the right. A flight of stairs twisted up to the left at right angles. It was non-descript and barely worth noticing.

"That's your real driver's license," George said. "You're really not Barry Lyga?"

"He could have had a new license issued in his new name," Mike pointed out.

"Guys, come on! This is getting ridiculous! Barry Lyga is dead. And he was older than me anyway. Do I really look that old?"

And the problem—as much as Mike hated to admit it—was this: Gayl did *not* look that old. Certainly not old enough to have been born when Lyga was born.

As he pondered, something amazing happened before Mike's mind's-eye, as he saw the letters of "LYGA" floating in the ether, gently moving as though pushed and tugged by soft, discrete breezes, rearranging themselves to re-spell "GAYL," and at the same time that the word anagrammed itself to and for his imagination, it seemed as though Barry Lyga himself reconfigured and transmuted before him into Gayl Rybar. The person before him had not changed at all, but Mike's perception and his belief shifted enough that what had been Barry Lyga was now Gayl Rybar. He believed.

"I'm . . . I'm sorry," he mumbled. "We started looking for Gayl Rybar because . . ." Mike trailed off, realizing how insane his premise was. It was not as though he hadn't had time to think about his situation—he'd done nothing but think about his situation for days now—yet when he had to explain it to someone who was not George, there was no entry point that did not seem lunatic. He thought of jumping in partway through, beginning with his discovery that he could edit reality. But was that a good place to start? It had a certain shock value, true, but was it believable? Was it a strong enough hook to get someone to pay attention to the rest of his story? He didn't know.

He looked at Gayl, who now had struck a defensive pose, arms crossed over chest, hip cocked, jaw set.

"We're not crazy. We're not here to hurt you," Mike said in what he believed was a kind, reassuring tone. "We just . . . I don't know where to start."

"Start with why you have my book and why you're in my house if you've never read any of my books," Gayl said. "Or, no, wait—start with why you think I'm Barry Lyga. I never even thought there was much of a resemblance, but maybe I need to look at some pictures again . . ."

"So you *do* you know who Barry Lyga is?"

"Well, yeah . . ." Gayl shrugged. "I read his first book in college. It had just been published—"

"*Inframan*," Mike said.

Gayl blinked. "Yeah. Not a lot of people know that book. Did you read it?"

"I couldn't find a copy."

"Yeah." A chuckle. "It's been out of print for a while. I still have my original hardcover from college." He leaned against the back of the sofa. "I just sort of stumbled over it one day in my college library and it was, I don't know, there was an old picto-novel once with a guy called Inframan in it, so I guess it caught my attention for that reason. I'll show it you," Gayl said. "Hang on."

He darted up the stairs for a moment, leaving Mike and George alone. "What are we doing here?" George whispered. "Does he know anything that can help us?"

"I don't know," Mike admitted. "But he looks like Lyga. And that's weird by itself, so maybe—"

He broke off as Gayl returned, clutching a beaten hardcover volume, the dust jacket to which was frayed and torn. He held it up to them; the cover was indistinct and blurry to Mike's eyes, but he could make out the words "Inframan" in an ominously-serifed font and the smaller "by Barry Lyga" at the bottom.

"They didn't print a lot," Gayl said, now thumbing through the book, which Mike could see was annotated with scribbles in the margins in various colors of ink. "It was a really small press to begin with; the editor totally believed in his work, so they kept printing his stuff even though he never really . . ." He cleared his throat. "Anyway. Sorry. I'm sort of a fan. Probably the world's foremost expert on this stuff—" waggling the book at them "—for whatever that's worth. So I go off sometimes."

"And you never realized you looked like him? Or that—"

Before Mike could finish, Gayl opened the book's back cover, showing the flap. There was a black and white photo of Lyga in younger days, specifically the early 1990s, when *Inframan* was published. His hair was long and unruly, down past his shoulders, and he was clean-shaven. He bore no resemblance to Gayl Rybar, nor to the older, more heavyset photo Mike had seen on Wikinformation, the photo he now wished he had printed out and brought with him.

As if he could read Mike's mind, George said, "Hang on," and touch-typed his preference for mint-chocolate ice cream over Rocky Road into Gooleg on his wIphone, then brought up the photo of Lyga, dated in early 2004. He held out the phone to Mike first for acknowledgment that this was, in fact, the proper photo, then showed it to Gayl.

Gayl shrugged. "2004? Yeah. Ten years is a long time, guys. So he put on some weight, cut his hair, grew a little beard-thingy there . . ."

"You don't think he looks like you at all?" Mike asked.

Gayl stroked his own little beard-thingy as he stared at the picture. "I don't know. Maybe. There might be some resemblance. He was the same age as me in this picture. We were born exactly eight years apart. I don't know."

He handed the wIphone back to George and smiled. "OK, guys, look. It's been fun. In a weird sort of way. But you've got one of my books right there, and if this is just your method of trying to find the strangest, most involved way to get me sign it for you, then you totally win."

Mike took a deep breath. "My name is Michael Grayson," he said.

Gayl arched an eyebrow and passed *Inframan* from one hand to the other. "Right. I think it's my turn to see some ID."

Mike showed Gayl his driver's license. George did the same, even though he wasn't asked.

"Grayson isn't such an uncommon last name," Gayl said, handing back the license. "And you're too young to be the guy from the book. And you're not a student at Yale. Are you?"

"I'm not sure."

If the response was odd to Gayl, he didn't show it. "It's an interesting coincidence, but that's all. You happen to have the same name as the main character in my favorite author's first book. So? That doesn't explain what you're doing here."

"He's your favorite author?"

"Yeah. I'm actually working on a . . . Well, it was going to be a biography of him, but it's turning into a novel."

"*Unfinished*," George blurted out, then grinned in embarrassment. "We read your Wikinformation page."

"Yeah, OK. *Unfinished*. Because he died leaving his final book unfinished. Still. Why are you here?"

Mike took a deep breath and told Gayl almost everything that had happened so far, getting so far as ". . . so we decided to go to Maryland to figure out what really happened to Barry Lyga," before Rybar interrupted, saying, "Whoa!" over and over in a mounting tone of urgency, the hand without *Inframan* in it held out to slow him down.

"Editing reality? Like the guy in *Redesigning You*? And the whole chocolate syrup thing, which is straight out of *Inframan* . . . Seriously? You expect me to believe this?"

As Mike struggled with the right tone and words for his response, George interrupted, speaking for the first time in many minutes to say, "Dude, it's all legit. It's real, you know what I mean?" and then explained how he had come to believe Mike's story of editing reality at the point of his own remembered knife.

Gayl shook his head. "There's such a thing as shared delusions, guys. It's even a part of *For Love of the Madman*."

"We haven't read that book," Mike protested.

"Yeah, it's convenient how you guys haven't read any of *my* books *or* any of Lyga's books, but you're somehow experts on both of us."

"The Internet—"

"Please." Gayl waved George into silence. "Do you think you

can learn what's in a book by reading about it somewhere in the Cloud? That insane One Book bullshit hasn't quite happened yet. There's still room for people who don't want to be subsumed into the collective 'literature' of a Gooleg search—" He broke off. "Never mind. Fuck it. You guys . . . You guys," he said at last, having given up on finishing the sentence, as though perhaps "You guys" sufficed to describe the depths of his confusion and annoyance.

They stared at each other, the three of them, locked in a tripartite glare. Gayl—once cowed by them—now seemed merely uncomfortable and exasperated. "If you want me to sign your book, cool," he said with finality. "Otherwise, it's been fun, but it's time for you guys to go."

"But we didn't even get to tell you how we found you," Mike said. "We went to Barry Lyga's grave—"

"Yeah, yeah, I've seen it," Gayl said dismissively, gesturing to the front door. "Time to go, guys."

"Then you know," Mike said excitedly, holding to his ground. "You know about the anagram."

"What anagram?" Gayl was still oriented to the front door, but the urgency seemed to have bled out of him, replaced with curiosity. "What are you talking about?"

"'alas, my Ca—'"

"'—Caring name,'" Gayl finished. "An anagram?"

"'Clean is my anagram,'" Mike explained, jumping in and describing the dream logic that had led to unscrambling the phrase on the headstone, which caused Gayl to chuckle and stroke his chin, nodding first, then shaking his head.

"If you took any collection of words, you could anagram it to *something*. It's kind of neat, I guess, but it doesn't mean anything. 'Clean is my anagram'? So what?"

George looked at Mike, who looked back. In the moments of their gaze, Mike made a decision.

"You never realized?" he asked Gayl.

"Never realized what?"

"His anagram. Barry Lyga's anagram. You never thought about . . . You don't realize what it might be?"

"What do you mean? 'His' anagram? People don't own anagrams—"

"What if it's an anagram of their name? Couldn't that be said to be 'his' anagram in that case?"

Gayl shrugged. "I guess. So?"

Mike was silent for a moment, unbelieving.

"We found your old website," George said. "From college. When you were gaylwriter."

"Oh. Oh, yeah. My first Internet handle. God, that was pretentious of me. I hadn't published anything yet—who the hell was I to call myself a writer?"

"You're missing the point," George went on, gently prodding with his words. "That gave us your first name. And we had *his* last name. And . . ."

Mike watched and waited for George's clues to unite in Gayl's mind, in his eyes. But . . . nothing.

"You really don't realize?" he asked Gayl. "You never realized?"

"What are you talking about?"

"You're a fan of his books?" Mike went on, incredulous, his voice rising. "You read all of his stuff. You studied him. And you never realized?"

Gayl blinked and in the microseconds of the blink, his entire expression changed from indulgent to stony. "It's really time for you guys to leave."

"You're the anagram!" Mike shouted. "Barry Lyga anagrams to Gayl Rybar! How could you not realize that?"

Gayl pursed his lips and shook his head. "You're nuts. My name is *not*—"

"Jesus!" Mike said, but George stepped up, pulling something from his pocket. It was a slip of paper, on which he had worked the letters of Barry Lyga into Gayl Rybar. He thrust the paper at Gayl, who fended off the offer, only to have George re-thrust it, this time more insistently, such that Gayl—whether by reflex or self-defense or intention—snatched the paper as George said, "Look at it! Look at it!"

Gayl looked at it.

His eyes grew wide and his nostrils flared and his lips trembled.

"This doesn't mean anything," he said, sounding as though he had a collapsed lung.

"You mean you knew?"

"No. No. I didn't . . . I never realized."

"How could you never realize that?" Mike asked, incredulous. "It's your *name*!"

"I don't know," Gayl said defensively. "I just never noticed."

"Right," Mike said.

"It's a coinci—"

"No," Mike said, as George shook his head emphatically and supportively.

Gayl stared at the paper, his eyes darting back and forth and up and down over George's work as though in so doing he could reverse the work, re-scrambling the letters of his name, uncreating the connection and editing reality on his own to make it so that not only had George never discovered this fact, but also that the fact never had been and never was true, that by some quirk or loophole in the very physics of language that the letters in "Gayl Rybar" and "Barry Lyga" were no longer identical and interchangeable.

"Get out," he said, and while it was not the first time he had ordered them out of his home, it was the first time Mike and George truly believed that they would be in danger if they did not heed him. So shocked were they—mutually—by Gayl's sudden aggression that while they fully intended and wished to move, they could not, causing Gayl to scream his command again, shouting, "Get! Out!" in hard-bitten, staccato syllables, his face twisted into a panicked rage that terrified them both and propelled them out the door as Gayl bellowed it behind them over and over, his cries of "Get out! Get out!" following them out the door and past Unit B and Unit A and onto the street as they ran as though for their lives.

That should have been the end of it, Mike thought as they ran. If this had been a book, a chapter—at the very least a scene—would have ended then and there on the drama of the two of them running from the ranting madman that Gayl Rybar had become. There should have been white space and enough of a hook to get the reader to turn the page, wondering *Did Mike and George get away? Do we pick up with them later on the subway once again, panting with exertion and relief? Or maybe on the porch behind George's house, which we have not seen in hundreds of pages/many months of novel time. Did Gayl run after them? Did he call the police? Or perhaps the nosy, suspicious neighbor mentioned in passing, in a tone too casual to be ignored, had already called the police and Mike and George ran straight into them, the next chapter (or scene) beginning with them in custody?*

He ran, thinking these things, asking himself these questions, his breath coming fast and harsh, George just slightly ahead of him as the residential neighborhood gave way to the library and laundromat and senior center again, the café hovering into view on the horizon, a safe haven, an oasis marked not by water and date trees, but rather by the single blue lamp denoting a subway station.

They tumbled down the stairs, oblivious to the looks of fear, astonishment, aggravation, and anger belonging to those whom they shoved aside in their haste. A Morrison train pulled in on the platform just as they burst through the turnstile and they launched themselves through the open doors.

As the doors slid shut and the train pulled away from the station, an old man sitting nearby sniffed derisively and enunciated in a voice that carried to every ear in the entire car: "Fucking kids."

****

Awkwardly, Mike found himself at home, alone, where he had not expected to be at this particular moment. And yet here he was, there he was, at home, eating dinner alone, the rest of the family having eaten hours ago, Mike arriving home quite late due to his and George's trip so far north and the seemingly wasted time spent with Gayl Rybar.

As he finished eating, his mother invited him to join the family in watching a movie, but Mike demurred. He did, however, stand for long moments in the archway leading from the kitchen to the family room, watching his parents and his brother as they in turn watched the TV, their attentions wholly captivated by whatever transpired on the screen.

He loved them, he knew, but at a remove. He loved them in the way children loved grandparents they never saw, relatives who lived far away and visited infrequently, randomly, capriciously. Yet they were his immediate family, the people closest to him on the planet in terms of DNA and relations, in terms of both nature and nurture. Why, then, did he feel closer to George than to them? Why, then, did he feel closer to Phil? Why did he feel that he knew more about Barry Lyga and Gayl Rybar than he knew about his own family? His love for them was abstract, unproven and untested, assumed and stipulated. A fierce loathing aroused deep within him, and Mike realized with no shock at all that the loathing was directed at himself: He had been so obsessed with Phil that he had neglected his own family, had treated George shabbily—he realized, belatedly, in retrospect—and had dragged his best friend along on a mission to a dead man's grave and then to disturbing the peace of a man they'd never met before.

Should he say something to them? He felt he should. The world seemed to have changed in some manner both subtle and monumental today, and Mike felt as though he'd moved from one chapter of his tale to another, the delineation only visible and knowable in retrospect. Furthermore, he felt another change coming, the way the ground hums to one's feet at the approach of a train that is still invisible around a corner, another change, this one perhaps irreversible, this one perhaps leading him to a world where he would never see his family again, never hear his brother play his preferred instrument.

"I love you guys," he said into the family room.

"Shh," his mother admonished.

That, Mike decided, was not wholly undeserved and was entirely appropriate.

****

His bedroom was now a welter of notepads and drawings, papers scattered and strewn everywhere, sketches of Phil staring back at him from the floor and the bed and the desk and the walls, where he'd pinned them, his own handwriting inscribing their multiple realities in a chaotic ring around the room, a hydra-headed tale that had not yet ended, not if Mike had anything to say about it. In the midst of it all was the original drawing of the elevator building, the sketch from eighth grade that had—in every reality thus far—drawn Phil to him at the lunch table, in this one for his manic declaration of love that ruined everything. He'd kept it all these years.

Of course he had. It was his totem. His Phil-summoner.

There were no other architectural drawings. This version of himself had never drawn such again after Phil's panicked, wholly understandable, freak-out.

He lacked the energy to clean up the papers or to organize them, so instead he simply cleared a spot on his bed and lay back, staring up at the ceiling, thinking how clever, foresighted, and symbolic it would have been if he had affixed something there as a child—perhaps glow-in-dark star decals mapping out the southern sky (everyone loves glow-in-the-dark stars on the ceiling)—that he could see now, something that would add some color and history to this moment, and yet his child-self disappointed him, for the ceiling was nothing more than a generic, white pebbled texture, with a black scuff where Mike had once thrown a shoe in anger over some parental infraction he could no longer recall.

Perhaps he could imagine the scuff to be a comet.

He stared at the comet and wondered—what if Gayl's shock was a charade? What if Gayl Rybar was, in fact, Barry Lyga, having faked his own death years ago and somehow rejuvenated himself (no doubt a man who rejects his old life sheds years and gains fresh vitality in the new one) into an existence which he felt would . . . would . . . Would what? Would allow him some success or happiness he'd not had under his own name? If he merely wanted to write different books—better books? more successful books?—why not simply use a pen name? Why go through the complexity and stress of faking his own death and building a wholly new life in the city? And now—in what was surely the world's pre-eminent example of self-absorption and egoism beyond the wildest dreams of Narcissus—he was pretending to be someone else while writing a book about himself. What a fucking egomaniac! What monumental self-indulgence!

But no. Gayl's anger and shock had seemed real. As real as anything else Mike could sense. As real as anything he could touch. Gayl really had had—prior to George's forcing of the sheet of paper on him—no idea that his name was an anagram of Barry Lyga's, meaning that Gayl Rybar and Barry Lyga were two separate and distinct entities, different and discrete people, separated not only by eight years of life, but also by the distance between the city and Maryland, as well as by the nearness/remoteness of death. And if that were true—and Mike suspected it was with a brawny suspicion that toed the border into absolute certitude—then it raised the disturbing question of how and why Gayl's name ended up as an anagram of Lyga's, and, further, how and why Lyga (or whomever had inscribed the headstone) had left a clue to Gayl at his grave. For what purpose would a dead man direct people to someone he'd never met, never spoken to, never, indeed, known existed, as Gayl's first book had been published more than a year after Lyga's death?

Was it possible that Barry Lyga wasn't merely a writer of obscure fictions? Was he something more? Mike had, after all, the power to edit reality. What if Lyga—like Mike, like (apparently) Inframan—had this power as well? What if he was a cautionary tale, having edited reality to the point that he died years ago, leaving his dark doppelgänger, the Untermensch, to roam the world with an ice cream cone, leaving Gayl Rybar—perhaps a clue; perhaps a leftover remnant of some whimsical edit—to walk among the rest of what Lyga may have come to see as nothing more than "characters" in some tale he was telling.

While he knew many things *almost* for sure and suspected that he was sure of them, deep down, there was one thing Mike knew that he knew for sure: That Gayl had been genuinely shocked and distraught at the revelation that his name was a scramble of Lyga's. Clean was Lyga's anagram, but dirty and low and mean was its revelation to Gayl. Mike didn't know what any of it meant and despaired of ever finding out, as Gayl would certainly never speak to George or Mike again, thus closing off that avenue of inquiry and knowledge, forcing Mike to think fiercely and futilely about what his next move could possibly be, despairing that there were, in fact, no further moves possible, at which point the phone rang, with Gayl Rybar at the other end.

CHAPTER 24

"How did you get my phone number?" Mike asked.

"From *Inframan*," said Gayl.

Something about Gayl's voice was slightly different in some ineffable way that Mike could not identify. "You mean the book?" Mike asked. "Or are you just emphasizing the name of the guy?"

There was a protracted, breathing-filled pause that concluded with Gayl saying, in a strangled voice, "There's a scene in *Inframan* . . . where Mike's phone number . . . I called it. And it was you."

Mike sat up straight in his bed, rustling a particularly lascivious sketch of Phil reclining in a wanton pose of charcoal concupiscence conjured from the horniest depths of Mike's memories of the history-made sheets.

"There was a real phone number in the book? And it's mine?"

"It could be a coincidence," Gayl said in a tone that communicated both his own disbelief in that particular theory as well as his fervent, pitiable yearning to believe it.

"I don't think so," Mike said, wondering how on earth an

author who had died when Mike was a child, years before he ever had a cell phone, had managed to predict the phone number, "and neither do you."

"No. No, I don't," Gayl said, his voice surrendering. "I don't know what to think anymore, Mike. I can't even believe I'm talking to Mike Grayson, of all people. You say you're not a student at Yale?"

"I'm not sure," Mike said. "I go to College Y. Or did. Sort of. Is it the same place?"

"Do you want to be a police officer?" Gayl ignored the question and pushed through commandingly in a new tone of assertion—Mike had the distinct impression that he was reading off a list of questions and thoughts, that even though making this phone call forced him to question his own sanity, he was determined to work his way from the top of the list to the bottom, no matter the consequences.

"A police officer? No."

"Do you have a sister? Preferably adopted?"

"No."

"A brother?"

"Yes," Mike said quickly, tiring of this game, "and he's not dead. He wasn't killed by a drunk driver. I don't think I'm the Mike from the book."

"I have more questions—"

"Look, Gayl, we're not . . . What are you thinking? Do you think we're . . ." He laughed suddenly at the thought that occurred to him; he resolved not to vocalize it, not to let it out into the open air, yet his mouth was already working, running ahead of his brain: "Do you think we're somehow *living Inframan*? That we're inside Lyga's book?"

He expected a hearty return laugh, but was met with silence. "I don't know what to think," Gayl said eventually, his voice broken and no longer commanding. "I . . . I spent the day with that goddamn piece of paper. Staring at it. Scrambling the letters. I was on a website for hours, some kind of anagram engine, trying to find . . . Trying to find other things my name could . . ."

A swell of pity and fellowship burgeoned within Mike; he knew how disorienting, how devastating this could be, this discovery that the world was not, in fact, as had been assumed and that—further and worse—while being different from its hitherto assumed form, the world's new form was not in any way immediately comprehensible. A notion—long-held and life-long—had been ripped away, with nothing to replace it.

"But there's nothing," Gayl went on, and Mike thought he detected a sob in the older man's voice. "There's nothing. This has been my name my whole life, Mike. It's on my birth certificate. I checked with my brother, Liam—he doesn't remember any other name from when we were kids.

"Barry Lyga was eight years old when I was born, Mike!" Gayl thundered. "He was a kid! Why would my parents name me with his anagram? They wouldn't," he bulled through, cutting off Mike, who had been ready to say nothing more helpful or insightful than "I don't know, man," "and they couldn't, which means it has to be a coincidence, but that's just an insane level of coincidence. For me to have his name as my anagram, then to grow up and study his work and never—not once, not a single goddamn time—to realize that we're anagrams for each other . . . Mike, it just . . ."

He trailed off, leaving Mike to step into the vacuum.

"I've been thinking," he said, and told Gayl his theory that Lyga, too, had developed the power to edit reality and had done so in such a way as to lead to his own death.

"Meaning I'm what?" Gayl asked. "A clue? A warning?"

"I don't know," Mike admitted. "Your name could be anything, almost."

"What if . . ." Gayl offered tentatively, ". . . it's not just my name? What if it's me? What if I didn't exist at all until Barry Lyga created me?"

Mike shivered. "That's crazy talk. When I was editing reality, I wasn't creating anything. I was just changing the things I did and said at certain points in my past. I wasn't creating anything. That's how it works, right?"

As he said it, his own words jostled loose something he'd read on Wikinformation, in the description of *Inframan* and of Inframan:

> Inframan turns out to be another version of Lyga (or, perhaps, a split personality) who exercises strict editorial restraint to counterbalance Lyga's creative whims.

Inframan's power was not to create. It was only to edit. The same as Mike. Did that mean that Mike *was* Inframan? Somehow? Had he—

A sob broke loose from the other end of the line; Mike swallowed hard at the sound of it. When had he last heard a grown man weep? He couldn't remember ever experiencing that. An old song flitted through him: *Big boys don't cry . . .* a falsetto warbled.

Gayl recovered. "I'm saying, what if I didn't exist until just now? I think . . . I mean, I remember my childhood, but what if I didn't really exist until you came to see me?"

"Barry Lyga is dead. You're a real person." He thought back to his conversation with George at Crimson Rocks, where he had proposed exactly what Gayl now proposed—that he and

George had no pasts, no histories, that they had come into existence only recently. Somehow, he now found himself arguing George's position, and he realized that he wasn't just trying to persuade Gayl of his own reality; he was trying to convince himself as well.

"You just told me that you remember your childhood, right?" he went on. "That's a good thing."

"But what if those memories are just made up?"

"Gayl, look: Tell me one of your memories. Tell me something that's uniquely you. That will prove that you're real."

He could imagine Gayl nodding his head slowly. "OK. OK, sure, that makes sense." He chuckled. "OK, this is the first one to come to mind. This might be a little before your time. Have you ever heard of Daredevil Levi?"

Mike laughed with relief. "Yeah. Of course. I even had a Daredevil Levi action doll when I was a kid."

"So did I!" Gayl exclaimed. "That's actually what this story is about. See, when I was a kid, I had Levi and the stuntcycle and there was this thing—"

"The Stunt-er-a-tor," Mike guessed.

"Exactly! Anyway, we had this driveway that sort of sloped down to the road. And one day I decided to crank up the Stunt-er-a-tor and see if I could get Daredevil Levi to zoom down the driveway and all the way across the street at one shot. So—"

Mike, suddenly cold and gritting his teeth to keep them from clacking, moaned unintelligibly into the phone, unable to form words worth speaking or hearing until—after several such moans—he managed to say, "Stop. Just stop."

"But I was telling you—"

"The man with the ice cream cones didn't hit you," Mike said.

Gayl said only, "Oh, Jesus."

"I think we need to sit down together," Mike said.

****

They met at Books-A-Go-Go, which turned out—in a coincidence that none of them even bothered expending the energy to note or question—to be equidistant from all three houses. "Three" because Mike asked George to come along as well, thinking that George's perspective might be helpful, especially since Mike and Gayl's perspectives seemed to originate in similar—if not identical—circumstances. Books-A-Go-Go had a smallish coffee bar near the Gifts and Coolness section, and there the three of them gathered around a triangular table, each wearing his own expression of grim determination and bafflement.

"From what you've told me," Gayl said, bobbing an herbal tea bag up and down in his tea cup, "it doesn't sound like you're the Mike Grayson from *Inframan*. Not exactly, at least."

"Why would I be?" Mike asked. "I'm not in a book."

"But—"

"Wait," George interrupted. "Wait. What are we thinking here? What do we know for sure? Before we get into theories and shit, shouldn't we figure out what we know for sure? You know what I mean?"

Gayl nodded warily and—Mike thought—grudgingly, as if he'd made up his mind already and could not be bothered with facts or information or the scientific method.

"Go," George said, cocking an imaginary pistol at Mike.

Mike took a deep breath. "OK. I can edit reality. At first, it was easy, but the more I did it, the more I started smelling and then choking on the smell of chocolate syrup."

"In the book," Gayl interjected, "Inframan smells like chocolate syrup."

Once again, Mike wondered: Did he have Inframan's power? And why?

"It was too much," Mike said. "I know this sounds sort of silly, but the smell of it . . ." He choked a little with the memory of it. "The smell was like a physical thing. Like something lodged in my throat. I couldn't breathe. The last time I did it . . . The last time I did it, it nearly killed me."

"And on top of that, you were fucking things up worse and worse every time you tried," George pointed out.

"Yeah, that's true. So the upshot is that I'm not editing anymore. I'm done with that," Mike insisted. "But maybe it's possible that Lyga had the power to edit reality, too—and he put the bit about chocolate syrup into *Inframan* because it's what he experienced."

"Why chocolate syrup?" George asked. "Is there anything in the book about that?"

Gayl shrugged. "It's never explained explicitly, but I always thought that it was a metaphor for the way something that's assumed to be good can be detrimental as well. Chocolate syrup seems harmless, but if you had enough of it, yeah, it would be cloying. Sickening."

George thrummed his fingertips on the table. "Dude," he said to Mike, "are you sure you're not subconsciously editing things right now?"

"No. I mean, yes, I'm sure; no, I'm not editing."

"You're positive?"

"I'm positive."

"Look," Gayl broke in, "recapping what we know isn't going to help us. We need to figure out something new. Somehow, Mike and I share an identical memory from childhood."

"So are there any other similarities between us?" Mike asked, leaning forward.

"I guess you're not married," Gayl joked.

"No. Are you?"

Gayl shook his head. "No. I'm not even seeing anyone."

"Neither am I." They looked at each other. "Why aren't you seeing anyone?" Mike asked.

Gayl sighed and leaned back, clearly stalling. "Have you guys seen this report that came out a couple of days ago? From the Department of Homeland Statistics?"

Mike and George exchanged a look. "Go on," Mike said cautiously.

"It says that . . . Well, it basically says that no one's falling in love anymore. It doesn't come right out and say it, but that's what you get when you read between the lines. They culled all this data from the census and from advertising patterns and from Gooleg data-scraping. I sort of became obsessed with this. I started looking into the underlying research and there's something in the report that they never really brought to light: The downturn in people falling in love started in 2007." He gazed at them, his voice rising, his expression more animated, almost desperately so. "It all started after Lucky Sevens, don't you see? After Lucky Sevens, people stopped falling in love. And maybe someday there will be no more love in the world. And maybe—"

"Gayl," Mike said quietly. "You didn't answer my question."

Gayl opened his mouth as though to deny it, but then nodded slowly. "Yeah. Yeah, I know."

"Why aren't you seeing anyone?"

"After Lucky Sevens—"

"No. No more about Lucky Sevens and the DHS report and love leaving the world. Why aren't you—you, the individual—seeing anyone?"

"I broke up with her," Gayl admitted, struggling with the words. "It was stupid. My dad died; I had a big movie deal fall through . . . I was in a bad place and I didn't think I could handle the relationship. I moved here and I broke up with her." He rubbed at his eyes. "When that report came out, I thought maybe that was my excuse. Maybe it wasn't my fault that I broke up with her. Maybe—"

"I broke up with my girlfriend, too," Mike said. "And it was stupid, believe me. She was amazing, and I lost her, all because I was moving away."

Mike and Gayl stared at each other, neither one willing to speak.

"What was your girlfriend's name?" George asked.

"Phil," Mike knew Gayl would say in the instant before Gayl actually said it. "But that was her nickname. Her full name was—"

"Philomel," Mike said.

Gayl tilted his head. "No. Philomena. Like the saint."

"Whiskey Tango Foxtrot," George said.

"Was her hair blue?" Mike asked.

Gayl laughed loudly enough that other patrons turned their-table-ward in ill-disguised annoyance. "Blue? No. I'm not into the punk scene. She was a blonde. Sorry if that's not exotic enough for you, kid."

Mike ground his teeth in frustration, wondering if he should bother explaining that *he* wasn't into the punk scene either, that Phil's blue tresses were natural, wondering if it was worth even discussing.

"I guess it doesn't matter," Mike said at last, though the idea of claiming that anything Phil-related did not matter rankled him. This was all about Phil. Every detail of Phil mattered. "It's close to the same thing with me. Broke up with her. Probably shouldn't have. *Definitely* shouldn't have. And now . . . We're both in similar situations, though. It's a hell of a—" He bit down before he could say "coincidence."

George leaned in close enough that Mike could smell the cinnamon on his breath from the Giganto MochaCinnabomb he'd been nursing all along. "Are you *sure* you're not editing this and making Gayl's story like yours, Mike? That would explain everything."

Gayl nodded slowly. "He's right, you know. That would resolve everything."

"No. Editing was making me puke up my guts and I feel fine. Plus, well, look, Gayl—if I were doing it subconsciously, you'd be a woman. Before we met you, George and I were both expecting a woman."

Gayl kept dunking his bag over and over into the hot water. Mike realized that he had yet to see Rybar take so much as a single sip of the tea, as though he'd ordered it not to drink, but rather to have something to do with his nervous hands while they talked.

"Let me tell you my theory," Gayl said. "It's going to sound sort of crazy, but hear me out, all right?"

Both George and Mike nodded.

"I want to talk about how the universe works," Gayl began, and Mike huffed a laugh and said, "You're assuming the universe *does* work," which prompted from Gayl a sad, acknowledging smile as the author twisted to retrieve something from the messenger bag hanging from the back of his chair. It was the well-read, beaten copy of *Inframan*.

"Are we getting homework?" George asked with something caught halfway between boredom and terror.

"No. I just want to illustrate a point. You've heard of this One Book nonsense, right?" When they nodded, he went on: "They claim we're rushing towards this One Book, where all texts will be smashed together into one. But look." He fanned the book open, allowing leaves to fall in dull sequence, words rushing by like a corner flip animation. "Pages, right? You can't do this with an e-book. You can't fan like this. So you miss out on the basic structure of the book—they can mimic pages on a screen, reproducing length and height, but they can't reproduce that third dimension, depth.

"Now, how do we believe the universe works? The universe moves in one direction, right? It moves forward." Gayl held up a hand to stop Mike, who was about to interject. "Wait. Let me finish. Each second exists in the present moment, right? And we experience that second and then it becomes the past as we move into the *next* second, which is now the present for as long as it lasts before *it* passes us by and transforms into history, and so on and so on, right?"

Mike nodded. George shrugged and signaled the barist that he wanted another Giganto MochaCinnabomb.

"Well, look:" Gayl propped the book on the table so that it was open to Mike and George, the title page showing. Mike could make out:

INFRAMAN

or,

The Coming of the Unpotent God

a novel

by Barry Lyga

"Now watch," Gayl said, turning that page. "A second goes by. That page, that second, is now in the past. And another." He turned another page. "And another." And another. "Each page is thin, one-dimensional, until you stack enough of them together in sequence that you get something multidimensional. Again, you can't do this in an e-book. The precious 'One Book' will have height and width, but no depth. Literally and figuratively. See what I'm saying? We get to look at all of the pages, but only one at a time. And while we're looking at one, we can't perceive the others. We're aware of their existence, but not of their content. This is the structure of the universe. It's the way reality works. Imagine Heaven is just another set of pages, buried deep in the back of the book of your life. You can sense it there because of the book's heft, but that's all. You don't know what's written on those pages and you won't know until you get there. And if you skip ahead to look, it won't necessarily make any sense because you haven't read the pages leading up to it."

It made a strange sort of sense to Mike: He imagined each second as an almost-dimensionless sheet of paper, then an endless number of seconds piling up. It was, he thought—and he knew Gayl thought as well—the fundamental structure of the universe: Moments, pages, seconds, particles, call them what you will. Piling paper on top of paper. This was how books are created, but it was also, Mike saw now, how reality was created—one dimension, one layer of reality at a time. "You can look at any single page or moment," Mike said, "and you'll comprehend it, but you won't really understand it until you look at *all* of the pages, in the right order. Otherwise, you lack context."

Gayl shut the book triumphantly. "Exactly. Time is the fourth dimension, moving in one direction. Paging through a book is analogous—it's the time travel aspect of writing. But in your case, you gained the ability to . . ." He riffled the pages randomly, shuffling them back and forth, flipping willy-nilly through the book without even looking at the text.

"You're saying the universe is a book?" George asked doubtfully.

"I'm saying more than that," Gayl pressed on. "Are you guys familiar with fractals? A fractal is a mathematical construct that looks the same on the microscopic level as it does on the macroscopic level. Every time you cut a fractal into pieces, each piece is identical to the original, only smaller. You use an equation to generate them, and the equation undergoes a sort of recursive iteration."

Mike blinked. George shook his head. "Dude, you're talking to two guys who hated calculus."

Gayl shrugged. "Me, too. But my brother Liam is a math genius and he explained it all to me. It's something the One Bookers don't understand—they think information looks the same in every direction, that it doesn't matter where the information comes from or how it starts, only that it's accessible on Gooleg. But the thing is, fractals exist because, yeah, the equation is repeated over and over, but each time there's a tiny difference to it that jogs the end result. Sound familiar?"

Mike nodded. "That's what's happening when I edit. I keep doing the same thing over and over, but getting different results."

"Right. Because there's something called 'sensitive dependence to initial conditions.' Which basically means that the outcome of a fractal equation is pre-determined based on how it started. You started things not in a relationship with Phil; that's the initial condition, and everything that proceeds from it is affected as a result. The entire universe has a fractal structure. If you took our world, our reality, and started cutting it in half, then in half again, eventually you'd get millions of identical copies of it. And you know what I think they'd look like?" He didn't wait for an answer, but instead simply held up the book again. "I think that *Inframan* is an example of fractal mathematics at work. The kabbalists believe that God encoded the keys to the universe into the Torah; this isn't the Torah, but it's a microcosm of reality, and the keys to our universe are encoded in here. It's Lyga's clue to us, the clue that he's more than just a writer."

"You're talking about him in the present tense. But he's dead," Mike reminded Gayl.

"Well, in a manner of speaking. Look, I've been researching him, reading his stuff. My new book—*Unfinished*—started out as a biography, a sort of dry, academic piece because I was influenced by his writing and because he left his last novel unfinished. But then—in the writing—something happened. That happened with my second book, too, where it started out as one thing and sort of transmuted into another while I was working on it. So I started out writing a biography of this guy and it turned into a novel instead."

"A novel about a dead writer," Mike scoffed. "A dead writer no one's ever heard of. Who writes something like that?"

"Exactly!" Gayl leaned forward, his eyes dancing. "He was working on a book about a teenager when he died. And here I am, with his name scrambled into mine, and I write books about teenagers."

"What are you saying?"

"I'm saying that all the things we think are coincidences, all the similarities, are nothing of the sort. They're deliberate. They're encoded into the structure of our universe." Here he brandished *Inframan* triumphantly, as if the book contained all of the answers.

"And a book is the structure of our universe?"

"Not just *a* book. Not just *any* book: A book written by Barry Lyga. *Inframan* is the clue. It's a fractal representation of our entire universe, hence the repetition of the name Mike

Grayson, the reappearance of the Inframan character, the recycling of ideas and tropes. It's all the same. Our universe *is* a book, a novel to be precise. There may be more pages beyond this novel—I suspect there may be infinite pages—but for us, our universe is circumscribed by the narrative we belong to. For most people, a book is accessed in a specific manner—reading one page at a time, starting with page one, chapter one and working through the end. But for you, Mike . . . For the namesake of the lead in *Inframan*, the universe is randomly accessible. You were able to go backwards in our book and—more importantly—change things. Editing reality."

"So you're saying we're just, what, characters in a novel? Like in *Inframan*?"

"*Exactly* like in *Inframan*," Gayl crowed. "Do you guys know what gematria is?" At both shaken heads, he went on. "It's an old kabbalistic practice, a Hebrew sort of alphanumeric mysticism that teaches that when you mix up letters, you can reveal secrets encoded in the holy scriptures. They say that you can even reveal the name of God. Well, you did it, George." Gayl chuckled and flashed George an ecstatic grin. "You did what millennia of kabbalists couldn't do: You deciphered the name of God. My name, anagrammed: Barry Lyga."

Gayl slapped both palms on the table, causing George and Mike to jump. "Barry Lyga is God!"

****

"Barry Lyga is dead," Mike insisted.

Gayl shook his head wildly. "No. The character of Barry Lyga in this particular universe is dead. But the author of this universe is still alive, of course, still creating it. In fact, I bet . . ." He grinned. "I bet Barry Lyga had a Daredevil Levi action doll when he was a kid. I bet he raced it out into the street and when he went after it, he almost got run over by a car driven by a guy with two ice cream cones. That's what writers do—they recycle their own memories and life experiences into their fiction. Oldest trick in the book." He paused, then laughed at his own humor. "Literally."

Mike opened his mouth to speak, but George got there first, breaking in tentatively and tremulously. "Like Jesus, you mean?"

"How do you mean?"

George fumbled with his explanation for a moment. "I mean, God didn't come straight to Earth, right? He sent his son. But Jesus—"

"Of course!" Gayl interrupted. "Christian mythology teaches us that Jesus is the son of God, but also—paradoxically and concurrently—one and the same *as* God. It's the mystery of the Holy Trinity. Three-who-are-one. Lyga, Lyga-who-died, and Inframan. A Trinity."

"If any of this is even remotely true," Mike said, "Barry Lyga must be the most egotistical fucker in the universe. *Any* universe. To make himself God? *And* Jesus. I mean, Christ!" he said, unaware—for a split-second—of his blasphemous irony.

"I don't think it's egotistical at all," Gayl said. "I think from all the evidence we have before us, we can only assume enormous self-loathing on the part of Barry Lyga."

"How do you figure *that*?"

"First of all, in the book, Inframan is more than just a force of editorial control. He also claims that *he* is the real Barry Lyga. That the author of the book is an errant part of his personality, obsessed with itself, writing the book to placate its own urges. And Inframan is the real Barry Lyga, trying to wrest control back from the pretender."

"That's not fucked up at all," George said with quiet irony.

"Plus, look around you!" Gayl gestured out into Books-A-Go-Go proper, where displays, posters, and standees for *INsight* competed with tables piled high with copies of the book and its sequels. "If Barry Lyga were as egotistical as you believe, then wouldn't he have made *himself* the most successful author in the world? Wouldn't the shelves be piled high with this"—he waved the copy of *Inframan*—"instead of that *INsight* bullshit?"

"Why kill himself off?" George asked. "He didn't have to make himself as successful as Monika Seymore, but why kill himself off?"

"I don't know," Gayl admitted. "That's where the self-loathing comes in, I guess."

"This guy is God," George said, "and he hates himself? What the fuck kind of God is *that*? If Barry Lyga is God, he's the shittiest God I could ever imagine."

"This might not all be his fault," Gayl said. "In *Inframan*, Lyga's creative efforts are constantly frustrated and turned around by Inframan. That's the purpose of that character—he's there to tear apart the book even while the reader is reading it. Inframan is convinced that he is the real Barry Lyga. He believes that the Barry Lyga who has written the novel is actually a pretender, a version of himself that got out of control with delusions of, well, of authorhood, I guess. Inframan is like pure id, a powerful child gone amok. You've had a run-in with him already, right?" Gayl tilted his head questioningly to Mike, who nodded once in acknowledgment. "Some of these problems could be caused by Inframan, mucking around in the mechanics of the universe, screwing with the story."

"Some little kid Mikey saw on the subway is causing all these problems?" George drained the last of his second Giganto MochaCinnabomb, jittery and aggressive in his caffeine haze. "I don't buy it."

Gayl shrugged. "Based on the book, I have a theory that Inframan can take whatever form he likes. He's described at one point as 'the Dragon,' which has all sorts of allegorical implications, and also probably accurately reflects how Lyga feels about him. A sort of corrupted demiurge to Lyga's classical God. But whatever form Inframan takes, he usually isn't entirely successful at it because, well, he's the God of Failure, you know. If he ever succeeded entirely at something, that would be an abrogation of his duty."

"So you're saying," George said, jazzed, "it's impossible for him to win? We can beat him?"

"Well, no. He's the God of Failure. He can make you fail."

"But . . . If we fail, then *he* wins. Which is success. Which is—"

"I know. It's a paradox. Clever, isn't it?"

"No, not really. It just sounds like this Lyga guy threw a bunch of bullshit together and twisted it all together in such a way that he would never have to explain it."

"It's complicated," Gayl argued, brandishing the book like a Bible. "Inframan sometimes seems to be a mirror image of Lyga, sometimes a split personality or demonic possession. It's difficult to explain. There's even a whole part of the book written from Inframan's point of view. It's called 'The Gospel According to Inframan.' That's where Inframan claims that *he* is the real Barry Lyga and that the one writing the rest of the book is an impostor."

George threw his hands up in the air. "It's bullshit!" he roared so loudly that a barist came over to ask him to be quiet, took note of George's sculpted musculature, and changed his mind before saying a single word. "It's all bullshit, man! You say this guy is God, but he's a self-loathing, self-obsessed, schizophrenic God. How the fuck are we supposed to deal with a crazy God?"

"It's not—" Gayl started.

"Bullshit!" George insisted.

"You can't just—"

"—a bunch of made up crap that—"

"—structure of a *story*—"

"—metaphysical shit and—"

"—don't expect *you* to understand—"

Mike had been silent for entire minutes, for a time that—if Gayl was right and the universe's structure was pages and words—would no doubt have translated to many pages. Now he slapped the table once and stood up, not caring who in the coffee shop glared at him or stared, only caring that he had Gayl and George's attention.

"Let me get this right," he said, starting slowly, but accelerating as he went along, becoming more and more comfortable not only with the initial conditions of the premise before him, but also—as he went along—with the conclusion at which he had arrived and was about to arrive, a conclusion that now felt as inevitable as a child's love for a parent. "If the universe is a novel and Barry Lyga is the author, then that means he's the reason I'm not with Phil anymore. And he's the reason why *you* aren't with *your* Phil."

Gayl considered for a moment and then nodded reluctantly. "I suppose so. In a manner of—"

"Then this is all his fault. And I plan to tell him that."

George and Gayl stared. George spoke first: "Dude, what do you mean?"

"You know what I mean," Mike said with finality. "I'm going to find Barry Lyga. Not the dead guy buried somewhere in Maryland. Not him. He's just a character in a book. I want the real deal. The one who created all of this, the one who made this world, the one who made me and you. The one who gave me Phil and then took her away from me."

"Wait," Gayl said. "Wait a second—"

"No. No, I won't wait. You said there's no such thing as real. That's what this all means. No such thing as real. Just stories, just pages piled on top of each other. No one page is any more or less real or important than any other. But someone made those pages. Wrote them. Barry Lyga. Which means he's responsible not just for me and for Phil and for all of that. He's responsible for everything else, too. For Lucky Sevens. For GWB and the financial collapse and everything that followed. For love leaving the world. All of it. The whole world. All the suffering. All the craziness. It's all on him. He started it. He made a damaged world. He wrote a damaged story. That's not cool."

Mike took a deep breath. "I'm going to find that motherfucker and I'm going to make him fix it all. I'm going to make him give Phil back to me. And I don't care what it takes or what I have to do."

CHAPTER 25

Gayl hustled George and Mike out of the coffee shop and out of Books-A-Go-Go, leading them past the tall piles of *INsight* and *SightLESS* and the others before the barist—now propelled by the sudden outrage and discomfort of the other customers—could throw them out.

Outside, he steered them to a bench near the subway entrance. "You guys have to keep it down in there," he insisted, pacing back and force before them. "I do signings at this store sometimes. I can't have them thinking I hang out with a lunatic who shouts crazy shit in the coffee shop!"

"Fuck off," Mike said mildly, almost pleasantly. "This isn't about you and your books. It's about something bigger than that. Don't you want your Phil back?"

"Of course I do. So what? I fucked up. I lost her. Maybe someday when you grow up, Mike, you'll realize that this happens. Relationships end. Every couple doesn't get a happy ending. Life isn't a . . ." He trailed off, going pale and shaky as he felt around for something to steady himself. George gallantly stood and helped him to the bench. "Oh, God. Oh, fuck."

"Life isn't a what?" Mike asked quietly, tenderly.

"No," said Gayl, and buried his face in his hands.

"Life isn't a book. That's what you were about to say, isn't it?"

"A story. I was going to say . . . Oh, God."

"But it is."

Gayl's frame shook. He could not speak.

"Life *is* a story," Mike went on. "We just figured that out. So why shouldn't you have a happy ending? Why shouldn't I? It's a story. The only thing we need in order to have a happy ending is for the asshole writing it to *give* us a happy ending. That's all it takes."

Shaking his head, Gayl drew in a shuddering breath and wiped tears from his eyes. "It's not that simple. It never is. Stories are complicated. The story has to—"

"It's the easiest thing in the world," Mike said. "It's not like architecture, where there are building codes and the laws of physics to deal with. It's just a story. He could do it right now. He could write: 'And then they looked up and saw Phil and Phil coming up out of the subway, smiling and waving at them.'"

All three of them looked over at the subway entrance. A homeless woman loitered there, a businessman in an off-green suit loped up the steps while a young mother with a baby in a sling made her way down, but it was utterly Phil-less, lacking both the blue-haired teen and blonde adult varieties.

"God," said Gayl. "Until you did that, I didn't know how badly I . . ."

"Listen." Mike grabbed Gayl's hands, stared into Gayl's bloodshot, watery eyes. "Listen to me. We can do this. There has to be a way. The Mike Grayson from *Inframan* did it. He found a way to confront Barry Lyga."

"No, he didn't," George chimed in.

"That's right," Gayl said. "He gets to the real world; he goes to Lyga's college dorm, but he never actually sees him or talks to him."

"But he got *close*," Mike insisted. "We can do better. There's more of us. I'm a newer Mike Grayson. I'm different. I edited the world all on my own. And you . . . You're an author. That means you have power, right? You have God's power in you. We can do this. We can make it happen. We can find Barry Lyga. You want to know the truth? I think he *wants* us to find him. He's left all these clues. I bet *he's* the one who made that crazy-detailed Wikinformation page that kicked this all off. He wants us to find him. You said before he was self-loathing. Well, maybe it's time for some of his creations to kick his ass a little. Take him to task. Make him fix this fucked-up world he invented. Or, hell, I don't know—maybe he finally lost his battle with Inframan and he's not in control of the universe anymore. Maybe he needs us to find him and help him. But either way: Don't you want to know? Don't you want to know why we were made? Why we suffer? Why the world is the way it is?"

Gayl shook off Mike's grip and stood up, gazing around at the park outside Books-A-Go-Go. It was as if he was seeing it for the first time, noticing the details he'd never noticed before. The place was thick with the homeless—he'd always known that, of course, but never had it seemed so real to him. The fallout of GWB wasn't just in the villages and bombed-out shelters overseas; the fallout was right here, right here in the park in the city, as the homeless struggled and begged and implored, scrounging in the garbage cans for the dregs left in cans and bottles, snatching cold, limp freedom fries from the trays being bussed at PopeYes!, then running off before the Cops™ could seize them for junk-theft. For the first time, Gayl realized that the world had not merely stumbled into this perdition—it had been pushed. "Like Angia Eiphon," he mumbled.

"Who?" George asked.

"She's from the book, right?" Mike asked, pointing to Gayl's messenger bag, where he'd stowed *Inframan* before escorting them from Books-A-Go-Go. "She's supposed to be my—I mean Mike's—sister. And lover."

"Guh-ross," George opined.

"She wasn't really his sister," Gayl said. "It's complicated. In the book, she's described as a 'pushed angel.' She didn't fall from heaven—she was pushed. Apparently . . . You have to read between the lines, but it seems she started as a sort of perfect apotheosis of all girls. But as he wrote her in the book, she became more real and less perfect. And he felt guilty about that."

"She was a pushed angel, not fallen," Mike murmured, remembering his dream, snuggled next to Phil on the new historical sheets during a Spring Break that had now never happened, dozing. *Once my hair was blonde*, she had said to him, *and then I was pushed.*

This, Mike realized, was how Barry Lyga treated his creations: He pushed them into a hell of his own devising.

Gayl sighed. He looked around the park one more time. "Barry Lyga has a lot to answer for," he said. "Let's do this. Let's find him and make him fix it all. Or at least give us a damn good reason why he won't."

****

"What's our first move?" Mike asked at length, his mind afire with the possibilities and potentials of his immediate future. The world was about to change—for him, for Gayl, most especially for Phil, beautiful Phil, his darling Phil, who had lived the past years not knowing that she had once loved him. That part, Mike had to admit, was his fault, his own clumsy editing, but who had given him that editing power in the first place? Who had made him and his entire universe? Barry Lyga, that's who. So it was ultimately all Lyga's fault, and Mike planned on making Lyga fix it.

George gestured to Books-A-Go-Go. "Wouldn't a bookstore be, like, church to a writer? Do we go back in there and, I don't know, pray?"

"I don't think it's that easy," Gayl said ruefully. "We only have *Inframan* to follow, but in that book, that Mike Grayson only got as far as he did because he was clinically dead. He gets shot by the Shadow Boxer towards the end of the book and his heart stops. That's when he ascends to Heaven, but it turns out Heaven is just a stage with cheap, two-dimensional backdrops and some props. He goes backstage and finds a door that leads to some stairs and when he takes the stairs, he ends up in the real world, on Elm Street in New Haven. The intersection of Elm and College, actually, where Calhoun College is located.[55] That was Lyga's dorm at Yale."

George slapped Mike on the back. "Dude, all we have to do is get you shot, then, you know what I mean? Are you insane?" he added, aimed at Gayl. "I'm not letting anything like that happen to Mike."

"Thanks, man." Mike fidgeted. If nearly dying was the only way to see God and fix the universe, the only way to reclaim Phil, then shouldn't he be willing to do it? He'd been willing to risk so much when editing reality—was this really any riskier? Couldn't he take the chance? Maybe there was a way to bring him to the brink of death safely, in a hospital somewhere.

"Don't worry," Gayl said. "I don't think we'll have to rely on

55. Now Grace Hopper College. Long story.

anything quite so dramatic. There's something I didn't tell you guys." He hesitated. "Mainly because it sounds sort of crazy."

George and Mike both snorted laughter. "Yeah, because up until now it's all been completely sane," one of them said.

Gayl leaned back against the bench, his hands folded before him as though in casual prayer. "I went out to the desert one night. I don't know why. I was just drawn there, I guess. This was after a rough night, when I was missing Phil—my Phil—so badly. I was trying to forget her. I really was, guys. That's what adults do—you lose someone, you try to push them aside, try to push the memories away and move on with your life. But it was just impossible for me. She kept saying she wanted to be friends, but every time I called her or wrote to her, her responses were . . . well, perfunctory at best. Desultory. And I would get to a point where I would swear that I was over her, where I would say that I was done with her and could finally forget her and then—as if she had some kind of direct tap into my brain and my heart—I would get a random e-mail or text from her. Nothing major or exciting or meaningful. Just something like 'Saw your mom at the store today' or 'Your book is mentioned on this blog' or something like that. Something innocuous that nonetheless cemented her further in my mind and made it impossible for me to move on."

Mike's jaw tightened. Once upon a time—many edits ago, perhaps even in the original draft of reality (he could no longer remember, could no longer distinguish between them, the memories and universes folded over and intermingled in his mind like origami) his own Phil had done the same, refusing to allow him to forget her.

"So I went out to the desert. I knew I couldn't get a cell signal out there, and I knew that for a few hours at least, there would be no chance in hell that I could hear from her. Or from anyone else, for that matter. So I took the Fox line all the way out to the end."

"Near Crimson Rocks?" Mike asked, remembering his own trips out there.

"Yeah. Right around there. It was late at night—too hot to go during the day, you know? Have you ever been?"

They both nodded.

"Then you know what I'm talking about. It's just desolate out there, not like it was originally. You guys are too young to remember it, but before Lucky Sevens, Crimson Rocks was like a way-station to the Other City. There was always something happening there. And even right after Lucky Sevens, there was always a memorial service or a wake or some kind of celebration or remembrance out there.

"This time, it was just me, though. Just me and the darkness, with a little light from the stars, but not much. I stood there for a while and then . . . This woman showed up. Out of nowhere. One minute I was alone, the next she was there. I don't know where she came from. It couldn't have been from the subway station because that was behind me and she appeared in front of me. And it couldn't have been from the desert because I was looking out into the desert and I didn't see her approach. She just appeared."

He eyed them both warily, as if expecting them to gainsay his story and/or his recollection, but neither of them said anything—they had accepted madness into their lives already and were not going to stop now.

He went on: "She was quite beautiful, in a strange way. I don't know how to describe it, except to say that she seemed . . . idealized. Like someone's idea of a beautiful woman, not an actual beautiful woman."

"Like Angia?" Mike asked.

Gayl stroked his beard. "Maybe. Not exactly, but it seems to be a trope, a consistent trope, doesn't it? Women who are idealized in some way . . . Anyway. She told me her name was Courteney. She told me she had a schemata for me. Do you know what a schemata is? It's a word for systems used to define and organize information and experiences. And she said she had one for me. But first she claimed that she was nothing more than a character in a story. Written by a character in a story."

"So . . . She was from a story within a story?"

Gayl massaged his temples. "It was more complicated than that. I don't even know how to explain it anymore. It made sense when she said it, for just a brief moment, and then I didn't understand it anymore. It's like trying to remember a dream. You get the sensation of it, but not the details. She was a character from a story that was written by a character in a story; now she was in a pastiche of that original story written by a character in a story that was written by the author of the first story." He laughed. "I think. I don't know. It doesn't matter, I guess.

"And then . . . I don't know how to explain this next part. It's like she cupped her hands together and . . . Something came out of them. It was like a TV picture, but it was three-dimensional."

"A hologram, you know what I mean?"

Gayl nodded reluctantly in George's direction. "I suppose. Anyway, it showed me . . . It showed me everything I was afraid of. It showed me everything I ever wanted or needed. It was all there, in the palm of her hand: Success or failure as a writer. As a man. As a person. My need for Phil. My love for her. All of it. Right there, in the palm of her hand. And then she told me that I would go on a quest. That I would not be alone. And that I would . . ." He tapped a foot. "Guys, this stuff is kind of . . . I was exhausted that day. Dehydrated. For all I know, I imagined the whole—"

"Tell us," Mike said, leaning forward. "I went out to Crimson Rocks, too, and I felt like something was waiting for me, trying to communicate with me. Please. Tell us."

Gayl sighed. "She told me . . . She told me that only the Word of God can destroy God. And that I would walk through the wreckage of a broken heart—"

"I was told that, too," Mike said quietly. "In my dream. Inframan said it."

Gayl swallowed. "She said . . . Anyway, I would walk through . . . you know. And that I would . . . that eventually I would encounter God. There." He slapped his knees and leaned back, arms crossed over his chest as if to protect himself from the imminent barbs he knew would come.

But Mike said nothing, fell silent for so long, staring at Gayl, that George finally nudged his shoulder, first gently, then hard enough that Mike had to brace himself against the bench arm with his other hand to keep from falling onto Gayl. "Dude. Dude, are you OK?"

"A quest," Mike whispered. "That's how we find God, isn't it? Isn't it?" His voice rose in excitement.

"Probably," Gayl said, and Mike pumped the air with his fist.

"Dude," George said, "a quest is all well and good, but does anyone have any idea where we start?"

Mike deflated. "That's true. Where are we going? Where are we starting? We could go anywhere in the world, but that's no good if it's the wrong place. So where do writers hang out?"

"I'm telling you," George told him, pointing again at Books-A-Go-Go. "You know what I mean?"

"And libraries," Mike said, ticking off the possibilities on his fingers, "and coffee shops," he added, recalling how many times he'd been unable to find a table at the local coffee shop because all of the seats were taken up by jean-clad, unshaven hunt-and-peckers hunched over their laptops and webbooks and pad computers and—on rare occasions—tablets and pens, "and the park," he added again, gesturing to encompass the space around them, "because I see those guys sitting under the trees and shit during the day, listening to their music and typing away. Where do *you* work, Gayl?"

"Me? At home. I hate those pretentious fucks who cluster in public, like they're trying to prove something to the world. 'Look at me; I'm a writer.'"

"Monika Seymore started *INsight* at a used bookstore," George said.

"Fuck her," Gayl said with a savagery that surprised both Mike and George.

"In any event," Gayl said a moment later, no longer savage, "none of that matters. I know where we have to go. To start, at least. Courteney told me."

"Where?" Mike asked. He and George gathered around the bench, and when Gayl said, "The Other City," they both turned on Gayl with bug-eyed astonishment, as though he had just calmly and rationally suggested that they each—in order to understand each other better—saw off the tops of their own heads and exchange brains.

"The Other City?" Mike spluttered. Of all the things known by every man, woman, and child in the country—nay, the world—this was surely the best and most fervently known: That the Other City was a ruin, a devastation, a danger, and that it was utterly and forever off-limits.

"This all started on Lucky Sevens," Gayl said quietly. "Things went bad then—the DHS report says so. GWB started because of Lucky Sevens and then the world went to hell."

"But no one is allowed to go there," George complained. "It's impossible."

"There's a way," Gayl said. "A way to the Other City."

"We would never make it across the desert," Mike protested. "Even going at night. We couldn't use vehicles because the military has the Other City cordoned off and they would hear us coming. We'd have to walk and you can't make it in one night. The sun would kill us. Or the scorpions. Or the snakes. Right, George?"

George hemmed and hawed, contemplating his (limited) Marine training before pursing his lips and saying, "We don't have good odds. You know what I mean? Especially you two," he added with slight apology in his voice.

"Even if we could make it, we'd never live through it. The Other City is poison. It's radioactive. It's—"

"Which is it?" Gayl asked, rising to stand before them, his uncertainty now replaced with a quiet, unobvious sort of confidence that nonetheless was very obvious to the two teens, who actually took a step back each in surprise. "Is it poison? Or is it radioactive?"

"It's one of them," Mike said. "I'm not sure which. But the government says it's dangerous and that no one can go."

Gayl laughed softly. "The government. Do you know what actually happened on Lucky Sevens? Do you?"

"We were attacked," George said, earning a fierce, agreeing nod from Mike, "by terrorists, who destroyed the Other City. That's what happened."

Gayl looked up at the dark sky, speckled with starlight. "You guys were kids. I was an adult. I remember it. Early in the morning and the news broke in on all the TV channels and radio stations. They said we were under attack, that the Other City was under bombardment. I remember that very specifically—the word 'bombardment.' You don't hear it a lot. So I remembered it. But the funny thing is that later they stopped using that word. They just started saying 'attack.' The Other City went from being 'bombarded' to being 'attacked.'" He glared at them. "Words have meanings, guys. 'Bombarded' means something very specific and the government doesn't want you to know what specifically happened that day."

"You're one of those conspiracy nuts," George said. "One of those guys who thinks the government was behind Lucky Sevens!" He shared a look of horror with Mike.

Gayl waved off their mutual terror. "I don't know what I *believe* about Lucky Sevens. But I know what I *know*, which is that the official reports started out specific and then became very vague. That the government used Lucky Sevens as an excuse to launch Global War B, and GWB is sure as hell the worst thing that ever happened to this country." He glanced around at the homeless people in the park, mute testimony to his assertion. "So if the government tells me not to go to the Other City and that the Other City is dangerous, I'm not one hundred percent sure I'm going to buy any of that. How about you, Mike? You said you were willing to challenge God to get Phil back. You'll do that, but you won't challenge the government?"

Mike kicked at the cobblestone path on which he stood. "Shit," he said under his breath. "Can you give us a second?" he asked and did not wait for an answer before pulling George several yards away, near a grassy strip on which several homeless people had made camp.

"George . . ."

"What?" George stared at Mike with an intensity that Mike could not identify. It was familiar, but—for the moment—unnameable.

"I think I have to do this, man. I really do. But I can't ask you to come along. It's going to be dangerous. Hugely dangerous." Somewhere deep down in Mike's psyche, in his spirit, in his very being, he wanted George to say, "Fuck that. I'm coming with you," because he needed George by his side, for the very simple reason that George had always been by his side. But deeper down still—at the very deepest part of his core—he wanted George to stay, to refuse to go and refuse to come, for the even simpler and more elemental reason that perhaps—just perhaps—then Mike might somehow be worthy of being his best friend's best friend, that by sparing George this danger, by insisting that George not risk his life on the journey to the Other City (for Mike did not believe for a moment that he would ever actually gain entrance to the Other City, though his need to reclaim lost Philomel compelled him to make his best effort) that he would compensate for the years in which he had enjoyed the benefits of being George's best friend without ever repaying them.

"Fuck that," George said, though, thrilling a deep—though not the deepest—part of Mike. "I'm going with you."

"Are you sure, man?" Mike asked, though unpersuasively, for his desire to have George with him was powerful and deep, rooted in need and self-preservation, while his desire to have George stay behind was rooted deeper, true, but in selflessness, which in so many people (Mike included) is a less powerful force. "This is the government we're defying. And you are . . . You were . . ." He knew that "once a Marine, always a Marine" and that there were no "ex-Marines," only "former Marines," but did that count when one left boot camp under mysterious circumstances? While George had thought of himself as a Marine since a young age, how legitimate was his claim at Marine-hood right now?

"Dude, I went into the Marines to protect people," George said, still staring at Mike with that nameless intensity. "You think I'm gonna let you go with a fucking *writer* as your only protection? You know what I mean?"

"Thanks, man." Mike turned back to Gayl. "Are you sure about this? I'm ready to do this, but you better be sure. It's dangerous to go to the Other City. The trip—"

"Why can't you just edit us there?" George complained. "Just say, 'And then they were standing before God,' and bang! we're there."

Mike shook his head. "The last time I edited, it almost killed me. Remember me throwing up at the grave? And that was just a little edit, really. A tiny one. Nothing special. If I tried something that big . . . It's no good to meet God if I'm too dead to talk to him."

Gayl cut in. "Guys! Guys, I'm not going to lie to you. Yeah, it's dangerous. But you know what? Truthfully? I think it's dangerous for us *not* to go at this point. Things will just keep getting worse if we don't."

Mike couldn't explain how or why, but he agreed with Gayl Rybar. And so, to the Other City they would go. No matter what. "But how are we going to get there? Like I said before—we can't walk. We can't drive."

"You guys are too young to remember," Gayl said, "but there used to be a subway line that connected our city to the Other City. It went straight under the desert, right under Crimson Rocks, all the way out to the Other City, past the mountains. They shut it down after Lucky Sevens and stopped running that particular line. But if you take the Moore line to the Fox line, the Fox goes all the way to the Other City, where it becomes the Barth line."

"Barth?" George said. "Like our school. Well, our old school: Wallace-Barth. The WB, you know what I mean?"

"Named for the same guy," Gayl told them. "The Fox and the Barth are the same subway line—it just depends on what city you're in. The name changes."

"If the subway isn't running anymore, then that doesn't help us," Mike pointed out. He was thinking of the day before—or maybe it had been two days or maybe three, reality and time having become a confusing potpourri of days and hours and moments that jumbled together and moved independent of one another—when he'd taken the Fox line out to Crimson Rocks and been forced to wait until a returning train was available. Had there been something going on then? Had there been some mystery he'd missed, so caught up in his own drama and puzzlement?

"The tunnel is still there," Gayl said. "If we had to, we could walk, but I don't think we'll have to. I think that the government still runs secret shuttles to the Other City."

"Here we go with the conspiracies again!" George snorted in exasperation.

"It has nothing to do with conspiracies, George. It's common sense. There's a phalanx of soldiers surrounding the Other City. They have to be resupplied somehow. You could fly in supplies or drive them out over the desert, but why go through all of that when you can just shuttle them through the tunnel? I have a contact with the Department of Tracks and Tunnels; I think I can get us to the tunnel, at the very least."

And that was when it clicked for Mike: The delay at the final Fox station. The wait for another train. There *was* a hidden subway tunnel that went through to the Other City, and it *was* being used. By the mysterious bullet-headed train he'd seen and not been able to catch.

"That's it, then," he said with finality.

CHAPTER 26

They went their separate ways for the time being, agreeing to meet at the faux terminus to the Fox line early in the morning, at the same time Mike had noticed the delay in return trains, working on the (reasonable though by no means flawless) premise that the strangely shaped supply trains would go at the same time every day.

Gayl went home to his townhouse to pack a bag, reasoning that they would be gone at least a day, possibly more. How many pairs of underwear, he thought sardonically, does one pack on a trip to visit God? He thought, too, of the Tower of Babel, but mostly of the ending to *Inframan*, in which a different Mike Grayson finally reached the threshold of God, only to find no one home. In *Inframan*, Grayson was allowed the opportunity to write the last page of the novel and took that opportunity, giving himself and his friends a happy ending. But the true last page of *Inframan* was not Grayson's—it was clearly written by Lyga. So had God gone back on his promise? While the final page did not obviate or abrogate or undo or reverse Grayson's, its mere existence—that single page beyond the Epilogue—still meant that God had broken his promise. What were the implications of this?

It was, Gayl surmised, a warning, an exhortation against and about God, from God, proclaiming that God was not to be trusted, that God—thousands of years of accepted, rote theology to the contrary—was not good. He was, perhaps, not evil (no demiurgic power, he), but neither was he good, an elimination that left only one option—to wit, God was neither good nor evil, meaning that God was like any other human being walking the planet. Not neutral, but conflicted, perhaps bifurcated, dichotomous, capable of both good and evil or neither at any moment. If God made Man in his image, was this not to be expected?

It did not take long to pack the bag—Gayl threw some underwear and two clean shirts into a duffel, along with several pairs of socks and a lighter. He also packed his battered old copy of *Inframan*. He did not know if having it with him would help on this quest, but he felt it couldn't hurt.

He knew that he should sleep—the next day would be a welter of activity and he would need his wits about him—but even the thought of it seemed absurd. In less than a day, he had gone from his quiet, workaday world—a writing life that was, he knew, vastly more satisfying and interesting than the lives of the mass of his fellow citizens, yet still on average boring—to being . . . what? A knight? Is that what he was? Don Quixote or St. George? Was he off to tilt at windmills, or was he instead mounting up to slay the dragon that was Inframan?

More importantly, what awaited him at the end of his quest?

He roamed his house, which sheltered him, but never felt like a home. He'd moved to the city from a small town back East, where he'd felt stifled and—he admitted now—too comfortable. His relationship with Philomena had reached that natural turning point, that fulcrum where after long months of balancing with perfect equilibrium it must either tip over into the future or tip backwards into the past. Unable to decide which side he preferred, Gayl had delayed and forestalled and then the movie deal had fallen through; his first novel, long-optioned, was to have been his ticket to greater exposure, with a screenplay that hewed to a greater fidelity to the source material than Gayl could have ever hoped. But the financial ruin wrought by GWB had taken its toll even on the magical land of moviemaking, and he'd finally received the phone call that the option—lapsed for months—would be neither exercised nor renewed.

Gayl had been surprised to discover how much emotional capital he had invested in the dream of his first novel becoming a movie, surprised further by the sheer emotional devastation it wreaked upon him. His novels were well-considered, but not popular. Even within the tiny, tight-knit nonadult publishing community, he was more unknown than known, and the movie had seemed the perfect way to expand his notoriety and cement his reputation, to say nothing of his publishing future. He never entertained dreams of the fame and fortune of Monika Seymore—he just didn't write those kinds of books—but he had hoped for something a little more stable, something that would make him known enough that he would not have to struggle to publish each book and then wait with Thoreauvian quiet desperation for each royalty statement, hoping that his publisher would not regret its decision to publish him.

Phil had comforted him during the emotional market crash and he had both loved her and hated her for it. He both loved and hated her faith in him, loved it for it nourished him, hated it for he did not believe he deserved it; her faith proved her blindness. He wondered if Mike felt the same way about his

Philomel—had she had blind faith in him as well? Did he think it was deserved or undeserved?

Gayl's perambulation brought him to his office and his computer. He called up a picture of Phil, gazing at her. He had not thought of her in months, not until the boys came and made him think of her.

No. No, that was not true, he had to admit to himself. He thought of her every day. He didn't want to think of her, but he was powerless not to. He had not stopped thinking of her. He had stopped feeling the pain of her loss—for the most part—but the thinking went on and on. Each time his phone rang, he had a moment where he thought it might be her; it never was. He had once given her a custom ringtone, but after the break-up, he'd deleted it, thinking that he no longer wanted to hear it. Now, though, his standard ringtone could be her, with no custom tone to signal her call, so every ring of the phone made her possible in his life until he answered. For long months after their break-up, he'd felt a stab of loss each time he picked up and it wasn't her; now he felt only dull disappointment.

Wasn't that progress? Would there come a day where he felt nothing? Where he thought of her not at all?

He supposed so. He supposed that that was the natural evolution of things. Yet he realized now that he did not want to feel nothing for Phil. He did not want to think of her not at all.

Shortly after the movie deal collapsed into ruin and blank, Gayl's brother, Liam C. Grey, called to inform him that their father had passed away. It was not a shock so much as a relief—he had been in ill health for years and the shock had come every day that he lived, every day that his body had not yet given out. The true shock came in the days that followed, when Gayl found himself unable to think of anything but his father, a baffling position for him to be in, as he had thought little of his father in the previous years or even decades. There had been no animosity between them, no point at which one or the other had said, "I'm through with you." They had simply settled into the polite, casual sort of relationship reserved for people who have little if anything in common, despite their filial and genetic association. Until his father died, there was no reason for Gayl to think of the man at all.

Phil once again succored him and this time Gayl realized that the fulcrum on which he pivoted was threatening to force him to the future unless he pulled back to the past. He could not allow Phil to comfort him in his grief without an understanding that their relationship would somehow move forward. And yet, he could not bear to tell her that he could not see her anymore. And so, he'd taken the coward's way out, telling her that he felt the need to move to the city, to be closer to his family during this time of familial crisis. He never formally broke with her, never said the words, but he knew that she could not follow him to the city, meaning that the result of his decision and announcement would be a *de facto* break-up in which he could claim not to have broken up with her at all. They were simply on different tracks, tracks that had run parallel until now, when they split apart and moved into the mutual distance.

Staring at the picture of Phil on his screen, Gayl wished for the power to reach into the screen, to go to the moment the picture was taken. He'd been signing copies[56] of his second book, *Teacher's Pet*, at a local Books-A-Go-Go and Phil had come along. He'd snapped the picture of her, smiling and posing by a six-pocket dump for *INsight*, the copies of which she had

56. Truthfully, he had signed only one copy for a paying customer. The rest had been signed at the behest of the store's Community Liaison Officer, who then slapped "AUTOGRAPHED COPY!" stickers on them and whisked them away.

replaced with copies of *Teacher's Pet*, her expression in the photo mischievous and infectious, causing him to smile even now at the memory. She had loved him and he had loved her, and some ineffable, ill-defined fear had driven him away from her, and he wished for Mike's power to edit reality, even with its attendant dangers, for if he had it, he would surely go back to that moment before the *INsight* display and take Phil's hands in his own (as he had not in that moment) and draw her to him (as he had not) and kiss her (as he had not, instead sighing and telling her to replace the *INsight* books, lest the manager become annoyed) and pledge to be with her forever.

"What does my life mean now?" he whispered to the photo, as though Phil-from-years ago had the answer and could answer. "Am I just a creation? Am I even real? Are these really my thoughts and fears, or are they Barry Lyga's?"

And that, he thought, was a good place to wrap things up. For now.

****

George stood outside his house for several minutes before going inside. There were piles of wood—two-by-fours, sheets of plywood—stacked in the driveway, as always, like pyramids built to testify to George's mother's ongoing interior re-design project, the piles changing in size and shape and kind of wood (pine, then cherry, then oak, then hickory), but their existence a constant. Ever since the asshole had left—had been made to leave, was more accurate—Mom had turned the house into a perpetual re-design machine, flowing from the original contemporary design to Victorian to classic to neo-classic to neo-contemporary to modern to Georgian to whatever the hell it was now. Only George's bedroom had gone untouched, every other room in the house twisting and turning and reconfiguring under his mother's insistent and watchful and demanding eye. The hundreds of thousands of dollars she had spent over the years had not touched the outside of the house, only the inside. Even though George had lived almost his entire life in this house, he felt as though he'd hardly lived here at all.

That, he knew, was the point.

We should just sell the house, George had told her on more than one occasion during his youth, dodging contractors, trying to study while hammering and drilling and sawing whirled around him, safe in his cocoon of a room from the madness without. *We should sell it and move if you hate it so much.*

Hate it? she had responded. *I love this house. It's our home. It just needs a little work, is all.*

And so she had been doing "a little work" on it since the asshole had left. George understood—he, too, wished nothing more on certain days than to forget the horror of living with the asshole who'd contributed half of his DNA—but rejiggering the innards of the house would not change what had happened, nor would it exorcise the ghosts of 911 calls and kicks and punches and slaps; only leaving would accomplish that, but leaving was precisely what his mother refused to do.

George loved his mother—she had asked no questions when he returned from basic training and she had, other than the ceaseless remodeling, never interfered in his life to any appreciable degree, almost as though she were apologizing for the rigid hold of terror over his early years by overcompensating via laxity in his later teen years—and had no wish to bring her distress or cause for alarm. He could not tell her the truth, that he was traipsing off to the forbidden and foreboding Other City with Mike to look for God, nor could he tell her nothing and simply disappear, perhaps (likely, some tenebrous, urgent part of him insisted) forever, yet neither did he wish to lie to her.

I'm going somewhere with Mike, he could say in such a tone as to forestall any follow-up questions.

But Mom would not accept that. She would say, *Always going somewhere with Mike. I like him, Georgie*—for she persisted in calling him by his old childhood diminutive, despite his age, though thankfully only when alone with him, never in the presence of peers (hers or his) or friends (again, hers or his)—*but you're always off somewhere with him. Don't you think he takes advantage? Isn't he treating you like a sidekick?*[57]

He's my best friend, Mom, George would offer both as answer and as an avoidance of an answer.

He could tell his mother, he supposed, some variant of the truth, that his regular beatings as a child and the continual witnessing of his mother's torture at the asshole's hands had inculcated in him a desire not to be harmed or defenseless, but at the same time had also imprinted on him an extreme and almost bloodthirsty desire—no, *need*—to protect others, that the pain and shame he'd felt as a child after one of the asshole's beatings was nothing as compared to the shame, weakness, and helplessness he'd felt at being unable to protect his mother from

57. In truth, George did sometimes feel like a sidekick, as though the attention of the world were focused on Mike, not on George, as though he existed only as a way of casting light or shadow on Mike, depending on whether Mike needed shadow or light at a particular moment. The technical term for it, he knew, was *foil*, a word that came from the literal usage of foil backing to make somewhat dull gems sparkle and luster all the more, and now had common usage as someone, well, someone like George, whose mere presence made Mike . . . more interesting? More understandable? Relatable? Sympathetic? It's a convenient conceit of fiction that even "supporting characters" think they're the main characters in their own stories. But in real life, aren't there people who think of themselves as adjuncts to others? Political aides and trailing spouses and the like, people who see themselves as add-ons to someone else . . . and are also okay with that? George, perhaps, is too self-aware for his own good. Or, alternately, he's just self-aware enough.

that neverending torrent of abuse and danger and suffering. People needed protection, George knew from an early age, and while there had been no one to protect him, he could at least be there to protect others.

And now that the Marines were done with him, he would do what he could on his own. Maybe he was nothing more than Mike's sidekick—that was all right. Being a sidekick was actually a noble and time-honored tradition. Don Quixote needed Sancho Panza. Hamlet needed Horatio. Without the sidekicks, without the foils, the Mikes of the world would not and could not shine so bright, nor would they even survive to tell their tales. He would simply tell his mother that he was going to spend some time with Mike, and that was that.

His cell chirped for attention as he entered the house, a text from Seth, the former UPN linebacker he'd seen at The CW celebratory ball the other night. George stared at the text for a long time and felt as though two worlds were coming together, worlds that could either collide and destroy each other in a great fury of destruction or somehow mesh together and unite, becoming a new, single world in the process.

He couldn't imagine the latter happening, and did not want to picture the former, and so—after a long moment staring at the screen of his phone—he dismissed the text message and slid the phone back into his pocket.

****

Mike waited on the platform to take the Moore line to his house and was surprised when an empty car stopped right in front of him, its door sliding open like an invitation.

He entered the car and heaved himself onto a bench, bone-tired beyond any exhaustion he'd thought possible. While he'd slept more last night than in the past few days, he felt even more fatigued now than he had before on less sleep, his body taking its cue from his overtired and enervated mind. The insane decisions he'd made, the crazy moments of realization in the Books-A-Go-Go coffeeshop and on the bench outside had all settled into his physical form, depleting his muscles, draining his vitality.

But a part of him perked up, alive with the possibilities of what was to happen. Yes, it was the height of madness to essay a quest to the Other City for any reason, never mind for the purpose of finding God, but at least he had—for the first time—a definite goal, a target at which to aim his arrow. When he'd been gifted with the ability to edit reality, he hadn't known what to do with it, and so he'd arrived at his current impasse. Now, though, he had a goal. He had companions. He had a plan.

"Did you really think it would be this easy?"

Mike startled at the sound of the voice on the empty subway car, jolting around, looking in every direction until he spied the source. The kid was no older than seven or eight, brown hair cut as though someone had placed a bowl atop his head; he still had a sloppy, part-melted ice cream cone clutched in one hand, which reminded Mike of the shared memory of Daredevil Levi and the near-miss sedan.

"Were you the man?" he asked, narrowing his eyes. "Were you him? Have you been haunting me that long, since I was a kid? Since Gayl was a kid? Did you almost run us over? Did you want to, but you failed because that's all you can do?"

The kid shrugged, but his grin was predatory, self-satisfied.

"I know who you are this time," Mike said. "I know your name. You're Inframan." An electric shiver vibrated him as he said the word out loud.

Inframan laughed and licked the ice cream cone with a

long, languorous swipe of his tongue. "Do you smell chocolate syrup, Mike? I smell it all the time. I am failure. I'm the failure of aspiration, of hope, of dreams. So, yeah, I've been with you all along. I've haunted you your whole life. I haunt everyone. I'm the voice in the back of your head telling you that you shouldn't even bother trying to build the elevator building. I'm the voice telling you that you'll never build the underwater hotel room."

Mike swallowed. "No. That's not true. I'll build it."

"What makes you so sure?"

"Phil. Phil believed in me."

"Past tense, Mike. And even past tense isn't right. It's not something that happened in the past. It's something that never happened in the past. You did that. You edited that moment, that belief, right out of existence."

"I'm going to fix it. I'm going to find Barry Lyga and he'll rewrite it and make it all right."

Inframan burst out laughing, the sound surprisingly deep and rich coming from such a small child. "Barry Lyga! Barry Lyga! Do you really think you'll find him? And even if you do, what do you expect him to do? Do you realize how complicated this story has become already? Do you have any idea? I do, because I'm the God of Failure, and this whole story is a big, steaming pile of fail."

"I don't care about any of that."

Inframan shook his head and licked the ice cream with sinister intent. "You don't get it. Neither did the original Mike Grayson. The first one. This isn't about you. It never was. It's about *him*. His ego. You think I'm the bad guy, don't you? You think I'm the devil, stepping in to stop you from getting what you want. You idiot!" He shook his head sadly and gazed at Mike in a way that Mike supposed was intended to be sympathetic, but instead made Mike think of wolves. "I'm the good guy. Barry Lyga is the bad guy. He's the one who tortured you with the power to edit reality. I came in and tried to stop you from doing it because I knew that editing reality only leads to heartache. And I was right, wasn't I? Each time you edited, you thought you were making things better, but you only made things worse."

Mike didn't want to admit that it was true, yet it was, for each edit had taken the world not closer to the present and future he wanted—he and Phil together again and never having been apart—but further and further away, until he had ultimately broken things altogether, such that not only had they never been together, but that Phil was also terrified of him to the point of a restraining order.

"You made things worse," Inframan went on, "and you made it so that your whole story never even happened. Phil doesn't love you and never loved you. Lyga let that happen. I tried to stop it. What makes you think you're going to change his mind and make him fix it? Why would he go back and change everything now? That would be a cop-out, and trust me: this guy hates cop-outs. Almost as much as he hates happy endings."

"I don't believe you." Mike wasn't sure if he believed Inframan or not, but he also knew that succumbing to Inframan's seduction meant giving up, meant guaranteed failure. Inframan wanted him to give up now, leaving the *status quo* in place, leaving Phil's restraining order in force, her fear fixed firmly in her heart, that same heart undeniably given over to *him*. Mike could not abide that.

"You know what happened at the Tower of Babel, don't you?" Inframan asked. "It didn't end well for the mortals, and God didn't give a damn one way or the other. Do you think you'll do any better?"

His mouth gone dry, Mike worked his lips and tongue

for several seconds before he could manage to speak: "Things changed. One way or the other, Babel changed things."

Inframan goggled at him. "Really? That's your attitude? Anything is better than this? Do you have any idea how much worse you could make things? How much worse he could make things? You think this is rock bottom, but let me tell you something—" here, incongruously, Inframan swiped his tongue at the ice cream cone for a huge slurp of flavor "—it can go deeper. A lot deeper."

"I like Spanish," Mike said. "It's a beautiful language."

Inframan snorted. "You're going to fail, Mike. Trust me—I know these things. I've seen the plans, the outline. I've seen the ending, Mike. The final pages of the book. Spoiler alert: It ends with you. In a room. Alone.

That electric shiver returned, this time tracing static fingers up his spine and down both arms to the tips of his fingers; his back teeth clenched. "Spanish," he said again, shaking as though cold. "Beautiful language."

"Good luck, Mike." And for a moment, he felt as though Inframan truly meant it, as though the God of Failure actually wished Mike could succeed against all odds.

In that instant, Inframan vanished, the only memento of his presence a small splotch of intermingled chocolate and vanilla soft-serve ice cream melting on the floor of the car, the same car that braked now at a station two away from Mike's, the stop closest to Phil's house.

And then time stopped.

Mike could tell time had stopped because the doors to the subway train stalled while still partially open and the soothing almost-British voice of the subway announcement system did not click on to ask that "Passengers please refrain from blocking or holding open doors while the train is in service." Instead, the doors simply gaped as though thunderstruck, holding there for an endless second.

That time had stopped did not surprise Mike, not given his past few days/months/years (depending on how you counted), to say nothing of the just-completed audience with Inframan. A dearth of chocolate syrup lingering in the air convinced him that this was not some new, hitherto-unwitnessed and -unexecuted application of his ability to edit reality, but rather some sort of (super?)natural phenomenon, made all the more perplexing when a man strode through the gap in the doors and took up a stance just inside, placing hands on hips. He wore an old trench coat and a pair of wrinkled dress slacks with a button-down shirt and tie (loosened at his throat, the knot pulled partially down and to the left, revealing the top button of the shirt to be open).

For Mike, the man's appearance was more stunning than the time-stoppage, for looking at the man was like looking into some strangely trans-fourth-dimensional mirror, a mirror that warped like a very specific sort of temporal funhouse, allowing the viewer to witness several years' hence.

The man standing opposite him looked like Mike would in four or five years, allowing an assumption that they would be stressful, difficult years indeed.

"Who are you?" Mike said, the words spilling from him before he could stop them, for his mind understood and knew who the man was, though his eyes and lips apparently had not yet been converted to this particular truth.

"I'm Mike Grayson," the man said.

"You're me," Mike said.

Mike shook his head. "No. Not you. Well, maybe a version of some sort."

"You're the me from the book," Mike said, realizing. "You're a Cop™."

"A Cop™"? No. I'm just a police officer. A detective with the New Haven Department of Police Service. I was hunting the Shadow Boxer and then I found him and then . . ."

Mike thought back, remembering. "And then you went to an amusement park. And got shot. And ascended to Heaven . . ."

"I am not Mike," Mike said. "I am *a* Mike. I am here to talk to you, Mike."

"How can you be here? You're just a character in a book."

"How could that stop me? We're the same, you and I."

"How? I'm a college kid. Or I used to be. I want to be an architect. I'm in love with a girl I can't have—"

"I know a little something about that. With love, nothing is ever truly impossible."

"Oh. Oh, that's right." Mike grimaced. "You slept with your sister. Angia was your sister. She was pushed by God and her hair turned black and you slept with her."

"It isn't what it sounds like. She was adopted. We aren't related by blood."

"But you grew up together. You . . ." Mike shivered. "It's disgusting,"

Mike harrumphed and crossed his arms over his chest. "It's the most important and dearest relationship of my life. Thanks for your judgment."

"Look—"

"We're two consenting adults. Who are we hurting?"

Mike thought about that. "Are you really here to debate incest with me?"

Mike shrugged. "I guess not. Look, you're about to undertake something . . ." He glanced around the frozen air of the subway car as though the next words would be etched in the stillness, writ in the time-hardened relief of shadows and light. "This isn't a thing to embark on lightly. This ascent to the Real World."

"What was it like?" Mike asked. "When you were there?"

Mike shrugged again and gestured around them. "It was like this. This is my Real World. My author died years ago, just like the old saying goes: 'God is dead.' But I came here, ascended to your world, and I went to his Heaven. Which," he said with a chuckle, "looked a lot like a Yale dorm room to me."

"What do you remember?" Mike asked. "Anything could help me."

"Not much. It was . . . intense. That's what I remember. Overwhelming. Too many sights. Too many sounds. It was too powerful. Too potent. But I made it through . . . I found my way to his room . . ."

Mike thought of Inframan's warning: A room. Alone. That's how it would end. It had been like this for Mike, too, ascending to the Real World, only to find himself in a room, alone.

"And there I was," Mike said, as though he could read Mike's thoughts, "in a room, alone. God was absent. I found a single sheet of blank paper and a note from him that said, 'Finish the story yourself.' So I thought about it. I thought long and hard about it. And I used that single page as best I could, writing an ending that I thought would work for everyone. It left me alive and happy with Angia. It left my friends alive and happy. I did the best I could."

"I read what you wrote. The epilogue, right?"

"Yeah. Yeah, I . . ." Mike seemed on to be on the verge of tears. "I did my best. I tried to come up with an ending that he couldn't cheat. I wrote an epilogue because that's the last part of the book. And I made sure we were all OK, so that he would have to honor that, so that no one else would die."

"And then he," Mike said, remembering Gayl's web page, "came in and put something after it."

Mike nodded. "Yeah. It was just a little something.

Meaningless, really. It didn't change the character or the tone or any of the specifics of what *I* had written. But still . . . It bothered me. He had promised, you know? He told me to write the ending of the book; he left that to me. And then . . . I don't even know what the point of what he wrote was. It's like all of a sudden, after everything he put me through, he was saying none of it mattered. None of it had any consequence. It was all just a trick or a joke. And even though he didn't change anything, it just felt . . . It just felt wrong, you know? Why did he do that?"

"Maybe . . ." Mike hesitated. "Maybe it means that writers change their minds? Or maybe . . . Maybe he thought the story would go one way and then he got tired of it?"

They stared at each other, identical eyes meeting through the time-stopped subway air.

"Maybe so. But learn from what happened to me. If you do meet him—and you might—maybe you shouldn't trust him."

The peculiar time-deadened silence enfolded them.

"Inframan," Mike said quietly. "What about him?"

Mike shivered. "He's the one . . . I don't know. He's the one I worry about. Lyga is . . . Well, my Lyga. My Lyga was just a confused guy trying to write a story. I think he was pretty young. Inframan, though . . . Inframan is a *creature.* A force. He worships failure and he is failure. He wants you to lose. Everything Barry tries to create—everything that you are and everything that I am—Inframan wants to destroy."

"How do I stop him? Someone said that 'Only the Word of God can destroy God.'"

"I don't know. I don't know if he can be stopped. You think about gods, you know? Gods from ancient mythologies. And they all had their areas of expertise, their spheres of influence. But everyone fails, Mike. At some point, everyone fails. And everyone dies, which is a failure in and of itself—your heart fails, your liver fails, your kidneys fail, whatever. Something fails and then you die. If gods are made powerful by those who fall under their spheres of influence . . . then wouldn't that make the God of Failure the most powerful god of all?"

"Can you tell me what to expect?" Mike asked. "Can you prepare me just a little bit, at least?"

"I don't know what to tell you. I would say 'expect the unexpected,' even though that's just a bad, old cliché. But I was shot and then I saw Heaven and then I realized that Heaven was just a sham, so I kept going and I came to the Real World. You might go there, too. I don't know. If you do . . . You have to understand that the Real World . . . The Real World is different from what we're used to. At first it *seems* like it's the same, but then you realize it isn't. And the differences overwhelm you. I saw so much, but I feel like I only came away from it with a sense of what reality really is. Does that make sense?"

Mike didn't wait for Mike to answer, but just continued: "It's less that I remember the details and more that I remember the impressions, sensory impressions. I have a sense of being in his college dorm, sort of a Platonic notion of 'college-dormness,' but no actual memory of details. You get me?"

Mike nodded, and Mike continued:

"All I can tell you is this, Mike: Be damn sure this is something you want to do. Something you have to do. Because I had to die in order to make it work for me, and I guess if I hadn't written that last page the way I did, I never would have come back."

"I have to go. I have to do this. There's a girl . . ."

Before he could go further, Mike grinned for the first time and nodded knowingly. "See, and you got on me about Angia, but you understand, don't you? You get it. For love, we'll do the craziest shit, won't we? We'll track down God himself if we have to. We'll throw society's foolish taboos in its face. All for love."

"It's not like that—"

"If this is about love, then I'm for you. All the way. But you have to remember something, Mike," Mike said. "Remember that this is not a small, whimsical thing you're doing. Moses saw God and was stricken with age. Job bellowed into the whirlwind and lost everything. And we all know what happened to the guy claiming to be God's son, don't we?"

"What are you saying?" Mike asked Mike.

"I'm saying that this girl? This one you love so much that you'll go to God for her? Realize that by going to God, you may never see her again."

Mike opened his mouth to speak, but his throat and his tongue and his lips would not cooperate with his brain, permitting him only a low, guttural, wordless groan.

"Oh, yeah, one other thing," Mike said, backing out of the subway car. "I don't know why, but . . . Bring a crowbar."

Time resumed.

The doors slid shut.

As the train pulled away, Mike watched as Mike disappeared from view.

CHAPTER 27

Mike's heart—as though suddenly competing for his attention—thudded loud and hard, so loud and hard that he could hear nothing else, could feel nothing else. *Phil*, it thudded. *Phil*, it pounded, demanding, commanding.

I might never see her again, he realized, or rather continued realizing, the words wrapping themselves around his throat, constricting, making it impossible to breathe. If he went to the Other City . . . if he made things worse . . . He would never see her again. Never mind improving things—he would never get the chance to see her one last time . . .

With a cry torn from his closing throat, he lurched up from his bench and threw himself through the subway car doors as they hissed shut behind him, leaping to the platform, the wind of the departing train at his back, pushing him forward. He ran through a throng of straphangers waiting for the next Moore line, dodging complaining travelers with nary an apology or "excuse me," his breath greedily conserved for his mad dash to the stairs, his hurtle up the stairs and out into the open air of the night.

He had no muscle memory from months of walking the

path from this very subway stop to Phil's house, but his psychic recollection propelled him, his arms pumping, his breath coming in harsh gasps as he launched himself forward, crashing through pedestrians on the sidewalk, sidestepping baby carriages and dogs on leashes. He ran not like a man possessed, but rather like—precisely like—a man who wishes to possess.

Crossing against a light, he narrowly avoided being sideswiped by a tiny electric blue hatchback, then stumbled into the path of a metallic, cherry-purple sedan that honked its horn in annoyance. Waving a combination apology/thanks to both drivers, he leapt the berm to the sidewalk and kept running, turning down Phil's street, where the city bustle quickly gave way to an almost suburban calm. From the intersection of Phil's street and the nearest cross street, he could see her driveway—her mother's car was nowhere to be seen. But Phil, he knew, would be home. She would have to be home.

Gaining the front door, he pounded on it with both fists, not pausing to catch his breath, the momentum of his mad dash from the subway shaking the door fearfully. He had to see her one last time. She was the reason he was doing this, after all. It was all for her. If he saw God and wrecked the world or the timestream or—like the (cautionary?) protagonist of *Redesigning You*—ended up erasing himself from reality, he had to know that he'd done it all with one last look at Phil burned into his eyes and his mind and his memory and his soul.

The door yanked open, he brought his fist down again, stumbling over the now-unblocked threshold, colliding with Phil, who stood in the foyer with an expression of wonder that rapidly and heartbreakingly shifted to abject terror.

"Oh my God!" she shouted.

"Phil!" he bellowed, and found no breath for anything other than her name. "Phil!"

She shouted again, this time shouting *his* name, which stabbed at Mike almost literally, causing his wounded heart to twist and jump in pain. Mike shook his head violently, struggling to regain his breath, struggling to say all the things that now ricocheted and clashed in his mind, each claiming primacy, each trying to force itself through the bottleneck of his voice, which had yet to recover.

"Phil," he managed. "Please," but she only shouted *his* name again, stepping back towards the stairs where, Mike now saw, *he* loomed at the top, shirtless, no doubt summoned from Phil's bed, the combination of no mother and—he saw now—Phil's t-shirt-*cum*-pajama top all-too-familar to Mike as signs and portents of what he had interrupted; glee at having interrupted flared bright and hot within him, overpowering and blotting out any fear he may have felt at the sight of *him*.

"I'll just be a second," Mike promised, holding up a defensive, calming hand towards the stairs. "I just need to talk to Phil for one second, OK?"

"Are you insane?" Phil rasped, backed away further now, her arms wrapped around herself in terror and panic, causing Mike to want nothing more than to do what came naturally, to go to her, to put his arms around her and protect her from what frightened her, never mind that right now what frightened her—what terrified her beyond all belief—was Mike himself. He took a step towards her nonetheless, unable to stop himself, and she screamed, and *he* came down the stairs, and Mike thought that perhaps he was insane. It was likely enough, and he'd certainly considered it as a possibility over the past few days, but he no longer cared if he was insane or not. Insane or not, he wanted Phil. Insane or not, he needed to speak to her one last time, just in case it was, in fact, one last time. And so he took another step and by now *he* was down the stairs and *he* swung at Mike, *his* swing thankfully made slow and obvious by Phil's liminal placement, making it easy for Mike to step back and avoid the blow as Phil shrieked.

"Stop it!" Mike yelled, and his thoughts became more jumbled, more confused, his love for Phil and his anticipated words to her commingling with the memories of the fight(s) he had had/had had again/had not and never had with *him* in the bathroom at The WB ball, the blinding, the blood, the stark terror and the stark delight. "I'm not here to—" interrupted by a glancing blow to his shoulder, only half-dodged this time, the surprise of it hurting more than the actual pain, *he* throwing an unexpectedly weak punch, given all *his* past bravado and braggadocio, and Mike thought of *him* with her on the history-made sheets, obviating history, rewriting history, and he lashed out as Phil screamed again, catching *him* under the jaw with a blow that rattled both *his* teeth and his teeth at the same time. *He* uttered a single syllable—"Urk," it sounded like—and dropped to the floor, crumpled in an unconscious heap.

"I'll call the Cops™!" Phil cried, backed up in a tight corner of the foyer and clearly in fear of her life, either terror or blind hope driving her to her threat even though Mike stood between her and the landline in the kitchen and she evidently had no cell phone on her person. "I'll call them!"

"I'm not going to hurt you," Mike said, his insides twisted and blasted at the very thought that he needed to say such a thing to her, above and beyond the agony of the actual saying of it. "I'm just here to . . ." And he drifted off, realizing that no matter what he said or did, he couldn't possibly explain his presence, not in any way that would make her understand. He was here for her, in truth, but in order to be here for her, he first had to be here for himself. In order to restore the world—the universe, the *book*—to its original, prescribed form, to recapture her lost love, he had to remind himself of what he had lost, of what was at stake if he failed in the Other City, if he allowed fear and the unknown and unknowable to trump courage and love.

"I need you to tell me," he said slowly, aware that *he* could waken at any moment, "that you don't love me, you don't want to be with me, and you never want to be with me again."

Her eyes widened at "again," but Mike refused to amend or emend his statement—she had loved him before, in another time and in another draft of the universe. He knew it; he remembered it; he would not pretend—for her sake; not even for her sake—that it had not happened.

"What's the big deal?" he said into her silence. "It's what you're thinking, so just say it. It will help me a lot. Look, you've always told me the truth, right? So tell me the truth now. Just say it. Please."

But she shook her head. "Why are you doing this to me? Why? What did I ever do to you?" she begged, her eyes welling over with tears, the sight of which burned him like acid.

She needed him to go. She needed to feel safe. But he needed something more. He needed to know what he was fighting for and against in the Other City. "Say it."

"I don't love you," she blurted out.

"Say it again," he demanded in a mingle of pain and joy. His heart throbbed with anguish, but also soared at something to fight for.

"I don't love you." Choked through tears.

He leaned in further and almost kissed her, unable to help himself, caught in the moment, needing to kiss Phil when so close to her, after so many kisses and so many closenesses, hoping—even though he knew it would be impossible—that she would somehow remember, that her body would remember their closeness and their intensity and their history, that her body would respond, that she would press to him, the strong, yearning heat of her against him, wanting him, her tears trickling between their cheeks.

But instead he pulled away. At the last moment, his breath a caress on her cheek, his lips so close, too close. He pulled away from her. He denied himself that kiss.

"I don't love you. I don't," she sobbed. "Why are you doing this? Why?"

He wanted the next part. He wanted the rest. In that moment, his darkest, surely, he did not care what she wanted, only what he could take from her, what he could have, which he'd had any number of times in any number of pasts at her desire, often at her insistence.

"Please," she sobbed. "Please leave me alone. I never did anything to you. Please."

He watched the spill of blues in the dark light of the foyer, then gazed into her wet eyes. "Phil, I'll never hurt you. I promise. I want to tell you something, Phil. I love you. I love you so much that I will climb the Tower of Babel and confront God himself for you."

She shivered. "Mike . . ."

"No," he told her. "Don't say anything. I just want you to know . . ." and language forsook him, abandoned him. He swallowed, feeling that he was swallowing all the possible things he could say to her, the good and the bad, the effective and the useless, that he had now subsumed all possibilities, all the branches of the tree of the universe, the multitudinous paths the world could take or would take from this moment on, all of them now inside him and, therefore, protected. And his. And still very possible.

"You once told me that you couldn't bear the thought of leaving high school the same way you started it. And look at you now. Look at what you've done. You're out of high school, but have you changed at all?" He glanced over at the still-unconscious heap of *him*.

Back to Phil. She stared in terror. "What are you talking about? How do you—"

"You told me that and you gave me a wine cooler and we drank and we talked, and we . . ."

"You're scaring me," she said, very quietly, and he knew it was true, but he was helpless to stop.

He held her gaze and said the only thing he could say in that moment, the only words that came to him, nonsensical to her, he knew, but alive and heated with power for him:

"Back and forth and back and through: I am redesigning you, redesigning you."

And then he left the house, closing the door quietly and almost gently behind him before dashing back to the subway.

CHAPTER 28

On the subway, Mike suddenly found himself gasping, gulping in great, whopping quanta of air, as though he'd been holding his breath since first disembarking to run to Phil's and inhaling only now that he had returned to the subway. This car, fortunately, was packed with riders, and for the first time in his life, Mike did not mind standing and holding one of the support poles, heaving in and out his breath as the commuters around him studiously ignored him, having seen stranger and more disturbing sights. Mike laughed softly to himself, thinking of the stranger and more disturbing sights he himself had seen on the subway, from Inframan to the Electrostatic Man.

The car shook and squealed to a stop at his home station, and he filed out onto the platform along with a collection of others, then pulled away from the pack, veering around slow-walking couples and zigzagging children and package-laden plodders to get to the stairs quickly. He knew that what he had done was potentially—probably? maybe—dangerous and foolish. But how could he embark on this mad quest without saying goodbye to the woman for whom he embarked on the quest in the first place? Did not the knights of old spend one final night with their beloveds before setting out to slay the dragon/find the Grail/defend the Crown?

He was going to save more than just Phil's love. He was going to save more than just himself.

He was going to save the world.

Out of the stifling enclosure of the subway station, into the cooling-though-warm night air, he slowed his pace, thinking of what he would say to his parents and his brother. What could he say? How could he explain what he was going to do and why?

By the time he reached home, he had decided that he would not and could not tell them the truth, that he would simply tell them he was going away for a few days with George—camping, he decided, even though he and George had never gone camping before, as it would explain why he would not be staying in touch via cell phone—and that he would be back and that he loved them all. He would be sure to add that last part, even though they might wonder at it, for his was not an effusive family, not given to displays of affection or affectations of emotion. But it was true—he loved them all—and it needed to be said, so that if/when the inevitable happened, they would know that his last words to them had been words of love.

He went into the house. His parents were watching a movie on TV, as they always seemed to be doing when he needed to see them, and his brother was in his bedroom, playing his tuba/flute/harmonica; his skills had improved dramatically, Mike noted with brotherly pride.

"Mom? Dad? Got a second?"

They both looked up at him with mild interest, not expecting what was to come, nor expecting what lay behind what was to come.

"George and I are going camping for a few days," he said,

the lie so smooth and so easy that he stopped talking for a moment, surprised by his own believability, wondering for a moment if he was in fact merely going camping with George for a few days, if everything else was just a flight of fancy, fact and fiction careering on the highway of his mind, threatening to crash into one another. "He's going to show me some of the stuff he learned in basic training," he went on, as though they needed further convincing, which—he could tell from their guileless expressions—they did not.

"That sounds like fun," Dad said. "Always thought George was a good influence on you. Get out of the city; into the fresh air; clear your head out a little," he finished significantly.

"Right."

Mom came to him, took his face in her hands, and planted a maternal kiss on his forehead. "Be careful, OK? I know George won't let anything happen to you—"

"He won't. We'll be fine. And hey," he said, pulling back, "I just wanted to tell you guys that I love you."

Mom looked at him quizzically, but Dad just chuckled. "We know."

"Are you all right?" Mom wanted to know.

"I'm fine. I just feel like I don't say it enough, I guess." He couldn't say what he truly felt in that moment—that he felt as though he didn't spend enough time with them (for then they would ask why he was going away), that he felt as though he treated them as a backdrop to his life, not as an integral part of it. But he didn't know how to fix that problem, so bringing it up would be useless.

"We love you, too," Mom said, beaming. "Don't we, honey?"

"You betcha," Dad said in a jovial tone, flicking a thumbs-up at Mike.

"OK, I need to go pack," Mike said, forcing a light, jovial

tone in return, while deep down he felt a welling of horrible, dark import, as though this might be the last time he would speak to them. He shook it off, forcing himself to his bedroom, where he quickly packed a bag with a few days'-worth of underwear and socks, as well as a light jacket and—on a whim—a sheaf of blank paper. If Barry Lyga decided to replay one of his own tricks—and the man seemed determined to repeat himself at almost every turn—and offer *this* Mike Grayson the opportunity to write the ending to this tale, then Mike would be prepared with more than just a single sheet of paper. He looked around, feeling both powerful and impotent in the same moment; he was undertaking an astonishing adventure, the likes of which had been unattempted since the days of the Grail quest, and yet he had no idea how to prepare, what would be important, what would matter on his expedition.

His room was strewn with the drawings of Phil, the notes, the sketches from his orgy of remembering.

In the end, he could not take it all—indeed, had no desire to take it all—and so he chose one charcoal drawing of Phil (which he folded into loving and precise quarters), his initial attempt at redesigning/remembering the underwater hotel (folded this time into eighths, though no less precise and loving, as it was drawn on larger paper), and—after a furious search—the original elevator building drawing that had so riveted Phil and lured her to him so many years ago, this last folded once, hastily, and jammed with the others into his bag. The rest he left, telling himself that he would be back for it, that he and Phil would be back for it all, that they would sort through it together and laugh at his obsession, then kiss at his obsession, at the obsession that had brought them back together after eternities.

He slung the bag over his shoulder and on his way to his brother's room passed by the door to the storage room. Grayson's last words echoed: *Bring a crowbar.* Mike had no idea what that meant, but he decided that it couldn't hurt to heed the advice. He pawed through the toolbox in the storage room until he found a smallish crowbar, no more than a foot long, unchipped, unworn, the price sticker ($10.99) still intact. He slipped it into his bag.

He knocked gently at his brother's door, not wishing to interrupt practice, but knowing that he needed to take this opportunity. When his brother called out for him to enter, he went in, closing the door behind.

His brother sat on the bed, a music stand before him, sheets of music scattered on the floor and on the bed, his brother's musical instrument on the bed next to him. His face lit up at seeing Mike, and he rose to hug him.

Mike held his younger brother tight, and in that moment a profusion of emotions weltered within him—love and guilt and fear and indecision. Love for his brother. Guilt that he had not been there enough for him. Fear that he would never be there again after this one, pure moment of fraternal attachment. Indecision that he was doing the right thing. Would going on the path to see Barry Lyga mean fulfilling the askew prophecy of *Inframan* and sacrificing his brother's life?

"I know why she doesn't love you," Mike murmured into his brother's hair. "I know why and I can't explain it, but I'm going to do my best to fix it, okay? I wanted to tell you—" and then stopped suddenly at the sound of the doorbell, unexpected at this time of night.

His brother wanted to know what Mike wanted to tell him, but Mike only held him tighter and listened as footsteps went to the front door—his mother, from the tread.

The front door opened. Mike suddenly knew. He knew he'd made a mistake in going to Phil's.

"Mrs. Grayson?" a voice said, and Mike closed his eyes and saw the Cop™ in his mind's eye—two of them, actually, standing in the doorway, lit against the dark of night by the thin spill of light from the hallway lights, unless Mom had turned on the porch light before opening the door, one of them (or maybe both) flipping open a small leatherette wallet (or wallets) to display a badge (or badges), face(s) stern and resolute, eyes hard and determined.

"We need"—the voice said, Mike straining to hear it, vindicated by the "we" in his supposition that it would be two Cops™, not one—"to speak to your son, Michael Grayson. Is he home?"

"What's this about?" Mom said, in a tone of voice that told Mike—and, no doubt, the Cops™—that she knew exactly what it was about: the restraining order. And suddenly, to her, the world made sense. Her son's abrupt uncharacteristic decision to disappear for "a few days" with his best friend. His equally sudden, equally uncharacteristic expression of filial love, offered without prompt or inducement. For Mike, the "reality" of the restraining order was mere days old; its reality savored of a particular unreality, especially when stacked against the many realities in which it did not exist and never had existed. But to Mom and to Dad and to his younger brother, the restraining order was their only reality, and they had lived it for years now, years of wondering why and how Mike had "gone off the rails" and become obsessed with "that poor girl," years of wondering if he would snap, years of worrying, those years now funneled down to a single pinpoint moment—this moment—as the Cops™ stood at the front door, all grim and dour and official, with a whirlwind in Mom's mind, Mike was sure, a whirlwind shouting questions, throwing out horrific scenarios, all of which boiled down to *Oh, God, what has my son done to "that poor girl?"*

Mike pulled back from his brother and held a finger to his

lips, silencing his brother (who was very, very good at saying nothing) as the Cop™ explained to Mom that they had received a complaint that Mike had violated his restraining order for the second time in a week, this time actually going so far as to go to "that poor girl's" house and confront her and assault her boyfriend—at which Mom gasped while Mike climbed onto his brother's bed and carefully though quickly though quietly prized open the window—necessitating this visit from the authorities, ma'am, and please just tell us where your son is.

As Mike inched the window open further, cautious to avoid the slightest sound, looking back at his brother occasionally, whose attention shifted from the closed door to the opening window and back again, the whole time with eyes wide and anticipating, he heard Mom call for Dad, who came to the door, too, who haggled with the Cops™ another minute or so, which allowed Mike to ease the window open the rest of the way, but climbing out the ground floor window would put him directly in the line of sight of the Cops™, so he was grateful when he heard Dad say—after a moment more of discussion—that the Cops™ could come in and they would find Mike in his room, but "you're not taking him anywhere until I've called my lawyer," to which the Cops™ grunted noncommittally and then—leaden-footed—entered the house.

Mike held his breath. His brother said nothing still, now staring at Mike with an almost physical force, as though he could force him out the window to safety with the mere power of his gaze and nothing more. But Mike was frozen at the window, captivated by the sound of the Cops'™ feet in his own hallway, now outside his own room, now *in* that room, one of them saying, "Mr. Grayson, we need to— Oh, shit, he's not . . ." and drifting off, as Mike hauled half his body over the window sash, realizing that it wasn't so far and he had to go *now* or go not at all and never, as a Cop™ said, "Jesus! Look at this place! It's all about the girl! This kid is—" being cut off not by his partner or by anything other than Mike's departure, slipping through the window.

The last thing he saw in the house: The expression on his brother's face—terror mixed with urgent love. And then he was outside, rolling away from the house, the air *whoof*ing out of him, wanting nothing more than to stay and catch his breath, knowing that he couldn't, rising and running, running, running.

CHAPTER 29

Mike ran.

He knew that he had to find a place to hide. It was still hours before he was to meet George and Gayl, hours before he could safely disappear into the Other City (and his mind rebelled at the conflation of "safe" and "the Other City," two hitherto mutually exclusive notions that now seemed irrevocably conjoined), and he had to lay low until then.

The thought of meeting George and Gayl reminded him that the Cops™ would, surely, go after his best friend when they failed to find him. He slowed down, pulling out his cell phone, then stopped near a spindly cherry tree planted by the side of the road. George answered on the second ring.

"Dude, what?" he asked somewhat testily.

Mike gave him a heave-breathed, truncated version of what had just happened, concluding with, ". . . so maybe you should be on the lookout."

If George wanted to reprimand Mike for the abject stupidity of violating his restraining order (and Mike sensed in that way that long-time friends can that he did), he managed to suppress that particular urge. "They'll be coming to talk to me, you know what I mean?" he said.

"Yeah. You can't tell them about Gayl or about—"

"How stupid do you think I am?"

The answer to that question—"Not stupid at all, man"—had to go unspoken, for in that moment, Mike heard a car's engine gun to life. Looking back towards his house, he saw the bright white headlights of the Cop™ car, and realized he had to keep moving.

Slipping the phone back into his pocket, he ran, his mind outpacing him, thinking ten steps down the road, then a block, then two. He had to hide. He had to get away. On this street—this street he'd lived on for so many years—there was nowhere to hide, only mute and dark houses where the parents of friends from elementary school would happily turn him over to the Cops™, only stretches of desert between them, with the occasional Joshua tree or cactus, impossible to hide behind and among.

They were in a car and he was on foot. Sticking to the sidewalks or the street would avail him nothing, so he cut across a lawn, then hopped a cinder-block wall and dodged a pair of palm trees. Now he was on the main road, and ahead he spied the blue light that signified the entrance to the subway. Under his pounding feet, the pavement rumbled—a Moore car was approaching the station.

Mike thought he was running as fast as he could; now he pushed himself to run even faster. He threw himself down the stairs to the subway, leaping down the last half-flight, his breath a hot and ragged wind in his chest. He nearly collided with a man in a black jacket who jumped to one side and cursed under his breath, but did nothing more.

Mike surprised himself by taking a moment to swipe his

card at the turnstile. Fortunately, it was late at night and the platform and station were not crowded—he had no trouble making his way through.

The entire station vibrated and clattered, heralding the arrival of the Moore. Mike risked a shoulder-glance and saw, with horror, that the Cops™ were not far behind him, coming down the stairs, yelling and gesturing for other passengers to get out of their way. The Moore line ran both uptown and downtown, and while Mike didn't currently care which way he went (he would have preferred a sign for a train marked "Away from the Cops™" at that moment), he had to choose which ramp to run down—he couldn't afford to be trapped on the uptown platform while the downtown train clanked and clunked into position across the way, or vice-versa.

A shout from behind him alerted him that the Cops™ were through the turnstile. He made his choice blindly, racing down the uptown ramp, and was greeted with the welcome sight of a Moore train waiting for him at the platform. The doors were still open and he charged at the nearest one, flinging himself through so hard and fast that he flew across the width of the car and plowed into the opposite, closed door, raising a chorus of tsks and a flurry of head-shakes from the scattered few on the car with him.

A single Cop™ charged down the ramp, the other, he realized, having no doubt gone to the downtown platform, splitting up to cover both possibilities. Mike watched as recognition exploded in the Cop™'s eyes; Mike shrank against the closed door, watching through the open door as the Cop™ ran closer, and then a chime sounded and an incongruously English-sounding robotic voice intoned, "Stand clear, please. Doors closing," and the doors slid smoothly shut.

An instant later, the train chugged to life and pulled away, the Cop™ still a good five or six feet away from the now-closed door. Gasping, Mike dragged himself to the door closest to the platform and—as the train picked up speed—flipped the Cop™ off, pressing his finger against the window as the station and the Cop™ receded into the distance and the train vanished into the subway tunnel.

Moments after Mike—now seated and studiously avoiding the unwelcome occasional glares and haughty sniffs of his fellow passengers for his indecorous and potentially dangerous entrance into the car—caught his breath, the Moore line stopped dead in the tunnel. Mike was rubbing his side—when he'd crashed into the closed door, he smashed his bag between his side and the subway car, driving the edge of the crowbar painfully into his abdomen—and looked up as the car slowed and then came to a halt. The passengers, en masse (Mike included), held their breath, gazing up at the ceiling, the entire car frozen and silent for a moment.

The lights overhead flickered once, then died. Pale emergency lights blinked to life. The car groaned as one.

"FOLKS," a voice crackled over the inter-car intercom, "WE'VE BEEN TEMPORARILY DELAYED. WE'LL BE MOVING AGAIN SHORTLY."

"Son of a bitch," someone said bitterly and loudly to a murmur of agreement.

Mike knew that this was not a coincidence or a temporary delay. The Cops™ had stopped the Moore line in order to get to him. They would send a team into the tunnel, get on the last car and make their way to the front until they found him. Son of a bitch, indeed.

He stood, wincing slightly at the tenderness in his side, and quickly checked the doors on either side of the car. The door to his left—the one he'd banged into—looked as though it fronted to a wall with slightly more space before it than the one on his right, so he forced his fingers as best he could into the rubbery gap between the two halves of the door and strained.

"What are you doing?" a woman demanded.

Mike ignored her. The door stubbornly did not budge. His fingers were slick and kept slipping on the rubber. He could not find purchase, nor could he get his fingers deep enough between the doors for the requisite leverage.

"Just wait," the woman went on. "Are you crazy?"

"Probably," Mike admitted, realizing that he was also quite stupid, and zipped open his bag to retrieve the crowbar. A moment later, he levered open the door, the brand-new crowbar completing its virgin mission without complaint and with no more damage to itself than losing the price tag that had clung to it until now.

Several passengers called out to him; even more of them simply shook their heads or rolled their eyes. Mike ignored every last one of them and pressed himself through the opening into the tight, filthy space between the subway and the tunnel wall.

Just then, the Moore line shook and quaked and the lights came back on and the door behind him ground closed and the train began to pull away.

CHAPTER 30

Against his fervent expectations, Mike did not see his life flash before his eyes as the train blasted away from him. The tunnel filled with wind and soot and ash; he shut his eyes against it and held his breath and flattened himself against the tunnel wall. For a moment, he prayed to God that the train would not catch on him or his bag and drag him through the tunnel to his maimed, bloody death, but then he realized that God was, most likely, not listening. Or, if listening, caring.

The subway rattled and shrieked all around him, careening ahead toward uptown, the updraft from its departure threatening to pluck him from the wall like a leaf whisked away by a breeze. Mike probed and discovered with one hand a grimy pipe of some sort, which he clenched with all his might as he pressed himself flatter against the wall, his cheek turned to the disgusting concrete. The roar of the train filled him and washed over him, penetrated him, and then was suddenly and absolutely *gone,* so gone and so suddenly silent that he was certain he must have died and, on opening his eyes, was sure he'd landed in the blackest, blindest pit of hell.

He had survived. The last car of the uptown Moore receded before him, its lights disappearing even now around a bend in the tunnel, leaving him in total darkness.

He sucked in a huge gulp of air and immediately succumbed to a coughing fit that pried him away from the wall and caused him to stumble to the ground, tripping over a track and almost falling forward, pinwheeling his arms as he hacked his lungs out, the grit and grime of the subway having found its way into his body despite his best efforts. Something shifted, skittering, at his feet and he kicked out, connecting with absolutely nothing. His balance regained by the fruitless kick, he felt behind for the wall, then leaned against it, coughing and hacking up phlegm in the total darkness of the subway tunnel, spitting and gagging it out until he could breathe again.

The air in the tunnel was cool but stale and somewhat humid, a surprise in the desert. Still, he gobbled it greedily, glad to be alive, to be free for the nonce, though lost and trapped.

The Cop™, he realized. The one he'd flipped off in a moment of escape-induced adrenaline and exuberance. That Cop™ would have seen the number of the car he was on. Their first inclination would be to stop the train in the tunnel, trapping him. But then they realized they knew the train, the line, the direction, the car number, and the next stop. All they would have to do is wait for him at the next station. Mike's great escape plan—formulated on the run—now seemed pathetic.

And yet, he was still free. He could not go forward—uptown—as the Cops™ were waiting there already. The Moore only took five or six minutes to arrive. Even with the temporary stop and the need to ramp up to speed again, it would be there soon, and then the Cops™ would know that Mike was in the tunnels. He had a few minutes to get back to the previous station and find another train. Maybe a downtown Moore or a crosstown Bates. One or the other would do, and the usual schedules meant that one or the other should be arriving shortly, as they usually clustered around the arrival of the uptown Moore.

He looked around, seeing nothing but black in all directions. He was reasonably certain that he hadn't turned around too much since getting off the train, so going to his right should lead him back to his original station. But he couldn't see, and the thought of feeling his way along terrified him. Scorpions lived down here, he knew, and he had no desire to stumble into a pack[58] of them. Nor did he wish to stagger into the third rail or bang his head on a low-hanging pipe or walk into a curving subway wall or any of a plethora of other hazards that awaited him in the unfamiliar dark.

Tamping down his panic, he forced himself to breathe calmly, forced himself to think, then—with a slight smirk—he delved into his pocket for his cell phone and grinned at the smallish cone of glowing light that burst forth, illuminating a few feet in front of him. For a long time, he had kept a photo of Phil as his phone's wallpaper, Phil caught unawares while napping one day, tangled in the history-made sheets after the most recent chapter of their history had been written. Now, though, he saw that his wallpaper was a different picture of Phil—similarly unawares—shot at a distance, from a stalker angle, lovingly and assiduously zoomed and cropped, slightly pixelated. What would the Cops™ think if/when they saw this? More evidence for them. More proof. As if they needed more.

He was surprised to find that he actually had a signal down here—a single bar, but a signal nonetheless—but then recalled his father mentioned months ago how the various tele-cartels

58. A group of scorpions is appropriately called a "cyclone," but not because the rock band Scorpions became famous with the song "Rock You Like A Hurricane."

were jockeying for position in the race to bring connectivity to the last place in the city where it did not exist, the underground. Briefly, he contemplated calling George, but quashed the idea. He needed to conserve his battery life and, more importantly, he couldn't be certain that George was alone, his phone line untapped by the Cops™.

For now, he had only one option, and it lay both ahead and behind, the future and the past at once, returning to the previous station.

His path illuminated by the bright, purloined photo of his lost Philomel, he made his way through the tunnel.

****

George's mother—the internationally renowned and mega-bestselling author Monika Seymore—clearly wanted to interrogate her son as to his camping plans, but held her tongue, merely nodding and giving George a variation of the same smile he saw so often on television and webcasts and in magazines, the smile that she had practiced long and hard in mirrors over the years, the smile that substituted for her true feelings almost by default, one of the many unforeseen consequences of global stardom and scrutiny. George knew the smile well and since Monika was more than just a celebrity to him, he also knew what lurked behind it—the years of anguish and pain, of guilt and fear, of shame. He knew that she wanted to protect her son, her son who was old enough to be on his own, old enough to join (and to be dismissed from) the Marines, and that—simultaneously—she was convinced that her deficient protection during his childhood made her inadequate to the task even now, thus setting her fervent maternal urges in conflict with her fervent maternal guilt. The result, as George knew from long experience, was the fake smile, the smile Monika Seymore showed to the rest of the world with increasing regularity. Some days, George feared that Monika was becoming the smile, that the smile was transmogrifying her, growing like an out-of-control mole, sinking deep into her, sending malignant tendrils as far as her soul, threatening to consume that soul, such that all that would remain of the once and former Monica Singleton would be the sheen, the pleasing and empty varnish of her pseudonym.

"I'll be fine," he told her again, smiling reassuringly. They were in the kitchen, where Monika still wrote, even after all these years. She had begun *INsight* shortly after the asshole went away, starting in a used bookstore, then banging away on an ancient notebook computer at the kitchen table at night when she thought George was asleep. George, in fact, had usually been concealed just around a corner, daring peeks every now and then, listening as his mother pounded the keyboard and muttered under her breath (she claimed that the only way to get the dialogue right was to speak it aloud), fearing that she had lost her abuser and her mind at the same time. When she told him—eventually—that she was writing a book, he had assumed it would be some sort of autobiography or journal, not a novel that would spread throughout the world like a pandemic. As the house's kitchen changed and moved over the years, the one thing that did not change was Monika at its table, still pounding her old laptop's keys as if they were the eyeballs of her ex-husband, still mumbling her characters' words under her breath.

Now she said to him, "I know you'll be fine. I'm worried about Mike. And if something happens to Mike, it'll make you a mess, darling, and I don't want that." Still the smile. The words, stilted. Honest words, honestly felt, delivered with all the vigor and heft of a morning show interview answer.

"Don't worry, Mom," George said. "It'll be fine, you know

what I mean? We're meeting later," he told her. In truth, he wanted nothing more than to call Mike back, having immediately been deluged with guilt for snapping at Mike, for answering the phone somewhat . . . testily, he supposed was the best word to describe it.[59] While Mike had been difficult to understand, George had picked up the gist, that Mike had idiotically (he felt a pang of guilt for thinking it, but—like "testily"—it seemed the most appropriate, most accurate word) gone to see Phil and now was on the run from the Cops™. The police would have been bad enough—the Cops™ were worse. George needed to call Mike for more details, but he realized that if the Cops™ were after Mike, then there was every chance that they had already dropped a virus on Mike's cell. Which meant that now George's phone was infected, too, and the Cops™ would be able to listen in on him.

So, no, calling Mike was not an option. George would just have to hope that Mike could avoid the Cops™ and meet him and Gayl at the final station on the Fox line in—he checked his watch surreptitiously, hoping Monika wouldn't notice—six hours.

Six hours. A lot of time to run. George's cell phone seemed to throb and burn in his pocket, pulsing a Morse code: C-A-L-L-M-I-K-E! There was no Morse code for an exclamation point, but George imagined it nonetheless.

"Do you need the sleeping bags?" Monika asked, having failed at Concerned Mother (a role she relished, but never quite nailed) and segueing smoothly now into Solicitous Mom, a role at which she excelled.

For camping, yes, George would need the sleeping bags.

59. George actually spent a few moments thinking of a better word, but could come up with nothing. His initial "testily" thought turned out to be the best.

But for hijacking a subway car and hurtling under the desert to what was supposed to be the most dangerous place on the planet? He had no idea what he would need for such a journey,[60] but he imagined that he—and they—would want and need to travel light, so the sleeping bags, though welcome-sounding, would have to stay home.

"No. Mike's bringing sleeping bags. We're good."

Monika strummed her fingers on the closed lid of her laptop. She usually stopped work for the day at dinner, but there were days—and he could tell this was one of them—when she would, in a fit of near-possession, continue writing long into the night and morning. "I'll let you go pack, then. Just make sure you wake me up and say goodbye before you leave, OK?"

George knew he wouldn't have to wake her up; his mother showed all the signs of a woman who would still be at the keyboard when he left in—checked his watch; an hour on the subway to get to the last Fox station—less than five hours.

"Hey, Mom," he said, stopping at the kitchen door and reversing himself as a thought struck him. "Can I ask you a question? About writing?"

"I'm not going to tell you whose baby Siobhan is having," she said lightly, a true smile touching her eyes for the first time all night.

Siobhan, the underage protagonist of the *INsight* series, had found herself on the final page of the latest book (page 692) staring at a positive pregnancy test, and the world was dying to know who the father was. Was it Georgos the resurrected Knight of the Red Cross, her one true love, who had been forced at gunpoint to defile her earlier in the book, a heinous deed that compelled him

60. In truth, he had some idea, based on his (aborted) Marine training, but the materiél he desired was beyond his current capabilities to procure.

to seek purification by committing suicide?[61] Was it Finn Dredmôr, the blind wizard, who had claimed—in Chapter 16—to have cast a spell of impregnation upon her, forcing a demonseed into her young womb sans any sort of penetrative act? Or was it Connor, the visitor from the future who claimed to be Siobhan's husband from ten years hence, and who—in a moment of weak passion—had seduced his young, theoretical bride-to-be?

No one knew—except for Monika—and no one would know until the manuscript she worked on every morning from six a.m. to noon and then from three p.m. to dinnertime was finished and sent off to her publisher under armed guard.[62] In the meantime, the world suffered and ached and swirled in a mad cacophony for the answer. The furor had risen so high and so passionate that Monika rarely left the house anymore unless she was in disguise or accompanied by the two large, Samoan bodyguards her publisher kept on retainer for her.

"I don't want to know about that," George said. He pondered briefly. How to bring this up? If he was joining Mike and Gayl on a quest to find a writer, didn't it make sense to talk to another writer first? The Marines had taught him—however quickly and incompletely—the importance of reconnaissance. "I'm just wondering . . . This might sound a little weird . . . But . . . What would you do if one of your characters came to life?"

Monika blinked, and for an instant every part of her that she had accreted as protection and armor over the past few years fell away and George saw only the terrified, battered woman who had taken him to the emergency room that last time, the terror in her eyes not for the life of her child, but rather for the

61. Georgos had begun the series dead, so while fans were worried about him, there was an undercurrent of reassurance that he would be back.

62. No one even knew the title—*SightED*—except for Monika and George.

knowledge that now—this time, in this place, at this moment—she would have to tell the truth. She would finally, finally have to tell the truth to the young Indian doctor with the kind eyes and the lips resolutely pursed and the clipboard held to his side and the phone already held out. But then the instant passed and she was Monika Seymore again.

"Came to *life*?" She laughed. She had a good, throaty laugh that microphones picked up particularly well, developed over a rigorous six-month period with a publisher-hired speech therapist and marketing expert. "What do you mean? Do you mean I'd be walking through Books-A-Go-Go and turn a corner and see Siobhan standing there in the SpecFic aisle? Is that what you mean?"

It sounded foolish the way she said it. "Well, yeah. That's what I mean."

"I would assume I was losing my mind, Georgie." He hated the diminutive of his name. She used it infrequently and, as best he could tell, for no particular reason or set of reasons, but every time she did, it rankled. "They're just characters." She winked. *They're just characters* was on the list of phrases her media trainer had begged her to purge from her lexicon. Monika had uttered it early in her career at a signing, to the visible and audible horror and shock of those present. *People want to think these characters are as real to you as they are to them*, the media trainer had patiently explained. *No matter how you think about them, you always need to say something like*

"I mean," Monika said, pretending to clear her throat and recover from her "gaffe," "'sometimes I don't know where the fiction starts and stops, they're so real to me!'"

They chuckled at the canned phraseology. "But seriously, Mom."

"So, we're assuming I'm not crazy? We're assuming

that—somehow—Siobhan, my Siobhan, is standing there in the store?"

"Exactly."

"Well . . ." To her credit, she actually thought about it. "I guess it would depend on what she did. What she said. What she looked like." She paused. "Which book she came from. Which chapter in which book, you know?"

George nodded, thinking. That was all true. The first few chapters of *INsight* were not kind to Siobhan—the orphanage, the near-death experience at the hands of Father O'Culligan, the whole thing with the dog . . . But by the end of the book, she was pretty happy.

"Say it's Siobhan from the early parts of *INsight*, when things weren't going well for her. Say she's sort of pissed at you."

Monika blew out a breath. "So she knows who I am?"

"Yeah. She thinks of you as God. And she wants to know why you're doing all these horrible things to her. She wants an explanation."

"I don't know. I would . . . You know, the thing is, I *am* God to her. I made her. I can make her do whatever I want. So I would just tell her to go away, and she would have to."

"You wouldn't try to explain it to her?"

Monika laughed again. "Explain what? What's there to explain? She's not a person, Georgie. She's a character. She exists to play a role in my story. Stories, I guess."

"You wouldn't tell her that things will get better by the end of the book?"

A shrug. "I could do that, I guess. But then what? First of all, what if she didn't believe me? And second of all, what about the next book, where things get bad again? And the one after that? Am I supposed to lie to her?"

George wondered what Mike wanted to hear from Barry

Lyga. Did he want to hear that everything would be OK? Sure he did. But things could "be OK" and then not be OK again. What did anyone's assurances mean?

"Characters in books exist to suffer," Monika went on. "That's their purpose. They go through things so that we can feel along with them. They go through horrible things so that when they ultimately triumph, the reader gets to feel a . . . a . . . cathartic buzz, a vicarious victory. Oh, that was alliteration. I know. I want to leave it."

Ultimately triumph . . . "So they have to win in the end." That sounded promising for Mike. For everyone, really.

"I hope so. Most stories have happy endings. That's what people like. They don't like stories that make them feel bad or confused or unsure. They want to know that everything turns out well in the end. When they don't get that assurance, they turn against the book. If the book made them feel bad, they assume the book itself must be bad."

"Are you saying people are stupid?" Monika had never had any but the kindest words for her readers, even the ones who inundated her with letters and e-mails written in some prototype of an English to come, lacking proper capitalization and/or punctuation, using abbreviations in running text, substituting numbers like 4 and 2 for their proper words. He never imagined he would hear his mother disparage her readers.

"God, no!" she exclaimed, meeting his expectations and realigning his understanding of her. "They're not stupid. People just have expectations, and when those expectations aren't met, they're disappointed. See?"

"I guess." The conversation had diverged from George's original intention, which had been to assess what his trio might encounter should they actually succeed at this mad quest to find Barry Lyga. "So," he said, dragging the dialogue back to its purpose, "if you met Siobhan and she demanded a happy ending from you, would you give it to her or not?"

Again, Monika thought, taking very seriously a perfectly absurd and pointless question. "In the end, I would tell her to keep trying for her own happy ending, to keep fighting. That's what Siobhan does in the books, doesn't she? She never surrenders. She never gives up."

CHAPTER 31

Mike was ready to give up.

He had been on the run in the tunnels for more than an hour now, and everywhere he went he found only more and more Cops™. At first, he had emerged into the Moore station near his house as a crosstown Bates pulled in on another platform; he'd managed to sneak aboard. With no Cops™ at the station, he had breathed a bit easier once on the train, confident that he had escaped.

But as the Bates neared its first stop, a quick look out the window revealed—gathered on the platform—a cluster of Cops™, all gesturing quite excitedly at the oncoming and braking train. Somehow, they had gotten here ahead of him.

Fortunately, he was near the rear of the train, so as it lumbered into place at the platform, he used the emergency access doors between cars and nimbly and hurriedly hopped from car to car until he was at the last car, at which point he popped open the final emergency door and—as the car ground almost to a halt—leapt out into the darkness of the tunnel and ran as fast as he could, knowing that in mere moments the passengers on the train would be interrogated by the Cops™ and reveal that a teen matching his description had just leapt out of the Bates car. He had run until the dim light from behind melted into murk and black, then once again flipped open the cell and allowed the surreptitious luminescent photo of Phil to lead the way.

He turned down other tunnels, slip-walked tracks that ramped down, hiked tracks that ramped upwards, heart-hammeringly aware that a train could at any moment explode from the guts of the earth and smash into him, reducing him to a loose bag of paste and flesh and shattered bones. More than once, he heard the remote rumble of a train, and, assuming that it was still far distant, continued walking, only to be surprised moments later by a burst of light ahead or behind, then scrambling quickly to the wall, pressing himself there as the cars rattled and shook past him. Now when he heard that rumble, he made haste to find the nearest spot of wall. In between episodes of defying death-by-subway, he came upon other stations, but each time found Cops™ already waiting for him, alerted in some cases by their stiff, jargon-shot chatter, in other cases by a serendipitous glimpse of a boot or pant cuff before swiftly doubling back and fading into the tunnels again.

"Is this what you want?" he said quietly, his voice nearly smothered by the closeness of the tunnel. "Is this what you want, Barry Lyga? For me to die here in the dark? For me to make some kind of dramatic decision?"

He considered the situation, wondered about his options. He refused to believe that he was fated by God or Barry Lyga or by outline to die here in the tunnels of the city's subway system. Was he supposed to risk his life by editing one last time, by removing himself from this situation, or even by editing last night's visit to Phil?

No. That part of the story, he suspected, was done and over with. The edits had become progressively dangerous for a reason—they were a countdown, a steady drumbeat leading with inexorable precision to this moment where Our Hero, his powers exhausted, struggles for life in the modern-day Hades of a grimy subway tunnel. Mike thought of Orpheus and Heracles and Hermóðr and Ishtar and their travels and travails to their various underworlds.[63] This, he reasoned, was his version of Hades, Hel, etc., requiring a heroic level of cleverness or strength to emerge.

In his ranging and roaming, he had encountered doors set at regular intervals into the walls of the various tunnels, their surfaces laden with grime which, when wiped away, revealed in the pallid glow of his cell phone signage of the sort:

AUTHORIZED PERSONNEL ONLY!

and

DANGER!

and

WARNING! DO NOT ENTER!

and, further

TRAIN PERSONNEL ONLY!

NOT FOR RIDERS!

each one more declamatory and restrictive than the next, as though some urban planner decades ago had foreseen Michael Grayson's madcap race through the tunnels and sought to proactively piss him off.

63. cf. Joseph Campbell's *The Hero with a Thousand Faces*, an academic description of the common elements of mythological journeys throughout history, all of which involve a trip to an underworld of sorts, whether literal or symbolic. The book was, unfortunately, discovered by Hollywood and its tropes bastardized and literalized by generations of screenwriters attempting to add scope to their stories. Its basic premises, however, are sound and worth reading. In 1992, Barry Lyga (at the time working on *Inframan*) wrote a scholarly essay entitled "American Buddha" which mapped the Campbellian monomythic structure to American comic book heroes.

The signs scarcely mattered, though, as each door was firmly locked, and though specks of rust dotted the latches and locks and hinges, none of them would budge.

Until this one.

****

Mike tugged again on the door handle, feeling the slightest bit of give. He had almost given up hope of getting one of these doors open, but this one had called to him in some way. Exhausted and filthy, he had stopped to catch his breath and, looking over, spied the door, just one more of many that had mocked him already, but then noticed that there was no lock threaded through the loop near the doorknob. He attacked the door with a savagery that surprised him, twisting the knob, finding it turned, it actually turned! With no idea what lay beyond the door, he kept pulling, straining against the decades of grime and dirt and rust that fixed the door fast in its frame, caring only that he could—for a moment at least—get out of the tunnel, finally gather his wits without worrying about the next train dashing him to pieces.

He pried the door open and peered inside, casting Phil's light in each direction. The cell phone, he knew, was rapidly dying, its battery leeching away each time he used it, yet he had no choice. Now it revealed to him a tight corridor walled and ceilinged and floored in concrete. Desiccated scorpion shells—molted and sloughed off over the years—clustered in pyramidal piles here and there along the walls, and the corridor vanished ahead into darkness.

And then—deep in the darkness ahead—a light flickered.

Mike stepped into the corridor and eased the door shut behind him, closing it silently and without the firmness that would seat it in the frame again, just in case he had to come back through this way in a hurry, unable to take the time to struggle with the door again.

He made his way forward as the light flickered again in the distance. For ten or a dozen paces, the light flashed and danced, then finally persisted. Mike crept forward, slipping his cell phone into his pocket as the light became stronger. The corridor continued ahead, but the light came from a small room to his right, no more than a closet, really, lit by a smudged light bulb dangling from the ceiling. Metal shelves lined one wall, stocked with little more than empty space and a somewhat-familiar-looking ball cap that once upon a time may have been blue. A dirty sink, spotted with rust, cracked with age, jutted from another wall, and against the third wall (the fourth wall being barely large enough for the entrance through which Mike now peered) was a threadbare easy chair bleeding clouds of stuffing, on which curled a lanky, sandy-haired man in jeans and a trenchcoat. As Mike froze in the doorway, wondering whether he should enter or consider himself fortunate to slip away, the man opened his eyes and shot his brows.

"Hey!"

Mike stood rooted to the spot, part of him wanting to run down the corridor, another part grateful for a fellow human being, especially one who would know more about the labyrinth under the city.

"I'm not here to hurt you," Mike said, holding out his hands in a defensive posture. "I got lost. I just need to get out of here."

The man unfolded himself from the chair and the light overhead flickered in an on-off pattern for a moment before settling into a half-power, buzzing on-position. In the dim light, Mike could just make out the man's dirty face (no dirtier, Mike realized, than his own at this point), smudged as if by coal, scoured by the desert sand above. His eyes were surprisingly clear, a penetrating blue, as though discs of bright sapphire had been carefully cut by a jeweler and then set in place. The trenchcoat, long and filthy, was buttoned to his neck.

"John Hanson," the man said, and Mike suddenly recognized him—the homeless man from the subway, the one to whom he'd given a dollar, the one he'd thought . . .

The man stretched out an arm for his ball cap, jamming it on his head. When he moved, the light overhead crackled again, threatening to burn out. The man cursed and slid back into the chair; the light bulb, as if relieved, returned to full power.

"You gave me that fake dollar," the man said, curled once again in his chair. "In the subway."

"It's a real dollar," Mike said, exasperated, incredulous that he was even having this conversation.

The man waved it off. "No, no. It's OK. It was nice of you. Sorry I lost my shit like that back there."

Mike risked a step into the room, and when the man did nothing, he took another. He was aware of his own filth, and that sink beckoned him.

"Is it all right if I wash up?"

The man grunted something that could have been assent or denial. Mike took two more steps and, met with no resistance, put his cell phone on a shelf and twisted the faucet. Air belched forth, followed by a gush of rusty water, which moments later cleared enough that Mike risked dipping his hands in, then scrubbing them across his face. He felt vaguely human.

Turning to the homeless man, he gestured to the sink and the water, now running even more clear. "Do you want to . . . ?"

The man shrank into his chair. "Not a fucking chance, homeboy. Not a fucking chance."

"Sorry. I didn't mean to—"

The other shook his head. “I don’t get along with water.” He held up one arm, revealing a thin, bony wrist and forearm as the sleeve fell away. The flesh there was mottled with hideous, painful-looking electrical burns. Mike hissed in a breath of surprise and sympathetic anguish.

“Got a bunch more on my back from when I got caught in the rain back in New Haven,” the Electrostatic Man said. “That’s why I’m in the desert now.”

“You really are the Electrostatic Man,” Mike whispered.

“Who the fuck else would I be? I’m the spark/in the dark/make my mark . . .” He trailed off and sighed. “Nah, fuck it. Not gonna bother with that shit anymore. Too much work.”

“Look, I know it’s a lot to ask, but do you know how to get to the last stop on the Fox line from here? I’m supposed to meet some people there—” he checked his cell and gazed at Phil for a moment while checking the time—“in about two hours. I’ve been wandering all night.”

“You ain’t far from there.” The Electrostatic Man snorted laughter. “But you don’t got to walk. You can hop on a train. You got money, right?”

“It’s not that simple. The Cops™ are after me. Everywhere I go, they seem to know I’m headed there already. I need to get to the Fox terminus without them following me.”

“Hmm.” The Electrostatic Man extended one dirty hand and gestured.

Mike fumbled for his wallet.

“I don’t want your fucking money,” the Electrostatic Man breathed, then re-thought and said, “Well, no, fuck it, I’ll take your money. But I need your phone.”

Mike handed over a twenty, hoping that would assuage the Electrostatic Man’s needs, then gave him the cell phone. A massive jolt of electricity shocked him; ozone filled his nose as he jerked his hand back. In the Electrostatic Man's hand, the cell phone screen flashed once, then went dark.

"You broke my phone!" Mike yelled. That picture of Phil was the only one he had, other than the drawing he'd brought along with him.

"No shit," the Electrostatic Man said, handing the useless hunk back to him. "How you think they been finding you?"

Mike nodded slowly, staring down at the fried phone in his hand. He had been surprised to find a signal in the tunnels and now he knew the cost of that signal. Ever since Lucky Sevens, the Good American Act let the Cops™ track anyone anywhere without a warrant or warning. The Cops™ had used the phone's GPS to follow him through the tunnels, plotting his movements and predicting each station on his route. He had wasted fruitless hours in the tunnels when he could have just ditched the phone . . .

". . . or turned it off," he finished aloud.

"Battery still charges the GPS," the Electrostatic Man said, yawning and tilting his cap over his eyes for a nap. "Only thing to do is ditch it or kill it."

Mike dropped the cell in his bag, just in case. "Look, I hate to ask, but can you help me get to the Fox line?"

"You're pretty close," the Electrostatic Man said, sounding as though he couldn't be bothered. He looked at the twenty clutched in his hand as though just realizing it was there, uncrumpled it and lit up with delight. "Grant! That's right. That's real money. Cool."

"Who else would it be?"

"I don't know. But you fuckers don't have George Washington on the one, so who knows what the fuck you'll do with your money?"

Mike gave up. "Look, I just need to get out of here. Preferably to the Fox line. Can you help me or not? I have another twenty I can give you." In truth, he had three more twenties, a five, and six ones (which the Electrostatic Man would call fake due to the portrait of John Hanson, but which would spend just fine, Mike knew), and he was more than a little nervous at the prospect of revealing that he had money, for what was to stop the Electrostatic Man from just attacking him and taking all of his money? But thus far, the vagrant had been passive, with none of the aggression from the other day in evidence. He needed some direction, and clearly the Electrostatic Man knew his way around the tunnels.

"Look . . ." A thought occurred to him. "You said before you came from New Haven. In Connecticut?"

A yawn. The twenty disappeared into a pocket. "Where else?"

"That's where Yale is, right?"

"I guess."

"Did you meet a guy there . . . A guy named Barry Lyga?"

"Who?" A blank gaze, those blue eyes revealing nothing.

"What about Mike Grayson?"

This time the blue eyes flickered. "Mike Grayson?" The Electrostatic Man frowned. "Name's familiar . . ."

"What about—"

The Electrostatic Man suddenly bolted upright in the chair (the light bulb dimmed) and held up a hand for silence. Mike shut up and backed up a step, bumping into the sink.

"Shit," the Electrostatic Man whispered, and before Mike could respond, he became aware of what his companion had noticed only moments before—the slightest shiver-squeal of the heavy door to the subway tunnel scraping against the floor. Maybe, though, it had just opened due to its own weight . . .

No. Footsteps. Mike was sure of it.

"Police," the Electrostatic Man whispered. "Or Cops™."

He glared accusingly at Mike, who knew he deserved it—the Cops™ were coming to the last place they'd seen a signal from his GPS before it died.

The Electrostatic Man leapt up and grabbed Mike by the wrist; the light bulb overhead flickered, then burned out, plunging the room into darkness. The sound of footsteps went from sneaking to a rush as the Cops™—deducing (correctly) that the darkness meant they'd been made—ran towards their target. A negative flash of the room blazed in front of Mike's eyes as he allowed himself to be dragged into the corridor, the darkness and photo-negative image suddenly and spectacularly replaced by a great blaze of light—the corridor's ceiling was lined with darkened light panels that now erupted with illumination as the Electrostatic Man came closer. The Cops™—Mike's eyes (having an instant ago been in the light) adjusted quickly enough that he could see close to a dozen of them, some still squeezing in through the door—stopped, shielding their eyes from the sudden unexpected blast of light.

"Go!" the Electrostatic Man gritted through clenched teeth, pushing Mike further down the corridor, away from the Cops™. Mike could see now—with the lights on—that the corridor extended deep into the distance.

"But—"

"Now!"

And then the Cops™, recovered, charged, and Mike, looking over his shoulder as he ran, heard the Electrostatic Man bellow with rage and saw him reach out so that both hands were on opposite walls in the tight corridor, the left touching a light switch and the right touching what appeared to be a metal sign or plaque of some sort . . .

The circuit completed, the result was spectacular, as the overhead lights exploded in a shower of sparks and shards of high-impact plastics and glass. The Cops™ panicked, their sudden dives and dodges rendered into an epileptic stop-motion series by the on-off flashes of light from the erupting fixtures. Where Mike stood, the lights still functioned, but the effect was moving towards him, plastic guards shattering as bulbs overloaded and burst into a shower of hot, bright flares that burned in the air for tracery moments before fading. The Electrostatic Man stood between Mike and the Cops™, still bellowing, his body a black X in the corridor as light and dark warred around him.

Mike ran down the corridor, chased by darkening ceiling panels as he went, breathing hard and heavy. Lights flashed behind him, strobing the corridor ahead just enough that he saw the L-bend in time to adjust his path before colliding with the wall. He thought he heard gunfire; he knew he heard the laughter and the bellow of the Electrostatic Man, the sizzle-crack and pop of light fixtures. He smelled smoke and ozone and burning scorpion shit.

At last (or swiftly—it was impossible to tell), the sparks and fireworks from behind stopped, and he slowed to a walk, hands held out carefully lest he run into a wall in the dark. Straining his hearing to its utmost limit, he could discern no movement behind him and wondered how badly hurt were the Cops™; how badly injured was the Electrostatic Man? Was anyone coming after him?

Blind, he stumbled forward, arms extended, feeling his way in the pitch black, begging himself not to panic. The corridor turned left, then right, then left again, then seemed to double back on itself. By now he was thoroughly lost.

Finally, he came upon a door. Bracing himself (for he had no idea what would be on the other side), he twisted the knob and pulled. Nothing. Pushed. Still nothing. Threw all his weight against it, and the door flew wide open, as light assaulted him, blinding him. Voices raised in shout as he stumbled out of the corridor onto what he imagined was a subway platform, his eyes not yet adjusted, but perceiving a somewhat-familiar blur of concrete pad and turnstile gate. He fell to the ground, the light searing his eyes, one hand held up to shield them, as footsteps neared him.

Then he heard George saying, "Mike? Mike?" Hands were on him—too many hands to be just George and Gayl. Someone helped him up and he leaned into the person, grateful to have emerged from the underworld of the subway system, even if only to a station. As his eyes adjusted, he looked around wildly, suspecting that the Cops™ had them all, but it was only George, standing nearby, Gayl standing a bit further away, and a newcomer, the one who actually had gotten to him first and helped him to his feet, a man who grinned at him lazily and said, "My name is Joe Roberts. I work for the state."

CHAPTER 32

He had made it to the last station on the Fox line. "You okay?" Gayl asked once he'd stopped shaking long enough to sit down at the edge of the platform with him and George. "You ready to go?"

"I don't—I don't know." The shaking had subsided, but Mike was having trouble catching his breath and couldn't seem to focus. Maybe it was the brightness of the lights after the darkness of the tunnels.

"Give him a second," George said protectively. "He's been running from the Cops™."

"You don't know the half of it," Mike said, and began shivering. George threw a brotherly arm over his shoulders.

"Joe says—" Gayl began.

"Joe's the guy who's getting us to the Other City, you know what I mean?"

Gayl snorted. "Guys. Seriously. We need to get moving. The Cops™ are gonna be able to figure out roughly where you were headed. They probably already know you're friends with George and are tracking him through his phone."

"Back off!" George snapped. "Give him a minute, okay? Just one single—"

"We may not *have* a minute! We have to get on the train and—"

"Help me up," Mike said. "If I'm gonna pass out, I can do it on the train."

Gayl and George helped Mike along the platform. "There was a . . . guy who helped me," Mike said. "He might be hurt. Can't we look for him?"

"No time," Gayl said tightly. As if to underscore the point, Joe Roberts took that moment to hustle past them towards the access door through which Mike had come. Joe closed and then locked it with a hefty padlock. Just in case the Cops™ tried to come through there. "The Tunnel Police, they steadily increase," Joe mumbled under his breath. It wouldn't stop them, but it would slow them down for a few minutes at least.

"We have to move forward," Gayl said. "You want your happy ending? We go that way." He pointed to the train just ahead of them. It was a low, bullet-shaped affair, sleek and not nearly as dirty as the typical city subway train. There were only three cars, all of which had blacked-out windows, as though there was anything to see in a subway tunnel (as Mike knew from harrowing personal experience at this point). The design of the cars looked more like a concept design than anything in active use. Until recently, Mike had never seen its like in all his years traversing the city's subway system; but this was, he knew, the same train he'd seen the morning of his sojourn to Crimson Rocks, the train that had mysteriously entered and then left the station without giving him time to climb aboard.

Joe Roberts brushed past them and hopped in the first car. "This train carries saints and sinners!" he called. "So get in and get tough or get up and get out."

The three of them joined Joe in the car, the driver disappearing through a door at the fore as soon as they were on-board. The doors slid shut with whispered efficiency. "Are you sure about this guy?" Mike asked quietly.

"Who, Joe?" Gayl asked. "Yeah, he's solid. He talks a little funny and it takes some getting used to, but he's fine. He's one of the higher-ups in the Transportation Services Administration."

"What's that?" Mike asked as George lowered him into a seat much cleaner and more comfortable than any subway seat Mike had ever experienced.

"It's a branch of the *whoa!*" Gayl stumbled as the train revved and pulled away from the platform, catching himself on a pristine, sparkling-clean handrail. "A branch," he went on, "of the Department of Tracks and Tunnels. You've heard of them, right?"

George nodded. Mike, after a moment, nodded, too. Somehow, the motion of the subway was making him less dizzy and disoriented. At this point, he wasn't about to question it.

"Well," Gayl continued, "they're also known as the MTA—the Mystery Transit Authority. Ever since Lucky Sevens, they've been empowered to monitor and regulate all public travel in the country."

"Like the way the Theoretical Security Administration watches air travel?" George asked.

"Yeah, just like the TSA, only for public transportation. Joe runs the lines of the city's subway system; he's the Boss. And these little daily trips to the Other City are pretty important, so he pilots the Fox-Barth train himself."

"He's a government guy bringing supplies to government troops," Mike said. "Can we trust him?"

"He's a good guy," Gayl said. "I met him last year, when I was in the planning stages of *Unfinished*. Looking for information about some of the tunnel structures down here. There was . . ." He chuckled without mirth. "There was going to be a scene where the protagonist gets trapped in the subway tunnels, hunted by the police. I guess that's not a surprise, is it?"

Mike shook his head.

"What exactly happened to you?" George asked, so Mike told them everything, beginning with his confrontation with Inframan on the subway last night, his subsequent encounter with the other (original?) Mike Grayson, and concluding with his meeting with the Electrostatic Man and his run through the underbelly of the subway system.

Gayl sank into a seat near Mike, stunned. "You're sure about this? You're sure you actually met characters from *Inframan*?"

"Yeah. Mike and the Electrostatic Man and the God of Failure himself."

Quietly, George asked, "What does this mean? Does this have to do with the fractals you mentioned?"

"I don't know what it means." Mike could tell it pained Gayl to say that. "We're not living inside of *Inframan*, but somehow characters from that book are entering our reality. It could just be some sort of Godlike whim or it could be . . ."

"Could be what?"

Gayl shrugged helplessly. "Maybe the One Bookers aren't so crazy after all. Maybe all realities—all texts, all stories—are merging into one."

"What do we do about that?" George asked.

"I'll tell you what we do," Mike said. "We go find God and we make him fix it. That's what we do."

"Can Joe make this thing go any faster?" George asked.

"No. The trip to the Other City takes about two hours. And there's a Marine checkpoint where the cargo gets inspected." Gayl held up a hand and then explained: "Don't worry—we'll hide in the driver's cubicle while Joe keeps them busy. From there, it's a straight shot to the Other City.

"And then what?" Mike asked.

Gayl shrugged.

"We play it by ear, you know what I mean?"

The thought was both comforting and condemning at once. Mike stripped out of his filthy shirt and pulled on the clean one he'd packed in his bag. Somehow that simple action relaxed him even more than eluding the Cops™, and he curled up on a bench by himself, his overnight bag as a pillow, and finally—after a night and morning on the run—fell asleep.

****

He woke up an hour later, or so George told him. During his brief but powerful nap, George had moved from across the car to sit next to Mike, protective to the last.

"We're about halfway there," George said.

"So we're under the desert right now."

"Yeah. Gayl's been talking to Joe. Picking up some more info about the Other City."

"Like what?"

"I'll let him tell you." Gayl was sitting near the door to the driver's cubicle, which was propped slightly ajar by his foot, leaning in and talking through the gap. "Look, before we get any deeper into this, I have to ask you: Do you really think you're going to get to meet this guy?"

"You mean Barry Lyga?"

"Yeah. I mean, he already wrote one book about a guy named Mike Grayson who tries to meet him, and we know how that panned out: The guy ends up in a college dorm with a piece of paper and a note to finish his own damn story."

"That was a different book. A different Mike Grayson. And he managed to cross from his universe—his book—into ours. So maybe there's life after the book closes. Maybe there's more to this than we thought."

"Dude, I'm just saying that maybe you should prepare yourself for the possibility that Barry Lyga is never going to meet with you, you know what I mean? He doesn't give a shit about you. You're nothing to him. Words on a page. You're just a character."

Before Mike could respond, Gayl came over to them and slid into a seat nearby. "Did the nap help?"

"I feel a little less groggy. What did you learn from Joe?"

"He's been traveling to the Other City since about a week after Lucky Sevens, which is when they set up the system to resupply the military forces there. The biggest surprise, to me, is that there are people there."

Mike and George exchanged a shocked glance. "You mean," Mike managed, "people other than the military?"

"Civilians?" George clarified needlessly.

"Apparently so. I thought the whole place had been evacuated, but there are still people living there. Should make it easier for us to blend in."

"How can that be possible?" Mike asked. "The whole place is supposed to be radioactive. Poisoned."

Gayl raised an eyebrow. "We talked about this already. You believe everything the government tells you?"

"You believe everything Joe Roberts tells you?" Mike shot back. "We could be walking into a death trap."

"Dude, that was sort of melodramatic."

"I didn't know how else to put it."

"I don't know what to tell you," Gayl said with an expression of surrender. "Joe says he's seen civilians in the Barth station there when he helped unload the cars."

"Maybe they're like consultants or something. Or scientists studying the after-effects of Lucky Sevens."

"I guess anything's possible," Gayl said.

"We're gonna find out soon, you know what I mean?" George checked his watch significantly.

Mike gnawed at his bottom lip. "Hey, guys? Listen to me for a second, all right?"

Gayl and George both looked at him with concern.

"You guys need to decide if you're really going to do this, OK? I mean, I pretty much have to, but you guys—"

George shook his head with fierce conviction. "No. Uh uh. No way, Mikey. Not a chance, you know what I mean? I'm not letting you go there alone. Not happening."

"I have to go, too," Gayl said quietly. "I appreciate your offer, but I have to go. I don't know who or what I am anymore. I need to confront God or Barry Lyga or whoever or whatever it is that's waiting for us. And I need answers."

"And," George added, "this has gotten bigger than just you and Phil. It's about the whole world. It's about love, you know what I mean?"

"What about Joe? He could get in a lot of trouble."

"Joe's seen a lot. He's been ready to quit this job for a while. He'll be fine."

Just then, the door to the driver's cubicle slid open and Joe Roberts emerged. At Mike and George's looks of panic, Gayl reassured them, saying, "He told me once that the autopilot controls it from here to the Marine stop."

"How are we doing?" Mike asked Joe, who sat down across the aisle from them.

"The road is long and seeming without end," Joe said.

Mike gaped. "Wait, what? How far—"

Joe shrugged an apology. "Just a dirty mile down on

the borderline, past the playground and empty switching yards."

"There's still time for you, Joe," Mike told him. "You can have us get out at some point along the way. We can make our way back through the tunnel."

Joe shook his head. "Some people wanna die young and gloriously. And I was gonna quit my job too."

"Yeah, I know, but this could be rough."

After thinking about it for a moment, Joe nodded once and then fixed Mike with a confident, resolute gaze. "I wanna go out tonight," he said. "I wanna find out what I got."

Other than the fact that it was morning and not night, Mike couldn't argue with that. Who was he to tell Joe that he couldn't test himself, prove himself?

They sat in silence for a while as the train clacked along the tracks. Mike took a good look at Joe, the oldest of the group. His hair, though, was thick and wavy and dark, slicked back from a high, regal forehead. Threads of gray wound through the temples, noticeable only when the light hit a certain way. He had a world-weary air about him, a sort of tired vibe, and his way of speaking was at once laconic and poetic, as though he'd spent a long time thinking about his answer; years, perhaps. He dressed not in the standard gray coveralls and matching cap of most subway drivers Mike had seen over the years, but rather in a pair of black jeans, a black vest, and a white button-up shirt, the sleeves rolled to reveal muscular forearms.[64] All in all, he was fit, and a powerful energy lurked within him, hidden behind heavily-lidded eyes.

64. Mike wondered why Joe Roberts was allowed to wear whatever he liked as opposed to the standard uniform. Then again, he had said that he worked for the state, not the city, and so perhaps his dress code was more lax.

“Are you sure?” Mike asked him. “This might be your last chance to—”

“You asked me that question,” Joe interrupted. “I didn’t get it right?”

Mike shut up. He had done what he could to protect the people who were trying to help him. He could do no more.

They sat in silence for a while, for even though Mike felt that there were things that needed to be said, none of them seemed urgent enough to break the silence. The blacked-out windows had more of an effect than Mike had initially and sardonically thought—he missed the blur of the subway tunnel in the window, the sense and sensation of speed, of motion, of progress. This new train was so quiet and steady that—but for the occasional and rare bump or jostle—they could have fooled themselves into thinking that they weren’t moving at all, that they had gone nowhere since boarding the train at the Fox station. Mike actually worried that perhaps they *had* gone nowhere, that Gayl’s notion of scarpering to the Other City through some long-forgotten tunnel under the desert was the game of a madman, that after a couple of hours the doors would slide open to reveal nothing more exotic than the Fox station and a horde of Cops™ ready to haul Mike off to prison.

“It’s a gone-dead train rumblin’ down this track,” Joe said into the quiet.

And it was.

CHAPTER 33

Overhead, the speaker crackled to life and with the exception of Joe Roberts—who appeared to have slipped into a half-doze—they all startled as a polite and nearly-genderless voice announced, "LADIES AND GENTLEMEN. THIS TRAIN IS NOW ON THE BARTH LINE. YOU ARE ON THE INBOUND BARTH LINE."

"That must be an automated recording," Gayl surmised, and Joe nodded once in confirmation.

"We're almost there, then?" Mike asked.

"More than halfway," Gayl said, once again checking with Joe for agreement, which came immediately in the form of another nod. "Now that we're on the Barth tracks, we'll go a little faster." He held up his hands to illustrate, bringing one closer to the other slowly, then suddenly much more quickly. "The Fox line goes slow coming out of the city and going under the desert, then picks up speed once it crosses over onto the newer Barth tracks."

"Got it."

They passed a few more minutes in silence, and then Joe

Roberts ushered them all into the driver's cubicle. Now Mike had a sense of the speed he'd missed before, for the forward window of the driver's cubicle was clear and cleaner than he'd expected, the tunnel ahead illuminated by the car's single, enormous headlamp, which revealed a gray-blackness that stretched far ahead, pipes and cables whipping along on either side of them as they sped towards the Other City. The enormity of their velocity whisked their breath from all of them, save for Joe Roberts, who stood behind them as they all three stared into the onrushing darkness, which seemed almost violent and sentient in its scope.

Joe gave them a moment to adjust, then directed them to duck down behind the control panel. There was really only room in the cubicle for the driver and perhaps one other person, but the three of them flattened and contorted themselves into the cramped space as best they could, keeping themselves from poking up into that portion of the cubicle visible through the window. With a dark tunnel and station lights reflecting off the window, Joe assured them, they should be nearly invisible from the outside. He would speak to the Marines at the station, as usual, and get them on their way again as soon as possible.

"Be careful when you talk to them," Gayl warned him. "Don't talk too much. That's a dead giveaway. Just act normal."

"And I don't say nothin' unless I'm asked," Joe assured him, then winked and closed the door behind him as he stepped into the car.

Moments later, the overhead voice returned, this time to tell them that the train was stopping at King's Point, which Gayl had earlier explained was the first stop inbound to the Other City, an old commuter depot on the metropolitan outskirts that had now been abandoned, then repurposed by the military as a checkpoint.

The car drifted to a stop, its brakes hardly squealing or squeaking at all as it slowed into the King's Point station. Mike heard shouts and rhythmic, military footsteps come closer and closer. By circumstance of their compaction into the driving cubicle, his face was close to George's, and George took note of the fear on Mike's face, squeezing his thigh—the only part of him near a hand—reassuringly.

They heard the door to the car slide open and then the car shifted slightly as more people came on board. George squeezed tighter, as if pressure communicated *Don't worry; it'll be OK.* Mike realized that he was holding his breath, that he had been holding his breath since the train stopped, and became suddenly afraid to exhale, as though the slight sigh of his breath might be the clue that would lead the hunters to them.

A moment later, when a United States Marine opened the door to the driver's cubicle and saw them hiding there, he knew for certain that his exhalation mattered not at all.

****

Joe Roberts had betrayed them, Mike knew, a notion disputed almost instantly as two Marines dragged him out of the car along with Gayl and George, shoving them all into place next to Joe, who stood on the platform watched over by two armed Marines, his hands clasped in front of him, his eyes downcast. They were on a subway platform superficially like any from their own city, only this one had a cast-iron sign hanging from the ceiling that read "BARTH INBOUND," with a red arrow pointing in the direction they'd been traveling. Other signs abounded, though they were new, reading "CHECKPOINT ALPHA" and "QUARANTINE IN EFFECT." Stenciled on the far wall was an arrow pointing up a flight of stairs with the word "COMMAND." An old exit sign hung over them, its faded letters reading "TO BARTH OUTBOUND AND EXIT." Other signs pointed down tunnels to the Poe line, the Milton, the Brown.

Mike fell into line next to Joe and murmured, "Sorry, man." For putting Joe into a position to be arrested by the Marines he'd hitherto given no reason even to suspect him of wrongdoing. And for the however-fleeting assumption that the older man had betrayed him.

"Shut up!" barked a Marine, not much older than Mike or George, but certainly younger than Gayl or Joe, yet possessing all the authority necessary thanks to his uniform, his bearing, his superior numbers, and—of course—his M-17 assault rifle, slung casually over one shoulder, sleekly black except for the bright red and blue corporate sponsor logos on the stock and the vibrant yellow logo on the barrel.

Mike shut up.

The Marine in charge glared at them each in their turn, pausing for the briefest moment at George's ramrod-stiff posture, almost identical to the stances of the other Marines. For an instant, Mike allowed himself to fantasize that the Marine would recognize either George himself or something in his bearing that cried out as a fellow Marine, a fellow comrade-in-arms, and would induce him to let them all go, but the Marine merely took note of George's stance, then moved on to the others, fixing Mike with a glare he found particularly unwholesome and angry, as though somehow the Marine—"HUFF" was stenciled across the left breast of his desert camo, just to the right and above his standard-issue Macrosoft logo patch—knew that Mike was responsible for them all being here.

"You are all hereby on notice," Huff intoned as though reading from a teleprompter, "that you are trespassing on quarantined property, pursuant to U.S.C. 48-09, section J, subsection 2, paragraph B. You are being taken into custody in accordance with provisions of the Good American Act."

"I want to call a lawyer," Mike said.

Huff had been turning away from them. He paused mid-turn, then spun back to Mike, a joyless smile on his face.

"A lawyer? There's no such thing as lawyers. Not for you. You don't get a lawyer, man. You get nothing, do you understand?"

"I'm entitled to a lawyer," Mike said, realizing that Gayl, next to him, interposed between him and George, was shaking his head.

"Under the terms of the Good American Act, you're considered bad hombres," said Huff, now clearly enjoying himself. "You have no rights. You get no lawyer. You're not under arrest—you're just in custody. Got it?" Before Mike could say anything, Huff slashed at the air with one hand in the universal sign meaning, "Shut up."

"You guys are going into a long, dark hole," Huff said with obvious relish. "You're gonna be locked up somewhere so remote they won't even have to throw away the key because no one will be able to find you anyway."

The other Marines herded Mike and the others together and marched them to and up the stairs[65]. "Can't believe you tried pulling this shit, Roberts," Huff was saying. "Thought you were smarter than that. You've been running this line since before I was even a Marine. What the fuck got into you?"

Joe started to respond, but Mike didn't listen. All he could think of was Phil, and Barry Lyga, and the Other City, and how

65. The order being: Huff and two Marines, Joe, Mike, Gayl, George, two more Marines, the necessity of understanding which will become apparent in as long as it takes to read the next few sentences.

close they'd come. To come so far, to get within walking distance of the Other City, only to lose, to find themselves stripped of their rights and their freedom. It was a joke so cold and so evil that he almost wanted to shout his anger and frustration, but suddenly there was a scuffle from behind.

Mike whirled just in time to see George, wrestling with one of the Marines.

****

George knew that even under the Good American Act, the Marines weren't authorized to fire indiscriminately, especially when fellow Marines were in the line of fire. The stairwell up from the platform at King's Point was just narrow enough to make it impossible for the Marines at the top of the stairs to get a clear shot on the down angle, especially if Mike, Joe, and Gayl all stayed upright and—preferably—moving, as they all were now.

He disabled the closest Marine with a surprise kick to the left kneecap, feeling the patella slide away from the knee, stretching the tendons far beyond their natural elasticity. It was a good kick. Strong. Precise. There was a good chance he'd crippled the Marine for life; in any event, he didn't care to imagine the soul-numbing burst of sudden pain that had exploded in that knee.

The other Marine on George's end of the staircase moved quickly, but not quickly enough—George had already grappled with his first victim, wrapping an arm around his neck from behind, then back-stepping until he was against a wall. Anyone trying to shoot him would have to do so over the Marine's shoulder or straight through him. Not a chance.

With his free hand, George slid his captive's service revolver out of his holster.

It had taken mere seconds—ten or fifteen at the most—for

George Singleton to go from a suspect "in custody" to an outright criminal actor, attacking a United States Marine in the commission of his sworn and legal duty.

Most shocking was not that it had happened at all, perpetrated by a former Marine upon his brothers, but rather that George was not worried about it at all, had not stressed over the decision. Indeed, he was hardly aware of having made the conscious decision to attack another Marine. From the moment the door to the driver's cubicle on the Barth-bound subway had opened and he'd seen a Marine standing there, George had known how this would end, had assumed, in fact, that it could and must end no other way.

Some deep part of him understood this: That in order for Mike to persevere, in order for Mike to continue and to complete his mission, George would have to surrender a part of himself. He knew this and he complied without a moment's hesitation.

"Drop your weapons," he said now, pointing his recently-purloined revolver at the head of the moaning, pained Marine in his grip. "Drop them now."

"You know we can't do that," the guy in front of him said, raising his rifle.

George tossed a look to one side. Mike and Gayl and Joe still clotted the stairwell and the Marines at the top of the stairs hadn't yet pushed them away.

"Fine," George said, "then I'll shoot you instead," and aimed at the Marine aiming at him, now giving that same Marine a choice: Drop his weapon immediately or risk either being shot by George or killing his friend in trying to shoot George.

"Do *not* drop your weapon!" Huff shouted from above, but it was too late—the Marine had already dropped his rifle.

"Don't let them down here!" George shouted to Mike and the others. "They won't shoot you. They can't. You're not armed."

“That’s bullshit!” Huff yelled. “I can and will—”

“He won’t,” George said with grim confidence and then, to the Marine who’d dropped his rifle, “Drop your holster, too. And lose the knife.”

****

Mike trusted George. More than that, he figured that maybe—just maybe—it was time for him to start acting like George’s best friend. Maybe in acting like it, he would actually become worthy of the title. So he reached out and grabbed ahold of the handrails on either side of the stairs, locking his elbows into place, and stared up at Huff and the other two Marines.

“Don’t be a fucking moron,” Huff said, swinging his rifle around, the barrel less than six inches from Mike’s forehead and unshaking. “I *will* put a bullet in you, faster than you can blink. It will happen and it will not be pretty.”

“You’ll have to kill all of us,” Gayl said from behind, and Mike felt hands close over his as Gayl stepped behind him and took hold of the handrails.

“Drop your weapons!” George shouted from below, his voice carrying over a sound that Mike at first could not identify, but then realized was a low, steady moan of pain from the Marine George had kneecapped. “You have a choice to make, Sergeant Huff! Think about this!”

“Nothing to think about,” Huff responded. The barrel of the rifle did not waver, and Mike contemplated what it would be like when Huff stopped talking for the split-second it would take to pull the trigger. Light traveled faster than sound, with bullets traveling between the two. He doubted he would hear the explosive force of the bullet being fired, but suspected he would have just enough time to see the slight jerk of the rifle barrel, perhaps a flash of light and then nothing more as the bullet hashed his brains an instant later. It could come at any moment, the decision entirely in Huff's hands.

"You have a choice, Sarge!" George called. "I have two of your men down here disarmed. If you kill my friends, I guarantee you that Mendez and Johnsson down here die, too. So then you've got two dead Marines and four dead civilians on your hands."

"You're not civilians," Huff said. "You're bad hombres."

"And two dead Marines," George persisted. "At the very least. I may get in a last shot or two at you and those other guys up there before you nail me. So, two dead Marines and a bunch of guys who—when CID gets done looking into it—are gonna all come up clean. You'll have a fuckload of explaining to do, you know what I mean? Not to mention all the paperwork. A double-fuckload of paperwork. Maybe a court martial. Maybe not. But sure as shit, no one will ever fucking trust you with a command again. You'll be on latrine duty until you retire, and you'll be lucky to pension out still a sergeant."

Mike flicked his gaze slightly north of the gun barrel, refocusing for the first time on Sergeant Huff's eyes, which loomed large. He thought that maybe George was getting through to Huff, but that barrel still hadn't moved.

"So what's the alternative?" Huff asked. "Lay down my arms and let you kill all of us?"

"I don't want to kill anyone," George said, and Huff snorted.

****

"Dude, seriously," George went on. "I don't want to kill anyone. Especially not Marines. I'm one of you. Or I was."

"Bullshit!" Huff shouted, and George felt Mendez tense against him, despite the pain in his kneecap.

"I did boot camp at Parris Island eight months ago," George said. "Colonel Blackwater welcomed my class. You're not much older than me; you must have met him, too."

Huff was too far away and at the wrong angle for George to gauge his reaction, but Johnsson's eyes widened just a bit, and George imagined that he could feel something different in Mendez's breathing. Then again, maybe he was just adjusting to the pain.

"The first day, they didn't let us sleep," George went on, remembering. "For the first four days, we didn't get to shower or change our clothes. Not even our underwear. We ran. We ran like hell. And then we marched. And then we ran some more. And marched some more. And ran some more. And then they yelled at us and then we ran. And no salt, remember, guys? No salt for that first week, and then they switched us to saltpeter, which sucked. Remember that?" He saw the flicker of recognition in Johnsson's eyes, assumed it would be there in Huff's, too. Kept going. "When I got off the plane in South Carolina . . . They took us into that holding room, remember, guys? And there was a table piled high with food, but we all stood around and no one touched it because we were afraid to. And man, I wish I'd just eaten everything in sight because they didn't feed us again until the next day. And by then, I sure as hell wasn't in any condition to eat, you know what I mean?"

Johnsson spoke, a single word, tremulous: "Sarge . . . ?"

"Shut up, Johnsson!" And then: "What do you want?"

And that's when George knew he had them.

"You put your weapons down. The four of us get back on the train—"

"No!" Gayl said, speaking for the first time. "We can't get back on the train. They'll just stop it remotely in the tunnel or be waiting for us at the other end."

True. George knew that he could probably get the four of them out of here, but he couldn't expect the Marines to just let them go after that, to maintain radio silence.

"Then we go outside," George said, thinking fiercely. "We leave you guys here and we go for it."

"You're crazy," said Huff. "It's dangerous out there. You're outside the quarantine zone here, but a mile up the road—"

"A destination that can never be reached," Joe interrupted.

"Exactly," Huff agreed. "You'll never make it."

"We go on, as is our sad nature," Joe told him.

"That's the deal," George said. "We go. We tie you up and we go. Still a fuckload of paperwork for you to fill out, but not nearly as bad as a couple of dead Marines on your conscience."

He said it with finality. And then he waited.

CHAPTER 34

The sky was red when they stepped outside.

More than the sky, they realized—the air itself seemed steeped in a burnt sepia tone, as though seen through a sheen of old, stale blood. All around them, the King's Point Park'n'Go ranged, a dead macadam scab on the desert, with two stray Humvees sitting lonely and abandoned off to one side. The Crimson Rock mountains loomed to the east, and it was the first time in his life Mike had seen them from this perspective. A wind picked up, and the reddish sand blew at them, causing them to shield their eyes and mouths.

But to the west . . . To the west was the Other City.

More than a mile distant, it lay directly on a ribbon of red-hued highway that stretched west from King's Point and wound carlessly on its way. A large highway sign at King's Point read—when Mike craned his neck to read it—"NEXT EXIT: .9 mi." The buildings of the Other City loomed point-nine-miles distant, then, a collection of huddled skyscrapers, prickly black against the red sky, as though carved from obsidian or masoned with soot-covered stone. The Other City mirrored the city Mike had lived in his whole life, but now—after Lucky Sevens—did so darkly, its skyscrapers cracked and mottled, its skyline gap-toothed and ramshackle. Mike had seen pictures of the Other City both before and after Lucky Sevens, but nothing prepared him for seeing it in person, just before the horizon, as the sun rose in the east, casting the shadows of the Crimson Rock mountains towards it. The skyline looked ragged and unfinished, compared to the city's skyline in his mind, and where the Global Market Building should have stood high against the red horizon there was only a gap. The Other City's StratoSpire was the tallest building visible, its outline identical to the more familiar SkyTower from the city.

"All these years," Mike murmured. "All these years and no one's rebuilt."

"We have to get going," George said.

"We should have taken their weapons," Gayl grumbled.

"I'm not risking my life with a bunch of amateurs packing heat," George said. "Besides, I took the firing pins. Even if they get free sooner than we expected, they can't hurt us."

"But we should still get moving. We're not far." Mike pointed up the highway. "It's only a mile or so. We can make it pretty fast."

George shook his head. "We can't head straight there—that's what they expect. There'll be patrols along the highway and the usual entrance points."

"Then what do we do?" Gayl asked.

"We need to head north, then circle around. It'll take us a day, but by then they'll assume we've turned back or died in the desert."

"And, uh, is that because we might actually die in the desert?"

George grinned. "We'll be all right. Have a little faith."

Joe patted his pockets, then nodded. "I'm gonna bring along my switchblade, in case that fool wants to fight."

A switchblade seemed an unlikely and unhelpful asset in their current situation, but the energy and/or desire to question Joe's wisdom had drained from the others during their escape. With George at point, they marched off to the north, a column of dull, grayish stratus clouds scudding along the blood-red sky above them. The sand beneath their feet was hard-packed and Martian, breaking and crumbling at their tread. They trudged along for an hour before the flatness of the desert gave way to a phalanx of sandy hillocks and wave-like crests, into which they secreted themselves, the King's Point station finally disappearing from view and, thus, they themselves disappearing from the view at King's Point. Mike's bag grew heavier, but he knew leaving it behind was not an option. Ahead of him, George kept an even, steady pace, not faltering, not slowing, and Mike wondered not for the first nor even the second or third time, what had cast his friend from the Marines, and whether it related to the three secrets George had claimed his own so long ago on the back deck of his mother's house.[66]

The desert floor, now that they were among the hillocks and dunes, canted upwards, gone hilly and inclined, and despite the aridity of the heat, Mike began to sweat as they climbed. George tossed a look back at him, grinned, and said, "One foot in front of the other, you know what I mean? Just one foot in front of the other."

"It's the 'go back to step one' part that's causing a problem," Mike managed over his own gasps.

"We'll make it," George promised.

66. The first secret, of course, was George's proclamation that he could have and did not kill his own father as a child.

"How do you know?" Mike asked.

"It's obvious," Gayl said from behind. "It's what Barry Lyga wants."

That stopped George cold, for which Mike was grateful. In the pause, he said, "What do you mean?"

Gayl and Joe gathered around the two of them. "Look at it this way," Gayl said. "Look at it like a writer. It's all about set-ups and pay-offs, OK? It's about foreshadowing and then following through on something. When you write, you put details into the story early on that will matter later. It's the Chekhov principle—if you show a loaded gun in Act I, that gun has to go off by the end of the play. So, George is an ex-Marine—"

"*Former* Marine," George said, bristling.

"Sorry. Former Marine. But look—George went to Marine boot camp. He learned just enough to talk down those guys back at King's Point, just enough to get us through the desert. That's not a coincidence—that's a deliberate set-up. And then there's me. I know all about Barry Lyga and his career because I studied him. He set me up, made my name an anagram, and put me in your path in order to help you get this far. And hey—by coincidence[67] I just happen to be working on a book about Barry Lyga, a book that compelled me to research the subway to the Other City, which put me in touch with Joe Roberts, the only guy who could get us this far. So, he wants us to succeed. He's given us every possible tool, every conceivable advantage."

Mike considered. When put that way, it made sense, though only in the most linear and absolute fashion. Perhaps he should stop worrying about "what if" he were to meet God and begin, instead, to prepare for the inevitability of that meeting. They all

67. Gayl offset the word "coincidence" with air quotes.

four looked around each other, George nodding with thoughtful regard, Gayl smirking triumphantly, and just as Mike was ready to return the smirk and re-align his thoughts towards his (now definite) meeting with Barry Lyga, Joe Roberts spoke up softly, saying:

"Do you remember the story of the Promised Land? How he crossed the desert sands . . ."

"It's not the same thing," Gayl argued.

"It is," Mike said. "It's the same. God gave Moses locusts and blood in the river and the Angel of Death. He gave him the Ten Commandments and his brother Aaron and a column of fire to guide him. He gave him birds carrying manna from heaven and the parting of the Red Sea. But in the end, God held back Moses. He wouldn't allow him to enter the Promised Land. Moses fled Egypt and crossed the desert for nothing." He looked around the desert in all directions.

"Not for nothing," George said. "He got his people to safety, right?"

"But what does that mean for me in this case?"

"Dude, I don't know. But are you gonna stand around wondering, or are you going to find out?"

Mike opened his mouth to answer, but was cut off by George suddenly saying, "Oh, shit," very clearly and distinctly. They all followed George's line of sight, back along the way they'd come, skipping over the spines of the sand dunes all the way towards the King's Point station, now visible from their higher perch on the hillocks. As they watched, small figures they knew to be Huff, Mendez, Johnsson, and the two others clambered into the stationed Humvees. Exhaust fumes purled forth into the red, glimmering day's air.

"They're coming this way," George said.

"Can they see us?" Gayl asked. "We're pretty far—"

"If we can see them, they can see us. Plus, we blazed a trail right through the desert—every crack in the ground will lead them right to us."

Sure enough, as they watched, the Humvees turned north and blasted across the desert, plumes of sand scattering in their wakes, turning the red air into a black-pointillist painting.

"What do we do?" Gayl asked.

George hesitated only a moment, then said, "Run."

****

They ran.

They ran north, weaving through a maze of dunes and knolls. By now, the sun burned straight overhead, its light searing their shadows into the sand beneath their feet, those same feet a-blur with speed, a speed that was not enough. For behind them—in distance not far enough—they heard the gunning engines and the shushing sound of Humvee tires on sand. Mike dared throw a glance behind him, catching sight of Joe, who ran as effortlessly as the teens, and Gayl, who puffed and huffed, but kept the pace, and then behind them the first of the Humvees, erupting over a dune in a flurry of thrown sand, hanging for a split-second in the dead, red air before crashing back down to earth on the other side—the nearer side—of the dune, followed an instant later by the second Humvee, the two of them bearing down, plowing through or jumping over dunes and hillocks as they came.

"George!" Mike yelled, then yelled it again in his most desperate tone: "George!"

Ahead of him, George looked back and swore. "Keep going!" he cried.

"They're catching up!" Mike shouted.

“Keep going!” George insisted, and put on a burst of speed that carried him over the next hill.

Mike followed, stumbling and sliding as he went, the roar of the Humvees’ engines now blocking out everything else, even his own rasping, too-fast breathing. He picked himself up and kept running, not even checking to be sure that Gayl and Joe were behind him.

Suddenly, George stopped ahead; Mike almost collided with him, but pulled up in time. Before he could shove George back into action, George spun around, pointed to his right, and shouted over the Humvees, “That way! To the rocks!”

Mike ran, George now at his side, catching a glimpse of Joe and Gayl making the turn as well. Ahead of them now lay a field of rocks and boulders, most of which were small enough for the Humvees to bounce over, but a few of which—deep into the field—were large enough to prevent further passage. They charged into the field, their feet suddenly pounding on painful hard stone that shifted and jimmied under them. The Humvees turned and kept pace, racing towards them, and Mike could no longer keep from looking back, compelled, checking over one shoulder to see the Humvees bearing down on him, so close that he could see Huff grinning behind the wheel of one, Mendez shouting at the wheel of the other. But then, just as he thought he would be run down, he realized that he had gained the larger rocks in the center of the field. Following George’s flailing gestures, he ducked behind one of the boulders, joined in short order by Gayl and Joe.

They flattened themselves against the rock, breathing hard and heavy, the roar of the Humvees still vibrating the air until—a moment later—they stopped, first one engine cutting, then the other.

“Keep going,” George said, infuriatingly not as out of breath as the other three.

"They stopped—"

"Now they'll be on foot. They can still get us," George said, and took off running again.

After a moment to curse out loud, Mike followed him, trailed by Gayl and Joe. Doors slammed shut behind them, then the sound of boots on rocks, the measured quick-march of the Marines. Mike was ready to give up, to throw himself down to the ground and surrender to the Marines if it would only mean that he could stop running.

But then he thought of Phil. He thought of the broken and burned-out cellphone with its last picture of her, of the last time he'd seen her, terrified and panicked, and he swore that that would not, that could not be the last time he would see her; he thought of his brother, so young and fated never to know love, of George's mother, of George himself, who'd never even had a girlfriend. He thought of a city—a world—a universe—without love.

He thought it all and he put on a final burst of speed, charging up a hill made slick with grains of shifting sand, almost stumbling downhill, regaining his footing, then reaching the top of the hill, where George stood, staring straight ahead at a marker of some sort that shot up from the ground amid a cluster of scrub and cactus, a black flag dangling from it in the still air.

"Keep—" Mike began, panting, as Gayl and Joe scrabbled up the hill behind him.

George took a single step such that he was now on the other side of an invisible line extending from the marker post to another similar post a hundred or so yards away. Mike joined him, went to run further, and stopped when George grabbed his sleeve.

"Wait. I want to see."

"Are you crazy?"

Gayl and Joe did not stop—they blew past Mike and George and kept running. Mike tugged, trying to pull away from George, but George would not let go. "George! George, let go!"

"Wait."

The Marines came charging up the hill, Huff in the lead, murder in his eyes. They were weaponless, of course, but that meant little. In a hand-to-hand scuffle with six Marines, Mike could not see George and himself lasting long.

"It's like the magic fence . . ." George began, and Mike finally pulled away, so surprised at having done so that he staggered backwards and collapsed to the ground just as Huff suddenly and fiercely stopped running, as if he'd slammed full-tilt into a wall.

". . . in *INsight*," George finished.

****

There was a magic fence in *INsight*, Mike remembered now, an invisible shield of mystical energy through which Siobhan had to travel in the first novel, by proving herself worthy of entering the leprechaun city. Since the fence was invisible, its location could be divined only by its markers, a series of black flags planted around the city.

George and Mike were on one side, along with Gayl and Joe, who had turned and come back once they realized the chase was over. Huff and the Marines were on the other side, and no matter what they did, they could not cross the line between the markers.

"It's the border of the Other City, isn't it?" George asked.

The Marines tried for long minutes to get past the invisible barrier. They threw themselves at it, ran at it at top speed, walked backwards towards it, walked to it with their eyes closed. Nothing worked. They tried forming a pyramid, with Mendez—the smallest and lightest—at the top, but even a dozen feet in the air, there was a barrier he could not breach. Finally, exhausted and defeated, Huff sent two of them back to the Humvees for supplies and to radio for help. Mendez and Johnsson, after checking with Huff, sat cross-legged on the ground, staring through the barrier at Mike and the others. Huff remained standing, a wary intelligence in his expression, eyes darting from one marker to another, calculating, then finally shaking his head.

"What the blue *fuck* . . . ?" Huff demanded in a voice almost soft with awe. Like a child first watching and comprehending fireworks.

Mike stepped as close as he dared, so close that the space between him and Huff was measured in inches, so close that he could feel the Marine's breath and smell the sweat on him. Huff reached out to Mike, but his hand stopped less than an inch from Mike's face, as though a sheet of glass separated them. Mike reflexively put his own hand up, found no such barrier, and touched Huff's hand. Huff immediately grabbed Mike's hand and pulled at him. From behind, George looped a powerful arm around Mike's waist and tugged him free.

"We can reach through, but they can't," George said. "I don't understand. Why are we worthy and they're not?"

"It doesn't have to do with worthiness," Gayl said, coming up from behind. He stood on their side of the invisible wall, close, gazing through to the Marines. "Jesus. It's true. It's really true."

"What's true?" Mike demanded. "What are you talking about?"

Gayl shook his head. "You'll think it's crazy. You'll think *I'm* crazy. And maybe I am."

"Tell us," George insisted.

"You guys, you Marines," Gayl called out. "They made you take tests, didn't they? Before they assigned you here."

The Marines exchanged glances among themselves, as if

considering not answering, but then Huff shrugged a "fuck it" shrug. "Yeah. When we got assigned here, they did a whole series of interviews and stuff like that. We saw shrinks—three or four of them. It was all about our relationships. None of it made much sense. But now . . . It's love, isn't it? The wall blocks out people who are in love."

"That's crazy," Mike said. "For one thing, I'm in love and I got through—"

"It's not people who are in love," George said with confidence. "It's people who have loved and lost. People who are suffering lost love. They're the only ones who can get through. The people in good relationships can't."

"That's right," Gayl said. "One of those crazy conspiracy theories you guys didn't want to hear. Like the government being involved in Lucky Sevens."

"The United States government had nothing to do with Lucky Sevens!" Huff said hotly.

"I believe that now," Gayl assured him. "I think they just covered up what really happened."

"Which was?" Mike asked.

Gayl drew in a deep breath. "One of the theories I've seen is that there was no terrorist attack on the Other City. That something *else* happened. It sounds crazy, but the story is that the Other City was destroyed by love."

"By love?" Mike and George said at the same time.

Gayl held out his hands in protest. "I told you it sounded crazy, right? But it's the only thing that makes sense at this point. All of us—" he gestured to encompass Mike, George, Joe, and himself "—are victims of lost love. If there was some sort of . . . some sort of love catastrophe here . . . It sounds ridiculous to say it, but what if there's some kind of love toxin or radiation in the air? Like the aftermath of a nuclear bomb, but emotional? And we already have a tolerance to it because we've lost loves."

"You're crazy," George said.

"He might not be," Huff said. "I've never been inside the Other City myself, and that could be why. I can't go past this line. I can't enter the city limits. Which totally jibes with what I've heard over the years. There have been rumors. I didn't give them much credit. Guys in the service talk all the time. Bunch of gossips, you know? But, yeah, it would all connect. It would explain everything."

Mike looked around his fellow questers. Gayl, he knew, had lost his girlfriend, a different Phil. And Mike, of course, had lost his own Phil, had lost her again and again and again. He knew little of Joe Roberts, but what of George? Mike had known George his entire life, or almost so, and had never seen George in a relationship, had never heard George even bemoan an impossible conquest. George's entire life had been focused on the Marines and on nothing else, as though the part of his soul dedicated to love and to sex and to bonding had sworn *semper fidelis* rather than *amor vincent alia*.

"I don't get it," George said. "That doesn't make any sense at all."

"I miss Phil," Mike said, and it was the first time he'd put it in those words, the first time he'd said "miss," as opposed to "want" or "need" or "love." Somehow, missing her was worse than loving her. It was an acknowledgment that she was gone, she was vanished to him, and it pulled at his heart in a wholly new and unpleasant way. "I don't need to say that, I guess. That's the whole reason we're here."

"George?" Gayl asked.

But George had wandered a bit west, examining the marker pole more closely.

"Joe?"

Joe brushed dust and sand off his boots, then hunkered down into a crouch, gazing up and squinting against the sunlight. "I can remember how good I felt inside . . ." he began. "At night I get down on my knees and pray . . ." He sighed and then said, simply and heartbreakingly, "I know that girl no longer exists."

"But Joe said he's seen Marines in the Other City," George protested. "How could that—"

"Those must be the guys who failed the tests," Huff said.

"Or passed them," Mike said. "Maybe *you're* the one who failed. It all depends on what they're testing for."

"Regardless, they definitely don't want *me* going in there," Huff said. He held up his left hand so that they could all see the plain gold wedding band there. "Most of us are married. The other guys are all in steady, long-term relationships. Shit. Shit." He kicked sand at Mike—the sand shot through the wall easily, but Huff's foot came up short.

"We wanted to get you ourselves," Huff said mournfully. "Figured that would make it a little easier on us, come the court martial. Now we don't have a choice. We have to call it in."

A momentary tremor of guilt ran through Mike. His quest was for love, for love and for a chance to fix a world so badly broken. Ruining this Marine's life and career—to say nothing of the lives and careers of the men in his command—had nothing to do with that.

"I'm sorry," he told Huff, aware of the meaninglessness of his apology. "I really am."

Huff shrugged. "I always thought that this assignment would be trouble for me. I guess I was right."

George shook his head. "None of this makes sense. If the government knows about this then why would they even bother with the military presence inside? How many people are even trying to get—"

"I know," Mike interrupted.

Everyone looked at him, and whether Marine or civilian, they all leaned a little closer.

"It's for the same reason that we need to get there. Don't you see, guys? Gayl was right. Barry Lyga is in the Other City. God is there. And the government knows it and doesn't want anyone else in there."

****

For a long while, it seemed as though night would never fall in the Other City. The sun completed its journey and was engulfed by the horizon to the west, but the red patina on the air and the sky and the ground lingered, grown darker, but not extinguished, leaving the whole area bathed in a bloody swath of color. Together, the four of them migrated further north, then cut sharply west once they were out of view of the Marines.

"It's not too late for you," Huff had called to Joe Roberts. "You can come through the field and go back with us."

Joe had responded in his odd cant: "You know you ought to quit this scene too."

"Your choice, then. Your funeral."

They were the last words they heard from Huff, who soon faded into the background, his khaki camo gear offering little in the way of actual camouflage in this ruddy desert.

"So something happened on Lucky Sevens," Gayl said into the silence of their hike. "Something that—what?—dragged God down from Heaven? Yanked him into our world?"

"Maybe," Mike said, thinking. "Or do we have it backwards? We're thinking that Lucky Sevens brought Barry Lyga to us—"

"And started killing love," George put in.

"Right. But what if it's the other way around? What if Lyga coming here is what made Lucky Sevens happen in the first place? What if it's his presence that's causing the country to fall out of love?"

They pondered that for a while. Joe Roberts whistled a soft and surpassingly beautiful tune.

"If you knew where God was," Gayl said after a moment, "and you worked for the government . . ."

"You'd lock the place down," Mike said, nodding. "Quarantine it. Until you could figure out how to exploit him."

It felt like a charged moment, an instant of transubstantiation, as merest thought became genuine idea. But no one had anything to say in response.

"We can camp here," George said, looking around. The night had finally waged a campaign against the day and succeeded in tearing down the light, as the last glimmers of red shone around them. "We're protected on four sides"—he pointed—"so we can start a campfire without being seen. And that path there should take us southeast to the Other City when the light comes up."

"You don't think they'll find us in the meantime?" Gayl asked.

"Nah. There's a shitload of desert to search, and all they have to go on is our last known position and heading. They think we're headed straight for the Other City. They'll be looking closer to the buildings; maybe even in the Other City itself. They'll spread the search out in the morning, but by then we'll be heading in."

George had directed them all to scavenge for branches and kindling while they hiked, and now they dumped their armloads into a haphazard pile, which George then organized and constructed into a shape determined by some woodsy architecture Mike neither knew nor understood. Soon thereafter, with a book of matches from his overnight bag, George lit the stack. Mike had not realized how cold he'd gotten in the desert night until the moment heat poured forth and suffused his stiff, overworked muscles. The others gathered around the fire, legs bent to chests or crisscrossed like yogis or kindergarten children, silent at the four compass points of the fire.

"Dude," George said suddenly, his tone so light and so buoyant that for a moment Mike fantasized that he was hearing it in his sleep, that George was standing over him, shaking him awake after one of their sleepovers (for George was ever the early riser between them), meaning that, in turn, none of this could have happened, for their last sleepover had been in middle school, when they were still young enough for such silliness.

When no awakening followed, Mike said, "What?"

"We're camping out after all," George said, and laughed. "You know what I mean?"

Mike managed a weak chuckle, since it seemed to mean so much to George. "Yeah, well, it would have been better if we'd brought some actual camping gear. I don't suppose anyone thought to bring sleeping bags or blankets or anything?"

Gayl and George shook their heads. Joe shrugged. Poor Joe Roberts—he had not counted on any of this, and was the only one of them without so much as a change of clothes.

"What about food?" Gayl asked, prompting George to share out the protein bars he'd brought, as well as a bottle of water he'd snaked from a desk back at the King's Point station.

"There will be food in the Other City," Mike mused. "If there are people, there'll have to be food." He peered around in the dark. "I'm more worried about something eating *us*. Bobcat or something. Or getting stung by a scorpion or bitten by a snake or—"

"I bet there aren't any," George said.

"Why?"

A shrug. "I've never seen a scorpion or a snake that's lost love, you know what I mean?"

They all fell silent at that, pondering—each in his own way, each with the weight and the resources of his own memories and life experiences—the simultaneous absurdity and rock-solid logic of George's statement.

"We should talk about it." Gayl shifted into a new position, his legs uncomfortably cramped. "The love stuff, I mean."

Mike rolled up his protein bar wrapper and—after a split-second thought to simply tossing it on the ground—tucked it into a pocket. "Why?"

"You're here for love," Gayl said. "And we all got this far because of love. We might discover something important."

George and Gayl already knew Mike's story, but Joe Roberts did not, so Mike told the story yet again, in such a way that it took little time at all. Joe nodded sagely throughout, occasionally clucking his tongue in an almost musical fashion, his heavy-lidded eyes projecting that he had heard this story—or one like it—before, but never interrupting. At the conclusion of Mike's tale, Joe merely chuckled once, nervously, and said with confident, weary wisdom, "Fear's a powerful thing. Kills the things you love."

"I remember," Gayl began, "back when I was in high school . . . The first time I was ever in love."

They all leaned a little closer, Gayl lit by the flickering, lazy motion of the fire.

"God, I loved her! It was that teenage kind of love . . ." He broke off and nodded towards George and Mike, who had clustered closer together on the north side of the fire. "No offense. I'm just saying. It was that love you can only have when you're a teenager. I was something of an outcast in high school. I only had two friends, really—a guy and a girl, both of them charter members of the Chess Club with me." He let out a short "heh!" "'Charter members.' We were the *only* members. The three of us all alone in a classroom after school, playing chess against each other while our teacher/chaperone watched and graded papers.

"Anyway, they were my two best friends, really. I'd known him since elementary school, and I'd known her even longer, back to kindergarten. He was such a geek and a nerd that even I was ashamed to be around him half the time, but what could I do? He was my friend, right? The only one who'd have me. And she . . ."

"She was your first love," George said.

Gayl shook his head. "Who's telling this story? She was one of those girls who . . . When I was a kid, I used to wonder if somehow girls were just born with this innate understanding of . . . of girl things. You know? Like make-up and braiding hair and things like that. I thought they must just understand those things innately. Because I never saw anyone teaching them, you know? So I figured . . . Anyway, the girl in the Chess Club, if girls innately understood these things, then she was some kind of mutant girl who was missing that gene. Her hair was always disheveled and greasy. She had these huge glasses that took up half her face, and she always wore baggy jeans and men's shirts.

"And no, she wasn't my first love. My first love was the hottest girl in school. Most popular, too, because those things always go together, like, well, like any two things where one leads logically and irrevocably to the other. There was, of course, no way in the world that I could get her. There was no way in the world I could even make her realize I existed.

"Except there was. Something happened—I can't remember what; it was so long ago—that put me on the radar of the popular kids. Of the whole school, really. One day I was just another schlub in Chess Club (though the least schlubby of them, to be sure) and the next everyone was talking about me and I was hanging out with the football team and the cheerleaders, and then the most amazing thing happened: The hottest, most popular girl in school started calling me. Started coming to my house. Even kissed me. It was amazing.

"Of course, this whole time I was getting so caught up in my new-found fame that I ignored the Chess Club and my two friends. Stopped taking their calls. Just didn't have time. Forgot to fill out the paperwork to have the Chess Club renewed for another school year, which—honestly—I didn't care about anymore because I had bigger and better things to do."

"Wait, wait, wait," George said. "Let me guess what happened. I heard a story like this once. You found out that the hot girl wasn't really into you. She was just using you to get back at a boyfriend or something. And your new friends turned out not to be real friends. So you went back to the Chess Club and you apologized to your friends and then it turned out that the girl had been in love with you all along and when she washed her hair and took off her glasses and dressed like a girl, you realized she was really hot and she became your girlfriend for real. Right?"

Gayl tilted his head, a small wry smile twisted his lips. A forever of regret lingered in that smile. "Well, George, here's what happened. Yeah, the hot girl was just using me. But before I learned that, I came to realize that I really missed Chess Club and I really missed the girl in particular. So I broke up with the hot girl and I went to what would be the final meeting of the Chess Club, to apologize and to beg—on my knees, if necessary—for my two friends back."

"Ha!" George rocked back on his haunches in triumph.

"And my best friend spit in my face. He told me he hated me for abandoning him and to lose his phone number. And the girl? Well, yeah, it turns out she had been in love with me in secret, but when I confessed my love to her, she told me I'd hurt her so much by forsaking her, by going out with the popular girl. She didn't spit on me, but she did something worse—she told me she would never be with me.

"And then the school year ended, and I wish I could say that things changed over the summer or that one or both of them moved away in the interim, but you know what? Nothing changed. When I came back for my senior year, I was completely friendless, shunned by the popular crowd and by the kids who'd been my only friends for so long." Gayl slapped his knees. "And it was the most miserable time of my life."

Joe whistled, low and sustained.

"That . . . That's a terrible story!" Mike said. "Who would want to hear that story? Who would want to *tell* that story?"

"I know. But it's true and it's real, and sometimes people need to hear the stories where things don't work out well."

"Wait," George said. "That's not how I heard that story. Seriously, I heard the same story once, except it wasn't Chess Club, it was Matheletes. Or maybe it was Drama Club. But I've heard it and it had a happy ending."

Gayl fixed him with a look across the crackle of the fire. "You couldn't have heard it before because it's my story. My life. And that's exactly what happened."

"It's wrong," George said, unaccountably disturbed, his body rigid with a combination of annoyance and disbelief. "It doesn't end that way."

"It does."

"I don't want to talk about that anymore," Mike said. "Joe, how about you? Tell us your story."

Joe cleared his throat and tapped his foot, almost as though he were on-stage somewhere and counting out the beat. Then, with that odd drawl of his, he began:

"My life's the same story. My baby left, and she wouldn't say why. She just said, 'Joe, I gotta go. We had it once, we ain't got it anymore.' Now I hear she's got a house up in Fairview." He grimaced and shrugged. "Romeo and Juliet, Samson and Delilah. I told myself it was all something in her, but in the end I knew it was something in me."

"How long?" Gayl asked. "How long without her?"

Joe looked up at the sky, counting years, tears, who knew? "Feel like I been workin' for a thousand years," he said. "She went away, she cut me like a knife. Well if you can't make it . . ." He wiped at his eye, whisking away an invisible tear before it could become more. Gayl put a steadying hand on his shoulder and they were all quiet.

"Your turn, George," Gayl said, and Mike turned to look at his best friend.

George shook his head.

"Come on," Gayl urged. "The rest of us did."

George shook his head again. "No. It's pointless. So we've all loved and lost. Big deal. Everyone has, even those happily-married Marines."

"But we're all still caught up in the pain of it," Gayl said. "That's the only explanation. We can't let go. Maybe talking about it will, I don't know, give us some kind of armor or—"

"No."

Joe came around the fire and crouched down next to George, gazing into his eyes.

"Talk to me," Joe said, taking George's hand. "I know your heart is breakin'."

George shook Joe off. "Get off my back, you guys. I got

you this far and I'll get you the rest of the way, but no more of this bullshit, OK?"

He stood in a fury and stomped off into the darkness.

"He won't go far," Mike said. "He won't leave me."

The three of them sat around the fire and shared more stories. Joe and Gayl, being older than Mike, had many more tales of lost love to recount, though they each had that one big regret that had wrecked them for all time.

More accurately, though, they had wrecked themselves, for the common element in all of the stories was that some variant of male pride or sheer masculine stupidity had caused the men to forsake the loves of their lives.

"It's not just that we lost love," Mike said. "It's that we did something to drive them away."

"Or ran away ourselves," Gayl added.

They thought about that.

George returned to them, still refusing to speak of his own lost love. Mike wondered if had to do with the Marines and the words "fraternization" and "superior officer." That would explain a lot, up to and including George's sudden discharge from the service.

Still, if George wanted to keep his pain and his burden private, then Mike would not force him to open it to the air, just as he'd let George keep the pain and the details of the asshole's depredations within himself all these years.

"I think we should get some sleep," George said with finality.

Mike was beyond exhausted.

Gayl waved the battered copy of *Inframan* from his bag. "I'm too wired to sleep. I'll read by the fire for a little while."

Joe stretched out near the fire and immediately dropped off to sleep, his breathing rhythmic and somehow musical, distracting enough that George and Mike cleared a spot on the other side of the fire, far enough away not to hear.

As they lay there, George asked, "Dude, what are you going to say to him? When we meet him, you know what I mean?"

"Who? Barry Lyga?"

"Yeah."

"You're pretty optimistic, man. I'm not even one hundred percent sure we'll get to meet him."

"But you said he's definitely in the Other—"

"I'm sure he's there, but what if he doesn't want to see us? I keep thinking about the Tower of Babel . . ." Mike rolled onto his side, watching George in the firelight. "I know you'll say 'no,' but one last time—"

"I'm not leaving," George said with a finality that seemed to bare teeth and growl.

They lay in silence for a while, and then Mike said, "I sort of want to yell at him. I want to tell him he's a shitty writer and he's tormenting me for no reason. But you know what? I'm just gonna ask him to fix things. I'm going to remind him that he's the one who gave me those powers and ask him to fix things. Make people fall in love again. Fix the world. Put an end to GWB and make everything right. And, yeah, put me back together with Phil. That's all."

"What if he says no?"

Mike rolled to his other side, looking just past the fire to where Gayl Rybar sat reading *Inframan* by Barry Lyga. *Only the Word of God can destroy God.* "Then God had better hope that *God* has someone to pray to."

CHAPTER 35

Mike dreamed, but the dreams were entirely forgettable, disappearing as soon as he awoke to Joe Roberts shaking him by the shoulder. The sun had risen in the east, lightening the air, casting that strange red glow over everything, as though perpetually trapped in the crimson moment just before sunset.

Gayl was nowhere to be seen. Mike nudged George awake and thought of the book Gayl had brought, of the warning words from the mysterious desert "Courteney." *Only the Word of God can destroy God.* Was it true? Did they have the means to destroy God? Could that be the difference between this little band of God-seekers and the poor, devastated throngs who'd built the Tower of Babel?

Was the difference that this time they had a weapon to use against God?

"How'd you guys sleep?" Mike asked.

George shrugged. Joe said, "I slept the sleep of the dead, I didn't dream."

Together, George and Mike kicked the smoldering fire into dead embers, drowning it in red sand, then gathered their belongings and followed Joe along the path George had noted the previous night.

"Where's Gayl?" Mike asked. "What are we—"

Just then, Joe turned a bend in the path. The sky—blocked by the mountains and the ridge until now—suddenly opened up in front of them, the world falling away from the bluff they now stood on.

"Let me show you what love can do," Joe said, sweeping his arm in a ta-da! gesture, revealing the Other City, which lay below them in the valley.

Seeing it this way—from above—was an experience distinct and alien from seeing the skyline at a horizontal distance. From here, the Other City did not so much glow as simmer a deeper red than the surrounding environs; it gave the impression of still smoldering, all these years after Lucky Sevens, though no smoke and no fires were evident. The smolder was psychological. Emotional. It effervesced and throbbed on a plane beyond the visual, the physical. The Other City pulsated like a wound on the dry skin of the desert, its byways and boulevards—empty—now black varicose veins wending a tattoo along the cityscape.

Ghost city. Corpse city. City gone into rigor.

"Some punk's idea of a teenage nation?" Joe mused.

"I think Barry Lyga is a little old to be called a punk," Gayl said. He was waiting for them on the bluff already, gazing down and out to the wrecked skyline of the Other City. "In any event, there it is."

Breakfast was George's last protein bars, shared among the four of them with the solemnity of the Last Supper. Mike wondered if this would be the Last Breakfast.

"Are we ready?" Mike asked when they were done. "Are we going to do this?"

"Oughtta be easy," Joe Roberts said, grinning. "Oughtta be simple enough."

Together they clambered down from the bluff, following a dusty, worn trail that wended in a gentle series of ess-curves down the face of the mountain, the pathway so perfectly etched and preserved that Mike imagined it had been traced here by a finger, as though an enormous child had reached down from the sky and finger-painted down the mountain.

The Other City loomed in the near distance. Pictures of the Other City haunted the airwaves and old movies like particularly stealthy ghosts, leaping into the foreground to scream tragedy when least anticipated, but nothing could prepare Mike for the absolute devastation of it in person. He did not want to compare the jagged, damaged skyline to a mouth of rotted teeth, but somehow no other metaphor presented itself, and so he accepted it and moved on, grudgingly conceding that it was apt and descriptive, albeit cliché. Taken individually, no single act of destruction—no single missing tooth, to continue the dental metaphor—engendered the sense of contemplation and worry that brewed within him; only the Other City taken *in toto* did this, the overwhelming sense of *wrong* radiating out from the buildings, as if destroying or crumbling one or more buildings (or teeth) would result in a smile still acceptable to all social graces, but this specific combination of missing buildings (or teeth) meant a mouthful of distortion and disagreement.

He could not tell what enraged him more—that the Other City had been bombarded/attacked/take your pick, or that, in the years since Lucky Sevens, no effort had been made to rebuild. It offended his senses of national and local pride, as well as his every architectural sensibility. Whereas a layman might look to the Other City's amputated skyline and importune rebuilding and be persuaded into a grudging understanding that "these things take time," hence the caesura, Mike could not be so mollified. He knew exactly (well, not exactly, but certainly intimately) what was involved in rebuilding the Other City's structures, and even given a generous interval for the requisite politicking and back-and-forth-ing of the designs, the buildings could have been finished by now, the whole endeavor requiring nothing more than will and cooperation, two attributes allegedly much in supply in the wake of Lucky Sevens though there was no evidence of either in the skyline. All that was needed were a few charettes[68], the willingness, the will, the verve and the dedication.

As they gained the Other City, Mike's anger and disappointment inflated, as though proximately. How could they ("they" being the prevailing political powers of whatever stripe, allegiance, and constituency) have just left the place like this? How could anyone see the Other City in such a state and not want to fix it—immediately? Returning (ill-advisedly and reluctantly) to the skyline-as-teeth metaphor: How could anyone see such a smile—gapped and corroded—and not proceed to the nearest dentist? Was there a lack of agreement as to how to rebuild? Well, then, someone needed to step into the breach and *make it happen*. Mike knew that any architect seeing this blasted landscape would offer his or her services for free—anything to salve the wounded skyline and eradicate the blight. Since they were walking to the Other City and, thus, forced to stare straight ahead at it, Mike tuned out the easy and soft chatter of the other three and instead focused on reconstruction, his mind's eye laying in foundations, repairing damaged façades, erecting new skyscrapers in the place of old. Mike's gift—if he had any gifts at all—was to see the world not as it was or had

68. A French term that has been co-opted by the architecture field to mean an "intensive, all-night work session."

been, but rather how it should be, a gift that served him well now, as many architects would have been tempted to rebuild in homage to the past, old photos of the Other City pre-Lucky Sevens at their drawing tables as they slavishly sketched the past into the future. Mike—drawing table-less at the moment—chose the future, with designs that acknowledged the past, but were not childishly devoted to it. To continue the unfortunate (and surprisingly serviceable) skyline-as-mouth metaphor: Mike would not merely replace the teeth. He would replace them with better, more efficient teeth, a notion that now led him to think of environmentally-friendly teeth, his first (and conclusive) sign that the time had come to retire the entire metaphor.

They stopped at noon to rest, roughly halfway to the Other City by Mike's best reckoning (a reckoning he confirmed with George who had become—by dint of being the only one in the group with outdoors experience of any kind—the expert). The sun was a murrey blotch overhead and while the desert heat ranged all around them, it was not an oppressive heat.

They passed around the last bottle of water.

"What do you think it is?" Gayl asked at one point, in a way that told Mike that he had missed some crucial component of the conversation while freehand-ing a new freestanding skyscraper in his imagination.

Joe Roberts—noticing his puzzled look—took pity on him and pointed out a large chunk of . . . something just slightly west of the straight-line path they were taking to the Other City. Standing for a better look, Mike realized that there were many chunks of the something, some behind them, but more of them—most of them—along the path stretching out before them, leading to the Other City. Mike and George went for a closer look, Joe and Gayl pleading more advanced years and exhaustion.

"What is it?" Mike asked, echoing Gayl's question from a new vantage point.

George leaned in close. "Dude, I don't know." He extended a finger to poke it.

Mike grabbed his friend's hand. "You don't know what it is. And it looks wet."

"It," in fact, did look wet. It glistened in the sun, slick. It looked, Mike came to see, like nothing so much as a chunk of raw meat, still bloody, the size of Mike's head on the surface, possibly larger beneath, like an iceberg.

"It looks like blood," George said at that moment. "But this crazy red light is messing everything up, you know what I mean? It might be something else."

They walked to another chunk some ten yards away, Mike standing so as to block the sunlight as George crouched down and bent forward to scrutinize the thing. Their examinations were fruitless, though George did—darting a finger quickly—manage to touch it before Mike could stop him this time, proclaiming that the tack and scent of it favored blood, but he could not be sure, then—again, quickly, though Mike could not have stopped him for he could not have foreseen this next move—licking it, his immediate gagging and spitting confirming by taste that it was, in fact, blood.

As George hawked and spat, wishing for one more bottle—one more swallow!—of water to remove the rancid savor from his mouth, Mike turned a slow circle in place. There were similar chunks all around them, growing in density as they neared the Other City.

"What the hell is going on here? Did someone slaughter a whole ranch worth of cattle or something?"

They looked at each other and Mike shivered; his imagination—so wondrously fecund when repairing the Other

City—now turned its prowess towards the people in the city. Had they done this? Was it an offering to some capricious god? Was this what Barry Lyga demanded of his "subjects"—blood sacrifice? In Mike's mind, the Other City transformed from a damaged, wounded cityscape in need of a dedicated architect's skills into a postapocalyptic wasteland from every bad movie he'd ever seen and every nightmare he'd ever had, its cracked boulevards choked with roaming hordes of nigh-cannibalistic madmen.

"We should get back to the guys," George said quietly. He put a hand on Mike's shoulder. "We still doing this?" He asked it without rancor or condemnation, as though Mike could say, "I know we've broken a dozen laws and fought the Marines and come within sight of the Other City, but I've changed my mind—let's go home" and George would not reproach him, but would simply say, "OK, dude."

Mike tore his gaze from the Other City and tore his mind from its theoretical roving devastators. He fished in his bag for the sketch he'd drawn of Phil. It was a good likeness, but it was black (more gray, truth be told) and white. For a panicked moment, he could not recall the exact shade of blue of her hair, and he stared with all the fury he could muster until his imagination relented and filled in the proper hues.

"We're doing this," he said.

****

It took them less than three hours to reach the very edge of the Other City, the path becoming thicker with the strange, bloody chunks. By unspoken agreement, they looked straight ahead, trying to ignore the meat all around them, failing. The sun canted to the west, casting their shadows behind them as they neared the first building in their line of sight—a low husk fronting an access road that led directly into the Other City, with a three-car parking lot to one side—and could read its sign: CONVENIENCE. It was an old gas station with a mini-market, the gas pumps knocked down and dry, the word "STORE"—theoretically following "CONVENIENCE" on the signage—gone, scoured away by sand, perhaps.

If they expected something to change when they stood within the actual confines of the Other City, they were disappointed. After hours of walking on the shifting sand, the street's asphalt felt strange to their feet and they momentarily became sailors adjusting to life on land again. Although nothing (else) changed in that moment, they paused to mark it anyway, each of them realizing and all of them realizing that now they were irrevocable, that they had entered the Other City proper. While nothing indicated it to them, they somehow knew: They would not leave until they had what they'd come for. It was not that they *could* not leave; they simply *would* not.

They had talked on the way about what to expect and had been—to a man—spectacularly wrong. The Other City was devastated, true, but that seemed almost secondary now. What truly struck them was the sense that the Other City was worn out. Tired. There were missing buildings, their spots marked with piles of rubble like gravestones; there were damaged buildings, some of them bandaged with flapping sheets of plastic or nailed-over boards. But even the intact buildings exhibited a profound and weary sense of *age*, as though mourning their dead and wounded fellows had ripened them into a prematurely weathered senescense.

Surrender hung in the air like a shroud.

As they stood in silence, absorbing the sobering truth all around them, George took the first steps forward, made a slow circle, studying the buildings until he turned to face the others, and said, in a tone of quiet awe: "It's like the City of the Thunderstruck."

"Lost in trouble," Joe said in agreement, "so far from home . . ."

"The City of the Thunderstruck?" Gayl said in a tone of annoyance. "You mean from *INsight*?"

Mike shook his head. "No, man. It doesn't look—"

"Not from the movies," George interrupted. "The way it was described in the book. Well, in the second book."

Mike looked again. He could see it . . .

"'Now Siobhan knew what cities looked like when no one had the decency to put them out of their misery,'" George quoted. "Or close to that."

Gayl shook his head and crossed his arms over his chest. "Look, I appreciate that you dig *INsight* and all, but—"

"But what?" George asked. "What?"

"I just refuse to believe that we've come all this way just to find ourselves in some shitty city from a shitty novel by a shitty writer. There's a million light-years between Lyga and Monika Seymore."

Mike winced, but George showed no reaction. "Right," he said. "Seymore has sold enough books for every person on the planet to own two of them. Lyga . . . hasn't."

"That's not—"

"It has nothing to do with shitty or not," George went on, his tone never rising, eminently reasonable and relaxed. "It just is."

Gayl harrumphed. "Are you really into those books?"

At that, George cracked a small, knowing smile. "I guess you could say that."

"Well, then that's why you're seeing the City of the Thunderwhatever."

"Thunderstruck."

"Yeah, yeah." Gayl waved it off, smirking as though he couldn't believe George remembered the name. "You see that, but I see something from a picto-novel—"

"—which was probably influenced by *INsight,*" George said. "Almost everything is."

Gayl actually stamped a foot, so annoyed was he. "Not everything! Jesus! Those fucking books are ruining publishing. Between them and all the ripoffs, I'm lucky I can get anything on the shelves at all."

"People buy them," George said.

"So what? That doesn't mean they aren't shit. Do you really like them?"

George shrugged, as if that answered everything, a response which only drove Gayl into a further fury, throwing his arms up in the air. "So, you like leprechauns? That's your thing? Really? Little fucking magic midgets?"

"These are *different* kinds of leprechauns," George said. "They're not like regular leprechauns from mythology."

"Exactly!" Gayl said, his eyes flaring in rage. "Exactly! They don't have pots of gold and they're not even Irish! So they're *not leprechauns.*"

"But they are."

Gayl fumed. "Don't you get it? It's just . . . Her own story obviates itself."

"So you've read it."

Gayl laughed. "I read the first one, just to see what the fuss was about. Christ, that's fifteen hours of my life I'll never get back. The whole story just . . . just *dissolves* on a fundamental level. If the 'leprechauns'"—he made air quotes—"don't have a pot of gold to give, then the whole point of catching them is null and void. Which means that the whole story can't even happen because it's predicated on what's-her-face—"

"Siobhan," Mike supplied.

"—yeah, her. Her great-grandmother having a captured 'leprechaun'"—air quotes again, in case they missed it the first time—"is what kicks off the whole story. If no one would hunt them because they don't have pots of gold, then the whole story just falls apart."

"You're just jealous," George said confidently, managing the neat trick of saying it with no sense of malice or attack, such that even Gayl could not take offense. "No one reads your books, but everyone reads *INsight*."

"Look, people can read whatever they want. Even crap. And I get the appeal, but not for adults. Seriously. Anyone over seventeen who's reading those books is just . . . Can you say arrested development?"

"Whatever, dude," George said, clearly tired of it.

Gayl swore. "They're not fucking leprechauns!"

"But they are. They're just *different*."

"Guys." Mike stepped in between them, as though he feared they would soon come to blows. He didn't actually think that, but stepping in between them just seemed to be the thing to do. "That's enough. We all see the same thing, but we're interpreting it in different ways, OK? Like, Joe. How about you. What do you see?"

"Now our city of peace has crumbled," Joe said, craning his neck to gaze up at the StratoSpire in the distance. "The dust of civilizations."

The dust of civilizations . . . They could all agree on that one, and in the sobering moment that followed Joe's pronouncement, they stood in silence as though in memoriam or mourning.

"We should go inside," Mike said at last, gesturing to CONVENIENCE. "Maybe there are people. Didn't the Marines say there were still people?"

"And I could use something to eat. Even another protein bar," Gayl said.

It was just a convenience store. It was a tiny parcel of land, an empty parking lot, push-in glass doors gone grimy with red grit. And yet they stood before it for an endless interval before finally screwing down their courage and pushing open the door.

CHAPTER 36

The inside of CONVENIENCE, though red-dim and stale-aired, was a cool respite from the hot, dust-choked outside, some air conditioning unit somewhere still serviceable enough to drive off the worst of the outer heat. Most of the outside signage had decayed or dissolved or simply vanished years ago, but within the logo for the Kwik'r'Place chain was plastered on the wall behind the cash register. Rows of picked-over candy bars, packs of gum, bags of snack chips, and dried meats spilled their meager remaining contents into the aisles; shattered glass doors revealed freezer and refrigerator units that no longer functioned, but still stood spotted with a few bottles and cartons here and there.

They surveyed CONVENIENCE, craning necks to peer down aisles, peeking over the counter. "Hello?" Mike asked into the vacated space. "Hello?" The others called out as well, and when no one responded Mike shrugged and took a bottle of water from the (no longer) refrigerated unit and twisted off the cap.

"Hey!" Gayl protested. "You can't just take that. It's stealing."

"Stealing?" Mike quaffed from the bottle, slaking a thirst

that had been burning for hours now, basically since the last drop of water in their last bottle had gone down Joe Roberts' gullet during their hike here. "It isn't stealing if the place is abandoned."

"Abandoned? Are you nuts?" Gayl pointed around. "The lights are on. The air conditioning is on. It's not abandoned."

"He's got a point," George said, gesturing. "The cash register light's on, too."

Mike took another long, urgent swallow. "I'll leave some money. I'm dying here."

Joe scrounged around in the canned food aisle, coming up with a tolerable repast of room temperature pasta and tepid green beans, all of which they savored with a gourmet's gusto, their last true meals having been well over twenty-four hours gone, supplemented only by the few protein bars George had thought to bring. Mike leaned against a nigh-bare shelf, eating spaghetti and meatballs straight from the can with a plastic spork from a package George had found. "We're all leaving money," George had said in a vaguely threatening tone, and everyone agreed.

They ate in a swift, unself-consciously noisy orgy of starved, male aggression, speaking not at all, occasionally sighing in contentment and sharing satisfied grins before diving back into the pile of cans Joe had accumulated. George passed his pocket knife around and they used it to prize open the cans, careful lest they catch and slash a finger on the ragged tin edges. Finished, they stashed further cans and more bottled water in George and Mike's bags, then went to the counter, totalled up a rough approximation of what they'd eaten, and laid money down near the register, Mike contributing his last five, Gayl a pile of ones and fives, Joe Roberts a single twenty. George flipped open his wallet.

"Now it's your turn," Mike said.

Just then, a voice called out, "Hey! What are you doing?" and they turned to the left to see a man emerging from a door they'd hitherto not noticed.

He pointed a shotgun at them.

And he was the asshole.

CHAPTER 37

Now it was George's turn.

The other three put their hands in the air immediately and began a babble of overlapping excuses, apologies, and justifications. George did not move his hands, his wallet still grasped in the left, the right still in the process of removing a clutch of bills.

"Shut up," he said to the others, and they kept talking, hands still up and out, Gayl imploring George to raise his hands as well.

"Shut up!" George barked in the very best command voice he could muster, a tone he'd picked up in his brief time at boot camp, orders and invective hurled at him in equal measure by his sergeant, an effective voice to be sure, for everyone actually shut up.

CONVENIENCE went quiet. George took a single step towards the asshole, moving with calm assurance of his own and calm reassurance for the asshole. It was a step that was not aggressive; it did not threaten. Under ordinary circumstances, it would go unnoticed, or if noticed, noticed only as a momentary shift of weight and position for comfort's sake. In this extraordinary circumstance, it told the asshole that George was not afraid and also—incidentally—interposed George between Mike and the asshole, directly in the line of fire.[69] The others would have no way of knowing who this was, of what the asshole was capable. Of what he had done and done again and done again in George's childhood. Pleading for mercy or clemency or even simple human understanding would not prevail upon the asshole; it surely never had in George's broken-boned, contused childhood. Apologizing to the asshole, George had learned early on, betrayed weakness and invited further abuse. Retaliation, George had learned slightly later, further fueled the initial rage and again invited further abuse. Stoic acceptance, George had learned slightly later still, provoked a perverse urge to prove that the asshole could control your reactions . . . and invited further abuse.

In short, there was no way of dealing with the asshole, which George knew all-too-well.

He had fantasized this moment for years. He had fantasized it even before the asshole had gone to prison, awake in bed at night (George's childhood was a string of insomniac nights, lying awake either from the pain of a beating or—if one had not yet been administered—the apprehension of awaiting one), conjuring a world in which the asshole had gone to prison or simply up and disappeared one day, never envisioning a world in which the asshole was dead, for killing the asshole was George's favorite fantasy, and he knew as a child that he was incapable of doing this. He reserved that singular pleasure for himself.

When the asshole had been carted off to prison, George had asked his mother, "Will people hurt him there?"

69. No one ever asked George about this move, but if he had been asked later whether he intended this protective step, whether he would truly place himself in front of a scattering of buckshot for Mike, or whether it was an unconscious measure, George would have responded, with a thoughtful glance to the sky, "It was both."

And his mother—bruises along her jaw now faded enough that makeup could just about conceal them, her arm still in a sling, her subconscious already beginning to concoct the particulars of a universe of leprechauns and their hunters, a world in which abused children had a ready escape from pain—had told him, "That might happen."

George had responded, "That's good. As long as they don't kill him."

And his mother had put a hand on his head—he was still short enough that she could perform this maternal maneuver—and found herself wordless, stroking his hair and pulling her child to her and whispering, "You'll never see him again. Never, ever."

Now he stood before the asshole, a counter and seven feet of floor between him and the shotgun. In his fantasies, George had always been the one armed. He would have to improvise.

"Go, guys," he said to the three behind him, his gaze locked with the asshole's. "Get out of here."

"No one's going *nowhere*," the asshole growled, and the growl and the words themselves filled George with memory and rage at once. He remembered a time his mother had said she'd had enough (she hadn't—she had stayed married to the asshole two more years past this particular time of "having enough") and had gathered a terrified George and headed for the front door, thinking the asshole upstairs and passed out, having guzzled nearly a quart of booze and beer in his post-beating euphoric haze.

When she flung open the front door, he had appeared there with movie-suspense precision and perfection, grinning, bourbon and beer on his breath, and he'd said those exact words, with that exact inflection: No one's going *nowhere.*

That was the second time Monica (for she was not yet Monika) needed her jaw wired shut. George missed a week of school as the swelling went down around both eyes and the hairline fracture in his collarbone healed.

No one's going *nowhere.*

Control. It was all about control.

"No," George said evenly, surprising himself with his calm. Every fiber of his body—every cell, every mitochondrion within those cells—yearned to leap over the counter. He would take a shot in the leg, he knew, but he thought his chances good; the shotgun was old, single barrel. His leg would be shredded, but his momentum would carry him far enough to get his hands on the asshole. And then . . . Once he had his hands on him, no force in the universe could stop him from wresting that gun away and choking the asshole to death, even as George himself died from blood loss. No force in the universe: Not God, not Barry Lyga. Nothing and no one could stop him.

Except for his own in-born (or was it in-born? hadn't it actually come later in life?) compulsion to protect, to defend. He would take the brunt of any shotgun blast, but the pellets would scatter . . . What if the asshole missed him entirely? He was keenly aware of the three behind him, especially Mike, who would be in the direct line of fire if George attempted any trickery or attack.

"I said—" the asshole said.

"Get out," George said again.

"We're not leaving you," Mike said. George grinned. He sensed Joe and Gayl weighing their options—they would happily leave him, he felt certain, as was right and proper. George was no one to them. Just Mike's friend.

"You have to go."

"No one's going *nowhere!*" the asshole complained and gestured threateningly with the shotgun.

"It's the asshole, Mike," George said, still calm, his tone still even. Then, to the asshole: "You're not in charge here. You get it? You're not in control."

Mike said, "Are you sure?" (wondering, George knew, about his identification of the asshole, Mike having never met the man or even seen a photo of him) at the same time as the asshole said: "Yeah, then who's in control?"

"I am," George answered both of them. He realized he was still holding his wallet in one hand. Moving slowly, he laid it on the counter, freeing both hands for whatever might come next. He never moved his gaze from the asshole's eyes, watching the eyes, not the shotgun, betraying no fear, the shotgun a forgotten detail, unnecessary. "My friends are going to leave because you're not in control. You have one shot in that shotgun and I bet it has a hell of a kick. You might get lucky. You might take me down with the first shot. But by the time you've reloaded, these three guys will already be on top of you."

He said it with vastly more confidence than it warranted. He knew that if the shotgun went off and he went down, chest shredded to gobbets, the other three would most likely panic and give the asshole more than enough time to reload.

"All you'll have accomplished," George went on, "is killing me. And you never wanted to kill me, did you? I was too much fun to beat up."

The asshole's expression changed, going from snarl and anger to something George had never seen before, or, more accurately, had never seen on the asshole's face, something he'd seen on many other faces: Wonderment.

"Georgie-boy?" the asshole whispered.

"Holy shit," Mike said. "That *is* your dad."

"What?" Gayl exploded, his fear at being held at gunpoint submerged by his shock. "Are you *kidding* me?"

"Seems kind of hard to believe," Joe said.

"Not kidding," George said, satisfied now to see the asshole lowering the shotgun. "Go, guys. This is between me and—" he swallowed hard and said the words he hadn't said since childhood "—my father."

****

With the others gone, George stood alone with his father for the first time in nearly a decade. The asshole put the shotgun on the counter between them and they stood two feet apart. George was full-grown now, but still small, and he hated that he had to look up in order to meet his father's eyes.

Eyes that had begun to water.

It was a new tactic, one George had never seen before. At his trial and sentencing hearing, George's father had tried every strategem and tack in the vast repertoire of such he'd accumulated over his years as a drunken abuser: "I didn't do it" became "I did it, but it wasn't as bad as they say" became "I did it, but not as often as they say" became "I need to go into rehab—it's the booze's fault" became "I was beaten as a child, too" became "I'm so sorry; I'll never do it again" became "I've learned my lesson; I swear, judge, I'm a changed man." But in all that time, he'd never cried; George could never decide if it was that shedding tears was one step too far removed from his father's perceived masculinity or—and this was George's favored explanation—if the man was just constitutionally, perhaps congenitally, incapable of crying.

The favored explanation washed away in the stream of tears running down his father's left cheek.

The man looked good, George had to admit. In the nearly ten years since his father had been dragged off to jail, he had not aged significantly. Prison life must have agreed with him.

His hair—short-cropped—was now slightly salted, but otherwise unchanged. His stature was still impassive and blockish. George thought of the man who had struck him so many times over the years, then imagined that man spending his days in the prison yard, lifting weights. He suppressed a shudder.

"What are you doing here?" his father asked, echoing the question on George's lips. It was a tone of voice George had never heard from his father—pleading, anxious, worried. He didn't know how to respond, but then he responded anyway.

"Am I supposed to think you've changed?" he retorted, moving one hand on the counter closer to the shotgun. "Is that it? You've learned how to cry, so I'm supposed to forgive and forget? Is that what you think?"

"No. No." Waving his hands, his father took a step back from the counter and the shotgun. "No. I can't ask . . . I can't . . . Oh, God." There was a stool behind the cash register, and George's father slumped into it. As tears streamed down his face, he aged—in that instant—the ten years that he had thus far avoided, his hairline receding, the salt more pronounced, his cheeks cracking with lines, his jowls sagging, the entire transformation taking less than a second, taking place in the time it took George to blink, and George realized that he had only imagined the younger man before him, that his own fears and memories had conspired to buffalo his eyes, the sudden slump and utter weakness blowing through the illusion and allowing him to see his father as he was, not as George feared him.

He put a hand on the shotgun. Just a hand.

He did not pick it up. He simply put a hand on the smooth, polished wooden stock.

"What are you doing here?" he asked his father. "I risk my life to come here and you just happen to be the first person I see? I'm not buying it." He slammed his free hand on the counter to jolt his father, who was blubbering incomprehensibly. "Tell me! What are you doing here?"

His father jumped. "I got paroled years back. I moved here when I got out. I wanted to come to you, to apologize, but your mother had all kinds of security and restraining orders and I couldn't."

Mom had lied. She had told him his father would rot in jail for the rest of his life, and instead . . . Instead, he'd been paroled early. No wonder she only left the house when on book tour and surrounded by her bodyguards.

George funneled his mother-ward anger at his father. "Yeah, you wanted to apologize," he snorted. "Right. I've heard your apologies. They never stick."

"Believe what you want." He wiped his eyes. "I can't change what you believe. That's one thing I learned in therapy."

"Oh, so you had therapy in prison. That makes everything better." He tightened his grip on the stock. "Next you're going to tell me you found Jesus in jail. Or maybe Allah. Or did you join one of those crazy prison Buddhist sects?"

For the first time, his father smiled; it made George's heart race, for that smile—that sign of genuine joy—had always prefaced a vicious beating as a child. "Jesus and Allah and the Buddha don't need the likes of me," his father said. "No, nothing religious. I just did my therapy, behaved, got out. Came here. Tried to start over."

"Bullshit. You knew I'd be here."

"How could I know that?" His father threw his hands up in the air in surrender. Another gesture, another expression, he'd never seen with his father before, this one surprisingly childish, as though someone had just taken away a favorite toy. "How could I know you were coming here? What are you even *doing* here?"

"Mike's trying to fix the universe," George said. "We're all going with him."

"Well, sure, yeah. I guess that makes sense," his father said. "This is the place to do it. God lives here, you know."

Electricity ran through George in that moment, tingling thrills that skipped along his spine and sparked traces of lightning down his shoulders to his fingertips. For the space of several seconds, so great was his surprise that he forgot his hatred of his father and said, "God lives here? What? You mean Barry Lyga?"

"I don't know who Barry Whoever is. But everyone says . . ." His father hesitated, scratched his head. "Do you really want to hear this?"

George felt the reassuring, slightly warm shotgun stock under his hand. "I want to hear it."

His father took a deep breath. "Look, I came here a few years ago. Started working in this store, behind the counter. It was the only job an ex-con could get."

George fixed him with a hard stare. "I don't care about your sob story."

"Well, my second day on the job . . . I came in early to work the first shift. I was the new guy, so I got the earliest shift. Four in the morning. Get the place ready. Set up the coffeemakers. Bake the—"

"I don't care," George said through gritted teeth, "about your fucking job. You have no idea how much I don't care."

Swallowing hard, his father said, "My second day here was Lucky Sevens."

George blinked.

"Let me show you something." He pointed to the large front window, through which they could see Mike and Gayl, apparently arguing about something. Joe Roberts stood off to one side, tapping his foot to some music only he could hear. Three large panes of glass comprised the window, fitted together so that they appeared to be one.

"A piece of it came right through the window," his father said, pointing to a spot slightly left of center. "I was standing back here, making sure the register was loaded with change for the morning rush. And all of a sudden . . ." He made an explosive sound and spread out his fingers in a gesture of eruption. "Glass everywhere. And people started screaming outside. It was crazy. Crazier than anything I've ever seen."

"What crashed through?" George asked, searching his father's haunted eyes. "A piece of what?"

"I don't know. No one does. Some of the people around here—scientists, you know?—they call it σπασμένη καρδιά.[70] It's like . . . Bloody . . ." He swallowed. "It came from the sky, you get it? Great chunks of bloody meat, just coming from nowhere . . ."

George thought of the bloody chunks they'd found in the desert. "It wasn't a terrorist attack, was it?"

His father laughed. "You think terrorists gonna fly a plane overhead and drop . . . drop whatever-the-fuck on us? That sound like any terrorists you ever heard of?" He leaned toward George, his eyes alive with a light like that he'd had when he'd beaten George. George nearly plucked the shotgun up and fired, but his need to know what had happened on Lucky Sevens won out.

"It was everywhere," his father went on, no longer seeming quite so old and quite so chastened as he relived that day. "In the streets, smashing into buildings. It fell for hours. None of us knew what the hell was going on. And then . . . And then

70. Sounds like *spasmene kardia*.

people started disappearing. There were rumors that they'd all been taken by the government for some kind of experiment, but . . . I don't know. I don't know at all.

"All I know for sure is that the government sent some fellas around that night. It had stopped raining that . . . stuff . . . and they sent people in. Scientists. Military guys. No one could explain what the hell happened. They asked a lot of questions. Didn't answer any. Just asked. Stuff about relationships. I was like, 'The goddamn sky is falling and you're asking about my relationships?' And they were like, 'Mr. Singleton, this is our job.' They were trying to figure it out, but you can't figure it out. It was an Act of God. That means there's no sense to it.

"Eventually, things settled into a routine. We started cleaning up; the government took all the, all the *stuff* they could find. People say they have it in a big warehouse out in the desert somewhere. Then they left some scientist-types and some military-types and they told us the Other City is quarantined, sealed off, and that anyone trying to leave would be subject to arrest and all that shit.

"But no one tried to leave. See, we noticed something: The people left, we were all alone anyway. I thought about leaving to go to you and your mom, but I knew you wouldn't have me. And everyone else here was the same—all of us alone and with no one in our lives. So why not stay here?"

"You said God lives here," George prodded. "What's that all about?"

His father took a deep breath. "Soon after Lucky Sevens, the rumors started. I don't know where they started or why or who started them. I don't even remember where I first heard it. It was just a *thing*, a thing that you knew you heard and you knew that you knew. We all understood it: God had come to the Other City. First, He destroyed it and then He moved in."

"That doesn't make any sense."

"If you ask me, this was God's will. God destroyed the city and He kicked out the people he didn't want here anymore. Then he came down from Heaven and took up here." He got up from the stool and leaned in. George checked; his hands were nowhere near the shotgun. "You want to know a secret? It's a good kind of secret, Georgie. It's a secret *truth*. And here it is:

"I think God and the Devil are the same person. I think God made this place Hell and now he wants to live here for a while, with all the failed people, all the lost and lonely hearts, all the devastated and destroyed."

Something in his father's tone of voice snaked into George's heart and coiled around it, tightening. He had trouble swallowing, trouble breathing for a moment. It was, he knew, true. He wanted to see deceit and guile in his father's eyes, to hear those things in his voice, but all he saw and heard was earnest truth.

"I'd like to make amends, son. I've wanted to for a long time."

"You can't." It sounded like someone else's voice, but George knew it to be his own.

"I know. But I'm telling you what I'd like."

"Do you know what you did to me?" George's voice cracked. "What you did to her? Do you know?"

Hanging his head, his father said, "I was terrible. I was a monster. I know."

"You don't know." The words came before George could think them, welling up from some storehouse within him, words carefully tended by the child George, tended and cared for until they could finally be used. "It wasn't just the violence. If it was just that you beat the shit out of her and out of me, I might—*might*—be able to forgive you someday. But it was the fear." His father nodded, as though he already knew and understood, but he couldn't. His father—no, the asshole—could not possibly understand. "It was the *fear*," George said. "When you were around, I couldn't sleep, couldn't relax, couldn't watch TV or play or anything because there was always that fear, that fear throbbing in my head like a migraine, that fear keeping me on edge. And when you weren't around, it was worse because I would forget—sometimes I'd forget for as long as *five minutes*—and then, when I remembered, when I realized that you could be back any minute and pound the living shit out of me again, when I remembered it, it was even worse than the times I hadn't forgotten. It was getting a glimpse of something I couldn't have, something I could never have. And you know what the something was? Do you?"

The asshole said nothing. Did nothing. Merely watched.

"It was some fucking peace and quiet!" George roared. "It was just a fucking night's sleep! It was just a fucking *life*! And I couldn't have it because you wouldn't let me!"

"I'm sorry," the asshole said quietly, and the worst part was that George knew he meant it.

"Really?" George asked, finally taking the shotgun in his hands. "Are you really?"

CHAPTER 38

While George spoke with his father, Mike waited with Gayl and Joe on the street just outside CONVENIENCE. To the west, the Drag stretched ahead of them, straight as a bullet, its macadam skin pock-marked as though by a storm of meteors. On either side, buildings reared up like diseased horses pawing the air one final time before—blissfully, gratefully—collapsing. To Mike's eye, the entire Other City appeared rotted and tentative, as though a strong foot stomp could set up the radiating tremors that would bring the entire city crumbling down. Even the walls of CONVENIENCE seemed more dust and grit than actual cinder block. Mike ran his hand along one, gently, the solidity against his palm warring with the fragility his eyes perceived.

"This," Mike said, staring at the building, "is one hell of a weird coincidence."

"It's not a coincidence," Gayl said. "It's a contrivance, is what it is."

"What do you mean?"

"Oh, come on. We hike through the desert, avoid Marines,

show up at the forbidden, quarantined city, and the first person we bump into is George's long-lost father? That's a plot contrivance, Mike. If I put shit like that into one of my books, my editor would have an aneurysm."

"Everything's going to be all right," Joe assured him.

"A plot contrivance? Jesus. It's not like his dad's in there revealing some great secret to him or something. *That* would be a plot contrivance. They're just in there dealing with . . . dealing with their shit, you know? Talking."

Gayl harrumphed. "We'll see. I bet he'll come out of there knowing something."

"Like what?"

"I don't know. Something about the truth of this place. Something about how his father ended up here."

Just then, from inside CONVENIENCE, they heard an explosion, one that echoed and reverberated within the building as though the structure had suddenly acquired its own momentary heartbeat. None of them had experience with firearms, but in the silent look between the three of them, they all knew what it had been.

"Words were passed in a shotgun blast," Joe said in stunned disbelief.

Mike ran to the store and was about to throw himself through the door when Gayl grabbed him from behind and hauled him back. "Are you crazy? Don't go in there! You don't know what's—"

"George might need—"

"We should go get the Cops™," Gayl said. "That's what you do!" Gayl said. "You hear a gunshot, you get the—"

"We're not getting the Cops™! George can—"

"What if his dad shot him? What if—"

"What makes you think there *are* any Cops™, anyway?"

Mike struggled free from Gayl's grip. "There might not even be *police* here. Maybe they broke up when . . ."

Mike trailed off as the door to CONVENIENCE opened and George stepped out into the red sunlight, the shotgun resting on one shoulder.

Mike thought of how many times George had told him he would kill the asshole. Thought of how many times he had offered to help. And truly, if anyone deserved to be shotgunned to death in a broken-down convenience store in a broken-down city, it was George's father. Yet now, Mike wondered if anyone really, truly deserved that fate, moot though the point was.

George was not crying; he was, rather, in the immediate post-crying phase, his eyes swollen and red, the skin of his cheeks somewhat deeper and darker with blotted tears. He sniffed once, loudly, then tucked some shotgun shells into his pocket. "Let's go," he said, his voice hoarse and strained.

Mike approached him, unsure what to do. He wanted to hug George, pull him in tight for a clinch, but he was aware of the shotgun, which he had no desire to touch. Too, George's posture and demeanor said, Leave me the hell alone, even if his lips did not move.

"George. George, man, what happened?" He did not—could not—recognize the emotions in his best friend's eyes.

"Did you kill him?" Gayl demanded, his voice nearly hysterical. "Did you kill someone? Holy shit. Now we *have* to go to the Cops™. We have to—"

"Dude," George said in a tone of utter command. "No Cops™. We're moving on. God lives here. My fa— The ass—" He shook his head. "He confirmed it."

Mike turned. Gayl's expression had fallen, the writer torn between the quest and the law. "We can't just *go*," he complained. "Right, Joe? You're with me on this one, aren't you?"

"We keep pretending that there's nothing wrong," Joe said, and then shrugged. "Ain't nothing in this world I can do about it. The time has come to take this moment and . . ." He hesitated, looking from Gayl to George, then finally settling on Mike. "I'm going all in 'cause I don't care."

"The normal rules don't apply here," George said. "You said you came here to meet God. Are you coming with me or not?"

With that, he pushed past them all and walked across the parking lot.

Mike didn't hesitate—he took off after George.

"George," he said as he caught up. "Man, what happened in there?" Maybe it had been self-defense.

George's voice was tight with emotions Mike couldn't recognize from the jumble: Regret? Anger? Fear? Maybe a little guilt? He couldn't tell.

"Dude," George said. "I won't tell. So don't ask. You know what I mean?"

****

The parking lot for CONVENIENCE opened directly onto the Drag, the main strip of blacktop—four lanes wide—that bisected the Other City into northern and southern halves, similar to the Great Way back home. At the far end of the Drag, at its westernmost extreme, the StratoSpire thrust from the ground, tapering as it ascended, its aspect that of a syringe standing upright, ready to suck the clouds from the sky.

George led the way, with a stride quick and efficient that said he wanted no company, though he would permit followers. Mike, Gayl, and Joe lingered behind him, just out of earshot.

"You just don't know what he went through," Mike said. "What his childhood was like." He realized as he was saying it that he was advocating for allowing victims to execute their tormentors, even years after the crimes were committed, and wondered briefly if this was something he believed or if it was just a convenient defense of his best friend.

"And besides," he went on, "the only person we've even seen is George's dad, so who knows if anyone else is even—"

"I'm not thinking of that anymore," Gayl interrupted abruptly. "I have something else on my mind."

"Like what?"

Gayl hesitated, clearly not sanguine about the prospect of revealing his latest thoughts, but then said, "Mike, I've been thinking . . . Do you think there's a chance we're dead?"

"Dead?" Mike chuckled, but when Gayl and Joe did not join in, the chuckling did not last long. "What?"

"Well, this place sure looks like hell to me . . . And I've been thinking . . ." He held up the copy of *Inframan* as if he planned to thumb through it, then hesitated and thought better of it before just plunging ahead. "In the book, Mike Grayson—the book's Mike Grayson, not you—goes with his sister and his friends to this old amusement park. And they're attacked by the Shadow Boxer. Mike gets shot in the chest, and that's when his, well, his divine experience starts. He ascends to Heaven and then he goes beyond Heaven, to the real world."

"Where he doesn't get to meet Barry Lyga," Mike said drily.

"But it's the closest we can imagine!" Gayl said, almost desperate for understanding. "The novel presupposes that to the characters within it, the Real World is beyond Heaven. So what if we all died earlier? What if the Marines actually caught up to us and shot us down, and now this is Hell?"

"So you're saying Barry Lyga isn't God, but the Devil?" Mike mused.

Gayl seemed uncomfortable with the idea, no surprise given

that his name and Lyga's were the same. "I don't know about that. I'm just saying—"

"When I die," Joe cut in, "I don't want no part of Heaven."

"That's ridiculous!" Gayl exclaimed. "Why not?"

"It's a long walk to heaven and a road filled with sin. I've been there, too. It ain't no house on the hill, with a garden and a nice little yard."

"You can't just—"

"We're not dead," Mike said. "We got away from the Marines. We made it here. And we're going to make it the rest of the way, too."

With that, before the others could say anything, Mike jogged to come even with George, who strode ahead, the shotgun still on his shoulder, gazing straight ahead at the heaven-pointing StratoSpire.

"Is that the place?" Mike asked.

"Where else would you live if you were God?" George asked. "Tallest building in the Other City."

"Tallest building *left*," Gayl amended. He and Joe Roberts had caught up to the two of them. "And I told you so," he added, glaring at Mike.

"Told you what?" George asked.

"Nothing. Something about a plot contrivance. Doesn't matter. We're on the right path. I know it."

George suddenly, unexpectedly grinned a broad, flashing-white grin. "When we were kids, did you ever think it would come to this?"

Despite himself, Mike couldn't help returning the grin, chuckling. "What, you mean you and me on a hike to meet God?"

"In the Other City."

"In the *quarantined* Other City."

"Right. With an author and a subway driver—"

"—highly poetic and slightly brain-scrambled subway driver—"

"—in tow." Mike laughed. "Yeah, man, this is exactly what I pictured when we were kids." It was insane. It was beyond insane. The only healthy response—the only response that would keep his brain from leaking out his ears—was to laugh.

George laughed, too, and then Joe, Gayl reluctantly joining in last, his laughter completing the harmony, and they began to walk to the StratoSpire.

****

They saw other people.

If they'd had any questions or doubts about the Other City being populated, they quickly went away. It wasn't that the Other City wasn't populated—it was just dramatically *under*populated. Well over a hundred thousand had died on Lucky Sevens and in the immediate aftermath, with more emigrating or—according to George's dad—mysteriously disappearing shortly thereafter. The Other City, built and designed and rebuilt and redesigned for two million residents and another half-million commuters daily, now was home to less than a million. Whole sections of the Drag felt like a ghost town, but then they would advance another block and see people. On some blocks, they couldn't tell—other than the reddish haze in the air—that Lucky Sevens had even happened, so mundane seemed the people.

And yet . . .

And yet as they walked steadily west, they began to see that the horrors of Lucky Sevens existed everywhere, even when invisible, even when repaired or otherwise papered over. There was a slowness to the seemingly-mundane people they encountered, a *thick* quality to their movements, as though they had no purpose beyond basic animal drive, no reason. Some of them stared as the group walked past. Some—very few—shouted out encouragement. Some went so far as to say that they would join them . . . but none ever did.

Most, though, simply ignored them.

At one point, a man ran to them in the middle of the Drag. (Cars were abundant, parked along the street, and seemed functional, but they had yet to see one running. Gayl theorized that gas might have been embargoed by the government. George offered that people probably just didn't have anywhere to go. Mike leaned toward George's theory.) He waved his arms until he was sure he had their attention.

"Going to the StratoSpire, are you?" he demanded.

"Sure are," Mike said, amused. The man was squat and thick, a bushy beard erupting from his face with an aggression not usually seen in facial hair.

"You don't belong here," the man told them. "None of you do."

Mike tried to convince him, but the man would have none of it, stamping his foot on the asphalt and ranting at them. George shifted the shotgun significantly from one shoulder to the other, and when that did not dissuade the man, he testily pushed him aside. The bearded ranter scurried back to the curb and shouted invective at them from the sidewalk until they were out of earshot.

"This is fucking insane," George said, but his tone was mild.

"I'll tell you what's insane," Mike said. "What's insane is that it's been years since Lucky Sevens, and they cleaned up, but no one's rebuilt. Look at that." He pointed. "That's a church, for God's sake. And it looks like someone sat on it."

George shook his head. "Since when do you care so much about buildings, you know what I mean?"

"It's not that." Mike grimaced in frustration, trying to think of how to make George understand. "Architecture is the way we control our environment. But it's more than that. It's the ultimate expression of our humanity. Shelter is a basic need, right? But if that's all architecture was about, we'd all be living in lean-tos and tents and log cabins. We're not. Because we take that basic need—shelter—and we say, 'Hey, we're not just going to build a place to shield us from the elements. We're going to make it beautiful. Or tall. Or broad.' Or whatever. We turn our basic needs into art and we transform ourselves. Because once you've lived in a beautiful building, you'll never live in a tent again. Architecture pushes us forward as a species."

George had stopped to retie his shoelace. He stood. "What the fuck are you talking about? When did you become an architect?"

Mike gnawed at his lower lip. In this version of reality, he'd given up his dreams of architecture years ago. This iteration of George had never endured the endless lectures and observations, the attempt to memorize whole sections of Asher[71], the discourses on the golden mean[72], and more. As far as George was concerned, Mike was a lovesick, Phil-obsessed, nigh-dropout who'd never aspired to college, much less an actual career.

"Never mind. I just wish someone would do something here. Fix something. Rebuild. As a way of showing that no matter who you are, you can't just come in here and mess up one of our cities."

"You know what really sucks?" Gayl asked suddenly, coming up behind them. "What really sucks is that they told us terrorists

71. Benjamin Asher, who wrote the first book published in America on architecture, in 1797.

72. A 5:8 ratio, such that the ratio of the largest segment to the smallest is the same as the ratio of the whole to the largest segment.

caused Lucky Sevens. And we bombed the holy hell out of, like, four different countries in retaliation."

Mike and George fell silent, absorbing that. They had grown up in a world defined by Lucky Sevens and further defined by GWB and the resultant economic collapse[73]; they remembered little prior. Just as a child does not question the parental hand that offers sustenance and punishment, so too did Mike and George[74] not question the commonly believed details of Lucky Sevens or the government's bellicose insistence on the necessity of Global War B.

"And in reality," Gayl went on, "it had nothing to do with terrorism. Nothing to do with war. It was God. Or Barry Lyga. Whichever one it or he is. And that sucks."

"It's the government. They lie," Mike said.

"And we just accept it. They lie and we shrug our shoulders and say, 'Oh, that wacky government!' Like the government's a crazy neighbor in a sitcom. Hundreds of thousands dead from American drone bombers; cue the laugh track.[75]"

It should have taken them all day to walk from the east side of the Other City to the west, but they found themselves at the StratoSpire by noon, as though time had compressed, or as though they had fastforwarded through reality to this, the next most necessary moment in time. It made Mike think of the nature of reality, as Gayl had expounded on it back at Books-A-Go-Go only two days ago (though it seemed years),

73. Global War B's launch coincided with massive tax cuts; the combination of drastically increased spending and truncated revenues crashed the economy and led to unprecedented unemployment and homelessness among the population. Contradistinctively, those in power during Global War A had raised taxes to inflate the war coffers.

74. And their generation.

75. Hahahahahahahahahaahaha

how reality was a book, each page thin and almost invisible until stacked above and below with others, and he imagined them walking through the pages of a book—each page a moment, each moment invisible and ephemeral on its own, gaining bulk like atoms only in clusters and quantities—each page bringing them that much closer to the StratoSpire until someone flipped through the book suddenly, accelerating their trip, bringing them to where they now stood.

The StratoSpire loomed before them. At a distance, the skyscraper appeared needle-thin, but up close it was nearly as wide as any other building. Distance and the substantially wider bottom three floors conspired to create the illusion. Mike had studied the construction of the StratoSpire—and its twin from his home city, the SkyTower—in his earliest architecture class at College Y. In another life. It was, he knew, an internal conglomeration of carefully and precisely positioned triangular and polygonal substructures, designed to support weight and resist compression, the substructures diminishing in size as the StratoSpire rose to the sky, until the very top floor seemed a mere pinprick from below. The effect was that of a building vanishing as it penetrated into the sky. This was, indeed, a modern Tower of Babel, if ever there had been one. It was not the tallest building in the world—it was not even, historically, the tallest building in the Other City—but it was the one constructed with the specific intent to make people look up, to make them question.

The bottom three floors were clad in polarized glass that shrouded the interior of the building. A series of double-doors fronted the building and they could see themselves—their reflections smoky and indistinct in the polarized glass—in them. They hesitated some ten or fifteen yards from the entrance. It all seemed too easy, all of a sudden.

Mike walked forward to the center set of double doors; in

the glass, he noticed George following him and—as he reached out for the door handle—unshoulder and point the shotgun with a stance of menace.

"Seriously, George?" Mike asked, amused for reasons he could not articulate.[76]

"Dude, we don't know what's in there, you know what I mean?"

Mike shrugged and tugged at the door handle, expecting the door—locked—to resist; instead, the door easily came ajar a few inches, revealing in that crack only a dimly-lit, unknowable interior.

"I guess," Mike said slowly, "we can go in."

The others gathered around him, George still wielding the shotgun, which now no longer seemed quite so comical.

"I'll take point," George said.

"Last chance to back out, guys," Mike said. "I can go on by myself here. That's fine. You guys don't have to come."

George rolled his eyes. "Duh."

"How about you, Gayl?"

"Are you kidding me?" He cackled a brief laugh. "Kid, I was living a perfectly boring and acceptable life. And then one day you show up on my doorstep and tell me that the guy whose work I've been reading since college might be God. Are you kidding me?" he said again. "I can't stop here. I have to find out who I am. *What* I am. I have to find out what my life is about."

They all turned to Joe Roberts, who seemed oblivious to the conversation, staring up the great, long, and disappearing

76. It may have had something to do with the distortion effect of the polarized glass and the angle of the strange, red sunlight striking said glass, both of which conspired to generate a somewhat foreshortened version of a funhouse-George—a squat, thick dwarf wielding a comically bloated shotgun. It was an amusing sight.

column of the StratoSpire with an expression that suggested that he could find his answer—maybe every answer—if he could just see that exact point where the StratoSpire met the sky.

"Joe, are you—"

"I swear," Joe said, snapping his head down to look at them all, "I lost everything I ever loved or feared."

And then he surprised them all by taking a slim, silver harmonica from his vest pocket; he blew a single note—long, low, and mournful. There seemed to be infinity in that note. It made Mike see a river, rushing wide and foamy from some eternity to some endless abyss, the river the only thing in the whole of existence that was not the abyss, that was not the limitless tracts of black infinity. It made him think of regret. Of love that has soured like milk, curdled.

He found himself crying. But that was OK—the others were crying, too.

"Are we ready?" Gayl said when they'd finished.

"Yeah. Let's go."

Mike pulled open the door and they stepped into the StratoSpire.

CHAPTER 39

The lobby of the StratoSpire was dim and cool, silent but for the hum of some impressively-long-lived, still-running air conditioning unit. It was arrayed like an inverted doughnut, with empty space ringing a central column. Leather chairs and sofas clustered around coffee tables covered with magazines, and a bank of slot machines stood against one wall, their shiny, ostentatious chrome façades gone only slightly dull with tarnish, their displays dark and coated with dust. In the center of the lobby—at the central column—was a U-shaped marble counter, over which hung a gilt sign reading "WELCOME TO STRATO-SPIRE," below which depended a smaller but no less gilded sign that read "Reception." The air smelled vaguely of ink.

"Wow." Mike's voice was hushed. "This is like . . . I don't know."

"The last carnival," Joe Roberts said. "The devil's arcade."

The four of them drifted apart, spelunkers in a lost-now-found cavern. Mike traced a finger through a carpet of dust on the back of a chair.

"The light in here is strange . . ." George still had the shotgun at the ready, padding around the lobby, making occasional sharp

180° turns, lest something sneak up behind him. Mike would have laughed at the display, but something unsettling about the interior of the StratoSpire made him glad for George's wariness.

"Cinnamon sky's gone candy-apple green," Joe said, pointing. The polarized glass had transformed the reddish haze outside into a sour green.

"Red is stop, green is go?" Gayl didn't sound convinced.

"You mean we're supposed to stop, but then since we didn't, we go?" Mike asked with no small amount of sarcasm.

"I'm just trying to think in terms of symbolism," Gayl shot back. "If a writer is controlling all of this, he'll be using symbols all over the place."

"Yeah? Really? What does this symbolize?" Mike picked up a magazine from the nearest coffee table, a dust-covered May 12, 2007 issue of *You!* magazine. On the cover, a famous actress smiled past the words JOANIE'S REVENGE DIET![77]

"Well, I—"

"How about this?" Mike stalked over to the bank of dead slot machines and pulled one of the levers. The action was surprisingly fluid. Nothing happened.

77. Joanie (Joanie MacGillicuddy, also known as Joanie Mac and J-Mac in various tabloids and Internet chat rooms) had been a contestant on *Make Him Stray!*, a reality TV show in which a man married to a woman his own age is tempted with beautiful strangers who are twenty years younger. If he can remain faithful, he receives one million dollars. But if he strays, the woman who coerced him into a new bed wins the million dollars and a free plastic surgery of her choice (usually deferred until later years). J-Mac was the early favorite to win in her season, and in fact managed to seduce Brendan, a forty-two year-old advertising copywriter, during one of his business trips. He immediately regretted his transgression, however, and returned to his wife, leading Joanie to go on a quest to perfect her body and land images of said body on as many magazine covers and websites as possible in order to torment Brendan. When this did not work, she filmed a series of highly pornographic vlogs, each of which featured superimposed titles with the name of her former paramour and the legend, "Like what you see? You'll never have it again!" As of the events of this novel, she is one of the top hits on PornoTube.com, with millions of eyes on her, though no one knows whether or not Brendan represents two of them.

"I don't know, OK?" Gayl threw his hands up in frustration. "I'm just trying to help. Maybe it means that we never should have come this far, but now that we're here we might as well go the rest of the way."

Mike had no retort to that. None of them did.

They wandered the lobby, their mission not forgotten, but now lingering in the backs of their minds as they explored this relic, this strangely preserved habitat.

"This place must have been abandoned after Lucky Sevens," George said from behind the reception counter, the shotgun now resting on a shoulder. "There's a day calendar back here that's turned to the day after the, uh, the love catastrophe, you know what I mean?"

They gathered at the counter, peering over and around it. "I don't get it," Mike said. "If they know God lives here, why doesn't anyone come here? All those unhappy people. Or even the government people."

"They're afraid," Gayl said. "This is Old Testament stuff, Mike. Jewish stuff. Not the touchy-feely Jesus stuff from the New Testament. This is Eden and angels with flaming swords and Sodom and Gomorrah and Lot's wife and—"

"The Tower of Babel."

"Right."

George looked up at the ceiling. "How many—"

"Two hundred seventeen," Mike said automatically. "Plus the observation cupola, which is technically two hundred eighteen, though most people don't count it."

"So there's no one in the lobby . . ." George drifted off.

"But there could be people in the floors above," Gayl said.

"Or what's left of people." Mike shuddered.

"Jesus." Gayl flopped into the reception chair—a cloud of dust billowed around him and he waved it away as he coughed.

"Jesus. Are we gonna have to go through two hundred-some-odd floors looking for clues and shit like that?"

"I don't think so," Mike said. "I bet we just go straight to the top."

"See?" Gayl crowed triumphantly. "*That's* symbolic."

"Whatever," George said. "Let's do this."

"Wait." Gayl flicked the power switch to the computer at the reception counter; nothing happened. "Shit. I was hoping we could learn something about this place."

"Designed in 1971 by Fox and Barth," Mike said, ignoring the shocked stare from George, "under contract from the Two Cities Revitalization Project, which sponsored an architectural contest to enliven the skylines of our city and the Other City. Funding was approved in 1972 and construction on the Strato-Spire began in 1974, with the SkyTower starting in 1976—"

"Not *that.*" Gayl sounded exasperated. "I'm not interested in the history of this place. Just the present."

"Oh. Like what?"

"Like," Gayl said, heaving himself out of the chair, "do the elevators work, or are we walking up two-hundred-some-odd flights of stairs?"

Mike's calves hurt at the thought of it. They executed a quick counter-clockwise ramble from Reception and encountered—on the other hemisphere of the central column—a bank of elevators.

"One, two, three, four," Joe murmured, counting them.

"The air conditioning is still running," George said hopefully.

"You think it matters which elevator we take?" Mike asked, favoring Gayl with a glance.

"Why are you asking me?"

"You're the master of symbolism," Mike said lightly, though he meant it.

Gayl snickered. "Yeah, well . . ." He put a hand on the second elevator door, as though he could divine something through touch. "I don't know. Elevators. OK. Elevators. Elevation. Rising. Ascending. That's all good. I don't know. Going up." The others let him ramble as he closed his eyes. George noticed—with some amusement—that Gayl's fingers had begun to twitch as though he were typing on the elevator door. "Numbers. Right. Numbers. One through four. One's a good number. First. Primary. Primacy.

"Two, though . . . One is lonely. One is solitary. Two is congenial. Joining. Twins. Castor and Pollux? No, no . . . Two is also conflict—can't fight with only one person in the battle. So maybe not.

"Three. A magic number. Trinity. Father, Son, Holy Ghost. Three is the first real social unit: Mother, father, child. Trilogies. The three-act structure.

"Now four . . ." He stroked his beard. "Four is interesting. Not a lot of symbolism, but still—an important number. The first square. Time is the fourth dimension . . ."

Mike and George were rapt by Gayl's discourse, but suddenly Joe broke in.

"It ain't too complicated." He swiped his palm across a space to the right of the last elevator, scrubbing away a layer of dust to reveal a plaque. "Searchin' through the dust, lookin' for a sign."

The small sign said, "Express to Observation Cupola."

Gayl blushed. "Well, you know, I would have—"

"Let's do it," Mike said, and pressed the button for the fourth elevator.

For a moment the button did nothing and they all imagined the trek up two hundred and seventeen flights of stairs, but then the button lit up and they all breathed out their relief at once, then shared a look and a laugh at that mutual relief.

The elevator door opened with a jaunty and incongruous chime. The interior was wood grain and polished brass, well-lit. It looked like any other elevator in any other building in the world and suddenly none of them wanted to get in.

"Maybe . . ." George said. "Maybe one of us should try a test run, first."

The door slid closed, stopped at the last instant by Joe Roberts sticking his foot in the way. The door obligingly slid open again, chiming once more as if to say, "OK, no problem!"

"It's gonna be fine," Mike said, shaking himself as though he could physically cast away his doubts like a dog flinging off its fleas. "These elevators were re-installed just before Lucky Sevens to meet new building codes. They're rated for seventeen years of operation. They'll be fine."

"They may be rated for seventeen years, but they haven't been maintained since Lucky Sevens," Gayl said. "Are you willing to risk it?"

"Jesus, Gayl. You're the one who said before that Barry Lyga was making it easy for us to come to him. Do you think he set it up so we could come this far just to drop us to death in a faulty elevator?"

George shrugged. "Got a point."

"I don't know," Gayl admitted. "You haven't read his books; I have. He has a . . . an unusual sense of what makes for a good ending to a story."

The door slid open again. This time Joe stepped in. "Come on up. I can take you higher."

George nodded and hopped on. Mike followed.

Gayl grumbled as he got on, "If we all die, the last thing I'm saying is 'I told you so.'"

"I'm OK with that." Mike checked the control panel—there were only two buttons, one for the Observation Cupola, one for the lobby. He thought about giving them all one last chance to beg off, but that seemed redundant. Instead, he fumbled in his bag until he found the pack of gum, then shared out the sticks. "I didn't know why I packed this, but it'll help our ears pop when we ascend."

"Maybe that's why you packed it," Gayl said. "If Lyga is controlling this story, then he knew we'd end up here."

Mike shrugged and pressed the top button; the door slid shut, this time for real. Mike found himself holding his breath as the elevator jerked and began to ascend. No one said a word, instead simply staring at the digital readout above the door, which swiftly changed from L to 1, then 2.

And then a voice spoke from hidden speakers: "Welcome to StratoSpire! This express elevator will take you to the world-famous Observation Cupola in less than ten minutes, ascending through two hundred and seventeen stories at a rate of three stories per second.

"The StratoSpire was designed by the architecture firm of Fox and Barth in 1971, with construction beginning in 1973—"

"Oops," Mike said, but no one else spoke as the automated voice rambled on about the history of the StratoSpire; soon—in less than ten minutes, in fact—the doors opened to the sound of the chime once more.

"Welcome to the StratoSpire Observation Cupola!" the voice chirped with annoying friendliness. "Please enjoy your stay."

If before they had been reluctant to enter the elevator, they were now equally reluctant to exit it, the corridor before them ominous and dark, windowless and lit only by dull emergency lamps set into the ceiling at regular intervals. They stood in the elevator car, nervously sharing glances at each other and at the corridor beyond until Joe Roberts threw his hands up in the air and stepped out.

"Well, I hate to seem impatient," he said with a note of sarcasm in his voice, "but you'd be excited, too . . . if you want to come and see." When no one moved, he sighed and said, without a trace of sarcasm, "I wanna find me a world where love's the only sound."

Mike nodded and hopped out of the car, George on his heels. Gayl followed just as the elevator door slid shut, and Mike's heart sank at the sound of the car descending rapidly. He knew that the elevator system had been designed intentionally so, sending the express right back down to the lobby to pick up another cargo of tourists sightseers, but he would have felt infinitely more comfortable if the elevator had stayed here at the Observation Cupola, ready for a quick getaway if necessary. The air here felt electrically-charged and hot, as though something massive and slow were approaching, pushing thunderheads as its vanguard.

"Do you feel that?" he asked.

"Do you hear that?" Gayl responded, his head cocked.

"It's raining," George said.

"It sounds like rain and ee cummings," Gayl said.

"What do you mean?"

Gayl blinked in confusion. "I'm not sure."

A sign on the wall read "OBSERVATION" and pointed down the corridor, so they walked that way, clustered together, suddenly terrified for no reason they could articulate, save that they had gained the top of the Tower of Babel and who knew what they would see here?

The corridor opened into a windowed ring around the top of the StratoSpire, the glass flecked and spattered with raindrops that thrummed down in an irregular tattoo. The Observation Cupola was empty, the abandoned rail-mounted binoculars pointed at the floor like sleeping cranes. Yet there—in the exact center of their field of vision as they emerged from the corridor into the Cupola—was a comfortable-looking easy chair in which sat a very familiar-looking man, a man Mike sort-of, kind-of knew from the Wikinformation page and from the About the Author page in *Inframan.*

"Oh," Mike said. "Oh my God."

"That's about right," I said.

CHAPTER 40

Yes, "I." I, watching them all. Describing them all to the best of my ability, discovering them, often, as I go along. Sometimes—and this is true, I swear it—my fingers know the truth of a story or of a character before my mind does; the keyboard is the birthing chamber, the brain merely the . . . the . . . pediatric unit.

That didn't work. That was a shitty metaphor. Sorry.

But the point stands: My fingers type things sometimes before I am consciously aware of them. My fingers invoke plot twists. My fingers knew that George's mother was Monika Seymore[78] before I did, but as soon as it happened, I knew it worked. (Did it work for you? Had you been wondering how George's mother could afford the endless reconstructions and redesigns of her house in earlier chapters? I hope you had been wondering. I had certainly been wondering, and I was so happy that my fingers stumbled over an answer that worked. Before this

78. There is, by the way, no anagram to that name—"Monika Seymore" does not twist and contort to become some real-world author's name. Sorry. Are you disappointed? Were you hoping I was dishing on someone you knew of?

book landed at Blackstone with editor Dan Ehrenhaft, I worked on it with my longtime editor Alvina Ling at Little, Brown. She wasn't sure the George's-Mom reveal worked. She thought that Mike and George would talk about Monika being George's mom in the scene at Books-A-Go-Go. But I was like, "Why would they talk about something they both know?" Anyway, I did make some modifications to that scene, not to spill the beans, but just to make it a little more of an "Oh!" moment on a re-read.[79] Oh, and BTW: We haven't seen the last of Monika Seymore/Monica Singleton—she'll be back before the end of the book.)

You might be wondering what precisely I was doing, loitering there at the top of the StratoSpire, waiting for them. After all, I could have met them on the ground floor, right? That wouldn't have been too difficult for me, and I could have conjured a suitably dramatic moment around it, what with George prowling around the lobby with his shotgun at the ready. (And don't worry—I haven't forgotten about that shotgun blast in the convenience store back on page 547. We'll be coming back to that.) They could have come into the lobby, looking around, suddenly turned at a noise and . . . ta-da! There I am. End of chapter and you gotta turn the page, don't you?

But I didn't do it that way, and I'll tell you why: You didn't want it that way.

That's right. You. The reader. The audience. You would have been disappointed to have them show up at this tower—the tallest building left in the Other City—and *not* have to go to the top. It would have violated the unspoken, unwritten rules of quest fiction, which is that the heroes always follow the toughest

79. Because after getting this far, you're all planning on re-reading this thing, right?

path. I suppose I should have made the elevators out of order and forced them to walk up two hundred and seventeen stories, with all manner of mishaps and escapades along the way[80], but this book is so long already. It's so long. I can feel the end, so close, and I bet you can, too.[81]

So I put them in an elevator. And it started to rain while they ascended because I like the sound of rain and *she* likes the sound of the rain, too. She texted me one night and said, *come lie in bed with me and listen to the rain*. And yes, it sounds like rain and ee cummings right now, even as I'm typing these words in a garden apartment in Brooklyn. Why is it raining in real life just when I need rain in the novel? I don't know. I don't think I want to know.

Anyway. They all came in. Mike and George and Gayl and Joe.

"Oh," Mike said. "Oh my God."

"That's about right," I said.

And now you can turn the page for the next chapter.

80. That's actually a cool idea for a story—a tale set entirely in one tall building, with the characters working their way up from the basement to the roof, experiencing all kinds of adventures along the way. Has anyone done a book like that?

81. In my original plan for the novel, Mike and his *confreres* would have arrived in the Other City and then gone on a traditional quest, modeled after fantasy literature such as *The Lord of the Rings* and its ilk. They would have scoured the Other City for information about Barry Lyga, gathered traveling companions, etc., and then discovered that the elevators in the StratoSpire were not working. (I probably, in truth, would have killed someone off with a malfunctioning elevator at that point.) In ensuing chapters, they would fight and trek their way up hundreds of stories (and learn stories, get it?) in order to find me. But let's be honest with one another here: At this point, you're tired of reading. And at this point, I was so tired of writing. I had/have the energy to push to the end, but to recreate a fantasy universe and mimic classic fantasy literature in this world I've created? To spend 50, 60, 70 thousand more words on such a quest? No, thank you. I think we're going to wrap it up this way instead.

CHAPTER 41

They said nothing for an extended silence, so I said nothing as well.

"You're him," Mike said at last. "Right in front of us. You're Barry Lyga, aren't you?"

I shrugged and stood. The chair disappeared, mainly because I didn't feel like describing it in detail. "You could say I'm Barry Lyga," I told him. "But it's more accurate to say that I'm a version of Barry Lyga. An iteration. More like an avatar of a god than the god itself."[82]

I turned my back to them and looked out the windows. It became night and the rain stopped and the lights of the Other City—what few still lit up, given the decimated population—came up. From the Observation Cupola, the Other City at night looked like a circuit board arrayed below me[83], fanning out to the edges of the desert.

82. An inexact simile, to be sure, but I think you get the point.

83. I've waited ten years to use that simile in a story. Strange—it doesn't feel as good as I thought it would. Anyway, I hope it works for you.

"What are you saying?" Gayl asked.

"I'm saying that I'm not the one you're after."

"Who are we after then?" Mike demanded.

"You want Barry Lyga. The real deal. I'm just a version of him on a page in a book. The real Barry Lyga—the one in the real world—is the one you want. He's the one controlling all of this."

"Fine, then. How do I see him? How do I get to him?"

I turned back to them. "Gayl? You know this one, right?"

Gayl was having difficulty thinking just then. For him, this experience was eerily similar to gazing into a mirror that projected one's image into the future, for I am only eight years older than Gayl and—as he was realizing just now—we were essentially one and the same, he being merely another version/iteration/avatar of the One, True Barry Lyga, albeit one with a scrambled name and life.

"Gayl!" Mike nudged Gayl for attention.

"Oh," Gayl said. "Right. Seeing . . . Getting to the Real World . . ." He touched his bag, feeling the copy of *Inframan* there. "In the book . . . In the book, Mike Grayson gets shot. He dies. He ascends to heaven and then . . ." He drifted off, as if waiting for permission.

I nodded permission to him.

"Heaven turns out to be a stage, like in a play. The Pearly Gates, the clouds—they're just backdrops, paint on wood. He finds a way around and goes backstage and finds a staircase that leads to the real world."

"Very good," I told him. "That's exactly what happens in *Inframan*."

"So I have to get shot?" Mike demanded.[84]

84. He demands a lot, doesn't he? He's very angry.

"No, we won't be doing that this time around," I told him. "I just wanted you to get a feeling for the complexity of traveling to the Real World. Your path will be different from your namesake's, Michael. You'll be taking a different route. But one that's no less hazardous." I showed them all the wall to my left, which they'd never noticed before because I hadn't yet described it. There were four doors there, conveniently enough, just as there had been four elevators and just as there were four questers.

"Choose your path," I told him. "You have to go alone. Your friends get to decide for themselves what they'll do."

"And if I choose the right path," Mike asked, looking not at me, but rather at the doors. "If I choose the right door, do I get to see you again? In the Real World?"

I knew, of course, what he was thinking—that in the Real World, we'd be on equal footing and he could compel me to fix the world, to re-edit the story and fix Mike's own tragic edits.

"There is no right path," I told him. "There's no right door. There's just the door you pick and the consequences of it. And you'll never see me again, but if you're lucky and if you persevere, you might get to the Real World and then, yes, you might see the real Barry Lyga."

"That's all I needed to hear," Mike said, and then—as I knew he would, because I'd planned it this way—he reached into Gayl's bag and pulled out the beaten, well-read copy of *Inframan* and thrust it out before him like a crucifix before a vampire.

"What the hell?" Gayl said.

"Dude," George said, because George always says "dude."

"Well, surprise, surprise, surprise," Joe said.

"Only the Word of God can destroy God, right?" Mike said.

"Mike!" Gayl shouted. "No!"

But before anyone could stop him, Mike opened the book and I

CHAPTER 42

Barry Lyga was gone. In less than an instant.

"Holy shit," Mike whispered, looking down at the very mundane, very normal book in his hands. "It worked. The Word of God . . ."

"You idiot!" Gayl fumed. "What did you do? He was the one we came to—"

"You heard him. He was just a *version*. I want the real deal."

Gayl ground his teeth together. "I can't believe you!"

"That was pretty radical," George said. He slowly advanced on the spot where Barry Lyga (or at least a version of Barry Lyga) had sat, stood, paced, talked. "It wasn't like in the movies. There wasn't a sound or a special effect . . ."

"Gone, gone," Joe said.

Gayl joined George. There was nothing. Not even the dust was disturbed to mark Barry Lyga's presence and his passing. Outside, it began to rain again, the patter of raindrops on the windows of the Observation Cupola.

"He looked just like me." Gayl's voice trembled. "You all saw that, right? He looked just like me, only a little older."

Mike nodded. Joe looked away. George shrugged.

"How can that be possible? Barry Lyga died years ago. He never had a chance to be older than I am right now. And he . . ." Gayl ran a hand through his hair. "God. This is crazy. He said he was . . . He was an avatar. A version. An iteration. Is that all *I* am, too? He just took his name and scrambled the letters and—"

"Gayl, we thought that was possible—"

"That fucker!" Gayl screamed, interrupting Mike. "That piece of shit! I have a life! I had a life! And now it's what, just a joke to him? Just a way to play around in a fucking *story*?"

Gayl threw his bag on the floor and kicked it. It skidded along, plowing up a cloud of dust until it fetched up against the floor-to-ceiling window that offered a breathtaking view of the Other City by night. He ranted and screamed and then snatched from a caught-off-guard Mike the copy of *Inframan*, so lovingly read and re-read over the years, and opened the book and ripped out a handful of pages, then another, then another, scattering pages all over the floor around him, shredding the book from within until all that remained was the cover and the ragged edges of leaves that had not torn cleanly from the spine. Gayl sat against the window, breathing heavily, tears streaming down his face, surrounded by the remains of the book.

"Fuck him," he whispered. "Fuck him and his fucking books."

Mike and George crouched down on either side of Gayl as Joe started pushing the paper into a pile. "Hey," Mike said, "it's gonna be OK."

"Maybe for you," Gayl said bitterly. "And maybe for you," he nodded at George, "and him" nodding to Joe Roberts. "You guys are all distinct characters. I'm just a stand-in for the author. You don't need me anymore. I'm just here to play a part for him. Now that we've actually seen Barry Lyga, who needs Gayl

Rybar?" He buried his face in his hands. "I had a life! I wanted a life! I love cheddar cheese and jambalaya and ginger ale. Why can't I be real? Why can't I matter like you guys do? What did I ever do wrong? Why did he even create me if he was only going to make me miserable?"

George put a hand on his shoulder. "Dude. That's what we're gonna ask him. You know what I mean?"

Gayl sniffed back tears and looked up at them. "What do you think will happen?"

"I don't know," Mike admitted. "But I'll tell you this much: I think Barry Lyga—the real Barry Lyga—is an arrogant ass. I think he doesn't think we can hurt him. But we can. We're going to go through his challenge and get into the Real World and then we're gonna make him fix this. All of this." He gestured with a sweeping motion to the world around them. "You guys with me?"

George nodded. Joe grinned and said, "There's nothing I can say. I promise I ain't going to fuck it up this time. We got our own roads to ride and chances we gotta take."

Gayl blotted his cheeks with his palms. "Let's do this," he said, standing.

They stood before the four doors, each of which, they noticed now, was inscribed. The first said BROOKDALE. The second was a large X in a circle. The third said BOURING, and the fourth said CASTLETON.

"I don't get it," George said. "Are they place names?"

"What's with the X?" Mike wondered.

"My books are all set in a town called Brook's Dell," Gayl said after thinking for a moment. "If I'm a version of Barry Lyga, then maybe *his* stories take place in this Brookdale."

Mike nodded in cautious agreement. "But what about the other places?"

"I don't know."

George straightened. "Dude, here's the deal: Brookdale looks like the best bet. You go through that one, Mike. The rest of us will take the other three. And we'll meet you on the other side."

"Are you sure?" Mike ran a hand over the alien word BROOKDALE. The letters were shallow, but precise. "We don't know if they all lead the same way. We don't know . . ."

"We don't know anything," Gayl said. "But George is right. There are four of us and four doors. We go this way. That's all there is to it. Hopefully one of us gets through and finds Barry Lyga."

"And forces him to fix everything," Mike said.

They all nodded. They touched fists in a circle, swearing it to each other and to themselves.

Then they lined up at the doors: Mike/Brookdale, Gayl/Castleton, George/Bouring, and Joe/X.

"I'm countin' on a miracle to come true," Joe muttered.

"We all are," Mike said.

As one, they opened the doors and walked through.

CHAPTER 43

Astonishing Adventures/Unlikely Tales

Mike's door opened into a messy teen's bedroom: Picto-novels scattered, sheets torn from notepads and sketchbooks. Unlike in his own bedroom, the sketches and drawings were of people, not buildings.

"Guys," he said, turning back to the door, "this doesn't make any sense—" and broke off when he realized that the door behind him no longer led to the StratoSpire, but, rather, to what appeared to be a short, dark corridor.

Gayl took a step over the threshold, then hesitated, desperate to look over his shoulder for the reassurance of the others doing the same, but stopped dead, caught in the liminal space between one world and another, straddling the threshold between the room atop the StratoSpire and what appeared to be twilit outdoors. In his pause, he wondered if the others had paused, and then wondered if they hadn't what they would think of him for

George stepped through the door labeled "BOURING" without a second thought, the shotgun still clutched tightly in his hands and felt a jerk downward, a swift and unexpected gravitational tug of a descending staircase, but an instant later his foot did not contact the next step down and instead he found himself

Joe Roberts strode through the door marked with the encircled X and found himself in a wooded glade, speckled and tattooed with sunlight strained through the leaves and branches overhead. He executed an unhurried, considered three-hundred-sixty-degree turn, taking in the solitude and the foliage, which bunched and hunched around him like large, loyal hounds furred in greens, golds,

"What the hell?" he asked no one in particular. A complete circuit of the room revealed no other door. There was a desk, every last inch of its surface covered with an ancient computer and more artwork. Mike ran a hand over the keyboard. He thought of what Gayl had said about *Inframan*. Could this be the Real World? Could it be Barry Lyga's room? Did Lyga write on this very computer?

pausing. Fear of being judged and found wanting propelled him into the other world, the doorway evaporating once he was through. He stood on a bluff overlooking a small town. The stars glowed and glimmered; Gayl drew in a deep breath of clean, cool air, the likes of which he'd not inhaled since childhood.

I've crossed into another story, he thought. *Like in* Inframan, *when the characters end up in different short stories.*

plunging through the air, his arms flinging out reflexively to catch the sides of the door, releasing the so-tightly-held shotgun, which spun off into the clouds, his outstretched arms finding no purchase, no doorframe, nothing at all save empty air as he fell and fell and fell. His heart hammered in dual panic—falling!

and oranges. In the distance, a bird called—once, long, loud—before falling silent. Joe thought it was perhaps a bird he had heard before, though he did not know its species or name. He crouched down and ran a hand over the rough patch of heavy grass sprouting from the ground; it was uneven and ragged. Natural. Untended, save by the elements.

"Nothing on the computer will help you," a voice said, and Mike jumped back from the keyboard, spinning around to see a boy standing in the doorway.

The newcomer was younger than Mike by a few years. He wore glasses. "Are you Barry Lyga?" Mike asked. "As a kid?"

The kid shook his head. "Nah. My name's . . ." He thought

The memory galvanized him to the sort of action he understood—the written word. He fumbled in his bag for his copy of *Inframan*, then remembered with an abashed inward-directed anger that he'd shredded it. Thirty-two years old and he'd acted like a baby of thirty-two days.

He sat on the grass. The night was brisk, but not too cold, and the grass tickled his bare calves.

the shotgun, lost!—and he struggled for a moment to tamp down the blinding, distracting terror that squirted through his arteries.

His arms were already outstretched; now he spreadeagled his legs, the roaring updraft pulling at his clothes. His best

Something rustled in the brush. Joe spun around.

"Is there anybody alive out there?" he called.

Nothing. No response.

"Can you hear me? Can you hear me?"

Again, no response.

Joe stood, dusting his hands, brushing specks of dirt and clinging pollen from his immaculate black trousers.

about it for a moment. "I guess we're still playing it coy, so just call me Fanboy. Am I your first stop?"

"My first stop?" Mike felt behind him for the solidity of the desk and leaned into it. "What do you mean?"

"You're trying to get to the Real World, right? Sometimes it's called the Realm Above. My world's one step closer because it's based so heavily on the author's own life. He made my world

To the best of his recollection, the characters in *Inframan* had entered their short stories without memories. As the stories progressed, each character recovered memories, the final recaptured memories culminating in an explosive return to the world of the novel, just in time to save Mike Grayson.

Yet here was Gayl, in a new story, in full possession of his

chance of survival—and even that was, truthfully, minuscule—was to sabotage his own aerodynamics by increasing his surface area. This was not a survival skill taught to him by the Marines (though his ability to calm himself in such a moment of unexpected terror was), but was, rather, the

He straightened his bolo tie and ran his hands over his hair, still thick and lustrous even into his sixties, though his forehead was, he knew, more prominent than it had once been. A heavy vein stood out there, not from anger or stress, but simply from the vigor with which Joe approached the world.

He was beginning to sweat.

as close to the real thing as possible, but he made yours different." Fanboy sat on the bed.

Mike pulled the desk chair out and eased into it. "My world *isn't* based on the Real World?"

Fanboy thought for a moment. "It's like this: You have two mirrors. One is just a regular mirror, but the other is funhouse glass that distorts everything. My world

memories. Was Barry Lyga spinning a yarn in reverse now? Clearly (blatantly, Gayl thought with disgust), Gayl was meant to descend the slope, go into the town, and encounter . . . what? In *Inframan* the characters had to recover themselves; was Gayl here to lose himself?

In any event, Gayl was not going into that town. Mostly because it was what was expected of him, a trope as old as fiction

lingering result of a snatch of memory recalled from a TV show from George's childhood, a program titled *Could You Survive It?* which was hosted for its brief run by none other than Daredevil Levi. The show delighted in drawing "extreme danger" from "real-life situations" experienced by "real-life people just

The door *from* the StratoSpire was not a door *to* the StratoSpire, it having disappeared as soon as he passed through it. He was lost in an unfamiliar wood, with no companion, no guide. He looked to the sky in an effort to position himself by reckoning the movement of the sun, but the branches and leaves gave him no clear line of sight. He pursed his lips and whistled a short ditty that made him think of a man with is the Real World seen in the regular mirror. Yours is the funhouse."

"But my world doesn't feel like a funhouse mirror."

"Of course not. It's *your* world! Characters in stories never notice that they're in a distorted world. I'm from his first book, so I'm the closest representation to him there is. He made me a storyteller, just like he is."

itself. A wanderer discovers a town—of course that wanderer will enter said town! Otherwise, what is the point of the town? If Lucy walks through the wardrobe, well, you have to explore Narnia, right?

"Nice try," Gayl said to the sky, "but I'm staying here."

A cold breeze blew down and Gayl shivered.

"Trying to add a little drama, are we?" he muttered. "'As the

like *you*" and then—just before a commercial break—asking, "Could *you* survive it?" and then returning after commercial to show exactly how the "real-life person" in question had in fact survived.

On one episode, Daredevil Levi introduced the "astonishing

tattoos on his knuckles, a man rising from a bed at night to watch his young wife asleep beside him before walking out to the road, seeing nothing there but the blacktop stretching off into infinity.

Something rustled the bushes again. Joe turned around, then turned around again. He called out to the noise.

Nothing.

"You're from *Inframan*?" Mike asked. "So am I. In a way."

"*Inframan?*" Fanboy's face twisted in confusion. "I don't know what you're talking about. The first book was *The Astonishing Adventures of Fanboy and Goth Girl*." He grinned. "I get top billing."

Mike was beginning to understand. Gayl had explained the structure of reality as being comprised of pages, but

wind blew colder, he was grateful to see the town before him. He raced to the promise of glowing warmth in its windows . . .' Nope. Not me, buddy."

The wind grew steadily colder; it whined.

Gayl grumbled, retrieving his lighter from his bag. On a spot clear of grass, he pawed out a shallow firepit, dumped in some sticks, as well as dry grass for kindling, and soon had a fire going.

adventure" of Caldwell Blunt, a skydiver who discovered that his parachute would not open and his backup chute was damaged. With the word "RE-ENACTMENT" blinking fiercely on-screen, a stuntman dressed like Caldwell Blunt flailed and twisted in the air as dramatic music built to a terrifying crescendo. The image exploded into a shower

"Hi-yo silver-o, deliver me from nowhere," he murmured.

"Nowhere," a voice said, startling him. "That's a good way to put it. I call myself Nowhere . . . Lad. Yeah, it better be lad."

Joe cast about for the source of the voice, finding nothing but more empty air and trees and brush and scrub. He called out again and the voice responded:

Barry Lyga had created more than one universe—he had stacked moment upon moment and page upon page until he had Fanboy's world and Mike's world and who knew how many others. The other doors—they led to his other universes.

"This is our pathway to the Real World," he muttered. "We have to go through these universes first."

"Shouldn't have given me that lighter," he murmured.

"Talking to yourself?" a familiar voice said.

And there stood Phil.

Gayl knew he was being manipulated, granted this vision not out of altruism, but because it served a dramatic beat in the larger fictive rhythm of the narrative Barry Lyga was concocting. Yet, Gayl could not help but to rise,

of sparks, which then spun and resolved into the *Could You Survive It?* studio, where Daredevil Levi stood before a massive screen on which the scene with Blunt unfolded. Daredevil Levi gasped in incredulity, gazing at the screen, then turned to the camera just as it zoomed in for a close-up of his craggy face.

"You won't be able to see me. No one does. That's why I'm Nowhere Lad. But sometimes—if I try real hard—I can make people hear me. Like now."

Joe harrumphed and spat. Overhead, the tree branches swayed just enough to be noticeable.

"You're in the woods just outside Westchester, New York," Nowhere Lad went on. "This is a tough story to tell. There are . . .

"Sure," Fanboy agreed amiably. While Mike had been thinking, Fanboy had picked up a pad and begun sketching. Mike suddenly felt a strange but undeniable kinship with this boy—they were both artists after a fashion.

"Who's Goth Girl?" Mike asked.

Fanboy tapped the eraser-end of his pencil against his top

choking "Phil" pathetically, stepping towards her, then halting, as if—

"I won't fade away," she said in her slightly snarky, slightly annoyed way, that manner that would be off-putting if she weren't correct so often, her smile belying her tone.

Gayl had resisted as best he could, devoted to the prospect of foiling Barry Lyga's plans, but proximity to his lost Philomena

"Ten thousand feet above the earth!" Daredevil Levi barked. "No parachute! No backup! Tell me, America . . ."

And the studio audience shouted along with him:

"*Could! You! Survive It?*"

And the show cut to commercial.

George had watched the whole run of *Could You Survive*

copyright issues. Trademark issues. I can't go into too much detail. But if you listen closely, you might get a little hint or clue."

Joe started to speak, but Nowhere Lad hushed him. "Listen. Carefully."

Joe, as he was bade, fell silent and waited, waited beyond the point at which something should have happened, waited into the long quiet of the day, the rustling gone, the wind still, teeth. "She was just here. We had a fight; she stormed out. I don't know if I'll ever see her again. She was pretty mad."

"I know how that feels." Maybe this was why he'd been drawn to this universe—for the commonality between them. For loss of love. Fanboy, he surmised, could enter the Other City.

"The opposite of love isn't hate; it's indifference," Fanboy said. "My mom told me that just now, right after Kyra—that's

proved stronger than his devotion, and he lunged to her, fleetingly aware that she had last seen him not in the precincts of fidelity, but in the ghettoes of rejection.

Yet she opened her arms to him and they crushed themselves to each other, lips meeting, arms tight and strong around each other, pulling close, the feel of her lips, of her tongue, so new, so familiar, both at once, awakening memories forgotten,

It? to date (fifteen of the twenty-two episodes that would ultimately air), and no one had ever *not* survived it.[85] Still, such was the producers' skill at technical wizardry and emotional manipulation that George wondered if, indeed, "it" would or could be survived. The asshole watched the show, too, similarly discombobulated, and each episode was one of the few

the voice of Nowhere Lad disappeared, until at the last moment of his tolerance for the silence (Joe had ever despised silence, preferring instead life, sound, music) he heard something, a distant whisper-click of metal on metal, as of a blade snapping into place along a groove.

85. Whatever "it" happened to be, whether a crocodile attack in a bathtub, an exploding computer monitor, a necktie caught in an ATM, or a car suddenly and inexplicably filled with water, all "real-life situations" from previous episodes of the show.

Goth Girl—left. So maybe there's a chance. Because she was really angry at me, and if she can get that angry, then maybe she can be the opposite of that angry, you know?"

Mike thought of Phil. Maybe there *was* a chance.

"There's a girl," he said. "A woman, really. And I love her more than the world. I love her so much."

Fanboy yawned. "Yeah, yeah, and you lost her and you want

enlivening memories unforgotten, spinning out new memories yet to form.

And he wondered at how love—cerebral and emotional at once, contemplative and ponderable—could lead beyond thought, and then wondered no more as their heat took him away, everything else elided from that moment to this:

times in George's childhood when he felt any connection to his father.

"He'll never make it," the asshole proclaimed. "He's street pizza. He's a dead man."

George was convinced of this, too, and the particular psychological dynamic of the Singleton household conspired to

SNIKT

"There," said Nowhere Lad. "That's about all we can risk. You're here to learn. There's a school nearby, but you can't go to it. Copyright concerns again. He wrote a story that he doesn't own, so even though it's a part of his career and his body of work, he can't reference it directly or show you any of the elements. Fortunately, my . . . ability fits in her back. I know. I'm done with you, though. I'm supposed to pass you on to Josh now."

"Pass me on? What if I don't want to go?"

Fanboy arched an eyebrow. "Come on, Mike. Do you think you really have a choice?"

Mike sighed and stood up. "Thanks for your help, Fanboy. You . . . I hope you and your Goth Girl get together."

It was her, truly her, he realized as he held her at arms'-length. She laughed as they sat by the fire. He gazed at her.

"You're real," he whispered. "You're back."

Had she said, "Yes" and kissed him or "I am" and gazed at him softly, he would have realized that this was not Phil, but a simulacrum sent to tempt him from his path.

make him proud that he concurred with the man who routinely abused him and his mother.[86]

Back from commercial, *Could You Survive It?* lived up to its previous record when the "RE-ENACTMENT" showed Blunt's stunt double spreadeagling (as George did now, in recollection) enough to slow his descent to the point that a second skydiver

well. In the original story, no one ever saw me, and now you can't see me either. You can't trademark or copyright something that isn't there, right? You can't claim to own an absence of something. So that's me. And if you're lucky, you'll learn here."

Learn what, Joe wondered, but did not say. He had an

86. It involves the Stockholm Syndrome, post-traumatic stress disorder, and other complicated psychological jargon that we won't get into here.

"You'll meet her last, probably. You'll know her on sight, though—she'll be dressed in black. Black hair. Black lipstick. You can't miss her."

"You love her, don't you?"

"I might. She might be the love of my life. I don't know yet. We haven't gotten there."

"So am I in your book now, too?"

Instead, she smirked and said, "Well, yeah. No kidding," so necessarily piercing his ego, his wonderment at simple truth.

"I thought I'd never see you again," he said. "I thought you hated me."

She drew her knees to her chest, her body a shifting sculpture in the moving firelight, her blonde hair

could catch up to him (via the mechanism of reversing Blunt's tactics—pulling his limbs close to his body so as to descend faster, not slower) and deliver an emergency chute.

Plunging now to his own death, George did not expect anyone to swoop down and rescue him at the last minute; he expected nothing at all. Life had taught him that—for

understanding of this Nowhere Lad. Joe was intimately familiar with the poetry of the universe, with the idea that words could be used to illuminate not via direct light, but rather by casting shadows into sharper relief. Nowhere Lad was a poem, a song, a lyric—he referred to things not directly, but rather obliquely, as Joe himself often did. Words had meanings,

"Nah. This whole scene takes place between chapters and scenes for me. And since it was never written down in my book, I won't even remember it. But you will. Bye, Mike."

With a deep breath, Mike turned away and made for the door. "Wait a sec!" Fanboy called, spinning Mike around to see the kid offering him a sheet of heavy drawing paper.

cascading down her right side. "I did hate you. For a while. It was the only way I could deal with you leaving me like that."

"I'm so sorry—"

"Shut up. I'm talking. I hated you for a long time. And then I realized that I loved you. It was maddening because I felt them both. I didn't know what to do with all these emotions. And I

him, at least—there was no one to come to the rescue. Not as a beaten child and not now. He knew that slowing his plummet was nothing more than delaying the inevitable. George could not, in fact, survive it, and maybe somewhere Daredevil Levi was slowly shaking his head in dismay and disillusionment.

yes, but words seldom meant only one thing at a time, and often their meanings changed—intensified, in some cases—dependent wholly on the other words around them, or on the rhythm of their usage.

"Good luck," Nowhere Lad whispered, and Joe knew that he was alone again.

"For you," Fanboy said.

It was a beautiful charcoal rendition of Phil from the shoulders up, her neck a sweeping, graceful black line, her eyes and hair palest blue. It was so beautiful that before he realized it, Mike wept a single tear that fell in Phil's hair, softening the blue, making the picture absolutely perfect.

realized that my hate was a shield for love. I was using my hate as a way to block out that I loved you."

"And that's when you came here?"

She snorted and tossed her hair from one shoulder to the other. "No. I didn't look for you. Didn't call. You didn't want to be with me. What could I do? Once one person in a relationship says it's over, there's no point in the other person trying. I

George knew only one thing: Life was life and death was death. Life was good; death was not. So as long as he could cling to life, he would.

And just then, someone swooped down and rescued him.

It took George a moment to realize that he was no longer falling, no longer dropping in an inexorable straight line. Now

He patted his pockets, locating his harmonica, then played a brief, jaunty tune, the musical equivalent of muttering, "Buck up and move out!" to himself in a jogging tone of voice. Then he pressed forward into the woods, remembering as best he could the details of his life and of his love. A forest was, he knew, a place of remembrance, a

"Just in case you don't get back to her," Fanboy said. "I thought you should have something to remember her by."

Mike could barely speak, emotion throttling his voice. "How did you know what she looks like?"

Fanboy grinned. "Come on. She's perfect, right? I just drew someone perfect."

Mike walked through the door and found himself in a

accepted that I loved you *and* couldn't be with you."

"You make it sound easy," Gayl said, thinking of his own torment, of missing her. Needlessly, it turned out, as he could have called and rediscovered her love for him, if not for some alloy of love/shame/pride that had kept him from doing so.

"It sounds easy," she agreed, "but it isn't. So what have you been up to? Working on a new book, I hope?"

he was moving horizontally, his speed still great, but diverted. At first, he thought a strong wind must have blown him to one side, but his motion continued unabated and, more revealingly, he felt hands grasping him under his armpits.

"Relax," a voice called out. "You'll be fine."

Puffs of cloud smeared by. The arms under his armpits were

place where memories lurked in the shadowy undergrowth, where old friends and old lovers and old foes scampered in the overhanging tree branches like acorn-pelting squirrels.

He thought of Terry. His love. Of the words they'd spoken, the promises they'd made.

parking lot outside an apartment building at night. He sniffled back his tears and wiped his cheeks. He rolled up the drawing, rubber-banded it into a tube, then tucked it into his shoulder bag.

A door closed and as Mike turned he saw a guy roughly his age walking towards him, tall and handsome and carrying a baseball bat. From his expression, the guy was a welter of emotions;

"Yeah. Yeah, I . . ." Speaking of *Unfinished* seemed ill-fitting to the moment, overweening and arrogant; it seemed an overreach, ill-suited to his talents for the simple reason that his dreams had outstripped his abilities. He could see the completed *Unfinished* in his mind's eye, marvel in its perfection, flip its lucid and erudite pages, but his awe was counterbalanced by dread: the book would not be

slim, covered in blue sleeves with blue gloves. Below, he saw a smallish town with a circular road at its center that spun out spokes of streets in all directions.

"Welcome to Bouring," the voice said with a note of sarcasm. "Or at least, to the air space over Bouring. We're going to land in a second. It might get bumpy."

Joe had had many jobs in his lifetime: He'd been a mechanic, a police sergeant, a soldier, a guitarist in a rock band, a border patrol guard, a state trooper, a road crew, and more, before finally returning to one of his earliest professions: Train engineer. In his wild youth, he'd made the run to Georgia over and over again, rambling down those dusty tracks, often feeling like he'd never get home. Never had he worked in the wilderness like this, yet

Mike hesitated even to look at him, as though the mere act of watching would add to his load of troubles.

But the guy walked straight to the car near which Mike stood. He popped the trunk and dropped the baseball bat in, then slammed the trunk shut.

"You're the guy, aren't you?" he asked Mike, his voice low and gruff. "The guy looking for the Real fucking World."

as good as it could/should be. Because of his innate lack of ability. In the hands of a more skilled writer, it would flourish.

"Tell me about it," she urged him.

So he did, despite himself. He told Phil of his obsession with Barry Lyga's novels, his yearning to read *The Gospel According to Jesus*, how that yearning conjured a novel about an author

It didn't get bumpy. Moments later, George felt ground under his feet and gratefully lurched forward as the arms released him, stumbling to kneel on the earth like the Pope. He looked over his shoulder at his savior and was surprised to see a slim, smallish figure dressed head-to-toe in blue, including—of all things—a full-face mask. And, George now

he had an unerring sense of which direction to move, of which way lay his fate, and he walked that way without hesitation or concern.

He heard the river before he saw it, its wet burble and rush rising along the way ahead of him, greeting him as he parted a flurry of branches and leaves and came to the river's edge.

He and Terry (she'd gone by the name Mary then) had gone

"Josh?" Mike asked.

"Yeah, no fucking shit," Josh growled. "I don't want to do this now, OK? Do you have any idea what just happened?"

Mike shook his head. Fanboy had been easy to deal with. Non-threatening. But Josh was a human thundercloud. Violence lurked in every motion, spilled from every pore.

looking for a story that was never finished, a quest for a final work of fiction, the irony of the title plain.

Speaking of it now, the whole idea of *Unfinished* seemed pointless, meretricious, and—worst of all—*risible*. He faltered before describing the book's end.

"This is going to sound stupid and . . .self-involved . . ." In shame and self-pity, he shook his head, as though motion

noticed, a blue cape unfurled from his shoulders. It was clearly a child, no more than twelve or thirteen years old at the most, but he stood with confidence, his fists placed on his hips.

"I want you to tell people, you hear me?" the figure said, his voice muffled slightly by the mask. "Tell people that the Azure Avenger saved your life."

down to the river many times in their lives. From their first meeting, they'd arranged clandestine encounters there, skipping around their disapproving parents, entangling in each other along the shore, discovering each other in the wet grass and—on the warm summer nights—naked in the rushing waters. And nature followed its course and the world turned and the universe continued its perpetual exhale out into the infinite

"Love," Josh said, and brought a fist crashing down on the trunk. "Fucking *love.*

"I thought she loved me," he went on. "I don't . . ." His violence transformed into grief in such a powerful and sudden instant that it hit Mike like a physical thing as Josh collapsed to the asphalt. Mike could only watch as Josh crumpled on the parking lot against his car.

counterbalanced emotion. "But I thought that *Unfinished* might win the Kyng Prize."[87]

The fire crackled and sizzled and popped.

"Is that what matters to you?" Phil asked.

Gayl hmphed and smiled a small, sad smile. "When you're publishing your first book, you think about a lot of things, but I never thought about the Kyng. And then *Unlikely Tale* came

"The who?"

"The Azure—" The kid broke off and then said, in a tone both thoroughly annoyed and knowing, that did not seem aimed at George, "No *kidding*, Erasmus," before turning his attention to George again and saying, "I am the Azure Avenger. The media call me the Blue Freak, but my

beyond and Terry's belly grew with their first child while he and Terry were scarcely out of childhood themselves. But they'd made the best of it, and a series of jobs and lives followed, Joe doing his level best to build the kind of life suited to Terry and their children, studiously avoiding the lessons of his friends:

87. The Kyng Prize—named for renowned nonadult book editor, the late Joseph (Joe) Kyng—is the biggest, most important award in nonadult literature, given for Best Use of Onomatopoeia in a Nonadult Book.

"What do I do?" Josh begged. "I thought she loved me. I thought once I was old enough I would go to her and . . ."

Mike crouched down. "What do you mean *old enough*?"

"I was twelve," Josh began, "and then she went to jail and it's been five years and now I'm old enough, but . . . Do you get it? She told me, just now, that it didn't just *happen*. We didn't fall in love—she *planned* it. From the moment she

out, and I was at dinner with a bunch of big shots. I was just honored to be there. They sat me with Ian White and Jed Whale.[88] And Ian asked, 'Do you think you'll win the Kyng? You could, you know.'

"And that absolutely destroyed me. I'd never considered it, never thought it possible, but then here's Ian fucking White, the God of the Kyng, and *he* thinks I have a shot, and that . . .

real name is the Azure Avenger. If you could mention that along with the fact that I saved your life, that would be just great, OK?"

When George said nothing, the Azure Avenger said—again in that knowing, annoyed tone—"Right, right, I *know*," before going on: "This is Bouring." He gestured. "More

Ralph, who'd been laid off at the auto plant and gone on a shooting spree; Johnny, who'd gotten mixed up in a crowd of pimps and abandoned his one true love; Billy, who'd run off to the circus and vanished for years, finally reappearing in middle

88. Ian White and Jed Whale, titans of nonadult literature. White is famous for winning the Kyng three times in a row, with his first three novels. Whale wrote the definitive treatise on writing for nonadults, and was also the first author to use the word "fuck" in a novel for nonadults.

saw me in history class. She planned the whole thing. God-damn it!"

Mike froze. What was he supposed to do? Was he supposed to counsel Josh? He had no experience in that area. He didn't know anyone who'd been abused. Except for George, of course, but that was a different kind of abuse entirely, and Mike had dealt with it by . . . By . . .

messed with me. And I *didn't* win, but I thought I might because *he* . . . I started to care and before I'd never—"

Phil took his face in her hands. "Is that why you write? To win awards?"

"No. No, of course not. I just—"

"Then stop bitching about not winning one."

He stared into her eyes, covered her hands with his own.

specifically, what was once a coal mine outside of Bouring. The idiots who used to run things thought it was smart to put their houses next to their mine. Geniuses, eh? Anyway, that's where you are.

"My question to you," the kid went on, "is how you ended up in mid-air."

age, married and cautious, tentative, weighing his life in both hands and never able to chose one over the other. Their lives were the cautionary tales that informed his own, as if he'd been able somehow to live those lives, see through their eyes, take their experiences into him. He had hoped to be able to avoid their fates, and yet here he was.

He sat by the water and once again put his harmonica to

By doing nothing.

George is my best friend, but I'm not his, Mike thought for the nth time.

"Let me help you," Mike said. "Please."

Josh shook his head fiercely. "No one can help me. No one. I'll be alone. It's all I'm good for. Like in baseball—lonely man, lone swinger at the plate. No one else matters."

"Do you remember in my first book, how there are three things that Geekster wants? And you never learn the third?"

"Of course."

"Well, the third is . . ." Gayl paused, as though somehow aware that he would be revealing this long-held secret to more than just Phil, but then continued nonetheless. "The third thing is so sad and pathetic and . . . He just wants to be able to be

Given the situation, George could only imagine one way out of his dilemma—tell the truth. Lying would mean one more set of thoughts and complications to juggle. Telling the truth was much simpler.

"I walked through a door in the StratoSpire in the Other City," George said, "and the next thing I knew, I was here."

his lips. Blew a single, low note—mournful and sad. Followed the note with another, then another, building to a sad crescendo that wafted out over the water.

Then, in a voice deep and troubled and clear and heavy with hurt and clogged with gravel, he sang.

He sang that everything good in him had gone away when Terry left, his courage in particular. And maybe—just

Mike thought. "I don't know what baseball is like in your world," he said, "but in my world . . . Doesn't someone else have to *pitch* the ball?"

Josh said nothing for a moment, then wiped his eyes and chuckled, the sound mirthless and weary. "A pitcher. Ah, Jesus. Help me up."

Mike took Josh's hand and hauled him to his feet.

himself, to be with someone where he can be himself and not be afraid of rejection or being hurt.[89]

"And when I was with you, I had that. I could lay with you for hours, not worrying, not *doing*. We were two puzzle pieces. And I feel like I'll never find another puzzle piece."

She brushed her lips against his forehead. "Someone else needs to talk to you. You have to turn around."

The Azure Avenger stood perfectly still for a moment, then said, "Give me a second." He took a few steps away and George was positive he could hear him arguing with no one at all. Definitely split personality, George thought, until he noticed the kid lightly touch a finger to the side of his head. *An earpiece. He's talking to someone else.*

maybe—he could regain that courage if only God would send some task, some quest to him. Maybe then he could stop living life like a prisoner of his own guilt and loss, his bed at night a jail cell he could not escape, dreaming only of Terry, of holding her in his arms one last time.

Whatever it would take to get her back, he sang, he would

89. This is not Fanboy's third thing.

"You're right," Josh said. "I need a pitcher. Now I just have to hope she'll still have me."

"Pardon?"

"There's this other girl. She's, uh, age-appropriate. And I might have messed things up with her, but maybe not. Maybe there's still a chance." He grinned, and in that grin, Mike saw the child he had been—so wounded and so

He pulled away from Phil.

HI, THERE! MY NAME'S RYOKO KIYAMA. OH, WOW. YOU'RE ALL **WORDS.** THAT'S PRETTY COOL.

The Azure Avenger came back. "Try again. This time, tell me the truth. There's no such thing as a 'StratoSpire.' I memorized all of Wikipedia and there's no entry for it."

"What's Wikipedia?" It sounded like Wikinformation.

"Are you brain-damaged?" the Azure Avenger asked, in a tone not of concern or kindness, but more akin to a disgusted

do. Something as mundane as her shopping, even. Whatever the small, nuanced moments of life demanded.

And yet all he knew now were the dying and the damned. The broken, lost souls of the Other City and the poor, bedraggled knights who had brought him along to scale its walls. A part of him cried out to let them go, let them go, let them go—let them find their own tragic deaths and dance with the Grim damaged—as well as the man he would eventually become. "I need to get going. Sorry I didn't help you that much. But you helped me a lot."

"You helped," Mike assured him. "You let me help you, and I think I needed to learn how to do that. I've been so focused on myself that I never stopped to help anyone else."

Gayl could not understand how, but he now had a different understanding of the universe, his consciousness raised and opened in ways hitherto unimagined. He'd heard from drug-familiar friends that a new way of seeing the universe was a part of the drug experience. Now his mind opened *sans* drugs, as he perceived reality in a whole new way.

"What are you?" he asked.

curiosity, the tone and sentiment reserved for wondering precisely what one has stepped into or on.

George thought of pages flipping. "I think," he said, hesitating only momentarily, "I'm from another universe," expecting laughter or disbelief.

Instead: "Oh. OK. That makes sense." And a shrug

Reaper. He, he sang, would find Terry instead, would wrap her in his arms and bear her off to bed. While still, broken-down cars, burned-out hulks of damaged buildings and desperate lives waited on the edge of the Other City, roaming, nomadic, looking for their own lost loves and lost lives. But, he sang, they could not touch Terry. Not with Joe's love. With Joe's love, he and Terry could leave the Other City, return to something real,

"Well, you'll be meeting Kevin next," Josh told him. "He's a little . . . odd. But he's a good kid at heart. Good luck."

Josh climbed into the car and drove off. Mike realized that he now stood on an airport tarmac—before him was a small commuter jet and an airline crew hustling a mobile staircase to the side of it. A luggage trolley beep-beeped its way to the jet and a line of passengers waited with toe-tapping, watch-checking

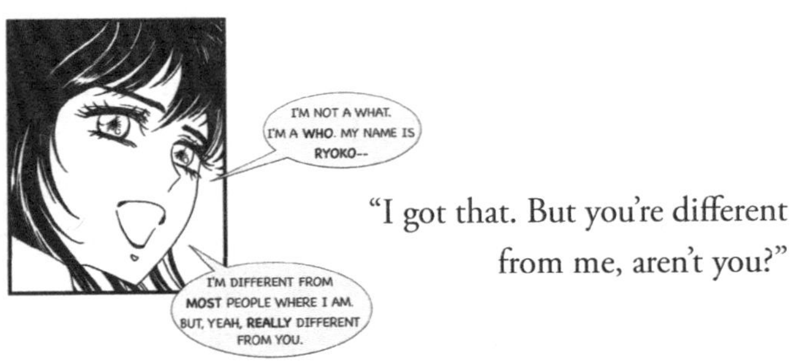

"I got that. But you're different from me, aren't you?"

that rippled the cape. "I've theorized that there must be other universes out there. Brane theory alone indicates that. Now I know for sure there are. Coolness. I'll have to visit one of them someday. Maybe I'll be appreciated there."

"People here don't appreciate you saving lives?"

something true. And nothing, he sang, could stop them. Not wind. Not rain. Snow, wind, rain—through it all, their love would carry them, would shield them.

"My love heart and soul!" he sang at the last, screaming it to the sky.

"I had it," Terry said softly, "and it wasn't enough."

Joe was not surprised by Terry's appearance. He understood

impatience. The last person in line was a kid with a backpack who, noticing Mike loitering near the airport wall, peeled away from the line and came over.

"Hail, Fool," he said, arching an eyebrow as if he fervently wished Mike would get the joke.

"What?"

"Never mind. I'm Kross. Let's talk."

"*Panel* borders?"

"You'd think. But, no. My name's Kyle," said the Azure Avenger, extending a hand. "So, you're from another universe. Excellent. I want to hear all about it."

George shook Kyle's hand, aware as he did so of the enormous strength in that grip. Kyle had swooped down in the air and plucked George safely from freefall without so much as a

the mystical byways of the universe. He'd seen the Other City in the early days after Lucky Sevens, after all, had watched as families and ex-lovers staggered the broken and ramshackle streets, looking for vanished mates and kin who had suddenly and irrevocably been removed from their city and their lives. Girlfriends shocked to find their boyfriends had never lost love. Parents stunned to see their children

"I thought I was supposed to talk to Kevin."

"Same thing. Kevin Ross. Kross. Get it? It's also symbolic because of the Catholic stuff in my book. But whatever."

"Catholic?" Mike held up a hand. "Is this all some sort of . . . of . . . Christian treatise? Because that doesn't make any sense. I mean, there's no religion in my life."

"But you *are* on a quest to find God, right?"

Something pressed into Gayl's hands: a brand-new copy of *Inframan*, crisp and perfect as the day it came off the presses back in 1994. And the moment he held the book, it seemed as though it had always been a part of him, as though he'd lost a limb and now had it replaced not by a prosthesis, but rather—miraculously—by the original limb itself.

grunt or a strain. Slim physique notwithstanding, Kyle's strength was tremendous.

"I don't know what to tell you. Except that I was in a place we call the Other City."

"Right, right, you said that before." Kyle waved him quiet. "There have been some strange goings-on in Bouring," he

gone forever, off in a world where they could live and love without the stinking, bloody reminder of Lucky Sevens and dead love. Terry's appearance here seemed, to him, poetic, almost musical, like a refrain or a chorus to a familiar song.

It had been ten years since she'd walked out on him, taking the children with her. She looked good. Unchanged except for

"Gayl says Barry is God. I don't know what to believe."

Kross chuckled. "Been there, done that. But we're not here to talk about me. We're here for you. So, uh, what am I supposed to be talking to you about? I've only got a couple of minutes before my connection to Burbank. Man, I didn't know I'd be getting into some little crappy commuter plane, you know? They should warn you. Like, put something

Gayl fumed. He did not *want* to want or need *Infra-man* in his life. He despised it with a true apostate's disdain. And yet he simultaneously yearned for the book. The book had claimed a significant swath of his adult life, its influences on him writ large and small. The first time he'd seen it, spine-out on a bookshelf in one of his college's libraries, something (Lyga himself? he wondered now) had compelled

mused, "ever since the plasma storm that gave me my super-powers. I wonder if the walls between universes are somehow thinner here, allowing you to cross over. That would make sense. Hmm." He clucked his tongue. "Has anything odd happened in the Other City?"

"No one knows for sure how, but the Other City was

the touch of happiness about her eyes. Younger than he did, for sure, and even Joe—he knew in a humble and honest way—looked younger than his sixty-odd years. He considered leaping up from his position and running to her, but did not. Instead, he smiled and nodded to her.

She approached him not slowly and not quickly.

"Hello, Joe. You look good."

on your boarding pass so you can be psychologically prepared."

"Oh. OK. Well, I guess I'm here to talk about love." It sounded so absurd out loud, but Kevin nodded very seriously, as if contemplating an exotic variety of quantum physics.

"I don't know what to tell you about love," he admitted. "I'm not the best guy to talk to about that. See, I thought I was

him to pluck it from its spot. As a thick film of dust fell away, the book creaked open stiffly as though new and unread.

He opened his new copy now; it creaked the same way, as if this could somehow be that same copy.

devastated. And now it looks like only people who've loved and lost can go there. No one else can get in. And there's this stuff all over the place—it looks like bloody meat." He tried to pronounce the words he'd heard in CONVENIENCE, but failed, coming out, "spasming cardio."

Kyle interrupted him. "Why were you even there?"

He shrugged.

"It's been a long time." She planted her fists on her hips and looked around. "Off on one of your quests?" she asked without the slightest trace of condescension or ire. She'd often accused him of being a dreamer (and had baffled him that one could be accused of such a thing, as though dreaming were a sin or a crime), but now seemed if not accepting, then at least resigned.

in love with this girl, Leah, but it turned out I was just kinda offloading all these unresolved feelings about my parents' divorce on her. Maybe your situation's like that?"

"No. My parents are still together."

"Wow. That's rare for this guy."

"This guy?"

Kross pointed skyward. "The big dude. God. Whoever. Four

"Looking for God."

"God?" Kyle scoffed. "If there is such a thing, then it's vastly more complicated than you would be able to understand, so why bother? 'God' is actually nothing more than a coherent 13-dimensional waveform with an energy signature that vibrates in multiple universes at once. Sort of a

He nodded. "Remember all the movies, Terry, we'd go see?"

She shook her head sadly. "We weren't those people, Joe. We weren't the kids up on the movie screen. We couldn't hide from the real world like they could, no matter how dark the backstreets we ran down."

Of course. He knew this already. Knew it all, even though he wanted not to know it. In some version of his life's story (he'd books, man, and not a single well-adjusted, happy marriage between them."[90]

"Really? What do you think it means that my parents—"

He waved it off. "Probably nothing. Look, are you sure this girl is worth everything you're going through?"

The question he hated. Why assume Phil *wasn't* worth "everything [he was] going through?" Missing Phil, losing Phil,

"No." It hadn't. Gayl had taken to *Inframan* with the complex and simple worship of a true zealot, surprised that none of his fellow English majors had heard of it. His professors regarded him quizzically with benign ignorance when he broached the topic of the novel and its author. *Inframan* was a child left to be raised by wolves or apes or whichever pulp fiction/B-movie cliché one preferred: It undeniably lives and breathes, but no one knows or cares.

fractal intelligence, if you will, that generates its own localized subgravity well."

"What?" It made literally no sense. None.

"I didn't expect you to understand. That's really the whole point. Your particular brain isn't developed enough to really comprehend God, which is why you shouldn't try. Don't take offense—it's just that you're only human."

imagined many of them in the past decade), she had betrayed him. In another version, he'd betrayed her. But what he'd come to realize and to acknowledge was that both versions could be true . . . and neither could be true. All at the same time.

90. Actually, by this time there are five books in the Brookdale "unseries." *Bang* came out in April 2017, long after I'd written *Unedited*. I considered adding that book's Sebastian to this sequence of events, but it was already running long. Still, Fanboy's point stands—Sebastian's parents are divorced, so that makes five interrelated novels without a single happy marriage among them. My record is intact!

had led him to the discovery that the world was broken, had sent him on a quest to fix that, too. Didn't that matter?

Simple answers to complex questions. The only way to survive, Mike realized. The more he tried to brain out the nature of Barry Lyga, the more difficult it became. He could become caught up in the metaphysics of it all, or he could just accept that an entity named Barry Lyga controlled his world and could

"I see. Right. Well, it's a long story,[91] but *we* think that God is actually a writer named Barry Lyga. He wrote our universe into being. And maybe even yours."

Kyle chuckled. "And you went to the Other City to find him. For love."

"Yes."

"Why?"

Terry had been sixteen when they'd met, and Joe not much older. Theirs had been a love of poetry and music and teenage fantasy and the desperation of those seeking escape from a small town and a small life, looking for an exit in the embrace and the lips of another. In that gentle summer of their meeting, they'd been first friends, then fire-breathing lovers, inhaling

91. 171,706 words at this point, in fact.

help rectify the errors Mike had made, the havoc he'd wreaked on his own personal continuity.

Similarly, he could examine and re-examine his feelings toward Phil, using flashbacks like time machines to revisit the small touches, the tender kisses, the laughing and gasping while tangled in the history-made sheets, the hours poring over his sketchbooks, the days on her sets. Or he could simply cut away

That was true. Gayl did not think of himself as a "success," but he sold well enough and had a big enough audience that his publisher continued to buy new books.

Gayl looked down at the book, open to the title page.

George opened his mouth, then closed it again, then—after a moment—spoke: "It's love. Love! True love. My best friend loved a girl and then he lost her and she's the biggest, most important thing in the world to him. And it really is a long story,[92] but we went to the Other City and then weird things started—well, actually kept on happening, and I ended up here,

and exhaling each other's glorious madnesses. The intensity of the love had taken them both by surprise, as though an anniversary they'd mutually forgotten. Inseparable, they danced to music only they could hear in back alleys and parking lots. Somehow, Joe had imagined it would last forever, even though he should have known better, was old enough to know that

92. Yep, up to 171,792 words now.

the details with Occam's Razor and leave the flayed truth open to the sky and the eye, the truth like bone, that he loved Phil, that he adored her, that if he could not have her back, he did not want to live.

"If you're sure you love her," Kross said, "then I guess you do whatever you have to do. But what do I know?" He glanced over his shoulder. "Oh. I have to board."

but kid, look, Kyle, Azure Avenger, please. Trust me. This is for a good cause. We're trying to save love."

"Love," Kyle snorted. "Love is for people who don't have better things to do with their brains." He thought for a moment. "Unless you're talking about loving pets. That's different. They don't take up as much time, so it's all right to love your pets.

the universe gives but takes as well, whether by death or infidelity or evolution. He dreamed, though, that he and Terry would not—could not—be like the others, like the friends they'd watched burn out on their love, combust with its intensity and proximity, young, foolish Icaruses entwined together, then exploded apart, all of them running away, some of them hurt, some of them dying.

"Wait!" Mike followed as Kross walked toward the plane. "What next? What do I do now?"

Kross turned, now walking backwards so he could watch Mike as he advanced to the plane. "You'll see Kyra next."

Mike chased him, but within two steps, the plane, the airport, the tarmac, and even the sun were gone, replaced by night and a parking lot and the chill of near-winter, clouding

"I want to think so," Gayl said. "I do. But there's so much more that I . . ." He trailed off, aware of Phil watching him, aware of the stranger from another universe, aware that he had almost revealed his deepest, most closely held secret: His ambitions had long ago outstripped his meager

I love my rabbit. Lefty. He's great. But another human being? What would be the point?"

For a moment, George's mind swam with the implications. Could it be that love was nothing more than a waste of time, a game played by those who had nothing better on which to spend their valuable intellects? What was the point of love, ultimately? Love had dragged Mike from

It had happened anyway, after years and children, it had happened anyway, as they cut loose from their love. Maybe it had been the lies—the small lies, certainly, the ones we tell ourselves and each other in order to eke out love and life in the quantities needed to survive—that destroyed them. Worse yet, maybe it had been the truth, catching up to them after so many years, the truth that they had not been the fated lovers, had not been destined for his breath on the air. A small cluster of cars sat near a grocery store, with a lone outlier—something called a "Toyota"—nestled against a lamppost far from the store. He shivered. He was dressed for a hike through the desert, not for this.

And yet here and now, he should meet "Goth Girl." Fanboy had said he would meet her last, and Kross had said that Lyga had written four books. This would be the fourth.

talents. He would never possess the intellectual strength to climb the mountains he craved. Failure, abject and utter and familiar, swaddled him like fog. Not winning the Kyng. Not even nominated. Never attaining bestseller status. Failed movie deals, advances that never met expectations, royalty

something approaching happiness into a world of constant devolution, under the desert, to the Other City and now to who knew where? It had dragged George along with him. Love had destroyed the Other City and set the lives within it to ruin.

George knew love. He hesitated to admit this—even in the privacy of his own thoughts and his own heart—but he knew

each other, that they had—perhaps—been only two scared and lonely kids alive in each other's arms so that they felt they could only be alive in each others arms, only to learn the truth after too many years and fears and tears. Or maybe, worse, they'd known the truth all along, had known they had an expiration date, but had persisted anyway, blithely and fatefully pushing ahead and ignoring what the universe had in store for them.

Four books. Four elevators. Four doors. Brookdale led to Lyga's books, just as a door labelled "Brook's Dell" would no doubt have led to Gayl's books. He wondered where the other three doors had taken the others.

Peering around, he spied a slim figure coming closer to him. As it came nearer, he realized it was a girl with no hair. Utterly bald and dressed in pure white. No Goth Girl, she.

statements that proved there were never as many readers as he hoped.

Against failure, he had only one defense, which he deployed now almost instinctively: An e-mail he'd received from a fifteen year old boy, saying:

love very well. He had loved and he did love, even now. And that love had brought to him nothing lasting. Nothing enduring. It had brought him disappointment and crushed his hopes and dreams. It had dragged him—

"Now this is interesting," Kyle said, his telling hand touching the earpiece once more. "Your entry point into my universe

But you could run down the backstreets all you wanted, hiding from the cherry-topped cops and the maximum lawmen and the tunnel police who sought to unpin your love and let it flap away in the breeze, but ultimately the universe caught up to you. The world had its rules and its laws, and it enforced them rigidly, if not fairly. In the end, there'd been nothing left for Joe to say. Terry hadn't blamed Joe for the divorce—she hadn't

The girl was shivering, too, but as she approached Mike, she dropped her arms and stood taller and more erect, unwilling—perhaps unable—to show weakness to him.

She wore a glittering red stone in her nose and a small ring in the corner of her mouth, a ring that tilted slightly upward as she sneered in defiance and contempt.

"So," she said, "you're him, huh? The asshole I'm supposed

ok so i recintly got your book and i belive you have saved me. i am like yor chartacers,i get picked on evry day,never had a girlfrend. i was almost to the pont of killing myself when i started to read this. what this book has done is shown me that.. hey maby my life isint so bad. maby i do have hope.

coincides with the longitude and latitude of the extrascientific event that mutated me."

"Excuse me?"

"You came to my world in the same location as the plasma storm that gave me my powers. Let's check it out."

Before George could protest, Kyle moved with preternatural

blamed herself, either; she'd blamed no one—but he would have allowed that, would have allowed her to settle the weight of it on his shoulders. Past the destruction of their marriage and their love, the blame hardly mattered to him, so if someone must bear it, why not him? There was nothing left in the wake of her leaving, nothing left but the hatred in Joe's heart, the hatred that flared like a black flame, reminding him of his love.

to talk to." Her words came out with an anger Mike usually associated with and reserved for people he knew, people who had wronged him in some way; this girl must have lived her life in a perpetual state of just-wounded, interlocked with a constant fear—no, not fear: *certainty*—that another undeserved and wholly haphazard injury lurked in the shadows, targeting her and ready to lunge at any moment.

you don't know how much this book changed my life

Gayl had written back, thanked the boy, hoped he'd sought help for his depression and was now doing better. But what he had *not* said was this: Gayl had changed the

speed, grabbing George under the arms again and lifting off in a swift, smooth motion that left George no opportunity to protest or even develop a lurching moment of airsickness before they were airborne, hurtling high over the town of Bouring.

Kyle slowed and descended, lowering George safely to a

"I'm not here to get back together," she said, telling him something he knew already, knew from the heart if not the head. Still, he let her talk. He had always adored the sound of her voice, the way she used words. "I came because you need to see me, I suppose. You're off on some kind of quest, looking for answers. Trying to figure out what happened between us.

"I'm waiting for someone else," Mike told her, relieved that he could send her away. "You don't have to talk to me."

"Don't tell me what to do, you effing idiot!"

Unbidden, a giggle escaped Mike's cold-numbed lips, the discontinuity between her hardcore attitude and nearly-Puritanical avoidance the closest thing to comedy he'd experienced in days. "You can say 'fuck,' you know."

boy's life, but the boy had changed Gayl's. He had given a despairing Gayl a defense against failure: No matter what, he could look to that e-mail and think, *I saved that kid's life.*

school football field, surrounded in three directions by cornfields, backing to a school in the fourth direction.

"This is where it happened," Kyle said. "I was out here at night and a focused plasma curtain of alien energy intersected with the planet right over there—"

George followed Kyle's pointing finger with his eyes and

"But Joe . . ." She knelt down close to him, and he stared into her eyes for the first time in ten years. "Joe, you already know the answer. And that's that there is no answer. It just happened, babe. You never understood that. You never understood that our love didn't fail ten years ago. Our love *succeeded* for thirty years before that. That's what matters. The good of it. The memories. Our children. They miss

She stepped closer to him, almost treading on his toes; he retreated a half-pace as she leaned into him and pinned him back with a glare from her hazel eyes. "Oh, yeah? I didn't ask for your effing permission and I don't *need* your effing permission. I say whatever the eff I want to say and if I don't want to say *that* word, then why don't you just get off my effing back about it?"

suddenly perceived the entirety of the universe in a new way. It was as though a blank spot had opened on the very air of the football field, and on that blank spot were written truths, important and hitherto-unknown truths, but truths nonetheless. He saw, inscribed there, that Kyle was wrong: Love did matter. It had its own heft and density and energy signature

you, Joe. They miss their father. Since the divorce, you've bounced from job to job, city to city . . . You need to settle down. You need to come to peace with yourself and with what happened. It wasn't your fault."

"Your sweet memory comes on the evenin' wind."

"Stop punishing yourself. What are you doing to yourself?"

"With a local bunch of do-good boys," he told her, then

Mike was no longer cold under the heat of her anger.

"OK," he said at last. "OK. Sorry."

"You know what?" she went on. "You know what? I just made up my mind about something. I'm not doing it."

"Not doing what?" He regretted asking as soon as his words became clouds.

"I'm not effing helping you," she said. "I'm tired of that

Ian and Jed had enough honors, awards, and sales for any dozen authors. How many lives had their books saved? It didn't really matter. Saving one life was enough. And as for those honors, awards, and sales, which Gayl knew he would never attain? What of them?

and import. It had, despite Kyle's assertions and rationalized confidence, a point.

The point of love, George realized, is love. That's it. Perfectly circular reasoning, sure, but no less true. One is one and love is love. Both are true.

And then in the blank spot, he saw more. He saw Mike.

hooked a sardonic thumb himself-ward, "and an old man from the West—"

"Yes. Yes, I know all about it. They're looking for answers, too. For solutions," she said. "And maybe Barry Lyga has answers for everyone."

Joe shook his head. "Oh but readin' words on a piece of paper," he told her, "it sure ain't gonna make no kind of sense."

shit. I did it for Fanboy, for a whole effing book and you know what I got out of it? I got sent to the effing mental hospital for six months! After everything I did to help—his stupid effing graphic novel and understanding women and I . . .I . . ." She pressed her lips into a line and shook her head. "After everything I did and said and . . .and . . .*was* for him, he never got in touch with me while I was gone. He forgot about me. Discarded

"I don't tell those kinds of stories. Those just aren't the stories I want to tell. And that's OK."

And then the strange boy was gone, and it was just Gayl and Phil, as it had been, as it should have been, as it was. He looked at Phil and smiled, a smile she mirrored.

"Got that out of your system?" she asked, as though his epiphany had been a tantrum.

And Gayl. And Joe Roberts. He saw, in some ineffable way he could not describe, himself and Kyle, standing in the field.

"It's like . . . It's like we were all on the same page," he whispered, "and I just realized it."

"Maybe he's about more than just words on paper. More than just writing. Did you ever think of that?"

He had thought it. Thought it, examined it, discarded it. He followed the boys (and Gayl, though Gayl was incidental—it was the boys he followed, their endless faith, their living in the moment) not because he truly believed that Barry Lyga had the answers or that Barry Lyga could fix his life, but me. So eff him. And eff helping people. And especially eff *you*. Just because."

She shoved past him. "And now I'm gonna go steal that Toyota over there because it's cold as effing hell out here and I need to get home. Don't even *think* about following me."

Mike gave absolutely no thought to following her. He watched her stalk to the car, so confident in her ability to cow

"Yeah. Yeah, I think so."

"Good. Then you're ready." The chill air of the night reclaimed him again. The fire swayed and guttered in the wind. Phil's smile went sad. "Look at the book," she said.

"How did you get here?" It was the first question he should have asked. But he looked; a corner of a sheet of paper stuck out from it.

"What are you talking about?" Kyle demanded. "What are you seeing?" He peered ahead as though sheer determination could suffice where his eyes failed.

"Can't you see him? I can see him. And Gayl. And Joe. Mike!" George shouted, waving, running towards the blank

rather because following the boys meant he at least had tried something.

But now, here, with Terry, he began to wonder: Were the boys right? Were miracles possible?

"Now you got no reason to trust me," he began.

"It was no one's fault, Joe," she interrupted, echoing her sentiment if not her words from a decade earlier. "I thought him that she never once looked over her shoulder to see if he was, in fact, following her.

"Who *was* that?" he asked himself. She had known Fanboy yet she did not match the description of Goth Girl.

Six months in a mental hospital. Things change.

He imagined her in black, painting her white over with black, conjuring matching black hair. But—the black of her

"I'm here to give hope," Phil said with belying sadness. "To sound a note of possibility before what is to come."

"Then why do you sound so—Oh." He tugged the paper out of the book. It was a single sheet, folded over.

He unfolded it, only to find that it was still, somehow, folded, so he unfolded it again, yet a fold somehow persisted,

spot, where a "plasma curtain" had changed this world. "Hey, Mike!"

"Wait!" Kyle called after him, his voice suddenly in a panic. "Erasmus is saying . . . What's that? Erasmus says there's a spike in . . . in . . . what? A spike in . . . something. In

we were going to last forever," she said now, sighing. "I truly did. And yet then there you were. I was suddenly confronted every day with the impossibility and the inevitability of you. Your you-ness. Your always-ness. When we were dating, you were my special thing. My retreat. And then we married and we were together all the time and suddenly you were real. And that meant that I was real. Do you understand, Joe? Do you?"

He hadn't understood ten years ago, and he did not

clothes against the black of the night. It should be white instead, the world should be *white*, so he imagined her as a single, slim black figure against a white backdrop, her hair grown back, a black splotch of ink atop her pale visage.

She would be a lowercase "i," he realized, set against a world like paper, and he thought of Gayl saying that "It sounds like rain and ee cummings" and he thought of the world of white,

and as he continued to unfold it, it grew larger and larger, its blank space filling the air before him, occluding Phil, now a silhouette, the paper now massively huge, becoming his world, Phil fading to a slender line topped by a dot, and then Phil's silhouette faded away, the entirety of the world before him nothing more than the white blank of a fresh page. He dropped the

something we don't know. You don't know what it takes to admit that. It's—"

"I'm going," George said, running faster. "Now."

"No! No, wait! The energy readings are off the charts. You can't just—"

understand now, but he lied now as he had then, not wishing to hurt her by allowing her to think—to know—that she'd hurt him. Lied to her with the words he held so sacred and magical and beautiful, saying, "Nobody knows, honey, where love goes. But when it goes, it's gone, gone."

And then there was a moment of mystery and power. In that moment, he knew he could make her stay (for evermore), with just the right combination of words and nuance. She of the letter i, of the rain that Phil had loved, the rain she'd wanted him to listen to, tangled with her in the history-made sheets, and he felt an urgent need to see her. He rummaged in his bag for the charcoal drawing Fanboy had made, but when he stripped off the rubber band and unrolled it, the page had gone blank as he shouted

paper, but it remained before him, upright, unfolding itself, conjuring new heights and widths.

"Phil!" he shouted. "Where are you? Can you hear me?"

He knew she could not. He screamed her name again, though, screamed it as he dove into the great white screen of nothing:

"Mike!" George screamed and ran towards him. "Mike!!!"

could be his again, but he knew that this would be his decision, not hers, and so he let her go.

"Terry . . ." he whispered.

And changed his mind. He did not want her back; he *needed* her back. He leapt to his feet, spinning around, looking for her, seeing nothing but the vast and enormous blank of the universe, and screamed her name:

KYRA!

PHIL!

MIKE!

TERRY!

```
 P
 H T
MIKE
 L R
   R
  KYRA
```

phltrrkrmk

ieyy

Perky Myrrh Kilt!

Retry Lymph Kirk!

Helm Kirk Pry Try!

Ethyl Kirk Mr Pry!

Elk Myrrh Kip Try!

Elk Myrrh Kit Pry!

Re Lymph Kirk Try!

Err Myth Kirk Ply!

Eh Kirk Ply Mr Try!

He Kirk Ply Mr Try!

Elk Thy Irk Mr Pry!

p
h
l
t
r
r
k
r
m
k

i
e
y
y

Why.
Why?
(The old joke says: Why not?)
Why I?

I

i want
she is i
not i
i is phil
mike is i
it looks like:

i

i need to go
to i
to her
to i
and I
i w
a
n
t
to
l
i
s
t
e
n
to
the r i
a
n
with
you
with i
l a r
o t a
o t i
k h n
e
l
e
tt
ers

spilling
it sounds like
rain and
ee
cummings
this is i
is him
is her
is us
the world is a page
and we are
letters
making
words
and look and see there are letters there are words that spell
C
    H
    A
    P

CHAPTER 44

Mike screamed, palms pressed to his temples as he stumbled forward, thinking there should be asphalt—parking lot asphalt—under his feet, knowing that having a psychotic break or an intrusive delusion or an all-consuming hallucination should not and could not in any way change the reality of pavement, and yet he became aware instead of soft carpet, padding, warm, motionless air, and the sensation of walls beyond his immediate range of touch. Opening his eyes, he saw white before him, white as blank as a page waiting desperately for ink and he opened his mouth to scream again, but a voice said, "Mike!" and he spun to see George and Joe Roberts and Gayl, but especially George, who rushed to him and unself-consciously threw his arms around him, saying, "Dude, I thought you were dead. I thought you were dead," Mike responding with a similarly unself-conscious return clinch, as though George had become his own personal gravity, the strong center of mass that could keep him from spinning away and spinning out into the wide and vast universe of still, dead space between galaxies.

"You made it," Gayl said. "You—"

"You're a lucky man," Joe Roberts said. "It don't take long for the good to get gone."

Mike wept with joy, with gratitude, with shock and surprise, and he reached around George to take hold of Gayl's hand and Joe's hand as they approached him, the strength in their hands good and powerful and nearly as convincing as George's gravity.

"I was stuck somewhere else," Mike said. "I met these other kids. I think they were from your books, Gayl, but they had different names. And then it's like the world went white. It's like I didn't exist anymore."

"You were seeing the fundamental structure of the universe," Gayl said quietly, stepping away and holding up a new copy of *Inframan*. Where had that come from?

Mike extricated himself from George. They all stood in a small, white-walled, white-ceilinged, white-carpeted room with neither door nor window. A box.

"We're in the real world now," Gayl went on. "We've crossed over. Crossed up. I don't know the right metaphor. Turned the page, maybe. Opened a new book."

They all looked around. "This is the real world?" George said. "Not much to it."

"I don't feel any different," Mike said.

"You know how this book begins?" Gayl asked. He flipped it open and read: "*In the beginning, there was light. And then God said, 'Let there be darkness.' And I said to him, 'But it's been there all along, don't you see?'*"

Gayl snapped the book shut. "It's like I said before: The page is the basic building block of reality. You were able to see what only God has seen before: The raw, white blank that precedes Creation."

"But it said there was darkness, too," George said. "That's got to be letters, right? Words. Black ink on white paper."

"But the darkness is already there?" Mike wondered. "How can you ever have a blank page if the darkness—the words—is already there?"

"I don't—" Gayl started.

"The darkness is me."

Mike knew even before he turned that the voice belonged to Inframan, so he felt no surprise—not even the shock of recognition—when he spied the child there, still holding that infernal ice cream cone, which had melted to the point that the chocolate ice cream threatened to stream down the cone and cover Inframan's childish fist.

"Can the rest of you see him?" Mike asked, mindful of his experience on the subway, which felt a century in the past, but was no more than a day or two, though by chapters or by words, who knew how long it had been? How long did it take—in word count—to traverse the desert to the Other City, to ascend the StratoSpire, to travel to other universes (other books, if Gayl's theories were correct) and back?

"We see him," Gayl said grimly, and then—to everyone's surprise—shoved George right at Inframan.

"Slay the Dragon, St. George!" Gayl cried.

George stumbled forward with the force of Gayl's push, stutter-stepping to a halt just before the child, over whom even smallish George towered.

"Dude!" George remonstrated, glaring back at Gayl. "What the fuck?"

"I was *sure* that would work," Gayl mumbled.

"Tired of the chatter," Inframan said, "so now you don't talk. I'm the God of Failure, Michael, and right now your friends are all failing to speak. It's just you and me."

Sure enough, George's lips moved again, but no words came out. Gayl and Joe were similarly mute. George gestured as if to say, *Screw it* and swung a fist at Inframan, who watched placidly as George froze in mid-lunge. Gayl and Joe also became statues, though the light of awareness still flickered in their eyes.

"And now they fail to move, as well," Inframan said, gazing levelly at Mike.

"What do you want?" Mike balled up his fists, almost unaware he was doing so until Inframan chuckled at the sight, saying:

"Do you think you can hurt me? Do you think you can even touch me? You'll fail at that, as you've failed at everything conceivable to you, everything imaginable."

"I didn't fail to get here," Mike said, now unclenching, then re-clenching his fists, as if waking them from sleep.

"True," Inframan mused and then took a swipe at his ice cream with an impossibly long and narrow tongue. "You made it here, but only with the help of your rather pathetic crew of hangers-on. If you go further, you may not survive. Believe it or not, I'm here to help. I've seen the ending of this tale. It ends with you in a room—"

"Yeah, yeah, I know—alone. I remember. I get it."

"More than that, Michael: It ends with a love unrequited. Can you bear that?"

Mike swallowed hard, thinking of Phil, thinking of her gone from him forever. "First of all, why should I believe you? Second of all, who's to say that it still can't be changed? Can't the ending be changed? God could change his mind about how to end things. Maybe I can convince him. That's the whole point of prayer."

Inframan snorted. "How often do you think prayers get answered?"

"Not often," Mike admitted. "Certainly not enough. But it only takes one time."

"You don't understand. You're acting as though this is all still in progress, as though you have the option of changing his mind and getting a new ending. I'm telling you that I've seen the ending already. It's written[93]. You, in a room, alone. Love, unrequited. It's a done deal."

"Then why," Mike asked, a delicious and thrilling notion occurring to him, "are you trying so hard to stop me from going any further?"

Inframan said nothing; he licked again at the ice cream, his tongue a menacing, threatening thing all of a sudden, as though it could dart the distance between him and Mike, wrap Mike like a fly and suck him into Inframan's maw.

"Do you have any idea," Inframan said in a slow tone of mounting malice, "what a God. Damned. Nightmare. It would be if he decided to change things at this point? Do you?" Mike said nothing and then Inframan roared—in a bellowing, hectoring blast of sound that far outstripped his size—"Answer me!"

Mike gulped and took a step back, coming up short against the wall.

"It would be a disaster!" Inframan roared. "This whole story—this whole universe, if you prefer—has one reason for existing! It exists to end with you in a room, alone! Do you have any idea how much work it would take to change that? Do you?"

"It's just the ending . . ." Mike stammered. "He wouldn't have to change anything else—"

"'Just the ending?' Just? Are you insane? The ending *is* the story! The ending is *every* story! There's no point to a story without an ending and the ending is all that matters. The ending is what you remember. The ending determines if you like the

93. Visit http://barrylyga.com/new/wa-writers-block.html for proof, if you like, that Lyga does sometimes (often) write his books out of order.

story or not. If it's satisfying, you're happy. If it's not, you figure the entire story must have been a piece of shit. So don't ever say it's 'just the ending!'"

Shaking, Mike pressed himself against the wall, forcing himself not to cower before the anger of Inframan, who leaned in close now, the familiar and overwhelming stench of chocolate syrup churning Mike's stomach. "Leave now. One last chance. Turn back. Go back to the city. Learn how to live your lives and forget everything you've seen and heard and experienced here. You'll be in a room, alone, but at least nothing worse will happen to you."

From some well of resolve he hadn't known he possessed, Mike managed a tremulous, "No," in nearly a whisper.

And Inframan became a dragon[94], an enormous, reptilian hulk, caparisoned in shiny, slick black-gold scales, his double-row-toothed mouth roaring wide and blasting out a noisome wind of bad breath and chocolate syrup. He filled the room; he exceeded the room, yet was contained within the room, though that should have been—was—impossible. He reared his head and clawed the floor with hard, horny nails the size of steak knives and the color of old shoes, the rending and shrieking sound of the floor rattling Mike's teeth, his bones.

"Turn back!" Inframan thundered, his voice as big as his body, crushing the air from the room and from Mike's lungs. "Turn back or be destroyed!" A curl of smoke wisped from Inframan's left nostril, an enormous cavern large enough for Mike to insert his fist without brushing the rim. "I am the darkness of ink and the light of all Creation! I am the God of Failure and

94. *The* Dragon.

though you have failed to worship me, I forgive you and will devour you in your defeat and in your foundering nonetheless."[95]

Mike squeezed his eyes shut tight and found his breath and his words, and spoke: "No."

He heard and felt Inframan shift in the room, that lizardly bulk sinuously twisting and contorting into a new position, and then another roar—more halitotic reek, more chocolate syrup—and flecks of spittle spattering him and the heat of a tongue so close, and he knew Inframan had leaned in to him, his maw gaping so wide that he could devour Mike heightwise with but a single snap-shut of the jaws.

"I haven't failed," Mike said. "Not yet. I'm not yours yet. I can still succeed. You haven't won."

The dragon harrumphed and Mike risked opening an eye, finding himself staring directly into one of Inframan's enormous eyes, a yellowish thing with a single black puddle floating at its center, gruesome and unblinking. He longed to put his fist through that eye, to blind the creature, but he knew, even half-blind, Inframan could still destroy him. He wished for Gayl's surmise to have been right, for George to be some avatar of St. George, slayer of dragons.

"Won?" More smoke curled out from Inframan and wafted to Mike, carrying with it the smell of carrion and chocolate. "You and I aren't in competition; I've been trying to help you. I'm still trying to help you. I'm on your side. Don't you understand?

"*You* caused this, Michael! I tried to stop you. I tried to warn you away from editing reality. Who knows—given enough

95. Alvina—the first editor on this book—thought Inframan's little soliloquy/threat was sort of ridiculous. I like it, though. It seems both frightening and childish at the same time, which is exactly what I was going for.

time, maybe you could have won Phil back the old-fashioned way. Maybe you could have gone to her and found that there was a place in her heart a bit emptier for your loss, a place she could not merely wall away and forget about. A place she needed open and filled. But no. You were too impatient. You thought you were special. You had power and you had to use it. It's your fault the universe is damaged, your fault history's been rewritten and fucked up beyond belief. Phil hates you and it's your fault and that's it."

It was true; of course it was true. It was true and Mike knew it to be true and yet he did not care. He had mangled things, bungled things, brought his oldest friend and his newest friends to this pass, yet he was helpless to do anything but to fight. To push on. To pursue the dream and the reality of Phil, no matter where or when or how it took him.

"You can't stop me," he said to the dragon. "If I go back now, what happens? I live without Phil. I get arrested for violating the restraining order. And—oh, yeah—the universe keeps bleeding love until no one can fall in love anymore.

"So, sorry, Inframan. I won't stop. I can't stop. I can't live the future you described to me. The worst thing that can happen to me is to be in that room alone." Saying those words, he realized their double meaning, their predictive quality and their reductive power. He laughed, despite the stench of the creature and the closeness of its baleful eye.

"Stop laughing," Inframan growled, turning now to bare his enormous, stained teeth. "Stop it!"

But Mike could not stop. Between gasps, he managed to say, "The worst thing that can happen . . . Oh, man! You said it yourself. I can do whatever the hell I want! The worst thing that can happen to me is to be in that room alone!"

"That will happen!" Inframan crowed.

"Right! Would he change the ending to make things worse?"

Inframan, for the first time, had nothing to say.

"I can't die," Mike went on. "You can't eat me or hurt me. The worst thing that can happen to me is that I'll end up in that room alone. So why not go forward? If Barry Lyga isn't going to change my ending, like you said—"

"He might. He might make it worse."

But the dragon's voice, for the first time, trembled with uncertainty. With ironic failure.

"Then maybe he's also willing to change it for the better, not worse. Maybe you don't know everything you think you know. But I'll tell you this much: I won't budge. I'm still not going anywhere. Except forward."

With that, Inframan became the little boy again, his ice cream cone magically replenished. Tears rolled down his cheeks.

"I tried," he whimpered. "I want you to admit that I tried."

Mike knelt before the boy and put a hand on his shoulder. He felt suddenly, tremendously paternal towards him, as though he had been there at this child's birth and sworn to protect and love him all his life. If he had had it in his power to give Inframan what he wanted, he surely would have in that moment, swooning to the child's final gambit of fat tears. But Mike knew now what he supposed he'd known all along, from the first moment he'd edited reality: He was powerless. Despite his power, he was powerless, helpless in the face of something greater than himself, of his own love. His love for Phil, but also his love for his brother. And his love for his parents. And for George. His love for love itself, for the universe's love.

Whether that love had come honestly or not, he could not say. Maybe it had been implanted in him artificially; maybe it was an outgrowth of some mistaken combination of words on a page. But for him, it was real and it was mightier than anything else in his life. Mightier even than the abrupt love he felt for Inframan.

"You tried," he told the child, and hugged him, careful to avoid crushing the ice cream cone between them.

"I failed," the boy bawled, nestling against Mike's shoulder. "No one likes me and no one loves me and no one will ever love me, even though I never hurt anyone and I just want to help. Really. That's all I want. I tried to help and I failed. I always fail. I always screw up."[96]

"No, you don't," Mike said, comforting him. "No."

"I do! I always do!" he blubbered, then pushed away. Mike anticipated some horrible light in his eyes, horns from his skull, fire from his nostrils, but no—he was still just a little boy, with tremulous brown eyes clouded by tears.

"I always fail!" he raged, and threw down the ice cream cone in a tantrum. He stomped a foot on the floor. "I'm the God of Failure!"

And he vanished, leaving only the melting brown smear of chocolate ice cream on the floor as a reminder that he'd been there.

Still down on one knee, Mike stared at the ice cream until George's voice came to him, saying, "What happened?"

Mike looked around. George, Gayl, and Joe had all come out of their trances, staring at him and at the ice cream.

"Oh," Mike said. "There's a door."

Yes. A door.

Mike stood and opened the door and the four of them came into my presence.

96. And here Alvina asked an interesting question: "Does Inframan ever wonder why Barry Lyga made him this way?" The answer is that—per previous discussions about Inframan among the characters—Inframan actually thinks *he* is the real Barry Lyga. So he might wonder why/how the false Barry Lyga was able to take over and fool the world into thinking that he's the real deal, but Inframan is probably more concerned with fixing what he perceives to be flaws in the continuum/story.

CHAPTER 45

I spent some time imagining how I wanted them to come into my presence. I had already done the throne bit in an earlier chapter, and it seemed tired now. I considered some crazy description of an abstract landscape and maybe choirs of singing angels and glowing balls of light in the air, but that seemed like an awful lot of work. Yes, yes, I know—it's just "words on a page," but I don't think you know how much work "words on a page" can be. I would have to design the environment in my mind, then figure out which details mattered. And let's say I decided that those singing angels were a good idea: Well, what are they singing? How loudly? How many of them are there? Will they keep singing during the dialogue scene to follow, and if so, how often should I intrude on the dialogue to point this out? Are they moving around? Interrupting and distracting with their motions?

You can see my dilemma.

In the end, I settled on another plain white room. Boring, yes, but be honest—at this point, you haven't read hundreds and hundreds of pages for the scenery of heaven. You want to know what happens next. You want to know if I could possibly be so cruel as to leave Mike in a room all alone at the end; if I could be so cruel as to leave a love unrequited.

We're getting there. I promise you. We're so close.[97]

****

"Is it really you this time?" Mike asked upon seeing me. I was standing in the white room, my hands clasped dramatically behind my back, waiting for him.

"Is it really you?" he demanded. "Because I want the real deal."

Tempted to do a Nicholson impression here, but I don't . . . "I'm an avatar, Mike. A version of Barry Lyga translated into prose. It has to be this way; trust me. You can't handle the real me."

"It doesn't matter what I can or can't handle. I came here, I fought to get here, to see God. That's what they came for, too." He gestured to his three amigos, standing slightly behind him, reminding me of bodyguards or superheroes, I'm not sure which.

"Mike, haven't you ever read the Bible? Don't you know about God and Moses? God showed his true face to Moses for like half a second and Moses aged a hundred years. Are we really going down that road? Believe me, kid, you couldn't handle seeing the real me."

"Why? Are you that magnificent?"

I laughed. "No, I'm just a guy pushing forty,[98] sitting at his computer. But trust me, you can't handle it."

97. Well, relatively.

98. Actually, by the time this damn book is published, I'm pushing *fifty*. Which, let me tell you, sucks. Remember way back on page 113 when I had Mike's architecture professor say, "Architecture is an old man's game?" Well, I'm an old man now. The things I dreamed of doing in my youth—my twenties, when I conceived of *Inframan*, my thirties, when I wrote this book—are now possible, but only now that I'm so damn old. And will anyone give a shit about the ramblings of an old man?

"I can imagine that, why can't I handle it?"

"Your universe isn't detailed enough. I see the world in hi-def; you're stuck in standard."

"I want to see the real you."

I sighed. "Fine. But don't say I didn't warn you."

I showed them the real me, from the real world. To them, it appeared like this:

Barry Lyga stands 5 feet 10.98351 inches tall when barefoot and standing fully erect. We will begin at the top and work our way down. His head is covered by 101,427 hairs, beginning at a hairline that recedes over the forehead. We begin by choosing, arbitrarily, a hair that is midway equidistant between the tops of his ears (as measured over the curvature of his skull) and midway between the nape of his neck and the lowermost jut of his chin, omitting for measurement purposes the perimeter of his nose and measuring, therefore, directly over his mouth, between his eyes, and over his forehead. This particular hair is 3.72 inches in length and .2 mm thick at the base, tapering to .1 mm at its furthest extension. It was cut approximately three weeks previous to the writing of this paragraph with a Braun electric razor with a Number 2 razor attachment at a small barbershop in the lower blocks of Court Street in Brooklyn, New York.[99] The hair is a reddish-brown in color, closely approximating a tone of CMYK 0-67-98-68, the red portion a recessive genetic trait from Scottish ancestors[100] that occa-

99. For simplicity's sake, let us stipulate that—unless otherwise mentioned—all of the hairs on Lyga's head were cut in such a fashion at such a place by such a gadget at such a time.

100. Lyga is one-eighth Scottish on his mother's mother's side, his maternal grandmother's mother's maiden name having been MacPherson. She was blessed with red hair and green eyes, and while interbreeding with Slavic, Germanic, and Mediterranean stock caused brown hair pigmentation to predominate, the Scottish genes occasionally surface, as now. In other words: Sometimes you can see streaks of red in my hair and beard.

sionally surfaces, as now. The second hair is located .5 mm to the right of the first, assuming one is observing Lyga's head from the top and behind, this second hair measuring 3.75 inches in length and .19 mm thick at the base, tapering to .11 mm at its furthest extension. The hair is a deep brown in color, closely approximating a tone of CMYK 0-50-74-70. The third hair is located .17 mm to the right of the first, still assuming one is observing Lyga's head from the top and behind, this third hair measuring 3.76 inches in length and .23 mm thick at the base, tapering to .09 mm at its furthest extension. The hair is a deep brown in color, closely approximating a tone of CMYK 0-51-72-71. The fourth hair . . .

And then I took mercy on them all.

"See?" I asked through my avatar. "Do you understand?"

You—as in *you, the reader*—probably don't really get it, but try to imagine what it would be like if everything you saw in the world were presented to you in exacting, exasperating, explicit, and total detail. So, you couldn't just pick up a glass, for example. You would have to burn through innumerable brain cycles noting the curve of its rim, the thickness at lip and base, the exact clarity, the albedo, the reflectivity, the weight and density and more, all in terms scientific and rote. Every action you take, every twitch, everything you see, taste, touch, smell, hear—*described.*

You'd go crazy, right?

That's what they got a taste of, just then. Mike and the others staggered backwards towards the door, their expressions uniformly dazed and worn, as though battered. It was a familiar sensation for poor George, but for the others, it was new and horrible.

"Oh, God . . ." Mike said without the slightest trace of irony.

"Now do you get it?" I asked. "This is just a simulation of the real world. You wouldn't be able to comprehend the *real* real world. That's why I have to fake it here on the page. That's why all writers fake it on the page. The real world is too detailed and too intense. And, honestly, too boring for prose. In the real world, we sort of automatically filter out the details that don't matter, but you guys are characters; you're used to living in a world where everything is described, not actually seen. Where everything that is described is important, so you have to pay attention to it. You don't have filters in place to help you figure out what matters and what doesn't, so when writing, I have to use metaphors instead. We don't have metaphors in the real world. We use them, but they don't actually exist. For this bit, I have to just say that I have short, brown hair. Otherwise, we could have gone for hundreds of pages just describing my hair." I ran a hand through it. "And I don't even have that much of it left these days!"

They looked at me as though . . . Oh, hell, as though they didn't believe me, OK? There's no point prettying it up for you with an analogy or a simile. I think you get it, right?

"Look, guys, writing is about reducing complexity, to a degree. Filtering out the stuff that doesn't matter and only committing to paper the stuff that does. You leave out everything else and let the reader's imagination do the rest of the work. Even for something as simple as: 'The dog ran.' Some readers will imagine the dog's tail wagging for balance, the tongue lolling out to cool it off.[101] Others won't see those things, but will see other details. And let's not even talk about breed! I haven't mentioned the breed of the dog, but everyone reading this book is picturing a specific breed or a specific sort of mutt."

"No two people ever read the same book," Gayl whispered. "The words are the same, but the story is always—"

101. And now you're probably seeing those details, whether you originally did or not, right?

"Stephen King says that stories are telepathy," I told them. "I say they're mind control, but mind control of an imperfect sort. When I write a story I can force you to imagine certain things, but there's always a level of control I can't attain. That is the flaw in storytelling. That's the flaw in creation, period. If what I imagine only communicates to you imperfectly, then how can we imagine that God created the world perfectly? My reality—the 'real world'—is nothing more than the imperfect reflection of God's imagination."

"I thought *you* were God," George said.

I ignored him and went on: "Or maybe it's more accurate to say that stories are time travel. I'm writing these words now, on August 24, 2010.[102] But they're being read a month or a year or ten years from now. Hell, maybe even a hundred years from now. I'm long dead, but the words I'm typing right now are—at the same moment—communicating with someone born after I died."

"So then the genesis of story," Gayl said, excited, "isn't just in the mind of the author. It has to do with a sort of collaboration—"

"An uneven, unequal collaboration."

"—between the reader and the author!" Gayl ran a hand through his hair, which wasn't thinning like mine yet, but would be soon. "Wow. Oh, wow, I never thought of it that way!"

"She died; he mourned," I said. "Shortest story in the world. Cause and effect. Action/reaction. Emotion. Two characters. Both of them change by the end. And the reader's imagination fills in all the details. Done and done."

102. Actually, I wrote most of this scene much earlier than that and this paragraph in particular was written possibly two years earlier, but August 24, 2010 is the day I sat down to revise this chapter, the day when I decided to add this specific paragraph to this specific exchange, so that's the day I'm using.

"This is all well and good," Mike said, "but I'm not here for some bullshit philosophy lesson. I want to know: Is this really you? This is what you look like?"

"Generally, sure. It's how I would describe myself at least: Average height, average build. Brown hair and eyes, unshaven with a chin beard . . . Close enough for government work, as we like to say."

He looked back and forth between Gayl and me. "You guys look a lot alike."

"Well, yeah. We're versions of each other. But, Mike—this isn't what you came here for, is it? You came for the reason all pilgrims visit their gods. You want a boon." I grinned in a manner I hoped was reassuring. Maybe it was, maybe it wasn't. "You all want something from me, don't you?"

They were silent.

"Don't you?"

George shrugged. "I don't want anything," he said very quietly. "Not from you."

Strangely, it was true. I knew, of course, the one thing that George wanted, for I was the one who had given him that impulse and that need and that drive.[103] Moreover, it was entirely in my power to give George the thing he wanted most and I had considered it, had been considering it for several chapters now. It would require rewriting the ending to the book (I had already written the ending months ago) and I really *really* liked the ending, but . . . If I pulled it off, giving George what he wanted would be a literary coup, a stunning

103. For a clue as to what George wants, see page 157 (Mike. Later.). Or simply keep reading—I promise I will tell you before the book is over. Yes, George has three secrets. Unlike Fanboy, I won't be keeping his particular "third thing" a secret. Some magic tricks only work once before the audience tires of them.

ending that would pull the rung[104] out from under the reader's expectations.

But I decided not to do this. Because it would mean imposing my will on George, and this is something I was not willing[105] to do. I liked George. He had begun as a cipher (as so many of my supporting characters do), although—conspicuously—he understood the nature of the novel from the very beginning.[106] Somewhere along the way, he'd grown on me. I'm not sure why; after all, for much of the novel, he's unaware of the progress of the plot, merely another piece on the gameboard that Mike keeps rearranging with his "editorial powers." And yet, at some point, he became very real to me, and I hated that he was drummed out of the Marines, hated that he lost one of the only things he cared about in the world, a goal he'd aimed for his entire life, a goal he'd accrued as his most potent and enduring form of self-identity. Maybe because on some level he reminded me of a friend of mine who, like George, wanted only to protect people, to defend them from enemies and keep them from being hurt, all because no one had been there to shield him when he'd needed it. George was important to me, and I hated what I had done to him and what I would do to him in the future.

But for now, I had to set George aside and move on. To Gayl. My doppelganger, after a fashion. Gayl was more like me than I cared to admit, just as I often said that Fanboy was "more

104. That's a typo, but I decided to leave it in. If you think about it, having a rung pulled out from under you would be just as shocking as having a rug pulled out from under you . . . and lots more dangerous.

105. No pun intended.

106. In fact, I even have a note to myself in the original manuscript at a point in the first fifty pages where George says something that connects to the larger meaning of the story. The note reads "Be sure to say later that George understood the whole thing from the beginning." So now I'm doing that.

autobiographical than I should admit in public."[107] Gayl was a version of me from many time periods, deconstructed and reconstructed repeatedly until he was almost—but not quite—his own character, hence the scrambled name. He was not a direct analog or avatar of me—he was an iteration. He had his own career that mirrored mine, but was different from mine.

"How about you, Gayl? What do you want from me? Surely you didn't come here just to provide moral support and the occasional convenient plot explanation?" I grinned because truthfully those were Gayl's primary functions in the story, other than being another in a fun series of ways to both mock and revere myself at once. "You've written versions of my books," I went on, "so you must have some idea of what you can get from me."

Gayl thought slowly and deliberately, just as I knew he would, just as I wanted him to, just as I would in the same situation. "I suppose I could ask for what Mike wants," he said, picking his words carefully. "I could ask for my version of Phil back, but I don't think you have any intention of giving her back. Because I wouldn't do it in your position. I would never give the reader or the character exactly what he or she wants. Also, even though we're just characters in a book, I'm uncomfortable with the idea of a woman being 'given.'"

"Because I am, too," I told him, somewhat hypocritically. After all, that was sort of the point of the book, right? Phil is a prize for Mike to seek. But it serves the needs of the story and

107. That's a line that, when used on panels and at signings, always gets a laugh. It took me a long time before I realized that it was a subconscious modification of something I had written in the unfinished *Inframan* back in college, when a friend of mine comments that my novel *His Darkness* (another never-to-be-written novel by the dead Barry Lyga) was "too autobiographical for your [my] own good." It's strange how something intended as a dark, dramatic, portentous line in one context can become wholly unconsciously revised and restructured, then delivered in another context that makes it comedic.

there's a point to it all, if you read closely. Anyway, back to my conversation with Gayl . . .

"Was that your way of asking for something?" I asked him, knowing it wasn't.

"Or I suppose," he went on, ignoring me, knowing that I knew it wasn't, "I could ask you to explain why I exist. Who and what I am. Why you gave me your name. Why you gave me a version of your life and career and books when there was already a version of you in the world."

"I can answer that," I told him.

"But I don't want to know anymore," he said, unsurprisingly. For I had already written a section to use at some point and now was the time to use it, and Gayl, I had decided, would be my excuse.

"I don't need to know those things anymore. I've learned they don't matter. So, I want to know what happened to Barry Lyga," he told me. "I want to know what happened on August 5, 2005 to the Barry Lyga in my universe, the one who wrote *Inframan* and *American Sun* and *Redesigning You* and the others."

"Of course you do," I told him. "And I can show you."

THE DEATH OF BARRY LYGA

AUGUST 5, 2005 . . .

Barry Lyga knew how the story ended.

It was his latest work in progress—*The Gospel According to Jesus*—and given the subject matter, the ending was preordained, perhaps in multiple senses of that word. It would end, as it must, with Jesus on the cross, with a final thought that Barry had kept locked in his imagination for years, ever since the idea of the book had occurred to him. That, he had come to realize, was how he wrote books—he knew the beginning and the ending and sometimes he knew something of the middle. But usually he started with a blank computer screen, an opening scene or handful of scenes, and an ending to work towards. In the middle was—he hoped—magic.

But there are different kinds of magic, different types. There's the magic of fantasy novels and there's the magic of the stage, and while he had spent his life fervently searching in his books for the former, he'd found only the latter, more accurately described as "illusion." And illusions may thrill or frighten or illuminate or awe, but in the end all illusions fade. Barry Lyga desperately did not want to fade.

Now, on August 5, 2005, he had come to a horrible crossroads. He had recently been released from the Sheppard Pratt mental health facility. His latest book had not done well, even by the lax and tolerant standards of his small publishing house (a tiny, four-man operation run from somewhere in Ohio). Each book, he had always said (both aloud to friends and to himself) needed only to supply enough money to his coffers to pay for him to write the next one. He cared not, he claimed, for the *New York Times* bestsellers list nor for awards nor for any of the other typical and standard metrics of success. He wanted only to keep writing, to have the writing be his life's work, without interruption, and so long as each novel allowed him the financial freedom to write the next, he would be happy.

He convinced himself of this early on. It was not a difficult conceit to swallow.

He had achieved this aim since college, beginning with the publication of *Inframan* and the others, leading up to the publication of *For Love of the Madman*, which had only been in stores for a week thus far, but which showed every sign of failure. Preorders had been "dismal" in the refreshingly honest parlance of his editor, and there had been no early reviews to speak of, save for the occasional mention on a blog or a few half-hearted attempts on AwesomeReads. No one was talking about the book. No one was reading the book. And sure as hell was hot, no one was buying the book.

It would be a year before *Sxxxxx Cxxx*, his latest novel, was published, and even if it did spectacularly well (and at this point, seven novels and a short story collection into his career, what were the odds?), it would be another six months after that before he could count on his first royalty check. He had stripped his lifestyle down to the bone. He ate frugally, adhering to a strict food budget each week. He'd stopped attending movies or sporting events; he did not even rent movies online, preferring instead to wait for the local library to offer the DVDs. He had canceled his Internet service, relying instead on a coffee shop some four blocks away, and had sold his car; he walked everywhere he needed to go, taking a bus when absolutely desperate to journey more than a mile or two from his home. He gave up on haircuts as a needless expense and his hair, though thinner, had become as long as he'd once worn it in college, down to his shoulders.[108]

And yet despite all this—despite these sacrifices—he still had not enough money to last him through the publication of *Sxxxxx Cxxx*, much less to that mythical royalty check.

He was a failure.

At his back, the creature giggled and changed shape. Sometimes it looked like Barry had as a child, always carrying an ice cream cone, perhaps from the now-defunct, long-ago closed-down Twin Kiss ice cream parlor on Reisterstown Road, where Barry had eaten his first soft-serve ice cream and learned how to love fried potato wedges.

At other times it looked like his father or his ex-girlfriend or the girl who had pulled his pants down on the baseball field in fifth grade, humiliating him.

Sometimes it looked like him, as though a mirror had pulled itself from the wall and decided to walk the world on its own.

But it always sounded the same and it always smelled the same. It smelled like chocolate syrup, like a bottle of Hershey's hooked up to an air compressor and fired straight up the nose.

It always sounded like a dragon.

In high school and in college, he'd been haunted, not by a

108. I'm not going to lie to you; this whole paragraph makes me extremely uncomfortable. So uncomfortable that I want to cut it . . . but that makes me pretty sure I shouldn't. Because if it make me uncomfortable, doesn't that mean it's powerful? Maybe even true?

ghost but by an idea, an idea of failure so large that it was its own God, the God of Failure, a creature he came to call Inframan.[109] He wrote a novel about Inframan, hoping that doing so would exorcise the idea, purge it from his consciousness, but all it did was make Inframan more powerful. Inframan whispered to him in his sleep, mocked him in his waking hours, tormented him.

He had tried to beat Inframan with words, and in the end, Inframan turned out to be made stronger by words. Every writer, Barry had been told by his acquaintance Art Holcomb, has a million bad words in him, a million words he had to write before he gets to the good ones.

Inframan was those million words times a million writers, then a million more. The very essence of failure, distilled down from a liquid to a thick, reductive . . .

. . . syrup . . .

It was time for things to be over, Barry Lyga thought. It was time, he thought and he knew. It was August 5, 2005. Bifurcation Day. Publication Day. He could no longer exist, this Barry Lyga, this author. *Inframan* had to remain on a hard drive, migrating from New Haven to Owings Mills to Hampstead to Hanover to Las Vegas to New York to New Jersey, unfinished like Gayl Rybar's masterpiece. *American Sun* was nothing more than a file of hasty notes and an idea for yet another inconclusive ending.[110] The short stories of *The Sunday Letters and Other Stories* were written, but unpublished, ill-suited for publication in any event. And

109. Imagine the horror Barry Lyga experienced when he discovered that comic book genius Alan Moore used the name "Inframan" for a throwaway superhero character in his *1963* comic book, published in 1993, years after Lyga had begun work on *Inframan* the novel. Would people think he had ripped off Moore, he wondered. Would he have to change the title of his opus because of a fucking background character in a comic book?

110. To be precise, the following sentence: "Cam pulled the trigger and realized that no matter what did or did not happen next, he had changed the world."

the other novels? *Emperor of the Mall* and the others? Nothing more than high concepts. Notions. A paragraph of description here. A character name there. A few fully-realized scenes never committed to paper or pixel, socked away instead in Barry Lyga's subconscious, whence they occasionally pop up, unbidden, like children given up for adoption stalking their birth parents.

On August 5, 2005, the phone call comes from a traditional inn in Japan at 2:00am local time. It comes from and to another universe, as another Barry Lyga's agent calls, whispering so as not to awaken the other inn guests sleeping behind rice-paper walls, informing him that Houghton Mifflin Books for Children has won the auction for his first novel, not the literary opus *Inframan*—an exploration and exploitation of the nature of textual realities and the relationship between reality and fiction—but rather *The Astonishing Adventures of Fanboy and Goth Girl*, a young adult novel about a fifteen-year-old sarcastic outcast (based on Lyga's own teen self) and the girl of his nightmares, the titular Goth Girl.

Inframan will never be finished. *American Sun* will never begin. And the Barry Lyga destined to write these books? The iteration of Barry Lyga who dreamed them and sculpted them to perfection in his mind's eye? Why, that Barry Lyga can no longer exist. His existence is an impossibility, for even if he someday *were* to write *American Sun*, to finish *Inframan*, to author all the others, they would come later, they would come after *The Astonishing Adventures of Fanboy and Goth Girl*, and they would be not of the Barry Lyga who dreamed them as his career, but of some other Barry Lyga.

And so that first Barry Lyga must—by force of logic, if nothing else—be gone. And if he must be gone, then he was here, and if was here, then he lived. And so, he must die.

This was not a difficulty or a complexity for the other Barry

Lyga, for the one on the phone with his agent on August 5, 2005. He gave—I gave—no thought at all to the first Barry Lyga. Not a single thought at all. Not a single regret. In college and for years after, he had fantasized himself the author of *Inframan* and the others, and now—in less than a heartbeat—he discarded that dream, that career, that legacy and that life, condemning the dream iteration of himself to death as he accepted the two-book deal from Houghton Mifflin, unsure at the moment what his second book might be, though the story of an abused boy had been nagging at the back of his brain for years now, and he had an inkling that maybe—maybe—it might be time to tell it. It might be worth his time, and the reader's time. Possibly.

There was so much to do. Death was merely an inconvenience, a detail to be ironed out, a T to be crossed.

An I to be dotted.

Many and various and—often—stupid were the times Barry Lyga should have died before this moment. Beginning—in his earliest memory—with the time he'd raced his Evel Knievel[111] action figure[112] on its motorcycle down the driveway and into the street, where a man balancing soft-serve ice cream cones with the mechanical complexities of driving nearly ran him over when he darted into traffic to retrieve it. In later years, he lost his grip while hanging upside-down from an exercise bar stupidly and precariously hung in the basement by his stepbrother and fell, landing on his head on a concrete floor.[113] Death had followed him down a flight of stairs where he almost impaled himself on his stepfather's motorcycle before catching himself on the

111. Not Daredevil Levi.

112. Not action doll.

113. I should have broken my neck or my skull. It should have caused brain damage. At the very least, I should have suffered a concussion. Instead, I was fine.

handrail at the last moment, and it had tracked him to Yale, where a car came within a page's-width of striking him one drunken night, and where a snowball made mostly of ice crashed through a glass window, driving a shard of glass literally between his eyes.[114]

He'd been lucky. Yet he did not see these close calls as good fortune or as a sign to change his life. He saw them, instead (when he thought of them at all) as the caprice of an indifferent universe, a universe very specifically and very strenuously capricious toward him. And even now . . .

It's not that he wished to die.

He simply no longer wished to live.

There was another Barry Lyga, he liked to fantasize. A Barry Lyga who had not made these mistakes. Call him, if you like, the Barry Lyga of Earth-2[115]. This Barry Lyga would be a bit older. A bit wiser. Maybe he would have wisely given up the pursuit of publication and would live to a ripe old age, surrounded by loved ones, beloved and content, having lived and worked some fulfilling career that this Barry Lyga could scarcely imagine.

Or maybe . . .

"Maybe he just wrote better fucking books," Barry Lyga said aloud to his cramped, empty apartment.

And died.

114. The glass caused a gush of blood that would not stop and required stitches; a scar remains, twenty-five years later. If my head had been turned a centimeter in either direction, I would have lost an eye at the very least.

115. A parallel worlds nomenclature lifted from the DC Comics of Barry's youth, once quite obscure to a mainstream audience, but now well-known due to its use on *The Flash* TV show on The CW. (Plug: I write a series of novels based on that TV show. Go buy them—they're fun, and I don't show up in them at all!)

CHAPTER 46

Funny.[116]

I never intended to write any of that. I never intended to describe my own death. If you want to know the truth, it sort of freaked out my girlfriend-at-the-time that I killed myself off at all. Bad enough I had the Wikinformation page and the scene at my own grave, but to actually describe the moment of death?

That really creeped her out.

I couldn't explain to her how liberating it was, how rejuvenating. It wasn't *me* dying; it was a version, an iteration, an avatar. It was a useless chunk of me that I had discarded long ago. It felt good to kill that Barry Lyga. It freed me from him, from his expectations and his needs. I never meant it to be a part of the book. I always intended to leave "his" death a mystery, but then one day it occurred to me how to write it, how to frame it, and I thought that it was very likely that Gayl—Gayl, of course,

116. "Funny strange," of course, not "funny ha-ha," the latter of which has been lacking in this book, unless you appreciate the sort of weird, obscure, intellectual and pseudo-intellectual in-jokes that I appreciate. For which I apologize.

of all the characters; Gayl the writer; Gayl the me—would want to know how it happened.

"I thought differently," Gayl said as I finished the story. "I thought the wrong things mattered. And I hated people for their success, and I hated myself for not having the same success. You made me in your image, didn't you?"

I said nothing.

"You made me in your image, and then you told me that story. Jesus. You killed yourself. You murdered yourself just because . . . just because you had some idiotic vision in your head from college about what it would be like to be a writer, what your career would look like, what it should look like. Do you really hate yourself that much? That you would kill yourself because the wrong fucking book got published first?"

"I don't expect you to understand," I told him. "You cannot know the mind of God."

"Yes, I can," he said, as I knew he would, his voice rising with tension and anger as he spoke. "Because God's mind is the same as mine. You made me to be you, or a version of you, because even though you saw yourself die, you knew you were still alive. So there had to be a representation of you, didn't there? Yeah. Because that's how I would have done it, too, I guess. Too much ego. Too much narcissism and self-indulgence. Twisting the name, the letters, hoping people will think it's clever, right? Changing the book titles. It's like copping a cheap feel, you know? Let the readers feel clever for noticing the little things, and you know that when the readers feel clever, they like more than the book—they like the author, too, don't they? God," he said, shaking his head, "you're disgusting. You're self-absorbed, solipsistic, batshit insane . . . I want nothing to do with you."

George and Mike looked stunned and terrified, as though they expected me to destroy Gayl for his impudence, and I certainly could have done so—it would have made for a dramatic moment, no?[117]—but I did not do so, instead finding myself amused that Joe Roberts did not look terrified at all, but merely leaned against a wall, applauding Gayl's strength.

"Listen to me," Gayl said, now ignoring me and speaking directly to Mike, who still looked as though he expected Gayl to explode into bloody chunks or evaporate into thin air at any moment. "Listen. You don't need him. You don't want anything he can give you. We came into this wrong. We thought this was your story, Mike, and that he had a reason to make it a good one. But it's not your story. It's his. It's his and it's been his from the first page. He isn't interested in anything but making himself look good."

"That's the first incorrect thing you've said this entire time," I told Gayl. I was disappointed, to tell the truth. Right up until his last sentence, he was making sense, but now . . .

Still, I did not destroy him.

"I'm not interested in making myself look good, Gayl. That was always you. Always. But you're done now. Your part is over."

"No!" Mike yelled, and he and George both leapt at me as if they could stop me or change the flow of the tale, but they could not and Gayl vanished before our eyes, reaching out for them, his last words hanging in the air for a moment (because it's a dramatic effect, not because it's particularly realistic): "Don't trust him."

"It's good advice," I told them, watching them as they stared in horror at the place where—a sentence earlier—Gayl had stood.

117. A part of me also considered leading you down a path whereby you would be certain I would not destroy Gayl, then destroy him anyway as a sort of Joss Whedonesque double-shock, but I decided against it, ensuring you here and now that I will not destroy Gayl.

"He had the book," Mike whispered in horror. "He had the copy of *Inframan* . . . Only the Word of God—"

"Yeah, well, it wouldn't have helped you anyway," I told him, waving off the threat of the book. "I just like the way 'Only the Word of God can destroy God' sounded, so I used it. And then my agent[118] pointed out that it never amounted to anything, so I had you use the book to destroy an iteration of me. But trust me, Mike—I'm completely in control here. You could have an entire library of my novels and it wouldn't do a thing to me."

Together, they stared at the Gayl-less spot.

"What happened to him?" George asked.

"Does it matter? His part was done. He said the things I needed him to say. And now he's gone."[119]

"Is that all we are to you?" Mike asked. "Just different mouths for words from the same fucked-up brain?"

"No, that's not all you are, but damn—I do like the way you said it!" If I do say so myself. Which I do. "But no—you all have different, important roles to play. The hero on a quest. The sidekick-slash-best friend. And . . . Well, you know what? I just always liked the idea of a character who only spoke in Springsteen lyrics."

"Well, I—" Joe started, but I was done with him and he was gone.

I watched them carefully. Where there had been four, there were now two, two who were keenly aware of how quickly and

118. Hi, Kathy! (That's Kathleen Anderson of Anderson Literary Management, for those of you wondering. Poor woman read the first draft of this book *twice*.)

119. If it helps, you can imagine Gayl back in his townhouse in the city, feverishly pounding away at the keyboard, desperate to finish *Unfinished*. When suddenly . . . the phone rings! It's Philomena! She wants him back! She's moving to the city to be with him! Aw, what a happy ending! If you want to imagine that, it's fine by me. But it didn't happen.

easily I had dispatched the older, more experienced members of their quartet. Touchingly, George gently pushed Mike back two paces, stepping between us, forming a liminal shield as he had done between Mike and *him* at The WB fundraiser so many chapters ago, and between Mike and the asshole's shotgun in chapters of more recent vintage.

"Do you think standing between us would stop me from hurting Mike if I wanted to?" I asked George, my heart aching for George's power, for his devotion. He was the best best friend I'd ever created, I decided. Better than Cal, definitely, and better even than Zik. Better than Howie from *I Hunt Killers*, pretty much the apotheosis of best friends in the Lyga *oeuvre* to date. A part of me wanted to let George defeat me, give him the ability to crush God himself. Maybe something about his devotion being so powerful that it affected even me? Or maybe I could drag out that old hoary authorial chestnut about "the characters just wrote themselves!" and claim that I had no control over the story.

But that's not true. I am in control. Every word. Every letter. Every punctuation mark.

"Life is good and death is not," George said. "I'm alive."

"Go away, George," I said as kindly as I could, and then I reached into the space where George had been, extending my hand to Mike, and he took it, for what other choice did he have?

"Tell me what you want from me, Mike."

He shook his head. "You know already."

"I think I know. But writing is funny business. Sometimes your fingers know something that your brain doesn't. So this is pretty much your last chance in the novel to surprise me. After you speak, it's all pretty well planned-out, so go for it."

He hesitated. "No matter what I say, it doesn't matter, does it?"

"Of course it matters. Look, you came here with some lofty

goals. When you started out, it was all selfish—you wanted Phil back. More to the point, you wanted her back and you wanted her to be a very specific way, a way that pleased you. Male Gaze much?

"But now you've had your eyes opened. You've seen how damaged your world is. Lucky Sevens. GWB. No new love. So it's simple, Mike—make your choice. Do you want the world fixed? Or do you just want Phil back?"

"I can't make that decision!" he cried. "How can you expect me to? I'm weak—"

"You're strong. Strong for her. Think of what you've endured to get her back."

He thought for a moment. He nodded to himself, steeled himself.

He said, "I want Phil back. That's what I want and I know you can do it."

I sighed. "You didn't surprise me, Mike. I was sort of hoping you would. You've been very single-minded throughout, though, so I guess it's not that big of a shock that you're still singing the same old tune. My agent thought you should demand I repair the universe here, insist I rebuild the Other City. And you know, she's probably not wrong. But you just couldn't ask for that, could you?"

"You *made* me this way. It's not my fault."

"In the end, you chose yourself over the universe. Over the Other City. Over your own brother. I expected that, though. So let's move on, shall we?"

And I made a door open behind me, and Mike said, "Another white room?"

And I said, "No, Mike. No more white rooms. Come with me."

We walked through the door together.

"I'm going to show you the beginning of the world."

"Oh, really?"

"Watch. Watch. I will show you perfection."

See

?

See

what the world

once

was?

Pure
L
i
k
e

f
a
l
l
i
n
g

r
a
i
n

Perfect

Dull

Dead

And then you/me

This world

mar

ked

in

black

Ask yourself:

Are the letters added to the page

Or subtracted from it?

Is this an act of creation

Or of reduction?

Hold
my
hand.

Tight.

We're almost

CHAPTER 47

there.

"Open your eyes, Mike."

I released his hand and watched him. "Bullshit," he said. "More blank pages. I get it, OK? There was nothing. There was blank, perfect order, and then you came along and . . ." He broke off, then looked around.

"Welcome, Michael. Welcome to the Real World."

"Where are we?" he asked.

"This," I told him, "is where I grew up."

We stood in the backyard of the house where I'd grown up in Hampstead—the overgrown woods off to our right, the barbed wire fence that divided our property from the cow field to the left. A single cow—I don't know what breed; I never cared and I can't be bothered to check now, quite honestly; the damn cow's just there for verisimilitude, OK?—chewed her cud just on the other side of the fence, watching us with dull brown eyes. The sun hung low in the west, melting the clouds along the horizon. It was the best I could do without going back in time and taking a picture.

"I can see all of this," he said. "I can understand it. It's not like before, where there was . . ." He shuddered. "Too much. Of everything."

"Yeah, that's because I lied just now: I'm just faking it again for you. You're not in the real world. The first Mike Grayson, the one from *Inframan*, he got to go to the real world because at the time, I (or the version of Barry Lyga who wrote that novel) didn't really understand what the real world would look like to a fictional character. Or maybe I just changed my mind about how to deal with that. Anyway, it doesn't matter. You're just in a facsimile of reality. There's all kinds of details I'm leaving out because they would just bore people at this point."[120]

"Oh. It seems nice here," he added after a moment.

"I fucking hated it." I turned him around, pointing him at the house. "I hated every last instant in this place. I was moved here after my parents got divorced. Didn't want to go, but I had no choice. This house and this town came to represent everything I wanted to escape in my life. Stupid hick town in the middle of nowhere in the 1980s. Before the Internet. We didn't even have cable TV. It was like living in another century. No wonder I read nothing but comic books and science fiction and fantasy. I was trying to escape the only way I knew how—with my brain."

"What does this have to do with Phil?"

"Oh, Mike . . ." I sighed. "It's not about Phil. It never has been."

"It's *all* about Phil!" he protested.

"You don't know what it's about," I chided him. "You have a child's view of romance, a bully's view of love. You want Phil to be a very specific, very constrained person, hemmed in by

120. In the original draft, I listed some of these details, but you know what? I was right! They bored early readers, so I took them out.

what works for you, what you need. That's not mature, Mike. And it sure as hell isn't love."

"Fuck you!" he yelled. "I just prioritized her over the goddamn *universe*. Don't tell me I don't love her!"

"Yeah, you love her. In your way. Maybe it'll grow and ripen and mature. I don't know. This'll all be over before then. But you didn't prioritize *her* over the universe; you prioritized *yourself*, and your happiness."

His expression softened the tiniest bit. "I need her to be happy," he said quietly.

"That's a pretty unclear statement. Are you saying that you need for her to be happy herself? Or that you need her in order to be happy?"

"Shit." Mike pondered. "Both . . . ?"

"That's great, but it's putting a hell of a lot on her, don't you think? And again—that's not necessarily love. Could be. Could also just be obsession."

He threw his hands in the air. "I don't care anymore! I have to be honest with you. I just don't care, OK? I didn't come here and do all of this to meet God! I didn't do it to learn the mysteries of the universe! I did it—"

"You did it for her. I know. I understand. You did it because you swore you would do anything to have her back. And I'm here to tell you that it doesn't matter. It doesn't matter what you say, what you think, what you feel. It doesn't matter that you're willing to challenge your God. Because in the end, she doesn't love you. And that's it. Nothing you do or say can or will change that. Accept it."

Mike glared at me, then—with defiance—sat on the grass, right on the spot where we buried Spacey, our black Lab/cockapoo mutt. He didn't know he was sitting there, and I didn't tell him.

"Make me," he growled. "Make me accept it. You're God. Make me."

"Stop pouting," I told him. "You're acting like a child."

"Well, so what? You've killed all my friends. You've taken away everything I care about. Why shouldn't I act like a child?"

I held out a hand to him. "Come on. Stand up. Let me tell you my story."

He crossed his arms over his chest. "I don't care about your story."

"Sure you do. You're curious, aren't you? Just a little bit? I made you that way. Let me tell you your first memory."

"What?"

"Your first memory. A neat little trick writers use sometimes, where they have a character think back to the first thing they can remember. You're about to experience yours, mainly because I just came up with it."

And sure enough, despite himself, Mike couldn't help but think of a time when he was four or five years old, a child in kindergarten. There were large blocks in the room, maybe eight inches long each, made of a light wood. They were stacked against one wall and while they had always been there, for some reason on this day, Mike became obsessed with them, to the degree that he could not concentrate during the daily recitation of the alphabet, skipping D and swapping the positions of M and N, when usually he could recite the alphabet backwards without missing a letter. Not today. Today he had eyes only for the tall wall of blocks that beckoned to him, and he swore that—come playtime—he would attack that wall, tear it down, reduce it to its component parts, then build a truly awesome fort for him and friends to use and play in for playtime. Yes, oh, yes, that would happen. Nothing would stop him.

At the onset of playtime, he beelined for the blocks, along

with George and two other friends, the plan already disseminated in hushed whispers during nap-time. They assailed the wall, tore it down, and began construction of a walled-in square, with an opening on one side for ingress and egress. They had decided on a game of Soldiers and Jihadists, with the jihadists holed up in a bunker (that suspiciously and conveniently resembled a square of large wooden blocks) and the soldiers attacking from without, just like on the Saturday morning cartoons they watched every week without fail. As they put the finishing touches on the fort, though, their teacher announced that playtime was over, the allotted time having burned through as they labored to build their fort. Grumbling and complaining, George and the others helped Mike reduce the fort to its components once more and then stacked them neatly against the wall, as though they had never moved, never reconfigured, never been anything more than a stack against the wall.

When Mike's mother came to pick him up that afternoon, the teacher recounted the story, saying, ". . . and I felt so bad for them! They spent all that time putting it together and it looked magnificent—I wish I'd taken a picture—and then they just had to turn around and tear it down. I felt awful."

But although Mike's mother clucked her tongue and joined in on the pity, clutching her offspring close to her in a comforting embrace that Mike secretly felt he was too old for but just as secretly enjoyed, Mike himself felt no disappointment at the day's events. Truthfully, some tiny inkling had opened up deep within him, some whisper of fresh air blowing into a hitherto-sealed cavern of his imagination: He had cared more for the building of the fort, it turned out, than for the playing in it. While George and the others had grumbled as they disassembled the structure, Mike had paid careful attention to the labor, to the way in which what had taken so long to build came down so quickly and so easily. He noted the way the boys stacked the blocks against the wall, and while he said nothing to push them in one direction or another, he realized that by placing *his* blocks in specific spots at specific times, he could force the other boys to place their blocks in a certain pattern, replicating precisely the original configuration of the blocks, pre-fort.

Building things and thinking of building things and tearing them down . . . It was the day Mike became an architect, though he did not know that word, could not spell it, would have mis-pronounced it as "archyteckt" had it been shown to him.

"Yes," Mike whispered. "That's it. That's my first memory." He wiped a tear from his eye. "I had forgotten. Forgot how deep it went. I always told people I loved the aesthetics or the art or the science or the precision, but it goes back—"

"Uh huh, yeah, I know." I stopped him before he could get too lachrymose. There was no point. "Wait. This next bit is going to be very dialogue-intensive. I'm going to switch over to a transcript style. I like that style and it's worked for me in the past. I'm getting tired of coming up with little things for us to do and little reactions for us to have during this conversation. It's one of the problems I've always had with dialogue. Trying to figure out how many times to say 'he said,' how many times to have someone arch an eyebrow. How boring is it to show reactions? How boring is it *not* to show reactions? So let's just switch over for a little while."

LYGA: There. That'll work. As I was saying: It's not a bad little scene. Or moment. There aren't Saturday morning cartoons anymore in my world, but in your world I think there are. So there are. But the whole memory is sort of based on something that happened to me as a kid[121], but I gave it some extra emotional oomph because of your architecture thing.

GRAYSON: Architecture "thing!"

LYGA: But do kids even get nap-time in kindergarten any more? I thought I read somewhere that they don't. Maybe my copyeditor will know[122]. I don't care one way or the other. Even if they don't, I'll probably still leave it in. The fact of the matter is, every story has some sort of anachronism crawling through it, regardless of how assiduously you scan the details. I like the nap-time bit and it's not going to ruin the story for anyone.

GRAYSON: Architecture "thing?"

LYGA: I'll probably leave it in anyway . . . What are you complaining about now?

GRAYSON: It isn't just some architecture

121. The fort was actually a boat and there was no war-play involved. And, obviously, it did not instill in me a desire to become an architect.

122. COPYEDITOR'S NOTE: I have no idea, sorry!

"thing!" It's my life! It's the most important thing in my life other than Phil, and the way things are going these days, I guess it'll probably be the only thing that matters to me, when it's all said and done. So don't minimize it like that.

<u>LYGA:</u> Oh, please. Mike, you care about architecture, but it doesn't matter. None of it's authentic. I did a bunch of research for you, but that's all. I don't know anything about architecture, so you don't, either. You just know the stuff I've made up and picked up here and there.

<u>GRAYSON:</u> I'm . . . I'm not really going to be an architect?

<u>LYGA:</u> You're not "really" anything. I can make you an architect, though. I can make you anything I want. All I have to do is write it and it's true. All I have to do is write it and then they read it and it's true. I mean, I could do this:

CHAPTER 53

Mike looked out at the audience, trying to find his parents and his brother among the hundreds gathered on College Y's New Quad. He didn't want to take long, but he was one of only a bare hundred graduating today from College Y's School of Architecture, so his momentary hesitation would hardly be noticed. He spotted them roughly midway between the stage and the archway leading out of New Quad and selfishly stole a moment of everyone's time to wave to them.

He'd done it. As of today, he was an architect. The diploma in his hand proved it.

"But what would that accomplish?" I asked, dropping out of transcript mode. "Come on. Walk with me."

He finally took my hand, and I helped him to his feet. Together, we walked around to the front of the house, where the long driveway made its unerring, straight-line way to the road. "Still feels weird to see the driveway paved," I told him. "It was a loose stone driveway the whole time I lived here. Shoveling snow from it was a bitch in the winter."

"Why are you doing this to me?" he asked. "Why are you showing me all of this? All I want—"

"—is Phil. I know. Why am I showing you all of this, Mike? Because just once I would like someone to understand, that's why. Do you have any idea what it's like to be God? To be all-powerful and powerless at the same time? God can do anything for anyone anywhere . . . except for himself.

"And that is the torture of being God. That is the dark secret of being God. God lives in hell, Mike. Why should you have it any better?"

Before he could respond, I turned around and pointed to the house. "This is where it all started. I have a memory of being about six or seven years old and wanting to be a writer, but it never really kicked in—I never started writing—until my parents got divorced and I had to move to Fuck-All, USA. But this is the house I lived in when I was in high school, which is when I came up with the idea for Inframan and for *Inframan*. Come on." I gestured for him to follow as I walked down the driveway. He waited a moment, then jogged to catch up.

"Where are we going?"

"The past," I told him. "With each step we take, the neighborhood around us decelerates into history, becoming closer and closer to the way it was when I moved here."

"Oh." A beat. "That's actually sort of cool. I mean, think of how you could observe architecture—"

"Mike, stop it with the architecture shit, OK?" I said wearily. "I'm tired of typing that word."

"Sorry."

"Anyway," I went on as we crested a hill and met the intersection of the street and the main drag through town, "this is what it looked like when I moved here."

Ahead of us was the empty road, two lanes of naked blacktop cutting through farm country. By now, we'd walked far enough that the history deceleration bullshit that I invented[123] had regressed the area to 1980 or so. Or at least, how I remembered it in 1980. A single gas station/convenience store waited across the street, looking suspiciously like the store on the outskirts of the Other City where Mike and his friends had encountered George's father. Other than that, there were just empty fields and—in the distance—corn and soybeans.

"This is what it looked like when I moved here. And this is what I wanted to evoke in *The Astonishing Adventures of Fanboy and Goth Girl*, this sense of isolation and desolation, of utter hopelessness for anyone who dreams of anything more. But somehow the little shitkicking town became bigger than I intended. And as quickly as the second book, there were all sorts of restaurants and even a mall with a movie theater. It still had a small-town feel to it—mainly because the characters kept bitching about how it was a small town—but for me it wasn't what I originally intended. What I intended was this, the way the town was originally. Just barren and empty and regressive and . . . Fuck, there wasn't even a Pizza Hut here until my senior year of high school!"

123. Be honest, though—it would make a kick-ass special effect in a movie, though, right?

I asked him,	"And this is where you came up with me?"	, he asked me.
He waggled a hand in the air in a "so-so" motion.	"Sort of. I came up with the other Mike Grayson, the one from *Inframan*. And when I went to college, I started to write *Inframan*. Got about a third of the way through it, too, and had the whole thing mapped out."	I waggled a hand in the air in a "so-so" motion.
I figured it couldn't hurt to pretend to be interested, so I asked,	"What happened?"	I can't decide if he's genuinely interested or just feigning interest to get on my good side. I created him, but I can't tell, and it's sort of bothersome. But I never give up an opportunity to talk about my writing.
He told me,	"The anxiety of influence happened. You know what that is?"	, I said.
I answered,	"Sort of."	He sounded convincing, but I didn't entirely believe him.
And because he can't just accept "sort of" as an answer, he had to go blathering on and explain it to me.	"It's when you freak out because you figure that what you're trying to accomplish has already been done by someone else."	Which is really boiling it down to the essence, but there you have it.
But I have to admit: I'm curious. A bit.	"Done better, you mean?"	he asked, and of *course* that would be his primary concern. I shrugged.

"Possibly. Maybe. Doesn't really matter. All that matters is that it's been done before, and that makes it less original, less innovative, less attractive. In my case, I had an idea for a book where the characters come to realize they're just characters in a book, and one of them even gets to meet the author. But then there was a comic book called *Animal Man*—"

"Animal Man? Seriously?"

"Just listen. The writer—Grant Morrison—did something similar, where the character realized he was just in a comic book and gets to meet Morrison. And I freaked out, wondering exactly *when* I'd come up with my own take on that. Was it really before I read *Animal Man*? Or was it after, and I was just playing memory tricks on myself? How original was I? Worse: would readers think I was ripping him off?

"And I have to tell you—it's not just the stuff that I *could* have ripped off. It's stuff that I couldn't *possibly* have ripped off. Like a scene in *Inframan* where Angia is eating breakfast with her husband and they're totally not communicating well at all and she's watching him concentrate on eating his eggs. It's similar to a scene in *Madame Bovary* . . . but guess what? When I wrote that scene in *Inframan*, I hadn't read *Madame Bovary* yet! That wouldn't stop people of accusing me of ripping it off, though, so what the hell was I supposed to do about that?"

"I can see that," he said with sympathy. "So you stopped working on *Inframan*."

"Yeah. For years. But you know what? It took me a long time, but I realized that there was nothing original in what Morrison did, either. People have been doing this kind of shit forever, in all kinds of media. Bugs Bunny cartoons where he looks into the camera or redraws the action. David Addison talks to the audience in *Moonlighting*. Old Justice League comics where Cary Bates or Elliot Maggin meet the superheroes they write about. John Barth's novels. Stephen King's *Dark Tower* series. All of it.[124] It's not the idea. It's the execution. It's all in *how* you do it. Hell," I laughed, "now I'm most worried people will think I'm ripping *myself* off because I just did something similar to all of this in *Mangaman*, my first graphic novel."[125]

Mike stared at me in disbelief. "You . . . You did this to someone else? You put someone *else* through this?"

"Well . . . Sort of. It was played for fun there."

"Fun! For fun! Are you insane?"

"~~Jury's still out on that one. Ouch. Cliche. I need to fix that in the revision process.~~ Depends on who you ask. And when. My point is, when we create art, we run the risk of overlapping those who come before us. Or even after us. Shit, when I came up with *Inframan*, I had an idea for a dramatic scene at the end where Mike Grayson dies, but the Electrostatic Man shocks him back to life with his electrical powers. And you know what? Ten fucking years later, the fucking *X-Files* did the same fucking thing. *After* I came up with it, but before I could publish it. So fuck it. That book will never come out."

"You curse a lot," Mike said.

"Yeah, I know. My editors always want me to tone it down, but I'm not doing it this time. Fuck it. Fuck fuck fuckity fuck-fuck. Annnnnd *fuck*."

I pointed to the west, towards the Hampstead town line and as we walked, the scene melted around us and we were suddenly in my senior year dorm at Yale. A massive Yale-issue desk with my old Macintosh Classic sitting atop it. Curtains that I never opened.

124. Which came after I thought of *Inframan* as well, but executed the "author meets his characters" trope so masterfully that I all but despaired of ever doing it myself. Clearly, I got over it.

125. Published in Fall 2011 by Houghton Mifflin Books for Children and available at bookstores and comic book stores everywhere!

Two doors—one led to the hallway and one led to an emergency exit that I never needed and never explored, lest I set off the alarm.

Mike gaped, twisting and turning to look around, as if the road from Hampstead would be right behind us instead of a closed door that led, when opened, to the stairwell landing directly across which lay the rest of my senior suite, perpendicular to which stood the door to the common bathroom.

"Where—" he said.

"My point—" I ignored him for now "—is that we all suffer the anxiety of influence. It's best just to get over it and move ahead."

"All of us?" Momentarily distracted from his new surroundings, Mike leaned close to me. "All of us? What about the ones who aren't writers?"

"You create things, Mike. Buildings. You're just as sensitive to—"

"What about my buildings? The elevator building? The underwater room? They're *mine*."

"Technically, they're mine. But the elevator building was inspired by the hotel in Dubai that transforms."

"No!"

"Yeah, sorry. I know you want to think you invented it, but you didn't. I heard about it and when I was trying to come up with something for you to obsess about, I just made it vertical instead of horizontal. And then I had a total Purple Cow Moment[126] because

126. A theory propounded by comic book writer Alan Moore, who claims that the variety of human experience combined with the sheer plethora of available information means that anything you can imagine can be supported by some sort of evidence. The example he uses: Say you decide one day that the universe was created by a purple cow. If you went and researched, you would find examples and anecdotes throughout history related to purple cows. Because someone somewhere thought of purple cows and it was written down. You just have to look for it and it'll be there, supporting your belief.

I read about this guy named Rem Koolhaas[127] who designed a home in France with a glass room that goes up and down like an elevator. It's in Bourdeaux and he built it for a disabled homeowner. So suddenly it was real, even though I have no idea how your particular version would work. It probably wouldn't."

"I could make it work," he grumbled.

"Mike. Please. You're not a fucking architect. Everything you know about architecture came out of a copy of *Architecture for Dummies* I got from a used bookstore."

He shook his head vehemently. "No. No. This isn't right. This is all wrong. Why are you doing this to me? Why are you torturing me? Nothing's real? Nothing at all? What about the underwater hotel?"

"Well, I'm not sure about that one, to be honest with you. It might actually be *sui generis*, though I doubt it. I sort of came up with it on my own one night, joking around with someone. And then I forgot about it until she mentioned it again a month later and I realized that I needed to put it in the book. It just sort of fit."[128]

"That's how you create the universe? You don't have a masterplan, you just come up with stuff and if it 'sort of fits' you use it?"

He was angry, fuming, in fact, going red in the face in a way I never have, really. One more difference between him and me.

"Well . . . sure. That's how everything is created, really. No one wants to admit it, but . . . It's like the Beatles song: 'While My Guitar Gently Weeps.'"

"The who?"

127. Doesn't that last name seem like it should be pronounced "cool house?" How fucking awesome a name is that for an architect? You can't make this shit up.

128. And somewhere between then and now, someone actually built a fucking underwater home in Dubai. Which is *not* the same thing as Mike's idea, but I just can't get into all of that right now. Goddamn reality, messing up a good story . . .

"Not The Who. The Beatles."

"I mean—who are the Beatles?"

I stared at him for a moment and then I remembered: I had decided that in his world, the Beatles had never formed. They'd remained the Quarrymen instead[129], so in this universe, poor Ringo Starr probably never had much of a career.

"Never mind. They're a rock band and they recorded a song called 'While My Guitar Gently Weeps.' The guy who wrote it—George Harrison—was fascinated by the *I Ching* and Eastern philosophy in general. See, Eastern philosophy teaches that there's no such thing as coincidence, that events occur because they are interconnected and meant to. I'm not sure I believe in that in the real world, but in your world, in the fictional universe . . . Man, it happens all the time!

"So, there's old George Harrison, at his parents' house, having just read the *I Ching*, and he decides that he will write a song based on whatever words he happens to see in a random book. He picks up a book, opens it, and sees the words 'gently weeps.' Bang.[130] Next thing you know, you've got this amazing song that *Rolling Stone* ranked #135 out of the 500 greatest of all time and seventh on the list of the 100 greatest guitar songs of all time. More than thirty cover versions. A really terrific piece of musical art, and it all came about because of coincidence. So, y'know, you ask me if that's how I create the universe, and, yeah, my answer is, 'Fuck, yeah.'

"Architecture became this really convenient metaphor

129. You may remember (but probably don't at this point) that DJ Tea at the party in Chapter 12 played a couple of Quarrymen songs.

130. I wrote that "Bang" roughly eight years before I actually wrote and published a book titled *Bang*. So, it's not a clever in-joke. Unless you think it is, in which case . . . it is!

throughout the book. I mean, we're talking about a discipline that has to do with building, with revising, with—literally—stories. It was a metaphor for the process I was going through, just waiting there for me. Remember when you sat with your professor? And talked about the underwater hotel?"

He nodded miserably.

"The underwater hotel . . . It was going to be just a mention, a little detail blip for readers, a handhold for them to cling to when understanding you," I said, "but then something really weird and sort of magical and serendipitous happened, just like that book falling open to the words 'gently weeps' for George Harrison. That was so big, man. When I wrote that. It was all about aspiration and inspiration. And I realized I was writing about myself, in a way. There were people—well, one person in particular—who was like, 'You shouldn't be writing this crazy book, this *Unedited*. It's too big and it's too ambitious. Who do you think you are to try something like that? What makes *you* so great?' Nice, huh? And you know, that's the sort of comment I used to get when I was trying to break into comic books and into publishing—'Don't even try this, kid. It's too much for you.'"

"'You're not Diller and Scofidio. And you're sure as hell not Frank Lloyd Wright,'" Mike mumbled.

"Right! Exactly! Goddamn!" I paced furiously. "I mean, how the fuck do *they* know? All your professor saw was a couple of sketches in your sketchbook. And when I was trying to break in, all those editors saw were a few pages of my writing. How the fuck do they know? You said that to your professor, remember?"

"'How do you know that? Maybe I am,'" he self-quoted.

"Yeah. Gave you that line because I once pitched a comic book idea to someone as 'Imagine Jack Kirby working on *Watchmen*.' And the response I got was 'Don't compare yourself to those guys. You aren't them.' And I wish . . . I wish I'd said what *you* said. That's why I gave it to you. I wish I'd said it, just once in my life."

"But it came from Phil," he told me. "You say you gave me the line, but it was only thinking of Phil that—"

"Ah, shit." Well, this is embarrassing. Fuck. Would any of you readers have even noticed? Anyway . . . "That's right. See, originally, you just said the line. But when I was revising, one of the problems with the book was that people were saying that Phil was a cipher. They couldn't figure out why you were so in love with her. So when I revised, I had her doing some cool shit—the plays, stuff like that—and also made her bad-ass enough to inspire you to stand up for yourself."

"But—"

"Anyway, look, now I'm all pissed off because this little digression has fucked up the flow of the conversation. So I'm going to take it back to 'Yeah':"

"Yeah. Gave you that line because I wish I'd said it, just once in my life. Wish I'd had the courage just once. But I didn't, so I gave you the courage, Mike."

He stared at me. "Do I thank you for that?"

Thank me? "Why start now? Look, my point is this: The architecture stuff started out as just little details for the reader and then became more important to me. And especially that underwater hotel. Something amazing happened there. Some truly amazing serendipity. Which is that I met this guy named Chris Cummings who actually designs aquariums—the big ones, not the ones for, like, tropical fish at home—for a living. So I sat down with him and asked him all sorts of questions, and suddenly 'your' idea became more important. So, thanks for that, Chris. I appreciate the time you spent with me talking about that stuff."

"Hey!" He waved a hand in front of my face. "Talk to *me*,

not . . . not some *reader*. Where are we? What are we doing here?"

"Oh. Right. This is my senior dorm at Yale. This is where I actually wrote about a hundred pages of *Inframan* and planned out my other books—*Redesigning You* and *His Darkness* and *American Sun* and all the others." I passed a hand over my face. "Jesus. I had this idea . . . I was going to take you on a tour of everywhere I lived, talking about the status of this book and of *Inframan* at each stop. Like how I decided George drank Stella Artois because when I was working on that part of the book, I lived near a bar with a big Stella Artois sign out front and I walked past it every day. But that just sounds so boring now. I don't want to write it, you don't want to hear it, and I don't think readers want to read it. So, look, let's cut to the core, OK?"

"And the core is . . . ?" He teetered between giving a shit and wanting to rip my head off.

I shrugged, probably the one thing guaranteed to piss him off even more. "The core is that Inframan always wins, Mike. I never finished *Inframan*. I failed. I worked on it in college, suffered the anxiety of influence, and stopped. Tried to get back into it sporadically over the years, but never could. And then on August 5, 2005, that version of me died and the book went away. Or at least I thought it did.

"Because then something happened that spawned *this* book, the one you're in right now. A new Mike Grayson. The same author, but different. Different world, similar problems. Different book, but . . . Somehow the same. A book that didn't shrink from the anxiety of influence, but reveled in it. Even there, though, he won. Because no one was willing to publish this thing. It took ten goddamn years. More failure."

He wasn't paying attention anymore, though. Earlier phrases had caught his attention, his imagination.

"Why did you come back to the book?" he asked. "Why did you reconfigure it into . . ." He gestured around us. ". . . this? What happened? What made you return to it?"

I smiled at him. "I lost her, Mike."

"Who?" he asked, but he knew. He knew and yet he asked anyway.

"I lost Phil," I told him, in a nice, suitably dramatic moment to break a chapter.

CHAPTER 48

"Come on, Mike," I told him, sitting at my old desk chair. My Mac Classic still sat on the desk, booted up and open to my senior essay[131] in Microsoft Word. I idly pushed the mouse, marveling at how slow and staid it seemed compared to the mouse on the iMac I'm using to write this book now.

"Come on," I said. "Don't tell me you didn't see that coming. That's the whole fucking point of the book: Losing love. You did. Gayl did. George did. Joe Roberts did. Didn't you think—on some level—that it was about me?"

"Phil . . ." His face took on the aspect of a man who's just seen proof of alien life or werewolves. He felt around for something to cling to, found the upright bar of the bunk bed[132] and gripped it for dear life. "You have a Phil. And you lost her."

And he thought, then, not just of my loss. But of his

131. "Transparent Eyeballs and Similar Dismemberments: The Body Paradox in Early American Literature"

132. I lived alone my senior year, but the room had originally been intended to be a double, hence the bunk.

own. Of losing Phil, yes, but also of losing George, best friend George, faithful George. George, whose only sin had been loyalty. Whose only crime had been steadfastness. George was gone now, lost to the whims of a mad god, Mike thought. Lost like the love gone from the Other City, like the love slowly leaving the universe.

"Let's be honest here, Mike," I told him. "It's you and me now. No bullshit, OK? We didn't 'lose' our Phils; we gave them away. Better put, we discarded them. Let me tell you what happened: I fell in love. I didn't realize it, but it happened. It sneaked up on me at a time in my life when the idea of being in love was the most frightening thing I could imagine, so I denied it and then I left her before it could become real to me. Oh, I had my reasons, reasons that had nothing to do with being in love. Bullshit reasons. Shit my mind made up to justify what I was doing, which was basically running like hell, like a coward. It made sense at the time, but later it didn't. And I wanted her back. She was . . . She was . . ."

"What?"

If God can be helpless (and I assure you—He can), I shrugged helplessly. "My only love, like yours. Does this sound familiar, Mike?"

He slowly lowered himself onto the bed, sitting on the edge of the blue-and-white stripped afghan that my great-grandmother knitted for me when she learned I was going to Yale.[133]

"It's what happened to me and Phil," he said, his voice that of someone who's barely avoided a fatal accident.[134]

"Well, yeah, it's what happened to you and Phil before you

133. I still have it.

134. Such as, perhaps, running into the street to chase a misdirected toy and being saved by the appropriate application of car brakes.

went and started mucking around with the fundamental structure of the story-slash-universe."

"You gave me that power!" He pulled himself up off the bed and loomed over me in what I assume was intended to be threatening. "You put it in my hands! What was I supposed to do with it?"

I sighed and fiddled with the old early-nineties-era mouse some more. "Isn't this always the way? You know, when God created Man, he got criticism. Everything was hunky-dory at first and everyone was happy, but then as soon as things started to go wrong, what happened? I'll tell you exactly what happened: Adam turned around and said to God, 'Hey, man, everything's turned to shit and it's all because of this woman that *you* gave me!' Check your fucking Bible—it's true.

"So I guess I should have expected to have criticism thrown my way for relatively innocent things, or things done with the best of intentions."

"Best of intentions?" He spun away from me, paced the length of the tiny room, then came back. "You wrecked my life with the best of intentions? Are you kidding me? Is this shit for real?"

"No, Mike," I said quietly. "This shit is not for real; it's for fiction."

"Stop that!" he yelled, and pounded a fist on the top bunk, then did it again. "Stop talking in riddles and . . . and . . . and . . ."

"Aphorisms, is the word you're looking for."

"Right! Aphorisms! Stop talking in aphorisms!" He kicked at the lower bunk, punched the upper, kicking and punching until he was out of breath and collapsed on the floor, leaning against the bed, gasping for breath.

"I don't even know what an aphorism is," he moaned.

"Doesn't matter. People will look it up[135]." I was distracted during his display of rage by my senior essay on the tiny, 9-inch black and white Mac Classic screen in front of me. I remembered, suddenly, calling Jenifer at beyond midnight to tell her I was using the word "apotheotic" in conjunction with Edgar Allan Poe's construction of libraries.[136]

"Why did you do this to me?" he whispered, now looking up at me, no longer looming, no longer threatening, now just another supplicant praying to God. "I get that you lost your Phil, but why did I have to lose mine?"

And for once, I decided, God would actually answer. Clearly. Decisively. None of these "signs and portents" that must be interpreted and divined. No, I was just going to answer the question.

"I thought of *Inframan* for years," I told him. "I wrote the first third of the book in this very chair, with this very computer. It's weird—I remember writing it. I have such powerful, detailed memories of it."

"Why is that weird? Shouldn't you?"

"No. Not always. When I was a kid—freshman year of high school—we read the poem 'Richard Cory' by Edwin Arlington Robinson. We had to write an essay about it. The strange thing is this: I remember getting back my essay, with an A on it. It was a pretty good essay and it referenced Freddie Prinze, who was a famous comedian in my world, a guy who killed himself

135. No. Seriously. Go look it up if you need to.

136. In the rarefied atmosphere of college, this seemed somehow romantic, important, and powerful all at once. I was an English geek . . . And Jenifer was a smarter English geek and I desperately wanted to kiss her, but never did.

at the height of his success.[137] I drew a pretty elegant parallel between Richard Cory and Freddie Prinze, and my teacher was impressed by it. And you know something? She was right to be impressed. I was thirteen fucking years old and drawing connections between poetry and real world recent events.

"Here's the thing, though, Mike: To this day, I have no fucking clue where I got Freddie Prinze. I had to ask my mother who he was when I read back my own essay. I don't even remember writing the essay. When I read the essay at the time, I didn't remember writing it *then*. It was like someone else had done it."

I grinned at him.

"And I think that's when I decided that someone else had done it, someone else living inside me, a creature named Inframan. Alan Moore was still years away from using the name for a comic book character, so I didn't rip that off. For me, it was a deliberate inversion of the Superman/Übermensch trope—instead of the 'over-man,' I was creating the 'under-man,' an insidious force that lived beneath my own consciousness. And then it occurred to me to write a book about the struggle between the two of us, but I never finished it."

"I know this stuff already," he said dully.

"Well, here's the thing: When I realized I would never get Phil back, I had to do something. I wanted to throw myself into work in order to dull the pain, but I had already finished one book and it was too soon to start on the next one on my schedule. I didn't know what to do with myself. I was just wallowing. And then I

137. Not Freddie Prinze Jr., dear reader, but his father, famous for playing the part of "Chico" in the seventies sitcom *Chico and the Man*, which was probably about as politically incorrect as you're imagining. Anyway, it was Prinze *pere* who committed suicide. Junior is still alive and well. (Well, at least at the moment I'm writing this footnote, he's alive and well. I'm not responsible for what happens after the book is published.)

went to a conference and ended up sitting in an airport in Nashville, Tennessee. I had just been on a panel at the conference and it had gone . . . eh." I waggled my hand for him. "I had a funny line I'd rehearsed, but it fell flat when I actually said it. I was sort of depressed, sitting there in the airport, and I decided that the solution to Phil, to my depression, everything was to move on to my next book. But at the time, I was planning to write a book titled *Sex + Violence*, about a kid accused of rape. And I just couldn't bring myself to work on it. I thought about maybe writing something other than a novel, like a play or a comic book. Or a movie."

Mike traced a dent in the metal frame of the bunk bed. But I knew he was listening.

"I realized that it had to be a book," I went on. "Books are the only way to really get into a character's head and experience their pain. You know, there are movies about heartbreak, but here's the thing: Their time is contracted. You can't do a movie that really exposes the endless, lingering pain of heartache. Movies make it seem like a dinner with friends, some decent dialogue, and a quick montage will make everything better, all in a sub-two-hour running time, as long as there's a kicky soundtrack, preferably by some up-and-coming band. Or a classic rock number. But real heartbreak is more intense than that. Real heartbreak will make you want to end the world and rewrite the world. Real heartbreak will make you want to confront God and take him to account for the world you live in."

He looked up at me at last.

"And that's OK. Yes, Mike. Yes, I wanted to do exactly what you've done: Go and find God and shake him by the neck and demand that that fucker tell me why he'd made the world the way it was, why he'd made me the way I was, why he'd made Phil the way she was. But that wasn't an option for me."

"So you made me," he said slowly.

"In my world, Mike, we can't edit reality. It's like a law of physics, like the laws that prevent us from creating matter or energy. But we *can* create art. I sat there in that airport, waiting for a delayed flight, and I thought about writing a book that . . ." I sighed. Hesitated. This next part was tough to admit. I had written it already—it was just a screen down on my computer—but actually linking it into the running text would make it real. And I didn't want to make it real. Not yet.

"I didn't have anyone I could talk to. Mainly because I'd already talked to everyone, told them so much, told them the same things over and over. They were all tired of it, tired of my endless 'what-ifs,' but I couldn't stop talking, couldn't stop dreaming and hoping. I realized that I was trying to edit my own life. Revising. 'What if Character A said this instead of that . . .' But we weren't characters, my Phil and I. We were real people. But that didn't stop me from torturing myself over and over with the thoughts. It's the only thing my brain knew how to do—I'd trained it my whole life to think in terms of editing and revising stories, and now it was trying to do that to real life.

"Somehow, it seemed to come together. All of these disparate elements from my life. They joined together with the old ideas from *Inframan* to make you. You love Phil. You lose Phil. One letter separates those ideas, Mike. In your world, the difference between loving and losing is a typo. It's simple. In fiction, it's simple to break and simple to fix. It's so much more complicated in my world. You think you have it bad? Think of us poor saps in the Realm Above.

"Anyway, I had always liked the idea of writing a book that was out of order, a book that started partway in, then jumped around, where chapters would be out of order. And I started thinking about that, started thinking about someone who could do that from within a book, someone who could edit from the inside. Because that, I realized, was what I was trying to do with my own life: I was always looking back at e-mails she'd sent me, things she'd said to me, things I'd said to her . . . Always thinking, 'If I had done/said *this* instead of *that,* then maybe she would have reacted *this* way instead of *that* way' and blah blah blah. It would be a perfect world. We would be together. I kept trying to read her tea leaves. Kept replaying conversations over and over in my head, poring over her e-mails and text messages, trying to find a logic to it all, trying to figure out when her character fell out of love with my character. But we weren't characters. And none of it made any sense. And, truthfully, that drove me a little bit crazy.

"So I decided to make it a story, a novel. It would be a big, ugly complicated thing, like love, like romance, like life. But here's the thing: Real life is messy. Complex. It doesn't make sense. The best we can do on the page is mimic that, but if you try to be too random, people get bored or get annoyed. So I needed some sort of force to show up and move things along, and that ended up being my old frenemy Inframan.

"So Phil started out as one woman in particular. One experience. And something happened in the writing. Despite my notes and my outlines and my planning, she began to merge with other women. So even though she's meant to represent/stand in for one woman in my life, she's somehow become *all* the women in my life, even though she doesn't represent them." I clucked my tongue and leaned back in my chair. It had been twenty years since I'd leaned back in this chair, but it felt like twenty seconds had passed. "Is there a literary term for that? There should be. Maybe it's reverse synecdoche."[138]

138. If there *is* a term for it, you'd think I would know it. Or take the time to look it up. But at this point, I honestly can't be bothered

Mike nodded, thinking. And then he went and did it: He stabbed into the heart of my shame. "Are you just doing this so that your version of Phil will read it and realize how much you love her and want you back?"

Damn. Why did I write that? Why did I let him say that?

"That would be pretty pathetic," I told him, my tone light at first, but then growing in anger. "Are you calling your God pathetic? Do you have any idea what I could do to you?"

"I'm sorry," he whispered.

"Sorry?" I stood from the chair and now it was my turn to loom over him. "Do you want me to make your Phil a lesbian? Or dead? Or have her forget you ever existed? Do you want me to make *you* forget *she* ever existed?"

His eyes lit with the rarest of horrors and he scrambled away from me like a crab. "No!" he cried. "No! I'm sorry. I'm sorry I said that."

I studied him, my Mike Grayson, my main character, my creation. "It's OK, Mike. I won't do any of those things. Because the truth? The truth is that when I sat down to start this book, yeah, there was a part of me hoping that she'd read it and come to understand how much I loved her. You know, we can tell people we love them, but they don't always get the depth of it. The power of it. Here's the thing: Actions speak louder than words. It's a cliché because it's true. I've never been very good at actions. But I'm fairly good with words. So I figured I'd give it a try.

"In the end, I just wanted one more conversation with her, one more chance to ask her so many questions. Not necessarily even in the hopes that I could make her change her mind. More in the hopes that something would come out of that conversation that would make me feel better, something that would make it all make sense to me, something that could help me deal with it."

"I understand that," he said, curled in the corner formed between my dresser and the far wall. "All I wanted was one last chance, too." He cleared his throat. "That should be present tense, right? All I *want* is one last chance. Please. I won't mess it up this time."

"But here's the thing, Mike. Here's the funny thing: I originally came up with the idea for this book because I wanted her back. But then you know what happened? Do you?"

He shook his head.

And I smiled. Truthfully, it was the first honest, happy smile in the whole damn book. "I met someone else. And that's the answer, Mike. That's the answer to your heartbreak and your heartache: You meet someone else. You don't re-design the universe to bring your lost love back. You give up. You give up on blue-haired Phil, you give up on the history-made sheets, and you move on with your life. That's how it works.

"At first, I thought writing this book would help me get through things. And then—before I even started the actual writing, when I was still in the plotting stage—I met someone new and amazing and wonderful, and suddenly that wasn't necessary anymore. But I wrote it anyway because I thought that maybe it would help kids who are going through losing their first loves. You know? Sort of show them that no one is worth all that angst. Or at least that there's a way to get through to the other side. And now . . ."

"Now, what? What?"

"I don't know. I've come all this way—a couple hundred thousand words—and I don't know anymore. I don't know what the point is."

"So you're saying this book you're writing, the whole story of my existence, my life—you're saying it's all pointless? That you're just going through the motions?"

"Maybe. What if I am? So what? If the One Bookers have their way, none of my words will be mine anymore anyway."

"There are One Bookers in your world, too?"

"Well, yeah, but . . . I sort of gave the notion of the One Book a doomsday-ish, cult-ish kind of flavor in your world. A zealotry. It's not entirely that way in my world. It's more a theoretical construct. But I hate it, man. I really do. This idea that texts are just interchangeable parts of some kind of apotheotic[139] One Book. There should be lines between books. Texts aren't just part of some big conglomerate. If you jam them all together like that, if you access them randomly and across the breadth of the available books without restraint, then you lose the individuality. And you end up with juxtapositions and contexts that may or may not be valid."

"Who decides what's valid?"

"Man, that's a question people have been asking for ages. The answer is: It depends. Sometimes it's the reader. Sometimes it's the author. But combining everything into One Book isn't the solution. Authors lose a lot of control when they put their books out into the public, and we accept that. But for fuck's sake—we shouldn't lose *all* control!"

"I don't care about any of that." He found the courage and the strength to stand up. "If you don't have a point anymore, then just let me have Phil back. End the book with the two of us together."

I shook my head. "Weren't you listening to me? That's not the point at all. You move on. You meet someone else."

"But I don't want to meet someone else. I want her."

"What is 'her,' though, Mike? Really. Do you want

139. Holy shit! I really love that word, don't I?

Phil-as-Phil or does she just represent something for you? If you go back and look at the whole of your relationship, you see that it's all very centered on you. Phil has little to no agency, which is super-un-feminist of me, I admit. But she had a very specific function in the story. In my defense, you *all* have very specific functions and you bump up against those limitations all the time. None of you have agency, really. I'm controlling the whole goddamn thing. You all exist to make a point. And I'm a random straight, white dude writing a book that is deliberately solipsistic and stridently unempathetic. Not because I think straight white dudes are awesome, but just because . . . If you're writing a book designed to show people what it's like inside your brain when you write, you have to limit yourself to what's inside your brain. The only character in the book who is fully realized and actually matters is *me*.

"Everyone else was a tough balancing act—like, you needed to be selfish, but at the same time, I had to make Phil cool enough that readers wouldn't reject your devotion to her. But Phil isn't really a person. She's a secondary character in the novel, man. She has blue hair because I wanted her to stand out. You objectify the living hell out of her because that's all you're capable of doing. It's all I gave you. It's no wonder your relationship fell apart: Her belief in you isn't enough. Her faith isn't enough. What did you guys have in common, anyway, besides, as one early reader put it, 'Lots of great fucking?'"

"It was more than that," he muttered.

"Yeah, but hey—about all of that fucking . . . Did you ever stop to wonder what was going on there? Like, maybe it wasn't all that great for her?"

"No. She said . . ." He stopped. Thought. Remembered.

"Right. She never said anything. She said sex with *him* wasn't good, but she never told you that sex with you *was* good."

"But she kept—"

"Of course she kept fucking you. But that doesn't mean it was mind-blowing sexcapades for her, dude. People have sex for all kinds of reasons. Maybe it was her way of being close to you. Or maybe she wanted to have sex over and over and over because she was trying to figure it out, trying to get it right. This is stuff I would have fed into the book in-line if I'd actually been trying to build you guys like traditional characters."

"This is all . . ." He shook his head savagely. "I know what I know, okay? Phil loved me. I love her. And you can ask for the reasons and you can point out the problems, but at the end of the day, that stuff's all bullshit. It's just bullshit. I don't have to have, like, a fucking spreadsheet of reasons to be in love with her. I just—"

"Right. You want her so badly that you . . . Look, did you ever think of maybe just trying to be cool to her? Or just talking to her? No, you just went ahead and tried to realign the fundamental nature of the universe in order to get her back."

"That's how much I love her," he said, not in the least bit defensive. Just matter-of-fact.

"Yeah. I know. I made you that way. A bit obsessive. Sorry. But look, why don't I do something for you? Why don't I show you the moment where everything could have changed?"

Mike froze.

"I know what you're thinking, Mike, and no—this isn't a joke or a scam. There really was an edit point—"

"An edit point?"

"That's what I called the moments in the story where I had you edit reality. I had to structure the story a specific way to make it work. Like early on, when you were in bed with Phil and then suddenly ended up on George's porch, talking to him.

That was me. I broke the chapter there because I needed you there at that moment in time because I was going to be referring back to it a lot."

He remembered, then, that sudden jump.[140]

"You've been controlling this all along," he said with miserable realization.

"Well, duh. I'm the author. Of course. It was easy, too. You had already been thinking of George when you were with Phil, so the reader was susceptible to making that leap in the next chapter to George's house. Cool, huh?"

"Yeah, real cool." He doesn't sound convinced.

"Buck up, Mike. Let me show you that edit point."[141]

He perked up. "Can I fix it this time? Will you let me?"

"No. That part's done and over with. But look at it this way: I promise you no chocolate syrup this time."

He nodded slowly, resigned. "OK, so what do I do?"

"Nothing. I'll do all the work. We're going to have a flashback to earlier in the book. I hate flashbacks, by the way. They're not real. They don't exist in real life. At least, not in convenient, discrete moments like in fiction. In real life, they're just memories and they flit and fly around us and through us all the time. Most of the time they're not even relevant to what's at hand. We just remember random shit for no reason and then it flies away just as quickly as it flew in. But in fiction . . . Fuck, in fiction, it's like every fucking character remembers all the important relevant stuff just when it works best for the author. Convenient, huh?"

"Can we go now?" he asked.

"Go? We're there. Here. Whichever."

140. It happens from page 24 to page 25.

141. Where did that come from? I've never said "buck up" in my life! Not even ironically.

UNEDITED

"I always thought it would be cool if flashbacks worked like this. Instead of just summarizing the moment, actually relive it. I guess that's similar to film, in some respects, but why not? It's sort of cool, I think."

"Someone has to be. So, check it out: Here's the moment where things could have changed. Right here."

"She wanted me to read to her . . ."

"You're really impressed with yourself, aren't you?"

"Yeah. She was ready. She was receptive. You could have read to her and then told her you loved her and it would have all worked out. And for your own reasons—creeped out by the paternity of it, comparing yourself to *him*—you couldn't do it. You wouldn't do it. So you lost her. Right there. Right here."

song is still strong) that we
other upon hearing Phil's mo
myself a final, half-hearted gr
ger-stroke down her naked flan
irt, watching as Phil shakes a s
her dress (I have decided in th
g) trumps watching her undre
hing, of shielding herself from
new meaning when I know tha
against, shielded against, tha
elf almost any time I want.
," she says, flinging herself on
What?

"*Read* to me." She curls up on the bed a
wall-mounted shelf I have noticed several times
books: *The Wind in the Willows*, A. A. Milne, Be
all the other old friends left behind in the old
of childhood when we packed our innocence o
moved to the new town of Growing Up. A sud
me: Phil dated *him* almost from Day One, hol
him from her second week in town until tw
junior prom. The terror is such: Was this *his*

Mike's voice was nothing more than a whisper. Well, words on a page and a whisper: "You mean, I could have done it? I could have actually fixed everything?"

"Well, maybe. I thought long and hard about that. I decided that it was a cheat not to have there be a way to do it. And I was rooting for you, man, I really was. But you just couldn't do it."

"You weren't rooting for me. You knew how it would end all along."

"Well, yeah, that's true, too. But let me tell you something, Mike: There's a problem with this scenario. Even with what I've just shown you."

"What's that?"

"You didn't love her. Not then. Not yet. You didn't love her until she was gone. And that's tragic and sad and stupid. But the only time you could have won her over was a time when you didn't really, truly *need* to win her over. And then there's the other problem with this solution. And as Alvina put it: 'And, frankly, at the end when Barry Lyga points out the moment that could have changed things . . . well, although I liked the fact that BL put in a solution, the truth is, I just don't believe that anything could have changed things—the timing just wasn't right for them.' And maybe she was right. She also pointed out that your ability to control her could be seen as misogynistic. Personally, I think it's more anti-humanist or anti-individualist because you were able to control *everyone*, including Phil's old/new boyfriend. But hey—you say potato, I say spud. Maybe it would have worked, maybe it wouldn't. Beats me."

He stomped his foot, as close to a temper tantrum as his self-respect would allow. "Is this all just laughs to you? You keep saying it's my responsibility, but you created all of it. You made me, you made her, you made me lose her—"

"Look at it this way," I said to him. "Take comfort in this: it's not like you ever really loved her. You just think you did. You're nineteen. You don't know what real love is yet."

He bristled and actually—I give him credit for this—took

a step towards me, an act of aggression in the face of unrelenting power that I didn't expect until I wrote it. "I do so love her! I love her more than myself. More than the universe."

"Yeah, that's not love, Mike. That's obsession. There's a difference. You're too young. Kids don't know what love is."

He flung his hands in the air. "We can know what love is. It's adults who have forgotten, so they cling to their poor substitute and yell at kids who dare to live with real love. Pure love. Love without compromise or distraction. Hell, when you're a kid you've got all the energy and all the free time in the world. You'll never have the chance to devote more to love ever again in your life."

I sighed. "Nice. Nice speech."

"Thanks."

"Yeah, that's not even your dialogue. I lifted it from my second book.[142]"

"Oh, come on! That's not fair!"

He said nothing after that and we stood in silence for a few moments, each of us thinking. I knew what he was thinking, of course, but dialogue will do a better job explaining it:

"Could you . . ." he said after a moment's hesitation, "could you make me a *different* way? Change me so that I don't want her anymore?"

It was a decent enough idea and sure, I had the power to do it. But . . .

"No. That would . . . Look, that would go against the reader's expectations, OK? The reader is invested in your story because you're a kid who loves a girl so much that you broke through the ends of the universe and challenged God for her. I can't

142. *Boy Toy*, published in 2007 by Houghton Mifflin Books for Children. The quotation in question comes on page 386.

just have you change your mind at this point. The whole story would fall apart."

"It's not a story! It's my life."

"They're the same thing."

"Fine, then it's my life story, but—"

"Life story?" I laughed at the absurdity of it, but also because I was finally using a line I'd written early in the planning days of the novel: "There's no such thing as a life story. Life isn't a story. Stories can be fixed and modified and changed and revised. Life is unedited."

Big tears rolled down his face and his shoulders—his entire being—slumped in the most abject defeat I've ever seen. "I've had enough, OK? I've had enough." He dropped to his knees and clasped his hands before him, his face tilted to look up at me in the familiar penitent's pose. "I am down on my knees, begging you, praying to you, please: Give me back Phil. Please, Almighty God. Please."

"Flattery doesn't do it, Mike. I can't give Phil back to you. It's just not that easy. Things have gotten too complicated."

"You met someone new," he pointed out, scrambling and desperate. "You got a happy ending. Why can't I have one, too?"

"Who says it was happy? We're not even together anymore. It was absolutely insane—the craziest breakup in my life. Holy shit." I shivered. "I don't even like thinking about it."

"Jesus!" he exclaimed, throwing his hands in the air in complete defeat. "God! Does *anyone* fall in love anymore? Is DHS right? Is love disappearing from the entire friggin' universe?"

"Stop being so melodramatic. Love's not going anywhere. Though, you know, it feels like it when the person you love doesn't love you anymore. Anyway, my kind of happy ending wouldn't work for you. I was able to move on from Phil. You can't. You're incapable. I'm not sure how I could give you a happy ending, if you want to know the truth. Not without wrecking the whole construct of the story. If I've done my job, at this point everyone wants you to end up with Phil. But you shouldn't, Mike. You really shouldn't. It would be a cop out. But right now, everyone wants that. They want me to find a way around the ending that Inframan revealed."

"The one where I'm in a room, alone." Still on his knees, but now slumped, staring at my feet.

"Yeah. That one. Endings are tricky motherfuckers. People are rarely happy with my endings, for example. People like everything tied up in a neat package; people like the kiss. They like the ride into the sunset. But I don't seem to be able to give them that. I don't know why. It's not that I have something *against* that sort of ending. I just can't make them work for me in my own books. They feel like cop-outs somehow. Here's something Scott Westerfeld said after reading one of my novels:

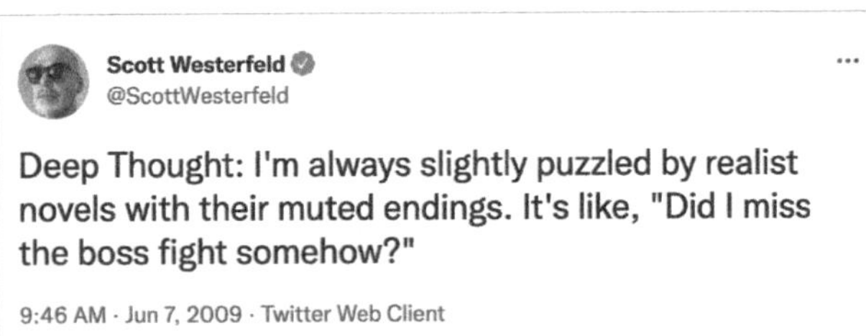

Scott Westerfeld
@ScottWesterfeld
Deep Thought: I'm always slightly puzzled by realist novels with their muted endings. It's like, "Did I miss the boss fight somehow?"
9:46 AM · Jun 7, 2009 · Twitter Web Client

"So, you see? Endings are problematic for me. I never do a good job with them. I'm always happy with them, but other people aren't. It comes down to this: I don't know *how* to give you a happy ending, kid. Fuck, I couldn't give myself one." I brightened and snapped my fingers as though I'd just realized something, though the next sentence was written more than a year before the current one. "That's the problem: We can't ask other people to fix our lives; we have to fix them ourselves.

Which, I've just realized[143], is the throughline for the whole book. You have to fix these things for yourself. You tried. You tried to edit the universe and you failed. So I can't do it for you."

He sat on his heels, still staring at my feet. "So there's nothing you'll do for me? You can't help me at all?"

I crouched down and put a hand on his shoulder, made him look at me. "Mike . . ." His watery eyes slew me. "I guess I could . . ."

Hope bloomed in his eyes.

I let out a frustrated groan. "Mike, all I can do is make you forget ever being in love with her. I can do that for you. Sort of an *Eternal Sunshine of the Spotless Mind* riff, I guess. Cheap and easy, but I can do that. It'll be a cruel, ironic ending, but it will end your pain."

"Is that all you can do?"

"Pretty much, yeah. I mean, there are other options, sure, but they take time. A lot of time. Like ten years or more."

"Ten years! I can't wait ten years to forget her. To get over her. Does it really take that long? God!" He twisted in on himself, clutching at his gut as though nauseated. "Ten more years like this? I can't handle that. How am I supposed to live with that?"

"One day at a time. Just like the rest of us." I gave him a few moments to think, then asked, "What do you want me to do, Mike?"

He shook his head, rocking back and forth, still cradling his urgent abdomen. "I don't know. I don't know what I want if I

143. No, really—this next part just occurred to me, even though I wrote the last sentence more than a year ago. How's that for coincidence and interconnectedness? After working on this book for more than a year and thinking about it for most of my life, the throughline just occurred to me.

can't have her." Then he sat up straight. "Wait. Wait a second. Aren't you writing both sides of this conversation?"

"Yeah."

"Then you already know what I want, don't you? What's the point—you know how it'll end. Just skip down the page or whatever and tell me what I end up choosing."

I chuckled. Not a bad idea, but . . . "I'm still figuring it out, kid. Believe it or not, I don't know what you're going to choose yet. I have some other stuff written already—future stuff—but it's not connected to your choice. Right now, there's just white space under these words on the page."

"You're a terrible God," he whispered.

"I might be. I don't even know anymore. We authors are Gods, but sometimes we . . . It's not that we lose control of our stories. It's just that it turns out there's a part of our brains working on the story we're not aware of. All authors have it. Some call it the back-brain, the lizard brain, the subconscious or unconscious. Some pretentious fuckers call it their Muse because if it's ripped off from the ancient Greeks, it must be impressive, right? And I was always of the school that people who said shit like that were either buying into some old authorial mystique or trying to propagate it or both, churning out bullshit pop mysticism in order to make themselves feel special or important or elevated above the unwashed masses.

"But you know what?" Mike stared at me with unwavering eyes—for a moment I thought he might be having a seizure (which is to say for a moment I considered *giving him* a seizure, but didn't know where I would go with the story after that), but then he blinked and focused on me. "You know what? On this book . . . Well, it's happened with books in the past, too, but this is the best one to use as an example. On this book, all sorts of crazy shit happened that tied in when I least expected it, stuff that I never thought would connect later. Like the whole thing with a secret subway tunnel to the Other City. I never really planned on that. I didn't have any idea that I was going to do that until it happened. I wrote that first scene where you went to the end of the Fox line and couldn't get a return train right away, which was really just an excuse to have you go up to Crimson Rocks and have your little experience there. But I didn't know that I would use that later. It was a nice bit of serendipity. And I wonder about things like that sometimes. Is it just a coincidence? Or is there some part of my brain—something far back and buried deep—that was setting it up for me? Because if that's the case . . . Well, that's kind of cool, but it's also kind of scary, too. The idea that I'm making plans somewhere, somehow, without even being aware of it. But then it's cool again because right when I need something, right when I desperately need a bit or a plot turn or something, it's just there. Someone put it there for me, and that someone was me, but also not me. Maybe it's Inframan. Maybe what we call a Muse or a subconscious is really Inframan. Maybe every author has an Inframan deep down inside, another author who's trying to make the story better, trying to make the story make some sort of sense. Do you think that's possible, Mike?"

"I, uh . . . I don't know what I think."

"Yeah, I knew you would say that. You know, when I told people about the book—this book, I mean—they all said, 'Wow, that must be some girl.' Meaning my Phil, not yours. No one knew yours yet. And you know what? I'm not sure if she is or not. So I have to ask you: Is she, Mike? Was she worth all of this? Your Phil, I mean now. Because yours and mine have become melded in some strange blending of fiction and not-fiction. I feel like the unreal world is intruding on my own world these days. I mean, I've been half-expecting to bump into *your* Phil—blue hair and all—on the subway or walking down the street. I saw a picture online of Katy Perry and she'd dyed her hair this amazing blue, with the most incredible, shiny lighter blue highlights . . . And it's exactly like I pictured Phil's hair. And I've been thinking to myself, 'Is the book becoming real? Have I broken some kind of barrier between the made-up world and the real world?'[144] I mentioned the idea of strip-searching women with breast implants before they get on planes—it was just an absurd (so I thought!) extrapolation of the security measures in my world. And then—the day I finished writing the first draft of the book!—I came across a story of how the security guys at an airport made a breast cancer survivor show them her breast prosthetic.[145] I've had horrible dreams where I wake up and I've never published a book and I'm still living in Maryland and working in the comic book industry. Or dreams where I really did kill myself back in 2005 and this whole thing, this whole experience I'm writing, is nothing more than a split-second fantasy as I die. And sometimes, Mike . . . Sometimes I wonder if I'm even writing this. I wonder if this is all being written by some *other* iteration of Barry Lyga, if the version of me sitting

144. It gets even crazier: Remember the kids on the subway in Chapter 23? That happened to me, only it was in a Starbucks and it was even more intense. They were talking about working on some project set in Las Vegas—I once lived in Las Vegas. And it was a book for kids—I write books for kids. And it was about magic powers—when I lived in Vegas, I wrote a draft of a book about a kid with magic powers. And their kid knew karate—guess what the kid in my book studied? Most frightening of all? As I was eavesdropping on them, simultaneously marveling and nauseated with horror at how closely their fiction hewed to my fact, one of them decided to call their advisor and checked the phone number with another kid. The area code was the same as *my* area code. I swear this shit is real.

145. Check it out for yourself: http://www.nbcnews.com/id/40278427/ns/travel-news/t/tsa-forces-cancer-survivor-show-prosthetic-breast/

in a garden apartment in a brownstone in Brooklyn[146] is just as made up as the iteration that died in 2005, just as invented as Gayl Rybar and Mike Grayson and George Singleton. I'm wondering, Mike: Am I real? Am I even a real person? It's the same thing Gayl worried about and why do you think I made him worry about it, Mike? Hmm? Why?"

I grabbed him by the shoulders and we stared into each other's eyes, the eyes identical. He is my child, my creation. He has my eyes.

"God made Man in His own image," Mike whispered. "That means God must be insane."

I stared at him in silence and then pushed him away, rearing back to laugh. "Insane? Maybe. Maybe I am. Maybe you are. Maybe we all are. I don't know. Why do you think I had your world's version of Barry Lyga spend time in a mental institution? I've been worried about my own sanity for most of my life. When you're a kid blessed with way too much imagination, it starts to get away from you. You start thinking things and then you start thinking they're real. You lose track of what was a dream and what wasn't. You realize that you don't fit into the world, that you're just an observer, and that fucks with you, big-time.

"And I've been writing this book for a long, long time. It started . . . God, the actual writing started almost exactly a year ago, the planning six months before that. But the idea of it . . ."[147]

I shook my head. Something had just occurred to me. An overt brainstorm, or more accurately a brain-thunderstrike, a

146. For the first go-round, I was sitting in a garden apartment, but by the time I got to the revisions, I was in a parlor-level apartment. And then, when I finished the book, I was in another garden apartment. But now I'm in a home office in the suburbs as I polish the book up for publication. What the hell is the point of this footnote?

147. Well, at the point of this draft, the actual writing actually began—oh, Jesus—MORE THAN A DOZEN YEARS AGO. I'm getting old.

bolt hurled by my personal Zeus—Inframan—from the cloudy depths of my subconscious mind. A memory. More accurately, a cluster of them from childhood.

"I always tried to put myself in my stories. Going back long, long before I ever read King's *Dark Tower* or Morrison's *Animal Man*. I remember being in maybe fourth grade and starting a science fiction novel, which was going to be about some kind of futuristic rivalry between my direct descendant and a direct descendant of Thomas Edison. It was probably the comic books. The fucking comic books. The ones where the characters cross universes and meet other versions of themselves. I was miserable as a kid, Mike. I guess that idea appealed to me, the idea that I was a wreck, but that there was another version of me out there that was happy. And that was just one step away from wanting to *be* that version. I never wanted to be real, Mike. I wanted to be *fiction*. I wanted to be make-believe because in make-believe . . ."

I trailed off.

No point.

"So what do you think, Mike? You met God. You did it. Was she worth it? Was Phil worth it?"

He didn't hesitate: "Yes."

"Well, of course you'd say yes. That's in your character. But what about your traveling companions? Was it worth it to them? For them?"

He tilted his chin in the air. "George believes in me. He came, too."

"Duh. George is gay, Mike.[148] He's in love with you.[149] Of course he came with you. You know how you'd go to the ends of the earth for Phil? Well, George would do the same for you. And

148. Second secret.

149. Third secret. (George would never tell it, but I will.)

has, in fact. You want to know what true love looks like? Try looking at George sometime and seeing more than just your sidekick or even your best friend. You went to the ends of the earth and climbed the Tower of Babel for Phil, who right now is safely at home, tangled up in her bed-sheets with *him*, none the wiser that you've risked your life and very existence to try to win her back. George went to the ends of the earth and climbed the Tower of Babel for *you*, Mike. He risked his life and very existence alongside you, and he did it for the most selfless of reasons: Love. Unrequited love, to be exact. He knew that if he helped you succeed, you would be with Phil again, but he did it anyway because more than anything else in the universe, George wants you to be happy. That's all he wants for you. And what do you want for him?"

The struggle played blatantly across his expression as he writhed internally, juggling childhood memories, promises, regrets, personal guilts. "But I'm not gay," he said.

"No one said you have to be. Just appreciate what he's done. And why. Think about how miserable you are and put yourself in George's shoes."

Stammering, he said, "I never felt . . . You know, I never felt like I was as good a friend as I could have—"

I flapped my hands impatiently. "Yeah, yeah, I know—loaded down with all kinds of guilt. 'He's my best friend, but I'm not his.' Blah blah blah. I know. This book isn't about the nature of friendship. I just wanted to give you something to think about, is all. Something that isn't and wasn't you, and you and Phil. So, you sit here—" I pulled over the chair "—and think about that. Meanwhile, I'm going to talk to Phil."

He looked up at me hopefully from the chair, his expression depressingly puppy-like.

"Not your Phil," I told him. "My Phil."

OK, everyone. This next part isn't for you. Unless you're

Phil. So, I guess this is like one of those Choose-Your-Own-Adventure Books. If you are Phil, turn to page 737. If you're not Phil, turn to page 741.

Ready?

Go.

HELLO, PHIL.

You know, I thought that when it came time to write this part of the book that I would have so much to say. But here I am, over 200,000 words into this draft, and it's not that I'm losing steam (there are days I think this book could be another 200,000 words, easily, and other days where I think I could spend the rest of my life working on just this book, could drop dead at a holographic keyboard some indeterminate day in the future with the ending still—always—a page away), but more that I've realized I have so little to say to you now.

But, yeah—I couldn't admit it to Mike, though I will admit it here: When I started cobbling together this book, taking notes and outlining, my primary thought was that maybe it would help me win you back. I would open my soul to you and you would be persuaded, convinced, and you would come running.

God, that seems so stupid now. Worse, it's a totally juvenile form of magical thinking, and you'd think that I'd be smart enough to avoid that. And yet, here we are: 200,000 words and counting. Why?

That's a question I've been asking myself a lot lately. Is my life perfect? Of course not. No one's is. But things are pretty damn good, if you want to know the truth. I told Mike that I couldn't give myself a happy ending, but I got one anyway. Somehow. I'm engaged now. Married by the time this sees print.[150] So why on earth am I still writing this fucking book? Why on earth am I opening up these old wounds and pouring all manner of literary salt into them?

There's the selfish reason: I have to. The story is inside me and this one in particular has been dying to get out since I was a kid, though I never in a million years thought it would take this particular form.

And there's the altruistic reason: Maybe it will help someone.

I don't think those reasons conflict. There doesn't have to be any sort of mutual exclusion between selfishness and altruism. Maybe that's a lesson Mike needs to learn. I think it's possible to have both motivations at the same time. It's possible to be selfless and selfish in the same instant. I suspect, in fact, that this may be the secret of God: That He created the universe not for us, but for Himself. That He made us because He couldn't bear not to, not out of love. But that doesn't mean that He can't also love us.

In any event, if I believed in God, that's the kind of God I would believe in.

Wow. How the hell did I get from you, Phil, to some sort of half-assed theology?

It's all tangled up in my mind and in my heart. You've transmuted into every woman I ever spent time with, every ex of every stripe. A part of me thinks I should use this space to apologize, to tell you—all of you in general, but you specifically, of

150. Not just married—we have two kids now, the lights of my life. That's how fucking long it's taken to publish this thing!

course—that I'm sorry for any pain I may have caused you, for any hurt I let linger. And then there's the part of me (I suspect it sounds like a dragon and smells of chocolate syrup) that laughs at that idea, that says, "Wow, Lyga—what a fucking egomaniac you are! Do you really think any of them need or want your contrition? Do you think you're so important that any hurt you inflicted lingers after all this time to any of them?"

And since that comes from me, it seems I've pulled off the neat trick of writing a book that manages to encapsulate utter self-loathing and unrelenting narcissism at the same time. That's fitting, I suppose.

Thanks for the ego-check, Inframan. I appreciate it. I probably needed it.

So, Phil. Here we are. You and me, connected by the strange combination of time travel and telepathy that is writing. Along with any number of recalcitrant readers who decided to ignore their instructions and read this anyway.

Phil, I loved you. All of the "yous" that there are and were. I was never able to say it or to prove it, I guess. I'm trying to be better. A better man. Person.

That's the lesson. The lesson Mike can't learn because I won't let him learn it. The lesson I want my readers to learn through his example, his cautionary tale.

Love is not fungible, but love is also not irreplaceable. That cute guy in gym class? That girl who was the first to let you reach under her bra for a magical moment? The guy who first said "I love you?" The girl who first said you were her world?

Yes, they are special. And dear. First loves are special and unique. But here's a secret:

All loves are special and unique.

Surrender is not failure when it serves to promote success. You let go of one swinging vine not because you can't hold it any longer, but rather to leap to the next one. And the next. And the next. Progress. The future.

That moment between vines? Where gravity says, "Oh, yes—I remember you!" and threatens to drag you down out of the sky? Oh, I know. I know. That moment is terrifying and horrifying and so awful that you'd rather just cling to that first vine forever.

But you can't. You shouldn't. You mustn't.

The funny thing, of course, is that Inframan has won once again. That little fucker always wins, even though he's the God of Failure. Because I've failed at what I set out to do.

I wanted to write something Truly Great. Something that was undeniably Art. Regardless of Zusak and Moore and Morrison and Bates and Maggin and Barth and Fox and King and all of them. I had to just plow ahead and tell my story the way I wanted to tell it. Fuck the anxiety of influence.

But I failed. I failed because it ended up being just another stupid love story.

Anyway, Phil, thanks for reading this long. If you even bothered. I wish I had some sort of grand answer for you here. I wish I could explain me or you or the book or anything. But I don't have any answers.

All I have is an ending.

Time to get there, I think.

Yes. Yes, it's time.

CHAPTER 49

Mike sat on the edge of the bed, picking at a stray thread on the afghan, staring straight ahead at the door. What was beyond that door, he wondered? Had Lyga bothered to write what lay beyond or would he see again—upon opening it—nothing more than the blank white of creation, of paper, of a blank word processing document?

He stood to find out and I reappeared in front of him. "OK, that's done." I brushed my hands together as though clearing them of chalk, as if I'd actually just done something physical. "Time for you to go. I have to get this thing wrapped up and move on to another book."

Mike blinked, gazing at me with an utterly guileless expression that revealed that he had never considered this, had never imagined me moving on to another book.

"Another one? Another whole universe?"

"Yeah."

"So are you like . . . the Monika Seymore of your world?"

I couldn't keep from chuckling. "Me? No. Not a chance. I'm just a guy who really loves writing books. And there are some people out there who seem to enjoy reading what I write. That's all. So for now I get to keep creating these universes, and playing in them, and doing fun stuff. In the time since I wrote this book, I wrote a trilogy about a serial killer, a book about a kid who accidentally killed his baby sister—"

"Jesus Christ! Who fucked you up as a kid?" His face screwed up in disgust and distaste. "People read this stuff?"

"Yeah, apparently. I mean, when I wrote the first version of this scene, the serial killer thing was still being worked on. But it's been published now and it seems like people liked it. It got me onto the *New York Times* bestsellers list, which—I'm not gonna lie—was pretty nice."

"Is that all you care about? What sells the most?"

I knew where he was going with this and decided to let it play out.

"Because if that's the case," he said, "then you should want to go for the romance, right? So it wouldn't be a big deal to change the ending to *this* one—"

"Nice try," I said, shaking my head. "But I'm sort of stubborn. I like to do things my way, even when that means the audience shrinks or the sales evaporate. Probably not the smartest, most career-friendly move, but I'm sort of an idiot that way."[151]

"I see. And 'your way' means torturing your characters. Or glorifying violence by writing about psychopaths."

I shrugged off his disdain and bitterness. "You don't understand. I'm living in a world in which a twelve-year-old can post a thirty second video clip of his cat falling down the stairs on

151. The truth of the matter is, the first thing I thought after making the list—well, after some rabid fist-pumping, let's be real—was "Will I even be able to publish *Unedited* now? Or will everyone expect crazy-ass bestselling thrillers from me?" Fortunately for this book (though not for my bank balance), I only lasted one week on the list.

YouTube and—in three days—have more people looking at that than have ever read one of my books. The competition is ridiculous. Sometimes you have to do crazy shit to stand out."

"Like write about serial killers and dead babies."

I shrugged. "I like playing in the darkness, Mike. Can't help it. But I also wrote some books about my favorite super-hero. And I co-wrote a book with my wife."

"Your *wife*? I thought you said you couldn't give yourself a happy ending."

"Well, that's true. We don't give ourself happy endings, Mike. They find us. And we just muddle along. Or maunder. I discovered that word in a story by my buddy Daniel Nayeri. I love that word. *Maunder.*

"Anyway, yeah, you have to do crazy shit. Like write about serial killers. Or write *this* fucking book. I mean, this thing's a young adult novel, man—people think I'm crazy for even trying this."

He tilted his head to a perplexed angle. "'Young adult?' What's that?"

"It's what I called 'nonadult' in your world. Books for teenagers. And there are these weird, calcified notions of what a young adult book is and should be. Like, the action all has to be from the point of view of a kid. And stuff like that. Rules I broke all throughout this book. Bad enough I put you in college, barely still in your teens, but I also have sections from Gayl's POV and my POV. Even the length—you're not supposed to do books this long. But I did it, and honestly, I have no idea if any kids are ever going to read this.

"Because let's be honest here—it's a long fucking book. I mean, I remember when I turned in the first draft of *Boy Toy*, it was a lot longer than what got published. And my editor on that one—hi, Margaret!—said to me, 'You can't publish a 650 page book in YA!' But I was ready for that, and I said, 'Oh, yeah? What about *The Book Thief*?' And she said, 'That was about the Nazis. Your book is about a kid fucking his teacher.' So I edited out some stuff to make it shorter.[152]

"So just the length alone is problematic, is breaking rules. There are all these tropes that have crept into YA, and people treat them like laws. Like, you have to have the best friend. Usually somewhat quirky. Almost always more socially adept than the main character. So I caved on that one and gave you George, but he really doesn't *do* anything in the book. He's just there for you to talk to and bounce things off of."

"And to love me," he said with quiet resentment.

"Well, yeah, and that, too. But honestly, he's a plot device. I came to enjoy him, but that's all he was in the beginning—a plot device. Then I decided he was black[153] and gay and he became much more interesting to me. And then I decided he was Monika Seymore's kid and he became *really* interesting to me.

"But anyway: After the best friend, you have to have the crush and then there's the person the kid is *really* going to end up with. That's how these stories are supposed to work.

152. That's a totally true story. I told it to Holly Black once and she said I should save it for a speech. But why not share the story with all of you, my readers, as opposed to the few people who happen to attend some speech?

153. There's an assumption on the part of most readers (especially white readers, but not exclusively) that if you're reading a book by a white author or an author of indeterminate race, that the characters are white unless otherwise stated. So I liked the idea of Mike not knowing George was black until something in the text specifically and explicitly clued him in. Like the reader, Mike assumed George was white. And, honestly, I'm not sure why I'm even explaining this. I always intended the racial thing to stand on its own, but my agent didn't get the "joke" when she read the first draft, and one reader thought it needed more explanation, so this is here to explain it. I think it stands just fine on its own, but hey—that's what footnotes are for, right?

But I said 'Fuck it. I'm writing a YA where the kid does *not* get the girl in the end, doesn't get *any* girl in the end, where it all falls apart.'

"It's everything you're not supposed to do. And I'm doing it."

"Just because." He snorted. "You've got a serious God complex."

"Or maybe I'm just a complex God."

"That's such bullshit!" He's off the bed now, making what will be his last stand. "That is complete bullshit! You're not complex—you're just . . . just . . . What did you say before? Calcified! You're calcified. You decided on an ending a long time ago and you won't give it up."

"Sorry, kid. I'm just *not* going to do a happy ending. And that's my prerogative—it's my story."

"No, it's not," he seethes, clenching his fists. "It's *my* story."

"Oh, shut up. It's not your anything. You're just a stupid character."

And even though it's my idea and even though I'm writing them, his next words still shock and hurt me:

He says, quietly, "I think I see why no one wants to read your books."

And shies away from me, as if afraid I'm going to destroy him like the others.

Instead, I just look at him, my creation, and I know how the Titans felt when the gods rebelled.[154]

Because what he said . . .

What he said is truer than he knows.

Because maybe you're reading this book and you're thinking,

154. My notes say "Ugh" after that line. And it *is* "Ugh." But I don't know how else to say it.

Damn, this Lyga guy has published a hell of a lot of books! He's living the dream!

But let me tell you: It's never enough.

Never enough sales to justify the things I want to do. Never enough readers to build a groundswell that could take me to the next level in my career. I'm stuck where I am, a minor "cult-favorite" as one of my editors put it once. A mouse with dreams of being an elephant.

"Before I signed the contract for this book," I begin, then hesitate. I never intended to put this in the book. And I'm still not sure it's the right thing to do, but here I am. I'm doing it anyway.

"Before I signed the contract for this book, I had a string of failures," I tell him. (And you, Dear Reader.) "*After the Red Rain. The Secret Sea. Bang.* They all *tanked*. Hard. Even the last books in the *Killers* series didn't sell particularly well. It's like I climbed a ladder with *I Hunt Killers*, just high enough that I could see what was next . . . and then fell off."

"Poor God," he says with mock pity.

And let me tell you something—that *pisses me off.* Because this is my life and my dream we're talking about here, and most days I feel like I've gotten *so close,* but I can never . . . quite . . .

"You know, I always wanted to write a story that was the prose equivalent of a Springsteen song. You would read it and it would make you feel the way listening to Bruce did. But I can't do it. I've spent my life trying and I can't. So I cheated with Joe Roberts. Because I failed. Because Inframan is right and all-powerful and I failed.

"I don't even know how I feel about this book anymore," I tell him (and, again, you). "It's a patchwork assembled from my life. And parts of it make sense to me and other parts . . ."

He doesn't like me drifting off. "Other parts what?"

I shake off the question. "There's stuff in here that I still feel intensely. And other stuff that I'm not sure about anymore. And still other stuff where I'm like . . . Damn, that's *dark*! I mean, there's shit in here I find sexist and uncomfortable, OK? But you scratch the human condition and sometimes it scratches back. I wanted this book to be my best ever and now I don't know what it is. And I can't count on it to change my career. Because every time I've thought, *This is the book that will really take my career to a new level!* it . . . hasn't. I have no reason to think this will be any different."

"God is a pessimist," he says.

I bristle. I've been called a pessimist most of my life, but the fact of the matter is that when you predict a negative outcome and you're right most of the time, you're not a goddamn pessimist.

"Oh?" I ask with a nastier tone than he deserves. He's just a character, after all. "You think I'm a pessimist? Well, let me tell you something: All those references to Lucky Sevens and Global War B in your life? Those are me taking potshots at George W. Bush and the response to 9/11 in *my* world. I thought Freedom fries and the recession and that bullshit was as bad as it could get. And then along came 2016 and Donald Fucking Trump, the Orange Traitor."

"Orange Traitor?" He was puzzled, but I was on a roll.

"I thought it couldn't get any worse than GWB and the depredations he committed on this country. But Trump's a goddamned nuclear bomb compared to him. So, you think I'm a pessimist? Fuck that. As bad as things get, they can *always* get worse.[155] God's not a pessimist, Mike—God is a realist. Even

155. Thanks for that line, Dan.

this book—this damn, impossible-to-publish book—is a failure. Damn, man, I had to make compromises to get it published at all.[156] And here I am. And here you are."

"Why me?" he implores. "Why did you have to do these things to *me*? Why couldn't I have been the kid with a serial killer for a dad?"

"Because you're Mike Grayson, that's why. Because I liked the character and the name from *Inframan* and decided to reuse it. You. It. Whichever. Both, maybe. At first I was just amusing myself, really, and then it became important. But it's actually pointless and stupid, because other than my brother and my writing adviser at Yale, no one has ever read—and no one will ever read—those original pages of *Inframan*. It was really the height of self-indulgence, I suppose. But I'm not going to change it now, so don't even ask."

"I wasn't going to ask."

"I wasn't talking to you."

"Will I see you again?" he asks, though whether in anticipation or in trepidation . . . I cannot tell. I truly cannot.

"Maybe. There's a chance we'll meet again in another city."

"You mean . . . my city?" he asks, puzzled. "Or the Other City?"

"Neither one. There's another one. It's a very special place and I've been building it for a very long time. Longer than I worked on the Other City or your city. It goes back almost as

156. The weird "companion/alternate" novel that came out at the same time as this book wasn't my idea. It was the brainchild of my editor, Dan. And it's not a bad idea at all—it's just not what I pictured. And since I'm a 47-year-old (51 by the time you read this) fucking man-child, I get all pouty when I don't get my way. Don't get me wrong: I'm grateful that this book is being published *at all*, and in terms of compromises, Dan's suggestions and ideas were consonant with what I was trying to do . . . and by any objective measure are probably absolutely the right call. But I'm a baby.

far as *Inframan*. I'll see you there, I promise. You may not see me, but I'll see you. And maybe someone will take a chance and publish that story, too, in which case everyone reading this book will see you again as well."

He absorbed that and nodded, his lips moving as he whispered something to himself that I've decided not to reveal.

"What happens now?" Fixing me with a strong, confident gaze. No longer afraid. No longer begging. Ready for it to end.

As am I.

"I don't know how much of this you'll remember," I told him. "Some of it you'll remember. I don't know how much. It doesn't really matter, though."

"Do I go to the room now? The one where I'm alone?" Eyes snapped wide as a thought occurred to him, and he gestured to the space around us. "Or is this where I end up alone? Are you going to leave me here in your senior dorm?"

I grinned at him. "No, Mike. It's not a half-bad idea, but no. It's time for you to go now."

And then I am alone in a room. Alone in my past. Irony and justice.

Mike

felt

the blank

all around
him.

He/I thought:

I

want to

l
i
s
t
e
n

t
o

t
h
e

r
a
i
n

with you.

And then he saw a sign.

With an arrow.

Pointing down.

"This way to **Chapter 50**," it read.

He followed it.

CHAPTER 50

Mike peered ahead and made out a flight of dimly-lit stairs, poured and dirty concrete leading down. A handrail—chipped black paint and rust spots—followed the steps down. Mike gingerly took hold of the rail, as though it could bite, and made his way down.

At the bottom of the stair, he noticed a sign overhead that said, "OUTBOUND BARTH." An arrow pointed to his left.

Could it be? Was it even remotely possible?

He bore left through a corridor tiled with filthy, cracked white porcelain, which then opened into a large waiting area with tracks and a tunnel to the right and another sign, this one reading "OUTBOUND BARTH TO INBOUND FOX." A bench was positioned against the far wall and three Marines stood there, watching over the bench's sole occupant.

It was George.

Mike's feet ran to George before his brain had finished processing George's presence, and he got there so swiftly that he hardly had time to formulate questions: Why? How? When? Instead, he pushed through two of the Marines and threw his arms around George, shouting, "George! George! You're alive!"

"Dude, obviously, you know what I mean?" George's calm, laconic reply belied the crushing tightness of his grip.

"Very sweet," Huff said from behind them. He was one of the Marines Mike had shoved aside, of course.

"What now?" Mike said. Reluctant to let go of his best friend, he nevertheless did so long enough to round on Huff.

The Marine shrugged. "We have our orders. From up high. *Really* high. We're to make sure you get on the subway and then we go back about our business. That's all."

"You're just letting us go?" Mike asked suspiciously.

"Dude, don't question it," George told him. "I was suspicious, too, but—"

"Not my call," Huff said, clipping his words. "Believe me, I want you guys arrested and put on trial for treason and a whole host of other things. But this one's above my pay-grade."

"What about Gayl?" Mike asked, looking around. "And Joe Roberts?"

Huff shrugged. The movement brought the barrel of his gun into alignment with Mike's gut, which clenched at the sight. "No one else has come through. We only have orders for you two."

"But I can't go back," Mike protested. "I have to stay here. I'll be arrested if I go back to the city." The Cops™ and the police and Phil's restraining order loomed large in his memory and in his thoughts—in his past and in his future. If reclaiming Phil was impossible, then better to stay here in the Other City, with his fellow love-deprived, and look for a new life here.

"You think staying here would be any better?" Huff asked.

"But—"

"What would you be arrested for anyway?"

Mike told him about the restraining order and his (clueless) violation thereof. Huff shook his head. "Mike *Grayson*?" he asked. "Are you sure?"

Whereas once Mike might have temporized, having spent a period of time unaware of his last name, now he did not. "Of course I'm sure."

"Because one of the guys was watching the news from the city a little while ago and they reported that a guy named Mike Grayson was arrested for stalking some girl."

Mike blinked, then looked over to George, as though for reassurance or understanding, but George could offer neither.

"It was a big deal," Huff went on, "because the guy was apparently a police officer. From somewhere back East. And they—"

He was cut off by the rattle-and-clank of a subway train clattering its way to the station. The dark tunnel lit up with a yellowish pall and then the outbound Barth clanged into the station, its brakes hissing and shrilling.

"This is it. All aboard, motherfuckers," Huff said and gestured with his rifle to the train door, which now slid open.

"But what about—"

"Seriously, kid," Huff said, and his stance and his expression and his tone of voice and his rifle—above all his rifle—left no room for argument.

Mike and George allowed themselves to be escorted to the train. They boarded.

They did not look back through the window as the door shut and the train pulled out of the station.

••••••••••

They sat on opposite sides of the train, looking at each other across the aisle in silence, each of them thinking of Gayl and of Joe and of what they'd seen.

"He says I won't remember all of it," Mike said.

George nodded, his expression thoughtful. "Yeah. Some of it is fading for me already. Not all. Just some of it."

"Yeah, it's like . . ."

"It's like the further the train goes, the more we forget."

"Yeah."

After a moment: "Dude, so what about this guy who got arrested . . ."

"It has to be him," Mike said, though he could scarcely believe it himself. "The other Mike Grayson. The one from *Inframan*. They got us confused somehow."

"Well, that's, uh . . . convenient. You know what I mean?"

Silence for an indeterminate time, broken only by the steady thrum of the train's engines and the occasional clank-smack of the wheels on the tracks.

"So," Mike said, clearing his throat, saying it because it needed to be said. "So, uh, you're gay."

"Yeah."

More silence.

"I'm not," Mike said. "I'm really sorry about that."

"Dude."

"No. Really. You're my best friend in the world and if I could be that for you, I would. I totally would."

George grinned. "Thanks."

"Probably doesn't help, does it?"

Head shake. "Not really. It's still nice, though."

Mike worried his bottom lip for a few moments. He had to ask. "When did you realize you were gay?"

George chuckled. "You know, I think I'm supposed to answer that by asking, 'When did you realize you were straight?' But I won't. Because there actually was a moment and I actually remember it."

"Really?"

"Yep. Do you remember when we were kids? When we snuck into the movies to see *Terrible Heart?*"

"Oh, God, yeah," Mike said, recalling. The movie trailers for *Terrible Heart* had led them both—at the tender age of ten—to think that it was a crazy shoot-'em-up, but when they actually got into the theater, they discovered they'd been had: It was a romance, rated D[157] not for violence, but for language and "brief moments of sexuality."

"It was a romance and we hated romances because we wanted to see blood and guts," George said. "But we watched the whole thing anyway because we kept thinking it was going to get better, even though it just got worse. But I remember watching the main character, whatever his name was, with the girl. Do you remember the scene where they kissed for the first time?"

Mike shrugged. He remembered it vaguely.

George leaned forward, elbows on knees. "Here's the thing: I wanted her to be a boy. That's what hit me. It's not that I wanted to be in the movie. I didn't even want it to be *me* kissing him. I just wanted it to be a boy. Any boy. And that's how I knew."

Mike pondered. "Is that right? Is that how it really works?"

"I don't know. For me, it did. I don't know about anyone else."

They fell silent again.

"I have to tell you about my father," George said suddenly.

Mike stiffened. He had managed to forget about that. It was one of the things he hoped would fall into some memory vortex and never leave, trapped by the inescapable gravity of trauma and horror. But here was George, hauling it out of a black hole with nothing more than words.

157. "D" stands for "Denied" and is roughly equivalent to the "R" (Restricted) rating in our world. This is a lame footnote. Sorry.

"George, I—"

"No. Listen. I know what you think. I know you think I killed him in that convenience store."

"We heard the shotgun . . ."

"Yeah, but—"

"You don't have to tell me. What happens in the Other City, stays in the Other City. No one has to know. I'll never tell anyone."

"No." He shook his head with a violence that frightened Mike. If it was possible to actually fling one's own head off of one's shoulders, George would have done it by now. "That wasn't me. I didn't do it. I swear. I . . ." He wrapped his arms around himself. "I wanted to, Mike. I wanted to do it so bad. It's all I've dreamed about my whole life, you know what I mean?" George stared at the floor of the subway car as though watching the tableau replay before his eyes. "I had the gun and I had him, and I knew I could do it. I knew I could kill him, so easily.

"And I didn't do it." Tears overflowed George's eyes, rolling down his cheeks, tracing dark paths along the curvature of his face. "I couldn't pull the trigger, no matter how badly I wanted to. Because . . . Because . . ."

"Because he was your father," Mike said with quiet compassion.

Another violent shake of the head. "No. No. Not that. Because . . . Because he was *there*. Because he was in the Other City!"

"I don't . . . I don't get it."

George groaned and mashed his palms against his cheeks, smearing the tears into wet patches. "Don't you get it? The only way to be in the Other City is if you've loved and lost, right? And if he was there, then that meant that somehow—deep down—he really did love my mom. Even after all the shit he did to us, after all the beatings and all the . . . He loved her, man. He really *loved* her." Still staring at the floor. Haunted. By exactly what, Mike did not know.

"And he took the gun away from me and turned it on himself," George whispered. "Did what I couldn't do. Last thing he said to me was 'I'm sorry.' And then his head was gone."

After a moment, Mike stood up, crossed the aisle, and sat down next to George. He paused, then put an arm around his best friend and let George collapse against him and weep, let him cry until the tears could come no more. It was, Mike thought, a poor substitute for the years George had been his best friend and Mike had not returned the favor. A poor substitute, but perhaps a good beginning.

"Dude, I love you," he said after George's last sobs had ejected from him and his body had settled into a normal breathing rhythm. "Just not that way, you know what I mean?"

George hiccupped and looked up at him, rolling his eyes. "Duh. Of course I know what you mean."

Just then, the speakers overhead crackled. The same polite and nearly-genderless voice they had heard on the way to the Other City announced, "LADIES AND GENTLEMEN. THIS TRAIN IS NOW ON THE FOX LINE. YOU ARE ON THE INBOUND FOX LINE."

"Almost home," Mike whispered. He took George's hand and gripped it tightly.

"What do you think happened to Gayl?" George asked. "And Joe Roberts? Shouldn't we go looking for them?"

"I don't know. I think . . . I think if he wanted us to find them, they would have been waiting in the Barth station with you."

"If *who* wanted us to find them?" George asked.

Mike thought for a moment. He had a vague recollection of a white room, of a man on a throne . . .

"God," he said, but that sounded wrong. There had been another name, but he couldn't remember it.

Well, it probably didn't matter.

The subway began to decelerate, its brakes shrieking and throwing out sparks in the darkness of the tunnel.

"So what happens now?" George asked.

"Maybe he'll write a sequel."

Mike hadn't meant it as a joke, but George erupted with a laughter so infectious and joyful that Mike couldn't help but to join in, and the two of them howled together, chortling and guffawing, wrapped in each other in their seats as the subway car slowed and stopped at the last and first station on the Fox line.

CHAPTER 51

Phil sat on her bed, a copy of A. A. Milne's *The House at Pooh Corner* unopened on her lap. She had a memory of reading the book and a memory of being read the book, but right now she was most concerned with this thought: Did the book actually exist?

She'd never experienced such an existential crisis before. Or perhaps *existential crisis* was too kind a way to describe it. Perhaps *psychotic break from reality* was more truthful.

The book weighed on the tops of her thighs. It had heft; gravity dragged it down. When she ran the pad of her right index finger along its edge, the smooth board of the cover indented her flesh ever-so-slightly. She knew that if she did the same with a page, she would inflict a paper cut.

This is a different world, she thought. *Did A. A. Milne exist in this world? Is that name an anagram for some other author? Pooh, we can be certain, is fiction, but is Milne fiction, as well?*

She knew that books written for children and teens and such were called *nonadult* books, to distinguish them from books written for, well, et cetera. And yet for some reason, she thought of this as a *children's book*, not a nonadult book. And the copy of *The Unlikely Tale of Geekster and the Vampiress* that had appeared on her bookshelf . . . It, too, was nonadult, and yet she couldn't help thinking of it as *young adult.*

According to quantum physics—about which Phil knew absolutely nothing except for what is to follow—the universe is not unique and solitary. There is/was a multitude of universes, each one with its own worlds and lives and loves. A staple of spec-fic (which, for some reason, her brain nagged her to think of as *sci-fi),* such universes existed in parallel to her own.

What, she wondered, if books themselves were portals to those other universes? Or at least representations of those universes? That would mean that every book—no matter its fidelity to reality—took place in a world that was *not* reality. And furthermore, that every book—no matter how *un*real—was, in fact, fact, not fiction.

The implications would have spun her, if not for the weight of the book in her lap.

She thought that perhaps her own world was not all it seemed, as though there could be more to it. And so she turned. And she looked at you. And she said this:

I'm Phil.

(Before you can ask: Yes, the blue hair is natural. No, I won't explain.)

More accurately, I'm an approximation of Phil, a version made of ink on paper as opposed to blood, bone, and flesh. And I'm also an approximation of the Phil who exists as a synecdoche—or perhaps more accurately, a metonymy—of the women he knew and chose to replicate, in cyborg-like pieces, on the page.

And so here and now, he is trying to write me as closely as a man can get to writing a woman. In fairness, he has an advantage—he created me, so technically no matter what he writes about me or for me, he can't be wrong. You can say, "Come on, Lyga, no woman would say that!" and he can simply sit back with a serene/smug expression and reply, "Phil would." And you can't say he's wrong.

But he's trying. He's trying very hard not to play the God card. Not here. Not now.

Because we're at the end. The end is where truths are revealed. No one solves a mystery in the middle of the book. The killer is never unmasked halfway through the movie.

You haven't heard from me yet. Maybe you think I'm paper-thin, a caricature more than a character. A weak female side character, developed purely as a prize for the male lead to pursue. An example of the male gaze in action and not much else.

Guess what? Yeah, I'm all of those things. And more. Some of it good, some of it bad.

Why? Because that's what fits the needs of the story. Because the story is about Mike and Phil, yes, but it is told via the mechanism of the quest for God, the pursuit of capital-l Love. Which is inherently unrealistic, and so you can't really expect all of the characters to be fully realized.

Even me, the most important female character in the book. As too often happens with female characters in male-driven stories, I become invisible and intangible to fit the needs of the story. No, it's not fair.

(This is where I'm supposed to say "Smash the patriarchy!" But this isn't that kind of book.)

You may be wondering: Do I love Mike? Do I not love Mike? Did I ever?

It almost doesn't matter at this point. Yeah, I know this is a love story, but so what? Love stories sometimes end in pain, in heartache. Sometimes they end inconclusively. Sometimes, like poor George's love story, they end unrequited.

Sometimes they end in a room, alone.

If you've read the book, you may wonder—love or not—exactly what I wanted from Mike. I felt as though my purpose in the book was to call Mike on his shit. And the problem, then, is that since he didn't like being called on his shit, he kept trying to edit the story to avoid those painful moments with me. Which ended in him editing our relationship out of existence entirely. Which, further, meant that I wasn't around to tell him how to fix it.

There's a moral in there, but you got this far—you'll figure it out.

What did I want from Mike? In the best of worlds, in the steadiest of timelines and iterations, I wanted him above all to be true to himself. To find that balance between selfishness and sacrifice. Because the world demands both from us. The only way to achieve and to proceed is by giving and hoarding. The trick is knowing when to do which.

Women know that better than men—we're the ones who get pregnant, after all, and you can't find a more potent metaphor for both sacrifice and greed than pregnancy. You have to think of only yourself, but of course you're also thinking of what's inside you. And then you have the baby and you have to let it grow up and become its own person, but it still feels like a part of you. You have to sacrifice your own life and happiness for that kid, while all along trying to steal moments for yourself.

Pregnancy is where it all starts. Everything else rolls out from there. All life, all politics, all art proceed from that. For good and for ill.

Look, I would love to live in a world where reproduction was considered so awe-inspiring that women were accorded respect and power and equality because everyone recognized that the whole damn shooting match begins right there in the womb, the one thing we haven't figured out how to replace with plastic and glass and stainless steel. Yet.

But instead we live in a world where reproduction—and the shit that gets you to reproduction in the first place[158]—generates hate, fear, contempt, misogyny, and lots and lots of fundraising for politicians.

At least, that's *my* world. I don't know what things are like in the pages of *your* book.

And speaking of the book—this doesn't even have anything to do with the book anymore. I'm just saying it because it's what I believe. And I bet someday Mike would believe it, too—he'd get there.

If he would let himself.

If he could get out of his own way.

Can he? Will he?

Well, like you, I don't know. What happens to characters after you close the book, anyway?

(Oh, and BTW: Smash the patriarchy. Smash that fucker to pieces, burn the pieces to ashes, and piss on the ashes.)

Phil stopped speaking. She lifted the Milne book from her lap and decided whether or not to read it.

158. I'm, uh, talking about sex, kids.

CHAPTER 52

Monika Seymore (née Monica Singleton) sat at her kitchen table, fingers poised on F and J on her laptop's ancient keyboard. Those two letters had worn almost entirely away, and some shivering superstitious part of her wondered if once those keycaps had gone worn-black, would she lose the use of those letters? Would she write books thenceforth without the benefit of F or J?

(She knew it to be a foolish superstition, but that knowledge had not prevented her from laying in a supply of replacement keycaps against that inevitable day when the letters would wear off entirely.)

It was past one in the morning and Monika was not the sort of author who felt the need to burn the midnight oil. She had achieved a level of wealth and success and fame (and, for some rare few, notoriety) achieved only by authors numbered in single digits. Such success, she had decided, meant that deadlines hewed to *her* schedule, not she to theirs. Sometimes she imagined herself as the hub of a wheel, her agent and manager and editor and publicist and all the others spokes that rotated about her, an image borne not of arrogance, but rather of simple fact. Her fingers on keys made that wheel turn. Nothing else. She would not let the wheel dictate to her.

And yet . . .

And yet here she sat, fingers on F and J, awake long past her normal bedtime, struggling with the words, struggling with the ending to the book.

There was no reason for it. She could go to bed and she could wake up in the morning and deal with it then. Or put it aside for days or even weeks. They would publish the book when it was ready and the book would be ready when she said it was ready.

And yet.

She was unsure how to end the book. Dramatically so. Injuriously so. It pained her that she could not conceive the ending to this book, that it eluded her like a jackrabbit in the wild.

She would never admit it to her editor or publisher or agent or to any of the others in the sudden entourage that her fame had caused to blossom around her, but she often wondered if she deserved her acclaim, if her writing and her stories really deserved the hundreds of millions of dollars they had secured for her. Such doubt made these moments of blockage all the more painful. They resonated with the savor of entitlement, as though she had earned her doubt and her literary constipation by virtue of her fame and success.

It was entirely possible, she realized, that this could be her last book, for reasons she could not completely enumerate or elucidate. It felt final.

Her fingers moved on the keys, typing words that did not fit into the story of Siobhan and Georgos and Connor, words she felt compelled to type anyway:

"Remember when we were younger?" she said to him, stroking the line of his jaw. "Remember you told me you would challenge God himself for me? You were so full of fire."

"I remember," he murmured, catching her stroking hand in his own. "Such was my love for you."

"Was?" she asked girlishly.

"Is," he said, and crooked a hand behind her neck and drew her lips to his.

The kitchen door opened and George walked in, his clothing dusty and filthy from his camping trip, his eyes haunted by something Monika could not identify, something familiar and old.

He hugged her tight.

"Is everything all right?" she asked.

"I don't know, Mom."

****

Outside the Singleton/Seymore house, Mike Grayson stood, watching the two shadows in the kitchen window blend.

Then, with a satisfied nod, he turned and walked back to the subway, alone.

EPILOGUE

Ten years passed then, ten years whipping by in less time than it took to say it or to write it or to read it. Ten years passed in the time it takes to turn a page.

Many things happened to Michael Grayson in those ten years, but looking back on them, they were blurry and indistinct, none of them standing out. They were just "many things" that had happened to him in ten years. His younger brother was still alive and this made Mike happy for reasons he could not quite articulate, as though he had once had a fear of his brother dying, as if he'd had a premonition of it or a certainty of it that had blessedly never come true.

He lived in the city still, had lived there since graduating with his degree in architecture. He had graduated years later than his contemporaries—having had to make up for his dismal performance in high school and then work his way through community college—but that no longer mattered. What mattered was that something had happened to him a decade ago, something that had compelled him to action, had compelled him to put his life together and rekindle the old dream of his childhood.

Now he worked for a firm that let him telecommute, so he spent many days just as he spent this one: Alone, in a room. Crooked over his drawing table or leaning towards his computer screen, doing that which he loved, building.

His current project was a shopping center, surely the most journeyman of architectural tasks, but this one in particular struck a personal and resonant note. It was the first new shopping center to be built in the Other City, recently re-opened for construction and reparation by the government.

Mike could not visit the site itself, but he could design it. He could take the first step toward rebuilding the Other City. And if that meant a shopping center, then so be it. A shopping center it would be. People needed to shop, after all.

On his computer, there were files in a folder marked "Dreams," files for a building made of elevators and a hotel room underwater. His boss thought he was insane, but tolerably so. Mike didn't mind that reputation. There was something to be said for an insane artist, he thought. Artists should always try to achieve the impossible, to construct the unconstructable. In short, to do the things no one else thinks they should even bother doing.

Time for a break. He stood up from his drawing table and stretched, cracking his back satisfactorily and soothingly. As he did so, he glimpsed a set of keys on the very furthest corner of the table. They were not his keys; they had been forgotten. Again.

At just that moment, the doorbell rang.

Mike grinned. He went to the door, thinking of nothing but the door. The doorbell rang again before he got there.

"Just a sec!" he called.

He opened the door. He said, "

Hello, Phil

—There are no quotation marks in dreams.

ABOUT THE AUTHOR:

Barry Lyga was the author of *Inframan, or the Coming of the Unpotent God*, as well as *American Sun, Redesigning You, For Love of the Madman*, and other novels. He died in 2005 with his last novel unfinished.

ABOUT THE AUTHOR:

Barry Lyga is the author of *The Astonishing Adventures of Fanboy & Goth Girl*, *Boy Toy*, *Goth Girl Rising*, and the I Hunt Killers series, among others. He lives in New York City. Or Baltimore. Or New Jersey. Or, possibly, Edinburgh. Or somewhere he hasn't imagined yet. It all depends on when you're reading this book. In fact, he might not live in any of those places, or he could even be dead by now.